ANNIE MURRAY

Family of Women

&

Miss Purdy's Class

PAN BOOKS

Family of Women first published 2006 by Pan Books.
Miss Purdy's Class first published 2005 by Macmillan
and simultaneously by Pan Books.

This omnibus first published 2008 by Pan Books
an imprint of Pan Macmillan Ltd
Pan Macmillan, 20 New Wharf Road, London N1 9RR
Basingstoke and Oxford
Associated companies throughout the world
www.panmacmillan.com

ISBN 978-0-330-45790-3

1 3 5 7 9 8 6 4 2

A CIP catalogue record for this book is available from
the British Library.

Typeset by Set Systems Ltd, Saffron Walden, Essex
Printed and bound in Great Britain by
Mackays of Chatham plc, Chatham, Kent

Family of Women

Family of Women and *Miss Purdy's Class*

Annie Murray is the author of ten successful novels, including, most recently *Chocolate Girls*, *Water Gypsies*, *Miss Purdy's Class*, and *Where Earth Meets Sky*. She studied English at St John's College, Oxford and has four children. She now lives in Reading.

Also by Annie Murray

Birmingham Rose

Birmingham Friends

Birmingham Blitz

Orphan on Angel Street

Poppy Day

The Narrowboat Girl

Chocolate Girls

Water Gypsies

Where Earth Meets Sky

There are always people who give generous help in the preparation for a book. On this occasion I would like to thank the following: Lewis Jones for his time, his wide-ranging knowledge, for the tour of the Kingstanding of his childhood – and for lunch! To members of the British Polio Fellowship who pointed me in the right direction, and especially to Sisters Maria Goretti Fitzgerald and Anna O'Connor of the Sisters of Charity of St Paul the Apostle in Selly Park, Birmingham, for help and hospitality.

Part One

1926–36

Chapter One

Violet was eleven when the first of the babies came.

A scrawny, cringing stranger appeared at their door and they had to peer out past Mom to see, she was such a big woman. She and her sister Rosina, who was eight, stood by the range, listening to the whispers.

'My sister ... Might be able to manage when she's better ... A few shillings, that's all we've got ... They sent me to you ...'

On the freezing air through the door came the smoke and stink of the metal-bashing factories and the sweet sawdust from the timber yard.

Violet's mother, Bessie, was a strapping matron of thirty-four. She stood with her hands on her hips in her white, starched apron, her face hard as granite, lording it over this poor woman. Bessie was gaffer of the yard here, and she knew it. Everyone looked to Bessie Wiles, but by God you didn't want to cross her. She'd take her time to answer if she wanted.

'I might be able to,' she said at last.

After a few questions – the sick mother of the child lived round in Summer Lane – she said, 'All right. Give it 'ere,' and held out her arms.

The visitor said 'Thank you' twice over in a grovelling voice and Violet knew her mother had never seen the woman before and wondered why she had come here.

It was only when Mom turned that they saw the baby, a pale, odd-looking thing. Its head seemed too big, and was topped with a fuzz of gingery hair.

Rosina ran straight up and peered at it. 'A babby! Whose is it?'

Violet held back, wary of Bessie's beefy, slapping hands and bullying tongue, and the cat o'nine tails she kept fixed to her belt. Violet was a frail girl, coltishly thin, with pale, almost luminous skin, straggly blonde hair and sad, blue eyes.

She saw a new glow in her mother's eyes.

'It's a little wench. Miserable scrap she is – look at the size of her! The mom's been taken bad so we're looking after her. There're worse ways of earning a few bob. Don't go poking her, Rosina, you'll wake her.'

Marigold came downstairs then and joined in staring at the red-haired baby. Charlie was out playing with his pals. Marigold and Charlie were twins, two years older than Violet, but Marigold wasn't quite 'all there', was what Mom said. 'She'll never amount to much.' She said that too, as if Marigold was a stone with no feeling. Violet saw some flicker of hungry emotion in Marigold's dark eyes and she clung on at her mother's side. Marigold couldn't seem to get enough of the baby.

'You going to give 'er your titty, Mom?'

Marigold had been old enough to see her mother feed Rosina, and Mrs Cameron next door was seldom without a child hanging off her little pimple breasts.

Bessie gave a harsh laugh, her big body quivering. 'Ooh no, I'm past all that, bab, more's the pity!' Violet had once heard her saying to Mrs Cameron and Mrs Davis out in the yard that after Rosina she'd had it 'all taken away'. She said it in a low, mournful voice, with a big sigh from the depths of her. Mrs Davis said that

4

she wished *she* could bleeding well have it all taken away too, that all these babbies would be the death of her, but Bessie looked at her with tears in her eyes. It was the only time Violet had seen Mom overcome like that.

'Ooh no, Clara – my Jack – God rest him – always liked me with a big belly on me and a babby in my arms. Nothing like it.'

'You daint lose any of yours though, Bess,' Mrs Davis said. 'Bring 'em into the world and watch 'em fade away – that's when it does for you.'

With a grunt, Bessie knelt down on the rag rug on the rough brick floor, barking out orders as usual. 'Pass my shawl over, Marigold, and we'll lay her on it for a bit, have a look over her. Violet – get the kettle on.'

Violet did as she was commanded, then looked grimly down at the child. She didn't want the puny thing there. There was barely enough to go round as it was.

'Mom. How long's it got to stay? *Mom?*'

But Bessie wasn't listening.

Marigold knelt over the baby. Her black hair was chopped into a bob, chin-length, parted severely down the right side and yanked back from her face with a couple of kirby-grips. She stared and stared.

Rosina, baby of the family herself, stood twiddling her long plaits, full of questions and jack-in-the-box energy. No one could ever miss the fact that Rosina was there. Violet stayed back, feeling outside it all, seeing her mother's thick, stockinged calves and the worn heels of her shoes as she knelt over the child.

'Mom?'

'Oh, shurrup, Violet – stop keeping on!' Bessie was peeling back the rags in which the baby was wrapped.

5

'Don't see why we have to have it,' Violet said sulkily. 'It's ugly.'

'Not half as ugly as you were. And it's a girl, not an it.'

'What's her name?' Rosina asked.

'The woman never said.' Bessie knelt back on her haunches. 'We'll have to think of summat. What about Daisy? Marigold – there's a tanner in the jug up there – run over to Mrs Bigley's and ask her for a tin of Carnation. I'll have to feed her, soon as she wakes.'

Marigold followed her orders, as usual.

Bessie scooped the child off the floor and stood looking at her, deaf to anyone else. She started humming a little tune and carried her through to the back, with Rosina following as if the baby was a magnet. Rosy wasn't frightened of Mom.

Violet stood scowling in the front room, in her old dress that was too short, socks sagging down round her ankles. She stuck her thumb in her mouth. As usual, she felt invisible.

Chapter Two

Daisy was the first in a long line.

There was nothing official about it, not then. In the seething, over-populated slum houses of north Birmingham there was many a mother at the end of her tether, worn down by having child after child. Bessie made her name in the district.

'Take the babby round to Bessie Wiles – number two, back of sixteen in Spring Street. She'll have it off you for a bit. And her house is clean as a pin.'

She was already a tough heroine of survival in their eyes. There was Bessie, widowed at twenty-six with four to bring up, worked like a Trojan, up cleaning pubs before dawn, taking in washing, carding buttons and pins for the factories. All the energy in the world, while weaker vessels fell along the way. And everyone came to her for advice. She had the neighbourhood just where she wanted them – respectful, fearful and under her thumb.

Bessie took in the babies of mothers who died birthing them, or were taken with infections or plain worn out. She kept them until they went back to their families, or handed them over to the orphanage and was paid for her trouble.

That wasn't the first time they had had other children living in the house. Bessie had once taken in some of Mrs Davis's children. Mrs Davis, a weak, cringing woman, lived two doors away then, and life was one long struggle. They were 'three-up' houses, with two tiny bedrooms on the second floor and cockroach-infested attics, and Mrs Davis had eleven children, nine of them boys, a wastrel of a husband and her father-in-law lodged with them as well. For two years, off and on, during the Great War, Bessie had taken the two girls in every night and they slept top to toe with Violet and Rosina.

'You're golden, Bessie,' Mrs Davis frequently said, with whining gratitude. 'I don't know what I'd do without you, that I don't.'

'Oh, I know what it's like in a big family, Clara,' Bessie would say magnanimously. 'What are neighbours for, bab, if not to help?'

Violet was four when the Davis children started sleeping in her bed. They were wriggly, vexing girls, prone to itchy suppurating rashes. Violet could remember the feel of little Ethel Davis's freezing cold feet if she stretched out, and Florrie Davis wet the bed. The room always stank of wee and every morning when they woke the mattress was freezing cold and wet. She was overjoyed when the Davises did a moonlight flit to dodge the landlord and she could sleep in a dry bed again without Ethel's scratchy toenails.

Now it seemed that a whole parade of babies couldn't do without Bessie either. As fast as one was sent off to a new home a new one arrived, and at times there were as many as three at once. Bessie rose to the occasion magnificently. She got Uncle Clarence, her brother who lived with them, to build cradles out of apple boxes. She knitted coloured squares for blankets. There were always kettles of water on for cleaning out babies' bottles and Bessie was seldom without a child in her arms. All life seemed to revolve round her.

8

Marigold and Charlie were thirteen then, and Bessie made a decision. One evening as they sat over tea in the sputtering gaslight, with a baby asleep in the corner, she said, 'I've been thinking about our Marigold, Clarence. There ain't no point in her stopping on at school – 'er's never going to be one for books and learning, not the way she is. You can stop at home and give me a hand from now on, Mari.'

Marigold looked dreamily up from her plate of liver and onions, barely seeming to realize what was being said. There was a thick streak of gravy down the front of her blouse. Violet knew that Marigold didn't like school. She could just about read and write but she was slow in every way, couldn't keep up with the running about, and all the teasing from the others.

'I don't know,' Clarence said. He ruffled a hand through his receding hair as he often did when Bessie asked his opinion. He was as thin and weedy as she was big and ebullient. Even in his early thirties he seemed like an old man, sitting there in his shirtsleeves, shoulders hunched. 'We'll have the bloke keep coming round from the Board if you keep her home.'

'Oh, I'll soon see to him,' Bessie said, drawing in a fierce breath that expanded her enormous bosom even further under her black frock. 'You'd like to help with the babbies, Marigold, wouldn't you?'

'Can I stop at home an' all?' Rosina asked.

'Don't talk *stupid*,' Charlie sneered at her.

Rosy stuck her tongue out at him when Mom wasn't looking and Charlie gave her one of his stodgy looks. He was like an old man as well, Violet thought.

Clarence wiped his chin on the back of his hand. 'Whatever you think's best, Bess.' That was what he alway said in the end.

9

So at thirteen, Marigold stopped going to school and stayed at home and learned about looking after babies. She never said if she cared either way. In any case, Violet never heard anyone ask her.

Chapter Three

1927

'Cat's got the measles, the measles, the measles...' Rosina was skipping ahead, dark plaits switching up and down.

'Cat's got the measles, the measles got the cat! Oi – ' She swivelled round, landing on both feet. 'Vi – d'you think Mom'd give us a tanner to go up the Picture House?'

'You'll be lucky!'

Violet stared at her in amazement. Trust Rosy! She'd never dare ask Mom for money, straight out.

'You ask – bet she won't.'

It was the end of the summer term and school was out. Eight weeks of freedom stretching ahead, and the day was hot as they trotted along in the blue shadow of the houses with the heady feeling of being set free from school routine into the wide, shapeless time of the holidays. Long days ahead to play out at hopscotch and tip-cat and hide-and-seek!

Violet was excited, because you couldn't not be excited at the end of term with all of them pouring out of the school gates on to the street, everyone running, shouting, cheering and tearing off home or to the park. But there was also a sad feeling because she liked her teacher Miss Green, who was about to leave the school. Miss Green was plump and comforting, with curly brown hair, and she knew Miss Green liked her and had

11

taken notice of her the way no one else had ever done, so she'd done her very best for her.

'You're my star pupil in arithmetic,' Miss Green had said a few days ago, smiling through her spectacles. 'You're working very well, Violet.'

These were words of very high praise from a teacher. Miss Green was very strict but she was fair-minded, and any words of praise coming Violet's way were rare indeed. She carried them inside her as if they were fragile birds' eggs. Clutched in her hand was the envelope containing her school report. Had Miss Green written something nice in there as well? If only she could get it out and read it, but she didn't dare – what would Mom say? She bubbled inside in anticipation.

Rosina adored the pictures. She'd sit through anything, laughing at Buster Keaton and Laurel and Hardy until she was nearly sick, riding in her seat through Westerns until people behind snapped at her to sit still, and most of all enjoying the ones with the actresses, with their big soulful eyes full of emotion and their lovely clothes like none they'd ever seen in real life. Rosina laughed, cried, trembled with them. She lived every second of it. She especially loved Lillian Gish and Mary Pickford.

They ran up the entry. Mrs Cameron was mangling clothes in the yard. The door was open as usual and they ran straight in. Charlie had beaten them home and was filling his face with a crust of bread and lard. Bessie stood, perspiring in the heat and rocking the latest orphaned infant in her arms, and the room was full of his wailing.

'Mom, Mom – can we go to the flicks?' Rosina demanded.

'I've got my report, Mom!' Violet thrust the envelope

12

towards her mother. She knew it was the wrong thing to do but she couldn't help herself.

'Can't you see this babby's running me ragged!' Bessie roared. 'Can't you see, you stupid wench. What's that flaming thing?' She looked at the brown envelope as if it was dirt. 'I don't want that – stick it on the mantel.'

Heart sinking, Violet did as she was told. Stupid – yes, to think Mom might want to know. Rosina carelessly put her report up there as well, then persisted with what she wanted.

'Mom, Mom – *can* we? It'll get us out from under your feet.' Rosina never gave up. If she couldn't get her way one way round she could think of half a dozen other avenues to try.

'You'd wear out rock, the way you keep on,' Bessie said crossly over the baby's screams. But she dug under her apron pocket, just near where she kept the leather cat o' nine tails which could switch stingingly across hands or legs. Instead she brought out a shilling. 'Go on then, all of you – clear off. I don't know what Clarence'll say though.'

Bessie always said this, even though Clarence never said anything of much note and she was firmly in charge and always had been.

'Come on, Vi!' Rosina cried.

Charlie and Marigold came as well and they sat in their threepenny seats through something all about the Alps, and then a Buster Keaton picture called *The Navigator*. Violet laughed along with Rosina and the others, but all the time in the back of her mind there was that envelope on the mantelpiece where things were written about her and she wanted to know what. Could she, Violet Wiles, be good at something – anything?

13

Had Miss Green seen something in her that no one else had?

That evening Bessie was snapping at them all, trying to feed the wretched baby and get the tea cooked. She stood by the stove in her huge flowery apron and the house stank of boiling fish. She'd obviously forgotten completely about the reports. Violet went over to the mantel and stared at them, hoping her mom would notice.

'Get to the table,' Bessie ordered.

'There's our reports – from school,' Violet said, perched on her rickety stool. 'You gunna read them?'

Bessie's face darkened. She gave a big, impatient sigh. 'Best get it over with, then.'

Violet scrambled eagerly to get them, heart thudding as her mother tore open Charlie's and looked at it. Bessie ran her eyes swiftly down the rows of brief comments from his teachers.

'Ah well, son.' She looked across at him. 'Not long now and you'll be out of there.'

Charlie and Marigold would be fourteen in October and then he'd be out to work. For Bessie it couldn't come soon enough. She had a shuddering dislike of schools and everything about them.

She picked up Violet's report and ripped it open so carelessly that she tore the paper inside. Violet sat, not eating, forgetting to breathe. What did it say?

Bessie eyed it in the same offhand manner as before, then moved on to Rosina's. Soon she dropped all the papers on the floor by her chair.

'Well, that's that. Get on with your tea. It'll be cold else.'

Violet shrank inside. She didn't want to eat smelly boiled fish. She felt sick and crushed. Course, Mom never took any notice of anything to do with school. She just thought this time she might have done well and Mom might say something. Her eyes filled with tears.

'What's up with you?' Charlie said.

'Nothing,' she whispered, and tried to swallow down the fish.

When they'd finished eating, Bessie got up and brewed a pot of tea. She plonked the bottle of sterilized milk on the table.

Violet still couldn't contain herself. She could sneak a look at the reports herself, of course, but if there was something special from Miss Green in there, she wanted to hear it, like an announcement. Wanted the others to hear it.

'Uncle Clarence – ' she whispered. 'Will you read my report?'

Clarence was sitting back, comfortable after his tea, and struggling to light his pipe.

'All right – pass 'em over,' he said indifferently. Clarence wasn't interested in anything that didn't centre on himself. Apart from two years in France in the Great War, he'd been looked after by Bessie all his life, and that suited him very well.

Violet's was on top. Clarence read, in his toneless voice, the remarks about her reading and sewing. They were ordinary enough. Violet's pulse quickened. Now he was coming to Miss Green.

'"Violet is very strong in arithmetic and geometry,"' he read. Violet sat drinking in every word. '"It would be a waste if she did not go on to greater things."'

The sweet honey words had not had a chance to seep into her when her mother gave a great mocking guffaw.

'Who the hell wrote that load of flannel?' She continued to laugh, shaking her head, her belly quivering.

'What "greater things" is she on about, d'you think? Tea at Buckingham Palace? God, they live in another world, these people. What bloody good does she think *geometry* – ' she put on a mock-teacher voice, 'is going to be when there's a babby in her belly and no food in the pantry, eh?'

She sat shaking her head. Violet didn't hear any more of her report. She tried to hold on to Miss Green's words. *Very strong! Greater things!* But every last spark of her brief glow of pride was snuffed out by her mother's scorn.

Chapter Four

1929

Two years later the gates of school closed behind Violet for the last time.

Miss Green had long left, with her words of encouragement. Violet tried to forget her excitement over that one school report. That little opening, those thin threads of light from a dream world not her own, was long in the past now. When she received her character from school, for arithmetic it just said, 'Good.' So, good enough, but nothing special. And now it was time to start looking for work, on a rainy April morning, two days after her fourteenth birthday.

'Marigold – look after the babbies.'

Bessie was putting her hat and coat on. Violet stared at her, a terrible realization beginning to dawn.

'Where're you going, Mom?' she asked, dreading the answer.

'You needn't think I'm letting *you* loose looking for a job by yourself,' Bessie said, doing up her buttons. 'You'll say yes to anything for slave wages – or you'll end up in service, skivvying for a pittance. I'm not having that. Come on – set your hat straight, wench. No good going out like a bag of muck tied up in the middle.'

There was no point in arguing. They stepped out into the Aston drizzle. Bessie cut a forbidding, matriarchal figure, striding out of the yard in her black winter coat which only just fastened round her. She always wore her hair, raven black like Marigold's, in two plaits coiled round her head, and over these she pulled a black hat with a narrow brim which curved upwards.

'Morning, Mrs Wiles!'

'Awright Mrs Wiles – off up the shops?'

'No – I'm going to find our Violet a job.'

These greetings were repeated several times, all with deference, a few with cringing timidity. Bessie, as the gaffer of the yard, was often consulted about quarrels which broke out with so many people living cheek by jowl under the stresses of poverty; she held the 'didlum' money, the savings people put in week after week to save for Christmas or to have some money put aside for an emergency, like paying the doctor. She was respected, for her dominant toughness as much as her immense capacity for taking things on.

Walking beside her, Violet felt any vigour of her own draining away. Her mother had this effect on her. Bessie's energy seemed to flatten her, like a steamroller. Bessie lived in constant terror of the poverty of her childhood and fought it even when there was no need. She never went out without a chunk of bread pushed into her pocket.

'You never know when lightning's going to strike,' she always said.

Violet trailed along after her. Her coat sleeves were too short and one of the blue buttons was missing. Although she had tied her hair back and tried to look neat and tidy, she felt scruffy and awkward and childish. All she wanted was a decent little job she could just slip into, with a few friendly faces around her. If only Mom could let her go out and do it for herself!

They walked a way along Summer Lane. It was a

notorious area, famous for its poverty and gangs of violent lads. Violet looked round. She was never out at night to see what went on. Everything looked normal enough now. She could just hear sawing from one of the mills round the back. The streets were busy with people, women with small children out on their way to the shops, drays from the brewery and the Co-op, one of the horses lifting its tail to deposit dollops of manure along the street. It had barely finished when a tiny lad, no more than four years old, was in the road scooping it into a pail. Its sale to anyone who wanted fertilizer brought in handy extra pennies. Another cart passed loaded with blocks of salt, its driver yelling his way along the street.

'Right.' Bessie paused suddenly, and from the house they were standing beside a cloud of dust and dirt was flicked all over them by a broom. ''Ere!' she shouted, brushing down her coat. 'Watch where you're throwing yer muck and mess!'

'Well how was I to know you was standing out there?' came a voice from inside. 'I'm not a bleedin' mind-reader you know. Why don't yer just bugger off and stand somewhere else if you've nowt to do?'

Bessie stalked away huffily. She was out of her own little orbit and people weren't showing her the same respect.

'Down here.' Bessie led her along several streets, all tightly packed with yards of houses leading off entries and front houses with their doors flung open to let some air in and, squeezed between them all, factories and workshops. At the end of one street they came to a bigger works. 'Steel Castings', it said across the front.

Without a word to Violet, Bessie went to the door and knocked. After a wait, a swarthy man with a moustache came to the door. Violet felt herself shrink inside. She didn't like the look of the place or the man's grim expression.

'What d'you want?' he demanded.

'I want a position for my daughter. You got any vacancies?'

Violet was very embarrassed by the aggressive tone in her mother's voice, and she had an almost physical sensation of the man running his eyes over her from top to toe. To her great relief he said, 'Skinny little mare like that ain't no good to us.' And shut the door.

'Huh,' Bessie said. 'Well, bugger him.'

Oh Lor', Violet thought, full of dread, what if she ends up shooting her mouth off? Bessie had a terrible temper on her when she got going. *Mind I don't lose my temper*, was one of her warnings.

In the next street, though, they came to a factory called Vicars which made brass hinges, and this time, while Violet prepared herself for being called a skinny mare again or something worse, in fact the middle-aged man who opened up to them looked kinder. He was certainly more polite.

'Er's got a good character,' Bessie said, thrusting the School Leaving Certificate at the man, which said that Violet was reliable and capable of hard work.

The man stroked his face as if he had a beard, although he didn't.

'You're young, but we can use you,' he said. 'You can start tomorrow. Seven and six a week.' He introduced himself as Mr Riddle.

It was only then that it really dawned on Violet that when she went out to work she would be earning her own money. Seven and six! It wasn't a princely sum, not by a long way, but it was still more than she'd ever earned before. She found herself beaming at the man, and Bessie said, 'Yes, she'll take it.'

On the way home, she said, 'You needn't get any grand ideas about your wages – you'll be handing them over to me, for your keep.'

The inside of Vicars was one big workshop, with long, grimy windows all along one side, a loud, dirty, stinking place with all sorts of different machines working at once to turn out brass hinges of a whole variety of sizes. However, Violet rather liked the atmosphere, especially as the first morning she heard someone singing 'Yes, We Have No Bananas!' in a cheery voice over the racket of the machines.

Mr Riddle came to Violet that first morning and handed her an overall.

'Don't worry, love – no one's going to bite you.' He smiled at her anxious expression. 'I'll start you off over here – in at the deep end, sort of thing. You look like a sensible sort of wench and I need someone with a bit of dexterity. Lil who normally works there's been taken poorly.'

He instructed her in the use of a drilling machine, set to drilling screwholes into tiny brass hinges which one of the other girls told her were for jewellery boxes. Though it took concentration because of the size, she found the work quite straightforward and after a few mistakes she settled in well. Over the next few days she learned about all the machines, for milling, drilling and countersinking, the capstan lathes and a big stamping machine for carriage door hinges. And she also got to know the faces behind them, some friendlier than others. She was relieved to find there was a jolly-looking girl

21

called Jo who was not much older than her. And she also identified the source of a lot of the singing – a stocky lad of eighteen with shiny black hair and a laughing, jaunty air about him, called Harry Martin.

Chapter Five

Marigold watched sparks flying from the knifegrinder's stone. Narrowing her eyes, she made the dots of light come into better focus. She didn't know she was a bit short-sighted, so it seemed normal to her that the gas lamps round the Bull Ring, the naphtha flares on the traders' stalls, even the match struck by a man close to her to light his cigarette were a soft-edged outburst of light and colour. Standing amid all the shouting as the traders vied to sell off Saturday night's cheap cuts of meat and fruit and veg, the glowing lights made her feel nice. A smile lit up her normally vacant expression.

'Want one?'

At first, she had no idea that he was talking to her. People hardly ever did talk to Marigold directly, except to give her orders. They talked round her and about her. *Marigold won't want one of them. Marigold doesn't do things like that . . .*

A few days ago she had turned sixteen. Under her old tweed coat she wore a muddy-grey frock from the pawn shop. Rosina, at eleven, wore the prettiest clothes because she had the nerve to keep on and get what she wanted. Violet was far too mousy to talk back to their mother, but at least she could save for bits and pieces with what was left of her wages. Bessie had relented and let her keep two bob a week now. But she wouldn't let Marigold go out to work. Oh no – she was needed at home. So Charlie and Violet were bringing in a wage, but not her. She never had any money to call her own. Marigold didn't complain because no one heard her if she did.

She was a frumpy sight in her old woman's clothes and flat shoes, wide as boats, her black hair chopped chin-length and kirby-gripped. Weighing her down were the carriers of meat and fruit. *Marigold'll go into town for the meat auction – she likes it.* For once Mom was right – she did like it. It was Marigold's one taste of freedom. But she didn't think for a moment that any man would bother talking to her or that her ripe, solid shape and dark brown eyes might be of interest to anyone.

'I said d'you want one?'

Marigold jumped, alarmed by the attention. He'd come close and was holding out a single cigarette. The face that looked out from under his cap was gaunt, tired-looking, but his pale eyes were friendly.

'All right.' She'd never smoked a fag before.

He leaned closer and pushed the end of the cigarette between her lips.

'Here you go.'

She saw that he opened the box of matches with one hand and then leaned down and struck the match on the ground, bringing the little flame carefully up towards her.

'Good job it ain't windy.'

She saw his left arm was missing, or part of it, and the sleeve of his jacket pinned.

Marigold was about to speak, but she breathed in a great chestful of the smoke without meaning to and coughed and retched until her eyes ran.

'First one, is it?' the man asked, grinning, once she'd stopped gagging.

Marigold nodded, gulping. She took another cautious

puff on the cigarette without breathing in. That worked better.

'What happened to your arm?' Her throat was stinging.

'Wipers, that's what "happened,"' he said sourly. She saw the muscles in his cheek clench for a moment. 'No one wants a bloody cripple working for 'em.'

'Oh,' Marigold said.

He seemed amused at her lack of pity. 'Oh? Is that all you can say?'

Marigold shrugged and puffed on the cigarette again. 'Tastes like tar,' she said.

He laughed. 'Does a bit.'

There was a pause. Sounds of the market surrounded them. The air was full of smells of smoke and cooked meat, mild ale and crushed oranges.

'Where're you going then?'

'Get a chicken,' Marigold said.

'Come on then.'

He told her his name was Tommy Kay.

'Tommy Kay,' Marigold said in wonder. 'You look quite old.'

'Old as the hills,' he teased. 'What's your name?'

'Marigold.'

She giggled with him this time, bubbly and excited. 'Violet, my sister, says it's a cow's name.'

He didn't ask her age.

Together they walked through the crowds to where a group were gathered round a chubby, red-cheeked man in a blood-smeared overall. There was a lot of pushing and jostling and shouting wisecracks. Tommy helped her buy a chicken, holding it up with laughing eyes.

'Look at the state of that – looks as if someone's sat on it!'

The chicken did look flat and dejected. Marigold giggled again. Everything seemed funny with Tommy Kay.

Tommy asked her where she lived.

'I live up Lozells. I'll walk up with you.'

Bessie always told Marigold to use a penny for the tram, but Tommy was insistent.

'No need – it ain't far. Give us one of your bags.'

'All right,' Marigold said, suddenly feeling shy and overwhelmed by the thought of walking all the way home with him. What she wanted now was to get on the tram and remember his smile, safely, like a picture from the front of those *Peg's Papers* that Mom liked Violet to read out to her, not have to go on with him. Why did he want to walk with her, daft old Marigold?

As they left the crowded Bull Ring she saw that Tommy walked with a limp. He didn't say much. Once or twice he whistled scraps of a tune she hadn't heard before.

'You're a nice girl,' he said suddenly. They were in a street with houses and factories, noise coming from the pubs.

Marigold giggled.

They crossed over a dark street and there was a factory with an alley down the side. Tommy stopped.

'Come and put your bag down a minute.' He was speaking softly suddenly. 'We'll have a rest.'

Marigold did as she was told. There was a lamp outside the front of the factory, and Tommy took her hand and pulled her into the deep shadow of the alley. Marigold thought it was a funny thing to do.

'You're nice, you are.' His voice had gone queer, low and tight. He wrapped his good arm round her and pressed her close to him.

26

'We're having a cuddle,' Marigold said. It was strange, but she found she liked it. It gave her an excited feeling in the bottom of her tummy. It was so dark she could barely see him, only feel him pressed against her.

Then Tommy started sucking at her lips and Marigold drew back, disgusted.

'What you doing?'

'Kissing you, silly.'

'That ain't kissing – that's dirty!'

'You never had a kiss before? I'll show you what it's like.'

The kissing was all right when she got used to it and it gave her all sorts of other feelings.

'Unbutton your coat for me,' Tommy breathed. 'And your other bits. This flaming arm – takes me an age to do buttons.'

She obeyed, not sure what was happening. It was frightening but exciting. The night wasn't too cold but she felt funny, undoing everything outside. Her large breasts lolled free under her threadbare old camisole and Tommy gave a groan of pleasure, running his hand over them. He teased up the edge of her vest and Marigold felt him reaching for her nipples.

'Ooh,' she heard herself say. Her body was flooded with feelings such as she'd never had before. She squirmed with pleasure and pressed against Tommy. It had an effect on him that she wasn't expecting. He pulled back and fumbled at his clothes.

'*Christ* . . .' He sounded angry. Marigold was confused.

'What's the matter?'

'I'm a cripple, that's what! Get your bloomers off for me – quick!'

'My *bloomers*?' She was giggling. 'What for?'

'Just get 'em off – you'll soon see . . .'

27

She never did see anything, in the dark, could only feel. Tommy groped at her skirt, trying to hoik it up, once she'd obediently removed her bloomers. He was panting and cursing, his breaths hot and frantic against her neck. Then she felt something jabbing at her thighs.

'Open your legs!'

There were a few moments of frustrated confusion and she heard him cursing, trying with one arm to find his way to her, to control himself. Then he was jabbing up between her legs.

'Christ!' he said again. 'Let me in . . .'

And she felt a burning and a hard thing up inside her and it ached and glowed with sensation and his jabbing in and out of her set something off in her body that started to rise and spread. It was the loveliest feeling she'd ever had and she didn't want it to stop. But it did stop, abruptly, because Tommy shoved into her very hard for the last time, gave a long grunt, and then all the urgent moving stopped and he pulled away.

'You can put your bloomers on again,' he said out of the darkness, and she fumbled to find them, confused by the warm burn of her feelings.

Tommy came up close again.

'Like that, did you, wench?'

Marigold decided she had liked it. 'Yes, ta,' she said.

'D'you come down here every Saturday?'

'I come for my mom – for the meat.'

'Well – I'll be here again.' He steered her out to the road and picked up the bag. 'How about it, Marigold?'

'All right,' she said.

She was met back home with a slap across the face.

'Where the hell've you been, you stupid good-for-nothing?' Bessie roared. 'How'm I s'posed to cook the tea if you don't bring the bleeding shopping home? Can't do the simplest thing, can you, you bonehead! Where've you been?'

'Nowhere,' Marigold's eyes were stinging from the slap. She felt wet and sore between her legs.

'Took you a bloody long time to go nowhere then,' Clarence observed. He was kneeling by the fire with his boot stuck on the end of a piece of wood, trying to fix the heel back on with weedy hammer blows. Violet and Rosina were sitting quiet, out of the way. There was no sign of Charlie. The room was full of steam and as usual a line of washing was strung across the ceiling so that they had to keep ducking under it to get around.

Marigold put the bags down wearily on the table, waiting for Mom's usual complaints about the stuff she'd bought and she didn't know why she didn't go herself. Bessie loomed over the bags of shopping.

'Is that the best you could do – look at that!' Bessie scoffed. The crushed-looking chicken hung limp in her hands. 'Looks as if a cartwheel's been over it!'

Marigold took no notice. She thought of Tommy's hands moving inside her clothes. She had a secret that was *hers*. Mom was never going to know that, however much she kept on.

Chapter Six

Violet liked working at Vicars. As the months passed she learned to operate the different kinds of machines, turning out brass hinges of all different sizes. It was very noisy and dirty, but the gaffer Mr Riddle was a quiet, fair-minded man and she found the other people friendly.

One of the girls, who had given her a cheerful smile when she arrived, was called Josephine Snell. Josephine was closer to Marigold's age than Violet's but they were the two 'babbies' of the works and ended up sticking together. Josephine had wild brown hair which she tied into a thick plait, and lively grey eyes. Her house was only round the corner from Vicars and she started asking Violet back for a bit after work sometimes.

'I can't stay long,' Violet said nervously, the first time. 'Mom'll go mad. I have to get home and help.'

'Just have a cuppa,' Josephine said. 'She won't mind that, will she?'

You don't know our mom, Violet thought, but she desperately wanted to go with Josephine. She was so happy that Jo was prepared to befriend her.

The Snells lived in a front house that opened on to the street, though in every other way it was almost identical to the one Violet lived in. What went on in that house compared to her own, though, was a revelation to Violet. She would never have taken Josephine back to her house, because of Mom.

When they got to Josephine's house, Mrs Snell was out at the front talking to a neighbour. She was a small, sweet-faced woman, and very kind.

'Mom – I've brought Vi home for a cuppa,' Josephine said.

'All right,' Mrs Snell said easily. She nodded in a friendly way at Violet. 'You the new girl at Vicars are you?'

'Yes,' Violet said shyly.

'Go in – the kettle's on, Jo. Cuppa tea'll set us up.'

As she got to know Mrs Snell, Violet found she was always doing little things to 'set herself up', a cup of tea being the chief among them. She was also a widow and had had a hard life.

Violet found herself visiting a haven of quiet, female company. She felt a pang of envy, seeing this gentle woman with her daughters and the obvious affection between them. And how peaceful and quiet their house was, not full of babies and all the washing and smells that went with them!

On the first day she had asked Josephine about the lad who was always singing. It always cheered her to hear him across the factory floor. He looked a good bit older than her and she felt rather intimidated by him.

'You mean Warbling Willie?' Josephine laughed. 'His voice is quite nice really, isn't it? That's Harry – Martin, I think his other name is. Why?' She asked coyly.

'D'you like the look of him?'

'Just wondered, that's all,' Violet said. She found she was blushing. She had barely known Jo then. Now they were better friends, Jo said, 'I reckon that Harry's taken a shine to you. He was asking about you today.'

'What? He never!' Violet really did blush then. 'You're having me on!'

To tell the truth she had barely thought about him. He seemed so much older and more superior to her – why would he even notice her?

'Ah well, you never know.' Josephine gave her a mischievous wink. 'You wait and see.'

Violet kept thinking a lot about Harry Martin after that. Was it true he had been asking about her? She deliberately didn't look in his direction or go out of her way to speak to him. She was very shy and blushed just thinking about him, knowing that she imagined talking to him, or him saying her name or giving her a look just for her with his dancing eyes.

Chapter Seven

It took months before anyone noticed, because no one ever noticed Marigold.

Her belly started to swell. She was already a large girl, in the mould of her mother, and she wore loose, shapeless clothes. But one evening Bessie came panting up into the girls' room and caught a glimpse of Marigold getting undressed in the narrow space between the beds, silhouetted in the candlelight.

'Christ Almighty!' she erupted.

Violet, who was just getting into the three-quarter size she shared with Rosina, turned to see Marigold's swollen outline in the candlelight. It had crossed her mind once or twice that Marigold was getting a bit stout. Now her belly ballooned out, forcing her camisole up.

'You filthy dirty little bitch!' Bessie loomed over her, seeming larger than ever in her fury. She grabbed the back of Marigold's vest and hauled her over to the door.

'Ow – Mom, stop it! What you doing?' Marigold whined.

'What's that when it's at 'ome?' Bessie ran her hand roughly over Marigold's belly. 'You're five or six months gone at the very least, you little hoower!' She gave Marigold a furious slap round the face.

'What you doing?' Marigold burst into tears. 'Don't hit me, Mom! Why're you hitting me?'

'I'll cowing hit you, you filthy little bugger! Whose is it?'

Violet and Rosina sat side by side, both hugging their knees. Rosina's hair hung loose down her back like a black shawl. In the gloom, Violet saw that her eyes were stretched wide with fright. Violet had a sick feeling in her stomach. What was Mom saying about Marigold? Rosina looked round desperately at her. *What does she mean? Why's Mari in trouble?* her eyes begged.

'I don't know what you're talking about,' Marigold was sobbing, knuckles in her eyes like a big, ungainly child.

'You've got a babby in your belly – that's what, and I want to know who the filth was that put it there. You've been with a man, Marigold – ' Bessie lowered her voice a bit. Violet imagined Mabel Cameron listening slyly the other side of the wall. 'Did 'e take advantage of you?'

'What d'you mean?' she wailed.

'Did someone force you, you gormless wench?' Bessie had Marigold by the shoulders and was shaking her.

'No! It was Tommy – he's my . . . We're courting!'

'Courting – you!' Bessie laughed, cruelly. 'Oh, very nice. You been out in the monkey run, picking up a fancy man, Marigold? I'd like to see that, that I would!'

'He meets me in the Bull Ring, Sat'day nights.' Marigold could never stand up for herself against the force of Bessie. Her mother could crush her to powder in seconds. 'He's my friend.'

'Is 'e going to marry you then?' Bessie demanded harshly. 'You'd better get down to the Bull Ring and see what sort of friend he turns out to be.'

With utter loathing she shoved Marigold back on to the bed. 'You filthy, disgusting little cow . . .'

Violet and Rosina sat, not moving as Bessie clumped heavily down the stairs.

'Tommy's my pal – he's nice to me.' Marigold's voice came out all muffled. She lay on her side, hugging her swollen belly, and sobbed.

Bessie put a stop to Marigold's jaunts to the Bull Ring. She wouldn't even hear of Marigold going to find Tommy Kay to see if he'd do the decent thing and marry her.

'You're staying here, where I can see you my girl. I don't want you out of my sight.'

Violet felt sorry for Marigold, but there was nothing any of them could do. Marigold was stuck, almost unmoving, at their mother's side now, handmaid to her every whim. She wasn't allowed to go out of the yard, but there was no hiding the fact of her ripe condition from the neighbours. She got bigger and bigger, had to resort to wearing dresses of Bessie's, and walked leaning backwards with a slow, lumbering gait. Bessie brazened it out with the neighbours – even managed to get some sympathy.

'Our Marigold's so simple – a man took advantage of her. My poor, innocent girl. Wicked isn't it, the things a man'll stoop to?'

When Charlie found out he looked at his twin sister with pure disgust, as if she was a bad smell under his nose. Violet wondered how Marigold felt. She didn't seem any different from usual, huge and passive, very little expression registering on her face.

Except once. One Saturday afternoon, in the heat of July, Violet went up to their bedroom to take her stockings off. It was too hot to stand them. Before she had even climbed the stairs she heard Marigold's voice, and she went in to find her sister on her bed in a great big flowery dress of Bessie's. Marigold was lying on her side, her chopped black hair a line across her chin and falling over her face. She was curled forwards, her hand stroking her belly.

'. . . and you're my little babby,' Violet heard. 'It's all right, 'cause I'm your mom and we're gunna be all right . . .'

'Mari? What're you doing?' She found the sight disturbing.

But Marigold raised her head and her face was full of a shining joy Violet had never seen in her before.

'I can feel it, Vi. I was talking to him. Here –' She rolled on to her back. 'Feel him.'

The baby had pushed her body up like a steep hill. Reluctant, but fascinated, Violet put her hand on the hard drum of Marigold's belly.

'Move it around,' Marigold ordered.

After a moment, Violet felt something, a little ripple, something independent of Marigold herself, moving in there.

'Oh!' Violet said. It was alarming. She hadn't let herself think too much about how it got in there. 'It feels funny!'

Marigold beamed, cradling her arms round herself. 'It's my little babby.'

Chapter Eight

August 1930

'Right, Violet – I want you over here today.'

Mr Riddle led her to one of the rows of Taylor's lathes at the far end of the workshop, their belts all looping up to the pulleys high above their heads. 'You've never worked this one, have you? I'll get Harry to show you – hang on a tick.'

Violet stood by the lathe amid the bashing, stamping and drilling of the other machines, her heart beating fast. Had Mr Riddle gone to get Harry Martin? So far the most they'd ever done was exchange a simple hello. What would Harry think, having to come and help her?

Don't be so silly, she ticked herself off, even as her palms began sweating. It was a warm day, and she was all nerves. *He's just coming to work the lathe for you. It's work, that's all.*

She saw Mr Riddle coming back, and Harry's striding walk and slick black hair. His dark eyes met hers shyly for a moment, then looked away. His face looked ruddy in the heat.

'Get Violet started on here,' Mr Riddle said. 'She's a fast learner – she'll soon get the hang of it.'

'All right,' Harry said. As Mr Riddle went off, Harry gave Violet a wink which made her giggle. She was surprised to see Harry's neck turn even pinker – did she imagine it? – and he turned quickly towards the machine.

'Right – I'll show you. Come and stand here.'

Harry was an expert. Violet watched in admiration as he turned out a perfectly drilled hinge, his fingers strong and precise, his movements quick and intelligent.

'There – think you can do that?' He turned to her.

'Think so.' She was a bit nervous but wanted to prove she could. She was also a fast, accurate worker and her first attempt was quite reasonable. Harry stood leaning over, watching her concentrate. She could feel his eyes on her. Her pale hair was tied back but she had to blow a strand of it out of her eyes, and shook her head back. Suddenly he reached forward and held it back for her.

'Ta – I need a kirby-grip for that.'

'That's not bad.' He turned her hinge over in his hands. 'D'you want me to show you again just to make sure?' And he winked again, his brown eyes full of laughter. Both of them knew she didn't need showing again, she'd got it right the first time, but she wanted him to stay and he didn't want to go.

'All right. Just in case.' She smiled back, cheekily.

Harry drilled the holes in another hinge, taking his time over it. He turned to her. Violet was watching earnestly. She liked Harry's hands. They looked like hands that should be good at playing the piano, although she didn't suppose he could. He looked round into her eyes and this time he was grinning.

'D'you want me to show you once more?'

A smile spread across Violet's face. This was handsome, cheeky-faced Harry Martin, going out of his way to stay with her!

'Go on then.'

'Blimey – ain't she got the hang of it yet?' one of the other girls shouted over to them. 'You forgotten how to do it an' all, Harry?'

'If he ever knew!' someone called with a ribald laugh.

'Better be off,' Harry said. 'See you, Violet.'

'See you,' she said.

'He *likes* you,' Josephine told her as they poured out of the factory at the end of the day. The girls walked the pavement, taking their time, heads close together.

'Who?' Violet asked, blushing.

'Harry Martin – who else?' Josephine teased. 'Look at your face – like a flaming beetroot! Want to know how I know?'

'No!' Violet protested, nudging Josephine in the ribs. 'Bet you do!'

'I *don't*!' Of course Violet wanted desperately to know every detail.

Josephine kept looking at her, eyes full of fun, until Violet could stand it no longer.

'Oh, all right – tell me then.'

'Cissy told me. One of Harry's pals told her.'

'Told her what?'

'Said he thinks you're really pretty and nice and he hadn't plucked up the courage to talk to you until today when he had to.'

Violet swelled with excitement. Had Harry really been watching her, wanting to talk to her? It had taken him long enough to get round to it! She dug Josephine in the ribs again.

'You're having me on – he never said that!'

'He did – I swear to you!'

'I bet he's been out with half the works already. What about that Mary Price?'

'Well, he may've gone with her but he doesn't want to any more, so what does it matter?' They reached the corner of the street where the Snells lived. 'You coming back for a cuppa?'

Violet hesitated. Josephine never questioned why Violet didn't invite her back to their house. The Snells' was on the way home, so it would have taken Josephine out of her way, but Violet sensed that Jo knew it was more than that and never invited herself. Violet was always glad to go to Jo's house; anything, in fact, to stay away from home. Charlie was courting with a girl called Gladys and was hardly ever at home. Rosina played round at her best friend's house as much as she could to keep out of her mom's way. And Marigold stayed in the house nearly all the time, quietly, disgracefully, swelling. Violet didn't want to go home.

'Go on then,' she said. 'Just a quick one. If your mom don't mind.'

She went to bed that night with her head full of thoughts of Harry Martin's laughing brown eyes.

Chapter Nine

Violet woke in the middle of the night to the sound of Marigold crying out.

'My belly – oh, it hurts!' This was followed by a frightening groan.

Violet went next door and woke her mother.

'You can stop making that racket for a start,' Bessie ordered grimly, standing over Marigold with a candle.

Seeing Bessie in disarray, in her nightgown, her plaits hanging down, felt almost as alarming as Marigold's strange cries. Bessie was always up before them in the morning, dressed, hair coiled above her ears, ruling everything with an iron rod.

'Rosina – run round to number fifty-one and get Mrs Barker.'

Wide-eyed, Rosina scampered off to do as she was ordered.

Marigold gave another moan of pain and Bessie tutted and yanked back the sheet covering her. It was a stifling, sticky night.

'Get your bloomers off, wench. You'll not get far in those.' She stared down disgustedly at her daughter as she tried to obey. 'Well – now you know. That's what you get for being dirty.' Bessie turned to Violet. 'You'd best get off downstairs. You'll only get in the way, as usual. Get the lamp lit and stoke the range – we'll need water.'

There was a commotion as Mrs Barker arrived. Violet had the kettle on and was hurrying round in the gaslight to find cloths and rags, bowls for hot water, carbolic soap, string. She opened the door to the yard to get some air, but even outside the atmosphere was syrup thick. She started to hear little growls of thunder.

Rosina settled in the armchair which was usually reserved for Uncle Clarence, his personal throne. But he and Charlie were asleep up in the attic. Violet thought Rosina would curl up and sleep, but instead she sat perched on the edge of the seat, bolt upright, biting her nails and cringing at every howl of pain from upstairs.

'Here – ' Violet gave her a cup of tea with plenty of sugar.

'Ta.' Rosina took it, with shaking hands. She looked scared, as if she was much younger than her twelve years and had woken from a bad dream.

'Will she be all right, Vi? I don't like it – it's horrible!'

'She'll be all right. That's just what happens, that's all,' Violet said, trying to sound experienced. She had never heard a birthing woman before either and it made her feel all peculiar. 'Trust Charlie to sleep through it.'

The hours crawled past. Once they heard feet on the stairs and thought it was all over, but it was Bessie demanding more tea. The thunder grew louder, cracking across the dark sky, and so did Marigold's groans. Every time she heard her Violet felt herself tighten with dread inside, and when it got louder Rosina started to cry.

'I don't like it! Why's she making them noises?' She kept putting her hands over her ears, screwing up her face.

'It'll be all right,' Violet snapped, jumping violently when there came an especially sharp crack of thunder.

'Oh God, Marigold, just hurry up and get on with it, will you!'

And then, just as Marigold's shrieks were getting louder and louder, the rain came, the sky emptying itself in a great swish of sound and coolness, and soon there was water pouring out of the broken gutters and splashing on to the grimy bricks of the yard.

'Let's go outside!' Rosina said.

They ran out in their nightdresses. In seconds Violet could feel hers clinging to her, and in the dim light from the yard lamp they could see the fast slant of the rain. She turned her face up, welcoming its coolness as it ran all over her face and neck, making her shiver as it trickled down between her small breasts to her stomach. She and Rosina were giggling and whirling round in the wet, nightdresses clinging to them. There was thunder still, but fainter, and the night's intensity was being released by the storm.

'What the hell're you doing? What's going on?'

Charlie had come down, was standing silhouetted in the doorway. They ran towards him, laughing.

'Ssh – we'll wake the neighbours,' Violet giggled.

Rosina's dark hair was like a dark, dripping cape over her shoulders. She was smiling now though.

As they stepped inside they sobered immediately. The screams from upstairs were high-pitched, horrifying.

'Mari – ' Violet said to Charlie. 'The baby.'

'Oh,' he said grumpily. 'Sounds like a pig being killed.'

Violet thought, not for the first time, that she didn't like her brother very much.

'I'll go back to bed then,' he said.

You do that, she thought. *You useless item.*

Soon after, there were more screams, even louder. Rosina grabbed Violet's hand and they gripped each other tight, listening, standing in their soaked night-dresses. After a crescendo of terrible cries there came a silence. Rosina's face was a mask of fear. Then came the alarmed squawk of a newborn child.

'The babby!' Rosina gasped. 'She's had it!'

'Thank God – at last.' Violet felt sick. The whole thing filled her with horror.

'Can we go and see?' Rosina was ready to run straight upstairs.

'Best wait. Mom'll only send us down.'

Some time later Bessie came down. Violet expected her to be all smiles, like she was when the orphanage babies (that was how Violet thought of them) arrived. Instead her expression was bitter hard. Violet shrank inside.

'What're you gawping at?'

'Has she had the babby?' Rosina asked.

'It's a lad, if you must know.' Bessie went to the range, looking for something to find fault with, but the kettle was full and near the boil. 'Could do with summat more than tea, I can tell you.' She didn't seem to notice the girls' sodden state.

'Can we go and see?' Rosina asked. She always dared to ask for things, not like Violet.

'No – best leave her.'

'Oh, Mom – please! We've been up all night waiting!'

Bessie wheeled round. 'I said no! Daint you hear me?'

'Why not?' Rosina persisted. 'We want to see him.'

Violet held her breath, waiting for the axe to fall. But Bessie stood, hand on hips, in silence for a moment. Then she shrugged and turned back to the range.

'Go on – go and see what happens to girls who don't keep themselves nice.'

Violet climbed the stairs behind Rosina. When they got into the room, Mrs Barker was putting all the bowls of water and red-stained cloths by the door to go down. Violet averted her eyes from the sight. She couldn't avoid the smell though, warm and bloody. It almost made her want to retch. She forced herself to stay in control and looked at her sister, propped up in the bed, hair lank with sweat and with a smile on her perspiring face.

At first she couldn't see the child because the sheet was pulled right up. When Marigold pulled it back, Violet felt another plunge of revulsion. Sucking on her sister's breast was a tiny, monkey-like baby. She could see Marigold's blue veins and the wet, slicked hair on the child's head. It all made her feel funny. Rosina didn't seem too sure either.

'You all right, Mari?'

'Told you it was a boy,' Marigold said.

Violet leaned closer and saw the tiny face, eyes and fists clenched shut, cheeks sucking in and out. There was white stuff rimed above his eyes and he smelt like cheese.

'What's his name?' Rosina asked.

Marigold looked severely at her. 'Tommy,' she said. 'He's mine.'

Chapter Ten

'Fancy walking out with me – Saturday?'

It was the next morning, and after a night with no sleep, Violet had been flagging with exhaustion until Harry found an excuse to come and see her, and whisper to her. Suddenly she was full of beans!

'He's asked me out – properly!' she told Jo during the dinner break and Jo's eyes were dancing with interest. Violet thought she'd never been so excited. First a pal like Jo, then this!

'Well, you said yes, didn't you?'

'Course I did – why wouldn't I?'

She was surprised that Harry seemed a bit in awe of her. There she was, only fifteen and he was already nineteen. But she was very flattered. Violet felt she had never had so much attention. And Harry was considered a bit of a catch in the works – a strong, good-looking lad, full of life.

That Saturday they went into town to the pictures at the Futurist. Violet had a row with Bessie before she went.

'What d'you mean you're going to the flicks?' Bessie demanded. 'No you're not – you've seen where gadding about lands you! You're going to the Bull Ring to get the meat, and let's hear no more about it!'

Violet was really fed up with spending Saturday nights traipsing back with heavy bags on the tram. She had had to take over this job once Marigold was not considered safe to be let out. For the first time, she found herself standing up to Mom.

'Why do I always have to go? Charlie never does anything – he can go tonight instead.'

'That's no job for a man.' Bessie was spooning a sloppy white gruel down one of the babies. Charlie was sitting by the door, jabbing idly at the sole of his boot with a penknife. 'You'll have to go, Vi.'

'I've told you – I'm not going!' She could hardly believe herself. 'Let that lazy sod do something to help for a change!'

'Don't talk to your mother like that!' Uncle Clarence's reedy voice piped up from his chair. 'Show her some respect!'

Violet felt as if she was going to explode.

'I'll go,' Rosy said. 'Let Violet go out.'

Bessie got up threateningly from her chair, slamming the money down on the table.

'You'll do what you're told!' She jabbed her stubby finger in Violet's face. 'And any more language like that and you'll be washing your mouth out with salt. Shift yourself – now!'

'I'll come,' Rosina whispered once Bessie had turned her back. 'I'll bring the shopping home.'

Violet was trembling with fury. She wanted to storm out, tell Mom to get someone else to be her slave for once, but she knew it was no good. She smiled at Rosina.

'Ta,' she whispered.

Snatching up her hat and the money she slammed out of the house. Rosina hurried after her. Violet was astonished at herself. She'd never gone as far as that before. But she was going out with Harry Martin. Nothing and no one was going to stop her.

'She's always on at you,' Rosina said. 'T'aint fair. Charlie *is* a lazy sod. Just 'cause he's a *boy*.'

Violet felt a warm gratitude towards her little sister for being on her side. They scurried round the Bull Ring and Jamaica Row, getting all the meat and veg, and Rosina bravely took it off her, even though she could barely carry it.

'Here –' Violet handed her a penny for the tram – 'I owe you a favour. Thanks, sis.'

She and Harry sat through the picture at the Futurist, watching the flashing images through a fog of cigarette smoke. Harry lit up and offered her one. Violet shook her head. It was so strange, sitting here beside him. She realized she knew almost nothing about him, other than that he worked at Vicars. She kept snatching little glances at him in the darkness. Solid, she thought. He looks strong. He had a thick, strong neck and there was an urgent sense of energy about him. He was very different from her brother, who just sat about and did everything Mom told him. Harry had life in him. And she liked his wavy, dark brown hair.

After a bit, Harry slid his arm round the back of her shoulders. She didn't know what to do so she just sat still, but she liked the feel of it. It made her feel protected. She didn't turn to face him as she felt shy, but she was acutely aware of being so close to him, his muscular legs beside hers in the gloom. Later, once he'd smoked his cigarette, he reached across with his other hand and took one of hers. They sat holding hands for the rest of the time and his hand was heavy and hot.

Afterwards they stood outside, unsure what to do next. Harry looked at her from under his cap. His buoyant, joking manner which carried him round the factory was all gone for the moment and he seemed uncertain. It touched Violet to see him look shy, and gave her courage.

'Shall we walk about a bit?'

Harry nodded. 'Fancy some chips?'

Violet grinned. 'Ooh yes! My tummy's been rumbling. Did you hear it?'

Harry smiled. 'Yes.'

He bought them a newspaper bundle of chips each and they walked across town, tucking hungrily into the chips, the smell of vinegar rising off them. Harry walked quite fast, with a restless kind of energy.

'What's the rush?'

'Sorry.' He slowed down, and once more she sensed he was nervous of her.

'Where d'you live?' Violet asked, and Harry told her the name of his street, not too far from the factory. She found out he was one of five children. She told him about her family, or the bits it felt all right to tell.

'My brother's an apprentice at Simmons,' she said. Simmons was a firm of toolmakers.

'Oh – our dad used to work there!' Harry said.

'Where's he work now?'

'Here and there – ' Harry was evasive suddenly.

'What's his name? I'll ask Charlie if he knows him.'

'He won't – it was quite a while ago.' Harry seemed sorry he'd mentioned it.

They finished their chips and threw away the papers, and walking on, found themselves in the square by the Cathedral, looking up at its grand bulk in the darkness.

'You ever been in there?' Harry asked.

Violet shook her head.

'We don't go to church – only Sunday School sometimes when Mom wanted us out of the way.'

Harry said he'd never been in there either.

There was a silence as they looked up, trying to see stars, but it was too cloudy. The sky just looked like a great, featureless shadow.

'I wonder if it looks like that in Australia?' Harry said.

'Why Australia?'

'Right the other side of the world – that's where I want to be. I'm gunna go there one day. Or somewhere. Just anywhere out of here. Don't you want to see the world?'

'Yes.' She'd never thought about it, not until that moment. But to get out, away from here, from Mom . . . 'I do.'

Harry slid his arm round her shoulders and she tingled at the feel of it. It made her feel excited and special. He liked her and that was a miracle! She wasn't used to anyone taking any notice of her.

'I've been looking at you,' Harry said. 'You're so pretty, you are. Thought I'd be afraid to touch you.'

Violet laughed in amazement. 'You're not, though.'

Her stomach lurched as he turned to face her. She looked up at him and his expression was very serious.

'Can I give you a kiss?'

Her eyes answered, and his face moved close to hers. With warm, vinegary lips, he gave her her first kiss.

Chapter Eleven

Marigold wasn't well after she'd had Tommy.

For days she ran a high fever and lay in bed, her breasts running with milk. The doctor had to come, and he told them to help her feed the baby.

'Trust her.' Bessie cursed her high and low. 'Always bloody trouble.'

She made Violet and Rosina help with Tommy's feeding. Bessie didn't seem to want anything to do with him or Marigold.

The two sisters were horrified at first, especially at the sight of Marigold's engorged breasts. She moaned when they latched the baby on. But soon they were fascinated by him. Violet started to see why Marigold thought he was beautiful, the way his little mouth opened at the touch of the nipple and the smell of milk. And every day he looked less like a shrivelled monkey and more like someone they knew. 'Little Tommy,' they started to call him.

The fever lasted for several days before Marigold began to get a bit better. But when Violet came home from work on the fifth day, the house was strangely quiet. She walked in to find Clarence in his usual chair with the evening paper, and Bessie in the scullery. Mabel Jones from next door was sitting at the table with her long face on and Rosina was next to her, her eyes red from crying.

'What's up with you?' Violet said, carelessly, thinking Rosy was having a blart because she hadn't got her own way about something.

'You tell her, Mom!' The rage and grief with which Rosina spat out the words halted Violet. She'd never heard Rosina speak to their mother in anything like this tone before. 'Go on – tell her!'

'Now, now,' Mabel Jones said, but she sounded rather uncertain.

Bessie came out of the scullery with a tin of flour. Her expression was hard, defiant.

'It was no good. You were all getting too bound up with him. It was never going to be any different, you know – not right from the start.'

'She *is* seventeen,' Mrs. Jones put in. 'I mean I had our Michael at that age . . .'

'She may be seventeen in years,' Bessie said, thumping the flour down on the table. 'But in her head she's a child – a babby herself. The girl's not all there.'

Violet looked at Rosina, still not understanding.

Tears ran down Rosy's face again. 'D'you know what she's gone and done? She's taken Tommy away and she's given him to the orphanage!'

'You didn't?' She whispered it, disbelieving. But she saw from Bessie's defiant face that it was true.

'You can't have – he was ours! He was one of us!'

'No he wasn't!' Bessie lost her temper completely. 'He were born out of a filthy act and he was a bastard child with no father. I'm not having a bastard child brought up in my house, and that's that. You conceive in filth and you live and die in filth, that's how it is. I've done the only decent thing and I don't want to hear any more from either of you.'

Rosina had got to her feet.

'He wasn't yours...' She was backing away from her mother, towards the stairs. 'You think you can tell everyone what to do – but he wasn't yours. He was Mari's!'

'Any more from you, my girl, and you'll have a damn good hiding!'

Violet followed Rosina up the stairs.

'Rosy!' Outside the bedroom she pulled urgently at the back of her sister's dress. 'Does Mari know?'

Rosina turned. Her eyes were burning with grief and fury and Violet could feel her trembling.

'She knows,' she hissed, clenching her fists. 'I hate Mom. I *hate* her.'

Marigold's face was turned away and for a moment they thought she was asleep. Both of them tiptoed over to her and she moved her head and looked at them.

'Oh, Mari – your little babby!' Rosina sobbed, and she flung herself on the bed, clasping Marigold in her arms. 'Your little Tommy. How could she?'

Violet stood watching, tears running down her own cheeks. She could see no expression on Marigold's face. She was blank, as if she had been rubbed out. She said nothing. But just for a moment, feeling Rosina's warm shape pressed to hers, she lifted her hand and gently stroked her little sister's dark hair.

Chapter Twelve

Marigold's mute misery was terrible.

They could neither take it away, nor stand to see it. It was as if no one could reach her. Sometimes she just started crying and couldn't be comforted. If she did it in front of the family, Bessie sent her upstairs.

'Can't stand all that carry-on,' she said. 'Time she got used to it, that's all.'

Violet couldn't bear it. Sometimes she saw Rosina looking at their mother in a way which almost frightened her. She could imagine Rosy getting a knife and sticking it in her, the way her face went.

For Violet, Harry had changed everything. Having Jo as her friend to natter to was wonderful enough, but this was different. Although she had occasionally heard people comment on her looks, that she was pretty, she had never believed it. Now, when she saw Harry looking at her, almost drinking in the sight of her face, she began to feel pretty as well.

In the one tiny looking-glass which Bessie kept nailed to the wall near the door, she began to notice that her hair *was* a nice blonde shade, and that the eyes which looked solemnly back at her were blue and remarkably large. She did something she had never done before during her reluctant glances in the glass: she smiled at herself. A sweet though sad face smiled back, the dimple appearing in her left cheek. She brushed her straggly hair back into a loose bunch and it suited her elfin features.

'You're the prettiest girl I've ever seen,' Harry would say, and Violet drank this in, heady at experiencing more attention than she'd ever had in her life before.

She revelled in it. All the wages that she kept off Mom now went on prettifying herself: a little pot of rouge, some stockings, a blouse with a little navy tie in the neck. She didn't tell Bessie about the pay rise Vicars had given her, so now she was two shillings a week better off. Anything was better than being at home, and she basked in being wanted and admired. She never gave a thought to what she felt about Harry. He loved her, so she must love him and that was that. It was like that tiny glimpse Miss Green had given her, making her feel she could be good at something, and special, only this was so much more powerful because with Harry came a real possibility of love, of a life of her own.

And Harry was full of dreams of escape as well. His loves in life, apart from her, were the Villa ground, where he spent every Saturday he could afford when there was a match on, his mom, who Violet soon learned lived a hellish life with Harry's drunken, vicious father, and his big dream of Getting Out. As the months passed and she and Harry spent more and more time together, this was his constant refrain.

'We've got to get out of this place, Vi. I've got plans, I have. Give it a year or two and I'll be on a boat to Australia to make my fortune. I want to see our mom all right. The old man's never looked after her proper, like. I want her to live like a queen.'

Sometimes, as they were walking, arms wrapped round each other in the dark, along the back streets of

Nechells or Aston, Harry would erupt with restless frustration.

'Look at this – bloody hole of a place! The state of these houses – crawling with vermin. They're hardly fit for animals.The filth – look at it!' He'd squeeze her arm, passionately. 'We've got to get out of 'ere, Vi – go somewhere better. There's got to be summat better than this.'

Excited, she'd nod, though she had very little notion of how you were supposed to achieve it. Getting out of two, back of sixteen Joseph Street felt quite good enough for now.

Months passed and they got used to each other, but there was always an understanding that they wouldn't go back to each other's houses.

'I want you to meet our mom one day,' Harry told her. 'But it's not a good time – the old man and that . . . Let's keep it as it is.'

And Violet was just as happy to keep Harry away from home. Harry was hers, her one bit of happiness, and if Bessie got in on it she'd only start taking over, spoiling everything. It was exciting having this secret. If Mom asked where she'd been she said she was at Jo Snell's house.

'Must be very nice over there,' Bessie would say, sarcastically. 'Don't know why you don't pack a bag and move in.'

When Mom started keeping on, Violet just didn't listen any more. She just thought about something else.

Everything about home got on her nerves. Bessie filled the house with her overbearing personality and the coming and going of babies. Violet was sick of it all. She didn't care if she never saw another baby, after all the screaming and wet nappies strung up flapping round their heads and Bessie sitting nursing them like a bloated queen bee in a hive, lording it over everyone in the house and yard. Rosina was hardly ever there, except to sleep and eat, and neither was Charlie. He was still courting Gladys, a shrew-faced redhead and the bossiest person Violet had ever met barring her own mother. Charlie was already talking about getting married. Lucky Charlie, Violet thought. As for Marigold . . .

'She's just let herself go,' Bessie said sometimes. 'She ought to pull herself together.'

Marigold hardly ever washed herself and her charcoal hair grew long, hanging lank and greasy. Her face was a mass of pimples, worse than it had ever been, and she had a pungent smell about her. Instead of being mutely obliging, she was silent, now, as if resigned. She followed Bessie's orders, sat for hours cradling the babies in her arms or pushed them out in the battered old pram that they kept in the brewhouse. Violet began to forget that Marigold had once had more life in her than this, had run with them in the yard playing tip-cat, that she used to laugh and smile. Her state became accepted, a way of life, and for Bessie she was a useful skivvy. The only thing that was different was that after a while they kept seeing her with scraps of paper at the table, and a stub of pencil, writing laboriously in her looping, childish hand.

'What're you doing?' Violet asked her, the first time she saw it.

With no change of expression Marigold sat up to let Violet see what she had written. The smudged line of writing read, 'If you were the only girl in the world, and I were the only . . .'

Violet hummed the tune.

'That's nice,' she said.

'Wasting your time messing with bits of paper,' Bessie said.

But Violet hoped Marigold was feeling a bit better.

And she had a lot else on her mind. One day during that winter after Harry Martin fell in love with her, he came to work one morning with his face in a terrible state. She saw him as they clocked in.

'Oh, my word – what's happened to you?'

There was a huge shiner all across his left cheekbone and the eye was swollen and bruised so he couldn't open it.

'Nothing. I'm all right. Leave it.' He shook her off, not wanting her sympathy in front of everyone else.

'But Harry!' She was hurt.

'*Leave it* – I'll see you later.'

He stormed off in his overall to start work at the other end. During the morning she kept glancing along the noisy factory floor to see if she could see him at his lathe in the light of the long windows. Harry kept his head down and seemed to be working with almost frenzied energy. In the dinner break she kept away from him and stayed with Josephine. She and Jo usually ate their dinner together in any case. She felt upset with Harry, pushing her off like that. If that was how he was going to be, then hard luck to him!

'Sorry about this morning,' Harry said when they got outside.

Violet was with Jo. She stood waiting.

'D'you want to come home – meet my mom?'

He asked the question almost shamefacedly, looking down to avoid her eyes. Violet was immediately appeased. She knew he was trying to make it up to her. She looked at Jo.

'Go on,' Jo said. She was so easy-going. 'You go with Harry. You can come to ours tomorrow if you like.'

Walking down the road, Harry took her arm and slipped it through his. Violet didn't ask anything. She waited.

'She threw the old man out last night.' The words erupted out of him at last.

'What – you mean, for good? Is that why he hit you?'

'He came home in his usual state – only worse. Set about Mom – with the poker. Tommy and me had to stop him. Mom's told him she don't want him back – ever. He never pays a penny of the rent or nothing. It's me and the lads do that – and Marj.'

'But – where'll he go? Won't he just come back?'

Harry shrugged. 'Dunno. Last night I told him I'd kill 'im if he did.'

'You never!'

Harry turned to her, his face set and intense. 'Bloody would, an' all.'

The force of his anger filled Violet with sudden dread.

'You'd go to prison.'

'It'd bleeding well be worth it.'

'It wouldn't, Harry!' She squeezed his arm. 'You want to get away, remember, go somewhere where there're open spaces – not be locked away. Don't talk like that!'

He took a deep, shuddering breath. 'I could've – last night. Easy.' He stopped abruptly and, turning to her, took her in his arms. Violet was moved.

'You're what I need,' he said into her neck.

She held him close, stroking his back.

'Let's get wed,' he said.

She pulled back, startled, but excited. 'But I'm not even sixteen till next month!'

'Soon – next year?'

She beamed at him, and kissed his cheek, the side which wasn't all sore.

'All right. But don't let's tell anyone yet.'

Harry agreed. He released her. 'Come and see our mom.'

'She won't want visitors – not after last night.'

'It's all right. Come on.'

The Martins' house was not on a yard, but one of a row of two up, two down terraces in ill repair, identical to the hundreds of others in rows stretching all round Birmingham. Violet knew that her mother could have afforded to move from the yard into one of these now, with all their wages coming in, and it would have allowed them a bit more space, but Bessie was well established and a move would have lost her her status as yard gaffer. She was used to being the big fish in a little pond.

When Harry pushed the door open, Mrs Martin started violently. She was standing by the range in the shadowy room, having just replaced the kettle on the heat.

'Lord love us, you made me jump, bab!'

Violet saw a slender woman in her forties with a lined, anxious face and what would have been wide, brown eyes like Harry's, except that one eye was badly bruised and swollen and her top lip was thick and had been bleeding.

'S'awright, Mom.'

'I thought for a minute . . .'

Then a smile flickered across her face for a second, but she winced and her anxious expression returned.

Violet could see she was looking at a very frightened woman.

'Mom – this is Violet. Works up Vicars with me.'

'Hello,' Violet said, nervously.

Mrs Martin stared at them both for a moment, wringing her hands as if she couldn't make any sense of the situation.

'We're courting, like,' Harry told her gruffly.

'I'm all at sixes and sevens today – don't know what I'm doing. We had a bit of trouble last night . . . Don't know if he's told you. My husband . . . I don't know what's going to happen . . .' She collected herself and stepped forward. 'Nice to meet you, Violet . . . Let's . . . let's have a cup of tea . . .'

She turned back towards the range but still seemed at a loss. Violet could see she'd had a shock. She seemed nice enough anyway. But she wondered why on earth Harry had brought her here today of all days.

They drank a cup of tea together but Mrs Martin sat perched on the edge of her chair holding her cup, rocking slightly, backwards and forwards. Violet could see all the tension was affecting Harry as well.

'Oh, Harry – what if he comes back?' Mrs Martin burst out at last. 'Every time I hear footsteps . . .'

'It'll be all right. He won't.'

Mrs Martin looked stricken. 'I can't take any more . . .' Her eyes filled. 'What if he does?'

'He won't – I've told you. And if he does, I'll see to him.'

'You're a good lad. He's good, my Harry. Always was.' Mrs Martin wiped her unblemished eye on her sleeve and tried to compose herself.

'D'you like working at Vicars?' she asked Violet, calm for a moment.

'Yes – it's all right. I've never worked anywhere else, though.'

'Oh, it's nice, Vicars is. Worked there myself for a bit once.' She looked anxiously at Harry again. 'Where's he gone? Where d'you think he is?'

'I dunno. Good bloody riddance.'

Violet was glad to get out of the house. Harry walked her down to the corner. It was already dark.

'Come 'ere,' he said, before they parted. 'Are you my girl?'

'Yes,' she said. 'Course I am.'

He held her so close and tight, as if she was the most precious thing in the world, and she understood that he had wanted her to see his mom with her bruised face, for her to understand. And she knew how much he needed her.

Chapter Thirteen

1932

'I s'pose it's all right if you want to look common as muck,' Bessie said, when Violet showed her the simple frock she had found for her wedding.

She unfolded her arms and twitched at the material with her fingers.

'Could do with a good wash, I should think. You don't know where that's been.'

The dress wasn't new, but Violet felt she had had a stroke of luck finding it on the market, in with all the other frowsty old rags. It was white and scattered with tiny blue forget-me-nots and had pretty frills edging the neck and sleeves. She was delighted with it and Jo said she thought it was perfect, but of course Bessie had to spoil it, nose in the air as if it was a dirty floorcloth.

'You going to give me the money for a better one then?'

'Don't you go getting uppity, wench,' Bessie snapped. She moved away, starched apron crackling round her. 'You're not marrying the Prince of Wales. Old man Martin's a drunk and a waster and it's like father, like son – I've never seen it go different. But you make your own bed – and you lie on it.'

On an overcast May morning Violet and Harry stepped, husband and wife, out of the little Congregational church a few streets from Vicars.

Nearly all the factory had come to see them marry and shower them with rice at the door. Their wedding photograph showed Violet in her pretty dress, with orange-blossom in her hair. Rosina was not in the picture, but she was Violet's bridesmaid, with her dark-eyed looks, her long hair plaited and coiled round her head and entwined with flowers, which Josephine Snell had done for her. Rosina adored any sort of dressing-up and revelled in the attention.

'You both look lovely!' Jo said, kissing Violet outside. 'You lucky girl, you!'

The church was one which Harry's mother sometimes attended. Bessie, who never darkened the doors of any church, was not in a position to influence the situation much and she sulked. She wouldn't take much interest in the wedding, offering only sarcastic remarks.

She'd been sniffy about Harry from the moment she knew they were courting, and she'd been just the same over Charlie's Gladys, even though she was a young, red-headed harridan in the same model as herself. Charlie had certainly married his mother. Bessie's children had all been under her tight control for so long that she didn't like Violet making decisions for herself or moving out of her orbit of command. Yet weren't marriage and children all that she had insisted was a woman's place, loud and clear? Violet ignored her comments and her sulking. This was her chance to get out and away.

Bessie came to the wedding in the enormous frock she'd had made for Charlie and Gladys's wedding the autumn before, in primrose yellow, dotted with little nosegays of blue and violet, and a big straw hat. Uncle Clarence was there to give Violet away, in a dusty black suit, his balding head glistening with perspiration.

Before they stepped into the church he said, 'You quite sure about this, wench?'

'Bit late to ask me that,' she said crossly. After all, when had either of them taken any notice of anything she did, so why should he care now? Violet felt strong. She was a woman now, still at Vicars, earning as much as eighteen shillings a week on piecework if she worked overtime. And she had Harry, and Harry wanted her.

Harry's father was not at the wedding. He had shown his face a couple of times in the early days after the family had finally turned on him, then disappeared. Mrs Martin gradually relaxed, knowing he was not going to come roaring back in through the door, but she was a nervy woman who depended completely on her sons. Violet saw in her all she didn't want to be herself, and thought the woman demanded too much of Harry.

'When we're married, are you going to go and spend every evening with your mom?'

She asked it teasingly. But Harry's mother was coming to feel like an obstacle in her way, always so tired and pathetic-looking and forever whining to Harry. He seemed to be round there every spare moment. Although she tried not to feel annoyed and jealous, Violet sometimes couldn't help it.

She would have liked to live in a different area, get right away from her mother and Harry's, and from the sad spectre of Marigold. She dreaded seeing Marigold now. She was eighteen going on forty in her frumpy old dresses and with her lank greasy hair. Bessie had taken to having some of the women in the yard – and men if she could get them – round to play cards in the afternoon, holding court at the table, dishing out tea and anything stronger that was going and eating, forever eating. Lardy cakes were her favourite, and bags of sweets, barley sugar and humbugs. Marigold joined in, bracketed in with the middle-aged, one of those buzzing round her queen bee of a mother. She had no friends her own age. All she had was her pretty soapbox full of songs, all scrawled on little scraps of paper. Rosina helped her with the spelling, when she could be bothered. For the wedding Marigold had tried to dress up, and there was something even more heartbreaking about the sight of her with her badly cut hair washed and hanging dead straight, and the dress of Bessie's which had been taken in for her. Like all her clothes, it aged her and made her look shapeless and sexless like a sack of spuds.

Rosina was causing trouble now. She was thirteen but, Bessie said, very 'forward' for her age, always wanting to make her face up and nagging for clothes and wanting to be out and about. She was a precocious little miss, not like Violet. She stood up to her mother and there were frequent rows.

'You can't get married, Vi!' she said when she first heard the news. 'You'll leave me here on my own!'

All Violet really wanted was to get as far away from it all as possible.

But neither of them wanted to leave Vicars. Harry was already twenty and was champing at the bit to be able to get out and follow his dreams. But he couldn't go. Not yet.

'I want to see our mom all right first. I'll have to keep working here for now – that's all there is to it. We're young yet – there'll be plenty of time.'

Of course it made sense not to rent a place too far away. And being in the Summer Lane area meant wasting no money on tram rides to work. All the money they could put away was for Harry's dream passage to Australia.

'Let's get the lowest rent we can,' Harry said. 'There's only the two of us. We don't need much.'

So they rented a two-up house in Ormond Street, a back-to-back, on the front facing the street, with no attic. There was the downstairs room and scullery and two tiny bedrooms. For water and the toilets they had to go down the entry and into the yard. Violet looked round it, the first day they were allowed in. The place was in bad repair, great cracks up the side wall, cockroaches and silverfish all over the place. It was gloomy and stank of damp and mould.

'Oh, Harry,' she said dismally. 'It's horrible. Can't we go somewhere a bit better?'

'It'll be all right after a lick of paint!' Harry said, ever optimistic.

'But what's Mom going to say? I can't have her here!'

'It's our house – not hers!' Harry came and took her in his arms in the dismal little room and his eyes were alight with enthusiasm. 'Look – the rent's only six bob a week – think how much we can save with your wages and mine. The more rent we pay, the longer we're going to have to stay in this rat-hole!'

'I s'pose you're right.' Violet was lifted by his dream again. It just managed to raise her spirits above the sight of the stained old stone sink in the scullery and the pile of mouse droppings by the grease-encrusted gas stove. That and a lopsided shelf in the scullery were the only things in the house.

Harry was full of energy. He moved into the house two days before the wedding and spent the evenings and half the night with his big brother Tom, fixing the hinges of the front door and painting the flaking walls – pale green downstairs and white up in the bedrooms. He bought a table and chairs from a secondhand shop, and a mattress, and Violet bought some bedding and a few pans and crocks.

When they arrived back there on the evening of their wedding it looked better. Marigold had bodged a rag rug for them and Rosina had hemmed a red and white gingham tablecloth, on which were laid their white cups and saucers. Suddenly it began to look a little bit like a home.

They closed the door behind them and Violet stood still just inside.

'Listen – '

Harry stopped, frowning. 'What?'

'Peace.' In fact you could hear the murmur of voices from next door, but that was comparative peace. No Mom booming out orders and Rosina backchatting, no babies and stinking pails of napkins. Nothing but their own place.

'It's ours,' she said.

'And you're mine.' Harry turned, and she was moved by the look of pride and happiness in his face. He came and took her in his arms and his eyes were solemn.

'My wife. We're going to make it better, aren't we? Better than we've had it. Better than my father . . .' He looked vulnerable, like a little boy, and she reached up and stroked his hair.

'Course we are.'

'Up and up.'

'Yes – up and up.'

He grinned suddenly. 'Now for the best bit.' He stroked his hand over her little round breasts. She'd been very determined about not going with him before they were married. Not after Marigold. She was afraid of it. Didn't really know what 'it' consisted of except that the consequences were so frightening. And what if he went off and left her? Then where would she be? So whenever Harry had got a bit too amorous she'd pushed him off.

'Oi – don't get cheeky,' she'd say.

'No need to wait any longer,' Harry said. He took her hand and led her up the narrow, twisting staircase and both of them laughed at the sight of the bare room with nothing but the mattress on the floorboards, the sheets carefully tucked under it by Violet.

'Not exactly the Ritz, is it?' she said ruefully.

Harry pulled her down on to the mattress, kissing her hungrily.

'We've got everything we need.'

He hurriedly unbuttoned her dress and lifted it over her head, then slipped off her camisole. She looked down at his dark head, stroking his hair in wonder as his lips fastened hungrily on her breast. Later, Violet worked out that she must have caught for a baby that very first night.

Chapter Fourteen

The first week after the wedding, Bessie had said to her, 'There's no need for you to go cooking a joint on a Sunday – it's a waste of gas. Charlie and Gladys'll be round as usual. You and Harry come here with us.'

It was almost an order, not quite, but you didn't gainsay Mom. And it was quite nice, just for a bit, to be back with everyone, Marigold helping with the cooking, Rosina on about the latest picture she'd seen at the flicks, and Clarence sitting there talking about the Villa with Harry (Charlie had always supported the Albion, just to be different), and the smell of a joint of beef in the oven. Harry wasn't fussed about going, so long as he had a good dinner, and Bessie's dinners were mammoth events, with big steamed puddings.

Violet was feeling queasy that Sunday when they went, six weeks after the wedding. She found it hard to eat much and could feel Bessie noticing. They were all crammed into the little room, Bessie, Charlie, Gladys, Violet and Rosina squeezed round the table, Clarence and Harry on the sofa. Bessie always went round the table with the pans of food, breathing hard, dolloping it on to everyone's plates in huge quantities. As she came round with roast potatoes, Violet said, 'Not too much, ta – that'll do.'

It was the same with the cabbage.

Bessie sat down with a grunt in front of her heaped

plate, face red and perspiring from all the cooking. She eyed Violet.

'What's up with you?'

Violet looked down at her plate.

'Nothing.'

'You got a bun in the oven?'

The tone of her mother's voice was so grossly blunt that it cut right through Violet. Her cheeks burned red.

'Well – have you?'

Blushing, Violet looked up. 'Think I might have.'

Her mother's face changed. She sat back, seeming to swell with smug satisfaction.

'Hear that, Clarence?' She was beaming in triumph. 'Our Violet's expecting. I'm going to be a grandma. Now I really have got summat to tell everyone! 'Ere – Marigold – pass us over some more gravy will you?'

For the first time in her life, Violet felt she had done something right.

Charlie's wife Gladys, who was taking a long time to conceive a child, had to put up with Bessie's constant boasting about Violet.

'Course – she comes from poor stock, you can see by the look of her,' Bessie said.

Violet wasn't taken with Gladys, who she thought was a narrow-minded nag. All the same, she was embarrassed by Mom talking about Gladys as if she was a farmyard animal.

Violet didn't like being in the 'condition' she was in. She felt sick, and when that wore off and her belly began to swell she felt invaded, frightened and out of control. Panic-stricken, she remembered Marigold, lying there like a great bloated cow when she got big, and the terrible sounds she made giving birth. Sometimes she wept with fright just thinking about it.

'I don't want to do it!' she cried to Harry one night, as they were lying in bed. 'I'm only seventeen – I don't want this yet. My life'll be over!'

'Don't talk daft.' Harry gave her a cuddle and stroked his hands over her buttocks. Her new, curving shape excited him. He started touching her and Violet sighed. She didn't want him messing with her, she wanted him to understand and reassure her. She felt very alone. Apart from his sexual excitement, she saw that he didn't really want the baby, even though he tried to pretend.

When she'd first told him was on a Sunday morning. She'd made tea and they were snuggled up in bed together, with the luxury of no work and the morning stretching ahead of them. Violet didn't feel very well, but she'd been sick and felt better for it. She lay with her head on his chest, tickling him lightly with her fingers, just below his collarbones. Close up she could see the strong black hairs curling up from his pale skin.

When she told him she was being sick because there was a baby, Harry lay still without replying. After a moment he gave a deep sigh.

'Don't!' she cried, tearfully. 'Aren't you pleased?'

There was a pause, then he turned to her, and she could tell he was making himself smile.

'Course I am. I don't s'pose it makes any difference – we can still go to Australia.'

'We'll be a family,' she said. But she felt a plunge of fear. Australia was just a name to her. All she knew of it was that it was hot and dusty, and there were kangaroos! And it was so far away. The thought was frightening. All she wanted now was safety and what was familiar.

Chapter Fifteen

'I don't know why you didn't marry your mother!'

Violet shrieked at Harry's back as he left the house once again.

There was no reply, but he slammed the door so hard that it sprang open again. Violet sighed sharply and banged it shut again.

I'm turning into a proper fishwife, she thought. She didn't like shouting like that. They seemed to be rowing so much of the time these days. And it was usually over the same thing. *But he's never here!*

'You might as well bloody live with her still! Why can't one of the others go?'

As soon as he knew about the baby, Harry seemed to spend more and more time at his mother's. Mrs Martin wasn't well; his two other brothers were married now so there was no man about the house. Harry was the dutiful son; she needed him. Violet had gone off Mrs Martin very quickly as soon as she was married. She thought she was a selfish woman who made herself constantly helpless to get her own way.

Even when he was at home, Harry never understood how she felt, that she needed comfort and reassurance. Violet turned to Jo Snell and her family. Her friendship with Jo had come to be one of the most important things in her life. She could pour her heart out to Jo, and often did.

'I expect he'll come round when the baby's born,' Jo told her. 'And if he doesn't, more fool him. You can always come and see us.'

It was marvellous to have a friend like that. But even Jo didn't know how it felt to have a baby. The one person who seemed to understand, for the first time ever, was her mother. More and more often after work she found herself slipping along Summer Lane and into Bessie's yard. Home. That's how she thought of it still, and it felt reassuringly familiar, although she lived with Harry and that was supposed to be her new home.

Suddenly though, Bessie was treating her with a new respect. Almost, though not quite, as an equal. Violet existed for her in a way she never had before and when she went round there her mother was welcoming in her aggressive way. Yesterday when she'd gone there, feeling lonely, Bessie greeted her with, 'Oh – so you've come running back again, have you? You'd better come in then. How's the babby?'

To Violet's relief, no one else was in.

'Rosy out with her pals, is she?'

Bessie scowled, banging the kettle down on the fire. 'When's she ever in, little minx. She's felt my hand a few times lately, I can tell you. There's some factory Jack hanging round her already – at her age! I've told her she'll come to a bad end. The lip she's got on her! I said to her this morning, you'll have mustard on your tongue if you carry on like that but it's like talking to the wall . . .'

Violet was surprised how little authority Bessie had over Rosina. The rest of them had always kowtowed and tiptoed round her. Rosy had always been different – now she was even more so. She was just fourteen and had started work at a button factory and according to Bessie spent as little time at home as she possibly could. Violet felt sorry for her though, left at home with Clarence and Marigold.

Bessie brewed up the tea and set it on the table. As usual, the room was as clean as a pin, plates gleaming on the shelves, the rag rug shaken out and laid back by the range. Bessie was obsessed with cleaning.

'Here – have one.' On the table were boiled sweets in a little pale blue bowl. 'Barley sugar – that'll make you feel better.'

Violet obeyed.

'You should be drinking raspberry leaf tea . . .' Bessie sat down with a grunt in the big chair by the range, smoothing her capacious apron over her lap. 'Helps with the pains . . .' She poured from the old brown teapot and spooned plenty of sugar into her cup.

Violet didn't need to say a word. Bessie sat back, holding her cup up close to her chin, her dress riding up to show inches of coloured bloomers, shoes off to ease her corns. She reminisced about her own childbearing days.

'Ooh now, you don't know what's coming to you, wench. I'll never forget Charlie and Marigold – sick as a dog I was! Just be grateful it's not twins. Jack's face when she told him there was two of 'em! Treated me like a queen he did, your father.' She gave a great sigh. 'My Jack, God rest him. Now he was a man, he was. Father of twins! He was cock of the walk!'

Violet could see her mother had felt like one of the seven wonders of the world for producing twins. It was the great event of her life. Details followed over the willow-pattern teacups about swollen legs and having 'trouble going' or, as Bessie called it, 'corkage', and piles and other gruesome delights of childbearing, until Violet felt even more sick with dread.

'Don't tell me any more,' she begged.

This made Bessie laugh, her huge body quivering. 'You'll soon find out for yourself, any road, Vi.'

'I don't know as I want to find out,' Violet said miserably.

To her surprise, her mother leaned over and patted her leg. 'Time of your life, bab – that's what it is. Makes a woman of you.'

Violet was overcome by all this sudden attention from her mother. For the first time she wasn't just the spare part, just one other girl stuck in the middle between the twins and Rosina, the pale, sickly-looking one whom no one ever noticed. Suddenly Bessie wanted her, and she was brought inside her mother's powerful orbit with a warmth and sense of approval she had never felt before and barely knew Bessie was capable of. Bessie marched her off to the doctor for a check-up, and when they went round for the big Sunday dinner which was becoming tradition, Bessie kept making mention of 'Vi's condition' and 'Vi and Harry's babby'. She knew Bessie didn't think much of Harry, but he'd given her a child and that was what mattered. Gladys was having no luck, and Marigold didn't count. At last Violet felt she counted in a way that so far none of the others did.

Chapter Sixteen

The baby was due in February. By the end of the summer Violet stopped feeling sick and began to enjoy being at work again and the fuss she received from the other women, which made her feel important. For the first time she felt like Someone. Her belly swelled and showed up quite early against her slim figure. She started to feel the baby move inside her and it aroused her curiosity as well as anxiety. Who was that in there?

But come January, it all went wrong. Violet woke in the middle of the night and knew something had happened. She had a feeling in her, not pain at first, just a sensation as if something had given way in her. Then she felt a trickle between her legs.

I've wet myself! she thought, horrified as the trickle increased to a gush and she couldn't control it. She leapt up in the pitch dark, but it was too late. She'd already soaked the mattress and more was running down her legs. It was a freezing night and the old shift she'd gone to bed in was soaked and hanging icy cold on her.

'Harry!' she whimpered. 'Wake up – I'm all wet. There's something happening!'

Harry groaned. It took her some time to rouse him and get him to light the candle.

'What the hell's the matter with you?' he asked crossly. 'Ugh – it's all wet!' he had leaned his elbow in the big, pinkish stain which had spread across the bed.

'I don't know what's going on. The babby shouldn't be coming yet, should it?' Scared, Violet started to cry. She realized that despite all Bessie's talk she had given her no real understanding of anything that would happen to her.

Harry lit the candle and, seeing there was something really wrong, came and put his arms tenderly round her. She was shivering with cold and fright.

'It's all right. Come on – get this wet thing off.'

'I don't know what's going on!' she wailed. 'I've just wet myself.' She cried out then, as a burning pain tore across her swollen belly. 'Oh, Harry, what's happening? I don't know what to do.'

She would always remember her husband tenderly for these next moments. He held her as the pain gripped her, then as it died away he said, 'Come on – lift up your arms.' He tugged the half-sodden shift over her head and, finding a dry part of it, wiped her back and legs.

'What else can you put on?'

In a drawer he found a camisole vest and a blouse and dressed her like a child.

'I'm still losing,' Violet gasped miserably, as more warm liquid seeped out down her legs. Another pain came then, sudden and violent as a crack of thunder.

'Oh God!' She clung to him groaning until it passed. 'The babby must be coming. What do we do?'

'I'd better go and get the midwife.' She could hear him trying not to panic and it made her feel stronger. 'Will you be all right?'

'Course I will. But be quick!'

Harry tore down the street like a madman and soon she heard him coming back and bounding noisily up the stairs.

'You all right?' he panted.

She was kneeling, recovering from a fresh bout of pain and nodded at him, trying to smile.

'Mrs Barker's coming. She said to get the kettle on ... Back in a tick.' And he fled downstairs again, tripping on the top step and having to right himself as he went down, stumbling and swearing. Violet managed a smile at this before the pain took her in its grip again.

'Am I having the babby?' she asked when Mrs Barker, a kind, middle-aged woman, appeared upstairs.

'Looks like it, dear.' She patted Violet's hand. 'Now don't you worry. I've seen hundreds of babbies into the world. This one's coming a bit early, but you'll be right as rain.'

The night passed in a swirl of agony. Violet lay on the mattress, which Mrs Barker covered with newspaper and then with an old sheet over the top. Violet kept hearing the paper crackling as she moved, and in between the roaring pain she was aware of Harry's voice as he ran for the things Mrs Barker requested.

As dawn broke she was becoming completely exhausted and the pain reached the point where it was unbearable, and soon the baby was born, cracking her open, then slithering into Mrs Barker's hands. There was a silence, then a tiny snuffling noise. Despite her exhaustion Violet was alert with a mother's need to hear a cry, to know it was all right.

'What's the matter?' She wanted someone to comfort her, to say things were all right.

Mrs Barker looked up, immediately trying to hide her worry. 'You've had a boy. He's beautiful, but he's a tiny little thing. We'll have to do our best to keep him warm. Let's see if he'll take any milk. You just sit up a bit, dear.'

She brought the tiny scrap of a child to Violet, wrapped up but not yet washed. Violet saw a minute face, the skin yellow, eyes tightly closed and rimmed with white, the whole tiny creature pulsating like a little bird. She was frightened of him, he was so small, yet her whole being flooded with protective feelings. A little boy – *my* little boy!

'Hello, babby.' She heard the soft tenderness in her own voice.

'See if he'll suckle,' Mrs Barker ordered.

Without any ado she pulled up Violet's vest and began to massage her nipple.

'Put his mouth to you. They know what to do.'

But the little one didn't know what to do. His mouth didn't move when Violet pressed it to her breast and his eyes didn't open.

'You can do it,' she whispered.

But there was no response.

'Hand him to me,' Mrs Barker ordered. I'll wrap him up well and we'll get the fire going downstairs. It's a bitter night. We'll keep him warm till he's ready and you can get yourself a bit of shut-eye.'

Violet reluctantly handed the baby over. In a minute Mrs Barker was back.

'That husband of yours has built up a good fire – he's ever so good with him, I'll say that. Sitting holding him, he is.'

Violet smiled wanly. She was so exhausted, her pale hair plastered to her head. Mrs Barker cleaned her up and kept telling her to sleep. But she knew she would never sleep. She felt jangled and full of nerves.

But the next thing she knew, the room was filled with hard winter sunshine. Her body felt bruised and scoured out, a sodden rag between her legs and someone had just weighted the bed down, sitting beside her. It was Harry, and there were tears running down his cheeks.

'What's the matter?' She jerked upright, heart pounding.

Harry started sobbing. 'He's gone. Passed on.'

'What d'you mean?' Her teeth started to chatter. 'No!' she cried, her eyes desperately searching his face for some hope. 'No ... No – he hasn't – you're lying to me!'

But Harry's shoulders were heaving with sobs.

'He was in my arms ... He was all right ...' She could hear the shock and disbelief in his voice. 'She said to keep him warm and we was by the fire. And then he gave a bit of a shudder, like ... He wasn't breathing any more ...' He broke down and cried then, hands over his face. 'He's gone, Vi ...'

'No – he can't have! You're lying to me!' she screamed. She leapt up and ran downstairs to find him for herself.

Mrs Barker was down there and she turned. It was too late to hide the tiny form, lying on the table, wrapped in a piece of sheet.

'I'm sorry.' Mrs Barker shook her head. 'You poor young thing.'

Chapter Seventeen

They named him Bobby.

He was buried from Bessie's house, carried on the hearse of an old man who had died in Summer Lane.

Violet walked behind with Harry, and her mom and sisters and Charlie and Gladys. The day was grey and cold as stone, and Violet felt as if her heart was being torn out as she saw the hearse and the black horses with their plumes begin to move off along the row of mean, soot-grimed houses towards Witton Cemetery, carrying her little boy in the tiny white coffin.

They had had to cajole her out of the house that morning. She'd been staying over at Mom's, just for that one night. She didn't want to be with Harry – she wanted her sisters, her childhood. Harry had gone to his mother too.

Violet barely slept, lying in the old three-quarter-size bed beside Rosina. Charlie had left home, and Clarence had been very poorly over the winter with his chest and had taken to sleeping downstairs by the range. So Marigold slept in the attic and Rosina had made the room her own, with her postcards of her screen heroines, Lillian Gish and Jessie Matthews in their finery stuck to the wall above her head.

'I want my picture taken like that,' she said to Violet when they went up. 'With fur collars and feather boas and lace and silk . . .' She hugged herself at the thought.

'I've missed you, Rosy,' Violet said, miserably. 'You hardly ever come round and see me.'

'Well, you're married, aren't you?' She sat down with a bounce on the bed. 'What d'you want me for?'

It's lonely being married, she wanted to say, but didn't want to admit it.

'You could still come. Harry's not there all the time.'

'I meant to – only . . .' Rosina rolled her eyes. 'I've been busy.'

Violet smiled. Rosina seemed older than her years. She was a proper handful, bad-tempered and lippy, and although Violet sometimes admired her for it, she'd felt she didn't know her any more, or even like her, sometimes. But as they'd got into bed last night in the candlelight, Rosina stood between the two beds, her beautiful long hair loose over her shoulders, and said timidly, 'Shall I get in with you, Vi? Like we used to?'

Violet nodded, eyes filling with tears. She shifted over as Rosina blew out the candle and her slim, curving body snuggled up close to Violet. It was a comfort.

'I don't know what to say to you,' Rosina said, and Violet could hear that she was close to tears. 'I don't know what it's like. But it's so sad.'

'I want him.' Violet let go then and wept, wretchedly. 'My little boy! I just want to hold him . . .'

'Oh, Vi!' Rosina was sobbing too, and Violet remembered then how sweet she could be. Knowing her sister felt some of the pain with her was a comfort. And as she grew calmer, another thought came which had been returning to her all week as she had lain at home, aching with grief. It was the memory of that evening when Marigold found out that her mother had taken her baby and given it to the orphanage. At the time, and since, she had blocked out Marigold's great, unearthly howl of anguish. She had not understood, not then. But now she could hear it in her head. And she could feel it for herself.

'Let go of me a tick – I need to get up,' she said to Rosina.

'You gunna be sick?'

'No . . . I want to see Mari.'

She lit the candle and padded up the attic stairs to Charlie's old room. It had not changed much, still plain white and bare except for the bed and a chair. She could see Marigold's lumpen shape curled on her side in bed. Marigold hadn't said anything to her about little Bobby. She'd just silently got on with all the household tasks that were forever expected of her while everyone fussed round Violet, even Bessie, who had shown real grief over the loss of her grandson. Bessie had just taken over, and made a great to-do to the neighbours about poor Vi and all she was having to do for her.

Violet looked down at her sister, lying there with her eyes closed. No one had made any fuss about her baby going.

'Mari?' she whispered.

Marigold heaved herself resentfully on to her back and opened her eyes. Her face looked like a white, square box, framed with black hair.

Violet perched on the edge of the bed, which dipped severely in the middle. Marigold stared blankly back at her with her flinty eyes, as if she was still asleep, but with her eyes open. Tears ran down Violet's face again.

'I never said anything – at the time – about your little babby. It was terrible for you . . . I didn't know – not till now . . .' She trailed off.

Marigold's eyes narrowed for a second, into what seemed such a vicious expression that Violet's tears

84

stopped. She was chilled. But then Marigold opened her eyes again and Violet wondered if it had been the uncertain light, that she'd imagined it.

'S'all right,' Marigold said stolidly, then added matter-of-factly, 'Your babby died.'

'Yes.' The tears soon came again. 'He was so tiny ...'

'Poor babby.' The words held no expression. There was a long silence. Violet wasn't sure what she had expected. When had it ever been easy to communicate with Marigold? She had wanted to say she understood about the baby, but hadn't she also wanted something back?

Marigold turned over again. 'I'm tired.'

'All right.' Violet got up and the bedsprings creaked slightly. 'Night, Mari.'

There was no reply.

Chapter Eighteen

1936

After Bobby, Violet had two miscarriages, the second very shortly after she knew she was expecting. It broke something in her for a time.

'I'll never be able to have a babby. There's something the matter with me!' she sobbed to Bessie, to whom she went for comfort while the griping pains still signalled the quenching of that little flame of hope that had been lit with her third pregnancy. When her body let her down again, expelling vivid red clots, it mocked her hopes so cruelly. And it was made worse by the fact that Gladys and Charlie had finally had a little boy, Norman, last year, and Josephine had married her sweetheart Percy and had a daughter with a beautiful mop of curly black hair, called Lizzie. Violet felt left behind as a wretched failure, a nobody.

She became nervy and couldn't seem to make the simplest decisions, and in her anger and sense of failure she took it out on Harry. All the things which she had put up with before, even smiled at – the way he was unpredictable and she couldn't rely on him being there, his wild, sparky energy, his refusal to be tied down – all seemed aggravating and hurtful. Now it all just felt as if he didn't care about her. He was either out with his mates or at his wretched mother's house.

'I don't know why you bothered getting married,' she raged at him sometimes, when he turned up late once again to face a congealing plate of food. 'All you want is a servant to cook your dinner.'

'Well, I'm here now, aren't I?' Often he'd come up and squeeze her round the waist, trying to win her round with teasing and kisses.

But these days she'd lost her sense of humour.

'Oh, get off – you needn't think you can get round me like that. Why don't you try coming home on time for once?'

She became a thin ghost of herself. All she could think of doing was to run home to her mom, like a child, lost in herself. She started smoking. It soothed her.

And the house was in a terrible state. The roof leaked badly over the little back bedroom and the cellar flooded, so when they went to feed the gas meter they sometimes had to wade thigh deep through sooty water. All that paint which Harry had applied so eagerly to the walls was soon discoloured and began flaking off, and the place stank of damp and mice. Violet was forever battling with infestations of bugs, but the mice were the worst. There was a constant need to place mousetraps in the scullery, and all the food like flour and sugar had to be kept in tins.

'Oh, why can't we move somewhere else, instead of festering in this bloody dump?' she would moan to Harry as she had to clean out the scullery yet again to get rid of the mouse droppings.

'We're all right,' he kept saying. 'Only a year or two now, and we'll be off . . . No point in paying more rent than we have to.'

He always seemed able to keep his spirits up, full of money-making schemes to boost their savings. His pal Goosey's dad drove a truck, and on a trip up to Stoke-on-Trent got hold of a whole load of damaged crocks. Harry and Goosey bought the job lot off him and set up with a barrow until they'd got shot of them at knock-down prices. They barely made any profit but it seemed to keep Harry happy. Christmas of 1935 Violet remembered as the 'snake' year. Harry learned from another pal how to make colourful snakes and dragons to sell as little toys. They were made out of strips of painted paper, cleverly folded back and forth again and again and attached to an empty cotton reel. When you released them and unfolded them they ran undulating along the ground, propelled by the cotton reel. For weeks the table downstairs was covered in newspaper and cheap glue and paint and Harry was begging cotton reels off the women at Vicars.

'What you up to, Harry?' they asked.

'Going to Australia!' he told them, chirpily. They humoured him.

'Oh yes, and I'm flying to the moon, darlin'!'

'You building your own aeroplane?'

Violet wondered if Harry really believed they would go. Sometimes she thought he just needed a dream to hold on to. As for her own dreams, she had none except one. A child of her own.

And then she found she was expecting again. All through the pregnancy she was frightened, on the alert for it all to go wrong. She could hardly bear to hope for better, in case the next day she started bleeding. And even if she got as far as giving birth to the baby, it might be like Bobby all over again and she would be burying it within a week. Harry did his best to be soothing.

'It's all right,' he'd murmur into her neck as she cried with worry. 'Don't worry, Vi.' And he held her so gently and kindly that she could forgive all the times they quarrelled. But most of the time she was locked into her own cold self and she knew she was gradually driving him away. After all, she knew she wasn't much of a wife to come home to. If only they could have a baby, things would be better, she just knew it. It would make everything all right.

'Look at her – she's a right bonny little thing!'

'Is she all right? Tell me she's all right!'

Violet gasped out her anxiety, now the final pangs of childbirth were over at last. Her gaze seemed to bore into the midwife, and Bessie, who had been present all through the birth.

'As healthy a babby as I've seen come into the world,' Mrs Barker said soothingly, tying the umbilical cord so she could cut it. 'Don't you fret, dear. You've had a bad time, I know, but she's your reward. A beautiful daughter for you – look!'

'She's a little peach,' Bessie said.

It was one of those rare times when gentler emotion broke through Bessie's usual bullying tones. She held up the baby, swathed in a piece of towelling, and through the blur of her own tears Violet saw a squashed, startled face, mouth beginning to open and roar. She was delicate-looking, and pale. Violet had an immediate sense of kinship with her. *She's like me*, she thought, startled. *I know her.* This, and the realization that at last she had managed to deliver a robust child, made her sob with relief and happiness.

'Let me hold her!'

'Let Mrs B. finish you off first,' Bessie said, cradling the baby in her arms. She put her face close to the little one's, crooning to it. Even though Mom was being nice,

Violet found herself brimming with rage at the sight of Bessie's huge, bulldog frame wrapping itself round *her* baby. All those babies Mom had held – four of her own and all those orphaned brats – and now she wanted to take hers as well! She couldn't stand seeing her looking into her baby's face like that as if she was the mother, taking over everything!

'Give her to me now – or I'll never let you hold her again – she's *mine!*' Violet was shrieking, tears rolling down her cheeks. She was still tightly clasping the end of the towel, hooked over the bedstead, which she'd gripped to help get through the pains.

'There's no call to carry on like that,' Mrs Barker said. 'Your mother's only helping.'

'You don't know what she's like!' Violet hardly knew what she was saying. She just felt powerless, at their mercy. 'I want my babby!'

'Here she is,' Bessie said. 'Pull yourself together, girl – no call for all that.'

She deposited the little girl in Violet's arms. Violet grew calmer and gazed at her. She had such a sweet, fine face, and when she unwrapped her from the towel, her body looked in good proportion.

'Let her feed from yer tit,' Bessie suggested, leaning over and pulling Violet's old shift away to reveal her breast, her huge frame blocking out almost all the light from the window. She went as if to latch the baby on.

'I can do it,' Violet snapped, pulling away.

'Suit yourself.' Bessie drew back, hands on her hips.

Unlike the last time, when Bobby had not had the strength even to begin feeding, the little girl latched on and began to suck.

'There you go,' Bessie said, sinking on to the chair.

The baby's suckling seemed to reach right through

Violet. Her innards contracted so strongly that she gasped.

'It doesn't half hurt!'

'You'll soon get used to it,' Mrs Barker said calmly, wringing out a rag over the white pudding basin. Bloody water ran from it over her workworn fingers.

'I want Harry to see her.'

'Bull's gone off at Mount's,' Bessie said. The 'bulls' or factory sirens had gone off one after another to signal the end of a shift. 'He'll be in soon. Time we all had a cuppa tea – more than time.'

'Joyce,' Violet whispered to the child as she suckled. 'My little babby. I'm going to call you Joyce.'

By the time Harry walked in, Mrs Barker had been paid and departed, and Violet was sitting up in bed with tea and biscuits on the chair beside her. She had Joyce cradled on one arm, would hardly let go of her for a second. Although the baby had had a good feed for one so young, Violet kept looking anxiously down at her, checking to make sure she was still breathing.

'You want to put her down for a bit and drink your tea,' Bessie said. She dwarfed the chair she was sitting on.

'No!' It was almost a snarl. 'No one's taking her off me.' Tears ran down her face and fell on Joyce's forehead. 'This time, *I'm* looking after her.'

Bessie heaped sugar into her tea. She liked three big spoonfuls. 'You'll have to put her down some time, bab,' she said complacently.

Violet stared at her with narrowed eyes. *What do you know?* she thought. *You never lost any of yours. Just keep your hands off mine.* She was startled by the violence of her feelings.

They heard Harry come in then, unaware of the surprise waiting for him. 'Anyone home?'

'Yes, son,' Bessie called, grinning. 'You'd better come up!'

Violet heard him running up the stairs two at a time. She glowed with excitement. She'd done it, at last, the thing a woman was supposed to do!

In the moment he came into the room, she saw he was afraid of what he might find, and her heart went out to him, seeing how worried he'd been, even though he hardly showed it.

'You've got a little wench,' Bessie announced.

Violet looked up at him as he came bashfully to the bedside. She felt proud, yet vulnerable, needing his approval.

'Look –' Gently she pulled back the covers and showed him the crumpled baby, sleeping so trustingly with her mouth close to Violet's nipple. 'I thought we'd call her Joyce.'

Harry leaned forward, his face intent, and very tenderly stroked the tiny creature's cheek with his finger.

'She all right?' He looked anxiously at her. His son had died in his arms and he was afraid.

'Just had a good feed,' Bessie said in the background, as Violet nodded, her eyes filling with tears again. 'Looks right as rain.'

'Joyce,' he said in wonder, and she heard the catch in his voice.

Part Two

1941–3

Chapter Nineteen

1941

Joyce was five now.

She was a thin, rather fractious child with slightly squinting grey eyes, rather like her mother in looks, with blonde, wispy hair. Soon after she was born, Bessie suggested that she look after her. At first Violet had resisted. But Harry said Violet would have to go back to work: they needed the money. Of course it made perfect sense for Bessie to look after her. Joyce would be there with her nanny and her auntie Marigold – what could be better?

So Violet handed Joyce over to Bessie and went back to Vicars.

'I'll be going back to work,' she said to Harry. 'I know I've got to – even if I'd rather stop at home and look after Joycie myself. But I won't stay a week longer in this flaming dump of a house. We've got to move.'

So now they were living only a couple of roads away from Bessie, so Violet could pop round and pick up Joyce as soon as Vicars was out. They rented another two-up two-down terrace which was not, like all the houses round there, in very good repair either, but it was a step up from the wreck of a house they had first lived in. Violet made it as nice as she could, gradually turning it into a home. She bought a remnant of pretty royal blue velvet to drape over the mantel, and Harry found a battered old dresser for them to arrange their crocks on. Violet loved that, seeing her few plates all shining and propped up in a row, the cups hanging from hooks. And Marigold came round more often now they were just round the corner and, when they first got there, she sat bodging a new peg rug for the house.

Marigold didn't have much to say, but she took to Joyce, and Violet was glad to be able to give her somewhere else to go for a bit instead of being forever at home under Bessie's thumb. She would stand and rock Joyce in her arms when she was a baby for as long as it took to get her to sleep. Marigold had reached a point in her life now where she never seemed to change. She looked roughly the same, always, with lank, shoulder-length hair, dressed in one of a couple of capacious dresses, one navy, one dark green. She never seemed to get any older or to do anything different, and lived at the beck and call of everyone else. Tucked in her pocket was always a tatty collection of paper with scraps of songs written down in her slow, looping hand. Always love songs: 'Apple Blossom Time', 'Somewhere in France with You'. Her favourite song was 'South of the Border'.

'Henry Hall made the record at the Hippodrome,' she would say solemnly. 'It's lovely, that is.'

The only times she smiled, it was usually at one of the children, but it wasn't a lively vivacious smile, more a vague uptilt of her lips, accompanied, in her eyes, by a dreamy look of affection.

'Thank goodness you're here,' Violet said to her at times, when she was most exhausted. 'I don't know how I'd manage.'

She was often worn out. Joyce had been hard work. She didn't sleep well and cried a lot, but even though it was a struggle, Violet loved the fact that she had a daughter. She could take her to see Josephine, who was soon expecting again, and little Lizzie liked being the bossy older one. And the days revolved round work and Joyce's baby needs and her mom. She had to surrender to Bessie. She knew best, Violet realized, what with all those babies she'd reared. And it was the easiest thing. Family mattered more now she had her own child, and it made her feel safe and reassured knowing there was Mom to go to, with Marigold to wheel Joyce out in the old pram every afternoon. And Harry seemed happy enough being a father. He didn't go on about Australia. Not any more. Soon after Joyce was born he came home looking excited.

'You know our bit we had put away? Well, I don't reckon we'll be needing it, so I've spent a bit of it.'

He'd bought a Norton motorcycle. Violet could see from his face how delighted he was.

'Just like a kid with a toy,' she said to Jo Snell. 'I couldn't be cross with him. I never wanted to go to Australia anyway. It's too blooming far away. What would I do in Australia without you, eh?'

When Joyce was sixteen months old, Violet took her round to the Snells one Saturday afternoon, full of excitement. She knew Jo would be there with her mom and Lizzie, as they always called in on Saturdays. The Snells' house was a home from home. Jo was heavy out front with another baby. As they sat drinking tea in their cosy back room, Violet said, 'Eh, Jo – I've got summat to tell you. I've another on the way as well.'

Josephine grinned, laying a hand on her swollen stomach.

'Must be out of our flaming heads, mustn't we?'

Linda was born in March 1938, in the small hours of

a bitterly cold night. Once again Mrs Barker was in attendance, but Bessie was not there. It was so cold, they laid a bed for her downstairs and kept the range going all night. Just as things were really getting going, the meter ran out and Harry had to go down and feed it with pennies. Violet always remembered those moments, the room suddenly drenched in darkness with only a dim glow from the range, and herself isolated in the pains of labour. Somehow it made her feel strong. A few moments later they re-lit the gas mantles and everything was back to normal, though she felt she had travelled to another world.

'This one's not like Joyce!' Mrs Barker exclaimed as Violet, groaning, pushed the baby out. 'It's got black hair!'

The child was a round-faced, black-haired little girl with Harry's stamp all over her and, as she grew older, dancing brown eyes, just like his.

'She looks like Rosina,' Bessie observed when she saw her the next day. 'She were just like that, born.'

Then her face hardened, lips twisting. For a moment she forgot that she didn't mention Rosina's name. Not any more.

She gave a bitter sigh. 'Wherever *she* is.'

Chapter Twenty

A few days before her eighteenth birthday in 1936, Rosina ran away from home.

They didn't hear from her for months after, but everyone was sure she had gone to London. She went so suddenly that she didn't even take her film pictures – Jessie Matthews and the others. Bessie ripped them off the wall in fury.

'She needn't think she's coming back here when her pockets are empty. Selfish little bitch, taking off without a word! Never gives a thought to anyone else – always been the same! Well, I wash my hands of her – she's no daughter of mine any more.'

Her rage simmered endlessly. She'd lost control of Rosina. It had been coming for years – Rosina's lippiness, her lack of fear of her mother, unlike the others.

No one had ever crossed Bessie like this before. Before her own mother had died at her own hand, she'd begged Bessie to take special care of Clarence, her precious boy. Apart from two years in France, Clarence had been with her ever since, content to be under the thumb, it seemed, rather than making a life for himself.

'He was never the same any road – not after the trenches,' Bessie always said. He did little jobs for a bit, then just as suddenly stopped and sat at home.

And she had her other three children well in her control still, circling round her like planets round the sun. But Rosina had had the temerity to break off and go spinning away on a path of her own choice and without a hint of warning. Nothing had prepared Bessie for Rosina's spirit, and the older she grew the more rebellious she became.

Violet knew Rosy had become a handful but she was too caught up in her own problems during those years to see how it was going. Rosina stayed away from home more and more, haunting the streets round the theatres – the Hippodrome and Alex in town – hungry to catch a glimpse of theatre people and life.

In the Lozells Road was a photographer's business by the name of Juggins. Rosina had heard that Alfred Juggins and his son were the official photographers for the Theatre Royal in Aston, and that actors and celebrities often frequented the place to have their portraits taken. Rosina took to hanging around the shop with some of her friends and occasionally came home radiant, full of the fact that she'd seen one of the names, great or small of the acting profession, going into the shop.

'Charlie Chaplin's been in there, when he was young!'

After she disappeared, they managed to prise out of one of the other girls the fact that Rosina had begun a passionate romance with a young actor called Michael Albie, whom she had met near Juggins photographer's. Albie was entranced by Rosina's pretty looks and vivacious personality, as well as her passionate ambition to be part of the life of theatre herself. Now, for all any of them knew, she had gone to London to be with Albie.

'She'll end up on the streets with a brat in her belly and nowhere to sleep but the gutter,' Bessie decreed, with vengeful satisfaction.

It wasn't until four months later that Rosina sent a

postcard from London, light-hearted in tone, to say that she was well and happy and not to worry. There was no address on it and she did not say what she was doing.

Bessie peered at the card, turning it over and over. It was a photograph of Buckingham Palace.

'I s'pose she thinks she's going to be living in there next.'

Violet was just relieved to hear that Rosina was all right. Running off like that felt such a daring, impossible thing to do! She could no more imagine doing that herself – even as far as London – than she could going to Australia. But Rosy had always had a spark in her. Violet felt hurt that she had not confided in her, and she missed Rosy and longed to be able to see her. But Rosina obviously didn't want to be reached.

Chapter Twenty-One

The war changed their lives.

Gas masks sat in their boxes by the door, houses were blacked out and the windows taped against blast. Air-raid shelters went up and all sorts of regulations came into force. The evenings seemed long and dark, shut in the houses, and Bessie and Clarence bought a wireless.

Groups of young men disappeared into the forces, but Vicars had gone over to making ammunition and Harry's and the others' jobs were reserved occupations. They sat out what came to be known as the 'phoney war'. It was when the raids started in the autumn of 1940, with all their fear and cruelty and destruction, that the war came up close. It was with them in the long, sleepless nights, the terrible drone of the planes over-head, thin searchlights sketching like pencils across the sky over the city, in the evil glow of fire, and mornings of dust and rubble and the stink of gas.

From August 1940 Birmingham was under frequent attack and you never knew, when dawn broke after a raid, what familiar landmark would have disappeared next. The Bull Ring was blitzed at the end of August, the Market Hall, loved by so many people as a place to meet and shop, which had seemed so permanent a part of life, was smashed to pieces. It felt as if nothing could ever be the same again. And it was this time of death and fear which started to change Violet's life.

She had settled to a small, safe existence which revolved round these few streets, with all the familiarity of their blackened bricks, smoking chimney stacks and neighbourhood characters. Life consisted of her job, her daughters and husband, and her mom.

Linda was very different from Joyce. Soft and rounded, with a sweet, fleshy face and thick black hair, she was as quiet and serious as Joyce was jumpy and jealous and easily put out. Linda had a solemn, penetrating gaze. As a toddler she would stand in front of her mother, quite close to her, and just gaze at her.

'What're you looking at?' Violet would joke, trying to make her crack her face. 'Lost your tongue? Ooh, she's making me feel quite queer staring like that! Stop it, pet! I wonder what she's thinking?'

If she was thinking anything she usually didn't have the chance to do it for much longer, as Joyce, agitated at being left out, would come up and pinch her or provoke her in some other way and make her cry.

The girls spent a lot of time with Bessie. When there were daytime raids, Violet fretted at work, in the basement of Vicars which they used as a shelter. She knew her mom took the girls under the stairs. Bessie wasn't going slumming it in any public shelter. Violet and Harry's house had a bigger coal cellar than Bessie's, so they cleaned it out and Violet went down there with the girls when it got bad. There wasn't room for all of them so Harry stayed under the stairs. It was miserable and cold in the cellar and the ceiling was very low. Violet hated it. All you wanted after that was a nice cup of tea to perk you up and sometimes the water was cut off!

'I'd rather stay in bed and take my chance with their bleeding bombs,' she complained some mornings that autumn.

But soon after, something happened that made her vow never to say such a thing again.

'Ey-up!' one of the lads winked and called to her as she clocked in for work that morning. 'Best bloody night's sleep you've ever 'ad, I s'pose?'

Violet laughed grimly. 'Slept like a babby, what d'you think?'

Like everyone else, she was exhausted. It was November 1940 and the city had been pounded night after night. The row of houses along from the works had been hit; they had scrambled into Vicars through the morning drizzle, over hosepipes and piles of timber and rubble and glass, and there was a stench of sewage. One end of the front of Vicars had been blasted. Some of the windows were out and Violet could hear the sound of glass being swept up. It was always especially unnerving when the destruction came so close.

'Trying to do to us what they've done to Coventry,' people were saying. 'Bloody kraut bastards.'

Mr Riddle looked just as worn out as everyone else. Apparently he had spent the night in the cellar of the factory.

Violet went to begin work. The engines were on, the belts turning on the lathes. She looked at her machine with some affection. They were beautiful things, she thought. Today seeing the heavy iron lathe was like seeing a steady, familiar face amid all the chaos. She looked round for Josephine, and saw with a pang of disquiet that there was no one at her machine. Jo was usually in before her, full of energy as always, calling out some clever remark like, 'Decided to have a lie-in, did you?' because she was quicker at getting up and getting her children ready.

Violet tried to tell herself that there must be a good reason – perhaps Lizzie or little Sam was poorly, or Jo was ill herself. But when an hour had passed and other people were asking, she couldn't stand worrying. She feared the worst, sick with dread.

She crossed the shop floor to find Mr Riddle. His face was pale and she could see the tired lines round his eyes.

'I can't think straight worrying about Josephine,' she said.

'Oh God – I know,' Mr Riddle said wearily. The gulf between the gaffer and everyone else on the factory floor had narrowed with all the troubles. Mr Riddle was a kind, humane man who looked out for his workers. 'It was a hell of a night last night. I've never known it as bad. Look, love – go and see. It's only up the road, isn't it?'

'Ta ever so much,' Violet said. She could tell Mr Riddle was worried too; he had a rather soft spot for Jo, who was one of his fastest workers and always cheerful.

Hanging up her overall, she hurriedly put on her coat and hat. It was still grey and drizzly outside. She thought she'd never seen such a dismal sight as that road, a great gap where five or six houses had been taken out. The end of a terrace had been destroyed; the bomb had smashed into the court behind, leaving what was usually an invisible yard of dwellings suddenly open to view in all its glorious squalor. At the end the three lavs were on full view, the door of one swinging open. The sight made Violet's heart sink. She felt sick.

'Oh God, Jo – please be all right!' she found herself muttering desperately. 'Why are you so late, you silly sod? Couldn't you have just got there on time today?'

She could hardly bear to turn into the Snells' street for fear of what she might find.

And what she saw when she did left her in no doubt. She stopped, stunned.

'Oh God above . . . !' Her hand went to her lips and her legs started to shake. She could hardly believe what was in front of her.

There were fire engines at the end of the road, and an ambulance. The right-hand section of the street, and the Snells' house, number twenty-two, was gone. There was nothing but piles of rubble, smashed sections of walls with stained strips of wallpaper clinging to them and the debris of lives – a smashed pram, a kettle, a rent book, sodden among the heaps of bricks. The mess was unbelievable. Everything was wet, and stinking and so, so sad-looking.

Numbly, Violet scrambled across the mess to one of the ARP team. He was a middle-aged man, his moustache grey with dust.

'Number twenty-two? They're my friends . . .'

Silently he waved his hand over the wreckage.

'Where was it?'

'About there.'

He shook his head. 'I'm sorry, love. This was the bit that really took it. There's no one alive in there. No chance.'

'But . . .' She couldn't take this in. 'They would've been under the stairs – Jo, her mom, the two kiddies . . .'

'They've brought them out already.' His voice was quiet and gentle, and he was shaking his head. 'All of 'em. I'm sorry. Poor souls.'

Violet stood in the road as he moved away, shoulders hunched. She was so much in shock that she didn't know how long she stood there, shaking and chilled to the bone. It was only when an ambulance turned into the street and hooted at her to move that she came to again.

It hit Violet very hard.

Days went by before she could even take it in or begin to cry over it. She had been very fond of all the Snells. They had been almost family to her. And worst of all was the loss of Jo, her best friend, whom she could tell her heart to, share all the everyday happenings of life with, and the laughter. She had always loved Jo's sunny outlook at work.

'Smile and the world smiles with you – weep and you weep alone,' Jo used to say.

But there'd be no more smiles now.

Once Violet's emotion began to release itself, she only had to look at Joyce and Linda and think about Jo's little ones and the tears would start to flow. Especially as Joyce kept asking about them.

'Why don't we see Lizzie? I want to go to Lizzie's house.'

'Lizzie doesn't live there any more,' Violet told her. 'I'm sorry, bab, but we won't be able to see Lizzie and Sam any more.'

Joyce's little face creased with displeasure. 'What about Auntie Jo?'

'Not her either.'

One day she'd have to tell them that the Germans had killed Auntie Jo and Lizzie and Sam. But not today.

Violet felt terribly lonely. 'I can't stand being at Vicars now,' she told Bessie. 'Harry says I'm being silly, that I know everyone else there. But it's not the same. It's getting me down.'

'Well – it's not the only place in the world to work,' Bessie said. 'They're all crying out for munitions workers – and the pay might be better than you're getting at Vicars.'

Violet stared at her. She realized that while she had needed to have a moan she had not seriously thought about changing her job. She wasn't good at changing things on her own, she realized. She just let things drift along and happen to her.

Chapter Twenty-Two

During that winter of the Blitz, Harry's mom fell ill. She couldn't swallow and the flesh was dropping off her.

Then one February night, in the small hours, when big flakes of snow were falling, one of Mrs Martin's neighbours came to fetch Harry. Violet listened to their footsteps dying away along the street. A train whistled in the eerie quietness. She knew her mother-in-law did not have long to live.

Before things had become really bad with his mother, Harry was walking along Summer Lane one Saturday afternoon with his pal Stan 'Goosey' Gosling. As they crossed over Asylum Road, Harry nudged Goosey and jerked his head towards a man walking away from them along the cobbled street.

'See that bloke? That's my father.'

Goosey's brow wrinkled. 'I thought your old man'd passed on?'

'Might as well've done.'

'Well, ain't you going to speak to him?'

'Ain't seen him in ten year or more. Why should I bother now?'

'I just thought . . . 'E's your dad, that's all.'

'Bugger 'im.' Harry's expression was mutinous.

But Harry dithered on the corner as his father moved away. He couldn't seem to leave it.

'You could follow – see where he goes. He don't have to see you.'

With an awkward nod, half making as if to reject the idea, then changing his mind, Harry said gruffly, 'All right. But he'd better not see.'

They dashed along Asylum Road after the man, who was almost out of sight by now. A woman pushing a pram laden with coal piled curses on them as they almost crashed into her.

'He must've been away and come back,' Harry panted. 'He can't've been round here all this time – we'd've seen him.'

Harry's father turned right into Alma Street. He stopped for a moment outside the Sheep Shears Works to talk to someone and Harry and Goosey shrank back, but then he walked almost to the far end near Six Ways, crossed over the street and disappeared up an entry.

Harry stopped, only then realizing how much his heart was pounding. Suddenly he wanted, overpoweringly, to know about his father. Where had he been? Who was he living with now? Did he ever give his family, his kids, a thought?

He gave a shrug and said indifferently, 'Oh well. Least we know where the silly sod is, any road.'

Two days after Mrs Martin had breathed her last on that silent, snowy night, Harry was standing alone by the entry in Alma Street only streets away from home. The road looked a mess, edged with filthy clods of frozen snow. For reasons he could not explain to himself, he had not mentioned to Tom and Marj, the brother and sister he was closest to, that he knew where their father was or that he was coming here.

'Right, you bugger.' His breath formed white clouds

on the freezing air. Harry's chest was so tight he could hardly breathe. Horrified, he realized he might cry, and had to walk up and down the road for a minute or two more to get himself under control. He braced himself, pulling his shoulders back, then strode along the entry. At the entrance, he stopped.

'*Christ.*'

He wasn't exactly used to living in luxury, but this place was among the most dreary and squalid he'd ever seen. It was small and dark, overshadowed by the back wall of a factory, and there were rubbish and filth all across it. In one corner lay a pool of stagnant water, half frozen today, and in a pile of muck round the bottom of the lamp he could see the remains of a sodden rag doll. Its grey face was turned sorrowfully towards him. There was a foul stench on the air, even in the cold. *It must pong like hell in here when it's hot*, he thought.

He stood at a loss for a moment, then a woman came out from the house behind him. She was thin and dreary-looking, not especially young, her hair roughly scraped back, and carrying a pail of ash. She stared at him with a hostile expression, pulling her black shawl round her.

'What d'yer want?'

'I'm looking for . . .' He stumbled over the words. 'For a bloke called Josiah Martin.'

''E's inside,' she said indifferently. 'Asleep – as usual.' And she walked away, the pail causing her to lean over to one side.

Harry walked into the house, as cold inside as out, as the fire was not lit. The stink of urine overpowered everything else. It was a stench he always associated with his father and he was overcome with shame. The stench was coming from another bucket, by the range, which was acting as a po'.

There was a ragged chair in the corner. Harry made sense of the shape sprawled in it, taking in first the feet, toes peeping through black socks like mushrooms pushing up through soil. The right big toe was showing, the nail yellow and gnarled. His eyes followed the short legs, stocky body, bloated belly covered by a stained shirt, the buttons straining. He could see dark hairs in the spaces where the shirt was forced open.

It was as if he was avoiding the face at first because he knew what he would see. He was very like his father. When he at last forced himself to focus on the jowly, unshaven face, with its drinker's hue, the unkempt hair, once black, like his, now grizzled, it was with the horror of seeing himself as he might be twenty years on. What he might – was even destined to – become.

Memories rushed into his mind: his father when they were young, and he used to take them fishing to Edgbaston reservoir or even right out to Sutton Park. But often he'd stop, long before they wanted to leave, and go to a pub. He and Tommy and the others spent hours sitting outside pubs waiting for him to come out. There was the Christmas when Mom'd scrimped for weeks to get them all a decent meal, carried a joint of beef to the baker's to be cooked in the oven, made everything as nice as she could – and then they couldn't find him. He rolled in at five o'clock, long after they'd all finished eating, and Mom had sat crying over the dirty crocks. Eventually, though, she'd said, 'Well, sod him. You kids are my family, not him.' And for once, the only time he could ever remember, they all sat round and played cards and I-Spy and all the games they could think of that afternoon. And when Dad came home, they showed him how they were laughing and didn't need him and Mom acted as if it didn't matter if he was there or not. Harry was nine that year. And the memory of Mom's face as Dad came through the door, barely able to stand, made him want to sob like a child now, standing over him. Then he wanted to take a rock and smash his head in. He looked older. So much older.

Harry took in a deep, shuddering breath. That miserable cow of a woman would be back soon. He didn't want her around, seeing this.

'Oi – ' He shook his father's shoulder and spoke very brusquely. 'You – Josiah Martin – wake up.'

He was quite surprised how easy the man was to rouse, when you considered how deep his drunken slumber could be.

'Wha – ?' He woke abruptly, the eyes snapping open, yawning and scratching at the salt and pepper stubble on his cheek. Sitting up, he gave a loud, rasping belch. He stared round, not seeming to make sense of anything.

'D'you know who I am?' Harry said. He could feel aggression rising in him. *You're my bloody father!* he wanted to shout. *You'd better know who I am or else! Where've you been all these years, you drunken bastard?*

Josiah's bloodshot eyes turned on him. Harry could see he was having trouble focusing. His hands were shaking and his whole body seemed to quiver. His breathing, through his nose, was very loud. Narrowing his eyes, he said, 'Tommy?'

'Guess again, Dad.' He'd at least realized it was one of his sons. He and Tommy were also alike. Harry's hands, in his jacket pockets, were clenched into fists.

Josiah stared at him, at a loss.

'You one of my sons? Can't remember yer name.'

'Harry. It's Harry.'

'Oh ar. Harry.' He considered this, staring into the dead fireplace. 'Why're you 'ere?'

'Mom died. Two nights ago.'

His head tilted round. 'Elsie?'

'You can remember *her* name then.'

The savagery in his tone seemed to cut the air.

Josiah was about to speak when the woman with the ash pail came back in. Harry loathed her on sight. She walked smartly to the fireplace and slammed the pail down.

'Who's this then? What's going on?'

'I'm his son,' Harry said. 'And it's none of your cowing business what's going on.'

She was about to have a go, Harry could see, her face puckering up hatefully. He strode out of there before he punched the miserable bint in the face.

'Funeral's Friday,' he said on the way out. 'Eleven o'clock. St Mary's.'

The day of the funeral he still felt all the time as if he was going to explode. It was freezing, and wet. Couldn't have been a nastier day if it tried. The snow was all gone but there was a mizzling cold rain and the wind was bitter. He felt everything was against him.

'Put that fag out,' he snarled at Violet as they reached the church.

Smoke, smoke – all she ever bloody did these days. Like a cowing chimney.

'All right,' Violet said carefully. She dropped the stub and ground it out with her heel. His feelings softened for a moment. She was a looker all right when she took the trouble. Her hair was shoulder-length and she'd curled the ends today. He could see glimpses of its gold against the black hat and coat. Her blue eyes, deep as pools, contained the sad, yearning look which had always made him feel protective towards her. She was even thinner now of course – tired-looking. Jo Snell going like that had knocked her, he knew. The sight of her moved him. He knew he loved her and wanted things to be right, but all he could feel was this tight rage and grief which blocked out everything else.

She was being gentle with him, he knew. Sorry for him because of his mom, even though he knew she could never stand the woman. She had Joycie and Linda hanging on to her skirts, all in their best clothes and bewildered by the solemn carry-on of a funeral. Little Linda looked up at him with those dark, inscrutable eyes, as if waiting for something.

'I've got to go,' he said, turning away.

He was a bearer. He had to carry his mom's coffin into the church. No good thinking about anything else. Nudging the edges of his mind all the time was the question: would Dad come? Did he care whether he did or not?

Twenty years Mom and Dad were married, he calculated as they sat in a row in the pews. The rain was still on his coat. He felt out of place in a church. It was cold and the pews were hard.

The coffin was in front of them in the aisle. He found it hard to take in that Mom was in there, that he'd never see her again. For a moment the tight feeling in him increased so that it was almost unbearable. It frightened him, the way he felt. He couldn't make sense of it. As if his whole body was about to break open.

'We brought nothing into this world and it is certain we will carry nothing out . . .'

The vicar's words passed by him, barely heard. Suddenly, though, Linda, who was standing beside him, reached up and with her little hand caught hold of the ends of his fingers. Harry looked down. The child was gazing up at him with such naked trust that he suddenly wanted to weep. He took her hand properly and squeezed it.

I'm her dad, he thought, as if he'd only realized it for the first time. He could see himself in her, the way she looked. The thought filled him with joy and fear. Whatever kind of father did he know how to be?

They were sitting and the vicar was reading: 'For a thousand years in thy sight are but as yesterday . . .'

There was a thump at the back of the church as the door opened and a bang as it closed. Harry felt the hairs stand up on the back of his head. Somehow he could not bring himself to turn round, not while they were all sitting facing the front. Whoever it was must have sat down and it was quiet again.

But within a couple of minutes, before the vicar had got to the end of the readings, they all heard it start, low at first, then louder and unmistakable; the lurching, indecipherable singing of a drunk man. A drunk man who was the husband of the woman being commended to her grave.

The eruption that had been waiting to happen inside Harry began then. He loosed Linda's hand and got up from his seat, charging down the long aisle of the church to where Josiah was sitting, slumped to one side in the back row.

'Get out!' He seized him by the lapels of his jacket and hoiked him to his feet. 'Get yourself out of here – now!'

Outside the church door, Harry had no words any

more. For the second time in his life he laid into his father, holding him pinned against the wall with one hand and punching and punching him with the other. There was no holding back on it, no reserve: all self-control was lost in the bursting floodgates of his rage and pain. Josiah made no sound except a winded 'urrgh' noise when Harry punched him hard in the stomach and he collapsed, sagging to the floor.

'Harry – don't, for God's sake, what're you doing?' Violet was beside him.

'Don't, love – stop it! You'll kill him!'

She was pulling at his arm, trying to prevent him doing any more. Josiah lay on his side on the wet path. He was straining to breathe, after the winding he had taken from Harry's punch.

'You could've killed him!' she said. He could see the horror in her eyes but could not really take in what he might have done in his rage. 'D'you want to go to prison? Come on – we'd better sit him up.'

They managed to wedge Josiah in a sitting position against the wall. He groaned and mumbled and his face was all cut about, but Harry had done no more damage than that.

For a moment the two of them stood, stunned, in the rain. The organ was playing inside the church.

'Christ,' Harry said, his voice beginning to crack. 'Just look at him.'

'Oh, love,' Violet said.

Her eyes were full of emotion and she went to put her arms round him, but he couldn't stand her affection, her pity.

'Don't,' he said. And pushed her away.

Chapter Twenty-Three

October 1941

Violet stood by the gas stove, grimacing at the pans of butter beans and boiling fish. Harry was bound to moan. What was she supposed to do? She'd never been a good cook but now, with all the shortages and rationing, it was harder than ever.

Eyeing the clock on the mantel she wiped her hands on her apron. Saturday evening, and she was alone, as usual. She never knew when Harry would come home. Most nights he went to the pub and she didn't know what mood he'd be in when he got back. He seemed to be always frustrated and angry. With petrol in short supply, he couldn't take the bike out much now and it was under a tarpaulin out at the back. It had all got much worse since his mother died. There were still rare moments of tenderness between them, but the good times had grown fewer.

'Let's see what you've got to say.'

She switched on the wireless which stood in pride of place with its accumulator on the sideboard. Harry had come home with it a few months ago and she loved having it. He was spending more money these days – had given up on saving all the time. The wireless was company and cheered the place up no end. She missed Jo Snell and the rest of the family horribly. The ache of it never quite left her. Without Jo as a friend and with Harry hardly ever in, she was very lonely.

Making friends didn't come very easily to her. But

she tried to make things nice and keep herself looking presentable. It seemed a bit daft, the war on and everything, all those ships going down and Russian names she'd never heard before. The raids seemed to be over. There'd been warnings, of course, but not much in the way of actual raids since the really bad ones in April. But you still had to keep cheerful somehow, put a face on, a bit of lipstick and powder. She had let her hair grow over the past months, put some rollers in at night so it hung in pretty waves on her shoulders.

Humming along to the wireless, she went to the back door. The girls were playing out in the little yard in the grey light. She could see the barrage balloon – 'our' balloon, as the girls called it. A sycamore tree on the scrubby bit of ground the other side of the wall had shed its papery brown leaves over into their yard.

'Joycie! Linda – get in here for tea!'

'Mom – they'm birds, they'm flying!' Linda cried, her plump hands releasing a drifting shower of leaves into the air.

'Birds,' Violet muttered, shaking her head. That child was a proper one for seeing things a queer way.

But she smiled and leaned against the doorframe, watching them. It had been a long day, nothing but hard graft and kiddies, but it was a treat to see their cheeks rosy in the biting air, especially Linda, whose round face seemed to glow. Whenever she stopped to look at her girls she was struck by the difference in them – Joycie, five now, was thin as a twig, with her pale, wispy hair, and Linda, three, was sturdier like Harry, with his brown eyes and thick black locks. You'd never guess they were sisters. Even the way they laughed was quite different. Joyce had a high, thin giggle and Linda chuckled with a rich gurgle in her throat.

Breathing in deeply, Violet relished the smell of fallen leaves, mixed with smoke from the house chimneys. Mrs McEvoy next door was shouting to be heard over all her children. *Eamonn, stop that – stop it now!* She was forever yelling. Violet felt a moment of contentment, standing there by the glow of sycamore leaves. Then Joyce kicked up a shower of them, lifting a stone with them which hit Linda on the side of the head.

'Owwww!' Linda howled.

'Oh, Joyce – what d'you have to go and do that for?' Violet snapped. 'Get in now, the pair of you.'

'Stinks in here,' Joyce said resentfully. 'Why do we have to have fish?'

Sighing, Violet sat them down at the table.

'Urgh,' Joyce whined, seeing the pale beans being doled out. 'Don't like those.'

'Nor do any of us,' Violet said sharply. 'But that's what there is today. That or go hungry.'

She felt the boredom that accompanied the children's mealtimes come over her in a wash, like fatigue, as if her limbs were suddenly too heavy. It was a constant struggle, keeping it all going with rations, let alone trying to cook anything they really liked.

Joyce groaned and picked up her fork, leaning on one elbow and pouting.

'How many beans make five?' Violet asked, trying to distract them.

Linda's dark brows dipped in a frown. 'Five, dafty.'

'You calling me dafty?'

'Don't *like* fish. And I don't want beans. They're nasty.' Joyce was moving them round the plate as if they were dead beetles. A couple of them flicked off the edge of the plate.

'Oh, shut your face and eat them, for God's sake.'

Violet got up and fished in her pocket for her Woodbines. They were in paper wrappers now – it saved on cardboard. She lit up and stood over by the wireless. George Formby was singing and she managed a smile, recovering her temper.

'. . . as a certain little lady passes by . . .' she sang, conducting with her cigarette so that the smoke drew circles in the air. 'Eat up, Joycie.'

The door rattled and Violet felt herself tense up. Harry! How much booze would he have put away this time? His dark, handsome features appeared round the door. Not enough, then, for him to be scowling and in a temper.

'Hello, ladies!' he cried jovially, flinging his cap at the hook behind the door. It fell on the floor.

'Missed by miles!' Joyce giggled. The girls immediately sensed his good mood.

Clownishly, Harry stooped to pick it up and try again. He missed two more times, messing about, and Joyce and Linda giggled. Violet relaxed a little.

'There!' He managed it finally and turned, swaying a little, an amiable grin on his face.

'How's my wenches?' He circled the table, shrugging his jacket off. He was strong and square, his muscular shoulders appearing about to burst out of his shirt, and he seemed to take up most of the room. Bending over the table, he tickled each of the girls under the chin and they laughed, squirming.

'Do it again, Dad!' Joyce got up and tugged at him. They were so hungry for his attention. Often he barely did more than grunt at them.

Violet doled out more of the beans and fish for Harry and herself. She felt light-hearted as well. At least for now it was going to be all right!

Harry stood across the table from her, and his face changed. He looked instantly sober and regretful, but behind this she could also sense an excitement. She would never forget the look on his face at that moment.

'Got summat to tell you, Vi.'

'What?' She was holding the plate of food out to him.

'Me and Goosey – we've joined up.'

'*What?*' She put the plate down with a bang. Beans spilled on to the table. 'You can't've – what d'you mean?'

'The army. We're going. The both of us.'

'But . . . You can't! You're reserved occ— Mr Riddle won't let you!'

'He's said I can. I've asked him – a few times. He was down the pub earlier on and he said, "Well, lad – I can tell you're just going to keep on and on and wear me down. If you're that restless you'll only go upsetting everyone – you'd better go with the others."'

Violet pulled out the chair and sat down, as her legs would no longer hold her.

'But – you don't have to go, do you? They want you in the factory! You mean it's what *you* want, to go off and leave us?' Her voice was starting to thicken with tears.

He came round behind her and put his hands on her shoulders; the warm feel of how he used to touch her made her weep.

'I don't want to leave *you*. That ain't it. I just . . .' He sounded completely sober now, and sad. 'You know me, Vi – I've always wanted to get out of here. I'm a silly sod, I know – itchy feet. Just want life to be . . . *bigger* than anything I've ever seen. Never thought I was going to do it, like, not now, with the kiddies and everything. But there's blokes going off and ... I don't want to be left behind.' He shrugged. 'Won't be for long, I don't s'pose.'

He sounded apprehensive, as if only now was it sinking in what he had done.

She turned to him, wiping her face. The girls were watching in silence and she didn't want to upset them.

'Oh God, Harry – why d'you have to go? I need you here – I can't do all this on my own. How'm I ever going to manage?'

'You'll manage.' He kissed the top of her head. 'You're my missis – and you're much stronger than you think.'

Chapter Twenty-Four

He left a few days later, for basic training. The night before he went, they lay together in their room with the leaking roof. It was raining and the drops fell with a metallic 'plink' into the pail underneath.

They made love with a tenderness that had been missing for a long time. She lay resting on his strong, stocky body afterwards, her cheek resting on the V of black, wiry hair on his chest. He curved his arm round her and laid his hand on her head.

'Wait for me, won't you?' he said quietly, and she could hear that he was frightened, although he wanted to go. Frightened of what was facing him, and that everything would have changed by the time he came back. 'I'll be able to think of you – in this house, the girls and everything.'

She reached up and kissed his cheek, her tears coming again. If only it was always like this – this closeness between them. For the first time in such a long time she could feel she loved him, and had a glimpse of a kind of heaven that she had always longed for. Why did it have to be snatched away now?

'I don't want you to go!'

'I'm no good to you.'

She raised her head. 'What d'you mean? Course you are!'

'Nah. Look at my old man. I'll be no better, in the long run.'

Whatever she said, that he wasn't like that, it seemed to make no difference and when he spoke like that his eyes were very sad.

He left very early the next day, when the girls were still in bed. Before he opened the door he took her in his arms once again and looked down at her.

'I just have to go. Don't really know why. But I love you. I do.'

Violet stood at the door in the dawn light, with her coat over her nightdress, and watched him walk away, past the run-down houses of the streets he had so long wanted to escape.

I'm all on my own was all Violet could think, for days. She felt desolate and frightened. What on earth am I going to do?

Out of habit, she did what she had always done. She turned to Bessie. There was no Josephine, no husband. Bessie was already looking after the girls, as well as Gladys and Charlie's two boys. It felt easier to go back to being Bessie's girl than try to do anything else for herself.

Every morning she was up early, pulling back the blackout curtains in the hope of some light to get ready by, though winter was coming fast now. She got Joyce ready for school and took both of them along Summer Lane to her mom's. Bessie made sure Joyce got to school all right and had Linda for the day. It gave Violet a soft feeling inside, seeing them playing in the yard with Colin and Norman, where she'd played out not so long ago herself. Somehow it made her feel safe, as if amid all the destruction there was something that wouldn't ever change.

'Give me your ration-book,' Bessie said, soon after Harry left. 'No point in us both making tea, is there? Waste of gas. We'll all have it together.'

Violet hesitated for a moment. Wasn't this just what she had wanted to escape from? From Bessie being in charge of everything? But it was so much easier, and nice not to go home to an empty house and know no one else was going to walk in through the door that night. Charlie and Gladys took the boys every night and went home for their tea, but Violet stayed and ate with Bessie and Clarence and Marigold and the girls. Even Clarence was working more now, in munitions, and was full of importance about it.

So Violet did as Bessie told her. The more she stayed away from home, the more she could forget how alone she was.

Chapter Twenty-Five

In December they all went to the flicks together and saw the Pathé news about how the Japanese had bombed America at Pearl Harbor. It had been all everyone talked about at Vicars for the past days.

'If we've got to fight the bleeding Japs an' all, there'll be no end to it,' Clarence said. He was full of opinions these days.

However, in the Wiles family even the news of the attack on Pearl Harbor faded into insignificance compared with the news received a few days later. Violet had just come in, after trudging along the dark street from work.

'Look at this –' Bessie, tight-lipped, went to the mantelpiece and fetched out an envelope.

Violet stared at the looping handwriting. There was something familiar about it. Bessie watched with her arms folded. As Violet turned the envelope round, something fell out. She gasped at the photograph which lay on the table. There, after a silence of almost five years: Rosina.

'Is that Rosy?' she cried excitedly. 'Oh, my goodness, look at her! She looks like Jessie Matthews!'

Joyce and Linda ran up, attracted by the excitement, and they all pored over the picture. Rosina was dressed in a white hat with a black feather in the band, the brim upturned at the front, and a white dress bordered with black at the neck. Lacy white gloves reached almost to her elbows. Her dark hair was bobbed level with her chin and her eyebrows had been plucked to thin, elegant lines. She looked at once provocative and sweet.

'Who's that?' Joyce demanded.

'That's your auntie Rosina,' Violet said, staring at the picture, still hardly believing it. 'It *is* her, isn't it? I mean you can see it is, only I can hardly believe . . . Oh, my word, look at her!' She felt a sudden surge of longing for her little sister. Marigold also stood beside them, quietly looking.

'It's her, all right,' Bessie said. Her voice was full of bitterness. Rosina had long escaped her control. Yet look at her! Violet thought. There she was, so beautiful and obviously making a go of it.

Joyce was pulling a letter from the envelope.

'Read it, Nana – read it to us!'

For a moment Violet saw a hunted expression cross her mother's bullish features.

'I ain't reading it!' The aggression was back.

'Can't you read, Nana?' Joyce laughed.

There was a terrible silence.

'Get your mother to read it. I can't be bothered with it.' And Bessie turned her back and busied herself by the range as if she couldn't care less.

'Give it here, Joycie. Ooh – ' Violet raised the blue paper to her nose. 'This paper smells nice!'

'Perfume.' Bessie tutted. 'Just like that one to drench her paper in perfume.'

There was only part of an address at the top. It just said, 'Clapham, London.'

'You might as well read it out to everyone,' Bessie ordered.

Dear Mom and everyone,

Thought it was time I dropped you a line to show you how I'm getting along. I have had a few parts lately and this is the best – running every night this month and I'm fit to drop! All going very well and I might be heading for wedding bells soon. I'll keep you posted.

Love to Violet, and Marigold and Charlie and Clarence. I'll drop by and see you all one day.

Rosina. xx

Violet looked up through her tears and to her surprise saw that Marigold's eyes had filled up as well. It was the first time she had seen her sister display any real emotion in a long time.

'Oh, Mari – It's so nice to hear from our Rosy again, isn't it? If only she'd come back. I don't half miss her!'

Marigold nodded and blew her nose.

'Little madam – if I saw her again I'd have a thing or two to say.' Bessie banged the frying pan down hard on the hob. Her body seemed to vibrate with fury.

It was maddening, of course, like Rosina always was, not giving a proper address and hardly saying anything. But she looked so pretty, so successful, and Violet ached to see her again and hear all about her life. Her own seemed suddenly so very drab and unadventurous in comparison. But Rosina wouldn't tell them where she was living or in which theatre she was playing. Was she so afraid of them coming to find her? Why? What had they done? And that hurt and made her feel rejected and angry.

'You'd think she could have let us know her address, wouldn't you?'

'Let me see it again!' Linda almost snatched the

picture from her. Her eyes seemed to drink in the sight of Rosina, but she was confused. 'Who's that lady?'

'Our auntie, stupid,' Joyce said.

Bessie shrugged angrily. 'Give it here, Linda. We'll put it away. She obviously don't want anything to do with the likes of us any more. Thinks she's far too good for us.'

But Violet noticed that she did not put the picture back in the envelope. Instead she propped it back behind the jug so you could just see Rosina peeping out from behind it, full of dark mischief.

'It's time I shook myself up a bit,' Violet decided, after they got home that night.

All evening, Joyce and Linda had been agog for stories about their mysterious auntie Rosina, whom neither of them could remember. As they walked home, feeling their way along in the darkness, Linda said, 'Is it dark where Auntie Rosina is?'

'Yes, I s'pect so,' Violet said absently. 'She's only down London.'

Yet the question didn't seem such a silly one. London, and Rosina's life, were another world to her altogether, one where she could imagine that the sun shone all the time.

Once she'd got the girls to bed, she sat downstairs, the windows blacked out. She felt restless and turned on the wireless. It was Thursday, *ITMA* day, and she distracted herself laughing at the antics of Colonel Chinstrap, Mrs Mopp and Sophie Tuckshop. But when the show was over her unquiet feelings had grown rather than quietened. She clicked the wireless off and sat there, hearing the tick of the clock and the murmuring of the McEvoys next door. She thought about Rosina, all her impatient, bounding energy.

'Oh, Rosina,' she whispered, 'you're the end, you really are.'

The sense of exasperation with her sister was still strong, but mixed with the powerful desire to see her was a deep longing of her own. Hadn't she once wanted more from life? How had she spent these years? Having her girls, it was true, but running round after Harry, appeasing his every mood, trying to keep him and his love. Had she anything left now of herself?

I'm only twenty-six, she found herself thinking. That's not that old. And Harry's gone. What's going to happen to my life? Am I just going to go to work and come back and sit here like this now, night after night? The war could go on for ever!

Turning the light off, she went upstairs and in the dark pulled back the curtain. There was not much to see except darkness and the even denser black of houses picked out by the thin moonlight. She slid the window up and stood shivering in the cold air, elbows on the sill.

What is there out there? she wondered, her thoughts wheeling like a bird. Beyond Aston, and Birmingham, way beyond to the sea, to other countries, other sights. She had never seen any of them, and knew she probably never would, but tonight she wanted to fly out over the rooftops, to spread herself into something, anything different and bigger. She stood there for a long time, the cold air stinging her face.

The image of Rosina in her finery stayed peeping out from behind Bessie's jug. Violet saw it there every day when she had tea with the girls. It seemed to haunt her.

That was when she started really to take notice of the recruitment drive for more women to staff the factories.

'Conscription for wenches now, it says 'ere,' Clarence read from the paper one evening. He showed the paper to Bessie, who looked up from her knitting to run an eye idly over the page.

'You read it – I've got my hands full.'

The government were conscripting women between the ages of twenty and thirty for war work.

''Ere – that's you, Vi,' she said.

'I'm already *doing* war work.' Violet was wiping semolina off Linda's hands.

'It says unmarried women, any road,' Clarence said. 'They ought to be doing their bit.' Though only forty-six, he was already stooped and full of ponderous statements.

'What about Marigold?' Violet said. It seemed odd no one had thought of it before.

Marigold was bent over one of her scraps of paper. The song sheets, Violet called them. Her puffy face looked across at them as if roused from a deep sleep.

'What?' she said.

But Bessie was already dismissing it. 'Don't talk daft. What use would she be? They don't want the retarded ones.'

'She could do summat,' Clarence said. 'They take all sorts now.'

But Bessie wasn't listening.

'If you take my advice, you'll go in search of better wages, Violet,' Clarence said, eyes still on the paper. 'At one of them bigger firms. Dunlop pay better'n what you're getting.'

Within days, three people had talked to her about the big works at Witton, not far away, where Kynoch's, the ICI factory, were recruiting munitions workers. And there was a smaller firm not far from Kynoch's called Midwinters, looking to recruit women to train. It felt like a sign. She had to do *something* to make life different. And Vicars had never been the same without Josephine. Every day there was a reminder of what she had lost.

By the next week she had handed in her notice at Vicars, despite the protests of Mr Riddle, and been taken on at Midwinters.

Chapter Twenty-Six

'Right, then – I'm the lucky so-and-so who's been given the job of training you lot.'

The man was tall and gangling, with a comical, thick-lipped face. He rolled his eyes in theatrical despair, looking over the six women before him, and added chirpily, 'What a shower. Old Adolf'd be shaking in his shoes at the sight of you lot.'

Of course they all giggled, and this provoked more eye-rolling and a contemptuous waggling of his head.

'Saints alive. Bunch of girls. I'm Gilbert Cook. You can call me Bert – just so long as that's the only thing you call me!'

They were standing in the yard at the back of Mid-winters, and not far away from them were two tanks in varying stages of assembly. All of them kept blowing on their hands in the freezing cold, though Gilbert Cook seemed oblivious to the arctic temperature and didn't offer any sympathy. They were all kitted out in scratchy brown boiler-suits, including Gilbert, who was so tall that the trousers dangled comically round his shins. Violet felt drab and lumpish in this get-up.

She eyed the other women. The one nearest to her was so skinny and frail she looked as if she'd snap, and had red hair and scared rabbit eyes. One was big and sullen-looking, with thick black hair and mannish hands that looked as if she might break your neck without much provocation. The third one had pretty chestnut hair and seemed rather posh and confident and the other two ... Violet had blinked the first time she looked at them. They must be identical twins! Both small and mousy and very young-looking, with thin brown hair and exactly the same pale, squinting faces.

Violet's heart sank. She was shy at making friends and none of this lot looked very promising.

Gilbert was telling them that the main works were over in Washwood Heath, making tanks – Cromwells, Valentines, Tetrarchs ...

'... but we get to finish some of 'em off. So – it now befalls me to drum into you lucky lot, the rudiments of welding ... Come on – inside. I s'pose we'll have to start somewhere.'

As they turned, almost rigid with cold, to go back inside the works, to Violet's surprise the red-haired girl came up to her and, nodding mischievously at Bert's swinging trouser legs, murmured, 'D'you think our wee man's expecting a flood?'

Violet giggled. She'd have liked to think of something clever to say in reply but nothing came to mind. The girl had a strong accent.

'We could sew a bit of gold braid round the bottom for him!' The red-haired girl was wearing bright red lipstick which clashed with her hair but the overall effect was very cheerful. 'I'm Muriel, by the way. Who're you?'

'Violet.'

'Well – nice to meet you, Violet.'

The girl's blue eyes were full of real friendliness. Violet immediately felt better.

*

They spent the next weeks being trained in the art of welding.

From the beginning the women seemed to fall into pairs. The twins, who were twenty-one but looked fourteen and had never been parted at any stage in their lives, were called Maureen and Doreen and seemed, as Bert put it, to be 'flaming welded together' themselves. Joan, the posh one, was from Sutton Coldfield, and she worked with the big girl, May. And Violet and Muriel worked together from the start. Muriel was from Ayr.

'My mother died last year,' Muriel told Violet the first day as they stood in the canteen at Midwinters, nursing mugs of tea with frozen hands. 'It's not been the same back home. I did nae want to leave my sister, but then they conscripted the both of us anyways. She's gone into the army, so I thought well, that's that then. I'll be on my way.'

'What about your dad?' Violet asked.

'Och no –' Muriel said grimly. 'I was nae staying home wi' that miserable old sod. And I was only working in the tobacconist's – it was just a wee little job so I could be near my mum. Not much for the war effort that. I would have trained up there, but they did nae like Catholics.'

Violet was overcome with admiration. Here was she, after being spurred on from a distance by Rosina, thinking she was making a break in her life, and she'd only gone up the road. Muriel had come hundreds of miles – and she looked such a fragile little thing!

'Have you got somewhere to live?'

'Aye – with a lady along the way. I only got here yesterday so I don't know what it'll be like.' She shrugged. 'Who d'you live with?'

'Just my girls – my old man's in the army.'

'You're lucky then.' Muriel's lipstick lips parted in a grin to show a line of uneven teeth. 'And you're bonny too – some people have all the luck!'

The two of them quickly became friends, thrown together by the work. Both of them soon became adept at welding. Muriel had little, nimble fingers and was given intricate jobs if there were any.

'It's no different from decorating cakes when you come down to it,' she said. 'My mother used to do them to sell – she taught me.'

'If you say so,' Bert said resignedly. He had quickly come to be know as 'Bert the Flirt', because despite his quaint manner he certainly had an eye for the girls. And despite the fact she was the only married woman among the group, he had a special fancy for Violet, the prettiest of them. He seemed to spend more time hovering around her, overseeing their work, than anyone else.

'Why d'you nae go and see how the doormice are getting on?' Muriel asked sometimes when Bert was once more lurking round them. 'They've got a lot more to learn than we have.' The 'doormice' was her name for Maureen and Doreen, who did scuttle about like two little rodents.

'Exactly so – it's a pleasure to watch you ladies work,' Bert said ingratiatingly.

'More like it's a pleasure to stare at your backside in those gorgeous slacks!' Muriel muttered to Violet, and both of them got the giggles.

'I don't think I've ever worn anything that makes me feel *less* gorgeous. And what with this on an' all . . .' She pulled her welding mask down over her face with a mock seductive air. Joan, the posh girl, wouldn't wear her mask at all and insisted on having a hand-held one, so as not to spoil her permanent wave.

Violet was at first puzzled, then slightly flattered by Bert's attention. He was an odd bloke, she thought, and she wasn't interested in him, but it had been a long time since Harry had paid her any compliments. She started paying more attention to her appearance, despite her jokes to Muriel about the welding masks. Since Harry left she hadn't bothered with make-up, but now she put on a touch of lipstick and powder again.

'You look pretty, Mom,' Joyce told her one day as they were getting ready in the morning. 'You've got quite a nice face really.'

Violet laughed, and heard a light-heartedness in herself that she had barely ever known before.

'Well – we all have to try and be cheerful,' she said.

Bessie took one look at her powder and lipstick and said, 'You want to go careful, my girl, going out looking like that.'

Her tone was so condemnatory, so offensive, that Violet immediately felt angry and crushed.

'What d'you mean? It's only a bit of lipstick!'

'You know what I mean. Going about painted up like a fourpenny rabbit. You want to watch yourself.'

Once again, Violet thought furiously as she went to get the bus to Witton, there was Mom going out to do her down! Going on as if wearing a bit of make-up made you into the Whore of Babylon! What the hell was the matter with her?

'Ooh, I say!' Muriel said when they clocked in together. 'Don't we look lovely today?'

'Don't you start,' Violet snapped. 'I've had my mom keeping on already this morning.'

'What – about your warpaint? But you look *gorgeous*!'

The compliment was made with such sincerity that Violet calmed down.

'Sorry. Mom just gets me worked up. She's such a bully – she has to rule everyone's life for them. Sometimes I bloody hate her!'

As she said it, she realized she'd never said that to anyone before – even to herself.

When she got home on Christmas Eve to find Harry waiting for her, it was a shock. She'd come in from Bessie's, not too late, but having no idea he was coming. Harry had lit the fire with the few remaining bits of coal and was sitting waiting.

'Dad!' Joyce and Linda ran to him.

'Hello, Joycie – 'ello, Linda.' He scooped them up and held them against his chest. 'Didn't your mother tell you I was coming?'

'I didn't know!' Violet said. It was a shock to see him. It took a minute to adjust, and then she was smiling. 'So you're home for Christmas? You never said! I mean I wondered . . .'

'I sent a wire . . .'

He put the girls down and came over to her, and she found herself pressed against his chest. He smelt of the smoky inside of a railway carriage. And it felt almost as if he was a stranger.

Chapter Twenty-Seven

Soon after Christmas, Violet asked Muriel whether she'd like to come to them for Sunday dinner. She was a bit nervous of it as Bessie was often very off-ish with strangers.

'Scottish, did you say?' Bessie demanded suspiciously, when Violet suggested the idea to her. 'I look after my own,' was one of Bessie's phrases. Anyone outside her small orbit didn't count as 'my own', and had to go out of their way to prove themselves, especially if they spoke or looked differently from her. Violet knew she'd better keep quiet about Muriel being a Catholic as well.

'She's nice, Nan,' Joyce said. 'She talks funny.'

In the event, Muriel charmed Bessie with her absolute respectfulness and sense of humour. Bessie said she was 'all right – once I can make head or tail of a word she's saying.' And Joyce and Linda loved her. With Harry gone it soon seemed the obvious thing to ask Muriel to move in as a lodger. Though Muriel put a brave face on it, Violet could tell she was finding it lonely where she was, as the one lodger of an elderly widow.

'I know it's not such a good neighbourhood as the one you're in now,' Violet said, nervous at asking. 'And I wouldn't charge you much rent. But if the girls move in with me, there's a room if you want it.'

Muriel was delighted. 'That'd be grand! We can have

140

a laugh – and I'll help you with your weans. Better than mouldering away where I am night after night, drowning in the smell of mothballs!'

Those months of 1942 were some of the happiest Violet had ever had. With Muriel in the house, she retrieved her ration-book from Bessie and said that they would now have their tea at home. She picked up Joyce and Linda from Spring Street while Muriel started on the cooking, and they spent cosy evenings together. Bessie sulked about this for a time, but Violet took no notice.

One of the other girls in the factory called Muriel a 'rapscallion'. She was always prepared for a laugh and a practical joke, often at the expense of long-suffering Bert. She also had an astonishing range of skills. Soon after discovering that the roof over her room in Violet's house leaked and she was going to have water dripping loudly into a bucket all night, she said, 'That's all right – I can fix it. You got a ladder?'

'Well, no,' Violet said. 'You can't do that, can you?'

'Aye,' Muriel said, without expanding on this any further.

She sweet-talked the use of a ladder off a builder's down the road and managed, from somewhere, to find several new slates for the roof. The next thing was that one Sunday morning in January, returned from Mass from which nothing short of an earthquake would keep her, Muriel was up on the roof, boiler-suit on, a green scarf holding back her hair, fixing the slates. It was drizzling lightly and the slates were dark and slippery-looking.

'I can't bear to watch,' Violet shouted as Muriel reached the top of the ladder and set off towards the roof ridge on her hands and knees, holding on to the chimney stack, tools in a bag slung round her neck.

'Don't then,' Muriel called down crisply. 'Go and do something useful like making me a cup of cocoa – it's cold enough to freeze a monkey's tackle off up here.' She twizzled round for a second. 'Sorry – forgot the weans were down there!'

Joyce and Linda watched, mesmerized, eyes full of sky. A few other people started to notice, the men shaking their heads in disbelief.

'For God's sake be careful,' Violet said, heart in her mouth as Muriel's wiry figure scrambled up the roof. In a moment she was straddling the ridge, making a thumbs-up sign.

Violet was supposed to have climbed up and passed her the slates, but one of the neighbours wasn't having that and insisted on doing it himself.

'Can't 'ave two of you killing yourselves,' he muttered.

But Muriel got the job done very proficiently and was soon sliding down towards the ladder, calling out, 'Got that cocoa ready for me then?'

Poised at the top of the ladder, she looked from her bird's-eye vantage point along the street.

'Oi, oi – new neighbours, look,' she called, pointing to her left. A baker's van had drawn up outside one of the houses and Violet saw two men begin unloading bits of furniture from in the back. She didn't take too much notice, being far more interested in the moment when Muriel's feet finally touched the ground and she felt herself relax again.

'Lord – you'll be the death of me,' she said. 'Can't you stick to cake decorating?'

*

They passed the evenings talking and laughing and telling each other about their families and Muriel's exploits with 'laddies'. Men seemed to like her and she was ever baffled as to why. Violet could see why. Muriel wasn't the world's greatest beauty, but she had such a lot of life in her. Her abundant energy and good humour lifted Violet out of her usual fatalistic and gloomy turn of mind. Muriel took life at the run.

In March, Harry came home for what turned out to be embarkation leave. The notice he gave was very short.

'Look – you don't want me about if your husband's home,' Muriel said. 'Let me see if I can find a place to stay for a couple of nights.'

'No – don't talk daft,' Violet said. 'Where're you going to go? It'll be all right.'

Muriel looked very doubtful. 'Well – at least let me take Joyce and Linda in to sleep with me.' She rolled her eyes comically. 'You'll not be wanting company in the bedroom department, will ye?'

In fact, Muriel and Harry got along very well and he seemed reassured that there was another woman in the house. As they lay in bed together the night before he went, Violet realized how different it would have been had Muriel not been there. She would have been insecure and grieved at his leaving again – this time overseas. Instead, she knew, guiltily, that although she was worried about where he might be going, she barely missed him at all.

And Harry had a new light in his eye. The army suited him. He had lost the girth that too much ale and lack of much purpose in life had gradually accumulated round him. He was trim and fit, his hair clipped short. She could see he looked and felt younger.

'Well – I never thought it'd come like this – all the ideas I had about seeing the world and that.' He squeezed Violet round the waist. They were lying close and warm after lovemaking. 'I'll miss all you girls. I don't even know where we're going. The lads all think it'll be out East. Got to be really, hasn't it?'

She nodded against him, unable to imagine it. He already felt far, far away from her.

'Promise me –' He turned over suddenly and in the dark she could feel his face close to hers, feel his breath on her face. 'You'll be here when I get back . . .' He ran out of words.

'Don't be daft.' She kissed his cheek. 'Course I will! Where d'you think I'm going to be off to?'

Chapter Twenty-Eight

March 1942

'Right, you two – up the wooden hill!'

Joyce and Linda, both ready for bed, were huddled close to the fire. It was a bitter night, the wind slamming against the windows and sucking the flames up the chimney.

'When's Muriel coming back?' Linda asked. She was very taken with Muriel.

'There's no telling,' Violet said. 'Come on – shift.'

Muriel was out with 'Dickie', a friend who she was being unusually coy about.

The girls were already upstairs when she heard knocking on the door. In the blacked-out darkness she saw a long, rather melancholy face under a cap. He was holding it on to stop the wind lifting it away.

'I . . . I live at number two . . .' He seemed distracted, or nervous. Violet recognized him – they were the family that moved in a few months back. She'd seen his wife about, a rounded, sleepy-looking woman. The man who stood in front of her was thin, and there was something gentle about him, but somehow intense at the same time.

'Thing is . . . the babby's sick – very bad. And the wife. And we've no coal. I've tried a couple of the houses, but . . . You got any to spare?'

'I've got a bit. You'd better come in a tick.' She shut the door. It was second nature now, the blackout, not letting light spill into the street.

Violet fetched the coal scuttle. She felt sorry for him.

'It's mostly slack, but there's a few bits in there. It's a bad night out.'

He took it absently, his thoughts obviously elsewhere. 'Ta. Very good of you. I'm Roy ... Keillor.'

His voice was nice, she thought. Gentle and quite well-spoken.

'How old's the babby?' she asked gently.

'Three months. Don't know if she'll last. And Iris, my wife. Cough, cough, fit to break her apart. I don't know what to do for her.' He trailed off again. She felt for him, could see how worried he was.

'What's the matter?'

'Pneumonia, the doctor says. Look – I'd best go. Very kind of you.' He tipped his cap. 'We've no fire, else, and the other kiddies're starving cold.'

'Is there anything else I can do?' Violet said, touched by this desperate picture.

He shook his head. 'No, ta. Can't do anything now but keep 'em warm.'

She watched his slim figure disappear into the dark street.

A couple of days later she learned, from other neighbours, that a tiny coffin had gone into number two. The little girl hadn't won her fight for life, but apparently Mrs Keillor was rallying. Violet felt for them.

'Brings it all back,' she said to Muriel. 'I lost my first babby – a little lad. We called him Bobby. It's the worst feeling there is, seeing 'em go like that. He died in Harry's arms.'

Muriel shook her head, her eyes filling. 'You poor wee thing. I could nae come through that, I don't think.'

'Well, there's no choice, is there? D'you think I should go round and see Mrs Keillor?'

But shyness prevented her. Later, she wondered if that might have made all the difference. In time, once Iris Keillor had recovered, Violet saw her in the street in passing and at first she made to pass the time of day. But Iris had a very shy manner. There was nothing haughty about her, she just seemed to go about in a kind of dream, although the neighbours on either side said that when you did speak to her she was always nice enough.

When Roy called the next time, Muriel was in as well.

'I've had this a while – sorry.' He held out the coal scuttle.

'Oh – ta.' Violet took it, expecting him to move away, but he just stayed, looking at her. She realized she had not said anything about the Keillors' misfortunes.

'Sorry to hear about your little girl.'

'Oh – yes –' He nodded. Again, this vagueness. Violet was starting to think that the Keillors were a pretty odd pair.

'Would you like a cup of tea?' Muriel said.

Violet could have crowned her. What on earth did she want to invite this strange man in for? They could have had a nice evening on their own!

Roy Keillor hesitated. 'Nice of you. All right.'

Muriel made tea and chatted on in her friendly way about how the two of them were welders and their work at Midwinters. Roy Keillor started to relax and he laughed at one or two things Muriel said. When he smiled, his thin face creased up and came to life. Violet thought how nice he seemed. He had laid his cap on the table beside him. He was wearing a black gaberdine which he didn't take off. Under it, Violet could just make out a maroon jersey.

'How many children've you got, you and your wife?' She sat down as Muriel brought the pot of tea over.

'Three – well, we did have. Two now. Two lads – they're twins aged three.'

There was a silence for a moment, then Muriel said, 'We've got twins at the works, haven't we, Vi? Like two peas in a pod they are – and there's no separating them. They'll both need to marry the same man!'

Roy laughed, and again Violet saw his features transformed.

'Oh – ours aren't like that. One's like me and the other's like their mother. No trouble telling them apart.'

They chatted for a while, about the families and work. Roy told them he worked at Kynoch's.

'I nearly went there,' Violet said. 'But where we are's smaller. Suits me better.'

'It is a big works,' he agreed. 'But you know – you soon settle into one section of it and get to know people. There's quite a few women now, of course.' He laughed suddenly, his face lighting again. 'Still can't get used to the idea of you two being welders!'

After he'd gone that night, Muriel said, 'He seems a nice enough fella.'

'Yes,' Violet said. She'd been sorry to see him go. There was just something about him.

148

Chapter Twenty-Nine

.

Every Sunday they went to Bessie's, pooling ration
cards for whatever meal could be scratched together for
them all. Everything revolved round Bessie's house.
Muriel usually came along too, now Bessie had accepted
her. Muriel was always polite and entertaining, but
sometimes she said things which later made Violet see
her family through other eyes. When they were walking
home with the girls one afternoon, Muriel said, 'Why
does your Marigold nae go out and get a job? She's
stuck there all the time. Would she nae like to get out?
She's the right age to be conscripted, isn't she?'

'She's twenty-nine this year,' Violet said.

'There you go.'

'Mom won't have it. Any road – I don't think
anyone's ever asked her. It was like that when Mom
took her away from school. No one ever came. It's as if
no one knows she exists.'

'Well, she must have her own ration book?'

Violet frowned. 'I s'pose so.'

Another time, Muriel simply said, 'Your mother's
got all of you just where she wants you, hasn't she?'

Violet was so used to things as they were that she
never gave it much thought now. Bessie was still taking in the babies from time to time and she relied on
Marigold's help. And where would she be without her
mom? She minded Joycie and Linda – if it wasn't for that

Violet'd have to stay at home or give them to strangers to be looked after. She didn't like the idea of that, and the thought of staying at home, without all the jokes and companionship in the factory, was a very bleak thought.

She had a brief letter from Harry, written on a ship. He wasn't much of a letter writer in any case and really didn't have much to say.

'I thought he'd at least tell me where he's going,' Violet complained to Muriel.

'They're not allowed to, nitwit,' Muriel said. 'Anyway – he most likely does nae even know himself yet.'

Her married life with Harry already felt such a long time ago to Violet. She could barely even imagine it now. All those evenings spent in waiting for him, with his dinner, while he was at the pub, the loneliness of it, his outbursts of temper, were something she realized she didn't have any desire to go back to. Thinking like this made her panic. Harry was her husband! The chances were he'd be back one day and they'd have to pick up where they left off. She didn't like to think about how glum a thought this was. Life had been so much happier and more fun since Muriel had moved in. They'd enjoyed so many cosy, laughter-filled evenings with the wireless, the children safe in bed. With a shock she realized she had experienced more love and support from Muriel, certainly more *help*, than she ever had from Harry. But when the war ended . . . No . . . She didn't want to think about it.

She hadn't given Roy Keillor any thought either, until one evening they met him on the bus on the way home. There were always queues waiting for the buses as the firm finished work. Now the spring had come there wasn't the bitter cold wait in dark evenings, huddled there, collars turned up, and it all felt more bearable. But Muriel was impatient. She was meeting Dickie for a trip to the pictures.

'Hurry up, will ye,' she muttered as the awaited bus remained stubbornly absent.

'Got your lipstick?' Violet teased.

Bert the Flirt had been outraged earlier to find Muriel fusing a broken scarlet lipstick together with her welding torch.

'What the bleeding hell are you doing? Saints alive – I've seen it all now.'

Violet giggled. 'His face!'

Muriel had turned, lifting up her welding mask, and with lips already well coated in red advanced on Gilbert, lips pursed as if for a kiss.

'Red as a beetroot he was.' Muriel laughed. 'D'ye think he's ever been with a woman?'

'I dunno, do I? You're awful!'

The bus came swaying along the street then and they were among the last in the long queue to squeeze aboard. Muriel managed to push her way further down to the back and Violet was left standing near the front. At the last minute someone got on just as the doors were closing and a second later Violet found she was standing squeezed close to Roy Keillor.

'Oh, hello!' he said. He had evidently belted along for the bus and was panting hard.

'This is a bit of a way from Kynoch's.' She found she was blushing. He was so close to her, his left arm and hip pressed to her. When he turned to her she had the strangest feeling, as if he could see deeply into her, and she looked down in confusion, focusing on the black weave of his coat.

'I had an errand to run over here.' He was still regaining his breath.

'Oh,' she said stupidly.

'Where's your pal?'

'Along there.' She jerked her head along the bus. She could just see Muriel's arm, reaching out to hold on as the bus swayed along.

They travelled in silence for a few moments and she didn't look at him for a time, but then she said, 'How's the family? The twins and that?'

'They're all right. You've got girls, haven't you?'

'Yes – two.'

'What about your husband? In the army, is he?'

'Yes. I don't know where he is for sure. Overseas, I mean, but he was on his way somewhere last time I heard. He doesn't write much really.'

He was listening intently. But so, she realized, were a lot of the people closely packed around them on the bus. It felt an effort to speak over the noise of the engine.

Roy looked away, then back again. 'I just want to say, that night – when our babby was poorly, and Iris – you were the only one who found any coal for us.'

'Oh. Well . . . I'd been at my mom's. There was a fire there, see, so I hadn't lit ours.'

'But it was kind. You could've said you didn't have any.'

She frowned. The thought hadn't occurred to her. 'But you needed it.'

When she looked up, he was smiling gently at her.

They didn't speak for the rest of the journey, except goodbyes as they got off, but all the way she was acutely aware of his presence beside her.

*

'There's someone at the door,' Muriel called up to Violet. It was a week later and Violet was settling Linda into bed. After a moment she hissed, 'It's that Roy Keillor bloke again!'

Violet felt a jolt go through her. She thought of his eyes looking down at her on the bus. What on earth was he calling for now?

'What're you looking like that for, Mom?' Joyce said, leaning up on one elbow in bed.

'Like what?' she said crossly. 'I'm not looking like anything. Get to sleep.'

From the stairs she could hear voices, Muriel's, joking as usual, and Roy saying something softly. It struck her then how different a man he was from Harry, whose voice always carried loudly all over the house.

He was watching her as she came to the bottom of the stairs.

'Oh –' she spoke rather abruptly, trying to cover the fact that his being there affected her in a way she was quite sure it shouldn't. 'Come for some more slack, have you?'

He smiled nervously. 'No – I er . . . Iris is getting the kiddies up to bed. I don't know why, I just . . .' He shrugged, and Violet noticed then that he was holding a thick little book with a worn leather binding.

'Tea?' Muriel asked. Behind Roy Keillor's back she gave Violet a comical smirk as if to say, *We've got a right one on our hands here!*

'Sit down – if you want,' Violet said, rather clumsily.

Roy settled himself at the table. He seemed shy.

'You'll think I'm a bit funny coming asking you this, but – do you like poetry, either of you?'

'I'm not much one for it myself,' Muriel admitted, tipping the tea grouts out. 'Cannae make head nor tail of it to tell you the truth.'

153

'Not even Robbie Burns?'

'Who?' Muriel said.

Violet, taken aback as much by the oddness of coming to ask such a question as the question itself, tried to think back to any poetry she had ever known. Bits at school of course, 'The Lady of Shalott' ... 'And through the field the road runs by To many-tower'd Camelot' – that was all she could remember. And something else about the boy on the burning deck.

'I know it's peculiar coming like this. It's just – there are things in here...' He held out the book. 'Just marvellous things. And if you don't read them at school, or afterwards ... I mean, no one talks about them – normally like, you know. I thought you might like to hear some of it?'

'All right then,' Muriel said politely. 'You carry on while I brew up.'

Violet, unsure what else to do, took a seat at the table. Roy opened the book and thumbed through.

'This is by William Wordsworth,' he said solemnly.

He began reading what turned out to be a long, long poem. Muriel filled the pot and brought cups over and dribbled milk into them and eventually, with a droll expression, she poured the tea. Glancing up at her, Violet saw the suppressed laughter in her eyes. Normally Violet would have laughed with her, but this time she found herself feeling annoyed. She liked the way Roy Keillor was reading to them, and she wanted to understand, but she had been lost almost from the beginning. It all seemed to be about meadows and birds and lambs, some of it very beautiful, she could tell, and he read it in a soft, slow rhythm. Sometimes she caught a bit of the sense of it, but then it kept slipping away from her. She listened to his gentle voice, affected by the fact that it evidently meant so much to him, but she just didn't know what he was on about.

And then in the middle of it, a few lines seemed to link up straightforwardly so that she could hear them, and she rolled along with them:

> 'Hence in a season of calm weather
> Though inland far we be,
> Our souls have sight of that immortal sea
> Which brought us hither,
> Can in a moment travel thither,
> And see the children sport upon the shore,
> And hear the mighty waters rolling evermore.'

She felt her skin prickle, as if all her hairs were standing on end, and the feeling that she had had sometimes as a child of being immense and spread out, and, as on that night looking out over the rooftops, that there was something in her that could fly and extend itself wide over the land. She felt as if in her soul she was a huge bird, or had been in another life, and the words reminded her of all that had once been and might be again that was bigger and grander than ever this life she was living now. She sat very still, feeling expanded inside herself by the words, and found that her eyes were full of tears as if for something momentous that she had lost.

A few verses later he finished reading and she had not heard much more of the poem. Just for once, she longed for Muriel not to be there. She looked up at Roy Keillor as he closed the book.

'S'pose I got a bit carried away,' he said. 'But can you see why I wanted to read it to you?'

Muriel was struggling to look polite, if not exactly impressed.

'I've never heard it before,' Violet said. 'I mean I couldn't follow it all, but . . .'

'It is long,' he agreed. 'But it's worth it.'

'Yes,' she said.

His eyes were searching her face. Violet met his gaze, and knew that no one had ever looked at her like that before and she had never looked back like that.

'Your tea's getting cold,' Muriel pointed out with just about concealed irritation.

'Oh yes.' He smiled and closed the book.

And they talked about other things.

Chapter Thirty

'Have these two weans ever seen the sea?' Muriel asked the next day as they hurried through the early morning routine.

'The sea?' Joyce piped up. 'Can we see it? I've never seen it.'

'Where is it?' Linda was four now. Violet was startled often by the life and intelligence shining out of her brown eyes, as if there was a powerful engine purring away inside her. Everything she did, even fastening her shoes, was done with intense concentration. Joyce was more vague and scatty.

'Here – eat up now.' Muriel placed a bowl of porridge on the table in front of each of them. The day didn't begin right for Muriel without porridge and she insisted on making it even though it meant getting up early to allow it time to cook. The girls were learning to like it – even salty, the way she made it – as they would have walked across hot coals for Muriel.

'The sea is round the edge of the country and we're right on the middle,' she told them. 'Where I come from in Scotland, we're only a stone's throw from the sea.'

Linda frowned. 'D'you throw stones in the sea?'

Muriel laughed, her jolly red lips parting. 'Aye, sometimes we do. One day, when the war's over, you'll have tae come up to Scotland and pay me a wee visit, won't you? Anyways – my auntie Jean married an

Englishman and she lives down in Brighton. What d'you think, Vi? We could make a trip?'

'I s'pose so,' Violet said. The thought had never occurred to her. She thought of the poem, the children playing along the shore, and wondered if despite all Muriel's mocking of Roy and his poems, that was what had set her off on thoughts of the sea.

'We cannae go on to the beaches now, so they say – but at least we could see the sea,' Muriel was saying, having to explain to the children that the beaches were mined and fenced off in case the Germans tried to get in.

'Are they trying to get in?' Joyce said, alarmed.

'Well, we hope not – they're not taking any chances. Vi – if we went one time when we have an early shift before a day off I'm sure Auntie Jean would put us up. You'd like her – she's my mum's sister. She and Uncle Mort have a wee bakery.'

The chance came within a couple of weeks. Auntie Jean had written back to say she'd be over the moon to see them, and if they sent a telegram to say when they were coming they'd come and meet them.

'I'll send Mort,' she wrote. 'He likes a little walk.'

It was the first time Violet had ever been out of Birmingham.

The girls were so excited they were hard to settle down in the carriage, wanting to jump about and kneel up on the seats, and Violet felt almost as frisky herself. She craned her head round as the train pulled out of her city, seeing its sooty factories and warehouses recede, its workaday yards and smoking chimneys, the barrage balloons still hanging over it like bloated guardian angels.

They all squeezed in close to the window, seeing the green expanses of spring fields and the farms and sheep and cows. Muriel kept pointing out things to them as they chugged along. The girls' excitement over the sight of a donkey or a farm dog was a cause of amusement to the middle-aged couple sharing their compartment. Violet was astonished by the orchards they saw full of pink blossom and the sheer prettiness of the countryside. She watched Linda, and at some moments, when she had seen something new, saw her face transformed in a moment of wonder, a glow which brought a lump to her throat.

At last they climbed down wearily in Brighton. It was only about nine o'clock but to Violet it felt like the middle of the night. She took the girls' hands as they walked nervously along the platform.

'Toot toot,' Joyce said, as the train let off a great sigh of steam.

Muriel carried the holdall into which they had squeezed all their clothes.

'Uncle Mort!' She raised her spare arm suddenly to wave. 'There he is!'

A short, plump man came towards them, smiling broadly.

'Well, hello there!'

As soon as she saw Uncle Mort, Violet's nerves started to subside. She could see she was going to like him. He was almost bald except for a ring of mousy hair and everything about him was plump and round:

his body, cheeks, chin. He had an old raincoat round him with the buttons done up wrong.

'Well – young Muriel!' He kissed her cheek, squeezing her hand. And this is your friend?'

'Friend – and landlady!' Muriel said.

'Very nice to see you, very nice.' He shook her hand, speaking in a deep, burring voice. 'Come on now – let's get home. Jean's on pins waiting for you.'

He led them through the dark streets, a little torch lighting their path. Soon they were in a row of terraced houses and Uncle Mort took them into one. He kept the torch on as they went indoors.

'Just follow me – up here.'

Violet knew that the couple lived over a bakery. There was a low counter on their left in the small room, and a strong, yeasty smell. They could see a light on upstairs.

'Is that you, Mort?'

The voice sounded so like Muriel's that for a moment Violet thought it was she who had spoken.

'We're all here – home and dry.'

'Bring them all up – quick!'

Violet and the girls were the last up the wooden stairs and she could hear the exclamations of 'Look at *you*!' at the top as Muriel was greeted by her aunt. Auntie Jean was in her fifties, and as round and comforting a person as her husband, with pink cheeks and her hair, still deep brown, tied back in a bun. She greeted Violet with a broad smile, then bent to speak to the children.

'I expect you little girls would like a wee piece of cake?'

Joyce and Linda nodded, wide-eyed.

Looking round fondly at Muriel, Violet was touched

160

to see that she was struggling not to cry. Auntie Jean resembled her mother very much in looks and Violet knew that for all her cheerful antics, she missed her mother and home terribly.

'I've got the kettle on – come on, sit down out here.' There was a kitchen built on to the house above the storeroom at the back. 'We have nae much room here but you're welcome to what there is!'

'We brought all our bacon rations,' Muriel said, wiping her eyes.

'Oh, you should nae have done that! Well – bacon butties in the morning for you! Here, you little ones – I hope you like a nice scone. I put a few raisins in . . .'

She offered Violet a scone, saying, 'You never said your landlady was so bonny! I was imagining some middle-aged matron!'

Violet laughed, shyly.

'Och – and you had it terrible with the bombing up there, didn't you? I should think your nerves were in shreds after that. I don't know how you all stood it.'

Jean and Mort tutted and shook their heads sympathetically.

'And you've a husband away in the forces, have ye, Violet?' Auntie Jean said.

'Yes – army. I don't know where, for certain.'

'Well, that'll be a worry too.' There was a silence. Everything looked so grim out East. It was hard not to feel pessimistic. 'Still – ' She smiled. 'We're so glad for you to come down here, both of yous, and take your minds off it all for a little while.'

They sat drinking tea with the comfortable couple. Auntie Jean asked after Muriel's father, from whom she hardly ever heard, then went on to bemoan the fact that the piers and beach were all off limits.

'These poor weans – I hope they haven't come thinking they can play on the sand?'

'They've never seen the sea before,' Muriel said.

'Have you not?' Jean looked at them in amazement.

'Well – you can see it,' Uncle Mort said, holding up his teacup. 'But you won't be able to get in it – not the way things are at present. You'll have to come back.'

'That's what I told them.' Muriel smiled at the girls.

'Come back when there's beach and ice creams!' Auntie Jean said.

'Mom! Mom!'

Violet managed to open her eyes with great difficulty. A crack of dim light was visible at the edge of the blackout curtains. She tried to think where she was. There was a strange, delicious smell.

'Mom – I want to go and see the sea!'

'Oh, Linda – what time is it? I'm sure you should be asleep.'

She realized then that the wonderful smell was of baking bread, and where she was, and that they only had one day here. Linda was right – they needed to get going!

Auntie Jean was already downstairs, in a big white apron, looking as if she had never been to bed. A row of newly baked loaves lay on the counter in the tiny shop.

'You go and have a look at the waves – it is nae far,' she said. 'And I'll have that bacon frying for when you get back.'

They walked down to the seafront in the misty morning. It felt very early. The breeze blew brisk and salty, bringing roses to their cheeks and ahead of them, grey waves heaved and shifted, breaking in a roll of frothy white.

'Is that the sea?' Linda's voice was barely more than a whisper.

'Aye – that's it. And that's the beach.' Muriel took them as close as it was possible to get. There were rolls of barbed wire stretching all along its margin. 'See – all the pebbles?'

They stared and stared. The sea sucked loudly through the stones.

'See those?' Muriel pointed at the two piers, extending out into the breakers, ghostly in the fog. 'That one's the Palace Pier – and that's the West Pier. There's lots of fun to be had on those – or there would be if it was nae for the war.'

'The war spoils everything,' Joyce grumbled.

'Aye – but we're having some fun together, aren't we?'

'We wouldn't be here if it wasn't for the war,' Violet said.

And she realized, guiltily, that she was glad.

The shop had a green and gold sign over the door saying 'Hall's Bakery'. They walked back into delicious smells, and Auntie Jean fed them on crusty white bread and the rashers of bacon. Violet knew it was one of the nicest things she'd ever tasted, and said so.

'That'll be the sea air,' Auntie Jean said, pouring dark tea from her big brown teapot. 'They say it makes everything taste better.'

Violet could already feel that the day was going to pass in a flash, and they had to be back on a late afternoon train to be at work the next morning.

They spent the hours they had walking round the town and seeing some of the grand buildings and looking in the shops, and the children played in the park and they had a dinner of fish and chips. As the day went by the mist burned off and though the breeze was cool, it was lovely and sunny. They enjoyed the town thoroughly, but all the time they kept being drawn back to the sea, sapphire blue now the sun was out, all of them fascinated by its immensity, its endless movement.

Joyce and Linda had a little bag of sweets each and they strolled along the front. There was only one sour moment, when they passed two rather smartly dressed women who spoke in loud voices, not caring who heard.

'Oh – ' one of them said, eyeing Violet and Muriel and the children. 'Must be some more of those dreadful evacuees. I rather thought we'd seen the last of them.'

'Well, we live in hope!' the other said. She turned for a moment, looking them up and down and said, *Ghastly!*' Then the two of them went off, laughing behind their hands.

Violet saw Linda staring after them. She saw herself and her children through her eyes: down at heel, poor, not respectable.

'Oh, ignore the snooty bitches,' Muriel said, catching sight of her face. 'I'd love to see them in a welding mask!'

As the last minutes of the time they had left in Brighton went by terribly quickly, they stood looking out at the sea, the sky patched with puffy clouds. Violet found herself drifting off almost into a trance, lulled by the waves' rhythm, her thoughts stilled. How could you take in, on a day like this, all the fighting going on in the world? She was filled suddenly with a deep sense of longing. She leaned on the railing, watching the waves break and break and all she could think of was the poem that Roy Keillor had read, and over the water, like a spirit presence, she seemed to see his face.

Chapter Thirty-One

Spring was turning into summer, and often when Violet passed the Keillors' house the two little boys were playing out at the front. One was, as Roy had said, dark and delicate-featured like him, the other was round-faced and fair. At times she saw the little girl as well. Occasionally she passed him in the street, once when his wife was beside him, and they all greeted each other with a polite nod.

At this time she was trying to ignore the effect that any meeting with him had on her, the way it seemed to mean far more than it should, the excitement she felt at any chance of seeing him.

It was some time before they spoke again. She was on her way back from Bessie's. It was still light and she saw him coming along the street, an old trilby shadowing his face. As they drew closer he looked up, and she saw his expression change. He smiled and lifted his hat. Violet felt a wave of something pass through her, the way she imagined a bomb blast might feel, only on the inside.

'Hello,' he said.

'Hello.' She could feel Joyce and Linda watching them.

Then neither of them knew what to say.

'We haven't seen you,' she blurted at last, realizing at once that it was an odd thing to say and blushing.

Roy seemed embarrassed. 'After I'd been round I . . . Well, you must've both thought it funny of me – coming along like that, with the poetry book . . . I don't know why I did it.'

'I liked it. It was . . . I've never heard anything like it before. Only . . .' Everything she said seemed to be coming out wrong. 'I mean, I couldn't catch it all.'

'I don't think your friend liked it much.' He gave a chuckle and she liked the way his face looked as he did it.

'She's not very keen on poems and that, I don't think.'

He was watching her, listening to her words as if everything she said was of the utmost importance. There was another silence. Linda tugged on Violet's arm.

'It was nice, finding someone who wanted to listen,' he said.

What she wanted to say was, please, come round again, read to me again, look me in the eyes the way you do. What she said was, 'I'd better be going. Come on, girls.'

'Yes, of course,' he said, putting his hat back on. 'Sorry to hold you up.'

'No – you're not!' Why couldn't she get the right things to come out of her mouth! 'Only I've got to get these two to bed.'

As soon as they were inside the house, she said, 'Go on you two, upstairs. Get undressed – quick!'

Muriel was out. As the girls clattered up the stairs, Violet sank on to a chair. It was only then that she noticed she was trembling.

*

He came round the next Saturday night.

'I bet that's our poem man,' Muriel said, hearing the door. 'I had a feeling he'd be back.'

'Don't be daft,' Violet said, but her heart went racing. And he was on the step, with his book, holding it out to her.

'You said it was too quick – hearing it read out. I thought you might like to borrow it for a bit.'

'Oh – thank you!'

She took the book from him, excited at feeling singled out, the way she had when Miss Green had told her she was good at something all those years ago.

'D'you think his wife knows he's coming round here?' Muriel said when he'd gone. She was sitting by the window, knitting in the last of the evening light.

'Um?' Violet fingered the binding on the book. It had been in his hands. He had stroked that cover so lovingly. Her skin prickled at the thought.

'I said, dreamboat, d'you nae think his wife might find it a bit peculiar him coming round here to visit a couple of women on their own?'

'No!' Violet said. This wasn't what she wanted to hear. More than anything, she wanted him to visit. He filled her thoughts, him with his longing, soulful eyes. It was getting so that she scarcely thought of anything else. 'He didn't stay, did he? I don't think she's interested, that's all – in the things he likes.'

'Vi –' Muriel put her knitting down. 'Can you nae see he's after you? That's why he comes round here – not to read his poems. I've seen him looking at you – it's written all over his face. And it's written all over yours, too. You're going to have to be careful.'

'Oh, don't be so stupid!' Violet erupted. At that moment she hated Muriel for turning all worldly-wise on her, for pointing out these hard truths. What did she know? She was younger and wasn't even married!

'How the hell can he be after me? He's got a wife and three kids – and he's not that sort, I can tell.'

'Really?' Muriel spoke in such a flat tone of disbelief that Violet lost her patience altogether.

'Oh, for goodness sake leave me alone.' She stormed into the kitchen and picked up the kettle, shouting, 'You're worse than my flaming mother!'

She took Muriel's words to heart, even if she wouldn't admit anything to her. Was it really so obvious the effect Roy Keillor had on her? She was even more struck by Muriel's observation that Roy was sweet on her. Could that be true? Could it really?

But she tried to stamp the feelings out in herself. She just mustn't feel like this! They were both married people – Harry was off somewhere fighting a war, in danger! She ought to be ashamed of herself. And sometimes she really was ashamed of how she felt and managed to put the thought out of her mind for a while, especially if she didn't see Roy. He would have forgotten about her by now, wouldn't he? And then sometimes it all came surging back, the simple longing to see him, to look into his eyes and see him look back.

She knew, as soon as she heard the knock at the door that evening after Muriel had gone out. It was only half-past seven, and she could still hear Joyce and Linda giggling upstairs, little monkeys.

Feeling strangely calm, she opened the door. The mild June air came in and the sounds of older children playing. It was the first time, she realized, she had seen him without a coat. He wore only a waistcoat over his shirt, and a cap.

'I saw your mate walking along – thought she must be going out.'

Violet wondered who was watching. Were the neighbours peering at them, wondering if there was some arrangement between them? And why did it already feel as if there was?

'Come in,' she said quickly.

He didn't hesitate. Taking his cap off, he tucked it under his arm. Once she had shut the door she turned to him, still calm. Somehow the fact that he had come to her made it easier for her.

'Did you want your book back?' She nodded towards the black volume, stowed safely on the mantel. She had tried to read some of the poems and liked a few of them, though most she found hard to understand.

'Not if you want to keep it for a bit.' But he went and picked it up, thumbing through it as if reacquainting himself with an old friend.

There was a pause.

'I like knowing it's here.' He looked across at her.

Where does your wife think you are? She knew she should say it, but that she would not.

'The girls aren't settled yet, but they should go to sleep soon. D'you want a cup of tea? Or there's a drop in here –' She held up Muriel's Scotch bottle. 'But it's not mine.'

'No – none of that,' he said abruptly. 'I want to keep my head.'

She avoided his eyes, but felt her heart rate quicken. *Oh God*, she thought. *What's happening to me?*

He stood by the table as she began to make tea, busying herself with teapot and cups.

'Sit down if you want.' She smiled across at him but kept her tone light. 'How's the family?'

'All right,' he said quickly, then in a more considered way, 'Yes – they're all right.'

'What're you going to read me today then?'

He stared at her for a moment, then with a more gentle expression said, 'I don't hold with religion, do you?'

Religion? Violet thought. Dark churches, boredom. She had barely ever been in church. Bessie had sent them to Sunday School, Sunday afternoons, to give her some peace and she'd sat through most of it in a dream. Otherwise it was funerals, the odd christening.

'No – not really,' she admitted.

'"Dover Beach" then,' he said. 'By Matthew Arnold. I didn't want to, sort of offend you, you know, if you'd been at all religious.'

'I don't know if I'll understand it.'

'You will. Some of it, anyway.'

They both sat at the table, and he started to read. She liked him reading to her, because she could look at him, at his brown eyes and thin, sensitive face. Now he had his cap off, a lock of his straight, black hair hung over his forehead. As he spoke, she saw the slight dimple in his left cheek. For three lines she was transported:

> *The sea is calm to-night.*
> *The tide is full, the moon lies fair*
> *Upon the straits'*

The sea again! And her mind wandered and soon after she was lost, as his gentle voice moved on, too fast for her to follow the thread of meaning. Instead she just followed the musical sound, beautiful because it was his voice. She didn't know why he thought she might have been offended by it. As he finished reading she sat quietly.

'Beautiful, isn't it?' he said. 'And I think that's how it is. There is no God, at least, not of a judging sort anyway.'

Violet didn't know, not about God. All she knew was that sometimes she felt lifted, that she could circle over everything, free and high as a bird but somehow part of all of it too. And it made her grateful.

She didn't realize she was smiling.

'Violet –' His words seemed to come out under pressure. 'I can't stop thinking about you. You're all I ever think about – ever since I first saw you. I don't know what to do.'

He sounded desperate. She lowered her head, her cheeks burning hot, hearing words from him that she longed to hear, could scarcely believe she was hearing, and yet was so frightened by what they might mean.

What about your wife? She never used the woman's name, not in her head. It made her too real. *And my husband?*

Then she looked across at him and they sat, locked in each other's gaze. He stood up and came to her, taking her hand from her lap and drawing her to her feet. There was nothing she could do to resist. Nothing else mattered or seemed real. The girls could wander downstairs, but even knowing that, she could not stop herself.

'You're shaking,' he said.

'Yes,' she whispered.

He just stood looking at her, as if he could not stop.

'Will you do something? Take your hair down for me?'

She had it pinned back, quite simply, and as she began to take the hairpins out he helped her, tugging them gently and laying them on the table until her pale hair was hanging all round her cheeks. He stroked it back from her face, then put his hand on the back of her head. She felt the warmth of his palm pressing her scalp, drawing her nearer to him, and his eyes never left hers. She could see nothing but his eyes.

'What're you doing?' She tried to protest.

'I don't know.' He stopped for a moment and she saw the struggle in his face. 'You're just ... I can't seem to see anything but you.'

'I didn't know I could feel like this,' she said, looking up at him. 'I *shouldn't* feel it, but I do ...'

He sighed, relieved. 'It's not just me then?'

Solemnly she shook her head, and he pulled her close to him, his body slim and strange to her as her arms wrapped round him. His lips were warm and hungry on hers and she felt as if she had come home.

Chapter Thirty-Two

It was something she couldn't stop now, as if she was falling and there was nothing to break the fall. She kept going over and over that evening in her mind, the way he had held her, their kisses, that look in his eyes. When would they be able to see each other again? That was her one longing.

The week passed, somehow, in waiting.

'How're things with Dickie?' she asked Muriel, in a light, teasing voice.

'Very nice, thank you,' Muriel said coyly. She wasn't letting on much, not as she had done before with some of her boyfriends. This made Violet think this one was more serious.

By Saturday, Muriel admitted that she was going out with Dickie once again.

'You're always going out!' Joyce accused her.

Muriel laughed. 'Only once a week! Tell you what – you can have my sweetie ration – how about that?'

She didn't see Roy to let him know. Although she had the day off, he was at work. But she knew he'd come – at least to see if she was alone.

All afternoon she was aflutter with expectation.

'Mom – *Mom*! You listening?' the girls kept saying. And mostly she wasn't. In her mind she was already with him, seeing him come through the door, to be with her.

And at last he did. She'd put on her favourite frock,

pale blue, sprigged with small, dark blue flowers, and brushed out her hair. As soon as she closed the door, they were in each other's arms. Now he was here she almost felt as if her legs would give way.

'Today's been so *long*! I thought it was going to go on for ever.' She pressed him to her, loving the smell of him, the warmth of his body.

Roy made a low sound of pleasure. 'I thought I might not get here. I couldn't really believe I would!'

'Roy – what're we going to do? I feel as if everyone's watching.'

'No – course they're not.' She felt his breath on her hair. He was stroking it as they talked. 'I've thought about you – all week . . . I've never felt like this before. I can't think of anything else . . .'

It was as if he didn't hear her question. They never mentioned his wife, her husband. It was as if they were insulated together in a place that outer realities did not touch, where life's responsibilities had no meaning. This was all that mattered.

They spent their few, snatched hours talking and holding one another. It became a pattern, every time Muriel went out. There were so many risks – who might see, the children coming downstairs – but they did not care about risks. Their passion for each other was too urgent. It was some time before they made love completely and then they had not planned to. She was sitting in his lap in the big armchair. It was just dark outside, but the window was open to let in the breeze as it was a sultry night.

Roy's eyes were fixed on her as she cuddled up to him, arms round his neck. She ached to stop the time speeding by before he would have to hurry off, back down the road. The clock said just before ten.

'We're safe for about another hour.' She sighed.

Roy gently ran his finger down her cheek, then wriggled it between the buttons of her blouse. She felt him stroking the little cleft between her breasts.

She undid the top button of her blouse, but he stopped her. 'No – let me do it.'

His hands looked dark in the dusky light, especially against the white of her breasts once he had removed her little camisole. He let out an excited rush of breath.

'God, woman, you're beautiful . . .'

She had never been touched like this before. Not with this gentle attentiveness. Harry was quite rough, keen to get his own pleasure over with. Roy took his time, stroking her nipples, his pleasure found also in hers.

Without a thought she whispered, close to his neck, 'Come upstairs.'

And they crept upstairs, holding hands like children, as if unable to let go of each other, and once inside he pulled her close, enveloping her, kissing her neck, her shoulders, his body taut with desire against her. When they made love it was a revelation to her, her own excitement, because of what she felt for him, the way every part of her, her body, her feelings, responded to him all at once. She lay with him afterwards, wrapped round him, awed.

'I've never known it like that before,' she whispered, eventually.

He made a low, joyful sound.

'It's amazing, isn't it? If you do it right.'

'It's not doing it right. It's you.' She nuzzled against his neck. 'I need it to be you.'

Chapter Thirty-Three

It was such a little time they had together, those precious hours in the summer months.

Violet had never been so happy. Her gaze, uplifted by love, saw everything differently. The old street which Harry had so longed to leave, with its sooty-faced houses and chimneypots, was now the most beautiful place ever, because it was Roy's street, and the place where they loved one another. She put out of her mind the fact that it was Iris's street as well.

'You look nice,' the other girls at work said. 'What're you taking – can I have some of it?'

Violet often wondered whether Muriel guessed. If she did, she never said a word. She was in any case courting with Dickie, a jolly, freckle-faced Catholic boy from Armagh who'd come to England to work in munitions. Even so, sometimes Violet caught Muriel looking at her with her candid blue eyes in a way which made her think, *she knows*. She didn't like keeping secrets from her, but what else could she do? All that she had with Roy, the talking, his love, was the most wonderful thing she had ever known.

And then it all began to go wrong.

Her two neighbours, Mrs McEvoy and Mrs Smith, were out that morning, aprons on, kneeling by their front steps with pails of water and scrubbing-brushes. Neither of them went out to work. As Violet came out with the girls, their talk stopped abruptly and there was a silent, frosty atmosphere. Mrs McEvoy put her head down and went to work vigorously with her scrubbing-brush, but Mrs Smith stared up at her. There was a spiteful, knowing expression on her face.

'Morning,' Violet said, shooing Joyce and Linda ahead of her.

There was no reply, and when she glanced back Mrs Smith was still watching her, saying something to Mrs McEvoy.

She knew then. Whispering had begun in the neighbourhood. But she didn't want to admit it. The next evening, after dark, a note was slipped under her door. It had obviously been written in a hurry:

Dearest Vi,
    See if you can meet me tomorrow night by the bandstand in the rec. I *must* see you.
    Yours, Roy.

The time was coming when she'd have to tell Muriel. If tongues were wagging she would hear something anyway, and Violet desperately needed someone to be on her side. Already every time she stepped out of the house she felt as if everyone was watching and the street was full of prattling tongues and pointing fingers, all condemning her.

She was in such a state the next night, knowing she was out to meet Roy later, that once the girls were upstairs she poured out the whole story to Muriel, who was standing by the table, washing up. She took this outburst quietly.

'I just can't help it,' Violet sobbed. 'I love him so much . . .'

Muriel laid a cup on the table to drain and wiped her hands on her apron, looking gravely across at Violet.

'I know you do. It's always been written all over your face.'

Violet wiped her eyes, sniffing. 'Did you know he's been coming here?'

'Not for sure. I had a feeling. How did you ... I mean what about the girls?'

'It was all right. They never saw.' She shrugged. 'What else could we do?'

Muriel came over to her and with unusual tenderness put her arms round her.

'I know. I can see. I mean, you and your husband, Harry – I could see there was not much between you. But he *is* your husband. And Roy's got a wife ... You're heading for trouble, darlin'.'

'Has anyone said anything?'

Muriel looked away, hesitating. 'I've heard the odd whisper. You know what people are like. If he kept coming along to the house, what were they going to think? Honestly, Vi!' For a moment, her exasperation flashed out.

'We just couldn't help it. Look, he's asked me to meet him – tonight.'

'Well,' Muriel released her. Solemnly, she said. 'Go on. You'd better get going then.'

By the time she reached the foundry round the corner from the recreation ground she heard footsteps, running behind her, and he caught up with her.

Without a word, they clung to each other in the dark street.

'What's happened? You're in such a state!' She could feel it before he said a word.

He kissed her face, feverishly, as if she was the most precious thing in the world.

'Let's go to the park – if it's open. We can talk in there.'

The gate was unlocked and they slipped in, across the moonlit grass. The night park smelt lovely, of flowers, and she ached for this moment to be different, for them to be able to enjoy each other instead of being gripped by this cold fear inside her. When they reached the bandstand he took hold of her again, wrapped himself round her.

'Iris knows, doesn't she?' Violet burst out. There was no point in waiting any longer.

'I think the whole flaming neighbourhood knows.' He gave out a sigh, almost a laugh. 'Goes round like wildfire. God, Violet... How can we have been so stupid?'

'You mean –' She felt as if he had punched her. 'You wish you'd never met me?'

'No! God, no – you're the most... I don't know what to say. You're the woman I love. I know that. It's about the only bloody thing I do know at the moment.'

'What are you saying then?'

'We just should've been more careful.'

'But how?'

'I don't know.'

For a moment they stared intensely at each other in the darkness, then Roy broke away from her and turned his back. She stood, bereft. A dog barked, somewhere outside the park.

'I can't go on like this, Vi, I know that. Lies, trying to be in two places at once. I'd leave, honest to God I would, if it was just her and me. She's all right, Iris is. She's a good sort really. But she's not you. She and I – I don't know – we've never had what we have, me and you . . . I'd leave now, for you. But there's the kids – and your girls and your husband. It's all too difficult . . . It's wrong.'

He turned to her again and she was rooted to the spot. She didn't want to hear what he was saying because it was true and therefore unbearable.

'We'll move,' he said. 'That's what Iris wants. She can't stand it any more. She can see it, see.'

'What d'you mean?' Her voice cracked.

'That I'm different. Feelings that . . . She can see what I feel about you, however much I try to hide it. It's no good.'

The last words were said with flat despair. He came to her again and drew her to him, pressing his cheek against hers. She was not crying, not yet. The tears were like a great wave, swelling deep inside her. Instead she felt shocked and cold. There was no hope now.

'I'll always love you,' she said wretchedly. 'Can't you stay near somewhere?'

'No. If I did I'd always be watching, hoping to see you somewhere, and it'd never end. I couldn't stand it.'

They held each other for a long time, silently, as if each engraving on them the feel of the other's body so it would never be forgotten.

Chapter Thirty-Four

The Keillor family moved out later that week and left the street.

For a few days number two was left empty, but by the end of the week another family had moved in and the whisperings and snide remarks to which Violet was subject died down for the moment. Muriel was her loyal friend throughout.

'Folk can always criticize,' she said. 'But I think no one ever knows what something's like until they've had to live with it. But now you'll just have to get over him somehow.'

Violet did not say a word even to Muriel during those anguished days after he left. She held the pain of it inside her in silence. It felt too much to put into words. And from across the world there was news of such terrible things, the human race in a spasm of agony on a scale to which she would not compare hers. She bore it alone, all her tears saved for night-time, clasping her pillow to her and aching for it to be him. She longed for him so completely that it felt like an illness. But after all, he was another woman's husband. She didn't deserve any sympathy, did she?

Sympathy of a different kind came much later when a letter reached her in February 1944 telling her that

Harry had been killed in action. They didn't tell her how, only that he had been in Burma.

Her mother appeared on the doorstep one day with rough words of comfort.

'I'm sorry for you, bab. I lost my man, and now you've lost yours. It's hard bringing up little 'uns on your own. But it makes you strong. I'll tell you that. Makes a woman of you. And strong is what you're going to have to be now.'

Part Three
1950

Chapter Thirty-Five

The machine was like a long metal coffin.

Violet's hands were trembling as she reached down with a convulsive movement and stroked the blonde head, the only part of her daughter not swallowed up by the iron casing.

'Don't cry, babby – oh, don't, you'll make it worse!'

The bellows pump sucked the air from the machine again with a loud *whoosh*, and the little girl let out a sob.

'I want to come home, Mom!'

You could almost smell the child's fear.

The nurse's heart went out to the mother, with her elfin face and poor, down-at-heel look. The disease was a horror, and a scourge, and this mother was taking it especially hard. It was her first visit, you could tell by her stricken face, and of course she'd brought her other two girls, not thinking they'd not be allowed in. There was far too much risk of infection. So the two lasses had gone to wait outside, with their forlorn faces and grubby summer frocks.

'You'll be little Carol's mother? Mrs Martin?'

'Yes – ' Violet pulled her gaze away from her little girl. The nurse saw a face pinched with anxiety, with clear blue eyes and blonde hair scraped back and carelessly pinned up. Hearing a note of sympathy, her eyes filled with tears. 'I've never seen anything like this . . . It's horrible!'

'I know – it's a shock when you first see it.' To give the woman time to compose herself, she turned to smile at the child.

'D'you know why it's called an iron lung?'

She stroked a hand over the curved metal surface. There were little windows in it so you could catch a glimpse of Carol lying inside, covered with something white.

'The disease attacks the muscles, you see. Carol's lungs aren't working properly at the moment and without the machine they'd collapse. It pumps air into the chamber here and presses the breath out of her body. Then, when it sucks the air out again – d'you hear it? – her lungs get bigger and she takes in a big breath, see? Don't you Carol?'

Carol's head with its tufts of blonde hair could be seen resting on a pillow at the end of the machine. She tried to nod. There were tears running down the sides of her face into her hair. She wanted to speak, but was forced to wait for the machine to give her breath.

'Show your mother what a brave girl you are.' The nurse touched the top of the girl's head for a moment. *Don't cry*, the pressure seemed to say.

'She's the image of you, isn't she?' she said to Violet, who nodded, absently.

The nurse wondered how old the woman was. There was something so worn and sad about her.

'How long will she be in there – in that thing?' Violet kept fiddling with the bottom edge of her cardigan as if to fasten it, but the button was missing. The cardigan had once been white.

'I'm afraid I can't tell you. Not yet. It does take time though, and it depends how well her muscles come back to her. Some of the children do very well.'

'I don't understand it . . .' Violet's emotion bubbled to the surface again. 'She only had a bit of a headache. One minute she was all right . . . She said her neck was getting stiff, that was all, and then . . .' Her face contorted. 'She won't die, will she? Oh God, she can't die – she's only seven! My little babby, just look at her . . .'

'That's how it is with polio.' The nurse spoke abruptly, as if panic-stricken by Mrs Martin's emotion. She turned on her heel, flicking her white veil over her shoulder. She had other patients to attend to, after all. 'We just have to wait and see.'

Chapter Thirty-Six

'Linda? Wake up – we're coming into Birmingham.'

'All *right*. Ouch – leave us alone, will you!'

Linda shoved her sister's sharp elbow away. She wanted to push Joyce all along the aisle and off the bus in her baggy blue frock and never see her again, ever! In any case, she hadn't really been asleep. She'd sat with her eyes closed, head resting against the throbbing window, to block out Joyce and her moaning about how even when they got into town they still had to get all the way out again to the estate.

'Have we got to do this every week? It' s *miles* away and it takes up the whole day!' Joyce had bad adenoids and always sounded as if she was holding her nose when she talked.

Linda felt as if she was going to explode. There was Mom on the seat across from them, turned away as if she was looking out of the window, even though the panes were filthy dirty. *Like staring into a sandstorm.* That was what Johnny Vetch said – in the desert there were storms of sand, whirling in the air and you couldn't see out.

She knew Mom was crying and that was why she wouldn't look round. Linda gripped the edge of the seat. All that they'd seen that afternoon kept burning through her mind. That hospital, the stink of it, and glimpses of sick children before the nurse had told them to get out and they'd stood around outside, feeling lost and stupid.

When Mom came out she looked as if someone had hit her. Carol was inside a big tank thing, she said. It was called an iron lung and it stank of rubber and made big sucking sounds of the air going in and out. She said there was a little mirror by Carol so she could see a bit more of what was going on. Linda decided that *not* seeing it was worse than seeing it. Every time she thought of being inside there she felt panicky and had to take in a deep breath. She could feel sobs rising in her and she forced them down. She wanted to see Carol so badly she thought her heart would burst.

If only it was me instead! She'd give anything for Carol to be all right – anything. To see her running round again in the garden with the rabbits, or with her skipping rope, her long golden hair lifting as she jumped.

Not that polio was to blame for the cropped state Carol's hair was in. Linda's mouth twisted in fury. It was Dad who'd done that.

'I'm starving,' Joyce moaned, slouching along once they'd got off the second bus. She found something to complain about all along Bandywood Road, one of the main arteries of the Kingstanding estate where they lived. 'These shoes're pinching me rotten!'

'What d'you wear them for then?' Linda's feet were sore too, the black pumps worn wafer thin on the bottom and rubbing her toes, but *she* wasn't moaning was she? Joyce was tripping along in that stupid pair of sandals which had never fitted properly in the first place.

'Look –' She displayed one foot. 'There's blood *pouring* down my heel!'

'Oh, shut it!

'Shurrup yourself miss bloody know-it-all!'

'Just wrap up, the pair of you,' their mother snarled exhaustedly. 'For God's sake let's just get home.'

They were walking down the row of municipal houses, doors all painted green. Theirs was number ten – the one with the garden that stood out for having nothing in it except Dad's old Norton bike, rusting away under a ragged tarpaulin amid the forest of dandelions, where it had been since he crashed it three years ago, leaving him with a deep scar on across his left cheek. Reg Bottoms next door, who grew prize-winning dahlias, took the presence of the wrecked Norton as a personal insult, which was the main reason Dad left it there.

They went along the cracked little path and Violet stopped at the front door and listened. Linda's eyes met Joyce's, all squabbles forgotten for the moment in the more momentous thought, *will our dad be in?*

He wasn't, of course, this time on a Saturday. Pubs'd be open. You could feel the house was empty. The dogs went mad when they heard the key in the lock, yowling, claws scrabbling at the kitchen door. The sour stink of parrot hit them in the hall.

'Mrs Martin!'

They were stepping inside when they heard Mrs Kaminski calling from the house the other side. The Kaminskis were Poles. They had the corner house, so the garden wrapped right round the side, and every inch of their land was covered in vegetables, potatoes right up to the front wall. Dad said they were afraid of going hungry. Mr Kaminski was a stocky, silent man who was out there almost every moment he was not at work, digging and weeding. Mrs Kaminski's face appeared over the fence, her lips a bright scarlet. She was a diminutive woman who seemed to hum with energy.

'Ze animals – again!' She hissed in warning. 'Mr Bottoms – very angry!'

'Oh . . . *no*!' Violet sagged against the doorframe.

Linda noticed how her mom never swore in front of Mrs Kaminski. She also kept the dogs well away from her because Mrs Kaminski was terrified of them. Everyone seemed to have a strange respect for the Kaminskis and she didn't really know why, but she'd heard whispers of '*After all they've been through . . .*'

'Thanks, Mrs K – girls, get out there now and catch those flaming rabbits!'

Linda and Joyce scuttled through the house, sore feet forgotten. The dogs leapt up, insane with joy when they went into the kitchen. The back of the kitchen door was all scratches from them, brown scars in the blue paint.

'Get in – now!' Violet shouted to them and all three, two brown mongrels and a beagle, shot through the house, only to be imprisoned in the front room.

'Right – get the bloody rabbits, and don't forget to shut the door.'

Linda and Joyce looked out through the back window. Over the fence they could see Mr Bottoms' head appearing and disappearing in an agitated fashion as he darted back and forth after the rabbits. Extending out of the chickenwire run in the Martins' garden was a seam of freshly dug soil. Moonlight and Snowdrop had burrowed their way out. Again. And were running riot in Mr Bottoms' perfect garden.

'Mr Bum's going to kill us,' Linda breathed.

The two of them stared in horrified awe at Mr Bottoms' bobbing head.

'I told you to get out there!' their mom shouted along

the passage. 'Go on – before they do any more bleeding damage!'

It wasn't often the sisters were allies, but they looked fearfully into each other's eyes. 'Here goes.'

Pushing open the back door, they stepped outside as if into the line of fire. Their own garden was a half-bald patch of badly scuffed grass, pocked with holes where the rabbits had dug. The only patch of colour was the scrubby clump of marigolds Mom'd planted up in the corner by the house once in a fit of enthusiasm. Linda went to the loose bit of fence and pulled it back, wishing they could just go in and catch the rabbits without Mr Bum seeing them. If only they were invisible!

She thought he was going to explode.

'About time! Get in here and get your bloody vermin out of my—' He lunged as Moonlight shot past his ankles, then stood up, puce in the face. Mr Bottoms was a short, compact man of military trimness, with mousy hair clipped to a military length.

'Sorry, Mr Bottoms,' Joyce murmured, putting on her most syrupy voice. 'Only we've been out to the isolation hospital. Our Carol's got polio . . .'

'I don't care where you've been! Those flaming hounds of yours've been howling all the afternoon . . .'

Linda thought Mr Bottoms looked like an angry hamster, his eyes popping, and she wanted to laugh. 'And these *vermin*'ve been at my lettuce. It'll never be the same! And droppings all over the lawn. Get them *OUT*!'

Linda managed to get hold of Snowdrop first, hoiking her out of the vegetable patch, which was carefully screened off by a flourishing set of runner beans. Snowdrop was so round and greedy that she couldn't be bothered to stop eating and run away.

'About time!' Mr Bottom's spluttered again. 'Now get the other one. Filthy animals everywhere – it's a disgrace!'

Mom just couldn't seem to stop getting more animals. It was as if she was running a refugee camp.

'You naughty, naughty girl,' Linda whispered into Snowdrop's quivering ear as she continued munching.

Walking with the warm bulk of the rabbit clutched close to her, she saw Mrs Bottoms watching from the window. She was a neat, darting woman, always full of cheerful comments. Her mouth was trying to smile even now, but Linda thought her eyes looked sad in a way that didn't match. She often looked like that.

By the time Linda had deposited Snowdrop in the hutch, Joyce had managed to get Moonlight. Mr Bottoms was pacing dementedly along the other side of the fence.

'How did they do it this time?' they heard. 'Where're the little so-and-so's getting in?'

Linda and Joyce collapsed into pent-up giggles over the hutches, hands clasped over their mouths.

'I can hear you!' Mr Bottoms roared. 'And it's not funny – like a bloody menagerie, your place. A slum. No wonder you catch diseases! I'll be having words with that father of yours . . .' In a lower tone he added, 'If he's ever sober enough to take in what I'm saying.'

The fuss over the rabbits made them forget everything for a few minutes, but when they went inside they found Mom at the kitchen table, hands over her face, tears running down her wrists. There was a milk bottle next to her, and a tin of jam. Polly and Bluebell, the two blue budgies, watched silently, hunched side by side in their cage.

'I can't think of anything to cook for tea,' she sobbed. 'I just can't think what to do.'

And Linda knew Mom was crying about Carol really, and all of it got up and hit her again and she felt too sick to want any tea anyway.

Linda lay in bed. She didn't like being alone. Normally Carol was in the other bed. Joyce slept in the little room next door. It was getting dark outside and a glow of light came from downstairs where the living-room door was open. In the end they'd had mashed potato and Bisto for tea, and a bit of bread and Stork. Joyce was the only one who seemed to be hungry anyway. It didn't fill them up for long and Linda could feel her stomach rumbling again now.

She wanted to think about anything but Carol lying there in the iron lung, but that was all that flooded into her mind. If she shut her eyes she could almost hear the sound of its air pumping in and out. Tears welled under her eyelids. She was so close to Carol she could feel her feelings. It had always been the same.

How had Carol caught polio? Why her and not the others? They'd all done the same things all summer: played with the rabbits, gone to Sutton Park, gone swimming down the baths. Why Carol?

The front door opened with a clatter. Dad. Linda tensed up straight away. At least he'd got the right house. More than once he'd been so kalied he'd gone crashing into the Kaminskis' by mistake and frightened the life out of them. Poor things were easily frightened too.

The door slammed shut again.

'Vi?'

'*Ssssh*,' she heard her mother. Dad had no idea about shutting up when kids were asleep.

'What's for tea?' He gave a long belch and Linda knew there'd be that gentle snapping sound as he pulled his braces down from his scrawny shoulders. He always did that, soon as he got home. Complained they rubbed. He had to have a cushion on the chair too. He was so thin, nothing was ever comfortable.

'There's not much – I kept it warm.'

'What d'you mean, not much?' He was almost shouting now.

'Keep your voice down...' It was always the same. 'We've carted all the way over to the hospital – to Carol.'

'Oh – yeah. The Lad.' His tone was twisted with sarcasm. He'd got a thing about calling Carol 'The Lad' for the moment. 'How is "he", then?'

'She's bad...' Linda heard her mother begin to cry. There was a rattle of plates. 'It's terrible – she's in this iron lung thing. I could hardly stand to see her...'

'Call this my bloody tea? Potato and nowt else? What d'you think I am, an effing fairy, living on air and gravy?'

The plate hit the wall and smashed down on to the floor. 'What does a man have to do to come home to a decent plate of food of a night?'

'Earn a decent wage and not pour it down your throat, that's what!' Violet flared at him.

Linda could hear the tinkle of broken crocks as she swept up.

'It don't make any difference what I give you for your tea, does it? You're still a bloody skeleton whatever I do!'

'Don't keep on, woman! Always keeping on...' There was another smashing sound and Violet's voice rose to a scream.

'Stop it! Just stop it, will you? There'll be no bleeding plates left if you carry on. Coming in like the Lord God Almighty and carrying on – after the day I've had! Why can't you just eat it and shut up, coming in that time of night with your boozing and carrying on, you selfish bastard?'

'Shut up, you nagging cow!'

Linda lay, hardly breathing. She could hear Mom was crying again.

'Well, you can do without. You'll have a roast dinner tomorrow!'

'I don't *want* a roast dinner . . .' There was a crashing sound, something hitting the table. 'Not if it means going to your sodding mother's week in week out. *Christ.*'

'But we always go to Mom's. You should be grateful . . .'

'Well I'm not going to "Mom's" any more – all right? D'you think I want to sit staring at her old bloomers all afternoon? That old cow thinks she owns the whole lot of us, lock, stock and barrel!'

'Don't talk about my mother like that. You'll soon come when you want summat to eat. Everything just so long as it suits you, isn't it? Harry Martin – the one person on this earth who matters. You don't give a monkey's if your daughter's in hospital in an iron lung . . .'

'My *daughter* . . . ?' He was snarling now. Linda turned on her side under the cover, forcing her fingers into her ears. Saturday nights . . .

It hadn't always been like this. So far as Linda was concerned she'd only had a dad for four years. Before, when the war was on, Saturdays nights had been her and Mom and Joyce and Auntie Muriel when she was living with them, and it had been safe, and fun and cosy. And then the new babby came. Mom was happy then.

'I know you don't remember your dad . . .' That day the telegram had come, she'd been six years old. Carol was crawling around by then, head a mass of blonde curls, too young to understand anything. Her mother's face had been ghostly white.

'Your dad's been a brave soldier, but it says here . . . . . .' She choked on the shock of it, couldn't say it for a bit. 'He won't be coming home.' *Killed in action . . . Harry Ernest Martin.* She didn't take in that they'd got his middle name wrong, that her Harry was Harry Arthur Martin. She didn't think it was important at the time.

Mom was upset, of course, but Linda had heard her say some funny things to Muriel. 'The terrible thing is, I feel *grateful*, almost . . . He'll never need to see her . . .'

And life had gone on without him.

Then, in 1946, while they were still living in Aston, this spectre appeared at their door. A knock one evening, her mother's scream of shock.

The man on the doorstep was horrifying to see, sinister, like a puppet. He was emaciated, his head too big for his body, thin grey hair, sunken eyes, stooped over. Mom's hands went to her face and she backed away, moaning.

'Vi?'

His voice was high and reedy.

'No! No . . .!' She couldn't think of anything else to say.

'It's me, Vi, for God's sake. It's Harry.'

Someone else had got killed, not him. Harry Arthur

Martin had been a POW of the Japanese. Even now he didn't weigh much more than when he came home, and food often didn't agree with him. They said he'd been so malnourished that his body had lost the knack of absorbing it. His head had lost the knack of fending off memories and dreams, and if Mom and Dad had ever loved each other they seemed to have lost the knack of that too. Drink was his anaesthetic and on Saturday nights he took as much of it as he could manage.

Linda screwed her eyes tightly shut as the voices raged on downstairs. She thought about the gates of the grammar school, seeing them open in front of her in her mind like the gates of heaven, safe and tidy and full of promise.

Chapter Thirty-Seven

'Mom – Linda's in the lav again. Tell her to get out!'

Linda scowled, perched on the toilet seat with her copy of *Great Expectations*.

'Lin, hurry up – I need to go!'

'Linda!' she heard Mom's voice. 'Out – now!'

It had always been the same, as soon as she could read. Going to Nana's meant perching in the outside lav with her books, the one place you could get a bit of peace.

Since Nana moved, after the war, to a two-up two-down in Spring Street, they had an outside toilet not shared with anyone. It felt like *her* place, with the cobwebs and slug trails and the nail with squares of newspaper hanging, or sometimes bits of coloured tissue from round the oranges and apples begged off the greengrocer. And best of all, the rusty bolt she could pull across and shut everyone else out – especially Joyce. From there she'd travelled to other worlds in her head with comics and some of the books Johnny Vetch lent her. Most of Johnny's books were about rocks and fossils and birds, but he did once hand her a dog-eared copy of *Treasure Island*. She was completely taken up in it, scared to go to bed every night for ages after, thinking she was going to hear Blind Pew's stick tapping along Spring Street, coming to get her.

They'd left Spring Street for the estate soon after, and

now they had a bathroom inside. It was warmer, in the winter anyhow, but it just wasn't the same. She still slipped out to the outside lav in Aston when she had the chance. In any case, it got her away from Nana and the others. Of course Nana didn't like Johnny Vetch. She said he was queer in the head. And she had no time for books because she couldn't read herself. She kept that quiet out of shame. Even Mom said she'd gone all her childhood without realizing Bessie couldn't read.

'No wonder she wouldn't read my school reports,' she said.

Sundays meant dinner at Nana's house in Aston the way morning meant the sun coming up. She was famous for it in the street, the way she always had the family there every week.

'Going to Bessie's, are yer?'

'Awright Violet – off to your mom's?'

It was always the same, voices greeting them as they walked from the bus stop. Bessie hadn't moved far, and everyone knew her.

The smell of dinners wafted out to them and they could hear the wirelesses playing through open windows where curtains wafted in the breeze. The old man was standing on the corner with string tied round his jacket, Mr Baffin was tinkering with his bike a few doors along from Nana's and kids were playing out with soapbox carts and marbles.

But today there was something else.

'Where's the little 'un? Where's your Carol?'

And Linda heard her mother keep explaining with tears in her eyes about the polio and how Carol was over at the isolation hospital and everyone saying *ahh* and oh, bab, what a shame and how sorry they were, so it took quite a time to get along the road. It made Linda feel all upset again too, so she held on tight to her book and tried to block out the voices which reminded her. It seemed terrible to forget about Carol, but if she didn't her tears would come. What was happening to Carol was like an ache, always there.

It was always the same, Sundays. Same smells of cooking and Uncle Clarence with his pot of ale resting on the arm of the chair, Auntie Marigold in her baggy old frocks following orders in the kitchen, cutting up cabbage and carrots. And Uncle Charlie and Gladys came with the cousins – Norman didn't always come now he was almost sixteen, but Colin came. And once it was all cooked, Nana always commanded one of the girls to knock for old Mrs Magee who lived across the street to eat dinner with them. She'd long been a widow and Nana said no one should have to cook for one on a Sunday, it wasn't worth the gas.

The kitchen was Nana's kingdom, ruled with a rod of iron. Uncle Clarence stayed in the front doing nothing much as usual and moaning about it.

'The country's going to the dogs,' was one of his favourite moans. He didn't work any more, now the war was over.

''Allo wench!' he said lugubriously as Linda ran in ahead of Joyce. 'How's the world treating you?'

Uncle Clarence always said that as well. In fact Uncle Clarence mostly said the same sorts of things over and over again, like 'Bottoms up!' when he drank his ale, and, with a jerk of his balding head, 'You'd best ask the kitchen,' which meant Nana was in charge and what was the use of him saying anything?

'Come 'ere and give us a kiss!' Linda kissed his

stubbly cheek and he rumpled her hair, but then, his eyes mournful as a hound's, he said, 'Did you get up the hospital to see her?'

Linda nodded. 'She's in an iron lung thing. They say they don't know how long she'll be there.'

She saw something in Uncle Clarence's eyes, as if he was flinching inside and he shook his head and looked away and picked up his ale. Everyone loved Carol, even Uncle Clarence, who mainly loved his allotment. 'Poor little bugger.'

Gladys and Charlie were listening, and even Colin, who was thirteen, didn't look quite so much like a spotty sack of potatoes as usual.

'Is that them here?' Nana's voice boomed through from the kitchen.

'Our Linda's here,' Uncle Clarence called.

'What about Joyce?' Linda made a face. Joyce was always the favourite.

'She was always like that with us,' Violet told Linda once. 'Only ever had eyes for Charlie.'

'I don't care,' Linda said, shrugging. Nana was even worse now, after the grammar school.

'She'll 'ave to do then. Get in 'ere, Linda – I can't leave this pudding. Marigold – pass us that cloth!'

The kitchen was full of steam. Bessie was in the process of dropping a pudding basin, tied firmly at the top, into a pan of boiling water. It would steam away for two or three hours, to be eaten draped in custard as the dinner ran on into cups of tea and Nana's games: canasta and cribbage and ludo for the kids, and the week's sweet rations from the grown-ups, all pooled together. Nana always ate as if it was the last day there'd ever be food.

She turned, her fleshy face puce and running with

moisture. She was enormously stout now, just past her sixty-fourth birthday, but very strong-looking, hair in plaits coiled round her head. Her hair was white but it always had a yellow tinge because she smoked one cigarette end on from the last, sucking the life out of each one. She always wore big frocks in dark material, blue or black, and tight black shoes, her feet appearing small because the flesh of her ankles bulged out over them. Her voice could fill a parade ground and when she laughed it shook her whole body up to her chins. Linda had heard Dad say Nana was 'like an effing battleship and someone ought to torpedo her'.

'Don't be so rude about my mother,' Violet would shout sometimes when the beer was in and they were at it again, bicker, bicker. 'She's done a lot for us, she has – more than yours ever flaming well did. You should show some gratitude.'

'*Gratitude?* She's worse than bloody Hitler ever was!'

'There –' Bessie settled the basin triumphantly. 'I've got a nice treacle suet in today. Linda – get over here!' She mopped her face with the corner of her huge white apron, stained all down the front with beef juices. 'Give your auntie Marigold a hand or 'er'll never get done today, this rate. 'Ow's Carol? Poor little beggar.'

Without waiting for an answer, Bessie waddled into the front room.

'Violet? How's our Carol? What've they done with her?'

'D'you want some help, Auntie?'

Linda sat across the kitchen table from Marigold, who was working on a pile of carrots. She smiled at Linda in her rather vacant way.

'You can do some of these.' Very deliberately she

wiped the blade of her knife on the floral breast of her apron and passed it to Linda. 'You be careful now.'

Marigold's hair, once liquorice black, was already fading to grey and hung limply round her collar, held back with two kirby-grips, and her fringe dipped into her eyes. Mom had told her that when Marigold and Charlie were born, Marigold came second and they hadn't got her out quick enough so her brain had been starved. Linda never really understood for years how you could starve a brain. But now Carol was having to be kept in the machine so she wasn't starved as well. Whatever exactly had happened to Marigold, she could talk to you all right and do a lot of things, but she wasn't quite like anyone else.

'Our Marigold's not the marrying sort,' Bessie had decreed for years, and no one questioned it.

Then there was Auntie Rosina, whom no one ever talked about much except to say she'd 'gone to London' before the war. If anyone even mentioned her, Nana looked fit to blow up. Auntie Rosina had wanted to go on the stage and ran off with an actor. There was that one picture she had sent, of herself all dressed up, and it stayed behind a jug on the mantelshelf. In the picture she looked very pretty and had dark eyes and hair. Gone to the bad, no doubt, Nana said.

It sometimes seemed to Linda that her mom and Charlie, despite being married and having homes of their own, were like Marigold and had never left either. They danced to Nana's tune like puppets. It was only Rosina who had ever really left.

Linda cut the end off a carrot and began to scrape off the dirt, dipping it in a bowl of water. Marigold was shelling peas, with her funny, secret smile on her face. Violet could hear the voices from the other room, Mom describing going all the way to that hospital, two bus rides away.

'I don't know how I'm going to go carting over there all the time,' she was saying.

After a moment Linda saw that Marigold had stopped doing the peas and was reaching furtively into her cleavage. With a swift movement she pulled out a little bottle full of clear liquid, took a quick swig which she swallowed with relish, then replaced the bottle with a wink at Linda.

'Don't tell on me, will you?'

'No,' Linda said, looking away, at the steam curling from the cooker over to the sink, in front of the window. There was a packet of Bird's custard on the draining board. Nana must smell the drink on Marigold's breath, but it seemed to please Marigold to think she had secrets.

'Where's little Carol?' Marigold said, as if she couldn't hear anything that was going on in the next room. When Linda explained, Marigold looked at her and said, 'Oh. Shame,' but without emotion.

They put the carrots on to boil and Nana came back in then, grunting as she hoisted the beef out of the oven with the potatoes sizzling round it and basted them.

'Vi, Gladys – set the table!' she bellowed. 'You go and get Mrs Magee,' she ordered Linda. 'You needn't think you're going to get out of doing anything.'

'I *am* doing something. It's Joyce who's sitting on her backside . . .'

'Don't you give me that lip or you'll be washing your mouth out . . .'

Linda shrugged.

Usually she had Carol to help. Mrs Magee loved Carol. Linda slipped out the back and along the entry, where the air was cool and her skin stood up in goose-pimples, until she reached the bright street. She walked into Mrs Magee's mothball-smelling house, bracing herself for the struggle.

The old lady was long and lean and sitting defiantly in her chair. She'd worked as a seamstress for years and her black clothes were old and wafer thin, but beautifully made.

'I'm not going. You can't make me.'

Her voice was high and scraped the air. She had her teeth in a teacup. They pinched her so badly that she hardly ever put them in.

'Please, Mrs Magee. It'll be all right.' Linda knew her twelve-year-old reasoning was no match for Carol's pretty charm. Carol could always persuade Mrs Magee.

'No it won't.' She clamped her knees together. Her shimmering black skirt flowed over them.

'But dinner's ready.'

'I don't care. Blasted thug of a woman. Thinks she runs the street, that she does, pushing me around, coming after my sugar ration and acting as if it's charity!'

Linda sympathized a great deal with Mrs Magee, but what could you do?

'She's just trying to be kind.' This was what they were supposed to believe.

'You can kill people with kindness,' Mrs Magee said, beginning to surrender. You could tell by the way her voice went quiet. She looked up at Linda. The whites of her eyes were bile yellow. 'I s'pose you'll be in trouble if I don't?'

Soon she was dressed in her black coat and hat to go across the road, cup of teeth in hand.

'This is the last time I'm doing this.' She said that every week.

Linda took Mrs Magee's stick of an arm so that they could shuffle across the road. The elderly lady was soon seated mutinously at the table and never took her hat off.

The afternoon passed as it always did on Sundays, with the huge meal which they ate until they were all stuffed full.

'Tummy Touching Table – that's what you want,' Bessie said, ladling out spuds.

Belly Busting Buttons, Linda thought.

When Harry had first come back, every week Bessie went on about how they had to fatten him up. She never said anything now. Even Bessie, who knew every trick there was to get around rationing, was no less defeated than the rest of them by the ravages the Japanese camps had wrought in him.

Harry ate his dinner in silence. It was Nana who held court, family her captive audience, full of her neighbours' doings, memories of Grandad Jack, her husband, who died of the influenza at the end of the Great War.

'Worshipped the ground I trod on, Jack did,' she sighed, between mouthfuls of beef. 'There's not many have a husband like I did.'

Occasionally someone else got a word in. Mrs Magee champed away resentfully with her troublesome teeth and the children listened and poured as much gravy over their potatoes as they could.

Today, though, a lot of the talk was about Carol. Linda didn't want to hear it. The others ate mainly in silence, Joyce and Colin looking sulky. Gladys nagged Charlie – 'Don't hold your knife like that, it's rude' – Charlie barely ever said a word and Harry answered in monosyllables if Nana said anything to him.

'Got enough spuds there, Harry?'

'Yes, ta.'

Afterwards, Linda took Mrs Magee back to her house – 'At last – I'm not budging next week!' – and when she got back, her dad was asleep as usual, his thin face sagging with exhaustion.

'Look at the poor bugger,' Uncle Clarence remarked.

He soon fell asleep too, the paper spread across his chest, so that the only sounds in the front room were their snores. The women went into the kitchen and talked over the first round of washing up and Violet made a pan of custard. Then Nana got her cards and boards and cribbage pegs out and they all played until it was time to put the kettle on and get the treacle pudding dished out.

'This is a good 'un, Bess – one of your best,' Uncle Clarence told her, and it was beautiful, thick and sweet and gooey with treacle, the custard not too thick or too thin.

'Very nice,' Gladys murmured. She came along with Charlie every Sunday, no question. This was what the Wileses did on Sundays and if you married one, then that was that. Bessie was the matriarch and no mistake.

Linda tried to sink into the familiar, over-fed drowsiness of Sunday afternoon with them all crowded in there together. She sat by the hearth, on the old peg rug. She knew the bright red bits in it were from a skirt she'd once had. Colin and Joyce were over in the corner, whispering. Linda wondering what they were saying. Colin never whispered to her, but she'd never found cousin Colin very interesting anyway. All he ever thought about was football. She missed the dogs, shut in at home. Nana wouldn't have animals in the house. She said they were dirty.

She tried not to think about Carol but her thoughts

kept going back to her. She was so poorly. What if she never got better? What if she died . . . ? No! Don't think about it!

She jumped up. Nana and her mom were in the kitchen, she thought, but it was quiet, and when she went through the back she saw that the door was open and they'd gone out into the yard.

Before she'd got across the kitchen she could hear Mom crying. Linda stood in the kitchen, looking out through the door. They were out there by the mangle, Nana with her arms folded, Mom wiping her eyes.

'That's why she's poorly!' she was saying. 'I can't bear it – seeing her like that, knowing she's lying there in that thing. What am I going to do? I've always tried not to show anything – not to treat her any different. It's a punishment, I know it is. But it's me should be punished, not her!'

Linda stood on her left leg, trying to balance, right leg bent up at the knee. She stood there, balanced, like a stork, listening to her mother crying outside.

Chapter Thirty-Eight

The week before Carol fell ill with polio, Harry came home drunk, on a weeknight.

'God almighty, hark at him!' Violet jumped violently as he came crashing in through the front door. The dogs all leapt up, barking frantically.

'Get away from me, stupid hounds! Violet – get 'em off me!'

The dogs were supposed to be outside at night, once the rabbits were safely stowed away.

'Why're they in the house? I've told you . . .'

'They're company – all right? Molly, Dolly – out!'

'Company – drooling bloody mongrels!'

'Well, they're better company than you ever are!'

Harry didn't mind the dogs when he was sober, was even quite fond of them. But now was a different matter because with the drink in, everything was hateful to him, himself especially.

Linda, Joyce and Carol scuttled into the hall to help Mom get Dolly, Molly and George out. George the beagle was leaping up, tongue lolling, at their dad, who was propped unsteadily against the dirty, scratched wall. His sunken eyes were glassy and he was still barely more than a skeleton draped in clothes. In the shadows his scar from the bike accident looked more pronounced than ever.

'What kind of house do I have to come home to, eh? Like a sodding zoo. Look at it!'

He pushed himself off the wall. The girls each seized hold of a dog – Carol had Molly as she was the easiest – and were dragging them by their collars towards the back door. Linda had George, who struggled mightily, his brown and white body like a ball of muscle.

They all ended up in the back room, dogs scratching at the kitchen door. There was something about Dad tonight. Linda felt her innards go all tight. It was never knowing what was going to happen, that was the worst thing.

'You aren't going to last in that job if you keep on.' Mom's voice was low and weary. 'The dairy've already warned you – they're only keeping you on . . .' She bit off the end of the sentence.

'That's it – go on!' He was holding on to the back of a chair, swaying. His voice grated out. 'They're only keeping me on 'cause what? 'Cause I'm a wreck, that's it, isn't it? "Poor old Harry, look at the state of him? Can't even shit regular like other blokes any more . . ."'

The three girls stood there, Linda pressing her shoulder against Joyce's arm, and she could feel that Carol had grabbed hold of the back of her dress and was clinging on. The fear in their eyes enraged him further.

'Go on – have a good look at the wreck!' He was trembling suddenly, as if he was freezing cold. 'Keeping me on out of pity! I'd like to've seen them . . . They didn't have to see what I . . . They've no idea – none of 'em . . .' He stuttered the words out, his face working, arms twisting at his sides as if fighting something.

'Oh, Harry – ' The sadness in Violet's voice brought him to tears and he stood there gulping in front of them, hands with their bony wrists pressed to his face.

'I couldn't bear it . . . there . . . in Burma . . .' he gulped. 'And now I can't bear it here neither . . .'

Linda felt herself twist inside and none of them knew what to do.

Mom looked as if she was going to cry as well. She went to put her arms around him, and worst of all were the little crooning noises she made as if he were a baby, the way they had heard her doing at night when he woke screaming. Suddenly, though, he pulled his hands down and his face was contorted with rage.

'You don't know!' he screamed. 'You don't know, none of you – don't touch me, woman!'

He turned on Violet. 'Wait for me, I said. And you couldn't even . . .'

The girls all jumped as he strode over to them suddenly and grabbed Carol by her wavy blonde hair.

'Found yourself a proper man, did you?'

'Harry, don't!' Violet moaned. Her hands moved in protest, but she stood helpless.

'Ow! Dad, don't – it hurts, it hurts!' Carol shrieked. He was twisting her round by her hair, her legs pedalling to keep up. Linda felt as if every hair on her own head was being ripped as well.

'Dad – stop it!' She went to try and get him off Carol. She'd do anything for Carol. 'You're hurting her! Bloody stop it, will you!'

Harry backed away, dragging Carol with him as she sobbed and screamed and tried to get away.

'Get me the scissors, Linda, *my daughter* . . . She's the only one I can be sure about, isn't she, looking like that?'

Linda stood at a loss.

He bawled at her, 'Scissors – *now*!'

'Harry, no – leave her alone . . .' Violet tried to tackle him again but he pushed her away.

'Shut up –' He pulled Carol even closer to the door. 'Linda – hurry up!'

Linda came back from the kitchen with the big, blunt scissors with black handles.

'Right – now then...' Harry was swaying slightly. He took the scissors in one hand and pulled Carol's hair all up above her head.

'For Christ's sake, what're you doing – not her hair! Leave her!' Violet was screaming now, trying to get near, to stop it. Drunk as Harry was, he kept twisting round, dragging Carol with him, fending her off.

'You know what they did with faithless fraternizing bitches, don't you? The ones who went whoring with the Krauts? Well – *my daughter* – I could cut your mother's hair off...' He dragged Carol by her hair again and she cried out, sobbing, hysterical with pain and fear. Linda clenched her fists; her body was so tense she felt she might snap.

'I've always fancied having a lad, though...' He snipped off a chunk of her hair, having to work hard with the blunt blades. The gold locks fell to the floor.

'Dad, don't!' Carol was crying. 'Stop it – don't cut my hair off...! Ow – you're hurting me!'

He sawed and chopped at it, hunks of it falling and Carol crying even more at the sight of it. Once the heavy length of her hair was all gone he carried on and on. The room was full of the sound of women crying. Joyce and Linda clung to each other, helpless as Dad reduced Carol's bright hair to uneven tufts all over her head. All Violet could do was hold Carol's hand.

'There you go – *lad* – ' He pushed Carol away from him and she fell into Violet's arms trembling and crying. Violet stroked her shorn head, sobbing heartbrokenly herself.

'You bastard, Harry. You pathetic, cruel bastard! Oh,

babby – my beautiful babby, I'm sorry. Your pretty hair ... My lovely one, my little love ...'

Joyce and Linda huddled together, shocked and crying.

Their dad stood looking at them, his own face wet with tears, but wearing an expression of terrible contempt.

'It's only a bit of bloody hair,' he said, disgusted. 'It'll grow again, for Christ's sake ...' He sank down into a chair. 'Go on – sod off out of here, the lot of you, with your blarting, and leave me alone.'

Violet took the girls up to bed. In Linda and Carol's room she sat on Carol's bed, holding her on her lap, Carol's scrawny little body still convulsing with sobs even after she had finished crying.

'Why did he do it, Mom? What did he mean?'

'Ssssh,' Violet held her close, rocking her, weeping into the stubbly remains of her hair. 'He's just poorly, and he's had too much to drink. You know your dad when he's had too much – he doesn't know what he's doing.'

Linda watched from her bed, hugging her knees, face swollen with crying. Mom was clinging to Carol, distraught, quite different from normal. She'd always been distant from her, fending her off as if she was a nuisance, so that Carol had learned to turn to Linda for comfort and they'd grown close as close. But now, there was Mom sobbing over her as if she was the most precious thing in the world. It stirred Linda up. She didn't know how to feel. She could never make Mom out. She hardly ever showed much emotion, and when she did, it was over things that didn't matter, like in the war when that family across the road, the Keillors, had moved away, when she hardly knew them: Linda had barely ever seen Mom speak to Mrs Keillor at all, but there she was, crying as if her heart was about to be snapped in two. Nothing ever made sense, like the things Dad was saying downstairs about Germans.

'I'm sorry,' Mom was saying, over and over again. 'It's all my fault. Oh, Carol, I'm sorry.'

Linda couldn't bear it. 'Mom!' Her voice cracked. 'Mom, don't!'

Her mother looked across at her, as if she had forgotten she was there, and her face changed. She wiped her face, as if stunned.

'Come here,' she said gently.

Linda crawled out of bed and sat beside her. Violet put her arm round her and she stretched one arm round Mom, the other round Carol. They sat quietly for a moment, then Joyce appeared in the doorway and came and sat down with them as well.

'I'm sorry, girls,' Mom said.

And she started crying again.

Carol came into bed with Linda that night. Linda put her arms round her.

'I'll look after you,' she whispered as they drifted into drowsiness.

A week later Carol came in from playing out on the estate saying she had a bad headache and felt giddy. Before long she couldn't get up at all.

Chapter Thirty-Nine

Carol's illness had a strange effect on the neighbours. Or at least the women. Everyone was kinder for a start, kept asking if they needed anything.

A few days after the rabbits got into their garden, Mrs Bottoms came round to see Mom. The front door opened on her anxious face. She had on a pale blue shirtwaister, her hair was tightly curled and she held out a bunch of pink roses from the garden. Joyce and Linda stood in the shadow of the hall.

'Here, dearie, these're for you. I hope you don't think it funny of me coming round ... Only I heard your Carol had been taken poorly.'

There was a pause, then Mom stepped back. 'Come in.'

Edna Bottoms talked agitatedly as she came through the door. 'Reg said I shouldn't bother you – should mind my own business. So I thought I'd come round while he's at work. Men don't always understand these things, do they?'

'Joyce, Linda – outside. Go on.'

They scooted out to where the dogs were lying out on the strip of concrete at the back of the house, basking in the warmth. Tufts of grass spiked up through the cracks in the concrete.

Linda was wandering off to see Snowdrop when Joyce hissed, beckoning. 'Come 'ere – see what she wants!'

The kitchen window was wide open. The girls squat-ted under it, backs against the hot wall. Violet was making tea. There was a clink of cups and they could hear snatches of her telling Mrs Bottoms about the hospital, the iron lung, and Mrs B's concerned noises.

Joyce and Linda mimicked her, under the window. *Oh dear, oh Lord ...* They mouthed like goldfish, crossing their eyes and pulling the grievous expressions they could picture on Mrs Bottoms' face. *How terrible ... Poor little thing ... Dear oh dear ...* until they were helpless with giggles and had to move down the garden to explode into laughter, tears running down their cheeks. Linda felt a bit better after it.

'Come on – we're missing it!' Joyce dragged her back by the arm.

They squatted down again. The breeze blew the women's drifting words back and forth in snatches, but they could catch the sad, confidential tones. Mrs Bot-toms was talking about a baby. She and Mr Bottoms had one son, called Frank, who was married now, but it wasn't Frank she was talking about.

'She only lived six days. Not even a week.' Mrs Bottoms was speaking in a tight, hiccoughy way. Her voice became a squeak. 'My little Daisy. She was just lying there in the cot ...' There was a long silence until they heard their mom say something: '... ever so sorry ... terrible ...'

Linda's eyes met Joyce's. They were solemn now.

'The worst of it is – it's Reg!' Words seemed to come out of Mrs Bottoms like a cork from a bottle. 'If we could talk about her, it might lay her to rest. But he won't let me. It's as if she never existed. I don't even know where they buried her – I was in that much of a state at the time. The police came. They thought ...

They took her away and I've never known . . . Reg said he didn't know – never asked . . . And he's not the same since the war. If I ever say anything he just says you have to forget everything. Put it behind you. But I can't . . . I try, but . . .'

When she started crying, really crying, they moved away. Linda went down on to the scrubby grass and picked up Snowdrop out of her run. She hugged the rabbit's big, robust body, stroking her cheek against the smooth white fur.

They didn't overhear when the next visitor came. Mom told Dad about it at tea, the four of them round the table, window open and a breeze blowing in.

'I met Eva up at the shops today,' Violet said.

Harry looked up, without much interest. 'Eva?'

'Kaminski. Next door.'

'Oh ar.'

'We were just going home, both of us, with the shopping and she said she'd walk with me. She asked about Carol – she was very nice as a matter of fact. Then all of a sudden she just came out with it. "You know, Peter and Alenka were not our only children." I mean, I don't always understand her – her accent and that – and I wasn't sure what she meant.'

Linda mashed her grey, boiled potato into the gravy. Glancing up, she could tell her father was listening now, elbows on the table, rubbing his hands together as if they were cold. And she could tell also that her mom was pleased he was listening, as if just for once they were talking like people who might like each other.

'What'd she say then?'

'She said they had four – another boy and girl. One was called Karol – but I think that was the boy. I didn't catch the girl's name. They were younger, she said.

Anyway, the whole family were taken off to a camp, in Russia somewhere. Nineteen-forty-one I think she said. Cutting down trees – even the kids working morning till night in the freezing cold. The boy died in the camp and then – it was a bit hard to follow – but the little girl died somewhere else, after – I think she said in *Persia*? Died in her arms, she said, in a truck they were crammed into. Nothing she could do. Couldn't even bury her. They just had to leave her.'

Her eyes filled. Everything seemed to make her cry these days. Linda felt close to tears herself.

'Terrible,' Harry said. He stared ahead of him for a moment as if seeing things none of them could see.

When they'd finished eating, the girls got down.

'Go and check the rabbits,' Mom said. They were trying not to aggravate Mr Bottoms – as much for Mrs Bottoms' sake as anything.

Harry got up from the table and put his hand on Violet's shoulder. As she was going out, Linda heard him say, 'Sorry, love. I'm sorry – about Carol. What I did – her hair. I wasn't myself.'

And she heard the half-stifled sound of her mother bursting into tears.

'She's so poorly,' she sobbed. 'I can't stand the thought of her in that horrible metal thing!'

Chapter Forty

Linda went with Violet to the hospital for visits even though she had to wait outside.

At first, Carol was very distressed and homesick.

'I want to come home,' she kept crying. 'I don't like it in here.'

Violet found it terrible to see, and made even worse by the sight of her chopped hair.

'She looks like a plucked chicken. What must those nurses think?'

She seemed glad Linda was there: someone to talk to and relieve her feelings.

The second time they visited, the two of them were utterly miserable. On the way home, Violet took her into the bomb-scarred middle of Birmingham and headed for the Bull Ring.

'D'you want a hamster?' she said suddenly.

'Ooh, yes!' Linda said. She knew Mom was trying to be nice. Carol's illness had brought out a softness in her. And it was her way of finding comfort. She collected animals the way a bird feathers its nest.

'What about Sooty?' Linda said doubtfully. He was forever bringing birds in.

'You can keep it upstairs, away from the cats. Make sure you keep the door shut.'

They went home on the bus with two tiny hamsters

in a little cage, one for Linda and one for Joyce. The man said they were sisters and wouldn't fight.

'They should behave themselves all right – like you and your sister, eh?' he added with a wink.

By the time they'd reached Kingstanding, Linda had called her hamster Goldie.

'You can't call her that – she's not one bit of gold on her,' Joyce sneered.

'Can if I want.'

Joyce called hers Loretta because she thought it was pretty.

'They all right?' Mom came up to see them in Linda's bedroom. They all knew they were trying not to think about the hospital, and Carol stuck in that machine.

The hamsters turned out not to be a good idea. Within a fortnight Linda woke up to find that Loretta had set upon Goldie in the night and killed her. She was covered in bloody gashes.

'I don't think you're supposed to put hamsters in together, are you?' Mrs Bottoms said when she heard. 'He should have told you, really.'

And quite soon after, Loretta died as well. Linda found her curled up in her bedding, cold and stiff. At the time, she thought of it as a bad omen about Carol. Fortunately, she was wrong.

'Hello, pet.' Violet bent down and kissed Carol's cheek, stroking her hair. It had grown back a little now and was like a soft, fair cap all over her head, in varying lengths. 'You all right?'

Carol gave a little nod, drinking in the sight of her mother. Her father, of course, she did not expect to see.

'I'm all right. I'm going to get better.'

She spoke with such certainty that Violet gave a faint smile and leaned over her, eyes filling with tears of relief, though she tried to hide it.

'Is that what the nurses say?'

'They think I'm better as well. And I told them.'

Carol's face had changed somehow since the last visit. The look of sadness and preoccupation had gone. Her eyes were bright again.

'It's going to be all right. And I'll be able to walk. He told me.'

'Who told you? Have the doctors been?'

'Yes – but it wasn't them. It was him.'

Violet's hand stilled on Carol's head and she frowned. 'Who? What're you talking about?'

'*Him.* There.' Her eyes looked up to the wall beside her. 'He comes to see me – at night mostly. And he tells me things.'

'Oh, I see – you've been having nice dreams!' Violet laughed with some relief.

'No – not when I was asleep. He's just there, when I look up. And he smiled and told me it would be all right.'

Violet frowned. 'I think I'll go and see if I can talk to one of the nurses.'

She walked off along the ward, a slim, vulnerable figure in her old skirt and cardigan, mac over her arm. She was less intimidated by the nurses now. The thin one they saw the first day often came and talked to her.

'She won't believe me,' Carol told the nurse when they came back together. 'But you do, don't you?'

'What're you talking about?' the nurse said impatiently. 'Who's this "he"?'

'I dunno. But he's there, and he talks to me.'

'She's coming on nicely now,' the nurse said, ignoring Carol. 'This week she's really made quite a stride –

everyone's pleased with her. We think she could spend some of each day out of the lung soon. And of course we're starting on the physiotherapy with her.'

Whatever had happened, there had been a definite change. When they were in Aston for dinner on the Sunday – one of the last times Harry ever came – Bessie said, 'Our Carol was looking better. Summat different about her. I'd say she was on the mend.'

That week, for the first time in ages, things felt lighthearted, as if there was hope.

When Violet said goodbye to her that day, Carol was beaming up at her, dark eyes aglow. She looked like an angel.

By the time Carol had been in the isolation hospital for just over three months, she was spending more and more time outside the iron lung. Once they were sure she could manage without it, the hospital told Violet that Carol was to be transferred to St Gerard's, the Father Hudson's Hospital at Coleshill, where she would be looked after and given more physiotherapy. Though her arms were little affected, the muscles in her legs were badly wasted and they thought it would take some time. There was also a problem with contractions in her spine. They said she might need an operation when she was older.

Violet didn't dare argue with them and took all this in quietly, but when she reached Linda outside, she burst out, 'Coleshill if you please? That's flaming miles away – it's nearly Coventry! I don't know what our mom's going to say. She'll have a fit.'

Linda wondered why Nana once again seemed to be judge and jury about every thing that happened. Surely what mattered now was getting Carol better?

Chapter Forty-One

'Ticket?'

Linda fished in her pocket for her penny and the conductor grumpily shoved a ticket at her and moved on. She made a face at him behind his back and returned to staring out of the rain-streaked window. The 29A had left the estate behind and was grinding along in the cold, wet October morning. She felt very out of sorts.

They'd been to see Carol on Saturday, right over at Father Hudson's in Coleshill. She had a proper bed now, instead of the machine, and seemed much happier. She was in a long ward with doors all along one side that could be opened to wheel the beds onto a terrace outside when it was fine. The nuns who nursed her were kind, she said. Her favourite was called Sister Cathleen. And they were doing physiotherapy every day. It was the only time her face fell, talking about that.

'It hurts ever such a lot,' she whispered to Linda with tears in her eyes. 'I don't like it.'

Sister Cathleen, who had a round, freckly face, said Carol was 'coming on grand'. But she still wasn't home and it felt such a long time since she had been, and the place was such a long way away. Nothing felt right with Carol away all the time. And Dad was drinking more. She tried to pretend to herself that that wasn't true, but she knew really it was. You never knew how he was going to be when he drank so you could never relax. All she wanted was to get out.

Yesterday she had wanted to meet her best friend Lucy Etheridge in Sutton Park, but Mom had said no.

'We're going to Nana's – you know we are.'

'But why do we have to *every* week? Can't we stay here and do something different – just for once?'

'You know we can't – she'll be expecting us!'

'Dad's not going!'

'All the more reason for you to go,' Mom snapped. She was bad-tempered all the time, living on her nerves.

'I'm fed up with going there. It's always the same and it's *boring*.'

For once she and Joyce were in agreement. 'I want to stay at home,' Joyce said.

'Enough of your bloody lip! Course we're going – no arguments.'

Violet left Dad with a ham sandwich and a plea not to go to the pub. He didn't go to the nearest pub, which sold Mitchells & Butlers beer, but walked further for his Ansells. Linda knew Mom was just trying to make herself feel better – he'd be out the door seconds after they'd gone.

Mom kept saying, 'He's getting worse. It never used to be this bad.' She looked thin and wrung out.

Linda glanced down proudly at the uniform skirt she was wearing. King Edward's Grammar School! She said it over and over again to herself like a magic spell. Even after a year the wonder of it had not worn off.

When she took the eleven-plus she was full of nerves, remembering how Joyce had said it was ever so hard. Joyce had gone without a thought to the new secondary modern school close by on the estate. Linda got part way through the test paper and wondered if it was all a mistake. If she didn't find it too difficult, did that mean she'd not understood the questions and got it all wrong? Her hands began to sweat with anxiety and her heart was banging away. She didn't have any real idea what going to the grammar school meant, it was all unknown, but there was something glowing in her, like the little pilot light in the Ascot heater in the bathroom. She *wanted* it.

And they gave her a place! It was the one time in her life when she saw she had impressed her father.

'Let her have a go,' he said. 'She's earned it.'

Mum was unsure, Nana full of scorn.

'We'll never afford the uniform,' Violet said. It was all beyond what she knew, unknown territory, and she wanted to play safe. 'And it's two buses away. No – it's better if you don't go. You'll be worse than you are already, nose always in a book. That's not real life, you know. No – it's not for people like us.'

It took Linda all her powers of persuasion – that she'd have no other clothes all year and she'd do odd jobs to get the money, she would even eat less to save the money, she'd do *anything*, if only she could go! It was Dad who stood up for her and for that she was deeply grateful.

For the last year she'd entered the portals of this other world of the grammar school, away from their scruffy house with its stinks of the animals and cabbage water and Dad throwing up – to a place where the world opened up in books and maps and pictures, the way it had that day in Johnny Vetch's house in Aston when he showed her his cases of fossils and his book about the stars and she knew it was possible for someone else like her to care about learning. At school she was in heaven, even though she never felt quite like most of the others. There were only a very few who were poor and down at heel like her. At first she'd wondered if she could ever keep up. By summer she was among the top five in her form, and though a few of the girls were snobby, they weren't all, and she had Lucy, a best friend who was prepared to stick around with her.

'If you go there,' Johnny Vetch said to her in his gentle voice, 'you'll learn things you'd never dream of in the other school. You'll be another person. It's where they separate the sheep from the goats.'

Johnny was a quiet, thin man of twenty-three. He'd gone away to college and had some sort of breakdown. He lived with his mom still and did odd jobs that didn't demand too much of him.

'He overtaxed his brain, that one,' Bessie would say. 'That's what happens. Overtaxed it. You want to be careful, my girl. You don't want to end up like Johnny Vetch. Nose in a book and no wife.' She added something else behind her hand to Mom and laughed in a way which meant it was something crude.

Be careful, was all Nana ever said. The only safe thing, so far as her grandmother was concerned, was having babies and more babies and staying at home like a fat queen bee in a hive trying to keep everyone under your thumb. Like her.

'The world's a big place,' Johnny told her one day. 'Full of interest. One day I'm going to go on a boat along the Amazon river. I've read about it. There're spiders there as big as my hand.'

The spiders made her shiver. But Johnny didn't tell her just about spiders. He told her about the birds, the snakes and butterflies in the Amazon. And the deserts across the world, full of seeds just waiting for a fall of rain so they could burst out into the brightest, most radiant flowers you could ever see. And about rocks and crystals, and the Northern Lights dancing like chiffon in the cold night, and constellations of stars. Johnny loved the blackout. You could see everything better.

One winter night before the war ended, when Johnny was still all right, he came round while Linda was at Nana's.

'Tell Linda to come outside a minute,' he said from the doorstep. 'There's something I want to show her.'

'Don't talk daft,' Nana dismissed him. 'She'll catch her death.'

But Linda was already jumping up to get her coat down off the hook. Whatever was Nana on about? She walked home every night with Mom, didn't she? It was just because Nana didn't approve of Johnny Vetch.

'Be careful...' Nana said reprovingly. 'Don't go keeping her out for long. Her mom'll be in soon.' It was getting late. But Mom sometimes was late these days.

The night was cold with the promise of ice. The air made her cheeks feel slapped. Once Nana had slammed the front door huffily, the dark closed in on them.

'Your eyes'll get used to it,' Johnny said. 'Come on.'

He took her hand and led her down the street towards his mother's house. She thought they'd go down the pitch black entry and inside, that he probably had a new book he'd ferreted out of some musty old shop somewhere. Or a new rock to show her. Linda knew people thought Johnny was strange, and that he couldn't hold down much of a job or anything. He wasn't thought of as 'normal', but she always felt safe with him. They were in tune somehow.

'Best be quick,' he said. 'This is something special. I've got the key off Mr Jacobs.'

Linda thought this sounded exciting. 'Where're we going?'

'Wait – you'll see.'

Two streets away was a brick church. To Linda's astonishment, Johnny led her round to the side door and unlocked it. Leading her inside, he pulled a torch from his pocket. Once more, her eyes adjusted. She could smell the place, a strange sweetness of stone and paper and wax, and as Johnny moved the weak beam of the torch around them she could make out a vast, dark space, pews stretching in lines ahead of them. It reminded her of her grandmother's funeral, when Dad had got upset and fought with that rough old man who'd turned up. The school had taken them into church once or twice, but that was all. It gave her a funny feeling, as if she had stepped into somewhere quite distinct from the street outside. She realized that Johnny knew the place very well. Perhaps he went to church every week? She didn't know.

They walked along the side aisle to the back of the church. Johnny shone the torch on a little door at the back and when he opened it she saw steps.

'You're not frightened, are you?'

'No!' It hadn't occurred to her to be afraid.

'Best thing is, if you go ahead of me, I'll shine the torch for you. I'm right behind you.'

The staircase wound round and round and the only sound was their footfalls on the stone and their breathing, and all they could see were the shadows winding round with them from Johnny's torch. At the top there was another door, and when Johnny opened it Linda felt a rush of cold air.

'This is the bell tower,' he said. 'Mind your head.'

They were in a wide, flat space, in which hung the

dark shapes of several bells. Linda would have liked to look more. They seemed so big and heavy, hanging there. But Johnny was steering her over to the side, where there was a window. Fixed over it was a mesh.

'That's to keep the birds out,' Johnny said. 'You get pigeons messing all over the bells else and it'd stink. But . . .' He struggled with something at the side of the window for a moment. 'It's loose. Look – come up this end.'

He unfastened the wire at one end and folded it back on itself so there was a space at the end for them to look out. Linda leaned against the wall, her hands on the sill, which was level with her collarbones. Johnny had to bend to look out over her head. He switched off the torch.

'You can't see much down there. We're high up, you know – above everything. If it was daytime you'd see all the houses and factories – the roofs – from up here.'

'Can we come back in the morning?'

She heard him laugh, faintly. 'One day, maybe. But look up. This must be one of the clearest nights of the year. Just for once, no clouds and you can see past all the smoke.'

She turned her gaze to the sky. Johnny was right. Apart from a few faint streaks there was nothing to obscure the arc of sky, the great sea of stars. She had never seen it like this before. The more she looked, the more of them she could make out, as if they were coming out in their tens of hundreds just for her. Silently the two of them stared into the sky's vastness and after a time she had a strange feeling, the same that she had had in the church downstairs, that she was in a special place and all that was around her was somehow alive and in communication with her, making her feel she was awash with life, but she could never have put the feelings into words. Words might have made it disappear.

'See over there –' Johnny broke their long silence. He pointed out a shape of stars, guiding her, and eventually she could see what he was talking about. 'That's Orion, the hunter. See those three stars? Those are his belt.' He pointed out arms, legs, a sword. 'Oh – and that one's Ursa Major – the Great Bear. The Plough they call it as well.'

'Looks like a saucepan,' Linda said.

'Yes, I s'pose it does.'

He pointed out another shape which he said was a Greek lady called Cassiopeia, but she thought looked like a W on its side. She liked the pictures in the sky, but best of all she liked standing looking out in the quiet, high above everyone, in a place she'd never been before. It was some time before she noticed how cold she was.

'Best go now,' Johnny said, fixing the mesh back. 'Keep those pigeons out.'

'I like the night better than the day,' she said, and he laughed.

'Only when there's no clouds.'

When her mom asked what they'd been doing, when she finally got to Nana's, Linda said, 'Looking at the stars.' She didn't say where. Johnny didn't ask her to keep it secret, but it was *her* secret because it had been special.

'That Johnny's stupid,' Joyce said spitefully. He didn't pay Joyce much attention.

'Bats in the belfry,' Bessie said.

'He's not stupid,' Linda said crossly. 'He's clever.'

That night stayed with her; and Johnny's books and

interest in things that a lot of other people didn't seem to care about. There had to be more, she knew, than the life she saw round her. Working in factories, having babies. She couldn't have put that into words either, but the knowledge sat in her like a hunger. And going to the grammar school was part of that hunger, of answering the need for more.

Soon, Lucy got on to the bus. She was a quiet, serious girl with thick brown bunches lying neatly on her shoulders. Linda adored Lucy, but she'd never invited her round to her house. She was ashamed of the state of the place, the smell. Lucy lived in a nice villa in Sutton Coldfield with a neat front garden and clean, tidy furniture inside. She didn't have any brothers or sisters and her mom and dad were quite old and they took her to church every week. Everything about Lucy's life was gentle and calm. Linda had been to her house a few times and they were very kind to her.

'Sorry I can't really take you back to mine,' she said. 'My dad's not well. He has to have it quiet so we're not allowed to take people back.'

She didn't want home and school meeting each other anyway. At school she could be someone else, just like Johnny Vetch said.

'You done your French homework?' she asked Lucy.

'Yes. I got stuck on my arithmetic though – could you do it?'

'Most of it.'

Lucy pulled her book out, and for the rest of the journey they talked sums and lessons, heading for the hours at school, those ordered hours of timetables and routines and being sure when you will eat, in which Linda was in heaven.

Chapter Forty-Two

Rain lashed down in slanting lines. It was early in the morning, November and bitterly cold.

The men were harnessing the horses on to the floats in the Co-op Dairy, and loading them up ready for the day's delivery. The light was poor and they were cursing the cold and wet. Hot breath streamed from the horses' nostrils.

The supervisor came over. One of the carts was not being attended to.

'That Harry Martin's?' He nodded grimly at it.

'Yup,' the next man said. He rolled his eyes. 'Poor bugger.'

'We can't go on like this. Where the hell is he?'

It had been getting worse, week by week. His timekeeping, the drink.

'He's here!' One of the others called, relieved.

All the men felt for Harry Martin. Who wouldn't? Christ alone knew what had got him in that state. He'd been out East in one of the Jap camps, and it was written all over him. Anyone'd need a few drinks after that. They tried to keep him going, made excuses for him. But Harry was going down the pan, they could all see it. Must have had a night of it last night.

He was shambling along, a pathetic figure, clothes hanging on him and bareheaded, no cap, even in this weather. And what was worse, he wasn't even

235

sobered up now, his gait unsteady, lurching from side to side.

The supervisor tutted, shaking his head.

'Come on, pal,' the other bloke was saying hurriedly to Harry. 'I'll give you a hand.'

'Ta,' Harry said. He clung on to the side of the float to steady himself. His face was so thin and drawn it was pitiful to see.

'Look, Harry,' the supervisor spoke quietly, not wanting to make a song and dance about it all in front of the others. 'You've been late in every day this week. And look at the state of you! The other blokes've been covering for you, but you can't go on like this. For heaven's sake pull yourself together! I'm giving you one more chance, but after that – you're out. I'll have to let you go.'

Harry seemed to be listening but not taking in the import of what his boss was saying. A smile played round his lips. His coat hung open and they saw that clothes were only scantily buttoned up, the top of shirt hanging open, showing the bones in his emaciated chest. And he was soaking wet.

're you listening to me?' The supervisor was aggravated now. 'I'm trying my best for you, pal, but you're a bloody mess – look at the state of you! Come on – get yourself together!'

'I c't.' Harry was still smiling. His face and words didn't match.

'Come on, Harry,' the other man said, trying to shift him with briskness. 'Get to work.'

Harry was swaying, smiling, almost laughing now. 'Can't no more.'

The two other men looked uneasily at each other.

'Look – we can't go on like this. You can see that,

can't you? I'm going to have to let you go.' The supervisor felt a real heel doing it, the state the bloke was in. The last thing he needed was more punishment. 'I'm sorry, Harry.'

There was no reply. It was as if he hadn't heard.

'D'you hear what I said?' His tone was harder now. 'I'm sacking you. You're not doing your job. You'd best get off home now in any case.'

There came a dark trickle from Harry's nose, blood running down his chin, but he didn't appear to notice. Gashes of it fell on his shirt.

'Harry? You don't look any too well, mate. Go on – get yourself home.'

But Harry continued smiling and swaying from side to side. 'Can't. Can't go home.'

A moment later his legs gave way and he collapsed on the floor. His hands went over his face and he curled up on his side and lay there, his whole body trembling.

'God Almighty,' the supervisor breathed. 'This isn't just the bottle, is it? We'd best call an ambulance.'

Harry was taken to Good Hope Hospital and it was soon clear he would not be coming home for some time. He was in a state of collapse.

'It's terrible seeing him,' Violet sobbed to Bessie.

She'd taken them straight round there after visiting Harry, and sank down in Nana's kitchen amid all the napkins and the smell of milk heating in a pan. Violet had snatched up a piece of old rag which she was using for a handkerchief, and kept squeezing it into a ball in her hands.

Linda and Joyce sat at the table, pretending to play with Nana's toffee tin of old buttons.

'He's like a shell. As if he's got lost somewhere in himself and can't find the way out!'

'Terrible. Terrible thing,' Uncle Clarence kept saying over and over. For once he'd got out of his chair and was standing in the doorway, fingers hooked in his braces. 'He's never been right since them Japs.'

'I don't know what I'm going to do!' Violet said. 'What with him there and our Carol all that way away! I feel as if I'm going out of my mind with it all.'

Linda took a black coat button and ground it into a crack in the table. The button snapped in half.

'Look what you've gone and done!' Bessie roared at her. 'Can't you behave yourself for five minutes?'

Linda pushed her chair back and it scraped the floor. 'I don't want to play with the buttons!'

'Well, sit quiet and behave yourself and don't give us your lip!'

Linda would normally have taken herself off to the lavatory but today she didn't want to miss what was being said. She went and stood in the scullery, arms folded mutinously, where she could see them all, Joyce sucking up to Nana as ever, sorting buttons as if she was five years old.

Bessie poured the milk into a cup. The child she was looking after now was not far short of a year old and she was getting fed up with him. They were trouble when they got older. She only liked the young ones. She stirred a spoonful of sugar into the milk and put it in front of him.

'Ere – get that down you and pack in that blarting!'

'Where's Auntie Marigold?' Joyce asked.

Marigold was just always there, normally, like the gas stove and the table.

'We've just had a new 'un come – only a few days old. Marigold's got her in the pram.'

Linda could see her mother, sitting bolt upright, her eyes filling with tears again.

'You're going to have to pull your horns in, now you've lost your breadwinner,' Bessie decreed.

'I'll have to get a job,' Violet said flatly.

'You'll be out at work soon enough, won't you Joyce? I don't know why they keep them in till they're fifteen now, that I don't – waste of time, staying on at school for nothing. And *that one*,' Bessie interrupted, nodding her head contemptuously in Linda's direction, 'will have to stop getting big ideas – swanning off, wasting two bus fares to get to school. There's been quite enough of that carry-on. What use is all that lark going to be to her? Bad enough when you had Harry in a job, but now – well, that's the first thing can go . . .'

Linda felt the words stab her, like poisoned arrows. Her eyes narrowed with loathing towards her grandmother.

'I don't know,' Violet was saying. 'Harry quite likes her going there . . .'

'Well, he ain't in any position to have a say, is he? He was always a fool to her – and he's not the one left to bring in the money. It's time you faced up to things. All those fares you're paying out getting to see him, and to Coleshill – it's all costing you, Vi, before you pay the rent and put a crust in their mouths.'

As if reminded, she leaned over, reaching for a finger of bread to give to the orphan child. There was a bowl of orange boiled sweets on the table and she took one for herself, untwisting the wrapper and popping it in her mouth before sitting back, arms folded across her bosom. Her skirt rode up, exposing her scarlet bloomers.

'You want to get her out of that school – all these bloody fancy ideas, and get her ready for work. She'll be no use to anyone, else . . .'

Linda looked across at her grandmother, at her broad, rough face, cheek bulging with the sweet, her battering ram of a body and bullish face, always so sure she was right about everything. The rush of rage she felt finally propelled her outside to the lav.

Between the rough brick walls she stood with her back to the stained lavatory pan, shaking, as if she was going to burst with the great, silent scream inside her. *No, no! Mom couldn't listen to that advice, wouldn't take her away . . . She couldn't . . . Wouldn't!* The thought of it was too unbearable. Clenching her fists, she banged them down on her thighs until they ached.

She stayed in there as long as possible, perched fully clothed on the edge of the toilet bowl, staring at the cobwebs across the hinges and dreading going back inside. She wouldn't say a word to anyone, not while they were still with Nana.

On the way home she could contain herself no longer. Words tumbled out.

'Mom, you won't take me away from the grammar school will you? Like Nana said? You can't, *please*. You won't, will you?'

Her mother whipped round in the road, all her own fear and tension pouring out.

'Just bloody shut up, will you? Stop going on at me! I've had enough! I don't know what I'm going to do, so just shut it till I've had time to think!'

Chapter Forty-Three

12 Bloomsbury Road,
Kingstanding
B'ham
Nov 18th, 1950

Dear Muriel,

Sorry I haven't written – have been at my wits end lately. Harry was taken ill last week and he's in the hospital. All the back-and-to between him and Carol is taking it out of me and I don't know what to do for the best.

Harry's in a very poor way. He's never been right of course, so when he started feeling poorly we didn't think much of it but he shouldve stayed in bed and he kept on instead. He was taken bad at work his lungs are bad and he's feverish and doesn't always know me.

When I went up the hospital the first time he said the doctors said, Do you keep birds at home? (Well I thought he's gone barmy at first, coming out with that.) And I said yes, we had budgies and the parrot and they looked at one another as if to say, 'Oh, yes, told you so.' They told him he's got some disease you catch from birds on top of everything else that's wrong with him that is. So I said, but the parrot's not poorly or anything. But they said it can be sick and not show it and I should think very hard about getting rid of the birds as Ive got children in the house as well because you can catch it by breathing it in. I didnt like the way he talked to me as if I wear dirty or something. I suppose the dogs make a mess I might have to get rid of Silver and the budgies but the worst of it is Harry's not right at all. He can hardly do a thing for himself he's like a child and he keeps crying over the least thing. He kept hold of my hand all the time when I went the first time and kept saying, Don't go, Vi, don't leave me. He was frightened to death, I don't know where he thought he was and course I had to go home. The doctor took me aside and asked about the war and Burma and the camps and that and when I told him he said "I see." I just don't know what to do, Mu, which way to turn. I wish you lived closer.

Our Carol's still over at the hospital in Coleshill and at least she's getting better, there's no doubt. Her arms aren't too bad it's her legs. And they say her back's not right and she might have to have an operation not yet though. But I feel as if they're taking her away from me. She's fixed on one of the nuns who's looking after her she's called Sister Cathleen and I know she's very kind but it's as if they're getting their claws into her. Someone's put holy pictures by her bed and she said last week they took her to Mass and Sister Cathleen said Carol asked if she could go but I don't know if that's true. She's only young and it feels as if she's more theirs than mine now. Sometimes I feel very down.

Done nothing but moan, have I? Thanks for your card. Glad you and Dickie are getting on so well but your news came as a shock, you can imagine. Australia! Harry always wanted to go there but I don't think I'd be brave enough to start a new life. I can't say I'm glad you're going though. I miss you enough, all the way down in Brighton!

Keep in touch, won't you? Need any welding doing! Sorry if this is a bit miserable.

Best wishes, Violet. x

Chapter Forty-Four

'What're we going to do with him?'

Violet stared into the parrot's cage. 'He looks all right, doesn't he? You'd never know there was anything the matter.'

'He's shivering,' Joyce said.

Linda watched the parrot as he sat huddled up at one end of his perch. She'd thought of the name Silver after reading *Treasure Island*.

'I think he looks poorly,' she said. He had an air of misery about him.

'Don't breathe near him!' Violet said suddenly. 'Oh, I don't know! I can't give him to anyone, can I? Who's going to want a parrot with a disease?' Linda could hear tears coming in her voice.

Out at the front Mr Kaminski was working with a spade, turning over the soil in his vegetable garden. In need of another adult opinion, Violet went and asked him. Linda and Joyce stood leaning against the smelly tarpaulin covering their dad's Norton. Linda felt her head swim with tiredness. Last night Mom had been crying. It had gone on a long time.

'He is sick?' Joe Kaminski said, standing his spade up in the soil. In the winter sunlight his chiselled face was divided into planes of light and shadow. 'Then you have to . . .' He made a wringing motion with his hands.

'Ooh no – I can't do that – I just couldn't! I mean, we've had him a long time.'

Mr Kaminski shrugged. 'I do it if you want. Or you let him go. What else?'

Violet came in and shut the door with a slam. 'Fat lot of good asking him.'

Next day she decided to let Silver go. First thing, she was down there in her nightie with an old cardi over the top, the cage door open and the back room window. Silver sat stubbornly on his perch, not taking the blindest notice of this generous offer of freedom.

'He doesn't want to go,' Joyce said, eating toast.

'You don't say,' Linda retorted. They were both dressed ready for school, shivering as the frost-nipped air streamed in.

'Shut it, clever clogs.'

Violet tried moving the cage over to the window, a development that Silver looked no further impressed by.

'You'll have to get him out,' Linda suggested. 'He doesn't like the cold.'

'He's poorly. What d'you expect? How would you like to be turfed out when you've got the flu or whatever? Just hang on. Something'll happen.'

'Yeah – a wizard'll come with a spell book,' Linda said, sarcastically.

'That's enough of your lip!' Violet turned on her, wagging her finger, her eyes narrowed. 'I've had quite enough of it. You can pack in thinking you're better than the rest of us – and you needn't get ideas about staying on at that posh bloody school any longer. I'm going to tell them – after Christmas you can go to school here with Joyce like everyone else!'

It came so suddenly, like a slap.

'No!' Linda gasped. She saw Joyce looking smug.

In a fury Violet reached into the cage. Silver didn't make any protest which showed he was not well.

'Mom – Mom, you haven't said anything to them have you? You can't – don't, *please* . . .'

She was whimpering like a tiny child, so full of shock and betrayal at this attack on the one thing she held so precious.

Violet steered Silver out of the cage and hurled him out of the window. 'Go on, you silly sod – just go! Get out of my sight!'

'Mom!' It was Joyce's turn to be outraged now. 'You can't – the dogs'll get him. That's horrible!' She ran to the window. A great chorus of high-pitched barking came from the garden.

Linda could see nothing, think of nothing but the shock of her mother's words. She went to her, pulling on Violet's bony arm, her voice high and shrill.

'Mom, don't make me leave, don't, please! I'll do anything, just don't make me. I like my school – I don't want to go to Joyce's school, please, Mom, *please* . . .'

'Get off of me!' Her mother shrieked. 'Stop keeping on – you've heard what I've said so shut it, 'cause that's how things're going to be. Your dad might die and your sister's bad and all you can think of is your bloody school! I've put up with your airs and graces long enough. I said *shut up*!'

Her own nerves at breaking point, she shoved Linda violently across the room so that she staggered back and fell, hitting her head on the hard arm of the chair. The stab of pain through her temple floored her and she curled up, head down, sobbing, dimly aware of the cold, smelly lino under her and Joyce shouting somewhere in the room that Silver couldn't fly.

After a moment Linda realized she was alone, because

Mom and Joyce were outside trying to get the dogs off Silver. She raised her head and looked through her tears at the dirty floor, her arms resting on it, the woollen sleeves of her school jumper. She could still hear the dogs, wild with excitement outside. Somewhere in it all was the furious voice of Mr Bottoms demanding to know what was going on at this unearthly hour of the morning.

Linda couldn't think straight. Every nerve in her body seemed to scream NO to all that was around her: her family, the filthy chaos of her home, being taken away without any say from the one thing she really loved. She put her throbbing head down on her arms, nipped a mouthful of the sweater between her teeth and bit into it, while her body shook with helpless sobs.

Her one hope was that her mom would simply forget, or not get round to talking to the school as she didn't get round to so many things. But Mom had Nana behind her, nagging and keeping on. And Nana wanted to bring her down a peg. She always had. With despair, Linda knew that her mom was in a state and couldn't think for herself, that in the end she would always do what Nana said. No matter if Linda cried herself to sleep every night and begged and begged, Bessie's word would rule. By the end of that week Violet had been to King Edward's School and told them Linda would be leaving at the end of term.

On Saturday they all trekked over to see Carol. She had a wheelchair now and had made friends with some of the other children. Linda was so pleased that she looked better, but she could not hide her own misery. The journey over there had been silent and mutinous.

'You can't sulk for ever,' Mom said.

Sulk? Linda thought. She was too outraged to reply. Mom and Nana between them were pulling her whole world apart and Mom could call it *sulking*?

'I don't see what you're making such a fuss about,' Joyce said. 'After all, you've been to the grammar school for a bit – you can always *say* you've been there, can't you?'

Linda turned her face to the window. Joyce would never understand. The secondary modern suited her perfectly well. If you were a girl they gave you just enough to get a little job to fill in time before you got married. You weren't supposed to expect anything much.

'Oh, leave her,' her mom said. 'She'll come out of it.'

Linda's throat ached, and her body felt brittle, as if she might just break apart. She didn't answer either of them. If only she could see Johnny Vetch again. He was the one person who would have understood what it meant to have your dreams smashed. She thought of that night up on the church tower, seeing the stars, the greatness of it. But Johnny had gone away for a bit. They said he wasn't very well.

Carol was not by her own bed when they arrived. She was sitting beside a friend's bed, and Sister Cathleen wheeled her back when her visitors arrived. Carol beamed.

'Someone cut your hair?' Violet asked straight away. Now it had grown longer, it had been trimmed into a bob round her chin and it suited her. She looked very pretty.

'Sister Cathleen did it,' Carol said. She turned and beamed up at her nurse, whose freckly face smiled back very fondly at her.

'D'you like it?' Sister Cathleen said. 'Looks grand, doesn't she?'

'Yes. Thanks.' Linda heard the coldness in her mother's reply. She could tell Mom didn't trust Sister Cathleen. She didn't like Carol loving her the way she did.

'I'll leave you to have a good old chat,' Sister Cathleen said. 'She's had a grand week, though, haven't you?'

Parking the wheelchair, she moved off along the ward. Violet stared after her energetic figure for a moment.

'Sister Cathleen's been teaching me some prayers,' Carol said, as Linda and Joyce settled on her bed close to her.

'Oh, has she?' their mother said. Carol didn't hear the hostility in her voice.

'And look – she's given me some rosary beads – aren't they nice?'

From her hands dangled a set of pretty blue beads.

'She told me how to say it in Latin – it goes, *Ave Maria, gratia plena, dominus tecum . . .*'

'That's enough of that,' Violet interrupted, exasperated. 'She shouldn't be telling you all that mumbo-jumbo without asking me. Gives me the creeps, all that.'

'It's not creepy, it's nice. She says Mary is our mother and she's always with us.'

'What a load of bloody twaddle! *I'm* your mother. Aren't I good enough for you any more?'

Carol looked taken aback at the fierceness of her mother's outburst.

'Well yes, but . . .'

'Sorry, bab.' Violet stroked her hair. Linda watched. She saw the way her mother looked at Carol now. It was a peculiar thing. Carol was the one she had paid no attention to before. Now, though, it felt as if she was the only one of them Mom really cared about.

They had to tell Carol that Dad was poorly. And about Silver. Violet kept it light, so's not to upset her. Between her and Joyce they made what had happened with Silver into a funny story instead of a sad one.

'In the end, we had Mr Bum yelling over the fence on one side, and Silver was sitting there with all the dogs round and Mom lifted him up and he flapped over into the Kaminskis. I reckon he likes it in there.'

In fact, Silver had sat in the Kaminskis' garden for the rest of that day looking stunned and unwell. By the next day he had disappeared, and Linda imagined that Mr Kaminski had done what he'd suggested doing to Silver in the first place, but none of them had seen, so they all chose to believe that he had flown off into the cold blue air and found somewhere to be happy. At least that was what they wanted Carol to believe.

Linda didn't say a word all this time. Eventually Carol reached over and touched her hand.

'What's up?'

Tears came into Linda's eyes straight away. Trust Carol to be the only one to notice how upset she was!

'Mom's making me leave my school . . .' She couldn't stop the tears then. It hurt so much.

Carol's eyes widened. 'But *why*? You love it there, don't you? Mom – why?'

'It's just how it has to be,' Violet said, in a voice that said *don't argue*. 'Too much on our plates.'

'Oh.' Carol squeezed Linda's hand.

'She's making a fuss,' Joyce said. 'Can't you shut up about it now, Linda? It's getting boring.'

But Carol kept hold of her hand. 'Poor Linda,' she said, and her brown eyes were full of an understanding beyond her years.

Chapter Forty-Five

'Come on – time to go!'

Linda was up on her bed. Sunday, and time to go and catch the bus to Nana's for dinner, the way they did every week, as sure as eggs was eggs. She didn't move. Joyce was already downstairs. She heard Violet's voice, full of irritation.

'Where is that girl? Linda? Come *on!*'

Slowly, limbs heavy, she dragged herself off the bed and downstairs.

'Why d'you have to make me keep on?' Violet was hoiking the dogs into the kitchen to be shut in. She already had her coat on. She had shrunk very thin, like a dry twig, always ready to snap.

Mutinously, Linda put on her school coat and scarf. She didn't know she was going to do it, but as soon as they were out of the front door she ran for it.

'Oi – what the hell're you playing at?' Violet shrieked after her. 'Get back here!'

'No – I'm not coming!'

'What d'you mean, you're not bloody coming? Get here now, or we'll miss the bus.'

'I don't want to go to Nana's!' She stood some way off along the road, poised for flight.

'I don't care what you want – you're coming!'

'No!'

A furious Mr Bottoms erupted out of his house, newspaper in hand, practically frothing at the mouth.

'D'you think you could *possibly* conduct your family business somewhere else so the whole road doesn't have to hear it?'

'Oh, sod off,' Violet roared at him. 'Come on – we'll leave the little cow. You won't get any dinner then!'

'Don't care!' Linda yelled.

She watched her mother and sister disappear along Bloomsbury Road to get the bus. For a moment she felt bereft. It was the first weekend in December and freezing cold. Her breath was white on the air, the sun at a low angle in the sky. She didn't have a key and she'd have to be out for hours now until they all came back.

But anything was better than going to Nana's. She boiled inside every time she thought of her grandmother. It was all her fault she had to leave her school. Mom wouldn't have made her if Nana hadn't kept on. The way she made *everyone* do what *she* wanted. Like poor old Auntie Marigold. Why did everyone just do what she wanted? Why was everyone frightened of her? It was only Auntie Rosina, whose pretty, dark-eyed face stared out of the dusty photo on Nana's mantel, who gave her any hope. She'd got away, hadn't she? But where was she now?

Sunk in misery, she came to the bit of waste ground where there was an old see-saw and a couple of swings. Across the way was Mrs Nixon's house. She had a refrigerator with an extra cold compartment and she made ice cubes out of orange squash in the summer. Linda sat on one of the swings but she'd come out without a hat or gloves and the chains made her hands cold so she got off again. Her palms smelt of rust from the chains.

Soon she came to her old school, where she'd gone before King Edward's. Of course it was silent and empty. She looked over into the playground, imagining herself in it with all the others, the games of 'hot rice and cold sago', running, bouncing the ball. All the girls she'd known there went to the secondary modern except for her. Of course she still saw some of them round the estate, but there was a distance between them. She had separated herself off, going to the grammar school. And now she'd have to go back. It felt like a disgrace.

She stood listening to the echoes of shrieks and laughter, games and chants: *On the mountain stands a lady, who she is we do not know* . . .

Turning away she walked and walked to keep warm, a determined little figure, dark hair waving round her cheeks, hands pushed down into the pockets of her coat, bare legs and ankle socks. She felt defiant. Never mind the cold, and no dinner! Who cared? She'd refused to go to Nana's! It was time someone refused Nana something. She got her way over every single thing. It was Nana's fault she had to leave her school . . . At this thought she was full of rage again. *I hate her, I hate her, the bloody old cow! Just because she can't read or write!*

There was a place on the estate that Peter Kaminski had shown them, years back when he was still not above playing out. Peter was sixteen now, and an apprentice engineer. He had always been a daredevil, seemed to have no sense of danger. And he had shown them where it was. Behind a fence, tucked in out of sight, was an old Spitfire.

Linda went to the fence and peered through at the little plane standing there in the weeds, its shape unmistakable, the round-ended wings, the bits chipped off the propellors. No one seemed to know why it was there. Peter used to run round, arms out, roaring and sputtering, and they all followed and joined in, a childish squadron of Spitfires. She remembered one summer evening when they were all up here, her and Joyce, Peter and Alenka Kaminski, who was Joyce's age, with Carol laughing and straining against the straps of the pushchair as she watched them all playing. Linda used to push Carol all over the place when she was little, she never minded. And now they were having to push her again.

She hugged herself and stared at the sad, silent plane in its bed of nettles. All that cold afternoon she felt herself changing shape inside, shrinking back. No more King Edward's. No more hope of being something special. Fate hadn't chosen her for something after all. She'd go to the secondary modern and be like everyone else, leave school at fifteen, get a job. At the grammar school they talked about taking more exams, going to college or university. Another world, and it was not to be hers.

She thought about Johnny Vetch's words, 'If you go there, you'll be a different person . . .'

Her breath streamed through the fence towards the Spitfire, lying there in the citrus afternoon light. There it was, a battle hero, grounded and unseen. For a moment she felt like reaching out and stroking its wing for comfort. Instead, she picked up a big stone and hurled it, heard it thump off the rotting wing and fall to the ground.

Part Four
1953

Chapter Forty-Six

1953

'Pass me my shoes over,' Joyce ordered.

She was preening in front of the bedroom mirror in her white taffeta wedding dress, the veil a cloud of net over her shoulders. She was thoroughly enjoying the audience of her mother and sisters, who she assumed were rapt with admiration.

Without enthusiasm, Linda reached for the pair of white shoes with their two-inch stiletto heels.

Watching her, Violet was struck once more by the way that Linda was a mystery to her – quite different from the other two. She was getting tall now, curvy, with a sultry look to her, that black hair curling inwards in waves round her face. She could tell Joyce was getting on Linda's nerves – as usual. They'd heard about nothing but Danny and the wedding for months now and Linda was bored sick with it.

'God, Lin – I'm getting *married*!' Joyce gibbered. 'Can you believe it?'

'Not really,' Linda said.

'You could at least sound pleased for me.'

'I *am* pleased for you!'

'Well, you don't *sound* it.'

'You want to be careful in them.' Violet nodded towards the shoes. If you catch one of them heels in the hem you'll have a nasty tear.'

257

'Well, I won't, will I?' Joyce said pertly. 'I'm not that stupid, am I?'

'That's a matter of opinion,' Linda retorted.

'Oh, shut *up*.'

'Charming. Does Danny know what you're like?'

Joyce's pointy, narrowed-eyed face squinted back from the mirror, eyes filling with tears. 'You're horrible, you are! It's my wedding day and you can't even stop being a cow! You should be nice to me today!'

'Yes – cut it out, Lin,' Violet said, though half her mind was on the dogs in the garden. One of them was barking loudly and she eyed them through the window. Herself, she rather liked Danny with his stocky barrel of a body and naturally cheerful expression. Joyce had been climbing on to the back of his motorcycle in her skirts and high heels for over a year and now there were wedding bells. Joyce had struck lucky, she thought.

'You going to put your make-up on now?' Carol wanted to know. Violet and Linda had helped her upstairs and she was on the bed, watching intently. She'd been in her wheelchair since she came out of St Gerard's and was going back to hospital in the autumn, for the operation on her back which they hoped would make her able to walk properly again.

'Give me a chance!' Joyce winced as she squeezed her feet into the shoes. If there was a fashionable but viciously uncomfortable style of shoe to be had, you could guarantee Joyce would get hold of it. She looked at her meagre collection of make-up. 'D'you think blue or green'd be better?'

'Blue,' Linda said.

'Green,' Carol said.

Joyce tutted. 'Goodness *sakes*. Mom – tell them to

get out! They're getting me all mithered, fussing around me all the time!'

'Right – you two . . .' Violet was about to usher them out of the room, but Joyce, about to lose her audience, changed her mind.

'Oh, I s'*pose* they can stay,' she granted long-sufferingly. 'Only tell them to stop talking stupid.'

'No –' Violet was firm. 'Next door, you two – you need to get changed. Quick!'

She still had her old work frock and pinner over the top and needed to get on, but she lingered for a moment, watching Joyce put on her make-up. Violet's tired features broke into a smile. There was Joyce, seventeen and with her job at Bird's, and *getting married*! Joyce really thought she'd arrived. Violet saw herself on her own wedding day, at the same age and with similar hopes. Then she thought of the wrecked, disillusioned man downstairs whom she had to go and get ready.

Heaven help you, Joycie, she thought, the smile fading. But then she and Harry had had the war, their generation sharing all that grief and trouble. It had broken Harry. But it'd be different now – had to be.

'I hope you'll be happy, Joycie,' she said gently.

Joyce turned, eyelids brushed with blue, and for a rare moment she was a soft young woman, and solemn.

'I think we will. Danny's a good 'un, Mom.'

'I know. I can see.' She put her arms round her daughter. Joyce felt to her more solid and substantial than she was herself. 'You worried?'

Joyce shook her head. 'Nah. Mind my veil . . . Is Dad . . .? Is he really going to come?'

Violet wasn't sure if this was asked with hope or dread.

'He says so. Won't hear of staying behind. He wants

to see his little girl get married. Look, I need to go and finish him, or Danny's dad'll be along before I've got him dressed.'

Let alone me, she thought, hurrying to him. Mother of the bride. It's going to be a rush job.

Harry was still in bed. She'd taken him a cup of tea earlier, and he'd drunk half and left the rest to go cold on the bedside cabinet. He lay there with his eyes closed, one arm out from under the covers, so thin in its blue-and-white-striped pyjama sleeve. He looked so settled, so still, that she wondered, as she often did, whether he had slipped away. But then she heard his breathing. It was tempting just to leave him there. She felt exhausted at the thought of getting him up.

Like having my feet buried in concrete, she thought. *That's how it feels, living like this.*

He had spent months in hospital after he broke down completely. He was better in himself now, gentler somehow, as well. But his body was never going to get any better. She knew that. And in accepting that, things had become quiet and gentler within her. Those days, after the war, when she had paced the floor day after day, weeping in anguish, were past. For a moment, in the shadowy room, she could see in his wasted features and grey hair a glimpse of the vital, energetic Harry she'd married, and the tenderness which so often saved her rose in her again. She remembered that Christmas when he and his pals had made those paper snakes to sell, paper and paint everywhere, the drive he had then to get on and get out of Birmingham.

'You silly sod,' she whispered.

Harry opened his eyes. He seemed alert, and she saw that he hadn't been asleep at all.

'What're you gawping at?'

260

'You, sunshine.'

'Have I got to get up now?'

'It's about time, if you don't want to be late. Sure you want to?'

'If it's the last thing I do. Give us a hand.'

She went to assist him, feeling his skeletal form straining to perform this simple movement. He groaned, already panting from the exertion, and she felt a moment of despair at the effort required to get him to the church.

'Harry . . .'

'No – don't say it. I'm going to that church.' He looked round at her. Even in the gloom she could see the sallowness of the whites of his eyes. 'I'm a useless item, but I'm not missing our Joyce getting wed.'

'All right, love, I know. Let's get you sorted out then.'

These days she surprised herself, often, by the gentleness in her voice, by her own patience. Since those months in hospital, he'd never been able to work. Not much more we can do, the doctors said. His system had taken too much. But she hadn't always been patient. Not all the way through, in those days of fear and strain. Now, though, she could see that he was moving slowly, so agonizingly slowly, towards the end of the line.

So she washed him and painstakingly shaved him, quite used to running the razor over the sharp contours of his face, and helped him dress in his old Sunday suit.

'Look like a bleeding scarecrow, don't I?' he said, but with resignation.

'You're all right,' she said, thinking, surely he doesn't imagine he's going to walk down the aisle with her? He'll never make it.

Once they reached the bottom of the stairs, his

261

breathing was so laboured you'd think he'd run a race. Violet led him to his chair by the window, and he sank into it with a groan. The ashtray on the arm was full of stubs from yesterday, and she went and tipped it in the kitchen bin.

'I'll get your porridge.' He lived mainly on porridge now. That and fags. 'Then I've got to go up and get ready.'

She cut herself a piece of bread, daubed some Stork on it and took it upstairs with a cup of tea. On the stairs she heard the girls giggling together. It was a nice feeling, them getting on for a bit, happiness in the house.

The bedroom smelt stale, with that sickly aroma of Harry. The doctor said, 'His body is slowly eating itself, Mrs Martin.' She didn't know exactly what that meant, but after hearing it, the smell repelled her more than before. She pushed the window open and smelt newly cut grass. Mr Bottoms had been out yesterday with his mower.

'Now then – get going, Vi,' she said. 'Or you'll be in that church in nothing but your girdle!'

Her dress was simple, a pretty blue and white cotton print with a white collar and sleeve edgings, and it hung flowingly over the curves of her slim figure. She'd been taking more pride in herself again now she was out at work. It was Rita, a jolly newcomer from London, who'd taken her on at the salon, just to help out at first. She could not have put into words the gratitude she felt towards Rita.

'You can sweep up and wash the brushes and that – do some washes. We'll see how you get on.'

She settled in fast. Rita, big-hearted and generous, took to her like a sister.

'You're a natural,' she said. 'I bet you could soon pick up a few basic cuts, Vi.'

And the wages, though not handsome, boosted Harry's National Assistance and Joyce's wages from Bird's.

The salon was now called 'Rita's'. Violet loved being there, after the loneliness of home and being forever surrounded by sickness. Here was a pretty, sweet-smelling female world of chat and cosseting. It wasn't just frippery haircuts, she decided. It was a way of looking after people, making them feel better, and she loved washing people's hair. They told her she had gentle hands, especially after Rita, who could be a bit vigorous on the scalp.

Rita was big and exotic-looking, with long dark hair all swept up into piled, curling styles. She'd always give Violet a cut when she needed it. She'd had her hair long and scraped back for ages, with no time or money to think of doing anything else, and it had gone lank and split at the ends. Her skin had been pasty and tired, like old congealed porridge. Rita helped her learn to take pride in herself.

'Well, this mop needs a cut all right,' Rita had said, the first time, running strands of Violet's hair through her fingers. 'Lovely colour though. It's all natural too! Oh, I'd love to be a natural blonde.' She regarded her own swarthy features in the mirror. Her dad was an Italian, she said.

'Very straight though, isn't it? No good trying to look like the Beverley sisters. You need it quite short and smooth. I'll make you look gamine, darlin'.'

'What?' Violet asked, alarmed.

'You know – boyish. Cheeky, sort of thing.'

'Well . . . if you think . . .'

'Oh, I do, love. Very definitely.'

Rita snipped the hair into a neat bob round Violet's chin.

'Ooh, those cheekbones! You're so lucky,' Rita murmured caressingly. 'A face I'd give my right arm for.'

Violet listened in astonishment. No one had told her nice things like that before. Only Harry, but such a long time ago that it felt as if she had been someone else. And Roy . . . But as soon as thoughts of him came to her mind, she slammed the door on them. No good thinking about that, his face the last time she saw him. She couldn't stand the ache it gave her inside, even after all this time.

She combed her sleek hair, stroked a dusting of blue on to her eyelids and added mascara.

'You don't look so bad, for an old 'un,' she told her reflection. 'Better than our mom looked at thirty-eight, any road.'

She had a pretty white cardigan and sandals bought specially.

'Today I'm going to my daughter's wedding,' she told herself archly, then laughed at herself. Today, no matter what other troubles there were, it was going to be good. She thought about Harry. *Please let it be all right*, she thought.

Chapter Forty-Seven

Linda had helped Carol downstairs and they were drinking Vimto in the kitchen, Carol resting in her wheelchair.

'You look *nice*, Mom,' Carol said.

A rare smile spread across Violet's face.

'Am I all right? Petticoat not showing?'

They reassured her.

'Rita's made your hair look lovely,' Linda said.

Violet was touched by this moment of warmth from her daughter. The one she now thought of as difficult, strange to her.

'And aren't you two a picture? Linda – you've done it all a treat!' Linda also had style, she saw suddenly, a knack for making things look right.

The two of them had new frocks as well, both pink. Their hair was brushed out and Linda had pinned little pink and white paper flowers at the side. They both looked so lovely: Linda with her dark looks and also smiling, for once, and Carol, oh, sometimes the way those brown eyes looked at her, those bright, soulful eyes, she almost gasped. His eyes, Roy's eyes. For an instant, just for seconds, she was awash with longing. She forced those thoughts away. She seemed to be so full of emotion today!

'Joyce still titivating?'

'She says she's not coming down because it's bad luck if anyone sees her,' Carol said.

'I'll go and see your dad,' Violet whispered. 'You stay here, eh? Let him be quiet.'

Harry was sitting in the back room, the window open on to the garden to let the smoke out. The saucer he used for an ashtray was on the arm of the chair. Outside, Molly was still barking.

'Shut up, you blasted hound!' they heard from Mr Bottoms over the fence.

'You going to be all right, love?'

'I don't know, do I?' Harry mumbled. 'For Christ's sake stop mithering me, woman.' His sweet pliability on waking had now disappeared.

With agonizing slowness he pulled himself forward in the chair, each movement costing enormous effort. Violet looked away, out of the window. Harry found any change difficult. He needed things to be the same: the daily routine, fags, *Evening Mail* and the *Daily Mirror*, music on the radio, bits of meals that he could manage, then the dogs inside later in the afternoon so he could get a walk round the garden with his stick without them jumping up at him.

'A puff of wind blows him over,' Eva Kaminski observed sometimes. Violet and Eva had become close over the years.

'He's very sick,' Eva often said. 'He looks terrible. He's not going to last for ever.' She was never one to mince her words, but she was a relief to Violet, someone who didn't pretend things were otherwise.

Violet supported Harry by the elbow and helped him haul himself up, a pathetic, gangling figure. Taking his arm, she helped him towards the door.

'All right, love? Need the lavvy again?'

'No – I'm all right. *Christ.*' He patted his pockets to make sure his packet of Capstan was in place.

A horn pipped out in the road.

'He's here, Mom!' Linda ran to the front door. The rest of the family followed, painfully slowly, Carol on her crutches now. She could manage on those for short periods. My family, Violet thought. And just look at the state of us – talk about the walking wounded!

Danny's dad, a hulking great figure, had just drawn up in his white Austin, wide face grinning out through the window.

'All right, Linda!' he called, his beefy arm resting along the edge of the open window. 'Nice day for it, eh?'

Linda nodded, smiling. It was a beautiful May day, a deep blue sky, the estate bathed in sunshine, front windows open all along the road. Bessie had said, 'You ought to have a May wedding – you can have orange-blossom. And you'll get it over with before the Coronation.' So, of course, Joyce obeyed.

'Blushing bride ready, is she?'

'Think so.'

'Don't let anyone see me!' Joyce shouted, all in a tizzy at the top of the stairs. 'It's bad luck!'

'Well, stay there and they won't, will they?' Linda called up to her.

'Tell her it's not too late – I can run her to the docks instead if she wants to get away!' Mr Rodgers joked, his barrel figure coming up the path.

Harry made a wheezing sound, his attempt at a laugh. Violet had her arm through his, which felt thin and hard as a broom handle. Between them she and Mr Rodgers helped Harry shuffle out to the car. He was all wrapped up as if it was December, scarf and all. The walk made him pant.

'All right, mate?' Mr Rodgers opened the passenger

door for him and helped him sink slowly on to the seat. Other men were always gentle with him, Violet saw.

'Oh – Vi –' Harry gasped before the door closed. 'Get us my cushion. Them church pews're hard as hell.'

'You girls'll be all right, won't you?' Violet said anxiously, hurrying in to get the old blue cushion from Harry's chair. Linda was outside with Carol, who was perched on the doorstep. 'Mr Rodgers'll be back for you girls, soon as he can. Don't come without Carol's crutches and for God's sake be patient with *her*.' She rolled her eyes up in the direction of the bedroom, where Joyce was shouting something about her lipstick. No one took any notice.

'It's all right, Mom,' Linda said, and Violet saw suddenly how grown-up she was. After all that sulking about school, just for today it was as if the sun had come out and she was a different girl. 'You go – we'll be all right.'

For a moment Violet felt like a child, sitting in the car, with its special smell, being waved off by the two girls, all in their pink.

'Beautiful,' she heard Harry mutter, as if he was seeing everything differently today. Even Carol. The cuckoo child, whom he was prepared to call beautiful as if she were his own. Violet's eyes filled with tears. It was one of those days when the gruelling, lonely struggle of it all was lifted into something bigger, some pattern which made sense of her life. You're a good man, Harry, she thought. I married a good man.

The church was only a mile away. Mr Rodgers chatted to Harry. Violet could see his good-natured face in the little mirror. They passed people doing their Saturday things and it seemed astonishing to Violet that to them it was such an ordinary day. Then she wondered if they all smelt of dogs and surreptitiously sniffed her sleeve. She couldn't tell. Linda said people at school complained that she stank of dogs.

When they reached the church, Harry murmured, 'There's the old battleship. What's up with her?'

'Harry!' But Violet smiled.

Bessie was standing outside, smoking, grim-faced. She and the others had come from Aston on the bus. She had on a capacious frock, mauve with white swirls on it, and a straw hat. Her expression was grim. Beside her, Marigold had on a similar dress in pale yellow, covered in pale blue polka dots, and a dark brown hat that didn't match. Violet looked at her sadly. Poor old Marigold. She wouldn't have thought of asking for anything better. For a moment she thought of Rosina. She would always have asked! You wouldn't have caught Rosina going to a wedding in a hat that didn't match her frock! She ached for Rosy for a moment, or at least the eighteen-year-old Rosina she remembered, and sighed. You felt it on days like this.

Clarence, a stooped figure beside them, had on his old Sunday suit, which he could only just do up round him, and which for some reason now seemed to be too short in the legs. The remaining wisps of his hair were combed over like strands of seaweed on a rock. Of the three of them he looked by far the most cheerful.

'We've been here close on an hour already,' Bessie complained, as soon as Violet set foot out of the car.

'Well, you knew it started at twelve,' Violet said mildly. Her mom was always at her most aggressive when out of her usual home and street. 'Why don't you go in and sit down?'

Bessie eyed the church door warily. Marigold stood, impassive as ever, though Violet could sense an excitement in her. Anything different was a treat for Marigold.

'Let's go in, Bess,' Clarence said in his quavering voice. 'My knees're killing me.'

'*You* go in then,' Bessie snapped, stubbing her cigarette out on the wall. 'And take *her* off my hands, will you?' She nodded dismissively at Marigold. '*I'm* going to see the bride arrive.'

Bessie had always liked Joyce, who did all the right things in her eyes.

Violet and Mr Rodgers helped Harry into his pew at the front of the church, settling him on his cushion.

'No sign of Tom yet?' Harry asked.

His brother, Uncle Tom, was to stand in his place, giving Joyce away.

'He'll be along. I ought to go and watch for him, see a few people,' Violet said, patting the back of her hair, agitated.

'I'll be all right.' Proud, he sat up as straight as he could. 'Leave me be, woman.'

Some of their friends and neighbours had walked over. Joe and Eva Kaminski were just coming in. Eva, dressed in bright emerald green, kissed Violet.

'This is a good day. A good day,' she pronounced, in her spiky way.

Behind them was Edna Bottoms, in a sober little navy blue outfit. She smelled sweetly of talcum powder.

'I wanted to come.' She was all flustered. 'Reg wanted to as well, only . . .'

'It's all right,' Violet said, knowing Edna was covering up for him. Imagine Reg Bottoms coming to Joyce's wedding! 'It's nice of you, love.'

She was distracted by seeing Uncle Tom arrive at last, striding up the road. The sight of him always gave her a pang. He was so like Harry! All Harry could have been in looks and physical strength.

Soon after, Mr Rodgers drew up with the three girls, Carol in the front and Linda with Joyce at the back. The few left outside all stood back to admire as Joyce climbed out of the car, full of herself, fussing over her dress and making Linda rearrange her veil. She beamed regally at everyone. Violet was aware of the special, pitying smile people gave 'little Carol' as she struggled up the steps with her crutches.

At last they were all settled inside and Joyce paraded along the aisle, Linda and Carol behind. Joyce, holding her bouquet of blossoms, tried to look solemn but couldn't contain her grin of delight.

Danny turned to greet her, looking constrained and uncomfortable in a suit, the collar too tight and cutting into his plump neck. He was very like his dad and just as jolly. Violet watched Carol anxiously, but she was managing perfectly well.

As Joyce and Danny stood in front of the vicar, waiting to make their vows, Violet couldn't contain her emotion and the tears ran down her cheeks.

'You're so young,' she'd said to Joyce. 'Just leave it for a bit. What's the rush? You're hardly old enough to know your own minds.'

'*You* got married when you were seventeen!' Joyce argued fiercely. 'And anyhow, Danny's nineteen. We're old enough to decide and you're not going to stop us. If you won't let us, we'll run away and get married somewhere else!' There was no budging her.

All Harry said was, 'She's right, Vi. She's no younger than you were.'

As she watched them standing there she was back at her own wedding day, Harry beside her as he was now, but then upright and strong, full of urgent male energy. She skipped past this painful thought. What about her own family on that day? Bessie had been approving all right. Had she married to please Bessie, or to escape her? Marigold had been there, just the same, like a sealed jar, its contents ageing in airless secrecy. And Rosina, her lovely bridesmaid. How she longed for her.

'I never knew why she took off like that,' she said sometimes. But she knew really. She was the one who got out from under Bessie.

Back in the winter they had heard from her for the first time in years. There was no special reason they could make out that prompted her to write. This time she gave an address though, in London.

Dear Mom and all of you,

I feel I want to write to you, Christmas coming up and everything. There's too much to tell you though, to catch up over the years. We'll do it one day. I hope you're all doing well. These are my children, Clark and Vivianne. Clark's nine now and Vivianne seven. They're doing well and I wanted to show you them. Clark's really one of us, isn't he?

Love to you all – Charlie, Vi, Marigold – I've missed you.

Rosina.

Clark was very like her: the definite brows and the delicate, handsome features. The girl's colouring was lighter and she was round-faced and sweet-looking, with long, curling hair. With her, Violet didn't immediately feel the same sense of recognition, of affinity that she did with the boy. My nephew, she thought.

Once again the picture was propped on the mantel in Bessie's house.

'So she's remembered we exist,' Bessie said. Her tone was very hard. 'Does she think we're all going to go rushing down there now she's spawned a couple of brats?' She heaped scorn on anything to do with Rosina.

But I might, one day, Violet thought. I might see her. Rosina was her one proper sister. There was Marigold of course, but you couldn't really talk to her, her and her love songs and her closed-off life. Violet was never close to Charlie. He was always just there – Gladys, his kids, beer. You didn't get much out of him either. We're a family of women, she thought. The men are like shadows.

Light streamed in through the high windows. Violet looked at Joyce's slim back in her shiny dress. And Danny. *He* was no shadow though. He had a lot of life in him, and the two of them really did seem to love each other. When they kissed after the vows, she heard a big sigh from behind, everyone going 'Aaah', especially Bessie. Joyce turned round, blushing and looking very pleased with herself.

She's done it, Violet thought, wiping her eyes. Our Joycie – married. I might be a grandmother soon!

Joyce clung on to Danny's arm, laughing, and Violet could feel the pleasure of the moment in the people round her.

'She looks very lovely,' she heard Eva Kaminski say behind her.

Then she saw Joyce's face change, a sober enquiring expression come across it as she looked down the church, seeing something behind them all. She squinted, trying to see clearly, to make something out, and then as if uncertain, puzzled, her eyes met Violet's.

Violet turned and saw as well. Seated near the back of the church, a slim, smart figure in a large, peach-coloured hat with a sloping brim, from under which looked dark, defiant eyes. As if Violet's thoughts had winged her there.

Rosina.

Chapter Forty-Eight

Linda didn't notice Rosina until they got right outside.

Everyone was milling about, lighting cigarettes, talking and laughing like children let out of school, amid the whirl of confetti scattered by Joyce's workmates.

'Who's that?' Carol nudged her.

The woman in the peach hat and dress had collared Violet and pulled her away from the rest of the group.

Linda shrugged. But there was something about the stranger that drew her attention. She seemed familiar, yet Linda knew she didn't know her. The woman was holding Violet's upper arm as if to stop her moving away, and talking urgently. Linda saw her mother nodding in a bewildered way and then as the peach-dress woman started to pull back, Violet made a sharp movement to stop her. All this only took a few seconds and it was only then that anyone else began to notice.

'Who's that?' she heard Bessie say behind her. 'Someone come to see Violet. Looks posh. Fancy barging in in the middle of all . . .'

'That's Rosina,' Marigold's flat voice pronounced.

'Ros . . . No! Don't be so bloody silly, Marigold.'

''Tis. It's Rosy.'

'It's never . . . Is it?'

But the woman leaned forward, swiftly kissed Violet on the cheek and hurried away along the road on her high, white heels. She seemed almost about to break

275

into a run. Violet stood staring after her, a hand up to her cheek.

'Vi?' Bessie shoved through the other guests to where Violet was standing by the road. Linda followed. 'Who was that? Was that Rosina?'

Violet turned. Her eyes were full of tears. 'She wanted to come. But she wouldn't stay. I wish she'd stay . . .'

'Well, what's she playing at?' Bessie erupted, red-faced. She threw down her cigarette and ground at it with her heel. 'Go after her and make her come back! Swanning in and out like that after seventeen years! Not a word to her mother. What the hell did she have to say for herself?'

'Not much . . .' Violet was weeping now, in shock and disappointment. 'I want her to be here – to see her . . .'

'Little bitch! I'd like to get her here and put her over my knee. You should've got her and made her stay. There's a few things I'd say to her, I can tell you. She always was a selfish little cow!' Bessie's raging started to filter through to everyone else and they went quiet. Joyce came hurrying over.

'Nan!' she hissed, mortified. 'Stop shouting – everyone's staring. What's going on?'

'I'll tell you what's going on. That . . . that trollop mincing off down the road there were your auntie Rosina, looking down her nose at us and then taking off as if she was royalty and too good for us. Wants a good hiding, that she does.'

God, Nana, *shut up*, Linda thought, mortified. Making all this carry-on at Joyce's wedding!

'Nan, please,' Joyce begged. 'Leave it. Everyone's staring at you.'

Bessie wheeled round to face everyone on the steps.

'Go on then – have a good look. That's it – walk away. See you down the pub, you bloody miserable lot!'

'Stop it!' Joyce wailed. 'You're spoiling my wedding. Just stop it!'

'Mom,' Violet begged, wiping her eyes. 'Don't keep on. It's no good. Rosy's gone. Don't let her spoil Joyce's wedding. Not after all this time.'

Bessie quietened and sank down on to the low wall. For a moment she looked frail. 'She's upset me, that's all, turning up like that, ungrateful little bitch.'

Everyone else, unperturbed by Bessie's outburst, was moving along the road towards the pub.

'I must go and get Harry!' Violet said, gathering her wits.

'Mom –' Linda hurried after her, sorry for her. She felt different about everything, just today. Able to forget her own feelings. Mom never said how much she missed Rosina, but Linda could tell. 'Mr Rodgers's taken Dad home, remember? And your mascara's smudged.'

'Oh –' Violet stopped on the steps and fished out her hanky. 'Is Carol all right? I feel all shaken up.'

'What did she say? Auntie Rosina? How did she know about the wedding?'

'I wrote to her. Just dropped her a line. It was when I wrote to Muriel telling her about Joyce, as if *she* was my sister. I just thought Rosy should know. And she'd sent her address this time. I thought she might want to know us again. And she came up all this way . . .' Violet shook her head, sadly.

They reached Carol, who was waiting by the church door. Violet laid her arm round Carol's shoulders and in that absent-minded gesture Linda saw another of those unguarded moments of devotion, of something only Carol brought out in her.

'She just said, "I wanted to come but I can't . . .!"'
Violet said. 'Something about not being able to face it.
It was all so quick and then she went off. It's made me
feel peculiar seeing her.'

'Mom –' Joyce came flaming up to them, all upset.
'Nana's spoilt it – she's spoilt everything!'

But Danny was close behind.

'Don't talk daft.' He put his arm round her waist and
gestured at everyone strolling off along the road. 'They
don't look bothered, do they? Come on, wench – Mrs
Rodgers! Our dad's waiting in the car.'

He squeezed her close and kissed her ear, and Joyce
softened and giggled.

'Danny! Gerroff!'

The two of them went off down the steps arm in arm
and Violet managed a smile.

'Look at them – least they're all right, anyway.'

That night, Linda couldn't sleep. She lay in bed, just
able to hear Carol's breathing in the other bed. No
Joyce next door now, of course. She and Danny were
off for a few days by the sea before moving into the
tiny flat above Mr Rodgers' garage, where Danny
worked.

There were no sounds from next door. When they
got home, after the celebrations in the pub, Dad had
been asleep in his chair, flaked out and grey in the face.
Linda noticed her mom's face alter as she saw him, that
thought that went through her head from time to time,
wondering if he was still with them, if the wedding had
been the end of him. But he woke and managed a bowl
of chicken soup.

Linda could feel Sooty, a warm, reassuring bundle

curled up by her feet. She needed comfort. Soon after they got home her monthly period had started – thank goodness not in the middle of the wedding! She lay with the thick Dr White's pad between her legs and gripes low in her belly. She felt fragile and emotional. Not that it hadn't been a good day. They'd celebrated with Joyce and Danny, and things in the family had been more or less all right. Linda felt for once that she hadn't been out on a limb, angry and misunderstood the way she normally felt these days. She knew how difficult things were for Mom, what with Dad and Carol, and she'd wanted to do her best to help. And for all that she and Joyce had never been close, she could see that she and Danny made each other happy.

But then Auntie Rosina turning up had upset Mom. Pleased her in a way too, but brought out a lot of emotion. And the wedding ceremony itself came back to her now, all the feelings that had swept over her as Joyce and Danny made their vows, then swept in triumph out of the church.

There'd been that moment as they turned, just married, Joyce's cheeks flushed pink. She looked pretty, Linda could see. The prettiest she had ever looked. But all she could feel herself was a stony sensation in her chest.

She's done it, Linda thought, she's done the right thing – the thing every woman is supposed to do. As everyone went 'Aaah', all she could see was a vision of how Joyce's life would be, mapped out in children and meals and Monday washes and hanging Danny's socks out until she was old like Nana, sighing with memories at the weddings of her grandchildren. And this ought to have seemed a happy thing, yet it made her sink inside with dread at the inevitable vision in front of her.

I don't want that, she was thinking. *I don't, I don't . . .* Yet what else was there? Being old and a spinster like Marigold, or funny Miss Turpitt who lived a few houses down and talked to the starlings and pigeons in the garden as if they were her family?

And what else was there to want, anyhow? Her years at the secondary modern had brought no satisfaction. The lessons were too easy and she couldn't be bothered any more. She felt like a misfit, and became lethargic, sullen. What was the point of anything? If you stepped out of where you belonged you ended up like Johnny Vetch, in and out of the mental hospital.

The organ had started up and Carol was tugging on her arm, smiling up at her. 'Wakey, wakey,' she whispered. 'Daydreaming again!'

As they turned to walk back down the aisle to the last hymn, her father looked ashen and exhausted from the effort of it all and he didn't stand up. He was watching the couple with a haunted expression, and she saw tears running down her mom's cheeks and a soft smile on Bessie's plump face.

Outside, Linda found herself next to her grandmother and Marigold. Bessie's breathing was laboured just from walking out of the church, her lungs giving off a sound like rustling paper. Linda watched as her eyes followed Joyce and Danny, both laughing as their friends threw confetti.

'I'm s'posed to throw my flowers, aren't I?' Joyce cried. 'Come on, you lot – who's going to catch 'em?'

Bessie gave a low laugh. Soppy face, Linda thought, watching her. She was filled with a swelling sense of loathing, of panic. Look at her stupid, soppy face!

Bessie turned to her, watery-eyed.

'Well, I s'pose you're next on the list?'

And for a moment she wanted to run and run and never come back.

But lying here now, there was a weariness, a surrender, as if all her dreams were ashes and might just as well be. What did it matter? She had thought she might have a different sort of life, but she was cut out to be just like anyone else after all. This was her last term at school, and then she'd go to work in some firm or shop, meet some factory Jack, marry and settle down and that was that.

All right, she thought, her foot pressed against Sooty's warm shape. If that's what they want, they can have it.

Chapter Forty-Nine

June 1953

Linda ambled home from school along Bandywood Road, not in any special hurry to get there. Home, school, what was the difference? She felt numb about all of it, the days drifting by, always the same. She'd tried a bit, at the beginning, when she first went to the secondary modern, but not now. Mostly she felt as if her head was full of scraps of soggy paper. And at home, Dad was always ill and there was nothing to look forward to.

Along the street, gardens were in full bloom with lilacs and beds full of pansies and marigolds, phlox and lupins. Bandy Woods used to be just that – woods. But the estate was more than twenty years old now and the gardens were maturing, trees softening the lines of the houses. Most of them were still draped with streamers of coloured bunting.

She always walked part of the way with Maureen, but she'd turned off for home now. Maureen was a slow, spotty girl, but the one person who seemed prepared to hang around with her. The others thought Linda was stuck up. She'd known a lot of them at the elementary school, but she never seemed to fit in. Maureen Lister, though, was glad just to be anyone's friend. Linda had been like that with Lucy, at the grammar school: honoured to be her friend.

It hurt, remembering Lucy. On that last day at King

Edward's, on the bus home, she'd handed Linda a little parcel. Inside was a book with a red cover, with 'Autographs' embossed in curling gold script. It had pink and yellow pages and inside, Lucy had written:

> Roses are red, violets are blue,
> Sugar is sweet, and so are you.
> Best Friends forever – Love from Lucy xx

Linda had stared at it, a big lump in her throat. She felt rotten that she hadn't got Lucy anything.

'I'll get you a present,' she managed to croak.

'No – you don't need to,' Lucy said in her earnest way.

And Linda saw she was being kind because she knew Linda's family hadn't got much money, and she felt even worse. She looked at Lucy's pale, kind face and barley-coloured hair and saw what she had always known deep down: that Lucy *belonged* in the grammar school in a way Linda never had and never could. That was what Nana had always said, wasn't it? Not for the likes of us. Getting above herself, fancy ideas. And if you had fancy ideas, there was punishment waiting at the end of it. That was what her life felt like now – a punishment, with the lessons that never fired her with enthusiasm, and nothing about that school feeling right. And Dad was sick all the time now – really sick. Past getting drunk.

Linda dawdled into Bloomsbury Road. Just round the corner a man was up a ladder, taking down more bunting from a telegraph pole.

'Load of bloody fuss that was, weren't it?' he called down chirpily. 'Still – all over now.'

Linda didn't answer, nor did he seem to expect her

to. The new queen had just been crowned and Coronation fever had set in all over town, infecting every street
with the urge to have parties to celebrate. The occupants
of Bloomsbury Road shared out the jobs – who was to
set up tables, or make jelly, or ham sandwiches or cake.
At least eggs were off the ration now. Violet was talking
about getting chickens but hadn't done it. Sugar was
still rationed though.

Grass was mowed and the gardens trimmed and
watered. The Martins' garden at number 18 was still the
one to disgrace the street. Even though grass was sprouting in the old bald spot where Harry's bike had stood
for so long, the specimens in the front garden were not
the pretty flowers of the neighbouring ones (Joe Kaminski was growing flowers between the vegetables now),
but groundsel, dandelions and quitch grass.

'It looks a right mess,' Violet said, staring helplessly
at it. 'I ought to clear it up . . .' But they knew she
wouldn't. She was too bowed down by everything else,
and didn't even know where to begin.

A week before the great event, Eva Kaminski
reported that a Rumbelows van had drawn up outside
and two men carried a television into the Bottoms'
house. Reg Bottoms had kept mighty quiet about it
though. There was another family at the far end of the
road who had a television, with the tell-tale H-shaped
aerial on the roof, and it was a magnet for all the kids,
who they generously invited in for *The Flowerpot Men*
and *Rag, Tag and Bobtail* on *Watch with Mother*, but
Mr Bottoms didn't want the neighbourhood traipsing
into *his* house. The little drama of the television
unfolded as the week went past. Linda was home in the
afternoons when her mom came in from work and Eva
came trotting round to report from the front line.

'He is a selfish kind of man,' Eva pronounced with her usual energy, perched on the kitchen stool while Violet made tea and they both filled the kitchen with smoke. As usual Eva was neatly dressed, an emerald green skirt with box pleats and yellow blouse. Eva made all her own clothes and always dressed to dazzle. 'There's enough gloom in the world, without putting it in the clothes as well,' she'd say. She was tiny and tough and gristly, and wore mascara and lipstick, and had a deep, smoker's voice. 'Fancy not sharing with everyone around? It is not hurting him to share, is it? I mean I know my Joe is not a very friendly man, but he would do anything for someone who really needs it. Yes – I think Mr B. is very selfish.' She dragged emphatically on her cigarette.

In fact, on the eve of the big day, Edna Bottoms went round to the Kaminskis and asked if they'd like to come in and watch the Coronation procession on the television.

'But what about Violet?' Eva demanded. 'And her poor husband?'

As Eva reported it, Edna had gone as pink as a rosebud and said that she was very sorry, she'd like to invite everyone in, but Reg wasn't prepared to consider the Martins. They weren't his type, she said.

'So,' Eva told Violet, 'I said to her, "In that case, I say no thank you. Joe and I can listen to it on the wireless with our friends like everyone else in the street."'

Violet laughed in surprise. 'You never!' She sugared Eva's tea and handed it to her.

'Ta, baby.' Eva had never quite got the hang of the way people called each other 'bab' so she called them 'baby' instead. She took a sip of tea. 'Anyway – who cares about this stupid television? We will have a nice time.'

On the morning of the Coronation when the street was full of activity – bunting flapping in the drizzle and tables arranged up and down the road and people running in and out of houses – Edna Bottoms appeared on the doorstep at number 18, hair tightly curled and her apron over a shirtwaister dress the colour of broad beans. She seemed flustered and started gabbling the moment the door opened.

'Violet – I don't know if you've heard about the television.' She was blushing again. 'I mean, Reg really can be the end. I wish we'd never bought the blasted thing, I really do, he's been so difficult about it. We've had words about it, I can tell you. See, I wanted to invite everyone in – you know, make a bit of an occasion of it, and Reg ... Well, anyway,' she added defiantly, '*I'm* going to ask you to come and watch – that's if you want to ... In fact I'm going to ask anyone who wants to.'

'Poor old Edna,' Violet said when she'd flapped off home again. 'She's a good sort really – it's just him. D'you want to go in, Harry?'

'No, I bloody well don't,' Harry said. Speaking made him pant. 'Sitting there looking down his nose. I'm staying here. You can go if you want.'

After a conflab with the Kaminskis they decided that the women and children would go. Linda sat at her mother's feet on the spotless green carpet in the Bottoms' house looking round her in amazement. She had never seen a room like it: the walls decorated with immaculate flowery paper, shelves of little ornaments, the chairs new and neat and not a smudge on the walls or speck of dirt anywhere. She could feel that her mom, on the sofa behind her with Carol, kept twitching her feet in discomfort. She was not going to be able to relax. In the event, Edna had invited in quite a few people; the kids squashed in on the floor and she handed them little glasses of orange pop and arrowroot biscuits. After a while Carol slithered down on to the floor as well to be with all of them. Mr Bottoms sat regally in his chair, acting as if none of them were there.

The drama opened on the fairytale world of royalty, the young Princess Elizabeth leaving Buckingham Palace in her gold coach.

Sylvia Peters appeared in her beautiful gown to report on the day.

'Oh, she does speak nicely,' Edna Bottoms said wistfully, 'Wouldn't it be marvellous to be like that?'

'Shame it's not a nicer day, isn't it?' Violet said. The overnight campers lining the edges of the Mall had woken to rain.

'She's so pretty.' Carol sighed.

Linda watched, entranced. Going to the Odeon was one thing. It was like stepping into another life, a palace of dreams in front of that giant screen, from where you emerged back into real life with a bump. But this was different – to have the screen right here in your living-room – and Edna and Reg Bottoms' living-room was already a palace of dreams compared to their house! She thought of her dad, fragile as a bird, dozing in his chair next door, dogs at his feet. And then she gave herself over to the journey of the young princess, meeting her destiny in Westminster Abbey.

Now it was all over everything felt flat, with nothing to look forward to except leaving school in two months. And then what? Joyce had got herself a job at Bird's a few months before the wedding, at Nana's urging. Bessie had worked at HP's, the sauce factory, for a couple of years – that was where she'd met Jack.

'Sets you up for life, good firm like that,' she'd told Joyce, the week she had come back triumphantly, having been taken on.

They'd had the conversation over Sunday dinner again, when Linda had reluctantly agreed to go to Nana's. Mrs Magee had died two years back so at least there was one less person who didn't want to be there.

'It's a long way to go,' Violet said. 'All the way over there – two buses.'

'That don't matter,' Bessie said. 'An early start never hurt anyone. People come from all over to work there – always have done. And what's up with you?' She finished aggressively, seeing Linda's gaze fixed burningly on her.

There was a time when she would have kept quiet, but it all hurt too much now.

'The bus fare to Handsworth for me to go to school was throwing money away – so how come it's all right her going all the way to Digbeth?'

'Don't talk daft,' Bessie scoffed, taking another large mouthful of cabbage and talking through it. 'Our Joyce'll be earning good money, not like you and your fancy books! You should never've had anything to do with that waster Johnny Vetch, that was your trouble. Load of airy-fairy nonsense – he's never been right, that one.'

Joyce was soon full of her job at Bird's. The firm was expanding. The new entrance to the Devonshire Works was opened by Roy Rogers and Trigger his horse, and Joyce got to pat Trigger's neck. She started off packing custard powder.

'It's not austerity any more,' she lectured them over tea, as if she owned the factory. 'It's the proper stuff.'

'Bully for it,' Linda said.

Joyce slammed down her knife.

'Listen to her – you never give up, do you? You still think you're above us, don't you, Miss Lah-di-Dah! I'd like to see you get a decent job when you leave school, like I have. That'll soon sort you out!'

Chapter Fifty

Linda walked into the house that afternoon, shoved the front door shut with a bang and flung down her bag. Almost immediately she heard a voice she wasn't expecting – Bessie's. It didn't improve her mood. What was Nana doing out here? She hardly ever came out to the estate.

'Hello, love,' Violet said.

They were at the kitchen table with Carol. Bessie and Violet were both smoking and there was a saucer of ash in the middle of the table next to the milk bottle. Linda felt all of it grate on her. Rage rose in her for a moment. She remembered the little china jug Lucy's mom used to pour milk into at teatime in their house. Why couldn't Mom try a bit harder? Why was the place always such a dump? Why did she have to be born into this bloody family at all? She felt them all staring at her and was about to make a bad-tempered retort when she saw an odd expression in her mother's eyes, something both wary and sorrowful.

'Cat got your tongue then?' Bessie said.

'Hello,' Linda said woodenly. She had no warmth left for her grandmother.

Carol was looking at her funny as well, she realized. They all seemed to be waiting for something.

'D'you want a cup of tea, or some squash?' Violet said, getting up. She wasn't long home herself, having picked Carol up from school on the way from Rita's salon. She looked neat and fresh in her pink dress, hair gleaming and well cut as usual. She was the cleanest thing in the place.

'Squash,' Linda said.

'Forgotten how to say please and thank you, have you?' Bessie challenged her, aggressively.

Linda ignored her.

'Here y'are – sit down love,' Violet said appeasingly. 'There's Bourbons as well . . . Pass 'em over, Carol.'

Linda sat down and nibbled at the end of a biscuit. Now, suddenly, no one was looking at her. They were all staring at the blue Formica or at their cups. Something was up, it was obvious. Linda couldn't stand it any longer.

'Why're you here, Nan?'

'Well, that's nice.' Bessie sat back in her chair blowing smoke above her head. 'Can't I pay a visit if I want?'

Linda shrugged. *I only asked, you old cow*, she thought.

'Nana's brought some news,' Violet said cautiously. 'I mean, not just – you were coming anyway, weren't you? Only . . .'

Linda felt her heart beat harder. What on earth had happened? Something about the atmosphere in the room was making her very uneasy.

'Something up with Uncle Clarence?' she asked. 'Or Marigold?'

She saw Carol's eyes fill with tears.

'No, t'aint that,' Bessie said.

'Let me tell her,' Violet said gently.

Linda saw her mom at her best in those moments. Whatever else she was, she was kind. It was in her eyes, the way she leaned towards her as if wanting to shield her. She laid her hand on Linda's.

'Pet, it's your old friend – Johnny Vetch. He's ... well, he's passed away.'

Linda stared at her. Johnny? Last time she'd been to Johnny he had been full of energy and excitement. Yes, too much excitement. He'd scared her a bit, the way he hadn't been able to keep still, and talked like a galloping horse.

'What was up with him?' Her throat had gone dry.

She saw Violet glance at Bessie, a dreadful knowing look.

'It's no good – I'll just have to say it. Lin – Johnny took his own life. Day before yesterday.'

Linda was about to ask how, where, but then knew she didn't want to be told. Not yet.

'Maybe it's for the best in the end,' Bessie was saying. 'He always was a queer bleeder. Square peg. I know that mother of his worried what he'd do when she'd gone. Fancy having a son like that. All that *blood*. Think how she must've felt!'

'Sssh, Mom,' Violet protested. 'Not in front of ...' She gestured at the girls.

Linda heard Carol crying beside her and all she could think to do was to turn to her sister and take her in her arms, burying her face in her soft hair.

On Saturday she went to see Johnny's mother. She was frightened, and when she got off the bus she felt like running away again, but Mrs Vetch had always been kind to her, like Johnny was. She'd seemed grateful someone wanted to see her son. Linda walked along to the little row of terraces where the Vetches' house slotted in like one card among many in a pack, unremarkable today except for the sadness it contained. Johnny had an older sister who had long been married. He had been the only son of his widowed mother.

'Oh – hello, bab,' Mrs Vetch said, seeing her on the doorstep. She didn't look upset so much as stunned. She was a respectable, sweet-faced lady in her fifties, with a high, melodious voice. She invited Linda in and automatically made tea. They sat in her little front parlour.

'The funeral's tomorrow,' she said, as if she was talking about something far away and nothing to do with her.

She told Linda that she had come downstairs, two mornings after the Coronation, and found Johnny dead in the back room. After she'd gone to bed he had slit his wrists and thrust his hands into a washpail of hot water. She crumpled as she said it, starting to shake.

'He wasn't right. I knew it. But then he wasn't so often, was he? You remember, don't you, dear, what he was like last time you came? On and on, too wound up. I should have known. His mood used to break, like a storm. He tried something like it before – only it was such a long time ago. It was after he left the college, you know . . . I think it was those mountaineers . . .'

'Everest?' Linda asked. On the eve of the Coronation they'd announced that Sir Edmund Hillary and Sherpa Tensing had reached the top of Mount Everest, the world's highest peak. They'd actually achieved it on May 29th but the news was saved as an extra jewel for the British crown to add to the Coronation.

'Yes. On and on, you know what he could be like. Couldn't leave it alone. I mean it wasn't easy to be with him when he was like that. I couldn't stand it

293

sometimes – on and on . . .' She trailed off sadly, eyes full of tears. 'So I went to bed early . . .'

As Linda walked back along the road that afternoon her body felt leaden with sorrow for Johnny. She'd loved Johnny, she knew now. The way Carol loved Sister Cathleen at St Gerard's. She loved him for the vision he had given her of a bigger world that he wanted to explore, with its deserts and jungles and his longing to take a boat up the Amazon river. She could imagine him talking about the mountains, with their white, mysterious peaks wrapped in clouds like homes of the gods. She could hear his voice, see the burning expression in his eyes as he talked about the mountaineers.

Johnny never got his trip to the Amazon basin. Maybe that was the day he knew he never would.

Chapter Fifty-One

After the Coronation, life for Linda went back to the dead-aliveness of school.

She tried not to think about what had happened to Johnny Vetch, and barely knew how the weight of it crouched inside her. All she knew was that she just couldn't be bothered. Nothing reached her, not the teachers encouraging her, saying she was a bright girl and she could do much better, nor them turning on her and telling her she was lazy. They'd given up doing either now. She'd be gone from there in two months anyway.

She let her appearance go. Her hair hung in greasy hanks round her cheeks, her shoes were always scuffed and dirty and she wore a sulky, closed expression. Everyone just left her alone, except Maureen, who placidly accepted whatever she did.

Some days she didn't go to school at all. One day, a warm, beautiful June morning, she got on a bus right to the edge of Birmingham and got off and walked into the fields and farms and spent the day wandering aimlessly. She didn't think she felt anything except the glory of having escaped from the humdrum ordinariness of the day. No one ever asked her how she felt, so she didn't find words for it. But it was her secret, running away like this, and it made her feel strong. Once in a while she did it again, not often enough to attract too much attention. She just didn't feel well sometimes, she said. Often she thought about Rosina. She'd run away too. So many times after Joyce's wedding she'd asked her mother when they were going to see Rosina. Violet would shrug and say, 'Sometime I'll get round to it,' but she never did.

That day she lay at the edge of a field of young corn, watching white clouds sliding across the deep blue. It made her feel as if she was floating, and she thought about death and heaven.

Are you there, Johnny? Her lips moved. *Can you see me?*

She saw his gentle, tormented face in front of her eyes and wondered whether he was free now. Could he circle the world and see all his deserts and jungles, see the sea creatures and stars that he'd taught her about, without all the pain he carried with him in this life?

'I wish you'd taken me with you,' she said.

She lay on her side, curled up, and cried in a way she hadn't been able to before, from deep down. After that she didn't hurt quite so much for a while, as if she had dissolved a hard stone inside.

Chapter Fifty-Two

One day she came home after school, bag slung carelessly over her shoulder, this time with Maureen Lister
tagging along beside her. Coming along Bloomsbury
Road they saw the bulky shape of someone sitting on
the doorstep of number 18.

'Who's that?' Maureen nodded at the house.

It only took a glance. It was quite unmistakably
Marigold, her swarthy features shaded by her blue hat.
She was wearing a pale pink dress dotted with little
pink roses, lace round the sleeves and bodice, like a
pretty little girl's frock made up in a very large size.
With a slight frown on her face she watched them draw
closer.

'Hello, Auntie,' Linda said. 'You can go in if you
want. Our dad's in.'

'No,' Marigold said aggressively. She didn't budge.

Close up, they could see Marigold's dress was very
grubby down the front.

'Is she all right?' Maureen whispered. She'd never
met Marigold before, but Linda wasn't worried about
her seeing. Maureen had a kind heart. She'd helped get
Carol into town at Christmas, on her crutches, so she
could see the petting zoo at Lewis's and Father
Christmas.

'Yes. Course.' To Marigold, she said gently, 'Shall we
go inside?'

Marigold lumbered to her feet. Linda saw that her eyes looked glassy as they sometimes did, and she was not very steady on her feet. All of them knew Marigold tippled, but this time she seemed quite far gone.

'Did you come on the bus?' Linda asked. There was no other way to get out to the estate but she didn't know what else to say.

'Course I bloody did,' Marigold said.

Linda took her inside and they all stood in the hall. Sally and Sooty came and rubbed themselves round Linda's legs.

'I'm gunna see the dogs,' Marigold said, indistinctly.

'Oh – all right,' Linda said, praying Mom would walk in with Carol. She showed Marigold to the back door, expecting Molly, Dolly and George to set up a great rumpus. But watching through the smeary window she saw Marigold sink down on her knees on the scrappy lawn, and the dogs, after their initial yaps of excitement, all fawned round her. After a second she realized Marigold was feeding them something out of a brown paper bag.

'She all right?' Maureen asked, peering out at Marigold.

'Yeah.' Linda turned away.

She looked in on her father. He was in his chair with his newspaper, the room blue with smoke as usual.

'Marigold's here,' she said.

Harry rolled his eyes. 'Is she? Blimey – what's brought that on? Where is she?'

'Out the back, with the dogs.'

Harry tried to move, and groaned. Linda looked out of the window.

Even though she was so used to the sight of her father, sometimes she couldn't bear to look. People asked after him sometimes. She would meet men from the dairy who'd say, 'Haven't seen old Harry in a while – I must pop in. How is he?' And she always said, 'He's all right.' She knew they didn't really want to hear the truth, how he could barely eat and that his insides were never right and that he'd break down and cry right there in the living-room. They didn't want to face this ghostly wraith of a man, or the sweet, cloying smell that hung round him. No one came near now except Uncle Tom and Joe Kaminski. Joe would come in and sit at his side, just be there. And Eva came and chatted to Mom.

'They're such good people,' Violet said in wonder sometimes. 'I don't know how we'd do without them.'

It was Joe who had finally got rid of Dad's bike, which had sat out there all this time like a promise of renewed youth. But there was to be no renewal. The tarpaulin was rotted and covered in moss, and the cycle still smashed up from the accident. Early one morning Joe took the bike away and there was nothing to see but the patch of dead grass where it had stood so long, like a wound in the corner of the garden. Later, Joe quietly handed Violet the few bob he had got for it for scrap.

'Linda?' The front door opened and Violet was calling. 'Come and give us a hand.'

She and Mom helped Carol in and Linda brought the wheelchair up the step. Maureen stood in the hall staring.

'Mom – Marigold's here.'

Her mother stopped in her tracks, on the way to the kitchen.

'*Marigold?* But she never comes out here! What the hell's she doing here?'

Linda shrugged. She heard her mom go to the kitchen and call out of the window.

'Mari? All right are you, bab? Why don't you come in and have a nice cup of tea?'

Linda helped Carol into the kitchen and Maureen followed. Marigold came in from the garden, closing the door with a great slam.

'Go easy, you'll have the glass out.' Violet eyed her sister. 'You all right, Mari?'

'Why shouldn't I be?' Marigold's tone was still aggressive.

'Sit down then – I've got the kettle on,' Violet said cautiously, reaching for the packet of Tetley.. 'Linda'll find you a Rich Tea . . . That's it, sit there, love. Why've you come all the way out here then?'

''Cause I wanted to,' Marigold stated. She took off her hat, which had already been knocked to the side by the dogs. Her hair shone with grease. Linda tried not to make faces at the way Marigold smelt. She was breathing heavily through her nose. Carol and Maureen were both staring at her, fascinated.

'Everything all right with our mom?' Violet tried again.

'She's all right. Where's my tea then?'

Marigold started ravenously on the Rich Tea, crumbs dropping all down her chest. Violet brewed up a pot of tea.

'I wanted to go out,' Marigold said through a mouthful of biscuit. 'Why shouldn't I go out?'

'Course you should!' Violet smiled and sat down opposite her with the milk bottle. 'It's lovely to see you, sis. I wish you came more often. Come when you like and see the dogs – they all love to see you too.'

'She's gone, see?' Marigold said.

'Mom? Where's she gone?'

Marigold seemed to lose the thread of the conversation.

'She's gone to one of the neighbours – or the shops?' Violet prompted.

'Asleep,' Marigold said. 'Er's asleep.'

Linda saw her mother's baffled expression. She looked at the two sisters, her mom with her blonde hair, made pretty and fashionable by Rita, and Marigold's smelly locks which had never been near a hairdresser her whole life long. She found in herself, along with her sense of revulsion at Marigold's state, a sense of kinship with her, with her dirty hair and low sense of herself. That was how she felt. Sometimes she almost felt like rubbing dirt into her hair and skin to make her outside match how she felt inside.

Marigold asked a few more disconnected questions, about the dogs, and about Carol. She turned to Carol once and stroked her hand over her head, giving her a sweet smile.

'You're a pretty little thing, you are,' she said, with a genuine smile. Linda saw her features light up into someone who once might have been pretty in a handsome way.

After a while she stood up, unsteadily. 'I'm going to the bus now.'

'Linda'll come to the bus stop with you, won't you?' Violet said.

Marigold made a performance of putting her hat back on before they left. She was obviously far from sober, but seemed more mellow than when she'd arrived. Linda led her out to the warmth of the road.

They didn't speak until the corner of Bloomsbury Road. Then Linda took a chance.

'Auntie – d'you know why Auntie Rosina left the way she did?'

Marigold looked at her, seeming blank.

'You know – your sister, who was at the wedding. Then she ran off again.'

'Rosy – course I know Rosy. It was me saw her, wasn'it?' This clarity startled Linda.

'But why did she leave home – when she was so young?'

'She weren't like the rest of us,' Marigold said. 'Clever, she was.' She shook her head with apparent fondness. 'Good old Rosy. Anyway, she had a man so she left.'

Linda stood watching the bus as it rolled away with Marigold on it. She thought about Auntie Rosina. *Clever, she was* ... Clever? Or clever to get out? She, Linda, had been told she was clever, but where had that ever got her? *She had a man* ... The message was becoming ever clearer, from Marigold, from Bessie, from Joyce's wedding. Nothing counted, not being clever, or working hard. If you wanted to get out from where you were, what was needed was a man. And what stayed with her after Marigold had gone was the tone of deep wistfulness with which her aunt had said it.

Chapter Fifty-Three

Linda left school that summer without praise and without regret. She and Maureen walked out into the summer day and did not look back.

'That's that, then,' Linda said.

By the next week she had a job, the first one offered, for an electrical engineering works in Witton called Porteous's. It was somewhere her uncle Charlie, Marigold's twin brother, had told her about. The work meant standing in a line fixing a fiddly electronic part into power connectors for electric cables. It was repetitive, very boring and she didn't give a damn. That was what she'd been destined for all along, wasn't it? Why bother looking for anything better?

'What the hell d'you want to go there for?' her mom demanded when she came home and said where she'd been taken on. 'That's two buses – you'll have to be up at crack of dawn!'

'Well, I'm earning a wage now, so I can afford two buses, can't I?' she retorted savagely.

She was always rowing with Mom now. Everything about her always seemed to be wrong. Violet eyed her lank hair, spotty face and unkempt look, her old white shirt hanging out of her skirt, shoes all scuffed.

'I'm surprised they took you, looking like that.'

'It wasn't a fashion model they were after.'

'If you came to Rita's and had a trim – tied your hair back nicely, you'd get rid of those spots.'

'Well, I don't want to – all right? Just 'cause you've decided to pull yourself together after all these years, you don't have to keep on at me!' She slammed out of the back room and upstairs.

'Don't you talk to me like that!' Violet's voice followed her upstairs.

She knew what they'd be saying downstairs. What had got into that wench these days, cheeky bint? Needs her hide tanned (from Dad).

Not that he had the strength to do it.

Somehow, over the last weeks, Violet had ended up cooking Sunday lunches for everyone. Two weeks later she was standing in a kitchen full of the steam of cooking vegetables and the delicious aroma of roasting beef, complaining, 'Why the hell did I end up doing all this?'

''Cause Nana said so,' Carol said from behind her, sitting at the table, slicing up a lump of suet for the pudding. Carol often helped in the kitchen. She knew how to cook more things than Linda, who wasn't interested.

'And we always do what Nana says, don't we?' Linda said.

Violet turned on her. 'Don't you start off again! Nana made Sunday dinner for all of us for years on end and she's no spring chicken any more . . .' She lunged to rescue a pan that was boiling over, its water putting out the gas.

Linda looked at her through narrowed eyes. *So what're you moaning about then?* her expression said. But she didn't say anything.

304

Bessie, Clarence and Marigold arrived in time for lunch. As they came in, Bessie and Marigold's bulk seemed to fill the whole hall. Linda, who was taking Dad's porridge in to him, could hear Bessie giving orders.

'Hope you put the joint in early enough,' she started, loudly. 'I like a bit of beef well done, I do. Don't like to see any blood in it. Joyce coming an' all?'

'She said she was,' Violet was just saying, and then there was a rattle at the door and Linda heard Joyce and Danny being welcomed in as well. Linda's heart sank. She was hungry and wanted some lunch, but most of all she just wanted to run away.

'Here y'are, Dad – ' She put the tray with the porridge on his lap. It was sprinkled with brown sugar and looked nice and creamy.

'Ta, Linda.' He shifted himself to take the tray. He looked very ill. His face was so sunken, hands skeletal. *He'll die soon*, she thought. *He can't go on like this.* He was never angry now. Petulant at times, and jumpy, but real anger required too much energy. A kind of passive gentleness had come over him, almost as if there was nothing else now that could touch him.

He often seemed dreamy, not quite with them, but now he looked up into her eyes.

'Want to stay in here with me, do you?' There was a flicker of a wink. She knew Dad had never been able to stand Bessie.

She smiled back. 'Best go back in there, hadn't I?'

But she lingered in the hall.

'Where's the other 'un?' she heard Bessie ask, roughly. She never could seem to bring herself to use Linda's name. There was the sound of cutlery being laid round the table.

305

'Don't talk to me about her,' Violet said. 'Got the sack, she did, this week – sent home with no pay, the lot!'

'What'd they sack her for?' Bessie demanded. 'Looking a bloody mess?'

Linda's pulse raced. She tried to bite her nails except there was nothing left above the quicks.

'No – 'ere – put them cups round – they told her she was doing it wrong all the time. I mean it was electrics. Can't have it going wrong, can you? Could be dangerous, that.'

Danny came out of the kitchen, carrying Carol in his arms as if she was a damsel in distress that he'd rescued. Carol was giggling.

'All right, Linda?' Danny said cheerfully.

Linda managed a smile back.

'Coming in, then?' he said over his shoulder.

'Waiting for our mom. I've got to help.'

'. . . she went and got another job, at least,' Violet was saying. 'In some box factory.'

'Well – let's hope that one lasts a bit longer. I can see that one being a proper rolling stone,' Bessie pronounced.

'Oh, it's just a stage she's going through. She'll find a man, settle down properly, sooner or later.' Joyce's matronly tone grated on Linda so that she wanted to scream. 'Anyway, everybody – where *is* Linda anyway? – I've got summat to tell you all.'

Seeing this as a moment when attention was directed away from her, Linda came and stood in the doorway. Joyce, who was looking incredibly pleased with herself, glanced at Danny as if for approval, then looked round the table to make sure she had everyone's full attention.

'I'm going to have a baby!'

306

Drowning out Violet's gasp of pleasure, Bessie gave a crude laugh. She was in the middle of lighting another cigarette.

'Well, you two didn't waste any time! Conceived in wedlock, was it? Don't want any bastards in the family, do we?' And her shoulders shook.

Joyce blushed right down her neck. 'Yes it was, Nan, as a matter of fact. What d'you take me for?'

Bessie blew out a mouthful of smoke. 'No need to get on your high horse – I was only having a joke. Good for you, wench. Make a proper woman of you, that will. There's a few I know could do with a dose of it, the way some of the girls carry on these days . . .' She eyed Linda with vicious contempt.

Linda watched Marigold, whose face was a mask. She showed no reaction to the news at all, but Bessie saw the direction of her glance.

'Yes, and she's a fine one.' Bessie spoke to Violet, but nodded her head at Marigold as if she was a wanton child. 'Playing me up good and proper. D'you know, she's started sneaking in and out, sly as anything, and I said to her, "What're you playing at, Marigold Wiles? You needn't think you can keep anything from me – I can read you like a book, I can!" And what d'you know but she's been carrying on with some bloke she met down the Crown. Old enough to be a grandfather he is! I told her, I'm not having it, so she can pack that in right away.'

'Oh but . . .' Violet protested. 'Surely he's just a friend, Marigold? I mean why shouldn't she have a friend to go out with – it's nice for her.'

'Nice be damned – it's disgusting at her age, that it is – or any age, her being the way she is. No – I've told her, I'm not having it. You don't know what she's like,

Violet, what with her drinking and carry-on. You have to keep her in sight all the time. Worn me out it has, all these years, looking out for her. Don't think you know, 'cause you don't . . .'

Violet hesitated, never up to arguing with Bessie. Marigold didn't even blink, but Linda thought she saw something in her aunt's eyes, a dark flicker, nothing more. She felt sorry for Marigold, but she was like deep mud – everything seemed to sink into her without trace. She wondered if Marigold had her usual stash of gin tucked down her bra.

Linda was about to sit down when Bessie snapped at her, 'Don't you go parking yourself. Help your mother bring the dinner in – you might as well be of some use in the family.'

As she left the room, Linda saw Carol look at her and give her a quick wink. Tears filled her eyes for a moment and in the hall she rubbed them away fiercely. She wasn't letting Nana see she ever had any effect at all.

Throughout the summer she worked at the box factory in Witton, counting flat cartons into piles of fifty to be packed. There were some kind ladies working there, but at the beginning of one week she gave in her notice on a whim and left on the Friday. She didn't tell Mom, not until she'd got a job at Wimbush's bakery, where she had to wear a neat white overall and worked amid the smell of baked bread and cakes instead of breathing in the cardboard dust in the factory. She liked working in a shop better. It was more varied, people coming in and out and chatting. She'd cleaned herself up a bit to go and ask for that job – washed her hair and tied it back.

They wouldn't want someone dirty handling their bread. And it made her feel a bit better. She quite liked the work too – cleaning down the shelves where they arranged the bread and cakes, and bagging them up and selling them, chatting to the regulars.

Mrs Richards, the middle-aged lady who employed her, was pleased with her.

'You're good at working out the change,' she said. 'Bright girl like you. Why don't you do something else? Learn to type or do accounts or something? You could get a good job, you could.'

'I might,' Linda said, without enthusiasm. 'I quite like it here though.'

'You could be a secretary, if you put your mind to it,' Mrs Richards said. 'You get a good boss in that, and you're made. My cousin Doris did that. Worked for one of the top men at . . . what d'you call it? Some place to do with pensions.' She tittered. 'See? Wouldn't have suited me – proper muddle head, me!'

Linda smiled. She liked Mrs Richards. She was kind and didn't pretend to be anything she wasn't. And she didn't mind the work. In her long days amid the bread and cakes she had time to think. She thought about Rosina. And she thought, how can I get away from home?

Chapter Fifty-Four

Carol's operation was in September.

'I wish they could tell us how long she'll be in there.' Violet was up in their room packing Carol's few possessions into a little bag. 'They never tell you anything.'

It all depended how the operation went and how quickly Carol recovered from it.

'I hate her being in there,' she said to Linda while Carol was in the bathroom. 'And she'll be under that flaming nun's thumb again.'

When they were getting ready for bed she cuddled Carol to her like a baby, tearful herself.

'My poor babby,' she said, rocking her on her lap. Carol was still very small for her age. She snuggled up, enjoying the attention, but she was in a calmer state than her mother.

'I'll be all right. I'll see Sister Cathleen and it means I'll be able to walk better when I get back.'

'You're a brave girl,' Violet said tearfully. 'Isn't she, Linda?'

Linda, sitting on her bed, nodded glumly. That was the one thing they were ever agreed on – their affection for Carol. With Carol gone for weeks, maybe even months, she was going to be the only one left! It was a horrible thought.

Soon the two of them were left alone in the half

light through the thin curtains. Carol lay very quiet and still.

'You all right?' Linda whispered.

'Yes.'

'Thought you'd fallen asleep.'

'No – ' There came another pause. 'I was praying.'

'Were you?'

'Sister Cathleen taught me. She said if you talk to God he'll always be beside you.'

Carol hadn't talked about Sister Cathleen for a while. Now she was going back into hospital, it had reminded her. No one had ever told Linda about talking to God, not in her whole life. She wasn't sure what to say.

'Don't you ever think, you having polio and that . . . That it's not fair? I mean it isn't fair, is it? You being in a wheelchair or on crutches all the time. Not like everyone else.'

'I wish I could go swimming again. They said that's where I caught it, didn't they? And to go to the park and run about. And I'll miss Joyce's babby being born when I'm away. I don't want to go . . . But I know I've got to.'

Linda was struck once more by her sister's patience. They were so different! Sometimes she burned with so much inner energy she just had to run and jump. She couldn't bear the thought of being stuck in a wheelchair, unable to run about.

'Anyway,' Carol said. 'That's why I'm having the operation, isn't it? To make me better.'

After a few moments, Carol's voice came again through the gloom.

'Lin? Will you come and get in with me? Like you used to?'

'All right.'

Carol wriggled across and Linda climbed in beside her, the bedsprings squeaking loudly. Linda lay on her back and Carol cuddled up beside her, in the crook of her arm.

'Lin?' Her voice was muffled.

'Ummm?'

'Don't get our mom too cross, will you? She doesn't mean it.'

'I don't mean to.'

'I know you don't. It's Nana, isn't it? The things she says . . .'

'I *hate* her.'

She felt Carol raise her head, could feel her looking down at her. 'Do you?'

'I don't want to stay here, not on my own.'

'You won't be – I mean, I'll be back. Course I will.'

'You'd better be.' She tickled her, and Carol squirmed. She cuddled her arms round Linda. Such a skinny little thing, she was, like a fragile kitten.

'Don't worry, sis,' Carol murmured. 'Everything'll be all right.'

The ambulance came for her the next day. Linda hugged her goodbye before she left for work, trying not to cry. Once she got on the bus she let the tears come and arrived red-eyed at the bakery.

'What's up with you, duck?' Mrs Richards asked kindly as she buttoned her overall. She was a thin, gentle little woman. 'T'ain't like you to be miserable.'

Linda almost managed to laugh at this. She felt as if she was miserable all the time!

'They've taken my sister into hospital today for her operation.'

Mrs Richards knew about Carol, and about polio. She had a niece who had been badly affected by it.

'Oh dear, you poor thing. Well – it's for the best, isn't it? Come on – we'll brew up a nice cup of tea at the back and you can choose yourself a bun. I bet you haven't thought to eat this morning, have you?'

Linda shook her head. She'd forgotten all about eating and her mom hadn't given it a thought either. She'd been in too much of a state fussing over Dad and Carol before getting out to work herself. It was lovely to be taken under Mrs Richards' motherly wing and she felt like crying all over again, but managed not to as she knew the kind woman was trying to cheer her up.

The day after Carol had her operation, Violet went over to Coleshill and Linda was left to take care of her father when she got home.

She opened a tin of chicken soup for him and carried it through on his tray to the back room. Mom had gone out and bought a standard lamp to have next to him so he could see better. It had a wide shade with a fringe along the bottom and it was the newest, brightest thing in the dingy room. Harry sat in the ring of the lamp's light, which made his sallow skin look even yellower.

'Get us a drink, will you?' he asked.

'What d'you want?'

'Pint of Ansells.' He was so breathless he could hardly speak, but he tried to smile at the joke.

She smiled wanly at him and brought a glass of water. 'I'll put the kettle on.'

'Ta, wench.'

She sat with him as he ate, so agonizingly slowly.

Linda saw as he held the spoon that the tremor in his hand seemed to get a little worse each day, so that he often cursed to himself when he got it to his mouth and there was very little soup left on it.

'D'you want me to do it, Dad?'

He looked up at her, ashamed. 'No. I can manage. It's this stuff, see,' he gasped between breaths. 'Porridge don't fall off the spoon.'

He laboured on for a few more mouthfuls.

'Go on then –' Proud, he thrust the spoon at her. 'You give us a few.'

She felt old, suddenly, as if in seconds he had become the child, she the adult. She helped him eat, holding the creamy spoonfuls of soup to his whiskery lips. He slurped loudly. After a few mouthfuls he said, 'Not so fast.' And they stopped for a rest.

He looked at her, considering her. She felt somehow as if he was really seeing her.

'Don't live like me.'

She stared at him, almost wondering if she'd imagined that he spoke.

'D'you hear?'

'Yes, Dad.'

He looked away, closing the door on a conversation that had barely begun, and left her wondering.

'I'll have a bit more now.'

She was scraping the last of the soup from the bowl when they heard the front door. Violet appeared with her coat still on, looking neat and pretty, but there were dark shadows under her eyes and she'd obviously been crying. Linda felt herself clench up inside.

'Oh – you've done his tea,' Violet stated.

'Did you see Carol? What's the matter?' She got to her feet in alarm.

Her mother came and sank into the other chair, her tears coming again.

'I saw her. They've done the operation, but they say it's not gone right. I mean, they haven't made her better ... Oh, I don't know ...' She put her head in her hands and cried, shoulders shaking.

Harry tried to say something but was overtaken by a fit of coughing.

'What d'you mean?' Linda knelt by her chair, willing her to speak. 'Isn't she going to be able to walk again?'

Violet gulped and wiped her eyes. 'They say they need to let her recover and then do it again. I mean the doctor said ... something ... about plates in her back, her spine. Curvature or summat. I don't know. I only know it's not gone right.'

'Did you see Carol? Was she all right?'

'I saw her. She was all in a plaster case thing and having to lie there – I mean, you know Carol – she was cheerful enough. The only thing she was bothered about was that that nun she's always on about ...'

'Sister Cathleen?'

'Yeah. They've sent her away – back to her nunnery place. Carol was ever so disappointed. Keeps asking for her. She doesn't like the others nearly as much.'

Linda ached for Carol. She knew how much Sister Cathleen meant to her.

'How long'll she be there then?' Harry asked.

Violet shook her head. 'Don't know. Longer than they thought. Months probably. And then so far as I can see she might be no better for it. One of the nurses kept saying to me I had to be hopeful, the next operation would make a difference. And then there'll be all that exercise and stuff for her. I just feel so bad, the thought of her lying there all that time again and nothing we can do.'

Linda lay in bed that night full of painful thoughts of Carol and how she must be feeling. Dad was coughing next door. Once or twice she heard him groan. His body was so emaciated now that moving was painful for him and even a soft mattress could chafe him to sores.

She felt utterly helpless. Her father had been sick for so long, Carol was stuck in her hospital bed, and as her mom had said, they couldn't seem to do anything about anything, ever. She willed thoughts to Carol, lying there in her bed at St Gerard's, unable to move without help. Was she awake now, saying those prayers she set so much store by?

God help her, Linda thought, and wondered if that counted as a prayer. *And Dad.* For good measure, she added, *please*.

Before she drifted off to sleep, she realized there might just be one small thing she could do.

Chapter Fifty-Five

Linda stood outside the convent walls, her heart thudding painfully.

It was an overcast, chill afternoon. The trees edging the park across the road were turning fast, their leaves adding a copper glow to the greyness. Reaching Selly Park, her nerves had increased enormously at the sight of the big, red brick convent behind its enclosing walls. It looked forbidding, like a castle. All she knew about nuns was that they wore strange robes and prayed a lot, that some were nurses, some were kind and gentle like Sister Cathleen, and others, from frightening stories she'd heard, could be anything but. It seemed so strange that Sister Cathleen with her friendly, freckly face lived in this terrifying-looking place.

For a while she walked back and forth outside the wrought-iron gates, too frightened to enter.

Well, I can't stay out here all day, she thought, and forced herself to pass under the arch into the courtyard. She felt as if she was being watched from all the many windows, and she hurried to the front door and rang the bell.

After a pause the door opened. A plain face, of an age she could not have guessed, look out enquiringly from under a black veil.

'Yes? Can I help you?' It was a melodious voice, the tone neither warm nor cold.

Linda suddenly realized she had not a thought in her head of what to say.

'Um – I've come to find Sister Cathleen,' she blurted out.

The woman's expression altered not a jot.

'I see. Well, we have more than one Sister Cathleen here. In fact we have three. Would your Sister Cathleen be an older person?'

Linda shook her head.

'Ah. Well, in that case you must be wanting Sister Cathleen Donovan or Sister Cathleen Geraghty . . .' She stood musing. 'And Sister Cathleen Geraghty has gone home to Ireland . . .'

'She's a nurse,' Linda offered. 'She was at Coleshill looking after my sister.'

'Ah,' she said again, softening a fraction. 'Well, you're lucky then, because that's Sister Cathleen Donovan and I happen to know just where she is at this very moment. You'd better come in.'

Linda found herself ushered through a dark hallway to a side room where there were a few chairs and a crucifix on the wall by the door. It was very quiet as the nun disappeared and the great building around her seemed to absorb all the noise from outside. She didn't think she had ever been anywhere so quiet.

In just a few moments the door swung silently open and she saw Sister Cathleen's round, pale face, in which the blue eyes looked very big and deep. She was wearing black now, not the white habit the nursing sisters wore, and she seemed to glide across the floor.

'Hello, dear.' She came forward with a calm, but puzzled expression. 'I hear you asked to see me?'

Linda's mouth went dry. She stood up awkwardly. Obviously Sister Cathleen didn't remember her.

'It's all right – sit down.'

Sister Cathleen sat down beside her. 'How did you know my name?' She drew back a little and examined Linda's face. 'Ah, now I've seen you before, haven't I? Would that be at St Gerard's?'

'It's my sister, Carol,' Linda blurted, feeling foolish as the tears welled in her eyes. 'You were her nurse at Coleshill. She's got polio.'

She saw Sister Cathleen's face break into a smile. 'Oh, one of our little patients, I see!'

'Carol Martin.'

'Little Carol.' She gave a little gasp. 'Oh yes, God love her! I'd not forget her. Lovely-looking girl, and she's something about her, you know. She's one of God's own and no mistake. I've not met many like her. How's she going along?'

Linda began to cry now, all her pent-up worry pouring out.

'She's back in the hospital and they've done an operation on her back and they say it hasn't worked and she's going to be there for a long time. And she thought you'd be there and she wanted to see you and you weren't there ...'

'Oh, the poor lass ...' Sister Cathleen looked stricken. 'The operation's not been a success? Oh, I'm sorry to hear that. Will they do it again?'

Linda nodded, wiping her eyes. 'I think so.'

'Oh dear ...' She tutted, shaking her head. 'Such a delicate little thing as well. Now don't you be upsetting yourself, dear, I'm sure it'll be all right ...'

'She wants you,' Linda sobbed, feeling at that moment as if the wanting was all coming from deep inside herself, not Carol. 'She wanted you to be there.'

'Oh, you poor young thing.' Sister Cathleen's eyes

were full of sympathy. 'I can see how much you feel for your sister. But at the moment I'm working here – we have a hospital of our own, in the convent. I'd like to see her, she's a special child, your Carol. But I'm not free just to go, d'you see?'

She stood up and in doing so invited Linda to stand as well.

'Send her my good wishes. Tell her to say the rosary I taught her, um? And I'll see what I can do.'

She showed Carol to the door and smiled. 'God bless you, Linda. It was brave of you to come.'

Chapter Fifty-Six

The first time he came into the bakery was late one afternoon.

He brought with him a waft of the autumn smell of smoky mist from outside as the door closed behind him, tingling the bell. Linda was wiping over shelves in the window and didn't take much notice to begin with.

'Hello, duck!' Mrs Richards' tone was very warm. 'You ain't been in for a bit, have you?'

Linda turned to see a boy not much older than herself, dressed in a baggy blue sweater and grey flannel trousers. His hair was unusually long, dark brown and tousled by the wind, his face thin, with striking grey eyes. There was an intensity about him, as if he was deep in thoughts which Mrs Richards had interrupted.

'Afternoon,' he said gruffly.

'You all right, Alan? How's your mom these days?' Mrs Richards leaned towards him, speaking as if his mother's health was in some way a secret. She gave a meaningful nod of her head. 'She having a spell in there again?'

The boy nodded abruptly, not meeting her eyes. For a moment he glanced across at Linda and she felt her pulse speed up, caught in his gaze, just for a second. 'Yep.'

'Oh, I am sorry, duck. That why you're not at

school, is it? Here – what did you want today? We've not got much left, but there's Eccles cakes . . .'

'I'll have four of them – and a white tin, please.'

His voice when he asked for the cakes was low, and well-spoken. There was something about him that intrigued Linda. As Mrs Richards fetched the bread and cakes, Linda kept taking little glances at him. The boy was tall and slim, and he stood with one arm resting on the counter, tapping his foot nervously. For a moment he looked round at Linda again and his eyes met hers with some curiosity, then he turned away and she was glad he did because she felt herself blushing at this frank look.

'Thanks, Mrs Richards.'

He handed over his coins and was gone with an impatient tug on the door.

'That's Alan,' Mrs Richards said. 'Lovely lad. Clever. Went on to the grammar school, he did. He was in here a lot at one time – last time his mother was in the . . . you know, the asylum. She suffers with her nerves. No brothers or sisters to keep him company, poor thing. There's only Alan and the father.'

Linda stared after him, seeing him for a few seconds through a patch of glass between the window shelves. She felt sorry for him. His life sounded sad and lonely, yet he did not look downcast. Instead, he had that energy about him which had drawn her to look at him. Any mention of the grammar school always hurt, though. She wanted to say to Mrs Richards, 'Did you know, I went to the grammar school as well?' But what was the use? It had only lasted a year, after all. One dreamlike year of bliss, which seemed like another life now.

The next time Alan came into the shop he was in school uniform, obviously on his way home. She didn't recognize him instantly because he'd had a haircut and was wearing a blazer. Her eyes were drawn with longing recognition to the emblem on his blazer pocket. A King Edward's boy. There were a number of King Edward's foundation schools across the city.

'Ooh, hello, Alan!' Mrs Richards greeted him.

Linda busied herself behind the counter, though her attention was fixed entirely on trying to overhear anything that was said.

He replied with a distant politeness, asking for the bread and cakes he wanted.

'Partial to an Eccles cake, your father, ain't he?' Mrs Richards said, in a conspiratorial way. Then, in almost a whisper. 'And how's your poor mother, Alan?'

'All right.' Linda saw his shrug out of the corner of her eyes. She could also see his discomfort at being questioned and wished Mrs Richards would leave him alone.

'I haven't actually seen her,' he added.

'No – course you haven't. And these things take time, don't they? Can't rush anything.'

'Could I have a couple of jam tarts as well, please?'

'Course you can, my duck – Linda, bring the young gentleman a couple of those tarts!'

Linda bagged a couple up and reached out to give them to him. She felt very self-conscious. For the first time in a long time it seemed to matter how she looked. Wearing her hair tied back in a ponytail in the shop had helped her spots clear up, but she still felt scruffy, and frumpy in the white work overall.

'Are they strawberry?' Alan asked.

'Oh yes,' Mrs Richards assured him.

'No – they're raspberry,' Linda said. 'They've got pips in.'

'Course they are,' Mrs Richards said. 'Silly me. Trust you to get it right.'

Linda saw Alan's eyes focus appraisingly on her for a moment. She tried to hold his gaze, but looked down, blushing.

'Thanks,' he said.

'This is Linda,' Mrs Richards said. Linda felt her cheeks burn even redder and she was forced to look up and meet his gaze. 'She's ever such a clever girl.'

'Hello,' Alan said. He looked about to say something else, but moved awkwardly away. Linda saw that he was embarrassed too. She was furious with Mrs Richards. Why couldn't she just keep quiet? Someone like him wasn't going to be interested in her, was he?

She tried to have nothing to do with him when he came in the next few times. But she couldn't help thinking, trying to guess. Was he one of the ones who had gone to the grammar school whose family didn't take that sort of thing for granted? She wondered what sort of house he lived in, whether he was ashamed to take people home the way she had been. Could he be in any way like her?

One afternoon he came in with another boy wearing the King Edward's uniform. Alan, however, was not dressed for school.

'All right lads?' Mrs Richards said, with the slight air she put on of greeting royalty. 'You not been to school today, Alan?'

'No.' His tone was abrupt and he looked away, putting Mrs Richards off asking him any more. Linda hovered in the background, trying not to look interested in them. In a few moments they were gone.

Seeing them made her feel miserable. She knew, somewhere in herself, she was their equal. But why would they take any notice of her, a shopgirl who lived in one of the scruffiest houses on the estate and had just left the secondary modern with no qualifications to her name?

'He doesn't have a happy life, that lad, for all he's from a good background,' Mrs Richards observed. 'His father's a doctor. They've got one of those nice houses in Handsworth Wood. Young Alan's been coming in here for years.'

Linda let this information sink in, gloomily. Not like her then. He was another Lucy after all. Someone from another kind of life. Angrily she tried to push away the fantasy that she had barely even admitted to herself, that Alan Bray might ever want to take any interest in her.

Chapter Fifty-Seven

She always went with Violet to visit Carol in St Gerard's on Sunday afternoons. Now and then Joyce would come as well, full of herself with her belly beginning to show and talking as if she was a seasoned married woman who had founts of wisdom to impart to Linda.

'Nana's made me two matinée coats,' she would rattle on. 'And Danny's mom's helping me get my layette together. You have to make sure a new babby's kept nice and warm, you know. Danny's just bought a new heater for the bedroom to make sure. He's worried about the way the windows let a draught in. Thing is, Linda, if a young babby catches just a cold it can be fatal when they're that small . . .'

But this time it was just her and Mom. It felt very peculiar. These weeks were the first time in her life she'd ever had any time with her mother on her own. At first she didn't know what to say to her.

'Remember those hamsters we bought, first time we ever went out there?' Violet said with a smile as they sat on the bus.

Linda's lips curved up for a moment. 'Didn't last long, did they?'

'You wouldn't think something so small could be so savage, would you?'

There was a silence in which she looked at Linda, at

her old navy slacks and threadbare jersey, the tired green of old dry herbs.

'Look at the *state* of you! How long've you been wearing that jumper for?'

Linda shrugged. 'Dunno.'

Violet fingered one of the loose threads. 'One pull and the whole thing'll just fall to pieces! Why d'you go about looking such a mess? Anyone'd think you did it on purpose. I mean, your hair! You know Rita'd cut it for you – *I'd* cut it for you. We'll do it when we get back. What's up with you?'

'Nothing.'

But she felt angry and tearful. Being looked at was hard. It was easier in a way to carry on feeling invisible. That way she could hold on to her angry feelings and didn't have to answer for herself. All the hurt and disappointment in her which she usually directed at her mother was hard to keep up when they were just there together, side by side on the bus, and she could see Violet's tired face. That was when she would realize Mom was just a skinny girl who'd got bigger and older but still didn't know all the answers about how to deal with her own domineering mother or what to do when she'd been saddled with almost more illness and misfortune than she could manage. And it twisted Linda's heart so she could hardly bear it.

'I'm all right,' she snapped. 'Just leave it.'

But it got worse because Violet's eyes filled with tears.

'I've not been much of a mom to you. All of you – but you especially, Linda.'

Linda didn't say anything. She wanted to smash her hand through the window of the bus and jump out and run away.

'We'll go shopping, shall we? Just you and me?'

She shrugged. 'If you want.'

'Well, if you're going to be like that . . .'

'I *said*, didn't I?' She turned sulkily away. 'If you want.'

As they walked along the ward of sick children, she could see Carol's face turned towards them, alight with excitement. She was still lying almost flat, in the plaster cast, facing the long doors at the other side which opened on to the garden. It was too cold for them to wheel the beds outside today though.

'Guess what!' she cried, almost before they'd reached the bed. Her brown eyes were full of joy. 'She came! Sister Cathleen came today – just to see me!'

Linda smiled, watching her mother kiss Carol's cheek. She could tell Mom didn't want to hear about Sister Cathleen.

'She came specially for me! She said you'd been to the convent to find her Lin – '

Violet's head snapped round, astonished. 'Did you?'

Linda nodded, smiling at Carol's delight.

'When the hell did you do that?'

'A while ago – when she first came back.'

'Well, blow me – you're a dark one.'

'They said she could come over – her superior nun said. And she came and took me to the chapel to Mass . . .'

'Oh, *did* she?' Violet said, folding her arms tightly. 'So that's what she was after!'

'Mom!' Linda protested. Why did she have to be jealous when Sister Cathleen had such a kind heart?

'Well, how did you do that when you're flat on your back?'

'They've got these special beds in the chapel – sort of stretchers. They lie you on them at the front and you can see the priest and everything. And Sister Cathleen sat on one of the chairs behind me. Oh, and it's so pretty in there. They say I can go again next week if I want.'

'I brought you some comics,' Violet said, and out of her bag she fished *Girls' Crystal*, *Beano*, *Girl* and a little book of *Amazing Stories*. 'That keep you going for a bit?'

Carol beamed. 'Thanks, Mom. Least I've got my hands free – not like before.'

Linda thought of Mom's description of the iron lung with a shudder.

'Here's some sweets for you.' Secretively, as if it might not be allowed, Violet slipped some mints and Cadbury's Fruit and Nut on to the bed. Sweets had been off the ration for months now, so they could treat her.

Carol seemed very happy. Once more Linda was humbled by her sister's patience. She liked the girl in the next bed very much, she said. Her name was Bernice and she had had polio as well. Her mother was a lovely-looking, dark-haired woman who had smiled at them as they walked past.

'Guess what – Mr Bum's got a new car,' Linda told her. 'It's parked out the front and he has fifty fits every time we go anywhere near it.'

'I don't know what he thinks we're going to do to it,' Violet said indignantly.

'He'll be out there carrying on if a bird messes on it,' Linda giggled.

'Linda!' Violet hissed, but she looked reassured to see her laughing.

'How's my dad?' Carol asked.

For a second Linda saw a strange register of emotion in her mother's face, as if someone had probed a hidden scar.

'Harry? Not very good, is he, Linda? He's not been out for days now. Says he just hasn't got the strength. I mean the doctor's been in and that – a few times . . .' She stopped herself pouring out all her worries. This was not the place. She could do that to Rita, about how she didn't know how Harry kept going at all, the way he was, and Rita would say, 'He's a strong man with a strong will, love, that's what it is.' But she shouldn't burden Carol with it. 'I s'pect he'll pick up – he always does,' she finished, brightly.

They left Carol at the end of their visit, delighted with her comics. As they left the ward and turned to wave, Violet suddenly said, 'I don't know what I did to deserve her, that I don't.'

Chapter Fifty-Eight

It was closing time, a week later.

Mrs Richards told Linda she could go and get the early bus. It was already dusk, and quite foggy, when she closed the shop door behind her. Everything seemed sunk in grey except for the red lights on the back of cars, and she liked their scarlet glow, slightly fuzzy in the moist air.

'Hello!'

She was a good way along the road when the voice called out. Her thoughts were on whether she'd make the bus, and wishing she had some gloves, because the sleeves of her skimpy gaberdine were too long to pull down over her hands. She was hungry, and it was cold and raw out there, but at least it wasn't wet. She had bits of cardboard in both her shoes to cover holes in the soles.

'Hello – Linda, is it?'

Alan came hurrying up behind her and she stopped, cheeks burning in confusion. At least he wouldn't be able to see – it was too dark. Why on earth was he coming after her? He was huddled up in a duffel coat and scarf and under one arm was what looked like his usual parcel of bread and cake. He smiled at her in the gloom. She smiled back.

'She said you'd gone, so I thought . . . I don't know . . .'
He laughed. He was talking quickly, obviously nervous.

'I thought it'd be nice to talk to you, but when *she's* there you can never get a word in, can you?'

Linda liked the way he spoke. His voice was deep and smooth. 'No. She's all right though.'

'Yes, I know. I didn't mean she wasn't. D'you live far?'

'I have to get the bus.' She found she didn't want to tell him where she lived. 'It's quite far.'

'Well . . .' He seemed at a loss. 'Would you like . . . I mean, if you're not in a hurry we could try and find a tearoom, or if you like you could come back to my house? It's only down there and – there'll be no one else. My father won't be in.' He waved the bag. 'I've got Battenberg!'

'What – me?' she said stupidly.

He laughed. 'Yes – you! Only if you'd like, though.'

'But . . .' She couldn't think of a but. There was no Carol at home. Mum got in before she did these days and there was nothing at all to get back for. No homework – nothing.

'Yes, all right,' she said, not quite believing she was saying it, and added, 'please.' And thought afterwards she should have said thank you, not please, but it was too late now.

Why have you invited me? she wanted to ask. *You must know all sorts of interesting girls.* Then she told herself off for being silly. He'd only asked her for a cup of tea. Perhaps he even felt sorry for her, seeing how boring things looked in the shop? Or maybe he was the sort of boy who was always asking girls home for tea?

They walked side by side along the road. The shops were shutting up as they passed. Alan's walk was bouncing, energetic, as if he was full of barely curbed energy and she was having to walk abnormally fast to keep up. His nervousness gave her courage.

'D'you do all the shopping then?' She nodded at the parcel under his arm.

'Well, no. We have a woman in to help a bit. We muddle along, you know.'

'Yes.' She did know, exactly. 'Sounds like our house.'

'Oh – does it?'

He was quiet again for a moment. She liked him for not questioning her too much, for just letting things be.

'You been at school today then?' she asked. She wanted to ask him how old he was, but if she asked too many things he'd think she was nosy.

'No.' There was an awkward silence. 'As a matter of fact, they've kicked me out.' He swung his foot at a lump of something dark on the pavement and sent it skittering. It was a beer bottle. With venom, he added, 'Bastards.'

She gasped. 'What – the grammar school?'

Alan nodded. 'Doesn't matter,' he said quickly. But she could hear that it did. Somehow it made her spirits lift. Someone else who'd had it taken away! Someone who would know how it felt!

'But *why*?'

He reached out and touched her arm for a minute, steering her.

'We need to cross here . . .' He released her again. 'School? I was never there anyway. Hardly ever, anyhow. What's the point – all that algebra and Latin . . . Bores me to death. Won't be of any use to me, not where I'm going.'

For a moment rage flickered in her. All that algebra, and Latin and music and history – all the things she craved, that he had been given and seemed not to care about!

'Well, where're *you* going then?' *What makes you so blooming special?*, she wanted to add.

'America. I'm going to write for the movies. It's the only thing for me. I just know that's what I'm meant to do. D'you like them? Movies – the flicks, I mean?'

'Yes. I go to the Odeon sometimes.'

'I go as often as I possibly can. I'd live in the cinema if I could! D'you like Westerns?'

She looked at him, saw the intense set of his face. 'Well – a bit,' she fibbed.

'They're my life. They're just – *it*!' He made an emphatic gesture with his arm. It all takes you off somewhere else. Away from it all. Oh, that silver screen! I've written two scripts already. When I leave school, I mean, *properly* ... the old man thinks he can talk them into taking me back, saying I've been playing the wag because of my mother and everything ... But when it's over, I'm going to go to America.'

'How d'you know?'

'I just *have* to. My father goes there sometimes. He's a scientist – works in laboratories in Massachusetts.' He talked about his father's interest in a bored, offhand tone. 'I've never been, but one day I shall. I have a penfriend, the son of one of his colleagues. We're the same age – he's called Stanley...' He stopped and indicated that they should cross another road. They were in a nice area, the houses getting bigger, timber-framed, with tidy front gardens. 'Nearly there ... Stanley tells me all about the movies that we haven't seen over here yet. They're *mad* about the silver screen over there! Have you seen *High Noon*?'

'No.'

'It's the *best*. Absolute best I've ever seen. Stanley got hold of a poster for me – had it sent back with Dad last time he was over there.'

'Oh. That's nice.' She felt stupid, not able to think of anything to say. She didn't mind Westerns but they all seemed pretty much the same to her, all galloping about on horses and shooting. She liked the quieter bits when there were women in them too.

'Mrs Richards said your father was a doctor.'

'The old man? He is – but not of medicine. He's an industrial chemist. Researches things for various firms. Dunlop – I know he's worked for them in the past. It's all very useful apparently. He lives and breathes it but I'm not really interested. Shame for him really – only son and I'm not much good at science. Can't possibly follow in his footsteps.'

'What do you like?'

'Oh – history, English literature, French – that sort of thing. Music. I'm more like my mother, I suppose.'

Linda didn't like to ask any more questions about Alan's mother. A moment later he led her up the path to one of the houses.

It was very dark and Alan felt round inside the door for the light switch.

'Dad won't be back until goodness knows when – there!'

He snapped the light on and Linda found she was in a spacious hall. There was a deep red carpet with hectic squiggles of yellow on it. Opposite the door stood a coat-rack with various old jackets and macintoshes flung over it, and beside it a small table with a telephone. Around this there were chaotic piles of paper and notebooks. As well as a broken umbrella and some wellington boots near the stairs, there were more bundles of papers stacked in one corner. Under the front window, next to the door, was a little bookcase crammed with paperback volumes.

Linda was a little comforted by the mess. It was different from the down-at-heel, squalid, doggy mess of her own home, but it wasn't all immaculate like Lucy's house. At least he didn't live in a perfect palace of a place, even if it was big.

Alan took his coat off and threw it on to the coat-stand, from where it slithered off on to the floor again. Underneath he had on a sea-blue jumper, very large and baggy, and the sleeves hung down partly covering his hands. Linda watched, wondering what his mother was like and what was the matter with her. He stood at a loss for a moment, as if he'd forgotten why he had asked her to come with him.

'Oh yes – let's get some water on for tea!'

The kitchen, at the back of the house, was much tidier. There was a table in the middle with a teapot waiting on it and there was an air of cleanliness and order.

'Mrs P. sorts out the kitchen for us,' Alan said, putting the kettle on the gas. 'She seems to feel it's worth keeping the kitchen under control. I think she's given up with various other parts of the house.'

He looked across at Linda, who was standing by the table, and grinned suddenly. This lit up his face in such an extraordinary way that she felt herself lurch inside. He had high, prominent cheekbones, his pale face tapering to a quite pointed chin, and his normal expression was rather sombre. The smile, however, brought out his vivid, deep grey eyes. His teeth were even, and quite large. She liked his smile.

'Fancy some cake?'

'Yes please.'

'I don't think there's much else ... There might be some Rich Tea ...' He shook the biscuit tin hopefully but it gave off only silence.

'Cake'd be nice.' She felt so shy and awkward. It was as if she needed opening up to tell him things, say things, but she didn't know where to begin. She just knew that they were the same in some way, and that was why she felt drawn to him.

He cut the cake on the table and, as an afterthought, produced two pale green sideplates. She watched him, saw the way his hair curled a little, just behind his ears. He interested her, not like most boys, whom she found dull. But she still couldn't think of anything to say.

'There –' He handed her a cup of weak tea. 'I suppose we'd better stay here and have this. Sit down.'

She nibbled the sweet marzipan round the cake, feeling tongue-tied and self-conscious. She stared down at the table-top, its pitted wooden surface, surprised at how old and rough it was.

'I expect you're wondering about my mother. Everyone does, and they don't like to say anything.' He was talking rather fast, almost gabbling, stirring a lot of sugar into the tea. 'No one likes to talk about things like that. She's been in and out of the hospital for years. I can't remember a time when she wasn't. She goes mad, you see,' he said candidly. 'Some of the time she's all right and gives piano lessons. And then ...' He shrugged. 'She really can't help it. She says she's sorry and everything. It just comes over her.'

'Oh dear,' Linda said, helplessly.

There was a pause.

'Must be lonely. Being here on your own so much.'

'I'm used to it.'

'My dad's poorly,' she offered. 'And my sister.'

His thin face turned to her and she felt the force of his gaze. 'What's the matter with them?'

'Dad's just . . . never well. Hasn't been really since the war. He was in a Jap camp. And my sister, Carol – she had polio. She's in hospital now, having an operation on her back – she'll be there months.'

'Gosh,' Alan said. 'That sounds terrible.' He looked closely at her for a moment. 'There's something about you. I mean – I don't know how to say this without being rude, but you don't look quite right in the bakery.' Still gazing at her, he said, 'You're *so* pretty.'

'Aren't pretty girls allowed to work in bakeries?' she quipped. But her face was pink again, with mixed delight and confusion. He'd seen something in her, he had, despite her down-at-heel shoes and cheap clothes! 'Thing is – a lot of things have gone wrong in our family. Sickness, and that. I was at the grammar school too – the girls' one in Handsworth. Only I had to leave – family reasons really.'

'Oh, I see.' Somehow she had expected light to dawn in his face, for this to be important, a big statement, as it was for her. Oh – that explains it! she wanted to hear. I thought there was something different about you, something special. As if there were two versions of her, the one that had gone to King Edward's, the real her, whom everyone else had forgotten, and the other disappointed one who went to the secondary modern, the mask behind which she was forced to live now. She desperately wanted someone to recognize the first version of her and for a second she thought he had. But he just said it matter-of-factly, as if it didn't matter.

'So you were just there for a bit then.' As if it was as easy as that. It would have been for him. He'd just go back to the grammar school – of course he would.

'Yes.' No one but her knew her sinking heart. 'Maybe.'

He drained his teacup and pushed the chair back.

'Come on up – I'll show you my room.'

She followed his long legs as he bounced upstairs, and had a brief impression of the upstairs landing, flowery curtains at the window, more of the crimson carpet and a very straight-backed chair standing between two doorways, but otherwise bare.

His room was not bare – anything but. It was not very large, and the bed, chest of drawers, desk, chairs and bookshelves took up much of the space. But there were the books and papers and clutter of Meccano and tools, several replica guns and piles of clothes strewn on the bed and floor. Most eye-catching in all the mess was the big poster dominating the wall above the bed. It was all in a harsh brown and bright yellow, dominated by Gary Cooper's face looking out over his gun.

'"Gary Cooper's *High Noon*,"' she read.

'Fantastic, isn't it?' Alan even slid into an American accent. '"The man who was too proud to run." See –' His English accent returned. 'That's the great thing about knowing Stanley. He sent it me all the way over in a big cardboard tube. It's my most precious possession. He says he may be able to get me some more – *Red River, Shane, Rio Grande, She Wears a Yellow Ribbon* . . . Any of them! I want them all!'

As soon as he started on the pictures an almost quivering excitement came over him. He sank down on the bed and went off into a description of all his favourite scenes from *High Noon*. She sat beside him and listened, feeling proud that he wanted to tell her all this. Something about him touched her, so passionate, so alone here in this house with his enthusiasms. She noticed how thin his wrists were, as if they could so easily snap. After a time, he stopped.

'Gets me going,' he said, glancing shyly at her. 'Sorry. There's not usually anyone to talk to, you see.'

'That's OK. It's interesting.'

'You're very nice,' he said, looking at her properly. 'You really are. D'you know, I kept coming in to buy extra bread! You've got a lovely face – it's so kind and friendly-looking.'

Linda giggled. 'Don't be silly!' She would have liked to say how much she liked his face, and about how much he moved her, but didn't know where to begin without sounding daft.

'No – I'm not. It's true. I don't know any other girls, you see. No sisters – well, or brothers either. And school's all boys.'

'D'you think they'll take you back?'

'Oh, I don't know. Maybe.' He sounded weary suddenly, and rather wretched. 'I just can't keep my mind on anything.'

'Because of your mom?'

'Maybe.' He shrugged it off, not meeting her eyes.

'Don't you want to go back?'

'The old man wants me to.' What did he think of his father, she wondered? When he spoke about him it sounded as if he loathed him.

'But you – don't *you* want to?'

He looked down, said sulkily, 'Yes – s'pose so.'

Suddenly, after all his talk, things seemed to come to a standstill and neither of them could think of anything to say.

'I'd better go,' she said. 'I've got to get all the way home.'

'Where's that?'

'Kingstanding.'

'Blimey – miles away!' He jumped up. 'Why didn't you say?'

He walked her back to the bus stop and waited with her. She felt his loneliness, which linked hands with her own and drew her to him.

'Will you come again?' he asked, as the bus swayed into view. 'I mean, meet me?'

She smiled, full of happiness suddenly.

'Yes – course. If you want.'

Chapter Fifty-Nine

Even before she got out of bed Violet could tell it was foggy outside. The estate was still almost out in the country, and the thick, waterlogged air curled up from the fields and along the streets in a grey pall.

The clock said ten past seven – time to get moving. She didn't want to get out of bed. It was cold, and Harry was settled, still asleep. The nights were so disturbed that broken sleep had become a way of life to her, and she was tired to her bones, aching to lie and sink back into the warm darkness. She thought of Carol in her bed in the hospital, as she did every morning. Her poor little lamb.

'Come on – out you get,' she said to herself. Her old pink nightdress was covered in bobbly bits and one of the cuffs was torn. 'Proper glamour puss, you,' she muttered to herself, hurriedly pushing her feet into her shoes and pulling a cardigan on in the chilly room.

She slipped next door and to her surprise found Linda was already out of bed.

'Blimey – what's come over *you*?' she teased, in a low voice.

'Dunno. I just woke up early.'

Linda was half naked, standing shyly with her back to Violet. She probably needed to start wearing a bra, Violet realized. They still hadn't been shopping. For a moment she studied her daughter's shapely back, the long dark hair falling in waves down it. *She's lovely*, she thought. *When did she suddenly get so lovely, almost a grown-up woman like that?*

'Want a cup of tea?'

'All right. Yes.'

There was something different about that girl suddenly, Violet thought as she went downstairs. Linda, her mystery child. She was still a mardy little madam at times, but something had shifted in her. She wasn't so *heavy* in herself. In fact she seemed almost happy.

The cats were circling her legs in the hall, miaowing as if they hadn't been fed for a month.

'All right, all right . . .'

As she opened the kitchen door the smell of the dogs hit her, overpowering. The three of them leapt up, full of excitement and she shushed them, wrinkling her nose and hurried to open the back door.

'Go on – get out. You stink! And don't go making a racket.'

They tore out into the milky air like children dismissed from school. Violet left the door open to air the room and grimaced at the floor, all muck and dog hairs. Would there be time to mop it before work?

She stood by the stove as the kettle boiled, hugging herself. Linda had even agreed to let Violet trim her hair. A smile came to her lips. Amid all the struggle of her life, the best thing to come out of it lately was Rita. She adored going into work every day, getting out of the house, the edge of glamour it gave to life, the chatter and companionship. And Rita was warmth and generosity itself.

'I don't know how you do it, Vi, love,' she was forever saying. 'Keeping going the way you do with all your problems. I think you're marvellous. I've only got my Micky to deal with and that's quite enough, I can tell you!'

No one had ever told Violet she was marvellous before.

Rita seemed prepared to teach Violet everything she knew. Although they were about the same age, Rita mothered her and she revelled in it. She was learning how to cut in different styles, how to do a permanent wave and set hair in curlers.

'Ooh, you do learn fast,' Rita would say admiringly. 'You'll put me out of business, you will!'

But they laughed, both knowing that was the very last thing Violet wanted to do.

She didn't want anything about her work to change – she loved it exactly as it was. It was much better when Rita said, 'You're my right-hand woman, that's what you are.' She liked being someone's right hand: it wouldn't have felt right being in charge.

By the time she'd poured three cups of tea, Linda was already dressed and downstairs, hair tied back ready for work. Violet looked her up and down. Her skirt, blouse and jumper were all pretty long in the tooth, but she seemed to be dressing with more care.

'You look nice, bab.'

'Mom – can I get something new to wear?'

'I promised you, didn't I? How about we go for a bit of a shop – late Saturday after I've finished? Rita'd let me go early.'

Linda's eye wandered, as if she had other plans in mind. 'Maybe,' she said guardedly. 'Or I could go by myself . . .'

'Suit yourself.' Feeling let down, Violet headed off upstairs. Why was it she never seemed able to do anything right for that girl, even when she was doing her best?

Putting the cups down on the sill in the bedroom, she drew the curtains. It still felt as if she was trying to stare out through muslin, everything shrouded and indistinct. She rubbed a layer of mist off the damp window but that only made a small difference.

'Proper peasouper,' she said.

It seemed a shame to wake Harry, but she had to make sure he had something to eat and drink before she left. She'd pop back at dinnertime, of course. Rita was quite all right about it. Harry wasn't getting up every day now. One morning, only two or three weeks back, he'd looked at her from his bed with a defeated expression and said, 'I don't want to have to make the effort today, Vi. Just let me lie here for a bit.'

That frightened her. It seemed to bring the inevitable closer. Up until then he had fought on, battling his declining body and frail mind.

She heard the hooves of the horse pulling the milk float outside, the man calling 'Milko!' and it pierced her with sadness. He used to be out there, early mornings. He used to . . . But it was no good letting her mind run down the road of the things Harry used to be able to do.

'I've brought your tea,' she said, more brusquely than she meant to. It was a way of trying to keep her emotion at bay. 'Harry – time to wake up, love – I've got to go soon.'

She carried the cup over and perched on the edge of the bed, leaning over to switch on the little lamp between the beds. They hadn't shared a bed since he came out of the hospital.

'It's not fair on you,' he'd said ashamedly. 'I don't

want you to have to put up with it.' She tried to argue, just a little, but he was adamant.

'No – don't, wench. I'm done for. I'm horrible. Just sleep across the room from me so I can see you.'

'Harry?' His stony, deep-sleeping face brought out her tenderness. 'Your tea, love.'

She reached for his hand, felt its stiffness, and it was then she knew. Her pulse picked up speed. She heard the blood thump in her ears.

'Harry!' She touched his face, shook him, but it made no difference to the cold statue he had become. 'Harry – love! Wake up!' She didn't realize she was screaming.

'Mom?' Linda came running upstairs. 'What's happened?'

Violet was backing away from the bed, both hands to her face. She was trembling all over.

'He's . . . your dad . . . I think he's . . .'

Linda went to her father, hesitating for a moment as if too scared to touch. Then she leaned down and laid her fingers on his neck, feeling for a pulse.

How does she know how to do that? Violet thought.

As if she'd spoken aloud, Linda said, 'You can see it moving, the vein in his neck. Like a heartbeat.' She turned, eyes wide. 'It's not beating any more.'

'Oh God,' Violet whispered.

You could see now that he wasn't there any more. His body had been vacated, life's current lost. His face was even more sunken, the last sparks of him flickering off into the darkness of night while they were sleeping. They both stood staring for a few moments, too shocked to move. Then Linda took a step towards her and they were in each other's arms. They didn't say anything. Violet stroked Linda's back. Her daughter smelled of Lifebuoy, and her curving shape in Violet's arms felt a great reassurance. After a moment, they stood apart. Linda had tears in her eyes.

'Poor Dad.'

Violet shook her head, too full to speak. 'Tell you what. Go and put the kettle on again.'

She didn't know why she said it, except that she wanted to give Linda something to do, and before calling the doctor, and telling Joyce and her mother, before all the busyness of death, she wanted to be alone with him, with his body, to know more fully than she could so far that he was gone.

Linda nodded, somehow understanding, and went downstairs. Her footsteps sounded sad.

With tentative movements Violet pulled back the bedclothes covering Harry. She thought there might be something to dread, smells, that he had soiled himself in passing as people did, she knew, but there was nothing but the cold that now seemed to hang about his skeleton body in the dark blue pyjamas. He had worn little but pyjamas these last weeks. Maybe it had been obvious that the end was coming, but somehow life just went on and she couldn't let herself think about it.

She laid her hand on his chest, on the protruding bones, a hard ache in her throat. His shoulders, ribs, chest, were nothing but jutting bones. She was so used to him, to washing, dressing him – not lovemaking, that had ceased a good while back – yet today she saw it all afresh.

'What the hell did they do to you?' she whispered. And everything in her began to ache and tears ran down her cheeks. And following came the realization that he had never told her, never felt able to talk to her. The years in Burma were something he could not voice, not to her, perhaps not to anyone, and this seemed the most heartbreaking thing of all. Had he been able to tell Joe Kaminski? Joe, who had also seen horrors in Poland untold to anyone around him?

For one second, half closing her eyes, she made him once more into the robust young man she had married, but he was too altered and the picture slipped away. So long ago now, before the war, before . . . Roy Keillor's face rose in her mind and she pushed the memory away, fraught as it was with guilt and longing. No good thinking back to the things you could have changed. That Roy and she . . . No – don't think. Nothing could be changed now, not one second of it.

Wearily she leant down to rest on her husband's body, moving her head to find any softness in him, and the only yielding place she could come to rest was on the concave drum of his belly. She put her arms round his wasted frame as if comforting a child.

'I'm sorry,' she whispered. 'I'm so sorry.'

Why she was saying those words she wasn't sure. It seemed the only thing that brought together everything she meant. And she thought of the night their little son Bobby was born, when Harry tenderly undressed her out of her soaked nightie in between her labour pains.

I loved him then, she thought, as her tears began to come. And holding him now, she knew she loved him today as well, and that despite it all, she had done her duty to him. Sitting up, she stroked her palm over his stubbly cheek, then rested it on his forehead.

'It's all right, love, you can stop struggling now. You can have some peace.'

Chapter Sixty

It was the sweetest, most exciting feeling.

Alan had burst into Linda's life, filling her with love and happiness and hope like a shower of rainbows. After that first day, walking home, she had felt like dancing along the pavement from the bus stop. She liked him and he wanted to see her again and he had told her he thought she was pretty. *Her!* Scruffy little Linda Martin, *pretty!* And the way he looked at her moved something in her, and he was lonely and unhappy and she was drawn in by him immediately. When would she see him again?

He was lovely to her when her dad died. The burial at Witton cemetery felt unreal to her. She couldn't seem to take in what was happening. The family were there, of course, except Carol. Joyce sobbed uncontrollably through the whole thing.

'I can't seem to stop,' she kept saying afterwards. 'I think it's because I'm expecting.'

Eva and Joe Kaminski came of course and, to their astonishment, so did Reg and Edna Bottoms.

'Another old soldier,' Mr Bottoms murmured. 'Just wanted to pay my respects.'

Mom looked exhausted, and so thin, with dark crescents under her eyes.

'I've looked after him all this time,' she said as they got ready that morning, just the two of them at home.

'And it's been a burden, I can't say it hasn't. But now – I feel lost.'

Linda wanted Carol. At least she could look after Carol so that she didn't have to think about herself. Joyce had Danny to comfort her and everyone was saying what a shame it was, losing her father with a baby on the way. Bessie was there, of course, with Marigold and Clarence, and Charlie and Gladys, but Linda didn't expect anything from any of them. Otherwise it was just her and Mom. The family seemed to be disappearing. She couldn't take in for a while afterwards that Dad had really died, that he was gone for good. He had been fading for so long to a poignant whisper: now silence. It was only when Mom started rearranging things, cleaning the room, bringing the table back in from the front to where it really belonged, taking his chair out, tears running down her face as she did so, that it began to sink in.

'We'll burn this.' She looked down at the stained chair with his blue cushion on it, cigarette burns along the arms. 'No good to anyone, is it? I can't stand to see it.'

Somehow it was arranged that Joe Kaminski would deal with it. A few days later Linda saw him outside going at it with an axe.

The house felt empty. Mom kept saying she didn't know what to do with herself.

'You all right, Linda?' she kept saying. 'You thinking about that boy? Why don't you bring him home to meet me?'

She'd had to tell Mom about Alan. A bit about him anyway, that that was where she went sometimes after work. And was she thinking about him? Of course she was. She scarcely ever thought about anything else! He occupied her imagination, his pale face, expressive hands, his words, something she examined over and over again. Each time she thought of him, the intense, yet vulnerable way he looked at her, it made her heart lurch. But she wanted to keep him to herself.

When she went to Alan's house he was almost always alone. She had met his father, Dr Bray. He was a large, imposing man, almost bald, with a residual ring of fuzzy brown hair and little half-moon glasses through which he peered at her. Though he always wore a suit he was not a smart man, but had a rather dusty, sagging air about him which Linda supposed was partly because his wife wasn't there to do something about it. He also smoked a pipe and always smelt of tobacco.

She went there a few days after the funeral. Sometimes Alan came to the shop to meet her but that day she had walked there by herself, expecting to find him alone in the big house as he so often was. But it was Dr Bray who answered the door.

'Ah – hello. Come in.' He spoke impatiently through his pipe, which trailed smoke as he stood back to let her in. She didn't like the way he looked her up and down. Despite his brusque way of talking, his sludgy eyes seemed to linger on her for too long.

'Alan!' Dr Bray took his pipe out of his mouth and called upstairs. 'Your friend's here!'

She heard Alan's footsteps on the landing, then he appeared at the top of the stairs.

'Hello – why don't you come up?'

'That's not very polite,' Dr Bray said. 'Why don't you come down and welcome your guest, Alan?'

It came over as false the way he said it, trying too hard, like trying to force a rusty piece of old machinery.

Alan didn't say anything. He stared stonily down at his father. Linda went up to him.

'Sorry,' Alan said, as they went into his room. 'He came home early.'

'S'all right.'

He leaned forwards and kissed her shyly on the cheek. 'Thank God you're here.'

He was always so pleased to see her. His need of her thrilled her the way nothing ever had before. Very quickly she had begun to feel in conspiracy with Alan: the two of them against the adults with all their messy difficulties, against the world. It felt as if he was all she needed.

He closed the door and went to his cupboard, bringing out his packet of Silk Cut, and held it out to her.

'Ta.' She took one nonchalantly and they shared a match. The first couple of times she'd smoked with him she'd coughed and found it a bit strong, but she'd got used to it now.

'Won't he smell it?'

'He doesn't care what I do, so long as I don't bother him.'

Alan put his head back and blew smoke at the ceiling. But he slid the window open before coming to sit by her on the bed. They ended up in their usual position, leaning against the wall, Alan's arm round her waist. She cuddled up to him. Nothing else mattered when she was with him.

Alan always spoke about his father in tones of complete contempt. He didn't talk much about his mother, though Linda had shyly tried asking, but she knew Alan blamed his father for her being ill. He'd only talked about it once. They were down in the kitchen at the table, smoking then as well.

'Course, *he* wouldn't notice what state she was in,' he once said savagely. 'Not till it was too late, anyway.'

His mother had been all right, he said, until she got married and had a baby.

'So it's my fault too, I s'pose.' He said it as if it was a joke.

'How can it be your fault? You were a baby!'

'Oh, I dunno.'

He stubbed out the cigarette fiercely into a saucer. Then he wouldn't talk about it any more.

Today there was a heaviness about him, a mood of melancholy. They sat in his room without the light on. It was nearly Christmas and the daylight was almost gone for the day. Outside was cold and damp.

'What've you been doing?' she asked. All his days must be so long and boring, she thought, without school, or a job. Dr Bray had talked the school into taking Alan back – after Christmas they said, as the term was almost over now. 'I s'pose they think they're giving me time to stew,' he'd said sarcastically. 'Appreciate what I'm missing.'

'Nothing much. Playing a bit . . .' He indicated the guitar propped against his desk. 'Reading. Thinking.'

'How's your mom?'

'Dunno. I'm going to see her on Sunday.'

'Oh.' She wasn't sure what to say. 'That's nice.'

'Yes, a trip to the asylum's always rather jolly.' He blew out another swirl of smoke. 'Sorry – I didn't mean it. Not to you.' He looked at her. 'How's your sister?'

'They say she's getting better but it takes ages. But she's all right. That's the weird thing about Carol. She's happier than anyone. You could come with us one day – come and see her.'

She had taken herself by surprise, inviting him. She'd

never invited him home yet, although it would be all right now – there was only Mom. In a way she wanted to, but in another she wanted him to be her secret. She didn't want the family's comments. Mom'd be bad enough, but imagine Joyce – and Nana! No, she wanted to keep Alan all to herself.

'Yes – I could,' he said. He sounded unsure, but pleased. He took another drag on the cigarette.

'Let your hair down – will you?'

She kept her hair clean now and enjoyed the feel of it swinging in a high ponytail. Alan liked to stroke it so she pulled the ribbon out and it fell in dark, glossy waves over her shoulders.

Alan sat up and stubbed out his cigarette. Eyes fixed on her face, he took her head in both hands, stroking her hair.

Chapter Sixty-One

On the Saturday afternoons when she wasn't working, they mooched about in town.

Sometimes they went to the pictures, but Alan wasn't really interested if it wasn't a Western.

Birmingham was a building site, still recovering from the war, everyone managing their shopping round the mess, the banging noises and scaffolding. They sat in a coffee bar at the top of the High Street, where there were other people their age, and felt grown up.

Alan could be very funny when he wasn't being gloomy. He had a biting sense of humour, keeping up a running commentary on the people walking past outside – 'My God, look at that coat. D'you think someone should tell her? It'd be a public service wouldn't it?' And the faces he pulled were very funny. It felt good being with him, made her feel properly alive, as if she'd woken from the long uninspired doze she'd been in ever since Mom and Nana made her leave her beloved school.

He bought a pair of denim jeans, like the Americans wore, and Linda saved up wages to buy a pair as well, which she wore with a big black sloppy jumper. She wore her hair long and loose, trailing down her cheeks, when she wasn't in the bakery. Alan said he liked her with her hair down. And she managed to pick up a secondhand duffel coat. She felt excited about how she and Alan dressed and talked. It was different from

355

most people. Almost all of the girls she knew dressed exactly like their mothers. It meant something, being different. They were the young ones, making the future. Violet didn't seem to see it that way.

'It's not very flattering, is it?' she said, looking at Linda's new outfit. 'I thought you were going to go shopping with me – get a nice new skirt?'

'Well, I like it,' Linda snapped. 'I don't just have to wear what you want, do I?' *I've done quite enough of what you want already*, she wanted to add.

The other thing about Alan was that he talked about ideas. He liked philosophy. He talked about something called existentialism which he said was about getting past all the 'tosh' all the adults talked about, with their establishment values, their religion and politics.

'We have to carve out the way for ourselves – with the choices we make,' he said to her earnestly, as they sat at a little table and sipped dark, strong coffee. 'Not be trapped in systems made by other people.'

Linda listened to him, feeling ready to go off pop. It was exciting enough sitting here with him, the taste of coffee and tobacco in her mouth, feeling all grown up and sophisticated. But now she could feel her mind expanding as well, the way she longed for it to do. If she'd carried on at the grammar school, wouldn't she have been able to have ideas like this, instead of finding them out from him by chance? But then, wasn't it romantic discussing them in a coffee bar with your boyfriend instead of with a load of girls in a classroom? At last here was someone who felt what she felt!

'Everyone's stuck, aren't they?' she said passionately, nodding out of the window at the Saturday afternoon shoppers trailing past in the Birmingham drizzle. 'I mean look at them – you're born, you work in a factory, have loads of kids, get old and fat and boss everyone else around to make them do exactly what you've done, and then you die!'

She spoke with such vehemence that Alan stared at her and then burst out laughing.

'What?' She blushed. 'What's so funny? It may not be like that for you, but that's what it's like for me, what I'll be stuck in if I let myself.'

'Can't imagine you getting fat.' He was grinning.

Linda stared at him, completely enraged by the laughter in his eyes. She was startled by the force of her anger. He'd missed the whole meaning of what she'd said! How could he reply in such a shallow way when she was laying out all her feelings in front of him? She took a fierce drag on her cigarette and blew the smoke in his face.

'No. Well – it's different for you, isn't it? You can just go back to school!' She was on the verge of tears suddenly. 'It's all there for you, if you want it.'

He was startled by the force of her emotion. 'Hey – what's up?'

'You just don't get it, do you? And I thought you would.'

Holding back the tears made her throat hurt. Wasn't there anyone who would understand how she felt, locked inside herself with this enormous hunger to escape?

She was quiet after that, couldn't find words. Alan finished his cigarette. He looked uncertain.

'Shall we go then?'

Linda followed, mute. As they walked back to the bus stop she didn't say a word and he knew he had offended her. It was the first time they kissed, properly, that afternoon. They went back to Handsworth Wood, to his house, almost in silence. She felt as if there was a well of sadness building inside her that needed release, and suddenly, on the smoky, upstairs deck of the bus, for no reason she could name, tears began to run down her cheeks.

'Hey –' Alan sounded alarmed for a moment, then shyly slipped his arm round her shoulders.

She put her hands over her face and had a quick cry and all the time was aware of the warmth of his arm round her, the woolly smell of his duffel coat. After, she dried her eyes and looked out of the smudgy window, because something had altered. There were strong, charged feelings between them and she didn't know what to do.

Upstairs in his room, Alan stood in front of her, eyes anxious.

'Sorry. I don't know what to say.'

'S'all right.' She looked at the floor, miserable.

He came to her then, and put his arms round her, but in a way that also felt as if he was a child and needed her and they clung together. After a moment he drew his head back and looked into her eyes. She scarcely knew what a kiss was, except something that happened in the pictures, but Alan was moving his face closer to hers and she found herself responding. The feel of his lips on hers was new and strange at first. His lips were warm and soft. They kissed shyly, then more passionately, pulling each other closer, and it was all new, his warm tongue between her lips, his hands stroking her back until she was floating amid all these sensations.

He drew back and looked at her again.

'I love you.'

This caught her so unawares that she giggled. Alan looked hurt.

'I mean it!'

'Sorry.' She managed to straighten her face. 'D'you really?'

He nodded. 'I need you, Linda. I do.'

It seemed a big thing to say, like stepping out somewhere new, but she said it anyway. 'I love you too.'

He pulled her close again and she rested her head against his shoulder and closed her eyes. He was all that made sense in a lot of confusion.

'We don't need anyone else, do we?' he said. 'Just you and me.'

The next time she saw him was a couple of days before Christmas. As soon as he let her into the house, she could feel how low his mood was. He was alone and there were no signs of any Christmas preparations. She and Mom had at least put some streamers up together and planned presents for Carol and Joyce and Danny. In fact Mom was gradually doing the house up, bit by bit. She seemed to be full of energy. She'd painted the back room and put new lino down on the floor and was starting to clean up the kitchen, with Joe Kaminski's help. Alan's house, though, was dark and cheerless.

'What's up?' she asked.

'Nothing much.' His voice was surly as he led her upstairs.

'You look like a wet weekend.'

'Thanks.' There was so much aggression in his voice she felt quelled.

'Alan?' She faced him across the room.

'It's just . . .' He sat on the edge of the bed, elbows resting on his knees, chin in his hands. 'They thought my mother might be out for Christmas. But she's worse, they say. She's not coming.'

Linda sank down beside him. 'So – is it just you and your dad?'

Alan nodded. 'S'pose you've got all your family.'

'Umm,' she agreed. She'd been dreading it – Christmas dinner with Nana moaning about Marigold, and Clarence coughing and hawking and the first one without Dad. But compared to Alan's Christmas it suddenly all seemed quite cheerful. There was Carol to go and see for a start, and they'd get together with Eva and Joe Kaminski and there were cards arriving – one had come from Australia, from Mom's friend Muriel, that morning.

'Wish I could be with you though,' she said. 'That's all I want – to be with you.'

He put his arms round her and rested his head on her shoulder.

'My girl,' he murmured. He kissed her cheek. 'Come to America with me?'

She was startled.

'When?'

'When I've finished school. I could work – you could go back to school there. It's all easier over there.'

She turned to face him, eyes alight. Everything seemed to open up full of hope. 'D'you really mean it?'

'I'm going to write movies, I told you. I want you with me.'

'I'll come with you!' she cried. 'I'd go anywhere with you.'

Part Five
1954

Chapter Sixty-Two

The clock on the mantel struck with a mellow-sounding 'bong!'

Marigold sat in the chair by the fire, which was usually sacrosant. It was Bessie's chair. But now Marigold was basking rebelliously in it. She also had her coat on, belted tightly round her, and a new hat she'd bought from the pawn shop, blue like her coat, a soft wool circle nipped in at the sides to fit round her head, her black hair sticking out below.

She smiled at the clock.

'Tick tick,' she said.

She was waiting to make sure there was no more noise from upstairs. Bessie and Clarence had gone up to bed as they always did when the clock struck ten. Wireless off, cup of cocoa, regular as clockwork.

'Get up to bed now,' Bessie bossed her, struggling to her feet, wincing at the pain. Her feet were no good now. She had rheumatism and bunions, bandages round her stout, ulcerated legs, and she couldn't walk far. Once she was upstairs there was no getting her down in a hurry. How long before she couldn't get upstairs? But this was not a question Marigold was interested in. Every day was Mom's legs and Clarence's wheezy chest, her at everyone's beck and call. Now, though, she had only one thing on her mind.

She got up with a little grunt, patting the bottle in

her coat pocket. Gordon's gin – her favourite. Clarence saved a bit of his pension money every week, kept it in a sock under his mattress.

'What're you hanging on to that for, you silly old sod?' Bessie would ask. 'Your own bloody funeral?'

And Clarence would nod in an enigmatic way, as if he had immense plans no one else was to know about. He never remembered how much was in there, which was a lucky thing for Marigold, who extracted a small amount from his stash each week, to make sure she could always get more gin. The rest she took from Bessie's jam jar of coins in the pantry. Why not? Bessie never noticed, not like she would have done years ago. Too taken up with her aches and pains these days.

Marigold went to the window and pulled back the curtain. It was snowing outside, flakes seeping down into the street where they disappeared into dark gullies of shadow. It was only by the lamp you could see a thin layer accumulating on the pavement. She giggled at the sight, excited as a little girl. And she had her new hat. She patted it proudly. Time to go.

'Dirty girl, dirty girl,' she whispered, going to the door. She snickered as she opened it. 'Dirty girl's going out, and sod you.'

She could hardly contain her laughter: it was bursting out of her as she stood on the step she'd scrubbed that morning, and would scrub tomorrow morning and every day of her remaining life, it seemed. Scrub, scrub. Rub-a-dub. What was that song? *I'm gonna wash that man right outa my hair* . . . Mary Martin, *South Pacific*. She hadn't written that one down yet. Tomorrow she'd do it, with her pencil and pad. But wash him out? Her Fred – oh no! Mom thought she'd washed him out, but Marigold was cleverer than they knew.

She set out along the dark street with her little bag over her arm, her steps silent on the cushion of snow. It was that cold, flat time after Christmas. Christmas Day they'd sat in Violet's house, nice and clean now, for a beef dinner and there were decorations and a big pudding. Violet looked nice too, Linda hardly saying anything, Joyce there with her belly all out. Marigold kept looking at it, Joyce's heavy belly. Full, like a pod.

'Two months to go!' Joyce said. 'I can't believe I'm going to be a mom!'

'And I can't believe I'm going to be a nan!' Violet smiled. She was looking nice. Pretty, with her hair and that. Good old Vi.

Joyce's belly made Marigold feel funny. She didn't like it. All she wanted was to stick something in it and make it go down. But she couldn't stop staring at it either.

Babby ... new, sticky babby between Joycie's leggies, her scrawny white thighs...

And while they were eating beef and potatoes and trimmings, Mom said in that voice she used, 'Marigold had herself a fancy man – did I say before?' She laughed, belly wobbling, forkful of cabbage. Then her voice changed and turned hard, contemptuous. 'Huh! I soon put a stop to that, I can tell you. Bloody disgusting – and at her age!'

That's what she thought, anyway! Ha, ha, that's what she thought, the old cow!

The lights of the pub beckoned her. She felt warm inside.

'That you, Marigold?'

'Yes – it's me.' She giggled again, seeing Fred's burly shape come out of the pub door.

'Took your time! Just got time for a quick 'un before closing.'

He was big, Fred, fat and red-faced, owned a butcher's shop. 'How's my girl, eh?'

'All right,' she laughed.

'Quick drink –' Fred laid his hand on her left buttock as he steered her through the door. 'Then we can get down to business!'

She was welcomed into the den of the pub. It wasn't far off closing time now, the air heavy with ale and smoke, the sawdust sodden underfoot, spittoon holding a murky liquid with a thin froth on top.

'Your usual?' Fred asked.

He brought her half of stout and another brown ale for himself. The old piano was quiet now, no more music, but a couple of Fred's pals were there and they all welcomed her.

'Here y'are Marigold – she let you out, has she? Come and sit here, bab!'

Marigold felt like a queen. She had never had friends before, not like this. She didn't need to say anything. She sat in her hat and coat, snowflakes melting on her shoulders, enraptured simply to be there, amid the desultory conversation of half-soaked men, out of home, away from Bessie, with the promise of . . . She looked at Fred and he winked at her.

'Drink up, old girl!'

She was draining her glass as the bell rang for closing time and they all had to mill out into the white street. The flakes were bigger now.

'Won't last long, I don't suppose,' one of the men said, squinting up at the dark sky. 'Too bloody wet.'

They said their goodbyes and Fred immediately put

his arm round her. With his free hand he reached round and gave her breast a squeeze.

'Let's be off, wench.'

Fred was a bachelor who lived in two rooms a street away fom the pub. Marigold went back regularly with Fred and shared his bed, nice for both of them, until it was time to creep back into her mom's house.

She liked Fred, and he liked her, but there was no ceremony about it. As soon as they were through the door into his spartan man's abode, his hands were under her coat, reaching for her breasts. Marigold took her coat and hat off and got ready to luxuriate in a man's attention.

'Just a minute, girl . . .' He went fumbling into the bedroom and she heard him relieving himself noisily into the chamber-pot. He didn't bother to button up when he came out.

'That's better. Let's be having you then.'

Soon they were on Fred's unmade bed with its wrinkly grey blankets, only half undressed. He rucked Marigold's dress up, yanked her bloomers off, fumbling at himself.

'That's it,' he grunted contentedly, steering himself into her. 'Into the harbour – that's my girl!'

Marigold snickered, then moaned as he jerked back and forth, fired with her own pleasure. This was a bit of all right. She always got what she wanted as well, whoosh, like a firework all down there. Nothing like it.

'You're a fine wench, Marigold,' Fred said, kissing her affectionately when they'd finished. 'Glad I found you, that I am.'

'You're all floppy,' she giggled, eyeing his flagging manhood.

'That I am . . .' He yawned and teased at her nipple under her blouse. 'Till the next time, anyway – eh?'

Half an hour later she left Fred snoring and crept back home. No one was stirring. Nearly half past twelve and Mom and Clarence none the wiser, once again. She took a swig of the gin as a congratulatory nightcap and lit a candle to get upstairs.

The boards creaked on the upper landing. She stopped for a moment, but heard her own loud breathing, nothing else.

Something made her go into her mother's room. A sense of triumph, of wanting to crow. Creeping over to Bessie's bed she stood over her. Bessie was on her back, her thickened face tilted to one side, mouth half open and snoring, oblivious to the fact she was being watched.

Marigold held the candle high and stood, looking down at her.

Chapter Sixty-Three

Joyce's baby was born in Good Hope Hospital on a February day as the clouds sprinkled sleet upon the sodden streets. There was more falling later that evening when Linda got home.

'Where've you *been*?' Violet was in the hall the moment the door opened.

'Out.' Linda pushed the hood back and peered out at her mother between long curtains of hair.

'She's had it! Joyce – they've had a little lad! Danny came round earlier to tell us and he drove me over to the hospital to see her! He's ever so bonny – just like Danny. He's got footballer's legs!'

Linda peeled off her damp coat, a smile coming over her face at the thought of a baby looking like Danny, with little football boots on. And it had distracted Mom from noticing how late she was. It was nearly ten o'clock.

'Let's have a drink . . .'

Violet led her through to the kitchen and put the kettle on in a celebratory way.

'Joyce's doing marvellously. They told her she's a natural mom – gave birth easy and that. She's very pleased with herself.'

Yes, Linda could imagine. But she leaned up against the side in the kitchen, full of a sense of wonder.

'Our Joycie a mom!' Violet said. She couldn't seem

to stop smiling. 'Don't seem five minutes since I was having her!'

'You're a nan.'

Violet looked solemn for a moment, then giggled. 'Blimey – I am, aren't I? God – it makes you think!'

Linda walked over to the flat on the Sunday morning. They'd been to see Carol the afternoon before and she was very excited about the baby. The nuns said Carol was doing exceptionally well and might be able to come home the next month. She'd finished the scarf she had knitted for Linda, a brown and yellow striped creation with a few missed stitches and wonky bits, but Linda loved it. It looked scruffy and in keeping with her look.

'Goes with my coat,' she smiled, indicating her mole-coloured duffel coat.

Carol beamed. 'It's cold out. I wanted it to keep you warm.'

The wool was a bit itchy, but the scarf was cosy to wear. She had it on, her hood up in the rain, as she walked round the Kingstanding circle and turned off towards Danny's dad's garage and the flat which was up a staircase at the back. Danny let her in, face dark with stubble and still in his pyjamas.

'Oh – it's you.' He sounded a bit bewildered. 'What time is it?'

'Dunno. 'Bout ten.'

'Little 'un's been on the go all flaming night. I've lost my bearings.' But he grinned good-naturedly. 'He can't half blart when he gets going!'

'Who is it?' Joyce called. She didn't need to raise her voice too much. The flat was small – one bedroom plus a boxroom, a living-room, and tiny kitchen and bathroom.

'It's your sister.' Danny was lighting the gas.

'Come on in then, Linda,' Joyce called regally. 'You'll have to take us as you find us. That's how it is with a babby in the house.'

Linda went into the bedroom, most of which was occupied by a double bed. There was an oil heater in the corner and they'd got quite a fug up, bedroom stuffiness mixed with paraffin and an animal, milky smell. It was so warm, Linda took off the coat and scarf and put them on the floor behind the door on what seemed to be a pile of laundry. Joyce was sitting propped against a couple of pillows, in a nightgown with frills at the neck. Her hair was long and loose and there was something different about her, as if she, like the baby, had been under water for a long time and the water had washed her features looser in some way.

'Here he is!'

In her arms was a bundle of blanket, at the top of which Linda could just see a crown of fuzzy dark hair. Joyce sat him up and the bundle gave out a sneeze..

'Ooh – bless you!' Joyce giggled.

Linda heard a tone in her sister's voice that she had never heard before, a wholehearted tenderness towards something outside herself. She was humbled by it.

Sitting on the edge of the bed, she leaned forward and Joyce laid the baby across her arms. He was more solid than she had been expecting, with a swarthy complexion and strongly carved features, almost like a grown man already. His eyes opened a slit to show cloudy grey pebbles. He was the first baby she'd seen close up in a very long time and she was astonished. And it was Joyce who had produced this miracle of a creature!

'God, Joyce – he's lovely, isn't he?'

Joyce beamed, gratified by her sister's genuine enthusiasm.

'He's the most beautiful babby *ever*,' she pronounced.

'I mean – where did he *come* from?' she stuttered.

'In my belly, stupid!' Joyce laughed.

'No – but I mean – I *know* that ... But it's ... I mean it feels as if he's come from space – just arrived on a flying saucer or something!'

'You been watching too much *Quatermass*?' Joyce laughed.

'Fat chance. Mr Bum won't let us near that television again!'

'D'you want a cuppa tea, Lin?' Danny called from the kitchen. They could hear him clinking cups and spoons.

'Yes, ta! Here – I'd forgotten. I bought something for him.' She reached for her coat.

Danny came in then, with a mug for each of them.

'Ta, love,' Joyce said comfortably, taking the tea.

From her coat pocket Linda took out a beautiful pair of bootees she'd seen in a shop window, wrapped in white tissue.

'*Ah* –' Joyce seemed genuinely touched. 'Aren't they pretty? That was nice of you. Thanks. Look, Danny.'

Danny nodded. 'Ta. Very nice.'

He came and perched wearily on the other side of the bed with his own mug of tea and leaned forward to look adoringly at his son.

'Ya cheeky little bugger! You're going to have to learn to sleep a bit better'n this!'

'We thought we'd call him Charles – you know, after the prince. And then –' Joyce looked to Danny for approval, 'Harry. For Dad. Only we're not sure yet ...'

'Eh, Charlie, what d'you reckon?' Danny leaned over to tickle his son's nose.

'Careful – you'll spill your tea all over him!' Joyce chided.

'No I won't – don't talk daft.'

Linda shifted the little boy in her arms so they could all see him properly.

'Charles Harry Rodgers,' she said. And she drew him close and kissed his bulging cheek, surprised at the affection she felt for him already.

She left Joyce, Danny and the baby resolved to go and see them as often as she could. She was so caught up with Alan that the visit to Joyce's had been a surprise, like emerging from a darkened room. Alan was almost all she thought about, and every spare moment they had, they were together. He had become the centre of her life.

Alan had gone back to school after Christmas and she would see him after work, but soon after the baby arrived she went round there one afternoon to find him in a strangely excited state.

'Well – guess what,' he said after letting her in. She could smell drink on him and his eyes didn't look right.

'What?' she asked, uneasily.

'They've just chucked me out again.' He flung the information casually over his shoulder as they went upstairs.

She was shocked. 'Why?'

'Oh – not turning up . . .'

'But I thought you had been . . . haven't you?'

Alan flung himself down on the bed, and looked up

contemptuously at the ceiling. Beside him, Gary Cooper stared out enigmatically over his gun.

'Not much. And it wasn't just that. I had a skinful.'

She knew he was drinking, but hadn't realized it was that bad. He didn't drink much with her.

'What – just today?' She slid her coat off and flung it on the chair.

'Today, yesterday, last week . . .'

'Oh, Al . . .' She sank down beside him on the unmade bed and took his hand. He shook her off at first, then his hand reached for hers and he looked up at her, hungry for reassurance.

'Why d'you do it?'

He didn't reply.

'You've really torn it now, haven't you?'

'Come here.' He pulled her closer and she lay down in his arms. She reached up and kissed him and she could taste the booze on him.

'What're you going to do? What'll your dad say? He'll be livid!'

She felt Alan shrug. 'Let him. Who cares?'

'But you can't just stay at home.'

'I'll get a job. Hey –' He released her suddenly and leapt up. 'I got a letter from Stanley today – there's this new movie he's seen . . .'

He fished about on his desk for the blue airmail letter and sat down beside her. In Stanley's small, painstaking handwriting were pages of description of a film called *Hot Blood*. Alan ran his eyes over the page, though he already seemed to know the gist of it off by heart.

'It's about a gang of motorcyclists called the Black Rebels and the leader's called Johnny Strabler . . .'

'Sshh – you don't have to shout . . .'

'They ride in and take over this town in California.

Stanley says it's the most fantastic film, it's like nothing else! Everyone's talking about it and the establishment types think it's a Commie movie.'

As usual, when he started on the subject of 'movies' his voice was taking on an American twang.

'I hope they blasted well hurry up and show it over here.' He turned to her, as if a thought had just occurred to him. 'That's what I'm going to do. Get Dad to buy me a bike.'

Linda sat up, laughing in disbelief. 'You must be joking! After you've just been expelled from school, *again*!'

'I can use it to get to work.'

'Well, where are you going to work?'

'I dunno.' He sat down again and put his arms round her, kissing her passionately. 'We can get out of here – ride off together.'

And again she found herself caught up in his dreams, which in some way spoke to hers.

Chapter Sixty-Four

Within a fortnight, Mrs Bray was sent home from the mental hospital for a trial period.

When Linda went round one afternoon she was startled to find all the family there.

'My mother's here,' Alan said at the door. His face looked different, as if something had loosened in him.

'You mean – they've let her out?'

'Yes – she came yesterday.'

Linda started to back away. She was muffled up in Carol's woolly scarf, speaking through it. 'I'll go home . . . You don't want me there . . '

'I do – please!' Alan seized her wrist. 'Come on – she likes a bit of company and I've told her about you. I want you to meet her.'

Linda was very nervous. She didn't know what she expected Mrs Dorothea Bray to be like, but the idea of the 'asylum' struck fear and dread into everyone. She'd seen Nana shudder at the very mention of it.

To her surprise, she could hear dance music coming from the living-room at the back of the house. There was a radio in there, Linda knew, but Alan led her to the kitchen. Standing by the table was a slim, black-haired woman with Alan's wide grey eyes. Linda had an impression of someone neatly dressed, in a calf-length skirt, pale blouse and a long black cardigan. Her hair was parted in the middle and taken back in a rough bunch at the back. What was startling was how young she appeared, almost girlish.

For a moment her face was blank and then, mechanically, as if having to recall how to do it, she smiled.

'Hello. You must be Linda?'

Her voice was soft, well-spoken. Linda had to remind herself to free her chin from behind the scarf. She unwound it and took it off.

'Hello,' she said, feeling very shy and at a loss.

'What a nice name,' Mrs Bray suddenly spoke very fast. 'Did you know Linda means "pretty" in Spanish? I expect you did.'

'No.' That was the truth of course. 'I didn't.'

'Well – it's very nice to meet you. I'm glad you're a friend for Alan because his father works so hard and my poor boy is alone so much with me being . . . ill.' She leant forward distractedly and picked up the tin of tea from the table. 'You know I've been away?'

Linda nodded.

'They did something to my head, you see, and now I'm back.'

Linda could feel Alan's discomfort reaching her, almost smell it. He seemed younger suddenly, now his mother was here.

'I can't always . . . manage, you see.' Dorothea Bray smiled brightly. 'Would you like some tea? I can make tea now, Alan.'

'Thanks – that'd be nice,' Linda said.

As Mrs Bray turned to light the gas with slow deliberation, she whispered to Alan, 'Where's your daddy?'

Alan rolled his eyes upwards. 'I think he's working.'

It seemed to Linda very odd and unkind of Dr Bray to be up in his study when his wife had only just got home. But she was relieved he wasn't here. He was so stiff and hard to talk to.

'You sit down, both of you,' Mrs Bray said. 'Let me make you tea. I haven't made tea for a long time.' She stood as if thinking for a moment, then said, 'You see, they did something to my brain – to try and make me better. Everything takes me a long time . . .'

She was so transparently open, like someone whose skin has been removed, that Linda was disarmed and felt sorry and somehow tender towards her. She began to relax, and saw that she was helping Alan to do the same.

'That's all right,' she said. 'You take your time. There's no need to hurry, is there?'

'No.' Mrs Bray gave a sudden little laugh. 'No, of course you're quite right. No reason to hurry at all.'

Watching her prepare the tea was agonizing. She laid out four cups and saucers with the slow deliberation of a child.

'Sugar . . .' she murmured, and opened the cupboard to stand staring for an age, while Linda and Alan could both see it right in front of her but thought they had better let her find it for herself. The same rigmarole went on with the refrigerator.

Just as she had found the milk and was closing the door triumphantly, Dr Bray's voice came booming from the upstairs landing.

'Isn't that tea ready *yet*, Dorothea?'

The effect was terrible to see. Linda thought Mrs Bray was going to drop the milk bottle, which she had finally identified in the fridge, and she only just managed to steer it to the table. Her eyes were terribly frightened and she was all of a quiver, almost to pieces. Linda was appalled.

'Y-yes, Arn . . . Arnold. Just a moment, please!'

Alan got up abruptly from his chair.

'No – Alan, don't!' Mrs Bray protested, but he was already out in the hall. They heard him say something low and emphatic and he came back with his cheeks red.

'Oh dear – I'm so slow,' Mrs Bray said. 'He does hate things to be slow.'

'Why's he like that?' Alan erupted suddenly. 'Why does he always have to be like that?' His voice was tearful. 'How are you supposed to get better?'

'Don't, Alan . . .' Mrs Bray was weeping herself now. She was trembling all over and she went to Alan and took him in her arms, cradling his head. 'Oh, my boy, my lovely boy . . .'

Linda watched, her insides knotting tighter and tighter. It was like it had been when Dad was ill and you didn't know how he was going to react to anything, that sense of fear and dread at what might happen. She knew it was one of the things that bound her and Alan together. Poor Mrs Bray! And poor Alan! He was crying now, his sobs sounding too deep and manly for his slim body. Behind them the kettle boiled and boiled, filling the room with steam.

'Why don't you leave him? Get away from him – he makes you ill. You wouldn't be like that if it wasn't for him!'

'Don't say that, darling!' She pulled him from her and took his face between her shaking hands. 'That's not true. I would. I truly think I would be. It's how I am and it's very hard for Daddy.' She managed a brave smile. 'And where would I go? Who would want a person straight out of the madhouse – eh?'

She chucked his chin, trying to be brave, to lighten things. She seemed suddenly more self-possessed.

Linda got up, shakily, and removed the kettle from the gas.

'Oh dear, yes – look at all this smoke ... no, steam, that's it – steam. Like a Turkish bath!' Mrs Bray said. 'Thank you, Linda! What a way to welcome your lovely, pretty friend. Come on now, darling.' She poured water into the teapot. 'We must look on the bright side – umm? I'm home now. Now you take your father his tea to keep him happy. I don't suppose he'll want to come and drink it with us.'

They sat together drinking tea, with a plate of biscuits, and Mrs Bray talked about some of the other inmates in the hospital in Winson Green.

'Some of them are really very nice,' she said. 'One does make friends – even in the oddest of places. But still – ' she braced her shoulders. 'I mustn't linger ... I must be here now ... Look after my boy ... I've not been much good.'

She patted Alan's shoulder and, looking at Linda, she gave a terrible, sad smile.

'You'll help me look after him, won't you?'

Chapter Sixty-Five

Three weeks later they came to take Mrs Bray away again.

Linda didn't realize at first.

Alan was outside when she arrived that Sunday morning. It was March, sunny, but still very cold, the air whirling white with their breath, but he was outside without even a jacket on, squatting down on the front path by a very smart silver and black motorcycle. He was polishing the front mudguard, frowning sternly.

'Blimey! Is that yours?'

'BSA Star Twin. Smashing, isn't it?' He stood up, his expression lightening a little. 'Got her yesterday. I've been out a couple of times already.'

Linda thought of her dad's old Norton, rotting away in the front garden all those years. Poor Dad. For a second she had a glimpse of the younger father she could barely remember.

'Is it new?' It appeared to be in perfect condition.

'Nearly. Dad got it off someone in Sutton. Said he had a shed out the back with a whole load of them. The bloke collected them and tinkered about with them, but he hardly ever rode them.'

'So – did he buy it for you? Just 'cause you asked him?'

Alan shrugged. 'He's got enough money. I can

381

always get money out of him. He's stopped going on about school, now he knows I'm not going to get to university like he did, he doesn't care a damn what I do.'

She watched his face carefully, seeing how much he cared underneath all his pretence not to.

'What about your Mum?'

Avoiding looking at her, he rubbed his cloth along the line of the handlebars, then circled it over the BSA trademark.

Linda bent down and looked quizzically into his face but he looked away.

'She's not here.'

She tried to make sense of this.

'She went bonkers again,' he said harshly. 'They came for her – yesterday.'

'Oh, Al!' Mrs Bray had seemed distracted, it was true, and odd, but she hadn't realized it was that bad. 'What happened?'

He ignored her. 'So – d'you want a ride, or not?'

Once he'd wheeled the bike out to the road, they both climbed on and it started up with an impressive roar.

'Get your feet up!' he shouted, and they sped off along the road. Immediately she could tell he was in charge of the thing, seemed naturally to know how to handle it, and she relaxed, arms wrapped round him, the cold wind rasping against her face, making her eyes sting, but she didn't care because even on the staid roads of Handsworth Wood it felt like freedom and she just wanted to ride and ride. She let out a cry of excitement and heard Alan laugh. They didn't go far, not this time. It was so cold, and by the time they got back her cheeks were raw and stinging.

When they jolted to a standstill outside the house again, she laughed, exhilarated.

'That's the *best* thing I've ever done!'

'Told you, didn't I?' He took the bike in on to the path and started polishing it all over again. 'Now we can really go places.'

As the spring came, the bike was like their magic carpet.

They went to Sutton Park and beyond, out into the countryside, whenever they could get away, and it felt to Linda as if everything about her life that was sad and limited and frustrating blew away as Alan rode faster and faster along the country lanes with her whooping, excitedly behind him, and the wind tore through her hair, seeming to wash her mind clean.

One Sunday he said, 'You've got to let me meet your mother. It's not fair if I never see your family.'

Linda hesitated. There was something about bringing together this dream world of Alan with home that she didn't like. His home was not a happy place, that was true, but that was his, not hers. She could manage it with him, give him comfort. But taking him home to hers felt difficult.

'We'd have to go on a Sunday,' she said. 'She's at the hair salon every other day.'

'Let's go now then.'

They whizzed out to Kingstanding. On the way, Alan pulled up abruptly by the Maryvale Orphanage to stroke the pet donkey which grazed outside and was a friend for the children. She had never thought of him as loving animals before.

'Never been allowed them,' he said. 'Mum couldn't cope – not with anything else.'

Linda looked into the donkey's wise brown eyes.

'Carol would love this.'

'When's she coming home?'

'Soon. They say in the next month or two.'

Alan rubbed the donkey's face. 'Must be nice – having other people. Brothers and sisters I mean.'

'Sometimes.' Linda laughed. 'It's better with Joyce now she lives somewhere else though. She doesn't half get on my nerves if I have too much of her!'

It felt grand somehow, riding into the estate on the bike. Along Bandywood Road, she suddenly spotted Maureen Lister, whom she barely ever ran into these days, and waved, yelling, 'Hello, Maureen!' as they streaked past. Maureen got the message almost too late and Linda saw her gawping in wonder.

When they pulled up to the door in Bloomsbury Road the dogs started barking frantically. They heard Violet ticking them off, shutting them out the back, and then she appeared, in her apron. She'd been in the middle of cleaning.

'What the hell's all the racket about? Oh – it's you. Nice of you to put in an appearance,' she said to Linda. *You're never here*, she was forever saying. *For all I know you could be lying in a ditch somewhere. I mean you never know . . .*

'Hello, Mrs Martin,' Alan said. Linda heard how polite he was, how he could put that on when he wanted. Somehow she felt proud of him, although she was anxious about him being here. She became aware just how desperately the front door needed a new coat of paint.

'Brought you out of hiding then, finally, has she?' Violet said. 'I was beginning to think she was making you up.' But her tone was friendly.

'Can we come in?' Linda said, trying not to sound irritated. She didn't know what it was with Mom these days. Sometimes she felt really sympathetic to her, what with being a widow after all that had happened to Dad and Carol being in hospital and everything. At other times it was as if devilment rose in her and she couldn't stand anything about home and her mom and all she could think of were rude, bad-tempered things to say.

'Course you can. Aren't you going to introduce me first?'

'This is Alan,' Linda said, grumpily.

'Come on in, Alan,' Violet said. 'I'll put the kettle on, shall I? We've got some cake over from yesterday, haven't we, Lin? We've always got cake, with her working at Wimbush's.'

She turned and smiled at them and Linda saw her suddenly. *Mom's pretty*, she thought. Maybe she always had been and she'd never noticed. She was certainly more relaxed and happy-looking than she had ever known her.

'Where d'you work, Alan?'

'Nowhere.' A hunted look came over Alan's face. 'Not at the moment.'

'Oh well –' Violet put a plate of sponge slices on the table. 'Never mind, love – you'll find something soon. Plenty of jobs about if you're ready to knuckle down, aren't there?'

'Well – yes,' Alan said. And Linda saw him relax. At home he felt a failure, but Violet accepted him just as he was.

She watched him getting on with her mother. He asked her about Carol and her job and then if he could see the dogs.

'Oh – you don't mind if I let them in again then?'

Violet was delighted. 'Some people don't like them –
Mr Bottoms next door doesn't, does he, Lin? If you're
all right with them, I'll bring them in.'

Alan loved the dogs and made a big fuss of them.

'They like you,' Violet said. 'They can tell when
someone really takes to them, can't they, Lin?'

Once Alan had ridden away that afternoon, though,
Violet said, 'Seems a nice enough boy. Bit posh for you,
though, isn't he?'

Without answering, Linda left the room and slammed
the door. *Trust Mom to want to drag me down as usual!*
she thought, thumping up the stairs. She'd keep Alan
well away from here, she decided. They were better off
without anyone telling them what to do and who to be
– just the two of them.

The next Sunday was a bright day and they rode right
out to the countryside and sat out of the breeze behind
a blackthorn hedge, looking across a sloping field where
tiny shoots of green were sprouting like hair. Clouds
came and went across the sky.

'Smoke?' He held out a packet to her.

Linda took one and enjoyed the trail of it on the
fresh air. They were huddled, side by side. She fished
out ham sandwiches and they munched in silence for a
time, alternating with puffs on the cigarettes.

'Here – ' Out of his bag he pulled a bottle of Bell's
whisky.

Linda wrinkled her nose. 'Don't like it much. Got
anything else?'

'No – go on. It's Dad's. It was in the cupboard in his
office.'

'Won't he want it?'

'Probably. He'll just have to get some more, won't he? Get out on his footsies and buy some for himself.'

She unscrewed the bottle and took a swig, gasping as it burned down.

'It's horrible!'

'You get used to it.' He drank himself, grimaced, then wiped his mouth.

'D'you know what?' He was full of indignation suddenly. 'The damn film censors...' He swigged again.

She pushed her fingers through the dropped stitches in Carol's scarf. The smell of the damp earth rose up between her knees. 'What're you on about?'

'That movie – the one Stanley told me about? It was *Hot Blood* – the one about the bikers, Marlon Brando...? They've renamed it *The Wild One*. But they've banned it – they aren't bloody well going to show it over here! The mealy-mouthed reactionary bigots in this pathetic small-minded country won't let us see it because it's too *controversial* for us. As if we're kids and can't make our own minds up! God, I was *dying* to see that. I was looking forward to it. Stanley's got a leather jacket – like the guys in the movie!'

'Stanley seems to get everything,' she remarked. She got a bit tired of hearing about Stanley. He was older than Alan, and already a college student.

'That's what comes of living in the US of A. It's another world from here. Everything here is so *staid* and tired and unexciting.'

'Mom says it's because of the war. Austerity.'

'It's not just that – it's the way we are. I don't want to be British. I don't want to be *me*!'

He flung himself over on his side, impatiently, as if trying to escape from his own skin. He was still holding the bottle and she could hear his voice getting louder, the way it did when he drank. She reached over and took it from him, standing it down beside a big thistle.

Suddenly he leaned over and kissed her on the lips. She wrapped her arms round him. At least when he kissed her he stopped being angry. She saw the tender side of him then, and he moved her. She loved him so much, the feelings seemed to fill her whole body.

Chapter Sixty-Six

A row of bright red tulips along the garden fence swayed in the spring breeze.

Violet stood by the sink, looking out.

'I planted you,' she whispered.

They were the first thing she had ever planted. Now and then there had been marigolds and pansies which she'd bought ready-grown to try and brighten up their patch of garden, but these tulips she had put in as dull, dry bulbs and now look at them!

She held her cup of tea clasped in both hands, and could feel the steam warming her chin. Today was special: she had taken the day off – 'Of course you've got to be at home, darlin'!' Rita said – because it was the day Carol was coming back from St Gerard's.

Linda had only just left for work, the door slamming shut to leave the house with this strange miracle of quietness. The cold tap was slowly dripping and she tightened the faucet to shut it up. She could dimly hear sounds from next door – the Kaminskis must have their radio on.

Out beyond the tulips, at the bottom of the garden, was a freshly dug patch with a little wooden cross on top made from slivers of the broken fence. This was Dolly's grave, one of the two old mongrel sisters, who had died last week. Violet's eyes filled with tears looking at it. Linda and Alan had buried her, taking turns with the spade, Joe Kaminski occasionally peering over the fence, baffled by such sentimentality. Violet knew she wouldn't get any more dogs. They still had the cats, and Snowdrop, and the budgies. Before she had craved animals, had gathered them round her for comfort. Everything was different now.

She had watched Linda and Alan burying Dolly. Sweet together, they were: Lin, with her long hair all round her face, both of them out there in those sloppy clothes they seemed to want to wear. One moment they had their arms wrapped round each other, the next they were down there scraping at the earth like little kiddies digging on the beach . . . She couldn't believe she already had one daughter married with a babby – and now it looked as if Linda was heading the same way. Linda of all people! But it was the natural way of things, wasn't it? She'd worried about Lin when she was younger, knocking about with that queer bloke Johnny Vetch, and all that business about the grammar school. It was as if her girl had taken off into a foreign country where Violet couldn't speak the language. Lin had been angry for a bit of, course, when she had to leave, but it had been for the best, hadn't it?

Only gets you into trouble, pushing out into water that's too deep, Violet thought. Best stick with your own and what you know. When it came to marriage – well, that she *did* know something about! What good ever came of kicking over the traces? For a moment she thought uneasily of Rosina, her agitated departure from Joyce's wedding in those fancy clothes. She should do something about her, get in touch. But there'd been so much else to get through, no time, no energy left. And who was Rosina now? The truth was, she wasn't sure she could face it.

For a moment she pictured the future, with her still living here in this house she was now licking into shape, month by month, room by room. She felt proud of it now – she'd done a lot of it by herself, with odd bits of help from Joe Kaminski and Danny. There were things left to do, of course, like the garden and their mess of a front door. But she'd made a real home of it. The girls would live nearby with their husbands, grandkids over at the weekend, her cooking, queen bee at the middle of her family. She smiled, in the direction of the tulips. It had all been such a struggle – making ends meet – where would she have been some weeks without the Divi stamps from the Co-op? But at last she felt on top of things a bit, could feel she was the driver in her life instead of always riding pillion on events and letting them happen to her.

Not like Muriel and Dickie, upping sticks and going all the way to Australia! They'd had Christmas on the beach! She did wish Muriel hadn't gone so far away. Sometimes she ached to see her, with her crisp Scottish accent and her jokes, to talk over old times. But the two of them sounded happy, that was the main thing – even if they hadn't managed to have any kids of their own.

I must write to her, she thought. Finishing her tea, she put the cup in the sink and sat down at the table. It felt like the first time she had sat down for twenty years and she smiled at this thought. God, there'd been some hard times! Considering that, she wasn't in bad nick, was she? She looked down at herself, trim in her blouse and skirt and stockings. And Rita had done wonders with her hair. In fact she felt better than she'd ever done in her life before.

Sitting back in her chair, she looked round the room, dwelling on familiar objects in a way she never normally had time to. This kitchen was a luxury compared to anything Bessie had ever had. She could have had it by now, of course, if she hadn't been too stubborn to move. Everything looked beautiful today, the sink with its wooden drainers, pans on the stove, handles all pointing the same way, the colander, sieve, potato masher, big metal spoon all hanging from hooks beside the sink, her life, with its mundane tools for feeding them all day by day. And on this day there would be a feeling of rightness, of gathering everything in, because, after almost seven months, Carol was coming home. Roy's Carol.

A bar of weak sunlight slanted across the floor and she watched it lazily, allowing herself to dream. How much had she ever really got to know Roy? Did he love that wife of his? He had seemed to, and loved his children, of course. His life had gone on, somewhere, children growing up, he getting older, and all she had of him were those pictures, frozen in her mind, of those ecstatic days when they had loved each other during the war. Real life wasn't like that, she reminded herself. Things change. Roy and his wife would be a middle-aged couple living out their life somewhere . . .

'And I,' she said, pushing herself up from the table, 'had better get on with it, not sit drooling here.'

But even now, at the thought of his lips on hers, a pang went through her almost as deep as the day he left.

They came with Carol soon after midday. Violet heard sounds outside and opened the door to see her getting carefully out of a car, not an ambulance this time. Her hair was long now, a gold blaze over her shoulders.

'Hello, Mom!'

And Carol walked, beaming, towards her carrying a little cloth bag. Violet saw that the limp was still quite bad. Her left leg was slightly withered, and though St Gerard's had done everything they could on her spine, her leg was not likely to get better than this. But Carol was delighted.

'It's lovely – I can walk properly!' That first time she had paraded up and down the ward to show them. One of the nurses clapped.

Violet still felt a mother's sadness at any disfigurement to her child, but of course it was true – she was walking, and without even a stick or a caliper! Her life could be much more normal now. Violet's eyes filled. Carol could have died, she could have been crippled for life, but here she was, walking up the path, almost right as rain.

Once they stepped inside, Violet took her girl in her arms.

'Hello, babby – ' She lifted Carol off the floor. She was eleven now, but still a little scrap of a thing. 'Oh, you're home at last.' She closed her eyes, feeling Carol's arms gripped round her convulsively.

'We've done up Joyce's room for you to have,' Violet told her excitedly. 'Linda chose the colour for you – it's ever so pretty.'

Violet showed her the new bedroom, pink walls and curtains, a teddy waiting for her on the bed. Sooty was asleep on there curled up as well. Then she wanted to see the rest of the animals and Violet made her a sandwich.

Carol was quiet at first, then talked in a constant stream, all about her friends at St Gerard's, Bernice and the others, the daily routine, what they'd be doing now. When she'd finished her sandwich she limped over to fetch the cloth bag. It was made of faded green velvet.

'That's nice,' Violet said. 'Who gave you that?'

'Sister Maria,' Carol said. She sat down at the table and from the bag pulled out a black book with a worn leather cover. Violet was startled for a moment. It looked almost like that poetry book that Roy had brought to show her!

'What's that, pet?'

'Sister Cathleen sent it over for me.' Carol hugged it for a moment as if it was a doll. 'She came to see me on Sunday because they told her I was going home, and she said it was hers. It's called a Missal – ' She flicked through the delicate pages. 'It has all the readings in that they do at Mass every day.'

'Oh,' Violet said. She felt resentful. Why give a child something like that? It seemed most peculiar – and why on earth was Carol so pleased with it? Thank heavens they were out of there and had seen the last of that meddling Sister Cathleen!

'I'm going to read the readings with them,' Carol said.

'I've got some chocolate biscuits,' Violet said. 'D'you want one?'

'Umm – yes please!'

'And shall we have a game of Ludo?'

Carol beamed. 'Yes, OK. When's Linda coming home?'

'She'll be in – soon as she's finished work.'

It was so lovely to have her back and Violet spent the afternoon close by her, wanting nothing else but to drink in her presence, and trying to understand that Carol had been away for a very long time and that she was full up with chatter about the day-to-day rhythms of the hospital because she had known nothing else.

When it was nearly dark, they were sitting together

in the back room and heard noises at the front. Carol gasped.

'Linda!'

A moment later, Linda appeared. Violet saw the two sisters' eyes meet and the joyful smile which spread over Linda's face.

Chapter Sixty-Seven

They were laughing. Linda had never heard Alan laugh that much before.

They were not laughing about anything in particular: it was the drinking that made all the difference, cider this time, a big bottle of it standing half empty in the bright summer grass by Alan's head.

'God – it's flaming strong!'

Linda started tittering after only a few mouthfuls. The stuff licked its way down into her stomach, and in no time she felt floaty and blurred in the head as if all she could ever do was lie in that spot for ever, unable to move.

'What the hell's that made of?'

'Apples,' Alan told her, taking another huge swig.

'No – it's never!' She giggled.

''Tis!'

The field started to swerve around her.

'I think I'm going to have to lie down!'

All she could see was the sky like a blue saucer, smell the heavy scent of cow parsley, waving close to their heads. Behind them, the bike was propped against the gate. Just for once she'd taken the denim jeans off as it was hot and put on a checked frock, and fronds of grass tickled the backs of her legs.

The more they laughed, the more they set each other off.

'You sound like a girl!' She laughed even more, hearing him.

'No I don't!'

'You do . . .'

He drank some more, wiping his mouth on his bare arm, then lay down beside her and they held hands.

'It's like standing waiting for the bus,' he said.

'What?'

'If you tipped us up, so's we were standing up. You're standing next to me . . .' His voice was slurred. 'Christ – it *is* strong, that stuff . . .'

He raised his arm and pointed two fingers at the sky.

'Bang . . . Bang!'

Then he pedalled his legs in the air. 'Roger Bannister! Four-minute mile!'

Laughter seemed to come out of Linda without her asking it.

'Stanley's going to get me a picture – Marlon Brando on his bike. *The Wild One.*'

He leaned over and kissed her on the lips. It was then he told her about the job.

He'd hung about for a few weeks in the spring, never seeming to get round to doing anything but tinker with the bike and go to the pictures. Linda liked him coming and meeting her from work, and Mrs Richards was always ever so pleased to see him.

'He is a nice lad,' she said frequently to Linda. 'You are lucky – you hold on to him, duck.'

Course, Mrs Richards could think about nothing but wedding bells and babies either. Linda didn't know why she felt stifled any time anyone talked like that. Even Carol had asked her if she was going to marry Alan. Carol said she hoped so because she liked him.

In May he'd announced he'd got himself a job, in a

foundry near the middle of town. At the time, they'd quarrelled about it.

'What d'you want to do that for?' she said. 'You can do something better than that, surely?'

Alan became suddenly hostile. 'What d'you mean, *better*? What – you think you're above an ordinary working-class job, do you?'

'No, but you could get a better job – in an office or a shop or something.'

'Maybe I don't want that kind of job – and anyway, what are you doing, eh? Are you going to stand there with Mrs R selling buns for the rest of your life?'

That stung. She didn't want to talk about her limiting of herself – she wanted to criticize him for doing the same instead!

'I dunno,' she snapped. 'But I'm not you, am I? I don't have a dad who works in a university . . . You could do better.'

'Well, maybe I don't *want* to. Maybe I don't think it's worth the bother. I don't want to be like him.' The anger in his voice went so deep that she was silenced by it.

So he went to work in the foundry. She could never get much out of him about it. Of course he didn't come and meet her out of Wimbush's any more, and he seemed tired by it. Otherwise, if she asked he just said, 'It's not too bad. It'll do.'

Now, he said, 'I've finished – at the foundry.' He was looking down at her, his face quite near hers, and she saw a flicker of something in his eyes, a strange, closed look. His eyes already had the glazed look that drink gave them.

''Bout time you gave that up,' she teased.

'I didn't give it up – they sacked me.'

'Alan!' she half sat up. 'Why?'

Offhandedly he said, 'Didn't get there on time. Didn't always turn up.'

'I thought you wanted to do that job!'

'Nah. It's a bore.' He lay back, reaching for his fags in his pocket and lit up. 'I've started writing a script.'

'What did your dad say?'

'Nothing much.' He handed her a lit cigarette. 'Usual sort of lecture ... got to learn to knuckle down, bow to authority ... the British Empire didn't get built by this sort of attitude ... rolling stones gather no moss ... blah, blah, blah ...' He hurled the match away into the grass. 'He's covered in so much bloody moss he can't see out.'

There was silence.

'Did you hear me?' It was a shout, almost. 'I'm writing a script.'

'Yes – I heard you.'

He rolled over, aggressively. 'D'you love me?'

'Yes, I love you.' But suddenly she was afraid.

They lay smoking and staring up at the sky. Linda felt the harsh smoke in her throat, the breeze on her face, and a floaty feeling as if they were not attached to the earth but on a raft, floating on a wide, empty sea, all alone, just the two of them. And the raft seemed to spin faster and faster and she wanted to put her hand out to stop it. She had no idea where they were floating off to, the two of them. None at all.

Chapter Sixty-Eight

Bessie and Clarence were in their chairs either side of the range.

Bessie never sat down, of course, not an actual 'sit down' like some idle old bag of bones with nothing better to do. When she did sit she was always about something – darning, knitting. She had a great-grandchild to knit for now of course, a boy, no less, and little Charlie was going to have nothing less than the best.

The half-knitted matinée coat in pale blue wool lay on the stool next to her chair. *I'll get going in a minute*, she thought. Opposite her Clarence was asleep, head tilted back, snoring. So he wouldn't be checking up on her. *That's it, Bess – you have a rest.* That would have made her pick up her knitting right quick. She wasn't having anyone thinking she was slowing down, starting to grow barnacles, oh no.

The back door was ajar to let the breeze through but she fanned her face with her hand. She was perspiring heavily. It was too hot! She could never remember a day as hot before. Flies circled round the ceiling, stubbornly dodging the curl of flypaper hanging from the light cord. They were after the waste bucket in the kitchen. She thought about going to tip it outside. Later would do. No need to move now.

It was the heat, that was what. That was why she couldn't seem to get going today. It made her dead tired, with a heaviness she'd never felt before except in the last month before a baby. A moment of deep longing went through her and she sighed. Those were the days all right. Her and Jack, babbies coming. The only really good time of her life, that was the truth, like a picture with a shining gold frame. And twins! Boy and a girl all in one! She'd felt like one of the seven wonders of the world, all the fuss from everyone when Charlie and Marigold arrived.

Marigold. Her mouth twisted bitterly at the thought of her slow, lumbering daughter with her sly ways. Out gadding somewhere, no doubt. Bloody disgrace she was, a woman of forty, stinking of booze and out round the pubs the way she was, like a bitch on heat. Thought she had secrets, didn't she? Thought her mother didn't know she pinched money off her, when Bessie could read her like a book, the silly little cow, with all her carry-on. She should say something – course she should. Kept putting it off. Her mind slid away from the thought, from the look she saw sometimes in Marigold's eyes that made her keep her lip buttoned. It was only a few bob she made off with, after all. Easier to keep the peace now.

Any road – I wash my hands of her, Bessie thought. I've done more than a mother should have to, over the years, that I have. Not just for her either.

She rested her head back in the chair. It was so seldom that she just sat. Her hands were resting on the arms of the chair. She stared at them for a moment, misshapen, puffy-knuckled. They weren't her hands, were they? *Old woman's hands.* Then down at her wide lap, capacious flowery frock falling in a curve between her thighs, at her old woman's feet, all swollen, the ankles bulging out of her sloppy old shoes. Better than being scrawny, though. Quite enough of that as a child. Years she'd spent, thin as a broom-handle.

'You're not bad for sixty-two, Bess,' she whispered. 'Better nick than *him*.'

After all, if she didn't give herself a puff up, who would? Sixty-two years she'd lived in this area, Aston born and bred, worked like a dray horse all her life, brought up four kiddies by herself and fostered scores of other women's brats. *Fostered*, they called it now – had to find a posh name for everything these days. In her day you just took them in out of pity and did your best. And a fat lot of thanks anyone had ever given her when you came down to it. Oh, there was the odd remark, and the money, of course. But not real *gratitude*, not what she really felt she was owed for all those nights she'd turned out of bed for a screaming brat and the mess and nappies everywhere. No real credit for the way she'd managed everything. *They owe me*, she thought, her mouth twisting bitterly again. *This neighbourhood owes me.* Not that anyone cared. No one cared about anything these days. You had to make sure you thanked yourself – no one else would.

She eyed Clarence malevolently. His face was parchment pale, cheeks sunken and his hair was almost gone now, except for a few strands which clung across his bald pate like the last survivors in a shipwreck. Looking over him she saw the white shirt, clammy-looking and stained with food, his skinny old shanks in shiny black trousers and his mouth hanging open like a bird waiting to be fed.

That's all he's done all his bloody life – wait for me to feed him.

Like the rest of the family, she decided, rage swelling in her. Take, take, take. Violet with her fancy ways now and her frippery little job mucking with women's hair. Thought she was too good for them now, she did, and that Linda, like something the cat dragged in. Serve her right, miss smartypants. Never did to get above yourself, did it – grammar-school airs and graces. She'd never seen it come to anything that a bit of hard collar couldn't do just as well.

As for Carol – well, who was the father of that one, eh? So it served them right really. Polio – Vi knew it was her punishment.

Behold I was brought forth in iniquity, and in sin did my mother conceive me . . . The words jumped into her mind, startling her. Where did she know that from? Somewhere way back – Sunday School? Any road, Joyce was the only one with any sense, getting on with life the way it should be. Like Charlie and Gladys – they'd done it right, never been any trouble.

Not like Rosina. Her picture and the two letters were still gathering dust on the mantel. Bessie never looked at them – not to take out and really look at. The letters were no good to her – she couldn't make head nor tail of them. But Rosina's face was there, always present behind the jug. She'd catch sight of a dark eye or the shoulder of her frock as she moved about the room. The scene at Joyce's wedding replayed in her mind. Rosina's glamorous get-up, her nervous, haunted expression and then her taking off along the street without even a glance at her mother, holding that hat on with her skinny arm, the ungrateful, scheming little bitch . . . Bessie realized her heart was beating so hard she had to push herself up in the chair and take in some deep breaths.

Oh, I mustn't think about it . . . I don't feel right today, that I don't . . .

If only there was someone to make her a nice cup of tea. That'd sort her out.

'Clarence?' It came out in a hoarse whisper. 'Clarence? Oh, wake up, you deaf old bastard you. You useless, stinking old bag of bones, you're no use to anyone, are you? Saddled with you all my bloody life . . .'

Rage engulfed her like a wave and she had to sit and concentrate on breathing until she felt a fraction calmer. All right, she'd have to make her own tea then. There'd been no one to help all her life – she wasn't going to cave in now.

As she got the things together to make tea she realized her hands were shaking. The teaspoon clattered on the saucer. She steadied herself, holding on to the edge of the sink as the kettle heated. That stinking waste bucket! The stench of it seemed overwhelming. Sweat was running down her face.

She didn't remember walking into the front room, sitting back down in her chair. A blackness spread through her head. When Clarence woke up, the kettle had boiled dry.

Chapter Sixty-Nine

'Get on.'

Alan yanked the bike away from the wall outside the pub.

It was a few nights later and they had been drinking with two of his old school friends. The two of them had been on at Alan. What was he playing at? Why didn't he pull himself together and get a proper job? Alan had lost his temper and stormed out, Linda following through the press of bodies, into the sultry evening.

He was trembling with fury.

'I said get on!'

'Alan!' But she obeyed.

Before mounting the bike himself he reached into his bag and took out a bottle, swigging from it.

'Al – be careful.' Fear slithered like worms inside her. He was more angry and unpredictable than she had ever seen him.

He mounted and started up the engine, revving it furiously. Luckily she held on tight to him, because he shot off very fast along the road.

Frightened, Linda shouted out, not knowing if he could hear her. It made no difference so she pressed her cheek to his thin back in his leather jacket and held on tight as they roared along the Birmingham roads, taking corners very fast so that her stomach lurched with dread, and he headed north. She only had on a thin cardigan, with her jeans and short-sleeved blouse, and the air felt much cooler as they tore along, but she was sheltered by him. She closed her eyes, fighting the fear. The bike swerved from side to side, leaning right over as they went round corners very fast. There was nothing she could do except cling on and wait until it was over.

Finally, right out in the country he took them up a hill and stopped by a gate. Linda peeled herself shakily off the bike.

'God, Al!' she raged at him. 'You scared me. You go too fast!'

'Don't be daft. I know what I'm doing. Come here.'

He took her in his arms and kissed her hard on the lips, then drew back, and she could see him looking intently at her in the darkness.

'D'you love me?' he said.

'Course I do.'

'No, I mean really – do you?'

The intensity of the question took her aback. She did love him, didn't she? She tried to quell in her the sense of unease that was growing. The voices of his friends had come back to her as she clung to him on the bike. *What the hell are you doing? You're messing up your life!* And she was angry and insulted by them because she knew they thought she was part of the mess, that she was beneath Alan. But her anger left her and she felt very tender towards him again.

'I do love you.' She kissed his cheek, tears in her eyes. 'I *really* love you. But you scare me sometimes.'

'I don't mean to. Look – let's go up there.' He nodded at the gate, behind which the field sloped up a little further, topped by a small clump of trees.

They climbed over and walked up in silence, holding

hands. They had to leave the edge of the field and walk through the wheat to get to the top. They could hear it swishing against their legs. Once they reached the top, they sat in front of the trees. The moon was coming up, half full, and its light showed the pale wheat falling away in front of them and the darkness of the lower-lying ground beyond. You could just make out more trees at the far edge of the field, the warm night air mingled with the smell of wheat.

'Those two, in the pub – were they your best mates at school?'

'Yeah – I s'pose they were.' Alan tore off a head of wheat and fiddled with it. 'Not sure I see eye to eye with them now though. They seem – I dunno – as if we don't care about the same things. Don't speak the same language any more.'

Linda thought of Lucy Etheridge from the grammar school and how hard it would have been to keep that friendship up once she left.

Into her silence, he said, 'I've got you, though.'

She smiled, though there was a moment of unease at the island the two of them seemed to have become, dark sea all round, no boats in sight.

'Haven't I?'

'Yes – ' She took his hand again, but he pulled away and put her arm round her shoulders instead, pulling her close.

'My Linda – God, I don't know what I'd do without you.'

He rested his head against hers for a moment.

'Look – ' she pointed – 'Stars.'

It was as if they suddenly became aware of them, as if they all came out at once.

'I knew this bloke when I was a kid, called Johnny

Vetch. He took me up a church tower to look at the stars.'

'Why?' Alan sounded puzzled.

'He was just like that. It was in the war, when it was all dark. Johnny saw things different from everyone else. He was nice – to me, anyhow. But he killed himself.'

'How?'

'Cut his wrists.'

'God. Why did he do it?'

'I don't know.' She wanted to cry suddenly and had to swallow hard. 'Everyone said he wasn't right in the head. But he was nice. He knew a lot about things.'

After a moment, Alan said, 'I don't want to be like my father.'

'I don't want to be like my mother.'

'Your mum's nice!'

'Yes. But I don't want to be like her.'

'I just want to get away.' Alan stared up at the sky, the great distance of it. 'Be somewhere else. Be someone else.'

Lowering his head, he said, 'I'm so glad I met you.' He kissed her and, passionately, she kissed him back.

She hadn't given any thought to how far it might go that night. Neither of them had. They lay back at the edge of the wheat, flattening a swathe of it like a bed and clinging to each other. They had done very little before except kiss, but now neither of them was completely sober and she felt his hand slip under her blouse.

He hesitated. Neither of them knew what to do. 'Can I?' he said.

She nodded, wide-eyed, not knowing exactly what she had said yes to.

She had a moment of panic at the newness of what was happening, his warm fingers on her skin, and then nothing mattered but the sensations of his hands and their lips, which carried them through the unbuttoning and sliding off of jeans and their skin against one another's until she could feel him between her legs, pushing into her, and though she barely understood what was happening she didn't want to stop him. She wanted the feelings, and what would happen next. As he lay still on top of her afterwards, her arms and legs round his back, she felt awed, a bit afraid, almost unaware of what had happened. Alan made a small sound of contentment, and she kissed his cheek, stroking his back. Their faces were close together, his breath on her neck.

'You scared me,' she whispered. 'Don't scare me, Al. On the bike. You were going too fast.'

'Sorry,' he murmured. 'Didn't mean to. You're everything . . . The whole world to me . . .'

She could hear that he was sleepy, overcome by the drink. He slid off her and they lay close. She held his slim body as they slept, naked on their bed of wheat.

She had never seen her mom so angry.

'Get in here.'

Violet opened the door to leave for work as Linda crept up to the house after Alan had dropped her off. Once the door was shut, she got the full force of her mother's ire.

'Where the bleeding hell've you *been*? Out all night without a word, you selfish little cow – I thought . . .' Violet raked her hand through her hair, which for once did not look immaculate.

'You thought I was dead in a ditch,' Linda mocked sarcastically. She'd felt a bit sorry on the way home, until Mom started on her. Now she just felt fed up.

'Well, I don't need to ask who you've been with, but God knows what you've been up to! I'm glad your sister's at school so she doesn't have to see you coming in with the bloody milk. You look as if you've slept in a field!'

'I have slept in a field, if you really want to know.'

'Oh yes – slept and what else – eh? All I can say is you're running out of control – as if I haven't got enough on my plate, with your nan having a turn ... I'll have words with you later, young lady – you're making me late for work. Go on – out of my way ...'

Violet yanked the front door open furiously.

'What's wrong with Nana?' Linda asked.

'I don't know – she had some sort of blackout. Marigold came over last night – not that you care 'cause you weren't even here. I've got to go over after work.'

Violet flurried out of the door, then turned, eyes narrowed, and as an afterthought hissed, 'You just better not have been up to anything – that's all.'

Chapter Seventy

Bessie was smiling.

Violet stood by the range, looking at her mother's sagging body sprawled wantonly in the chair. She felt a sense of discomfort, disgust even. And shame, because she wanted to feel kinder. But Bessie was not a kind woman. She was strong and in charge, or she was as nothing, Violet saw suddenly. Like a candle with no wick.

Marigold sat silently by the table, watching. She had a pencil in her hand, although there was no paper on the table.

'She won't stay in bed.' Clarence's stooped frame hovered behind her. Violet's nose wrinkled at the smell of him. His voice was high and quavering and if you heard it without seeing him it would have been hard to tell if it was that of a man or a woman.

'I said to her, Bess, you stay in bed today after a turn like that, but she wouldn't have it. I said I'd make her a cuppa tea and she did let me, and I took it up . . .'

'What happened?' Violet interrupted.

Clarence sucked his gums for a moment. 'Well, I helped her sit up in bed, and . . .'

'No – *yesterday.*'

'Oh!' Clarence stood wavering, supported by his stick. 'Well, I woke up, see, and there were these noises – the kettle . . . And Bess was – well, much like she is now only there was summat different. I mean, I can't

411

say really. I tried to wake her and she wouldn't come round . . .'

'The doctor's been, then?'

Clarence nodded hard. 'Oh ar – well if it wasn't for Mrs Jenkins calling in – I mean, she got the doctor. Marigold weren't here, you see . . .'

'What did he say?'

Clarence stared back at her with his rheumy eyes. Violet was seized with a longing to shake him by the shoulders.

'Well . . . He daint say much really. 'Cept she'd had a turn, our Bess . . .'

Violet tutted. 'Well, that wasn't anything we didn't know, was it?'

'She'd come to herself again, more or less, by then. Said her head was hurting—'

Bessie's eyes opened then, so suddenly that Violet jumped. But she did look dazed for a moment. She leaned forward muzzily in the chair, looking up at Violet.

'What're you doing here?'

'I came to see you. They said you had a turn.'

Bessie stared up at her so blankly that for a moment Violet wondered if she had really lost her mind. She put one hand to her forehead and rubbed it.

'Oh ar,' she admitted vaguely. 'I came over a bit dizzy.' She began to rally, to take charge. 'That's all though. As if my head went a bit numb. No need for a fuss. Marigold – put the kettle on.'

Silently, Marigold obeyed.

'The doctor just said to rest a bit and see.'

Violet went into the scullery where Marigold was lighting the gas.

'I wasn't here,' Marigold whispered emphatically, as if she'd been accused of a robbery.

'I know, Clarence said. You all right, Mari?'

Marigold nodded, and Violet saw that she did really look all right. Violet smiled at her, then got the cups down from the shelf.

There seemed nothing much to be done. Mr Bottoms had given her the impression that all this was an emergency, but now she was here, her mother just seemed a bit off colour and there was nothing she could do. She drank her tea with them and set off home again.

On the bus though, like a delayed reaction, emotions set in. She hardly ever went to the Aston house now. Life was too busy and, she realized, she had been avoiding it. But going back there, as soon as she walked into that house, so full of her mother's overweening presence, she shrank inside into a younger, more timid version of herself, who felt unsure and invisible, fit only to be pushed around.

Habit, that's what it was. It had always been like that with Bessie. She had to take up all the room. She could make you feel like nothing, as if you didn't exist.

I've changed, Violet thought. It came as a revelation, because she had not seen it before. All that had happened, Harry, Carol, everything, had made her stronger. And now there was Rita, her ebullient kindness. *You go off early, Vi, if your mum's been taken poorly. Course you must.*

All those years she'd been almost afraid to breathe without her mom to tell her what was what. But not now. She didn't need all that now. She inhaled the hot, smelly air in the bus, lost in her own thoughts, which were suddenly full of satisfaction.

I'm me now, she thought, smiling to herself. Really me.

Chapter Seventy-One

Linda stood at the back door, looking out at the sun-browned grass.

Carol and two little friends, all in little pastel frocks, were playing with Snowdrop. The two dogs were stretched out fast asleep by the back wall. Linda sat down on the step and stroked their hot, smooth fur. Next door, Mr Bottoms was hammering something, *chink, chink*, in his little lean-to at the bottom of the garden.

Linda poked at the frayed hole in the knee of her jeans. She hardly wore anything else now, when she wasn't at work, even in this heat. Her hair had grown very long, falling most of the way to her waist, and she wore it loose today.

She smiled wistfully at the sight of the three girls crouched over the fat old rabbit. Being little like Carol seemed such a long time ago. Now she was sixteen it felt as if parts of her life were spinning too fast, out of her control, and for a moment she wanted to run backwards into childhood again. It was as if she was locked into the separate world she and Alan had made, and couldn't get out.

'You coming to see Snowy?' Carol called to her.

'Nah. Going out in a minute.'

Carol's face fell. 'You going out, *again*?'

Linda didn't answer. She felt guilty. Of course she

loved spending time with Carol, but she had to do other things as well. Carol was in with all her little friends, and Mom took her out to those polio things – the society where they all met sometimes and had nice parties. Carol had made some pals there as well.

'Is Alan coming again?'

'Yeah. In a minute.'

The three girls stared at her for a moment, then turned away and continued chattering.

Linda sighed. Alan couldn't come earlier because he'd been to see his mother. Since that one last visit home, she hadn't been allowed out at all. Alan went about once a month now and she knew how much it affected him. She found herself at once full of tenderness for him, yet also dreading what mood he would be in. That was the trouble with Alan – he was so much pain and pleasure all rolled into one and she couldn't make out which she felt most.

Another twinge of panic went through her. All week she'd been so worried, trying to put it out of her mind. She couldn't believe now what had happened that night last week. That she'd actually gone all the way with Alan! Afterwards it had seemed like a dream. She'd barely known what was going on at the time, not to start with, all hazy from the drink. How could she have! She'd lost her virginity at sixteen! Didn't that make her cheap and dirty? A blush rose up her cheeks thinking about it, and about how it had felt. They'd got carried away, that was all, or Alan had. It had been over so quickly . . .

But what if . . .? What Mom had said – about babies? This was what was really making her panic. Surely there wouldn't have been time for anything to . . . well, have *happened*? With a feeling of despair she realized she knew nothing about any of it. And there was no one she could ask, was there? Certainly not Mom – God, no! Even if she asked the most innocent-sounding question Mom'd be off, carrying on. Joyce was the only one who had given her any clue.

She'd gone round there a couple of days ago. Little Charlie was six months old now, a real bruiser of a kid who looked just like Danny. Joyce was besotted with him, but she was also tired and bored and a good deal fatter than she had been before she had him. She looked pale and exhausted and was wearing a shapeless pink frock.

'He's everything to me,' she said, pushing her unbrushed hair out of her eyes. 'But I don't half wish I was back at Bird's sometimes. I'm just stuck in all day long – Danny's hardly ever here.'

Linda thought she looked a mess. She didn't understand what it was like to be Joyce, she just knew it was the last thing she wanted. As Joyce brewed up some tea, Linda perched on a stool in their tiny kitchen and tried to steer the conversation round so she could ask what she needed to. As it turned out it was easy, because Joyce turned and with desperation in her eyes said, 'I had a scare last week. Thought I'd caught again.'

'What d'you mean?'

'You know – thought I was going to have another one. I mean, it's too soon – we need to wait a bit.'

'Oh.' She didn't know anything about how you might choose to have or not have a baby. 'So . . .' She spoke casually, trying not to sound too interested. 'How d'you know you're not?'

Joyce gave a mirthless laugh. 'If you come on. You know – your monthly. Turned up yesterday. I've never been so pleased to see that, I can tell you!'

Linda digested this quietly and with great relief. So

416

all she had to do was wait and see if her monthly visitor turned up and she'd know she was all right. She'd been so afraid she'd have to tell someone, or even go and see the doctor! She calculated when she might be due – not until next week. And she wouldn't say anything to Alan. She just needed to make sure they didn't do anything again. Even so, she felt deeply ashamed. What if anyone found out?

A sound brought her out of her thoughts, the bike revving outside.

''Bye, Carol – see you later!'

Alan lined the bike up alongside the kerb, his slight figure dressed in jeans and leather jacket. His face looked tense, the jaw clenched.

'You'd better not be late!' Violet's face appeared at an upstairs window as Linda hurried down the path, pulling her cardi on. 'I want you back by nine o'clock, miss – at the latest!'

'Oh, Mom!'

'Nine or nothing,' Violet said adamantly to her upturned face. 'I'm not sitting here wondering where you are all bloody evening! All right, Alan? Bring her back on time, won't you?'

Alan raised a hand in salute, though he didn't smile.

''Llo,' he said gruffly.

'Hello. How's your mom?'

'All right. Same really. Let's go, eh?'

She swung her leg over the saddle and soon they were speeding north out of the estate, up past Pheasey and out into the country. Linda was filled with the usual sense of elation, the two of them like king and queen of the world, the rushing air, like flying away from everything, the sun, hanging between zenith and evening, hot on their faces.

'Where're we going?' she yelled.

He shouted something back that sounded like 'Anywhere', but she couldn't hear. Now he had the bike he always seemed to want to get right out of town, to the middle of nowhere. Fancies himself as the Lone Ranger, she thought. Only he wants me there too. *Needs* me, as he kept saying. She hugged her arms tighter round him.

He had his canvas bag resting on his thigh, the strap across his back. She slid her hand down and felt the hard bottle shape inside, and was immediately uneasy. The bike swerved and she quickly held on tight round his waist again. That fear again, like it had been with Dad. *Don't let him drink too much . . . Please don't let him.*

Chapter Seventy-Two

They passed the last of the sprawling new estates and headed into the countryside. It was such a beautiful afternoon, wheat and barley ripe and gold in fields stretching away from the road and tucked around green hills and clumps of dark trees. She saw that they were back close to where they had been last week, and soon Alan stopped and they found a beautiful sloping spot, where they left the bike tucked in by the hedge and walked a bit further up.

Alan took her hand and it felt nice, that they belonged together, just the two of them.

'Did your dad go with you today?' she asked as they found a place to be.

'Nope.' Alan swung the bag round and lifted the strap over his head. He put it in his lap and uneasily she saw him take out the bottle. For a moment she thought it was a bottle of water, then read the label: Vodka, this time.

'He's not here,' Alan said, unscrewing the cap. He spoke in a tight voice, as if he was keeping angry emotion under control. 'He's in America.' He took a swig from the bottle.

'*America?*'

'Some institute in Boston. He's working with Dr Rutenburg – Stanley's dad. He wouldn't take me with him, the mean old sod. Said I didn't deserve a free trip

419

at his expense after all the trouble I've caused. That I need to knuckle down and stick it out with my job.' He gave a harsh laugh. 'In a sweet shop!' That was the latest thing.

'Maybe next time he goes . . .'

She felt so angry for him. There he was, alone in the house with just that housekeeper coming in. Dr Bray acted as if he didn't even have a son! Even her own father had paid a bit more attention to them all. Once he was sick, anyway, and couldn't drink. She thought of him staggering to Joyce's wedding, looking like a ghost. Dr Bray probably wouldn't even notice if Alan got married.

'He won't ever take me,' Alan said flatly. 'He just won't – I know it.'

He swigged at the bottle, drinking as if it was water. Linda didn't want to see. She stared down between her knees. There were ants, a tobacco-brown line of them.

'Your mom,' she said gently. 'Did you tell her your dad was away?'

There was a long silence. Alan twitched one knee up and down. Tersely, he said, 'No. It wasn't much of a conversation.'

She dared to touch his arm. 'Why not?'

'She just – what she was saying. It didn't make any sense. And her face . . .' Suddenly he was struggling not to cry, his face working. 'I've never seen her as bad. I don't think she'll ever get better . . .'

'Oh, surely she will!' Linda said, because she didn't know what else to say.

'What do you know?' he snarled. 'It won't happen just because you say so!'

'I know . . . sorry . . . I didn't mean it like that.'

After a minute he rubbed his arm across his face and said, 'Sorry.' Anxiously he turned to her. 'I love you.'

'Love you too.'

In the hedge, close behind them, were flowering nettles. She picked one, thinking of Lucy Etheridge who had told her the stems of the flowers taste sweet, like honey. There had been some in Lucy's garden.

She plucked the pale flowers and sucked.

'Here – try,' she said to Alan.

He put the ends of two in his mouth.

'Can't taste anything. Too much of this.' He patted the bottle and drank again. She wanted to tell him to stop, but didn't dare.

'Want some?' He held it out to her. She shook her head.

'Have you finished your script yet?'

'No.'

Something in the way he said it stopped her asking any more. She wanted to talk about being out here last week, about what had happened and how it mustn't happen again, but his mood was so low and he felt so distant from her that she didn't dare.

After a moment he put the bottle down and put his arms round her, lips searching for hers. He kissed her hard, desperately. Sometimes she almost felt he was trying to suck the life out of her. His arms were tight round her and they tumbled back, lying there wrapped round each other.

'Don't ever leave me, will you?' He stared deep into her. He had 'drink eyes' already, glazed, too intense.

'Not if I can help it,' she said. But she felt helpless suddenly, and frightened. Whatever he needed from her it felt too much. She loved him so much that it was an

421

ache inside her, but now, when he was like this, she just wanted to get up and run away from him.

They slept for a time, in each other's arms. When Linda woke and stiffly sat up, the sun had sunk to orange, a last half-circle of it disappearing as if into the fields in the far distance. The sky was turning a mauvish blue. Alan was still asleep. She picked up the bottle, holding it up in the dim light. He had drunk a good half of it and she could tell by his breathing that he was very deeply asleep. He looked as if he might stay that way for hours. She looked at his sleeping face, feeling like a mother looking down at a baby. Even Mrs Bray had asked her to look after him.

Then she panicked. What time was it? She was really going to get it from Mom if she wasn't back on time tonight! Alan had a watch and she leaned over him to look at it. A quarter past eight. They'd better get going.

'Al – Al!' She tugged at him, shook him, wondering in panic for a moment if he was actually unconscious and she wouldn't be able to rouse him. Eventually he opened his eyes and stared ahead as if he was blind, then up at the pale sky, not seeming able to focus. How were they going to get back with him in this state?

'Alan – come on. It's getting on for half past eight.'

His eyes rested on her and to her relief he seemed more alert.

'How long've I been asleep?' he asked, muzzily.

'I dunno – an hour? Maybe more. But we need to go.'

Alan sat up and reached for the bottle again.

'No!' She tried to snatch it but he pulled it out of her grasp. 'Don't have any more, for God's sake!'

'Need a drink.'

There was something lost about him, as if he had let

422

go and fallen from a great height and was now lying crushed with nothing else to lose.

He drank, then got up, staggering.

'Come on then.'

She didn't feel too well herself, especially once they were walking. Everything seemed distant and her head hurt, a hard ache in her left temple, and she was queasy. The thought of the ride ahead was dreadful. *I don't feel safe*, she thought hazily. But how else was she going to get home from the middle of nowhere?

He started off slowly. It was going to be all right, she decided, relaxing, her cheek pressed to his back. He was talking, but she couldn't hear him. He started to pick up speed, and she could feel he was flinging out words with a violence which vibrated right through him.

'What?' she yelled. 'I can't hear you!'

He didn't turn or say anything to her. Then she realized he was cursing and swearing, she could feel the force of the words, and knew he was in a world of his own and she might just as well not have been there. She was really frightened then.

'Al – slow down!'

Instead they were picking up more speed, the bike going full throttle so that it began to judder, the light of the lamp jerking in the dusk.

'Al – for God's sake – you'll kill us!'

She was tugging at him, her legs gripping so tightly to the saddle she felt as if the bones in her groins would crack.

'Al, please – you're scaring me!' She started sobbing, hitting at his back, but he didn't seem to hear whatever she did, and her cries cut out to a terrified gasp as the bike bumped into a hole in the road and he only just managed to keep it upright.

'Stop . . .!' She hated him suddenly for making her so afraid, just wanting to get off and be anywhere but on this hellish machine where she had no control and he didn't seem to care about her at all. But there was no getting off, as they swung along the curved road up a hill, the night air beating against them and hedges, trees, gateways flashing past in a blur. She closed her eyes and buried her face against his back, crying to deaf ears for him to stop.

She felt, rather than saw, the bike reach the brow of the hill, and with a lurch inside her she knew that on the downhill it would go even faster. There was a bump at the top which left her stomach hanging sickeningly somewhere in the air, and then she felt them pick up speed even more, rushing downwards, ever faster, terrifying.

At the point when Alan lost control of the bike, she felt it at once. All she saw, opening her eyes, was the blur of faint outlines and darkness, but she felt the bike veer and hit the verge and a cry come out of her mouth and then she was wrenched away from Alan, being flung through the air, her arms and legs heavy, out of their element, then falling until the hard ground slammed into her from below.

Chapter Seventy-Three

'You can see him now – just for a few minutes.'

The nurse led her along the ward to a bed where Alan was lying with his eyes closed.

'He's very drowsy,' she whispered. 'I doubt you'll get much out of him.'

It was a shock. They'd told Linda what his injuries were, but the right side of his face was so bruised and swollen she could barely recognize him. There was something under the bedclothes, holding the weight of them off his legs, and above the line of the sheet she could see bandages round his left shoulder, up into his neck.

'He's in a mess,' the nurse added disapprovingly. 'He's broken both legs, there are at least three cracked ribs and he's dislocated his shoulder. He's lucky it's not worse.'

Linda sat on the chair by the bed, nursing her left arm in its sling. She had got away with scratches and bruises and a broken wrist, on which she had landed after being flung high away from the bike as it crashed. Alan had evidently clung tightly to it and gone down with it, he and the bike cartwheeling over together, and Alan ending up with it on top of him.

The ward was full of evening bustle, but she was oblivious to it. Her arm ached inside the cast and her head was throbbing. She had to move about very cautiously. Of course, they'd drunk a lot last night. When she came to, lying on the lumpy surface of the field, it had been pitch dark. All she could hear were night sounds: an owl, a car in the far distance, and her own heart. She was sure she'd heard that, thumping like a drum. She could remember lying there in the dark, gradually feeling colder. Nothing hurt, not until later. She was numb. Her head was all foggy, and although she thought about getting up, she never could seem to make her limbs move to do it. Vaguely, as if it was a dream, she wondered where Alan was. After a time she fell asleep, half waking on and off through the night, cold, but sinking back into unconsciousness again.

All she knew next was that it was dawn, and misty and she was wet. When she opened her eyes, everything seemed white – the sky and air – except for the black trousers of the man standing over her, accompanied by the hot breath of a brown dog.

'Hello?' the man was saying. 'Miss – can you hear me?'

It seemed a queer question.

'Yes,' she said impatiently. 'Course I can.'

'You've had an accident – you and your friend. You look in better nick than he does.'

His car was parked by the road and he went and called an ambulance. All day she had been in Good Hope Hospital, getting patched up, sleeping. Her hands and face were scratched and she felt bruised all over. They said the police would tell her mother what had happened. And Alan's father. But of course, she remembered, Alan's father wasn't going to be back for two more days.

She was about to lean forward and speak to Alan,

but stopped herself. She wanted to let him sleep – he'd be more hung-over than her – but it was more than that. She wanted to look, to *see* him, while he was not looking back at her. Last night, on the bike, he had cancelled her out as if she wasn't even there. He hadn't cared about her fear. It had cut something off in her.

He looked fragile, that was her first thought. Such a skinny boy and so defenceless lying there. A wave of tenderness went through her, wanting to stroke his forehead, his dark hair, to comfort him, but she still held back. Mixed with her tenderness was a great sense of weariness. There were so many thoughts she had not allowed herself while she was with Alan. About him, and even more about herself. She had felt wanted, honoured, by the way he clung to her, needed her help, her love, to heal him. But all that had happened was him sinking, drinking more and more. She could never truly help, never be enough. Something caved in in her as she stared at him under the bald light of the ward. All his dreams were his escape from pain, but he would never finish a script for a film, never go and work in America. Would he ever be able to make something of his life, or just spiral down into the hurt of it, taking her with him? And hadn't she taken shelter in him, used him as a reason to limit herself? It had felt so right, so exciting to begin with. Now all she could feel was the hurt and hopelessness of it.

If you stay with him, it will always be the same. It was almost as if she heard a voice whisper it. *Save yourself.*

Tears welled in her eyes. It felt like a door opening on to light, from the darkness in which Alan lived. Only lately had she noticed how dark it really was. And though her guilt and sorrow were overwhelming, so was her sense of relief.

'Oh, Al, it's no good – I can't stay. I can't do this any more. I've got to get out.'

She spoke the words aloud, but he couldn't hear her.

Chapter Seventy-Four

'What's up, Lin?'

She heard Carol come limping into the room and felt her sit next to her on the edge of the bed. She lay on her bed, facing the wall, crying. She couldn't seem to stop crying.

'Mom says d'you want a cup of tea?'

Linda nodded. 'OK.'

She wiped her face and turned to sit up, wincing. Carol went to the door for a moment and called down to Violet.

'I'll bring it up,' Violet said.

That made Linda cry again. It was something to do with feeling looked after, and the way she knew that Mom would have been furious, the night before last, when she didn't come home, and then her shock when the policeman appeared and told her there'd been an accident. Mom had come up to the hospital. When she saw Linda with only the sling on her arm and no other damage, she put her arms round her and wept.

'I thought something much worse had happened. God, girl, don't ever do that to me again. That boy deserves a good hiding . . .'

She spent money on a taxi, of all things, to get them home. Linda had never been in a taxi before.

And since then, there had been such a feeling of gentleness in the house, of the preciousness of her being alive. When they were children, Linda realized, Mom had been so full of worries, looking after Dad and Carol, she hadn't had much left for anyone else. She'd had so little attention for them. It wouldn't go on like this, Linda knew, this special feeling, but it was something while it did.

That morning, when Linda woke, she'd also come on with her period. At the sight of the rusty blood she sat in the toilet and burst into tears. It was only then she realized how much she had been worrying, deep down, that she might be expecting a baby, even though the thought didn't seem real. Now there was a gripey but reassuring ache in her belly.

'Is your wrist hurting?' Carol asked.

'A bit. Aches.' Linda looked at the plaster cast. It still felt an alien thing on her. 'You've had much worse though.'

'I got used to it,' Carol said.

They sat in silence. Linda wiped her eyes. The window was open and a warm breeze blew at the flimsy curtain and they could hear some kids playing out at the front. They didn't need to talk. Carol just sat with her. She could always do that, sit with you, very still, just being there. She looked at Linda and smiled her dimply smile.

'Must be nice, not being in that chair any more,' Linda said.

Carol nodded. 'I can go down the park on my own.' She picked up the old rag doll on Linda's bed. 'Poor old Polly. She needs new eyes.'

They heard Violet coming up the stairs.

'Here you go. Brought you a couple of bits of toast.'

The toast smelt delicious, real butter melting across it. Linda's eyes filled with tears again. 'Ta.'

'You feeling bad?' Violet asked anxiously. 'D'you think you had a bad bang on the head?'

'No. I'm all right.'

'You'll want to go and see Alan, I s'pose?' Violet asked.

Linda didn't reply.

'You can't go back to work yet,' Violet said. 'We'll have to let her know.'

For two days Linda stayed around the house, happy to withdraw, just to be there with Carol and the dogs while Mom was at work. And she knew she ought to go and see Alan, but didn't feel well or strong enough. If she went back she might never be able to leave him. She tried not to think about him, lying there alone. One afternoon she took a couple of towels and lay out drowsily on the grass. For a time she stared at Snowdrop in her run, at her confined rabbit life, her quick breaths and staring red eyes.

'Don't you want to get out?' she said to her.

Snowdrop stared back impassively at her. She never bothered to try and escape now, not like when she was young.

During those days, Linda started thinking again about Rosina. All she had ever seen were those pictures she had sent out of her long silence, and that glimpse of her at Joyce's wedding, so nervous-looking, so afraid of facing them all, it seemed. When her mother came home that evening, she said, 'Are you ever going to go and see Auntie Rosina?'

Violet sat down wearily. Lighting a cigarette, she took a drag and blew smoke at the ceiling.

'Oh, I dunno. Sometimes I think I will, and then I think: well, she could've come to see us, couldn't she? Properly, like, instead of how she was at the wedding.

431

I mean Rosy and me, we got on all right, as kids, you know – rubbed along. But she's made it clear she didn't want us.'

She drew on the cigarette again and frowned. Linda noticed how lined her forehead had become.

'Rosy was never like that – not stuck up. I dunno what happened to her.'

'Was she being stuck up? I thought she looked scared.'

'Well, what's she got to be scared of?' Violet said impatiently. 'We're only her flaming family, aren't we?'

Linda could see her mother was not going to tackle this.

But there was something about Rosina that tugged at her, goaded her on. It was the unknown, the enigmatic glimpses of her, and something about a sense of kinship with her, that Linda felt instinctively. They looked alike, it was true, but it was something more than that. Something of her spirit.

By the time she went back to work – something else she had to change, she realized – she had decided that whether Mom wanted to or not, she had to go and find Rosina.

Chapter Seventy-Five

'Are you quite sure Bernice is coming?' Violet said anxiously as they sat on the bus. 'I'm not sure I want to go if they're not going to be there.'

'She'll come,' Carol assured her serenely. 'You know she said she wouldn't miss it for anything.'

Violet was chewing the side of her finger. 'Well, I hope so.'

She was dressed in her best frock – white with pink roses on – and white shoes. She was really pleased with the dress. It was the prettiest she had ever had and flattered her slim figure. And she had treated herself to the little white bag which lay in her lap. Rita was paying her generously, and was talking about them being part-ners in the business. *You've got flair, love,* she told Violet. *And it'd take the pressure off me.*

'The other people are nice too.' Carol looked up at her. Violet was always taken aback by her daughter's trust in others. It was a precious thing, she decided. And she was getting better with people herself now, coming out of herself, with having to talk to customers in the salon.

They were on their way – a two-bus journey to Edgbaston – to an August Bank Holiday garden fête held by the Infantile Paralysis Fellowship. They'd been to a couple of their other fundraising socials. Carol loved going, because she saw old friends and there was the immediate understanding that the polios shared, even though some were much worse affected than others.

It was a fine day, although you could already feel the wane of summer in the way the light fell. The leaves had lost the fresh, expectant look of spring. As they walked from the bus stop to the imposing Edgbaston house, Violet plucked nervously at the edges of her white cardigan and ran a hand over her hair. She looked approvingly at Carol in her yellow sundress and little pumps, her gold hair in waves down her back. *My girl*, she thought. *That's my little girl.*

For a moment they stood uncertainly outside the house, in the shade of a tree. Then Violet heard a voice call, 'Come for the fête, dear? Do come in!'

There was a side gate to the garden and a tall woman in a hat was waiting to show people in.

'Here we are – you're very welcome. Hello, dear!' she finished, cheerily, to Carol. '*Don't* you look pretty!'

The garden was a long oblong, surrounded by a wall along which were climbing roses and hollyhocks, and they could smell flowers as soon as they walked in. All across the grass were stalls, run by women in cheerful frocks, and children, some in wheelchairs, others on crutches or with calipers on their legs, others their siblings, running about whole-limbed and unimpeded. A woman hurried past carrying a big metal teapot, smiling anxiously. Violet would have liked to see the garden with no people in it. It would be a sleepy place, she decided, full of the sound of bees.

'Come on, Mom – let's look at the stalls!'

Carol had half a crown's spending money which was burning a hole in her pocket. Feeling shy and uncertain herself, Violet was glad of Carol's self-assurance and followed her as she limped fast across the grass, eagerly in search of the white elephant stall and tombola. She was on home territory here with other polios.

Amid the bric-a-brac of old vases, a chipped teapot and embroidered napkins, she found a little china dog with soulful black eyes.

'Oh, Mom – can I get it?' She was almost jumping with enthusiasm. 'I'll give it to Lin – it'll cheer her up!'

The woman running the stall was elderly, with grey hair in a bun, and she laughed at Carol's excitement.

'It's very nice, dear, isn't it? I think you could have that for tuppence. Does that sound fair?'

Carol nodded and handed over one of her sixpences. Looking up again she cried, 'Oh, look – there's Bernice!' and took off with the little dog in her hand.

Violet rolled her eyes and accepted the change for her.

'She's not one of the polios?' the woman asked, with gentle tactfulness.

'She is,' Violet said. 'See how she's limping – it left her with one shortened leg.'

'Goodness though – you'd hardly know, would you? She's been lucky.' Her face clouded. 'My little niece wasn't so lucky, unfortunately.'

'Oh dear . . .' Violet said.

'Died within a few days with it.' She shook her head. 'Terrible disease. A scourge.' Her face cleared. 'Go on – you get after her. She's lovely.'

Bernice was still in a wheelchair, awaiting more operations at St Gerard's. She and Carol were nattering away while Mrs Miller, her mother, a slim woman with long dark hair, stood watching with a smile.

'Hello, Violet – lovely to see you. And what a wonderfully pretty dress!'

Violet had been very intimidated by Bernice's mother when she first met her in the hospital. She was a rather well-spoken, confident lady and Violet felt silent and awkward beside her, as if she had nothing to say. But they had had their daughters in common, and the terrible, long-lasting worry of polio, and all that had dissolved some of the social lines between them.

'Hello, Rachel – how is she?'

'They say she's doing well. She's due to go back in in two months.'

Rachel Miller smiled, though her eyes wore a wistful expression. She had a wide mouth, her face sensuous, with high cheekbones. 'It would be so nice if it was all over. I'm sure I get in more of a state about it than she does.'

Bernice and Carol were giggling and the two women smiled at the sight.

'I know,' Violet said. 'Carol's so calm. Just sort of takes what comes. I wish I could.'

They talked for a little longer and Rachel said, 'Come and see us, will you? We're not so far from you. Bernice would be so pleased.' She took a little oblong of blue paper from her bag and wrote down her address. 'May I take yours? Just in case we're in the area?'

'Oh – you'd be welcome to come,' Violet said, feeling remiss. She wasn't used to visitors, except Eva from next door. She jotted down her address in Rachel Miller's diary.

'Mom – Mom, look!' Carol was hopping with excitement. 'It's Sister Cathleen!'

In the distance Violet caught sight of a thin figure in black. For a moment she thought Carol had got it wrong, then realized that the nurses only wore white in the hospital. Carol had already darted away, dodging round the tables.

'I'd better go and say hello,' Violet said. 'I'm never sure what to say to her though, really.'

Rachel rolled her eyes sympathetically. 'She's very kind though. Don't forget – you're welcome any time. We're nearly always at home and I'd love the company too.'

Violet peered through the crowd, trying to see Carol, past a lady dipping her hand into a deep basket full of cloakroom tickets for a tombola, and the Guess the Weight of the Cake stall. The garden was getting quite crowded now.

A woman with two maroon velvet coathangers in her hand passed, saying, 'Don't forget there's tea and cake for everyone on the terrace, will you?'

Violet was more than ready for a cup of tea. She hesitated. Carol would be all right of course. She was quite happy. She caught a glimpse of her in the distance, being embraced by Sister Cathleen, her face alight with happiness. With the pang that she always had when she saw how much Carol loved this woman, she turned away, annoyed with herself for being jealous. She should be glad, after all. She turned towards the house, where, on the paving slabs at the front, there were chairs, and tables laid with teacups. She'd go and have a quiet sit-down with a cup of tea.

All she caught sight of in that instant was a tall man, just beside her, half turned away and helping a boy in a wheelchair to spin the dial on a game at one of the tables. It was his hands she noticed. There was a stab of recognition, as if by her body more than her mind. One hand guided the boy's as he could barely reach up high

437

enough. The sight of his long fingers rooted her to the spot.

After a second she dared to turn her head, trem- blingly afraid of him looking round and seeing her before she could be sure who it was, and how she might react.

That look left her in no doubt. The thin, gentle set of his face, the dark eyes, looking down at his son, the long, thin back. It could be no one but Roy Keillor. In those seconds she told herself to breathe, to move, to do something other than just stand there before he turned round. But she kept wanting to look at his hands, remembering his touch, which filled her with the kind of longing she had not felt in a long time.

'Excuse me – ' Someone wanted to come past and she was forced to step even closer to him.

'Sorry,' she said, and he looked round to acknow- ledge the remark, glancing at her, and away.

'Not to worry,' he said.

Deflated, she started to move past, and realized she was shaking. Tea, that was what was needed. But all she could think was that he hadn't recognized her, hadn't known her, instantly the way she knew him!

Before she reached the terrace, though, he caught her up, beside a flowerbed, full of bright blooms.

'Violet?'

He had hurried over without the wheelchair.

They looked at each other for a few seconds. He had spoken softly, his voice not giving anything away. Sud- denly she was coldly calm. There seemed no other way to be. There was nothing to expect.

'Your son,' she said. 'You've left him.'

'He's having another game. The lady's helping him.'

There were more seconds of silence, full of the

impossibility of beginning. She thought of his face that day they'd said goodbye, before she even knew she was carrying his child. How could they begin on this here?

'How are you?' He moved his shoulders in a way which acknowledged the lameness of the question.

'All right, thanks. What about you? The family?' She was finding it hard to look him in the eyes. Back then, she had looked so deeply.

'Yes. All right. Well – except for Philip.' He nodded back in the direction of his son. 'They both caught it, the twins. John had it much worse – he died of it after a few days. And Philip – well, they're working on him.'

'Oh, how awful,' Violet said. She could really look at him then.

'Yes – what with that and us losing one before, well . . .' The sentence petered out, implying something, but she was not quite sure what.

'Are you still living in Aston?' he asked.

'No. We moved out to Kingstanding – years ago, you know, after the war.'

The conversation felt so awkward, it was excruciating. She longed to be alone with him properly, to let go and talk.

Roy frowned suddenly. 'Why are you here? One of your two didn't catch polio, did they?'

The next couple of seconds seemed to stretch endlessly, as if her heart had stopped. She longed with every fibre of her to tell him about Carol, but she was so frightened by it. Eleven years had gone by – why did she need to tell him now?

'It's my youngest.' Carefully, she looked into his face. 'She's just over there. She's eleven.'

'Oh.' He nodded, and she could see her words had not registered. He had not worked it out.

439

There was more silence, the moment growing so awkward that he was starting to say, 'Well – I'd better go and get Philip. Nice to see you, Violet. You look . . . well, you look very nice.'

And they said goodbye and he turned back towards his son.

Violet went and got a cup of tea and sank down on one of the chairs by the wall, praying that no one would come and talk to her. She needed time to recover. There was both relief and a devastating sense of let-down at the same time. What else could she have expected, after all? But seeing him brought back all the feelings of those years, the only time she had had such feelings, as if he was burned into her in a way no one else could be.

'Ah – here she is now!'

To her disquiet she heard Sister Cathleen's cheerful voice, and she and Carol came up, Carol radiant and holding her hand.

'Hello, Mrs Martin – how are you?'

Violet stood up, trying to keep a grip on her dainty cup and saucer.

'I'm all right,' she said. Why was it that this nun always made her feel so awkward?

Sister Cathleen's pale face beamed down at Carol. 'Isn't this one looking a picture? Marvellous, isn't it?'

Violet smiled. 'Yes – she's going along well.'

'I should say she is! Quite the little miracle. Well I hope we shan't be seeing you back at St Gerard's again – not for treatment, anyways. Though it's always a treat to see you Carol, if you want to come to St Paul's . . . You take every care of yourself now, dear.'

She embraced Carol once more and said her good-byes. Carol stared adoringly after her.

'D'you want a drink?' Violet asked, brusquely. 'There are cakes, as well.'

Carol settled beside her with some home-made lemon in a glass and an angel cake, its little wings stuck on with butter icing.

'Why don't you make these, Mom? They're nice.'

Violet laughed. 'I'm not much of a cook. Perhaps we'll give it a try?' She put her cup down. 'D'you want to stay much longer? We ought to be . . .'

The rest of the sentence was snatched from her when she saw Roy again, coming towards them, pushing his son in the wheelchair. There was no sign of his wife with him. He saw her notice him and there was no point pretending she hadn't. He came towards her. Philip, the remaining twin, must have been about fourteen, she realized, though he seemed small for his age. As well as his legs he had one arm badly affected by polio.

'Hello again,' Roy said, and was obviously going to keep walking past. But then she saw him notice Carol. Everyone noticed Carol because she was so pretty, but this was different. She saw him stop and look, and Carol looked back in her usual open, inquiring way. Violet saw him take in her deep brown eyes, his eyes, looking back at him, and she saw the realization breaking over his face.

Part Six
1954

Chapter Seventy-Six

September

'All change please, all change!'

Linda walked along the platform at Euston Station. A lady in her carriage had taken her under her wing and explained about the Underground and what to do after that, very carefully, as if she was speaking to a class of six-year-olds.

But it wasn't just finding her way that she was nervous about.

She hadn't exactly planned to come today. She'd been secretly saving up the money for her ticket. This Saturday she knew Carol was out at a friend's house for the day and Mom was working, then going to Aston to see Nana. Bessie still wasn't right after her funny turn. The day was fine, and the only thing to do, it seemed, was dress in a skirt and blouse – she wanted to look not too scruffy and she didn't have anything very smart to wear – and go get on a train to London. She had to dare herself. It felt as if she was going to the other side of the world.

She had been determined to post the letter on the way. She stood by a postbox in town for minutes, after getting off the Kingstanding bus, trying to make herself push it through the slot. But the letter, with its Handsworth Wood address, was still in her bag. How could she just tell Alan that she couldn't see him any more? It seemed very brutal, especially when he was so injured.

She had not even been to see him because she was afraid that if she did, at the sight of him she would cave in and be dragged back into his strange, sad world and never escape again. And she knew now that she had to escape from that. But she felt terribly guilty.

'Dear Alan,' she had written last night, sitting up in bed, once Carol was asleep. At least it was her left arm in plaster, or she wouldn't have been able to write at all. She stared at the cast along her forearm for a moment. *He could have killed me . . .*

'I'm sorry for not coming to the hospital.' After that she sat for an age. How could she explain? *I don't think I can be with you – you make me feel sad and stuck and you're not good for me. With you I can see no real future.* How to say that to him? There wasn't a kind way to tell the truth. All she could say was, 'I don't think we can see each other any more. I'm very sorry. With best wishes from Linda.'

That was the note she put in the envelope. And she despised herself for it and that was why she couldn't bring herself to hand it over to the letterbox, to be free of this constant ache of dread and sadness because something had to be finished but it hurt too much to do it. As a result, the ache was still there, mixed with her nervousness at being alone in London, and looking for Rosina.

To Violet's surprise she had offered to go and call in on her grandmother in the week, to see how she was.

'This is a surprise,' Bessie greeted her, voice heavy with sarcasm. 'Bit like royalty showing up, ain't it, Marigold? What're *you* after?'

Marigold was knitting. She looked up at Linda in silence, but her treacly eyes held a twinkle and Linda sensed she was pleased to see her. She had a cup of tea with them – Marigold's with a drop of extra which she sneaked in behind Bessie's back – and put up with Nana's jibes about her clothes, her job, about anything at all that she could think to criticize. In the meantime she also managed to slip Rosina's letter out from behind the jug and into the scullery for long enough to memorize her address. She noticed that her grandmother really did look ill: puffy round the face, beads of sweat on her forehead and somehow simply changed, as if something had given way inside her. Not that it had sweetened her up in the process, Linda thought sourly as she left the house. It'd take more than a funny turn to do that. But she'd put up with it long enough to get what she needed. The address! She said it over and over in her mind and wrote it down as soon as she got home: Rosina Croft, 3a Brewer Street, London W1.

The lady on the train had frowned at the sight of the address. 'Are you sure that's where you want to go, dear?' She had an A-Z map book and, on a piece of writing paper, drew her a plan of how to get to Rosina's address from the Tube. On the Underground train Linda stared at the little map, hardly able to believe that soon the lines on the powder-blue paper would turn into real streets and she would be walking along them, moving closer to Rosina.

Until now she had two pictures of Rosina to hold on to. One was the pretty young woman in her stage costume whose face stared brazenly out of the picture she had sent to the family; the other was that glimpse of her peach-satin-clad figure retreating from the church at Joyce's wedding. These two images conveyed glamour, daring and mystery. The streets Linda found herself walking in search of her spelled something more ambiguous.

The country's on its knees . . . Uncle Clarence's whining words came back to her. Of course she was used to it in Brum, all the bombsites, mess and grime, all those years of Stafford Cripps, austerity and rationing, only just ending. And then came the building sites, the sense of old things giving way to new, but in the end always seeming workaday, functional, not glamorous at all. She had thought London would be different, even though they had the worst Blitz of all, that it would be cleaned up, smart and exciting. But she found herself in gloomy, seedy streets between run-down buildings strewn with rubbish and poky-looking cafés and bars. There was a life in it, it was true, people coming and going, neon signs outside clubs and theatres, and most passers-by in the street seemed to be speaking a whole array of languages she couldn't understand. She felt suddenly very young and overawed and out of place.

She stopped on a street corner and looked at the teacher lady's map to get her bearings. One more street and then she had to turn right . . .

'You working?' It was a gruff whisper in her ear and she jumped.

Behind her was a stringy-looking man in a singlet. He was not very old but his skin was deeply tanned, his face leathery and lined as if from screwing his face up against the sun and his chin covered in stubble. He stared at her suggestively.

'What?' Her heart was beating fast in shock at his sudden appearance.

'I said, are you *working*, love?' There was an edge of threat in his voice.

'No.' She shook her head vigorously.

'Fair enough,' he snapped, and walked off. She saw he had a limp. Linda looked round, hoping no one else had been close enough to hear. She didn't know for sure what he meant but she could guess. She felt dirty. Could he see she wasn't a virgin? Could people tell, somehow?

She scurried on and round the corner. Thank goodness she was nearly there!

Chapter Seventy-Seven

Standing outside number 3, from where Rosina had written her only letter in years to Bessie, Linda felt more and more nervous and foolish.

The house had a tall, forbidding frontage of red bricks darkened by soot. Linda was torn between her longing to get off the streets and fear that Rosina might not be there or would laugh in her face and turn her away. What if she told her to get lost? She'd have to go straight back to the station and go home.

There were four buttons. Two had names beside them, but the space next to number three was blank. She rang it anyway.

There was a long silence. She thought about ringing again, but then came faint sounds from inside of someone in heels clacking downstairs. After a moment she saw a movement through the clear spaces in the glass, and caught her breath. The door opened just wide enough for a woman to look out. She had dyed blonde hair, darker at the roots and scraped back into a ponytail, and her eyelids were laden with blue tints and mascara. She was obviously poised to slam the door shut again.

'Yes? Who're you?'

'I'm . . .' Linda lost courage. 'I thought I'd got the right house but . . . I'm looking for my auntie. Her name's Rosina.'

'Oh?' The woman looked taken aback, though some of her hostility faded away. She opened the door wider, letting out a strong, musty smell. Linda saw that she was dressed in a bright blue frock which barely reached down below her knees and high-heeled white shoes. She stared at Linda again for a moment, but in a different way from before, as if she had to calculate what to say.

'Does she live here?'

'She's not here – not at present,' the woman said. 'I mean, well, Rosy does live here. This is where ... I mean ...' She seemed oddly confused. 'Only she's not here at the moment, see. She's ...'

'I've come all the way from Birmingham to see her,' Linda said, desperately. 'I saved up for the ticket and everything and if I don't see her I don't know when I'd be able to come again.'

The woman was still staring at her in that odd way. Then she said abruptly, 'Look – hang on a tick.' She disappeared into the house and came back a moment later with keys, closing the door behind her. On the doorstep she pulled out a powder compact from her bag and used the mirror to apply deep red lip-stick.

'Can't go out without my face on, can I?' Rubbing her lips together, she clipped the compact shut. 'Come on, love. I'll take you.' She beckoned to Linda to follow her along the street. 'It's not far. Only, you're very young, see, only a nipper, aren't you? I know Rosy doesn't have much to do with her family. Not surprising really.' Casually she added, 'I don't know if you know anything about her?'

'Well, no.' Linda felt more and more bemused and nervous, although the woman was behaving in a more

451

friendly way now and she could see she was quite nice really. 'She's my mom's sister, that's all.'

'Well, you're in for a shock, love, I'd better tell you that now.' The woman laughed. 'I can hear you're from the same neck of the woods anyhow. Rosy still speaks like a Brummy even after all these years! My name's Irene, by the way. Reeny, I go by, though. Tried to get 'em to call me Irene – sounds better, don't you think? But I'm Reeny whether I like it or not – it's stuck to me. What's yours?'

'Linda.'

'That short for *Be*-linda?'

'No.'

'Oh – just wondered. S'pretty, anyhow.'

Linda had barely noticed where they were going, she was listening so intently to Irene, who took nervous little drags on her cigarette as she minced along on her heels.

'Now – Rosy's place is where we've just been. Her flat, I mean. She's got it nice up there – you can't tell from outside. But she don't get home till midday usually. I live with her, see, look after Vivianne and Clarkie – least when they're home from school. Almost like my own, those two. Not that she doesn't pay me well – she's a good 'un, Rosy is. We've been through some times, me and her – always stick together, see?'

Linda didn't see – not at all.

'Working the way she does, she has to be a bit careful – who she lets on to and that. Bit of a double life, but she manages. Ever such nice schools she's got those kids in. Clarkie's away boarding now. A real gentleman he's going to turn out. But all I'm saying is, she might be a bit put out to see you, just at first. You'll have to promise not to let on – to look out for her – OK? Then she'll be all right.'

Linda nodded, feeling even more worried.

'Whose wedding was it she went up for?' Irene asked curiously. 'Not yours, was it – you look too young?'

'My sister, Joyce.'

'Oh yeah, Joyce. Poor old Rosy – she got cold feet. Wanted to be there but she said she couldn't face it all in the end.'

After a time they turned left, and there was another line of very tall red-brick houses, rather wider than the ones in the last street.

'We're down the end here,' Irene said. 'Rosy's Palace, they call it – dirty old sods.' She gave a throaty chuckle. At the far end of the street, the last house, though not the smartest, still had an imposing air about it. All the windows were shrouded with curtains and blinds.

'Come on – round the back,' Irene said. She was clearly at home in the place.

Up some steps at the back, she rang the bell beside a black door, and after a pause it was opened by another young woman, also with long blonde hair.

'All right, Pol? Rosy up and about?' There was a noise from inside, voices on a radio. Then Irene lowered her voice and looking warily upwards, hissed, 'Is *he* about?'

'Nah. Not yet, thank Christ. But he'll soon come swanning down, no doubt. Rosy's in the kitchen doing him some breakfast. Who's this then?'

'Her niece. Name's Linda.'

'Oh,' the woman said, blankly. 'Well – I s'pose that's all right.'

Linda didn't understand the next part of the conversation.

'Is Rosy . . . down?'

Polly eyed Linda, and nodded. 'Yeah. Well – pretty much.'

Suddenly, Irene reached round and took Linda's hand, in such a naturally motherly way that Linda was touched.

'Right, love – come on.'

They went along a tiled passage that smelt of cigarettes mixed with a sweet, cloying smell, and frying bacon. Linda suddenly realized she was ravenously hungry. She'd had a bit of toast before she set out, which now felt like several days before. Irene took her into the kitchen. It was almost all too quick then, as if Linda was suddenly unprepared for the sight of a woman standing at the stove with her back to them, in a long, peach-coloured robe, a woman who was both shorter and more fleshed out than she expected. Her dark hair was lifted into a bunch and she was smoking and jiggling the handle of a frying pan with the other hand.

'Rosy!'

The first impression of her aunt's face, the brown eyes, strong eyebrows, still pretty, mischievous features was unmistakable, yet she was plumper in the face and older and she had a worn look, dark smudges under her eyes. She took the cigarette out of her mouth and frowned, though more with puzzlement than annoyance.

'Who's this, Reeny – brought me a new recruit?'

Irene laughed. '*No!* Chrissakes, Rosy – this girl's come to see you all the way from Birmingham. Says you're her auntie. I couldn't turn her away, could I?'

She really did have Rosina's attention then.

'Here – ' she jerked her head towards the pan of bacon. 'Finish this off for his nibs will you? He wants a couple of eggs thrown in as well.'

She stubbed out her cigarette on a saucer then came over, slowly, and Linda could feel she was being sized up.

'My God,' she said. 'Now – which one are you? You one of Charlie's?'

What a long time Rosina had been gone, Linda realized. She wasn't even sure who was who in her own family! Close up, her presence had a strong impact, fleshly, feminine, and perfumed.

'No – I'm Linda – I'm Violet's second girl. Joyce's sister.'

'Course you are!' Rosina put a hand over her mouth and to Linda's astonishment, she saw her aunt's eyes fill with tears. 'Oh – Reeny, get me a hanky, will you? I feel all ... Oh blimey, look at me!' And the tears ran down her face. She came close and leaned to kiss Linda's cheek, wetting it with her tears. 'Aren't you pretty, darlin'? How old're you then?'

'Sixteen,' Linda said. She suddenly felt like crying herself.

'She's the image of you, Rosy – I could see that straight away,' Irene said, flipping the bacon over, then going in search of a hanky and handing Rosina a square of checked cotton.

Rosina wiped her eyes and seemed at a loss for a moment. Someone else came in and asked her something about towels and she replied as if she had barely heard the question.

'Did you come all the way down today?'

Linda nodded.

'What – just to look for me?'

'Yes.' She felt foolish.

'Why? I mean ...' She laughed suddenly, good-naturedly. 'Well, you're a one, aren't you? You might not've found me! Little thing like you let loose in the big city.'

'Bit like you then, Rosy,' Irene reminded her. She

455

tipped the bacon unceremoniously on to a plate. 'Does *he* want fried bread an' all?'

'Yes – anything . . .' Rosina seemed to gather her thoughts finally. Almost formally, she said, 'Look, Reeny – I want to spend some time with my niece. Get Barbs to hold the fort, will you? She'll have to clear it with him. But this is family and it doesn't happen every day. All right, Linda? Give me a few minutes to get my glad rags on.'

Chapter Seventy-Eight

Linda sat in the kitchen sipping a strong cup of tea.

'Rosy won't be long, lovey,' Irene said, sinking down on to a stool with her cup. The plateful of food for 'him' had been despatched upstairs. Linda wanted to ask who 'he' was, but didn't dare. She was glad of the tea, and realized she had been almost faint from hunger.

Irene kicked off her shoes and rubbed her left foot. 'Bloody kill me, they do. Look nice though, don't they?'

She chatted about Rosina's children. Linda still had the picture in her mind of the two young faces in the picture tucked behind the jug on Bessie's mantel, but of course Clark was barely a couple of years younger than herself and Vivianne was twelve.

'Little beauty she's turning out to be,' Irene said. 'Course, she's a handful at times. Stormy, that's our Vivianne. Little madam. But clever – all she's learning at that school, sewing and that. Beautiful at it, she is. Rosy's got them at good schools out in the country. She couldn't have them round here – not with the business. Shame you won't meet them. Clarkie's a darlin' – soft as butter and always has been. He's a clever one and all. She's got high hopes for her kids, Rosy has.'

Linda felt intimidated by the thought of Rosina's children and their posh schools. How did Rosina afford it? she wondered. She had no clear idea of what Rosina

did or of her life. She just felt overwhelmed and confused, sitting in this stark, high-ceilinged kitchen.

Sooner than she expected, Rosina appeared, clad in
an apricot-coloured frock and with her hair brushed
and smoothed back into a stylish knot. Her heart-
shaped face was made up, lipstick and powder, and she
looked very pretty.

'Here she is – quick-change artist.'

'Is he taken care of?' she asked anxiously, rolling her
eyes to the ceiling.

'I'll ask Pol to tell him where you are. You go on
out, girl, and sod him.'

Rosina smiled faintly. 'Ready Linda?'

'I'll get back now then, Rosy.' Irene pushed her feet,
wincing, back into the shoes. 'You two have a nice
time!'

'Bet you've never been to town before, have you?'
Rosina said as they stepped back out into the street.

'No,' Linda agreed. She had a floaty, unreal feeling
now, as if this was all a dream.

'You all right, bab? You look a bit peaky. I s'pect
you could do with a square meal inside you. Come on
– I'll treat you.'

She felt safer now, walking out there with Rosina,
who knew the way. And she had liked her as soon as
they met. They went back to the main street and Rosina
stopped her, amid all the traffic and the great looming
buildings and lights.

'This is Piccadilly Circus,' she said.

'Down there's the Houses of Parliament – and Nelson's Column. Anyway –' She took Linda's arm and
looped her own through it. 'We'll go and see my friend
Mario.'

They took another turn, along a narrow street half

458

blocked by stalls selling fruit and veg and a churning collection of people of different colours. It was all very lively and noisy. They squeezed their way through and reached a place with a big white sign saying, 'Soho Café Restaurant – Food Served All Day'. Inside was a long room lined with bronzy tiles and yellow Formica-topped tables arranged all along one wall, opposite the serving counter. Most of the tables were full, a caco-phony of voices speaking various languages rising above the red lightshades on the tables, faces reflected in the mirrors all along the walls. Amid all the noise, a radio was playing as well. The man behind the counter, black-haired, with mischievous brown eyes, greeted Rosy immediately. 'How're you this fine day – eh, Miss Rosy?'

'Not so bad.' Rosina spoke quietly, as if not wanting to attract anyone's attention, but she smiled fondly at the man. 'This is Linda – my niece. She's come down to see me, all the way from Birmingham, and she needs the biggest meal you can make her – OK?'

'Birmingham, eh?' Mario gave a little bow. 'That's a long walk! What you want – eggs, bacon, chips?'

Linda nodded avidly. 'Ooh yes!'

'Coming up – what you want, Rosy?'

'Tell you what – I'll have the same. Celebrate! I'm all in, I tell you.'

'Sit – sit . . .' He waved towards the tables.

'We'll go down the end.' Rosina led her to the furthest table, down in the corner. 'Have a bit of peace,' she said, and indicated to Linda to take the seat facing back up the café. 'You can't hear yourself think in here sometimes.'

Linda liked the place. She'd hardly ever eaten out in a café or restaurant anywhere and this one felt exciting, with its swivelling chairs and colourful décor. In the middle was a coat-stand, a trilby hat stuck on one of the arms, tilted at an angle. As they sat down the tune on the radio reminded her, with a pang, of Alan.

'Sometimes they have a skiffle band in here,' Rosina said, lighting a cigarette. 'You know, with the washboards and that. I s'pect they'll roll in later.'

She sat back and looked very directly at Linda, turning the little tin ashtray round and round on the table. Linda blushed at this frank appraisal.

'You look like your dad,' Rosina observed. 'How is he? Looked very bad at the wedding.'

'He died – last year,' Linda said.

Rosina's face changed. 'Oh God – poor thing. Poor old Vi.'

There was a pause.

'How is she?'

'All right.'

'Good. Really all right, you mean?'

'I think so. She works in a hairdresser's, with Rita – she's the owner. Mom likes it. She's good at it.'

She hadn't realized that until she said it, but she saw that it was true.

Rosina laughed. 'Good old Vi. Time she had a life of her own. She was like a bleeding shadow at home with our mom. Hardly dared to breathe. None of us did.' Her tone was very bitter. She took a drag on her cigarette and looked at Linda sharply, weighing her up. For a moment Linda saw a steely hardness in her aunt's eyes.

'How's Marigold, poor cow?'

Linda shrugged. 'All right. The same. She's got a boyfriend, and Nana doesn't like it.'

Rosina burst out laughing, a chesty, smoker's laugh.

'I bet she doesn't! Christ alive – good old Mari. She must be gone forty now, ain't she? And what about Charlie? he still with that harridan Gladys?'

'Yes.' Linda couldn't think of much to say about him. 'He's all right. Norm's getting married in a while.'

'Little Norm! He was just a babby when I left.' She sighed, flicking the cigarette at the ashtray. 'Fancy that.'

She asked about Joyce and Carol, and Linda told her about Joyce and Danny's baby and Carol's polio and her operations and Rosina listened, looking alternately pleased and interested and wistful.

'Poor old Vi – she's had a plateful, she really has.' Then more quietly, as if broaching something difficult, 'And how's . . . Bess?'

'Nana? Poorly. She had a bit of a turn, a while back.'

Rosina digested this. Quietly, she said, 'And is she still the same?'

Their eyes met. 'Yes,' Linda said bitterly. 'She is.'

Without either of them having to say more, there was understanding. Linda didn't know why Rosina had run away all those years ago, nor anything much of her life now, but she sensed that they were in some way the same, that there was something they both needed. It was an exciting feeling. It gave her butterflies in her stomach.

They became aware of a thin man approaching the table. Rosina seemed to recognize him. Before she could stop him he unwrapped a piece of cloth he had taken from his pocket and showed something to Rosy. Linda couldn't see what it was but she could see the panic on Rosina's face.

'No,' she said sharply. 'Not now. Get lost, Pete.'

Suddenly her aunt was strange to her again. What

461

was going on? But the moment was interrupted by Mario swooping towards them with two plates of food.

'Here we are, ladies! Here you – clear off and leave these ladies alone!'

The thin man melted away. When Linda turned, she couldn't see him anywhere.

'Rosy . . .' Mario tutted at her. 'You gotta look after yourself better.' No more was said, but Linda saw, in the looks they gave each other, his affection and reproachful care for her.

'Thanks, Mario. That'll keep us going all right!'

He had cooked them a feast: rashers of bacon, two fried eggs each with perfect, gleaming yolks, sausage, fried bread and chips piled along the side. From under his arm, magician-like, he produced a bottle of ketchup. 'You want tea?'

'Yes – oh ta, Mario.' Rosina laughed. 'He's good to me, he is.' She smiled at Linda.

'You ladies got to keep your strength up!' He stepped back with a flourish. '*Buon appetito!* Tea coming up!'

'He's golden,' Rosina said as he strode off again. 'He's been like a brother to me – no funny business, nothing like that. Got a wife and four kiddies and he's good as gold. I'd trust him with my life, and there's not many you can say that about round here. Eh – tuck in, girl!'

Mario soon produced large mugs of tea, and as Linda ate, ravenously, she started to feel better. More colour came into Rosina's cheeks as well, and after a short time they ate more slowly, talking between mouthfuls. Rosina did nearly all the talking.

'Do they . . . I mean, back home . . . Do they ever say anything about me?'

'Mom wanted you to stay – after the wedding. They wanted to know why you ran away again.'

'I lost my bottle that day. Lost it bad.' She hesitated, kept looking at Linda as if unsure how much to say.

'Do they know you're here today? Did your mom send you?'

'No. I just came.'

'Where d'you get the fare?'

'I'm at work. It's my money.'

'You're at work! Blimey, yes, I s'pose you are! So you just took it into your head . . .?'

Linda looked up at her and nodded. There was another moment of unspoken understanding.

Rosina leaned forward, elbows on the table, lighting another cigarette. 'You want to know about me – is that it?'

Linda nodded slowly.

'Will you tell them?'

'Dunno. Not if you don't want.'

Rosina laughed suddenly. 'You've got a mind of your own all right, haven't you?' She sat back again, blowing smoke away at the ceiling. 'All right. I'll tell you. I've never told anyone – not the full thing. 'Cept Irene of course – she knows most of it. But you – ' she jabbed the cigarette in Linda's direction. 'You're a bit like me. Dunno how I know. I can just feel it. There's some in our family can't see over the wall and all they ever do's sit on their hands. That's Charlie, for a start, and Vi. God knows with Marigold. Probably she'd've been different, given the chance. And there's those of us who get up higher and can see over and we want something of what's over there. That's me – and that's you, Linda, isn't it?'

Goose-pimples came up all over Linda's skin. She

463

was filled with emotion suddenly, as if she wanted to cry. Someone could see her, see what she was like! But all she could do was nod again.

'Well, who I am's nothing to be proud of, believe you me. But you pays your money and takes your choice and this is me. OK?'

Chapter Seventy-Nine

'I s'pose you want to know why I left? I dunno – look at you. You're only a kid yourself. I shouldn't be telling you all this – but you want me to, don't you? Seems a whole lifetime ago now. I don't even remember you being born. '38? Yes, I was long gone by then. I remember Joycie arriving. Vi'd had all her problems with babies. I s'pose that's why I wanted to come for the wedding. And 'cause Vi'd written to me. She never has otherwise. S'pose she's had too much else going on.

'They probably told you I went off with an actor. Michael Albie was his name. I met him in my days hanging round the photographers and the stage doors at the Hip and the Alex. I was mad about Michael. Never felt the same way about anyone after him . . . All right, Mario? Yes, another cuppa'd be lovely. We'll be here for a bit yet, ta, love.

'See, I left Brum with Michael because I wanted more – I wanted life and the stage and I was in love with him. And I couldn't stand any more of our mom. There was no room for anyone in that house except for her and what she wanted. Sometimes you could hardly bloody breathe, and all them babbies and that carry-on. Always had to be queen bee, Mom did, never mind who she walked all over. I mean what she did to poor old Marigold. That was an evil, wicked thing she did. Don't s'pose you know all about that, though? No, I thought not. You'd've been too young . . . But you're just the age now that she was. See, this'll shock you, but Marigold had a child herself. A little boy. He was born at home – I'll never forget that night. It frightened me at the time, hearing it. But I can see him now. Beautiful, he was. But our mom upped and took him straight to some orphanage. Never would say where. She might as well have thrown him out with the rubbish, the attitude she had. Not a by your leave to Mari – she never had a say in anything. Christ, Linda, I can feel myself boiling inside even now, thinking about it. God knows who the father was – she was a poor old thing, Mari. But she loved that babby – you could see.

'Thing was, when I left Brum I was carrying Michael's child . . . oh, I'm going to get all weepy now . . . I mean I wanted to go anyway, but if our mom had known . . . I'd never have had a say either. And I loved Michael, wanted nothing else but to be with him. I'd only just found out and his stint at the Alex was ending and he was coming back to London. He wasn't poor, Michael wasn't. He was much older than me – gone thirty already and he had money from his family, not like a lot of the stage crowd, all living on a shoestring. He had a little flat – not so very far from here in fact. Anyway, when we got down here he started on me. If I wanted to be in the theatre it was no good thinking about carrying on with the child. He didn't want it, of course. Most of 'em don't – that's what I've found. They're not like us, Linda, men, that's one thing for sure.

'I gave in in the end. Course, I was frightened. I was only seventeen when we left, turned eighteen in the December. Michael took me to this woman . . . It makes me go cold now . . . Thing about it was how ordinary it all was. It was her flat, up some dark stairs, and her kitchen, a washing-up bowl and that. On her kitchen table in this flat. I s'pose that's where her kids ate their tea. She had a great big bottle of antiseptic stuff. It hurt, Linda. Hurt so much I fainted ... Phoo – makes me go all hot and cold to think of it. Michael had to get a cab to take me home and I wasn't right for weeks after. When I got better he started on me to look for work and I wanted to, of course, although I'd lost a lot of weight and was a bit too skinny. But he helped and I got a couple of parts – stand-ins in chorus lines. I can sing, see, as well. I've got a half nice voice, even now. And then he left me. Locked me out of the flat one night and he was going off to work up north some-where. Never said where. I was left with only what I had to stand up in. We'd only been together six months, altogether. That night, I slept in Hyde Park. Sounds bad, doesn't it? At the time all I could think about was Michael. Broke my heart, he did. I didn't care about sleeping on a bench in the park, only that he'd left me and I couldn't understand why.

'I was quite presentable still and I managed to get a job the next day. That was a miracle then. Jobs were hard to find and I didn't have a reference, but it was this woman, see, Mavis her name was, ran an eating joint off the Tottenham Court Road. I dunno if I reminded her of her daughter, or what, but I was bloody lucky is all I can say. She said I was pretty and that was good in a waitress as long as I could do the work. She worked me hard and tried to patch up my heart. Course, any time I could I was round the theatres, trying to get something else. I did get one little speaking part. That was the picture I sent you. I think my face's always been my fortune because I knew next to nothing. They said I had the right look and it was a play called *The Garnet Ring*. I had two appearances in it. I don't think it was much of a play but I can still remember the lines now! The first time I went on I had to say, "Mr Fellows, I do wish you could arrange to conduct your private business elsewhere . . ." Well, you can imagine what that was all about – yes, it was funny. And then later I had to say, "It's no good, I'm going to hand in my notice. Never have I had the misfortune to put up with conditions like these before!"

'Anyway, things went on like this for quite a while – can't say exactly how long. I had a few fellers come and go of course. Nothing serious. I was still in a mess after Michael. And then I met Johnny – just before the war. Hot and lovely it was, that summer. Johnny was an actor and he was no better off than me. Both of us had our rooms in seedy lodgings. But he was so handsome, Johnny was. Dark and *sleek* somehow, with thick wavy hair and sort of little boy looks. His eyes were blue as anything. China blue. He bowled me over. He was going to get somewhere with acting, I thought. With looks like that how could he not? He was quite young, see, not like Michael. He was only a couple of years older than me. I didn't want him to know how things had been. That I'd begun . . . a child, and that. I was very careful, held off from anything much in the love department. Very prim and proper I was – you should've seen me!

'Course, soon as the war broke out there was trouble – they closed the theatres and that, for a bit. But there were shows put on – Johnny got me into a few things. Bloody frightening it all was then – all those gas warnings, air raid sirens . . . I hated them public shelters. Stank to high heaven and you never knew who you were going to be with. Anyway – the thing was, I couldn't last out with Johnny. The Virgin Mary bit, I mean. By the time the Luftwaffe were hammering the guts out of us every night I was expecting again. Couldn't believe it – I mean I thought we'd been careful, you know, taken precautions. I'm one of them only has to look at a man, I reckon . . . Sorry, bab, keep forgetting your age. You seem older, you know, Linda. Well, you've guessed it – first hint of a babby on the way and Johnny was off. I mean I didn't tell him straight away, not after Michael. I thought, bide your time, Rosy, see how the land lies. I tried to get out of him whether he wanted to marry me. But you can't hide a babby for ever and I wasn't *doing away* with it . . . Sorry, I have to whisper that. I wasn't doing that again. It does summat to you, however much you don't want to keep the baby.

'Any road, Johnny guessed, in the end, saw my little belly swelling. "So now you know," I said. "And what're we going to do about it?"

' "I dunno," he said. "It's not me that's having a baby, is it?" Just like that. Couldn't care less. So I knew he'd be off and I took off first. Found a new room. He'd have come back for his bit of fun otherwise and I wasn't having that. I don't know what you must think of me – you're keeping very quiet. But it gets worse, Linda. I told you, if you've come to find someone to model your life on, you're barking up the wrong tree with your auntie Rosy.

'Any road – the best thing happened then. I'd finished working at Mavis's place a while back and I was in another joint in Soho. Course it was a bit different here then – not so many coloureds for a start – and the war was on. That's where I met Reeny. Irene Bartlett.

Best thing that ever happened to me – apart from my kids. Irene's bloke had joined up, gone in the army, and that was the best thing ever happened to her, an' all. Proper toe-rag he was. Joined up almost before Neville Chamberlain had finished telling us there was a war on, and good riddance, she said. He came back at the end, you know – but not to her. Had some bit of stuff somewhere. Reeny had her boy, Kevin. He was six then, and she had her mum up the road. We always hit it off, Reeny and me, and she was golden to me. Like a sister – always had been. "Don't you worry, Rosy," she used to say. "Us women'll stick together and sod 'em."

'And we did. Not half we did. She asked me to move in with her and Kev and we had some laughs. It was a godsend. But of course neither of us had any money. She was getting by doing a bit of waitressing while her mom was in with Kev. And I was all right till Clarkie arrived. Reeny was there with me, and her mom – one night when there was no bloody air raid for once! Had him easy, I did. I mean it hurts like hell, screamed my head off and that, but I mean it came natural to me. And Clarkie was big and healthy and – oh! Light of my life he is – and Vivianne. But that was later.

'Things got hard then, see, 'cause Reeny's mom took sick. It was so quick – she just wasted away in front of our eyes and by the time Clark was six months I carried him to her funeral. Poor Reeny. She always said, if she hadn't've had me she'd have gone off her head. Anyway, this is where things took a turn, as you might say. Reeny was working in the day, and I worked at night, doing what I knew best. See I'm blushing even now. When I'm here, the life I live – well, it's just how it is, day by day. I've got used to it, see? D'you understand what I'm saying, Linda? What it is I do to earn my bread? Course, it's not *me* doing it any more. Never – not now. I've got my girls and I treat them well. Come and work at Rosy's and you're as safe as you're likely to be – not on the streets, fair's fair ... You do know what I'm talking about now, don't you? But I couldn't come out to face you all, let you see what I was, not all at once. I've got a nice little flat, kids at good schools – that's all I want anyone to see, but it ain't the whole of me, see?

'I'm getting out of order now. There was a lot more road to walk before I got to this bit. Reeny and I kept each other going. She had her little house, kids upstairs, and I used the front room, nights, took the punters back there. The daytimes were another world – all kids and Reeny and me playing happy families and Kev at school. Clean, and nice.

'And then I met Humphrey ... I'm running out of fags. This is my last one – I'll have to nip out and get some more ... Anyway, this bit I'm ashamed of. It's different when it comes to friendship, see. I let Reeny down. Let her down bad. She forgave me, but that doesn't make it any better. Humphrey was this posh geezer. Not like the others. I never took old Hump back to Reeny's. Hump had money – *real* money. He had a wife and couple of kids. He was some top-notch city type – worked high up in a bank. Reserved occupation and all that and plenty of lolly to splash about. Only he had a taste for ... well, let's call it lower life than what he was used to. Wanted his nose in the gutter – it gave him a thrill. I met him when I was working the corner and he came and started the chat-up bit. Ugly sod he was really – one of them with a round face, looks about twelve years old still, all chin and no cheekbones.

' "I can take you somewhere nicer than this," he said,

all posh. "How much for the evening?" Well, I thought I'd up the score so I said "Ten quid" – well, what I really said was, "That'll be ten pounds to you, sir," trying to speak posh for him.

'He took me back to his place – over in Kensington. Lovely little flat, top of one of them big houses on a square, all trees in the middle. It became a fixture – every Tuesday night, all night. God knows where wifey thought he was, I never asked, poor cow. Or perhaps she didn't care. Thing was, Hump was fond of me. Sort of fell for me, in his way. Dunno if that sort can fall in love, exactly. Public school, sent away when he was four and all that. Always looked as if his shirt-button was done up too tight at the top – even when he was starkers!

'I met him – when was it now – sometime in 1941. I know it was pretty cold the night he came up to me and he had a nice little electric fire in the flat. I'd never seen such a nice one. And he asked me to move in there. "I want to think of you here, even when I'm not here. You won't be given any trouble – I've an arrangement with the landlady."

'"I can't," I said to him. "I've got a boy, not a year old."

'"Well," he says, "I don't mind that – so long as he's not there when I'm there. Thing about me is, Rosy, I don't like competition. I like to have my woman all to myself."

'And to my shame I went. I mean you should have seen the place! Me living in Kensington, all posh! Me and Clarkie, except for the times Hump was there – and that wasn't all that many – and Reeny had him then. I thought I'd arrived. I'd left Reeny, pretty much – after all she'd done for me. Told her it was an investment for

472

the future. Course I kept meaning to go back and see her more often, but it was a treat, living it up in Kensington. I felt like a lady and didn't want to think about what else I was. Not until I got lonely, anyway. Humphrey was hardly ever there and when he was, he wasn't much company, not really.

'We kept it up all through the summer. He kept saying, "I'll come and take you out for a day. We'll take a boat on the river." I liked the idea of that – even with him. I mean he wasn't that bad – quite easy to please really. Course he never did, though – take me out in a boat, I mean.

'Anyway, you've guessed – he was Vivianne's father. He got me up the duff. I told him, soon as I knew, and waited for him to run. I s'pose I just wanted to get it over with. That was men. I never expected anything of them – not by then. The soft bit of me that expected had all dried up with Michael. Everything hurts more when you're young. Course, he did run, but my God, Linda, he was all right, really, Hump was. He cried, you know, when I told him, went on about how he couldn't understand his children – they had two already – and he was a hopeless father and husband, unfaithful and no good to anyone and now he wasn't going to stay with me either. I mean I ended up feeling quite sorry for him, poor bloke. He seemed as if he was locked in a box and couldn't get out and I thought well, at least I'm not as bad as that.

'I went back to Reeny and asked her to forgive me. She was all right, she understood, she said. She'd've done the same. She wouldn't, though. She's more loyalty than that.

'Thing was, though . . . Old Hump waved me goodbye as if he'd never have another thing to do with me.

Oh well, posh bastard, I thought. That's how it goes, and you've had your fun, Rosy. Then one night I'm back at my post on the corner and back he comes, hat pulled down over his face.

'"I want you to know,"' he says, and he sounded quite tearful. Made me feel really sorry for him. 'That you've been a real light in my life, Rosy. You're all the things I'm not – courageous, strong, amusing. And I don't want you to remember me as a . . . as a complete cad . . ." was what he said, I think! "So I want you to have this."

'He gave me this envelope and kissed me on the cheek and off he went.

'Well, business wasn't looking good that night anyway and I went back to Reeny's and opened the envelope. And what d'you think was inside? There was a note, saying, *You'll need to set yourself up. This is for you and the child. With love from H.* He'd written me a cheque for *five grand*! Yes – well, I gasped even louder than that at the time! Reeny and me toasted him with champagne all that week, I can tell you.

'But I've got a good head for money, when I've got hold of any. I wasn't going to fritter it away. This was my main chance and I took it.

'First thing I did was buy us a house, number twenty, the one you've just seen. The flat didn't come till later. But Reeny and me and the kids had a bigger home and I ran my little business from downstairs. Vivianne was born in 1942 and that put me out of action for a bit, but Reeny was working – regular work, I mean, in a shop – and we managed. I bought the flat after the war. The kids were old enough then to notice what was going on around them and I wasn't having that. I can remember the day the war ended, everyone dancing and the tugs blowing their hooters along the river, V for victory! And dear old Winnie up there on the balcony with the Royals – we were there, Reeny and me. We took the kids. And as we stood there and everyone was drunk with happiness, I thought, I'm going to make a future for my kids. Whatever it takes, it doesn't matter about me, but they've got to have something better. Oh dear – where's my hanky? Soppy old thing aren't I, really? See, they don't know what I do, to this day. They go off with their little boaters on to their nice school and life's sunny and happy. Their dad was killed in the war, that's all they know. Their mum works for a firm and she often has to work late. But there's Reeny, you see. She's like a second mom to them, always has been. Happy as Larry they are, trips out and about, me all dressed up and coming along to the do's at school.

'They don't even know about Richie. He's my bloke – and he doesn't know about them. Proper Jekyll and Hyde, me, ain't I? Richie's not the sort I want round my kids. He's a love really, deep down, only he's got a temper and he's not the family sort. I just like to have a man about – for me and for the house, just in case, you know. I don't love him – nothing like that. I'm past all that. He's my night life, if you like. Only – I dunno. Coming to Brum, seeing you all, I was frightened. I admit it. I didn't want things brought together. Didn't want to admit that the left hand doesn't know what the right's doing. Yes – you're right, Linda. Sooner or later Clarkie and Viv are going to ask more questions . . . and honest to God, I don't know how I'm going to answer them.'

Chapter Eighty

They sat in Mario's café all afternoon.

'I don't want to take you back to the house,' Rosina said. 'You shouldn't be in a place like that – not a kid your age. Next time, you come home, properly, when Clarkie and Vivianne are here. You're cousins, after all!'

Later on she slipped out to buy more cigarettes and on the way back in joked with Mario and asked him for 'a nice bun or something', and he brought toasted teacakes to them, with butter and jam. Linda had barely digested the huge dinner, but she tucked in anyway, while Rosina continued to smoke endlessly, one cigarette after another. The whole afternoon passed for Linda as if bathed in light. She was overwhelmed by Rosina, shocked and impressed by what she had seen in her of steeliness and tears. And the feeling that she had always known her, not just the familiar dark eyes from Bessie's picture, but that she had always known that she would be like this, that she would feel familiar.

'What d'you do with yourself?' Rosina asked, sitting back and drinking yet more tea.

'I've got a job – in a bakery.'

Rosina stared shrewdly at her.

'Any boyfriends?'

Linda moved a blob of butter round with her knife on one half of the teacake. 'Sort of.'

'What d'you mean, sort of?'

She found herself spilling it all out, Alan, the accident.

'That what's wrong with your arm?'

Linda nodded. 'I was all right. It was him got the worst of it.'

'Serves him flaming well right, by the sound of it. It's no good, love – if he drags you down, ditch him. It won't get any better. What does your mom say?'

'Nothing much. She likes him.'

Rosina watched her for a moment, and Linda blushed.

'What're you going to do?'

'What d'you mean?'

'I mean, with yourself? Don't you want more than working in a bakery for ever more?'

Linda met her gaze, hungrily. *'Yes.'*

Rosina leaned forwards and looked closely at her. 'You could go far, girl, d'you know that?'

'Like you?'

'I think you are like me – in a way. Only, Linda love – don't be like me, eh? What am I when you come down to it? The madam of a whorehouse with two bastard children who she can't look in the eye and admit what she does, and who can't face her own family. God knows, sometimes I ache to see someone else who's flesh and blood. Maybe I'll get up the courage again one day. But don't be like me – be more than me.'

They left the Soho Café after Rosina had exchanged more fond banter with Mario while paying the bill.

'You're the best bolthole in town!' she told him.

'Eh – that's what they say about your place, Rosy!' he joked.

'You'll need to get back or Vi'll be doing her nut,' Rosina said. 'I'll walk you to the Tube, all right? But you come down again, girl – I'll pay your fare. That ain't a problem. Will you?'

'Yes.' Linda felt a smile break across her face. 'Course I will.'

Before Linda disappeared into the Underground, Rosina hugged her tight, and when she let go, Linda saw the tears in her eyes.

'Will you tell them, at home – about me?'

'D'you want me to?'

Rosina put her head to one side. 'No – best not. Not all of it. I don't want you lying – just hold a bit back, eh? One day I'll have to get out of all this – and then it won't matter any more anyway. Take care, love.'

And she turned, and walked away amid the crowds in Piccadilly, curvaceously attractive in her bright dress, and resolute, yet somehow the more vulnerable for it.

As Linda watched her, she caught sight of a postbox across on the corner of the street. She found a moment of resolution of her own. Making her way across the road, she took out the envelope, *Mister Alan Bray* ... on the address, and glanced at it for a second. The feelings Alan brought out in her rose up again – the longing and sympathy, the sense of hopelessness. *I do love you,* she thought. *But I can't stay. I need to live – properly.* She slipped the letter into the box. For a moment she felt stricken, then elated.

'Bye, bye,' she said.

Chapter Eighty-One

'Cold today, isn't it?' Violet said loudly. She was doing a wash and set for old Mrs Busby and had to speak up or the lady didn't hear a word. 'Feels like winter already, doesn't it?'

'Don't say that,' Rita said, pushing a trolley of rollers, pins and combs past her. As usual she had on the highest pair of heels you could find, in a bright shade of green to match her skirt. 'Gets you down thinking about it. One of these days I'm going to go and live somewhere where it's always hot and sunny.'

'Nice to have dreams!' Violet quipped, rolling a section of the lady's thin hair round a fat roller.

The girl Rita now employed to clear up and do some of the washes was sweeping up bits of hair round her feet. Violet stepped aside for her, feeling a sense of satisfaction. Not long ago that had been her job, salon skivvy, before Rita had made her a kind of apprentice, and now they were partners in their own little business! She eased her shoulders back, standing straighter in a gesture of quiet pride. For the first time in her life she was getting somewhere, being someone for herself!

'Cuppa tea, Vi?'

'Ooh, yes please – I couldn't half do with one. D'you want me to do it?'

'Nah – you're in the middle of Mrs Busby. I'll get it.'
Rita disappeared out the back and as she did so

Violet saw a familiar figure hurry past. Like everything else outside, she was stained yellow by the protective film hanging behind the windows to mute the sunlight. They looked out on a surreal, yellow world.

It was Joyce, with Charlie on her hip. She seemed flustered and pushed her way in through the door. Violet twisted round, still pushing pins through Mrs Busby's roller. Joyce looked pale, sickly. She had announced a couple of weeks back that she was pregnant and she wasn't feeling very well with this one and was none too pleased about the fact.

'Hello, babby – Charlie boy! What're you two doing here?'

'It's Nana,' Joyce panted. 'Danny's just had Clarence on the telephone – from the phone box. Nana's had another bad turn ... Marigold's with her but ... He said I should get you.'

'Well, how bad is she?' Violet, immediately tense, snapped out the words.

'I dunno, do I? And there's no need to take it out on me, I only came to tell you!' Joyce was almost in tears.

'Oh, for goodness sake,' Violet said. 'I didn't mean it like that.' She left Mrs Busby and went to kiss Charlie's squashy cheeks. 'Sorry, Joycie – don't get in a state. It's only that I'm in the middle of – you know, everything.'

'What's up? Oh – hello, Joyce!' Rita walked in with two mugs of tea. 'Ooh, look at him – you going to let me have a hold today?'

'It's my mom,' Violet explained.

'Well, you go – I can manage,' Rita said. She had taken Charlie's little hand. There was something so inviting about him, everyone wanted to touch him. 'Poor old duck – no good her being there on her own, is it?'

'I'll finish Mrs Busby . . .'

'Don't be daft – I can do her. Go on – scarper!'

On the bus over to Aston, Violet looked out at the grey sprawl under a heavy grey sky and felt her spirits sink low. In the background of her mind was the nag of worry about her mother, but she couldn't do anything until she got there and saw what was what. She'd deal with it then.

She knew the reason for her low spirits. After all, most things were going well. She loved her job, Carol was well and thriving and happy at school, and Linda was like a changed person. Quite a bombshell that, coming home saying she'd been to London – to Rosina! She had some nerve, Violet had to hand it to her!

Whatever had happened, a few days after Linda came home she announced she was going to start at night-school, learn all sorts, shorthand, typing, accounts – maybe even a language if she could. She was full of it!

'I want a better job,' she said. 'I can't stay doing what I'm doing for ever, can I?'

And that Alan lad seemed to have disappeared off the scene. Violet was half sorry about this – he'd seemed rather nice and obviously wasn't short of a bob or two, with that bike and everything, even if he did dress like a tramp.

As for the business about Rosina, she still felt stirred up about that.

'You should go and see her, Mom,' Linda said. 'I think she misses the family.'

'Why doesn't she come and see us – we're all up here, it's only her down there, all on her own. Is she all right? She's not in trouble?'

'No. She's all right.'

Linda had been quite cagey about Rosina, just said they'd sat and talked a lot and Rosina had told her about her children. Violet knew perfectly well she wasn't getting the full story.

What had kept her from contact with Rosina all these years? All her own troubles, the war, Harry, Carol, had all loaded down on her so there was no room to see out. And something else about Rosina herself: the distance she had created between them by taking off, accentuating a distance that had always been there somehow, the way it was with Linda, because they were so opposite to her. They were bold, hungry, they saw things very differently. *They've got guts*, Violet thought. Not like me – I've always been a stop-at-home. Not much about me really. That was how she had always felt, except for that brief, glittering time with Roy, Roy who had seen something in her . . .

And that was the source of the pain she felt now. For all these years she had turned her back on the memory of those months during the war, tried to see it as a time when she had been unfaithful, wicked, and that Carol's illness had been sent to punish her. How much more so, she thought, knowing what had happened to Roy and Iris's twins. A double curse! They had paid all right, both of them. Didn't that show how wrong they'd been? It was the war – all sorts of things happened, a chaos which sent people flying in all directions like skittles. And when peace came you had to settle back to what you knew, to the real commitment of your life. And she had done, hadn't she? She'd been a faithful, caring wife to Harry in sickness and in health – sickness especially. She had done her duty.

When she'd seen Roy she had not let herself feel

anything much – not at the time. It had all been too quick. Once she was alone, the reaction set in. She sat in the back room, smoking to try and calm herself, shaking. Eventually, out of the deep ache, the tears came. Roy, after all this time, those eyes, hands . . . and all the questions she wanted to ask, things she wanted to say – *This beautiful girl is your daughter . . . Do you remember? . . . Do you feel anything for me still? Because I loved you like no one else* – all these things echoed in her unspoken. There had been nothing she could read in his expression. She had had that one chance, in such a hopeless place with all those other people around them, and now he had gone. She had no idea where he lived. Of course, it was the best thing. What else could she have done? Yet ever since, she had been full of regret and longing.

All the way to Bessie's she sat staring through the window and ran the scene over and over in her mind, seeing not the streets they were passing through, but Roy Keillor's face.

Chapter Eighty-Two

Clarence was standing on the front step, peering anxiously along the road. He'd always been a bit short-sighted and still refused to wear glasses, despite the National Health Service. When he caught sight of her he waved agitatedly and took a few steps towards her with his stick.

'Took your blinking time!' he quavered at her. 'I've been waiting here . . .'

Violet didn't answer. No good getting cross: he was old and frightened. His hair was almost all gone now, barring a few wisps. You'd never think he was younger than Bessie, not even sixty yet.

'Go on up!' Clarence fretted behind her. 'Marigold's up with her, but she ain't no bloody good.'

Violet flung her coat on a chair on the way through and hurried up the stairs.

'Marigold? What's up – how is she?'

Marigold had lumbered to her feet from beside Bessie's big brass bedstead.

'She had a turn. This morning – before she ever came down.' Marigold's face was as blank as ever, yet Violet could sense something in her, a kind of suppressed excitement. Also, she stank of hard liquor of some sort. Poor old Mari, with all this going on.

She thought her mother was asleep. Her eyes were closed, hanks of grey hair on the pillow round her head, her face sunken. The left side of her mouth seemed tugged to one side, as if by an invisible thread. Violet could hardly believe her eyes. It was as if a huge tree had been felled. As she knelt down beside Bessie, though, her eyes opened and she gave a whimper of distress, nostrils flaring.

'It's all right – it's only me. What's up, Mom – you feeling bad?' There was no reply except for something Violet had never seen in her mother before: a look of utter terror in her eyes.

'Has the doctor been?' she asked Marigold.

Bessie made a loud, strangled sound.

'Can't she talk?'

Marigold shook her head. 'No. And she don't want the doctor. He'll make her go to the hospital.'

Looking at Bessie's frightened face, she knew Marigold was right.

'But Mari – Dr Cameron won't make her go. And we need to know what's wrong – how to look after her.'

Dr Cameron had known them all since they were children. He was about Bessie's age himself.

Marigold just stared at her sullenly.

'You've done everything right,' Violet reassured her. 'Only I think we need help. It's all right, Mom.' She squeezed Bessie's hand, struck by how cold it was. 'We won't let them take you away. But I'll get Dr Cameron to pop in and see you, all right?'

Violet walked down to the surgery to see old Dr Cameron. His rumbling Scottish voice had always been a comfort.

'I daresay she'll be averse to going near any hospitals,' he said jovially.

'She can't speak,' Violet said. She suddenly felt tearful.

'Can't *speak*? What, Bessie? Dear me – that does sound serious.'

Violet knew Dr Cameron was one of the people who had only ever seen the good side of Bessie, all the babies she'd fostered, pillar of the neighbourhood.

He came as soon as he could and stood looking down at her.

'Now, Bessie – what have you been up to? This won't do, will it?'

Bessie tried in vain to speak. Her eyes rolled with frustration and a sweat broke out on her forehead. All that came out were grunting, distorted sounds.

'You're worried I'm going to pack you off to the hospital, aren't you? You do know it's not the work-house any more? Things have changed, Bessie. You'd be better off there, you know.'

An agitated quiver was going on in Bessie's right hand and her face was working. Violet could see that every fibre of her was protesting. She took Bessie's good hand and was surprised how hard Bessie gripped it, face working.

'What, Mom? I can't make you out.'

Bessie was trying desperately hard to speak, but all that came out was, 'Arrr . . . arrr.'

'Clarence?' Violet guessed. 'You can't look after Clarence?'

She saw that she had guessed right.

'Don't you fret. We'll all look after him.'

Marigold's voice came from behind them. 'She wants to stay here.'

Dr Cameron turned to her. 'Yes. That's pretty clear. And I don't know that in terms of her health there's much to be gained from taking her in. But you're the one here, Marigold. D'you think you can manage?'

Marigold nodded, stolidly.

'We'll help you,' Violet hurried to say. 'All of us – I'll come over after work and Linda'll come sometimes . . . And the neighbours'll help, of course.'

'Is that all right then, Bessie? Are you happy now?'

Violet thought how kind Dr Cameron was, his smiling eyes looking down at Bessie, who gave a relieved moan in reply.

'Violet –' He spoke to her quietly, on the stairs, knowing Clarence was hovering about in the back room. 'You know, your mother may recover from this – but she may not. Another stroke and there's no knowing. If anything happens, we shall have to go against her wishes, I think. But we'll see for now – hm? She's not a well woman – that's all I'm saying. You'll all need to keep an eye on her.'

Chapter Eighty-Three

'Well, you sound cheerful this morning!' Mrs Richards said, smiling as Linda came humming through the bakery door, ready for work.

Linda nodded, pulling her hair back into a ponytail and putting on the little white hat. 'Cheerful' didn't feel a strong enough word for what she was feeling just now. In the weeks since she'd seen Rosina, she felt as if everything had changed, her whole outlook on life. She constantly bubbled inside with excitement. At her evening classes at the Commercial School she was learning shorthand and typing. She was very quick at shorthand. Her mind seemed to suck it in like a hungry sponge waiting for water. She practised at home, and Carol was fascinated by all the little Pitman squiggles and helped to test her. The teacher told her she was one of the best pupils she had ever had.

'If you carry on like this,' she said, 'you'll be faster than me! I'll be able to write you an excellent reference.'

She had no clear idea in her head about where she was going, only that she wanted to move on, to learn and make something of her life.

'I think you're marvellous,' Mrs Richards said, when she first heard what Linda was doing. 'Good for you, duck. Course, I could never have done it, not like you. And my Arthur wouldn't have liked it.'

Linda was so glad she'd found the courage to go and

look for her aunt. It was like finding a missing piece of a puzzle, a part of the family which she resembled, which could make sense of her feelings that no one else seemed to share. Even Carol, for all her clever liveliness, and all the love she felt for her, was not like her. She was a more settled sort, more like Mom.

Over those weeks she had thought a lot about things Rosina had told her – about Nana and her mother, and especially Marigold. The information that Marigold had had a baby, when she was only seventeen, had come as an absolute thunderbolt. She'd always felt sorry for Marigold, but now her heart ached for her. Her own baby and Nana had handed it over like a parcel! Hadn't the house in Aston always been full of babies? Always napkins and washing and a squalling bundle in Nana's arms. Always the neighbourhood hero, Bessie – *isn't she kind, what a big heart, isn't she marvellous?* – and yet her own grandchild! Her heart had not been big enough to take that one in. And there was Marigold, her pockets full of scraps of songs which she never sang.

She thought of how she'd felt when her monthly bleed arrived after that night with Alan, the tears of relief which showed her just how much worry she'd been carrying inside her. What if she'd caught for a baby then? It would have been the end of everything! It made her shiver even thinking about it. And Alan? It would have made no difference to him at all. She could have ruined her life for him, for nothing.

In all the weeks since the accident, she hadn't seen or heard from Alan.

At first, after getting home from Rosina's, amid all

the excitement that had raised in her, she felt ashamed of having written to him the way she did. Hadn't she been a bit of a coward? Shouldn't she have gone to see him instead, told him face to face? But when she heard nothing, she thought that was that. He had accepted it, maybe shrugged it off. She was free.

Of course she had had to explain to Mrs Richards what had happened.

'The thing is, I don't really see Alan any more.'

'Don't you?' Mrs Richards was astonished. 'Why's that then? He's such a nice boy, I thought.'

'Well, he is, but . . .' She shrugged.

'Well I never.' Mrs Richards looked deflated. 'That *is* a shame. I thought I was going to hear the sound of wedding bells before too long.'

Linda stared at her. 'I'm only sixteen, you know.'

'Well, I know, bab – but you don't want to go leaving it too long, do you?'

Once again Linda had that claustrophobic feeling. For a moment she wanted to scream. But she said nothing. Mrs Richards didn't mean anything by it. It was just what she was used to.

Late one afternoon though, at the time he used to appear before, Alan came to the shop.

'Ey-up,' Linda heard Mrs Richards say. 'Look who's here! How're you, dear? You have been in the wars, haven't you?'

He was on crutches, one leg still in plaster.

He pushed the door shut and came hopping over to the counter. Linda felt panic rising in her. What on earth were they going to say to each other? He looked very thin and frail, his dark hair quite long, collar-length and curling round his face.

'Hello,' he said to both of them.

Linda murmured a reply.

'I'll have a split tin and four doughnuts,' he said. It was strange to hear his voice again, quiet and well-spoken.

'Jam ones?' Mrs Richards said, sliding the bread into a bag.

'Yes please.'

'How're you going to manage, carrying them?'

He produced a cloth bag. 'I can use this with the crutches. It's all right. I'm used to it.'

Linda felt relieved. Alan talked only to Mrs Richards as she counted the doughnuts into a bag, and she thought perhaps he would not say anything to her, would just go. Perhaps he looked back on his time with her as some stupid mistake. But she knew how much this would hurt as well. It had hurt that he had not written back to her. And then he turned to her.

'Hello.'

She smiled, with her mouth, keeping her eyes neutral. 'When did you get out of hospital?'

'Only a couple of weeks ago. I've had a lot of trouble with this leg – ' He indicated his right leg, still in plaster. 'They've had to operate twice. I've got a metal pin in it now. They think it'll be all right, in the end.'

He looked up at her. 'Is your arm all right?'

'Yes.' She lifted it to show him, free of the plaster now. 'Thanks.'

'Go on, Linda.' Mrs Richards handed Alan his change and he awkwardly put it in his pocket. 'It's nearly closing-up time. You go along and help him carry the bag.'

'But . . .' Linda began.

'You'd like that, wouldn't you, Alan?'

Alan looked at her with injured eyes, and nodded.

Tersely, he said, 'I think a conversation might be in order, yes.'

He said it in such pettish tones that Linda felt immediately annoyed.

'Go on, Linda,' Mrs Richards urged.

'All right then,' she said, trying to sound indifferent. She didn't hurry putting her coat on.

Once they were outside, in the smoky winter afternoon, they started walking automatically in the usual direction they always used to.

'You could have visited. Just *once*, couldn't you?' His voice was full of hurt and rage. 'Wouldn't have killed you – instead of just writing that letter.'

Her own anger boiled up inside. 'You bloody nearly killed *me* – drinking and carrying on like that! Are you going to say sorry as well then? At least I wrote you a letter, which is more than you've bothered to do!'

'Well, I was having my legs smashed up and . . . and rebuilt, that's why. I wasn't in a fit state . . .'

'And I was worrying I might be having a baby – bet you never thought about that either, did you?'

There were tears in her voice, to her fury, and she choked the emotion down.

'After all we had – you just write to me like that . . .' They reached the corner of the street and he stopped, obviously tired from managing the crutches. They were close to the door of a corner shop.

Linda stood with her fists clenched in the pocket of her old duffel coat, the coat she had bought to look like him. 'You look like a real student in that,' one of the others had said to her at the Commercial School. She didn't want to let his emotion into her, to start feeling sorry for him.

'I had to. I can't stay with you. I don't think we're good for each other, Alan.'

'But I need you.' He sounded so pathetic now. He moved a little closer, as if he wanted her to put her arms round him. She kept them firmly by her sides.

'You don't.'

'I *do*. I've never loved anyone the way I love you, Linda.'

She pushed her chin down and looked at the ground. Their breath was white in the freezing air.

'How's your mom?' she asked abruptly. She didn't really want the answer.

'Bad.'

She nodded. 'Sorry.'

'Come back with me. I'm so . . .' He left her to fill in the words: sad, desperate, lonely. His eyes said everything without the words. 'I don't know what to do.'

Tenderness welled in her, and for a moment she imagined going back with him to the big, dark house, to the silence of a place from which his father was almost always absent and to which his mother might or might not ever return. And she would go up to his room, that brown space full of his Westerns and his fantasies of all he wanted to do and it would be just the two of them, the tight, enclosed world they had made together which needed no one else. And she would be with him and be stuck, rooted to the ground unable to get away. Her chest tightened and she had to take a deep breath.

'I can't.'

'Please . . .'

His face was distraught. He looked pathetic standing there with his crutches and his cloth bag of bread.

'If you needed me so much, why have you taken all this time to get here? Or not written?'

'I couldn't. I was upset.'

'I can't make things better. I can't. Even if I was with you, it wouldn't make any difference.'

'But it would! Remember – we were going to America together. I've been writing – while I've been in hospital. A script – I finished it. A new one.' He was speaking very intensely, leaning towards her, resting on the crutches. A woman came out of the shop and walked between them, giving them an odd look.

Linda looked at Alan. Would he ever go to America? Would he really?

'But it's not what I want,' she said. 'I don't want to go to America – not really. That's your dream, not mine.'

'I need you. I don't know what I might do if you don't stay with me . . .'

'I'm sorry Alan. I did love you, really I did. But everything's different now. I can't stay with you. I've got things I want to do.'

And she turned away and walked off, fast, along the road.

Chapter Eighty-Four

Violet closed the door of Rita's Salon behind her and locked up.

It was Rita's afternoon off and it hadn't been busy – Tuesday afternoon, and a freezing, late November day. She had had two ladies under the dryers until a few minutes before closing time.

'There – all done,' she said aloud, trying the door to make sure. She felt so proud, being able to take charge, to feel she could manage everything the day threw at her.

Rita, generous as ever, was talking about renaming the salon 'Rita and Vi's' – 'or d'you want it to be Violet? Vi sounds more catchy, don't you think?'

'Yes, it does. But there's no hurry – it'll cost us a bit doing that, won't it?'

She felt secure with Rita. Name or no name over the door, she was part of the business. Her life had a path now, and she had some say in it.

Walking along the road, past the shops and towards Bloomsbury Road, she felt contented. There was no need to feel ashamed of her house any more – even the front door was now a shiny green, thanks to help from Joe Kaminski. Linda seemed to have decided to take pride in herself – thanks, in some strange way that she didn't really understand, to Rosina – and Carol was well and thriving.

She pulled her scarf tighter round her neck. It really *was* cold. Must be snow on the way. She didn't want to think about Rosina. Not yet. Not that she ever had any falling-out with Rosina, but it had been so long with no contact, no knowing what bitterness or sadness might lie behind her silence. And Linda wasn't telling the whole story, that she was sure of. But she couldn't deal with that now. Not till a few other things were over. Not while she still had Mom to deal with . . .

Bessie would die. Sooner than they thought, by the look of her. She couldn't go on for long, not in that state. But it still seemed impossible that the huge, dominating woman who had ruled all their lives would not just get off her bed one day and take over again.

Violet'd told Marigold she wouldn't be over today, as she had to work on late, but Mari hadn't seemed bothered. She had to hand it to her, Violet thought. She was coping ever so well with Mom and Clarence. They always under-estimated Marigold, she realized – had done all her life.

Her mind ran over what she needed to do. Most days she did this on the way home: Linda should be back soon, Carol would be next door with the Kaminskis, where she went on the days when Violet wouldn't be home by the end of school. Get some tea on – mince tonight, the meat was in the fridge. Fridge! She was going up in the world! They'd get a television soon, she decided. Save up. It'd be nice to have a bit of chat in the house. She'd never thought she'd miss that when the girls were small, keeping on all the time, but it was surprising how quiet and lonely life could seem now. Mrs Smith down the road had hers on all day, even if there was nothing much on, just the test card. It was company, she said. Brightened the place up.

As she approached the house she met Mr Bottoms coming the other way, dressed in his neat little mac. It grieved him to speak to her, she could see, even after all these years. He still had them labelled as a 'problem family' even though they'd come through most of their problems. They didn't even have fights about the animals any more – Snowdrop and the dogs were too long in the tooth to cause any trouble. In any case, Reg's attention had shifted from next door to an anxiety about all the coloureds coming in. Sometimes he talked to her about it over the fence when she was hanging washing out. It wasn't like this before the war, he would say. Didn't she think it was wrong, things changing the way they were?

'They're letting too many in at once. We won't know where we are soon, if we're all mixed up together.'

Even now though, his whole bearing communicated fastidious disdain. As he came closer Violet found herself wondering what it must be like to go to bed with Reg Bottoms (still in his mac?), but the very notion made her want to laugh and she banished it fiercely from her thoughts.

Reg raised his cap with military precision.

'Aft'noon, Mrs Martin.'

'Afternoon, Mr Bottoms.'

No first names, even after all this time, no smile, even though her lips were curved upwards. She thought he was going to go straight past but he swung his arm back towards her house.

'Someone there for you.'

'Oh?' she frowned. 'Ta.'

She could feel there was someone else there, like a second sense, even from a distance. He was sitting, waiting for her, on the front step. She stopped at the gate, without going in, and they stared at each other.

Chapter Eighty-Five

Roy's brown eyes were fixed on her calmly, as if there was simply nothing else he could do but be here at this moment.

'I didn't know I was going to come.' He stood up, slowly. 'I was going home from work and I just had to.' He shrugged.

'How did you –' her throat had gone dry and she had to swallow – 'know where I live?'

'Rachel Miller told me. You know, little Bernice's mother. I've known her a while and she mentioned you.'

Violet walked towards him. Everything felt very strange, with an intensity that made it like a dream.

'No one's here. Not at the moment,' she said. 'You can come in.'

Automatically she led him through to the back, put the lights on, and the kettle, and felt pleased the room was newly painted and tidy.

'Sit down,' she urged him.

Roy sat on the edge of a chair, looking very ill at ease, far more so than the last time they met, as if there were things he had to say and didn't know where to begin, and seeing this calmed her. It wasn't just her then: there were things to say.

'Where's your daughter then? The little one?'

'Next door. My neighbours have her after school. I'll

have to get her soon. There's time for a cuppa first though. They're good to her – she likes it there.'

He looked at her in silence, really looked at her, as if drinking her in.

'How's the family?' she asked.

Roy nodded. 'All right. It's not easy, the wheelchair and that.'

'No. I know. It's a while since we've had that now. You still reading your poems?'

'Yes – well, if there's ever time. Actually, not much really.'

Violet carefully laid the pot and cups on the table, feeling the neatness of her own movements. She knew he was watching her and it gave her a powerful feeling, but she tried to keep herself calm.

Turning, she handed Roy his tea and he looked up into her eyes.

'Vi – she's mine, isn't she?'

They each had a thumb on the saucer.

'Your girl – Carol?'

Shakily she released the saucer and sat down, nodding.

'Yes. She is.'

'Did you know? Before I – before we left, I mean?'

Before Iris suspected anything, before he decided they had to move away, to do the right thing. He had to stick by Iris and the children, and she knew she would have to stick by Harry. She tried not to think of that last evening they had spent together, how she had cried and clung to him, trying to engrave the memory of his body on hers.

'No. I didn't know. And then, after, I didn't know where you were. Didn't think it would help if you knew anyway.'

'But your husband ... He must have guessed, worked it out?'

Violet looked down. For some reason, at the mention of Harry, a blush spread over her cheeks.

'He did. But he was in such a state, see. He said things happen in war, lots of things, and we have to go on and forget about it. It came out sometimes, now and then, and he'd have a go at me. But he was so poorly. He suffered a lot. He was in a Jap POW camp.'

'God ...'

'He was never right after. He passed away, last year.'

She sipped her tea, feeling like crying and trying not to. Roy watched her.

'You've had it bad. I'm so sorry I didn't know – about the baby, I mean.'

'Couldn't be helped. When I realized, I was frightened of course, upset. It's all passed now though, Roy. I'm just so glad to see her walking and happy after all she's gone through, in and out of St Gerard's and all that.'

'Yes, they're marvellous. Philip's going back soon.'

'How's Iris?'

Roy nodded. 'All right. It's not been easy, what with the polio and that, losing John, and then how Philip's been. She just ... well, as I say, it's not been easy.'

There was a silence. Even though they had been talking it was still impossible to say anything very much. Why exactly was he here? Violet wondered. He was still married to Iris, so it was not about her, he had not come back to revive what they had had. The only other reason he could be here, then, was to see Carol.

'Shall I go and get her?'

'Your daughter?'

She stood up. 'Yours, as well.'

'All right, baby?' Eva greeted her. 'Coming in for a drink of tea, or something stronger? She is fine, fine – she is playing cards.'

'Thanks, Eva, but I can't tonight. I've got a visitor and I need to pop back with her.'

'OK then. Carol! Your mother's here!'

Carol liked being at Eva's.

'She's teaching me Polish,' she had told Violet some time ago. 'I asked her. She said, "Why you want to learn Polish? No one speaks Polish except in Poland." But I said I wanted to.'

Violet had taken one look at some written Polish, which seemed to be all consonants and no vowels, and said, 'Oh, my word. I don't think I could do that.'

Eva said Carol had a good ear, and they parted from each other with a kiss and words in Polish.

'See you tomorrow,' Violet said. 'Sorry to rush off.'

'Why didn't you stay?' Carol said crossly. 'You normally do.'

'There's someone at home – an old friend from the war,' Violet said. 'I just wanted you to see him, that's all.'

'Oh,' Carol said, indifferently. 'Mom, when are we going to get a television?'

'When we can afford it.' Violet pushed open the front door.

Roy was standing in the back room and she could see he was nervous.

'Carol, this is Roy – we saw him at the garden party, d'you remember?'

Carol nodded, though she didn't seem very sure.

'I'm going up to my room. Isn't Linda back?'

'No – she'll be in any minute.'

She looked at Roy as Carol's feet were heard on the stairs. They smiled ruefully at each other.

'I s'pose I'd better be off,' he said.

She took him to the door, and as he was leaving he turned, as if about to say something more, then obviously thought the better of it.

'We might see you at one of the other parties,' she said. Then added, 'You can come again, if you want.'

Roy looked at her, and his eyes seemed full of sadness.

'Don't know if I should really. But thanks, anyway.'

Chapter Eighty-Six

Bessie lay drifting in and out of sleep, as she did most days now.

It was not a calm sleep but restless and full of memories. Sometimes they were of happier moments, of her marriage, when she felt light and lifted out of the prison of her body. When these visions faded she came back to the hard pillow under her head – her ears were sore now, chafed from lying there so long – and the burn of the mattress against her lower back. Sometimes when she was awake she lifted her good arm and peered at the hand which rose up in front of her face, wondering whose it was, that puffy thing with its cracked, yellow nails. How had she found her way into this old crone's body? Would someone come along and say a spell and let her out?

Faces came and went, Marigold's mostly. That it should come to this – being looked after by that sly, boozing half-wit! Violet came sometimes and asked questions. Was she all right? How was she feeling? Couldn't the girl see she couldn't answer? No bloody brains – never did have. Even that girl – one of the grandchildren – Linda, was it? Miss Hoity-Toity with her book learning. She'd been once or twice. Must be summat wrong if that lot were making an appearance . . . She would lie stewing in her thoughts until the dreamy, trance-like state came again.

There was one that was a real treat. If only it was like a machine, like one of those televisions and she could choose what to think about, she'd turn that on any time ... 1911, best year of her life. She'd had her job at the HP sauce factory then, one long whiff of vinegar, a big company, regular wages, and that was where she'd met Jack. They'd courted for a year, but it was 'let's get married' from the word go. Both nineteen they were, full of it. Worshipped her, he did, all their marriage – seven years when she was queen in her own house, with a man to feed and bed with and the babbies coming. And that day replayed in her mind. There she was, her hair long then, blue-black as a raven's and her still slender then, but strong as an ox. She was a sturdy mare, Jack said.

'I've had to be, you cheeky bugger,' she'd tell him.

'Well, you're my mare now ...'

She'd walked up to the altar in the prettiest lacy blouse, high collar, and a deep blue skirt. No father to give her away, no Mom. Her older half-sisters had scarpered by then and Mary'd died when she was fifteen. With that wheezing chest she'd never been built to last. There was only Clarence, sixteen and somehow old-mannish even then, to act as family and walk her up the aisle. And Jack stood there to greet her, beaming. This all played through her mind again like a beautiful, haunting piece of music, the spray of orange blossom she was carrying, the lace at her neck and her shoes, the smartest pair she'd ever had, in navy leather, and Jack's adoring smile. And then later, their first night. She'd saved herself for after the wedding. Not that it was her first time with a man ... But those thoughts weren't for this dream, this lovely memory. Shut that out, right out of all memory, back with all the other bad times, the dirt ... And she was back in Jack's arms, her man, her prize, with his lean, strong body and gruff, older-man ways even before he was twenty. He never cared that she couldn't read or write.

'That ain't no use to me,' he once teased her, running his hand along her thick thigh. 'There're other things much more important!'

God, he'd enjoyed her body – he'd revelled in it! He'd come home from work for weeks after they were married so hungry for her he'd let his tea go cold to have her first. And to crown it all, her first pregnancy had yielded two babbies! The midwife spotted it once she got big.

'You've got more than one in there, Bessie, I'd stake my life on it . . .'

'That's 'cause you're so flaming greedy,' she told Jack.

It all played in her mind, all those early days in Joseph Street, the little room with the range, their chairs close to the fire at night, the big brass bed she was lying in now – no, they bought that later on, but never mind. Then the babbies, Charlie and Marigold, twins safely delivered, wasn't she a miracle! Then Violet and Rosina, until there was a family, the house bursting at the seams . . . But of course before Rosina was born, Jack was dead. All those men killed out there in France and he gets Spanish flu. She sat that day she gave birth to Rosina and wept and wept. What a pretty one she was, right from the start, and just like Jack – and he'd never see her. She was no queen any more: her king had gone. All the bliss of the memories seeped away and once again she was back in the lumpy bed. Why did nothing good ever last? Everything was always spoilt. Always. And she was filled with hurt and bitterness, as if she might burst with it.

There was a beam of light in the room, dazzling as

she opened her eyes. Was it summer? Christmas, wasn't it, nearly, and cold? Where was Marigold? She wanted something, a cup of tea ... And then she was gone again, slipping away into a doze.

This time it was different. Not these memories, no, for God's sake no! But there was no way out, as there had been no way out then. She was trapped in her vision of the past ...

The accident happened in 1899, two days after Bessie turned seven.

April, what should have been the last days of the board school term, except that Bessie hardly ever went to school. She was Mom's skivvy. And she knew as soon as she came downstairs that her father hadn't come home again.

'You're not going nowhere!' her mother screamed at her. She was kneeling, sweeping ash out of the range, a grimy nightcap over her fading hair, which was scraped back severely from a face haggard from childbearing and disappointment. Her belly was heavy with the weight of another child, due any day now.

Bessie waited, in her ragged dress. It was brown and too short for her. Mary, her ten-year-old sister, sat hunched forwards on a stool by the door, each breath a wheezing agony.

'I don't know where that bastard is! No tea in the house, no milk, barely a crust.' Her mother reached out for the old coal pail. 'Nothing but a handful of slack and the cellar's scraped bare! You'll have to go and ask Mrs Preston if 'er'll borrow us some again ... And go and get Agnes before she bawls the bloody house down and wakes William.'

Bessie climbed barefoot up the twisting staircase. She was a scrawny child with a wide face and thick black hair. Her mother only ever had eyes for William. At last, after seven girls, six surviving, the longed-for son had arrived.

The stair treads were bare, but so well worn that they were not splintery. The house was one of Birmingham's thousands of back-to-backs, one room downstairs, two up and an attic, and they were on the yard side, down an entry from the front houses on the street. The houses were crushed in round the vast array of factories and workshops, poorly built, no water, little air, over-crowded. If it rained hard they flooded, sometimes right up through the cellar to the ground floor, and water dripped in through the roof and left tide marks all down the walls, and the battle against infestations of bed bugs, roaches and mice was endless.

Agnes, snotty-nosed and hungry, was sitting up in the big, deep drawer in Mom and Dad's room where she slept. She was nearly a year old.

'Oh, shurrup, will you?' Bessie said, hoiking her out. The back of her clothes was all wet, as was the bedding. William, who was three, was still asleep in the double bed which took up most of the room, one tiny hand a fist in front of his face, his hair brown and smooth. Mom's little angel. With Agnes on her hip, Bessie thumped downstairs again.

'Oh, bloody shut up, will you!' their mother snarled at them both from the grate.

The older girls had already left for work. Bessie's mother, Ethel, had been married to a man who'd deserted her, leaving her with three daughters. In desperation she set up house with Thomas Harris, who wasn't her husband at all though she called herself

Harris for the look of it. With Harris she'd had four more daughters, one buried soon after birth, and William. Harris was a carter, a charmer and a boozer who drank away not only any money he managed, intermittently, to earn, but also the factory wages of Ada and Rachel, the two oldest girls by Harry Marston, who were sixteen and fourteen.

Bessie spent most of the day out in the yard, doing as she was told and minding the babbies. That was always her job, looking after everyone else. When Ada and Rachel got in from work they did nothing but boss her around. That was her life, skivvy to Mom, maid of all work to her elder sisters and mother to all the younger ones. There were other children out there, playing around mothers who were taking their turn doing their washing, steam from the heated copper billowing out through the brewhouse door, chats and quarrels over the mangle. By midday the sun got round and shed some warming light into the dank atmosphere, drying out the blue bricks, the washing strung on lines.

Throughout the morning she heard her mom's voice inside, raised in bitter complaint. Ethel, exhausted and heavy with the next child, fell asleep in the afternoon, face pasty white against her black dress. There was still no sign of her 'husband'. Bessie heard the other women's gossip about Mom, how she was 'at the end of her tether' and would soon be 'on the Parish', and their opinion about her father, none of which was complimentary. No family on the yard had more quarrels about where the next meal was coming from.

'No use to anyone that one . . . Er'd be better off on her own . . .'

When the older children came home from school, two of the raggedy lads played with William. Bessie was bored, and relieved to have him taken off her hands. She and some other girls were in a corner, beyond the brewhouse, with a handful of pebbles, playing 'jacks'. They often sat there, out of the way, and it was in the lee of the wall where the stink of the gasworks wasn't so bad.

'We're going down Sheppard's,' two of the boys said to Bessie. 'Willie can come with us.'

'Awright,' Bessie said indifferently. Mom let William go with them to the shop. They might buy him a stick of liquorice to keep him quiet and she was fed up with him. The girls went back to their game. Mary sat near them, very upright against the wall, lips tinged with blue. She was having a bad day, but they were too used to it to feel much pity for her, her rasping breaths as much the background to their game as was the sound of trains, chuffing along, or their brakes shrieking a few streets away.

But then the shouting started. One of the lads came tearing along the entry in his bare feet as if his hair was on fire. His face was smeared with smuts and he looked frightened out of his wits.

'Quick! Quick! It's Willie . . . He's . . .'

'What?' Bessie felt as if her heart was a stone.

'He got on the railway. We daint see 'im, honest! And we daint know where he'd gone. And a train came . . .' The boy, who was eleven years old, began sobbing, his face twisting with distress. 'We never saw it – '

Ethel was beside them, pushing Bessie out of the way.

'What're you saying?' Seizing hold of the boy's scrawny shoulders she screamed into his face. 'What're you saying? Where's William? Where's my boy?'

Bessie knew then that she'd heard it, the moment he meant, when the train screeched to a stop... She already understood that William was dead.

A policeman came to the house and told them they could not bring William's body home. Not possible, he said. They wouldn't want to see. Not the way it was. Neighbours came and went. The girls tried to comfort their mother but she pushed them away.

'You're no good!' she howled. 'I want my boy – my beautiful little boy! You – ' She clawed at Bessie. 'You were s'posed to be looking after him. If it wasn't for you he'd be here in my arms!'

Bessie lay in bed that night with her sisters. Their father had still not come home.

'I want William,' Sarah sobbed. She was only four.

Bessie wanted him too.

Distantly, from the railway, they heard the whistle of a train, like the wail of an unquiet soul, and the panting noise it made building up speed. 'You're no good ...' it chugged out, 'you're no good ...'

Within the week the house was full of the cries of her mother in her labour pains. Bessie's job was to keep the other children out of the way. Their dad was home that evening when Mom at last gave birth to a tiny boy. She announced that she was going to call him Clarence.

Thomas Harris looked at the tiny, screaming form with no emotion.

'Ah well, there yer go – got another lad now, Ethel – tek the place of the other one.'

Ethel glowered up at him. 'Nothing can take William's place.'

Bessie stared at the round, contorted face of Clarence, pressed against the blue-veined pillow of his mother's breast. She felt something untangle in her, a rush of

510

relief that God had sent them another boy instead of William. It felt as if she was being given a second chance. She knew what she had to do now. With all her might she had to look after the babbies, and above all, she had to look after Clarence. Clarence was clean and new. That was what she must do. Then everything would be all right.

By the time she was eleven Bessie was left as mother and mainstay of the family. Thomas Harris was long gone. Ada, her oldest half-sister, was married, and Rachel came and went, didn't care for anything or anyone. Bessie was mother to Sarah, Agnes and Clarence, and to Susan, whom Mom had popped out, spawned by *him*. Arthur Seth Gibbins, his full name. It said so in the paper. One of the neighbours read it out to her after his trial.

'We're well rid of him now, Bessie. He's a madman. They'll lock him up and throw away the key.' He'd cut a woman's throat.

He might as well have cut Mom's throat. Did it for herself in the end, after Susan was born. Mom drank poison and left them all, and Susan only three months old.

It was by the grace of God he committed a murder or he would have been back, doing what he did to her that time. And she was there now, eleven years old, trapped under him on Mom's bed with Susan crying downstairs and his stink and him hurting her. He left her bleeding and she had to take an old blouse of Mom's and put it between her legs, lying curled up on her side, legs clamped together until it stopped. He had a beard with snuff trapped in it and sludgy grey eyes and ever after she never went near a man who wasn't cleanshaven. And while he was doing it to her his eyes were blind but it was her that felt invisible.

She was trying to get out of this vision of the past, but it paraded everything in front of her. Mom, that morning when she found her dead on the bed, body bent back, eyes and mouth open as if she'd had a terrible shock, her skirt rucked up, showing her white legs.

'Mom – Mom!' She had shaken and shaken her and then Clarence had come in. He stared and backed away, down the stairs again. She found him later in the brewhouse, curled up in the corner, his thumb in his mouth, and he was four then.

She woke, whimpering.

The sunlight was gone now and the room felt cool and grey. Her body was so heavy, like a mountain strapped to a bed, gross, impossibly big. She lay full of loathing and anger. Where was that blasted Marigold when you needed her? She couldn't even get up and sit on the po' by herself and she wanted that cup of tea. She wanted to kick and scream, like a helpless child.

It wasn't long before she heard footsteps on the stairs, Marigold's slow, cow-like tread.

Come on, come on, you great fat stupid trollop! Get yourself up here and give me my bloody tea. What's taking you so long?

There was a pause, and she heard Marigold catching her breath at the top of the stairs.

Bessie let out a shout of impatience which emerged only as a slurred groan.

Then Marigold hove into view, her square face appearing over the bedclothes. And no tea! *She hadn't even bothered to bring up the tea!* Was that the hard

512

stuff she could smell on her again – going about stinking like a distillery. *Filthy stinking trollop . . .*

Marigold stood, caught in her mother's glare of loathing. She looked down at her, hands on her broad hips, covered by her pond-green sack of a skirt. Her face was expressionless as it so often was, but there was a hardness in her eyes which even Bessie could see. *God, what's got into her . . . Help! Help me!*

Marigold's eyes narrowed. With a lightning move she snatched the pillow from under Bessie's head, which thumped down on to the mattress. Bessie gasped. What the hell was she playing at?

Marigold hoisted her skirt up with one hand to reveal the thick white thigh above her brown stocking, and half knelt on the bed.

She was holding the pillow up and her face was contorted.

'You think I'm going to keep on looking after you, don't you? Be your little slave for ever? Well, you're wrong. I'm not.'

Suddenly she lashed out and Bessie felt a sharp slap across her cheek. She moaned. The sight of Marigold's face was terrifying now, and she was trapped, trapped as she had been under Arthur Gibbins . . . She tried to move, to escape, but her body wouldn't work for her.

'All those babbies . . . You took in everyone else's babbies, but you wouldn't keep mine, my little Tommy.' She was howling. 'He was *mine*, not yours. *MINE!*'

Another slap, this time across the other cheek. Bessie heard herself mewling.

'You've had your life – and you've had all mine as well. Taken it away, and taken my babby away. And now you ain't going to take away any more . . .'

The pillow came down over her face with the force

513

of Marigold's whole body lying over it and Bessie managed to move her good arm, just for a second, but then there was no air, no breath, just the scream of a train whistle in her head coming closer, and closer, and after, all was dark.

Chapter Eighty-Seven

Linda was never sure, not absolutely, one hundred per cent.

'Can you go to our mom's this afternoon?' Violet had said. 'I need to work late.'

Going into Nana's house, Linda saw Clarence fast asleep by the fire in the back room, his mouth open.

She could hear Marigold upstairs, her voice, shouting, she thought. She'd have to go up, even though she was anything but looking forward to seeing her grandmother. Even in her depleted state there was something forbidding about Bessie.

On the stairs, she heard Marigold's voice again, saying something brief and emphatic, though she couldn't hear the words. As she went into the room she saw, or thought she saw, something. Did she? Was that how it was? Marigold holding Bessie's head up by her hair, as if she had a dog by the tail, and pushing the pillow roughly under her head. Marigold heard her and turned, straightening up, her face blank and guarded. And even after what happened next, Linda would wonder always, whether that was what she had seen in those seconds, or whether it had been a trick of her imagination. And yet she thought she knew, but didn't want to allow herself to know, what Marigold had done with that pillow in the moments before she got there.

Her aunt stood very straight by the bed, looking down, like a maid awaiting orders.

'How is she?' Linda said.

'I dunno.' Marigold seemed a bit stunned. 'Not too good.' There was a pause. 'Gone. I think she's gone.'

'Gone?' She started to feel shaky, like she had the morning she'd seen her dad lying there, dead. 'You mean . . . passed away?'

Linda went to the other side of the bed. She could see Bessie was dead. Her face was quite different. It was a bluish mauve, especially round the lips. She didn't look like herself any more.

She looked at Marigold and their eyes met. Linda remembered for ever what she saw in Marigold's eyes that afternoon. In that stolid, impassive face the eyes glowed, with defiance, and challenge and triumph. Linda met her stare. She thought of everything Rosina had told her. Her heart was beating terribly fast, but she spoke carefully to Marigold.

'Did she have another funny turn?'

Marigold nodded, still staring defiantly. They looked at each other in silent understanding.

Chapter Eighty-Eight

Violet walked through the gate of Witton Cemetery, holding her little bunch of flowers. It was the dead of winter after all, not a time for blooms.

'D'you want to come?' she'd asked Linda and Carol. Both of them shook their heads. They were playing Ludo, stretched out on the floor. Linda smiled up at her.

'I'll stay here with Carol – we could go and see Joyce.'

And Violet had been quite glad. It was the very last week of the year, the quiet, cold time before the new year of 1955 would break upon them. They'd buried Bessie before Christmas, after that final big stroke she'd had.

It was one of those still days when the sun never truly seems to rise. The path was edged with sodden leaves. Violet pulled her scarf further up, shivering as she walked between the rows of gravestones in the smoky light. She passed a middle-aged couple walking arm in arm, leaning into each other.

They had buried Bessie beside Jack, adding her name to the stone: 'BESSIE WILES – 1892–1954, A beloved wife and mother.' Charlie had insisted on organizing things, much to everyone's surprise, though it shouldn't have been surprising as he was the boy and the oldest. He suddenly came into his own.

Violet had brought a jam-jar of water, and put the little offering by the stone.

'Here you are, Mom.' Then as an afterthought added, '. . . Dad.' Not that she could remember Jack, or hardly. She had a dim memory of him being home, him being in bed, and sick, and then he was gone, like a shadow that had fallen on her life for only moments.

But Bessie going: it was going to take a long time to come to terms with that. She didn't feel sad exactly, not that. The state Mom had been in it was a blessing really that it came the way it did. *But I feel like an orphan*, she thought. *I'm lost.* Mom had been this big, dominating, endless presence in her life, inevitable, inescapable, at times cruel and unbearable but also comforting. And now it was like the roof being taken off. There was no counter-weight above her, no one to look up to. She was top of the ladder now, and it felt a lonely place to be. There was Charlie of course, and Marigold, who was still looking after Clarence, but she'd never been close to either of them. Now, more than ever before, she wanted Rosina.

A card had come at Christmas. She knew Linda had written to Rosy after Mom died. Violet felt ashamed that she hadn't written it herself.

'Did you ask her to come?' Violet asked.

'Course I did.'

'Did you say we really want her to be here?'

'*Yes.*'

But come the day of the funeral, there was no sign of Rosina. In the card she sent, she had scrawled – she always had bad writing, Violet remembered –

Dear Vi – sorry, sorry, sorry I flunked it again. I want to come and I thought of you all and said a prayer on the day. Thought I could do it but when

it came I couldn't face it there with everyone. I will come, quietly and just see you one day. Promise.
Rosina. xx
    PS Your Linda's a lovely girl.

'What's she doing down there?' she asked Linda. 'What's she so bothered about, coming back and everything? Anyone'd think she'd done a murder or something.'

But Linda just shrugged. (Why did she shrug all the time like that?) 'She'll have to tell you herself.'

'Well, she always was one to turn on the drama.'

But Violet kept thinking about her, and wondering.

Standing by the grave, she felt as if there was something else she was supposed to do. Were there some set words she should say? If so she didn't know what they were. No one had ever taught her anything like that. It seemed odd seeing Bessie's grave. It levelled her down to the same size as anyone else and seemed to have nothing to do with the mother she had known. She tidied the little jar of flowers and turned to leave, in the darkening afternoon.

Couldn't be bleaker if it tried, she thought, shivering. There seemed to be no one else around at all now, and she started to feel a bit uneasy. Why should the place give her the creeps? But it did, a bit.

Then she saw there was someone else up ahead, coming towards her, and felt somehow relieved. She squinted. Her heart began to beat harder. She was seeing things, surely?

The tall, thin figure came towards her. Even at that distance she could tell, somehow, that he was fixed on her, rather than anything else that was here. He had not come to tend a grave, he had come to find her.

'Hello,' she said, once he was near enough. She was surprised how calm and matter of fact she sounded. After all, she was used to pushing her feelings away. She mustn't let them surface, mustn't expect anything.

Roy smiled, nervously. 'The girls told me you'd come over here.'

'My girls?'

'I called at the house. I just ... Look, it's freezing out here. Let's walk a bit. They're not locking up quite yet.'

They turned back, along the main path of the cemetery, side by side, not touching. There was a silence which felt so full of feeling that Violet felt she must break it in case she was imagining it. She knew her feelings for him had not changed, that if she allowed herself to think about him and how they were together she was filled with such longing that it made her physically ache. But he was a married man ... She mustn't allow herself any thoughts like that. So, abruptly, she said, 'Why did you come to find me?'

Roy had his hands in his pockets. He gave a deep sigh.

'Seeing you again, seeing her – Carol, I mean ... I haven't been able to stop thinking about it, about you.'

She waited, watching her feet in their little black court shoes take one step after another, as he struggled to reach what he wanted to say. After a moment he stopped and turned to her.

'There's no point in me saying anything unless I say this.' Seeing her raise her eyes to look at him, and knowing that she could not hide the hunger in them for what he might say, he seemed encouraged. 'I've tried to do the right thing and got it wrong all the way along the line. I felt I had to stay with Iris ... Life doesn't come easy for her. She's never been a very happy person. What I know now is that she never will be, whatever happens. And you were married then. It was a mess, I know. But if I'd known about the baby ... I can't even say how it felt seeing you again. It was like ... I don't know, like the sun coming out or something. So's I didn't know how I've got through these years and not been with you.'

'Roy ... Oh God, don't ...' As he spoke tears began to roll down her cheeks.

'I've got to, Vi.'

'D'you mean it? I can't believe this – that you're here, saying this to me ...'

'I had to come this afternoon. I don't know why. It was as if—' He reached out and put his hands on her shoulders. 'I've thought and thought and tried to hold back, tried to think I could stay with Iris, when all I want is to be with you. I thought if I waited long enough and did the right thing all that would fade. But there's never been anyone like you, not for me. I can't feel for anyone else the way I feel for you. And I've just made such a mess of it all ...'

'No, you haven't. I mean, it was just the way it was, back then. And Harry was so poorly ... If he'd come back and been all right it might have been different. But you'd gone by then anyway, and you were with Iris.'

He looked longingly down into her face.

'Poor Iris,' he said. 'It's been bad for her. I mean, I let her down first of all. And then the polio. She's convinced it was a punishment, a sort of curse – on me, I suppose. Sometimes I've felt it myself. And John died of it so quickly, within a few days. It was like being struck by lightning. We thought Philip would die as well, after that. It was terrible to watch – well, I don't need to tell you. And then the iron lung and everything . . .'

'I thought it was a punishment too, when Carol got it. I remember looking down at her in that thing and thinking, if only I hadn't felt anything for you, if I hadn't found out what it meant to feel that much for someone . . . Maybe we're not meant to feel so much? Maybe it pushes everything out of balance or something. As though, if there's too much love and happiness, something bad has to happen to make up for it.'

'It can't really be like that, can it? Don't you think we've had enough of the bad already, anyway? Vi, I love you. For what's left of our lives, after all this, I want to spend it with you – if you want it too.'

His sensitive face was full of earnestness. She reached up and gently stroked his cheek.

'But what about Iris?'

'Iris isn't happy with me. Ever since the polio, she's turned against me. She's like a closed book. We hardly speak to each other, but we've just kept on, for the boys. And because that was what we had to do. And I could manage it, going to work, looking after Philip, not thinking or feeling anything else or that anything might be better. And then I saw you again. And I couldn't go on like that. Not any more. If you still feel anything for me . . . I couldn't tell if you did, that was the worst of it . . .'

He stroked his thumbs across her cheeks, wiping away her tears.

'Do you?'

She nodded, half laughing, though the tears were still coming. 'Yes. Oh God, Roy, I can hardly believe this! Are you really here?'

'I'm here all right.' He took her in his arms and she

rested her cheek against his chest. 'I'm here, my love, and I never want to be anywhere else.'

She breathed him in, the loved, familiar smell of him, stroking his back. 'Oh, I remember you. I remember every inch of you.'

She pulled back to look into his eyes and he lowered his head, his lips searching for hers, and she knew she had found again what she needed.

They walked in the cemetery until it closed, arms round each other, talking, catching up on each other's lives, kissing, holding each other, not even aware any more of the cold and wind.

'I feel terrible about Iris,' she said as they went out through the gate.

'I'll see Iris all right, of course I will,' he told her. 'But she doesn't want me, not really. Sometimes I think she hates me. I've made her unhappy all the way along – well, me and the way things have gone with the kiddies.'

'Are you going home now?'

'I'd better. When can I see you?'

'As soon as you can.' She hugged him, squeezing him tight. 'Don't go away again for long, will you?'

He began to walk away, but strode back to kiss her again. 'I don't want to go. Don't want to leave you.'

She was laughing now, her heart lighter than it had been in years. 'Go on – don't worry, my love. I'll be waiting. I've waited this long, haven't I?'

Part Seven

1960

Chapter Eighty-Nine

They stood on the deck of the huge liner, all four of them in a line, waving to their wellwishers, who all looked so small down there on the quay. Linda couldn't see the exact expressions on Violet and Roy's faces but they had their arms round each other, like a little island together.

They'll be all right, she thought, blowing them yet another kiss. She knew now all the story about their love for one another, and about Carol. It brought tears to her eyes thinking about it, and about her own dad and how things had been. Mom was happy now, happier than she'd ever seen her. No Carol down there to see them off, of course: she wasn't allowed out. But the few times she'd visited her sister, she'd seen the joyful light in her eyes and knew she was in the right place for her. When they'd first told Rosina that Carol was going into the convent, she'd thought she'd be horrified. But instead, Rosina looked quite wistful.

'Wish I'd been like that,' she said. 'Done something with my life that was straight and pure.'

The ship let out a long, sonorous hoot.

'We're moving – my God, we're off!' Rosina cried. 'I can't believe we're really going! Oh, at last – I can't keep this up! I shan't have any tears left!'

As they finally pulled away from the dock a silence fell over them all. Their light coats were pulled round them in the strong breeze, eyes narrowed against the glare, a row of hopefuls in a long line of emigrants leaving Liverpool bound for the far side of the world – for Australia.

Bye, Mom, Roy . . . Linda said in her head. It was too far to shout now. *I'll give your love to Muriel and Dickie, soon as I see them.*

She glanced along at the others. Rosina, beside her, hair taken up in a neat French pleat, despite her protests, still had tears running down her cheeks. Irene, dry-eyed, was still bright blonde, but instead of the ponytail her hair was blowing back in waves from her face as she leaned over, shielding the flame to light up a cigarette. She'd been waving to her brother and to her son Kevin and his wife, who'd come to see her off, but now they had moved too far away. And next in line was Linda's cousin Vivianne, a wholesome, peachy-faced nineteen-year-old, her mop of honey-coloured curls blown all over the place, cheeks pink from the wind. She was staring into the distance at the fading coastline and the cranes and gantries of the dock with her dreamy blue eyes.

'She's so like Hump was,' Rosina always said. She was plump, pretty and half the time seemed in a beautiful dream. But Vivianne was going to be the most crucial part of the business.

'They may not have taught her much at that posh school I forked out for,' Rosina sometimes said. 'But they didn't half teach her to sew.'

Vivianne seemed able to master anything that involved shaping and sewing fabrics and Rosina also had a natural flair for clothes. She'd had to pick up her sewing skills from her daughter though! With Linda's commercial head and training and Irene's shrewd ways with money and people, they were going to make this embryo business of theirs work when they got to Sydney all right! *Glad-Rags*, they called themselves. After years Linda had spent learning the ropes, slogging away in other people's firms, they were going to make it happen for themselves. Be their own bosses. Rosina's ambition was to make costumes for the stage as well.

'They have theatres in Sydney, don't they? We could do that, I know we could. Us girls together – we can do anything!'

Linda breathed in the sea air and gave a final, symbolic wave, as she could no longer see them, to Violet and Roy, to her old home.

Irene stubbed out her cigarette under her heel and threw it over the side.

'Ooh, I hate goodbyes. I know we'll see them all before too long but it's bloody awful, isn't it? Thank God that's all over. Let's go in and get a coffee, eh?'

Once the voyage was under way, the day sunny and calm, the ship fell into a slow, rolling rhythm. That first day seemed to last for ever, as they'd embarked early.

Late in the afternoon they were all sitting in one of the lounges, out of the tiring wind on deck, drinking cups of tea. Irene, already feeling queasy, was dozing. Vivianne was reading *Harper's*, paying careful attention to all the dress designs.

Linda got her book out, a love story she had saved for the voyage, but it lay unopened on her lap. Her head was too full of real life to escape into a story! She could tell that Rosina, sitting opposite her, was restless as well. She smoked one cigarette after another.

'What're you thinking about?' Linda asked.

Rosina smiled. 'Just having to pinch myself. I was

thinking about you, love, to tell you the truth. I mean look at you – twenty-two and gorgeous, with it all in front of you. You look fantastic, Lin.'

Linda blushed. 'Well – ta! So do you.'

She had dressed up a bit to begin the journey – it was a special occasion, after all! She had a red and white scarf over her hair to keep the wind from blowing it wild, and round white clip-on earrings with little tan dots on that reminded her of toadstools in a fairy story. Her dress was white with a full skirt and big red spots – she'd watched Vivianne make it for her – and red shoes. All in all it looked very striking with her dark colouring and a splash of red lipstick. Rosina's outfit was similar – in shades of emerald green and navy.

'I mean it, though,' Rosina said. 'You've come out like a flower and it's lovely to see. I was just thinking about that scruffy little kid who came to find me in Soho!'

Linda smiled fondly. 'Seems like a lifetime ago now – but thank God I did!'

Rosina looked serious. 'Yes – things were at their worst with Richie then. I'm surprised you caught me on a day when I didn't have a shiner on one eye or the other. I was in control back then – but only just. Irene kept trying to get me to see sense. I can't pick men, you know that.'

'Your blind spot.'

Rosina put her head on one side. 'You can talk.'

'I know – I'm keeping right away from blokes for the moment. It's only seeing Mom and Roy gives me some hope. And Joyce and Danny – I s'pose they're OK.'

Over the past few years she'd had a number of brief, unhappy affairs. She always seemed to go for men who told her how much they needed her and then fell into possessive depressions and wouldn't let her go. But she did go. Although they were bad experiences at the time, none of them had touched her anything like as deeply as Alan had. It was as if he had scorched her capacity to love into something charred and shrivelled.

Four months after she'd left him, when she was still working at Wimbush's and going to night school, Mrs Richards greeted her with tragic eyes when she came into work.

'I've got terrible news, Linda. That Alan Bray – *your* Alan – he's in hospital. Tried to, you know, finish himself. He took a whole lot of pills . . .'

Linda always felt as if Mrs Richards was reproaching her over Alan, as if everything that happened to him was her fault for leaving him. What did she think was the right thing to do? Stay with him and be dragged down into hell as well?

Alan lived, and recovered, she heard, from a distance. She only saw him once more, years later, in 1958 in a pub. By then the Beat craze had reached Birmingham properly and there were groups of teenagers of varying degrees of education 'dropping out' or putting on a dropping-out pose, wearing the jeans and sloppy clothes she and Alan had worn early on, disapproved of by their parents, reading poems by Allen Ginsberg and dreaming of taking off on the road like Jack Kerouac. She and Alan had been Beats before Beats really arrived, she saw. They'd wanted out of their families, wanted to be different, to talk philosophy, tear down what they saw around them. *Howl* was the Beats' favoured Allen Ginsberg book. Yes – that was it. They'd both felt like howling against all that was in their lives. Thing was – she didn't any more, not by the time she saw him again. There was Alan, in the pub with a group of them, no

531

one she recognized, and she hoped he'd found somewhere to be at home. He didn't see her, or pretended not to. But by then she was working for a big firm, had started to take more pride in herself.

Rosina knew the full story of Alan, as Linda knew her aunt's history, a pattern she now wanted to 'clean up', as she put it. They'd become very close over the years. Linda had finally got her to come home to the family.

She didn't make it to Bessie's funeral, but within two months Clarence went to bed one night and never woke up.

'I s'pose Mom was his life-blood,' Violet said. 'Poor old Clarence. She was like a mom and a wife to him all in one.'

Rosina had always been fond of Clarence as a child. She'd been able to get round him with her charms. And by then she had gained courage. She arrived the day before the funeral and Linda and Violet went to meet her at the station.

'I know it's ridiculous, but I'm shaking,' Violet said as they waited on the platform. 'I mean, she's only my little sister!'

Of course it was Linda who recognized Rosina and Vivianne. She'd been down to see them all several times by then. Clark was already away training for his pilot's licence. Rosina looked terrified, though she was dressed up to the nines, hat and all, with a brim that dipped down half covering her face.

'Come on –' Linda took her arm. 'Mom's more scared than you are.'

She watched the two sisters look each other up and down under the dim station lights. And then the tears came, and they were in each other's arms.

Chapter Ninety

She hadn't packed the album in her suitcase, because she wanted to keep it close to her.

That night, in the cabin, she sat on her berth and looked through it. Irene was already asleep in the other bed. She was not enjoying the voyage.

They'd bought the Brownie camera for the wedding, to have more photographs than the few professional ones. Linda had made sure of getting pictures of everyone, and arranged them, square white-edged images, carefully on black sugar-paper pages. Though she had not known, back in 1957, that she would be moving so far away, now the album was something very precious.

The main wedding picture was in pride of place on the first page.

'I'm not going to wear white or any of that carry-on,' Violet said. 'It's not right, not with how things are – and at my age!'

She wore a neat little suit in a soft cornflower blue, and in that picture, as she stood with her arm linked with Roy's, their smiles echoed each other's. Linda didn't think she'd ever seen two people look happier. There was such joy there, in her mother's eyes, in Roy's gentle smile. They'd been through such a lot to get there, what with waiting for Roy's divorce as well. Love hard won, Linda thought. Maybe that was the answer: you had to wait for it, long and slow.

Deep in her memory somewhere, like an old forgotten dream, she thought she did remember Roy. There was something familiar about him. When she found out that Carol was his, was only her half-sister, everything fell into place. It made sense of how Dad had been with her, how their mom had somehow withheld her affection, as if out of fear of how obvious it would be that she was favouring the child of the man she truly loved.

She and Mom got on so much better now anyway – understood each other better.

'I should never've let your nana talk me into taking you out of that school,' Violet said to her one day. 'I'm sorry, love. I was in such a state at the time, in a panic. I had no idea how much it meant to you.'

Linda turned the pages of the album, smiling. Pictures of herself and Rosina, of Clark and Vivianne. Clarkie was a handsome devil all right, though surprisingly shy. There were Charlie and Gladys, Gladys's mouth open in the picture, no doubt nagging as usual. And Joyce and Danny and the kids, three little faces all dark-haired and like Danny! They'd stopped at three – so far as Joyce was concerned anyway. Two boys and a girl.

'Danny'd have a whole nestful if I let him,' she said. 'But I've had quite enough of it, stuck here in the house all the flaming time.'

As soon as Charlie was at school, to the consternation of her friends she found someone to look after the children and went back to Bird's, on the Dream Topping. The firm were building a new site near Banbury, and Joyce and Danny were full of the idea of going, if they could. They could get a nicer house and Danny could have his own business, not just work with his dad. They were going up in the world, Joyce said.

Those kids'll be grown by the time I see them again, Linda thought, looking at Joyce's little brood. And she felt a pang of regret.

But turning the page again, a grin spread across her face. There was Marigold, her swarthy face beaming out from under the brim of a huge pink hat, and swathed in an equally huge pink dress. Marigold was having a whale of a time.

Now both Bessie and Clarence were gone, she had the house in Spring Street all to herself. She'd gone and got herself a job in one of the new launderettes that were opening up, paying her own rent and free to do as she pleased. She'd bought a little gramophone and some records. And what's more, she had Freddie nicely under her thumb. They went out and about together, to the pubs and clubs, the races or a show now and then. Freddie bet on the horses, winning quite regularly. Once he took them down to Rhyl with his winnings. They were, to all intents and purposes, a couple. Except, Marigold adamantly declared, 'I ain't marrying him and he ain't moving in here. I've had enough of all that carry-on, fetching and carrying for everyone else. He can keep his slippers in his own house.'

'Good for you, girl,' Linda said to the picture. These days the thought of Marigold made her feel very cheerful.

Carol had been at the wedding, of course. It was before she went into the convent. In fact she hadn't mentioned it to anyone by then. Linda realized it had always been on her mind though, beckoning. Her sweet, pretty face smiled out of the photo. The resemblance to Roy was so strong, seemed so very obvious, now they knew. It had been a hell of a shock to Carol, of course, when she first heard. It took time to come to terms with it and both of them had to work hard to get to know one another. And there was Roy's Philip, of course, who came sometimes. His operation had not been so successful as hers, and she was able to relate to him better than anyone because of having polio in common.

She entered the Selly Park Convent as soon as she was sixteen, to 'try her vocation' as the sisters called it. To her joy, soon after she arrived, Sister Cathleen was appointed Novice Mistress. Carol explained to them that for six months she would be there as a postulant, to try it out and see if the life was really for her. Then there would be a year in the novitiate before her first temporary vows. Perpetual vows came after five years.

It was then that Roy became her advocate. Violet was completely horrified by the whole thing. She cursed Sister Cathleen high and low, saying she had always wanted to get her claws into Carol and the Selly Park Convent was a horrible creepy place and Carol might as well be walling herself up in her own tomb. Roy talked her round.

'It's what she really wants, love. You can see it in her. No one's forcing her, are they?'

'But it seems such a terrible waste,' Violet sobbed. 'My little girl in one of those dark, dreary places, praying all day or whatever they do. And she's so pretty!'

'Are you really sure about this, sis?' Linda asked her the night before she left. They sat side by side on her bed. Carol reached out and squeezed her hand.

'I've been sure for ages. I just know it's where I'm supposed to be. I think God chose me, what with the polio and everything. He gives us all something we're supposed to do. That's why I can walk again.'

She wanted to be a nurse and work at St Gerard's.

Nearly a year ago, they'd been to her clothing ceremony after she'd been in the convent for six months. The nine novices of that year all filed into the high Gothic chapel dressed in white, as brides. That set Violet off before they'd even started. Some of the other mothers were crying too, seeing their girls all with their heads bowed in the white veils.

'You were given me as a surprise,' Carol had said to her, trying to offer comfort. 'Now you're offering me back.'

Midway through the ceremony they all filed out again and returned dressed in their black novices' habits, Sister Cathleen walking behind them. It would have been hard not to be affected by the solemnity of it all, and Linda found tears running down her cheeks as well. But at the celebration tea afterwards, Carol looked radiant. You could tell she knew she was in the right place.

Linda closed the album and lay back on the narrow bed with the book clasped to her chest. So the great adventure was beginning! It wasn't all uncertain – Muriel and Dickie would be there to greet them in Sydney. That was almost like finding another mom and dad.

Violet had told her that Harry had dreamed of going to Australia when he was young, but of course he'd never made it. The thought of her father's life, his broken dreams and shattered health, made her feel very sad.

I'm going for you, Dad, as well as for myself, she told him in her thoughts. *We're going to make it work, Rosina and me.*

Lulled by the motion of the ship, she fell asleep, holding the images of her family in her arms as they sailed the ocean to their new world, and a future of lives and loves of which she could now only dream.

Miss Purdy's Class

For Rose

Acknowledgements

Thanks are due to the South Wales Miners' Library, Swansea, the Labour History Archive and the Peoples' Museum, both in Manchester, to the Big Pit at Blaen-afon, to Tonypandy Library, Birmingham Central Library and Castle Vale Readers' Group, Birmingham.

To written resources – most especially Lewis Jones (d. 1939, RIP), to Hywel Francis, and to Peter D. Drake for his thesis on the Birmingham Labour Movement and the Spanish Civil War (1977).

To people – especially Alannah Darcy at Castle Vale Library, Sheila Ward, Jane and Lewis Jones for impromptu lessons in Birmingham's social history and to Susan Langford-Johnson for her hospitality in Wales.

Author's Note

The 'Federation' and the 'Movement' referred to in the text are the South Wales Miners' Federation and the National Unemployed Workers' Movement respectively.

Boxing Day, 1935

The bottle smashed through the window and shattered on the blue bricks of the yard.

'You filthy stinking whore!'

His father flung the door open so that the children's screams echoed round the yard. He lurched outside. Joey stood dry-eyed, paralysed in the one downstairs room.

There had been plenty of fights. He knew it was different this time.

'I'm not stopping 'ere one bleeding minute more!' Wally Phillips stood out in the yard, yelling back at the house. He was a thin, stooped man. 'I've had all a man can take. Four bleedin' whelps to feed and clothe, and that brat in your belly ain't even mine! I've put up with your boozing and your carrying on . . . I ain't slaving myself to the bone for you no more . . .' He stumbled backwards and cursed, just managing to regain his balance. 'You're in here with your legs spread for any tomcat who calls at the door . . . You're filth, Dora – there's no helping you.'

The children's crying did not abate. Joey froze somewhere deep inside. His father was circling the yard.

'That's right!' Wally yelled. 'You all listening, all of you? Call yourselves neighbours? What've you ever done for us, eh? Couldn't stop my wife being a fuckin' whore, could you? Lying here pouring my wages down her throat ... What did I do, eh? Loved 'er, I did. In the beginning ...' He lowered his voice. 'Christ, I did.'

For a moment he stood swaying, then he raised his fist and punched at the air so hard he almost fell over. He turned to go.

'Dad!' Joey fought to unlock his muscles. He ran outside, seeing his father striding towards the entry bare-headed, shoulders sagging in his threadbare coat. The boy tore after him.

'Dad – don't!' A great sob forced up inside him, as though his chest was ripping apart.

Wally pushed him off with the force of a drowning man. 'Don't, son. I can't. Just can't. Look after your mother, Joey. You'll have to be a man now. I can't live with it no more.'

Joey reeled back, clutching at the sill, his boots crunching on the broken glass. 'Dad!' It was a weak, childish cry now, of despair.

Through the broken window came the screaming of his brother and sisters, and his mother's coughing, on and on, from where she crouched on the bed they'd moved downstairs for her. She was in her twenties, her pale hair unkempt and straggling round her face. She coughed into scraps of rag which came away streaked with blood. Joey didn't turn to look at her or his howling brother and sisters. He had eyes only for the dark figure hurrying away from them down the entry. A moment later, his father turned the corner and was gone.

'You'll never make a wife if you carry on like this before you've even reached the altar!'

Her mother's bitter words propelled Gwen upstairs to the landing, where she stood in the darkness, hands clutching at fistfuls of her festive red skirt, her eyes squeezed shut. She could hardly believe herself! She had done the one thing the Purdy family never, ever did: she had made a scene. How had her inner feelings suddenly popped out like that in front of everyone? Their faces – how awful! Yet she could feel laughter threatening to erupt too. She'd *enjoyed* shocking them!

'However am I going to tell Edwin's parents? You're abandoning him on the eve of your wedding – heaven knows what the shock might do to an invalid like his mother!'

This was too much for Gwen. She stormed back to the top of the stairs.

'What are you *talking* about, Mummy? You're being completely ridiculous – I'm not getting married for eight months! I've taken the job for two terms, that's all. Until the end of the summer and then I'm coming home to marry Edwin. If it's too ghastly I can always throw in the towel. Whatever is the matter with that?'

'But *Birmingham*, darling!' Gwen's mother stood beneath the streamers criss-crossing the hall. Though colourful, they sagged joylessly. 'Gwen, what has come over you? You've taken this job without a by your leave and the school sounds...' Ruth Purdy gave a shudder, '... well, an absolute *disgrace*. There's no telling what kind of rough people you'll be dealing with! And there'll be no time to plan the wedding properly. You're being very selfish. You are my only daughter...' Her mother's voice was wheedling now. 'Your father thinks it's quite appalling.'

'Does he? Since when has Daddy ever cared what I do?' When she had made her announcement, carefully leaving it until after Christmas Day, her father had sat in the corner with his newspaper, opting out of family life as usual. His was the only unscandalized face apart from the baby's.

'Of course he cares.' Her mother lowered her voice to hiss up at Gwen. 'Don't be so ridiculous.'

Gwen clenched her fists so that her nails dug into her palms. 'Mummy, Daddy wouldn't notice if I did the dance of the seven veils in the middle of the parlour.'

'Don't be vulgar . . .'

But Gwen could not contain herself. She could not keep the bitterness from her voice. 'He's only ever wanted the boys! In fact, let's face it, he wanted Johnny to hand the pharmacy on to. Poor old Crispin hardly gets a look in either! All Daddy requires from me is that I keep out of his way and toe the line. Mummy – I am going to do this job in Birmingham. It's not for long, and whether Edwin likes it or not is not the point. I'm not a vicar's wife yet. I shall have the rest of my life to fall in with Edwin's plans. And we *shall* sort out the wedding, but it doesn't take eight months' continuous labour. I'm sorry, I've made up my mind. You're not going to change it.'

Ruth Purdy pushed her hands down into the pockets of her long cardigan in extreme agitation. She was a thin, faded version of her curvaceous daughter and was always terrified of what other people would think. And until now her daughter had been the sweet, biddable teacher at the local school of whom everyone thought so highly.

'You're a complete fool, is all I can say. You've caught a good man with a respectable profession, you're teaching at one of the best schools in Worcester and now you want to go and live in a slum!' She seemed ready to explode with anger.

'Well, maybe I'm just what they need,' Gwen retorted. 'I don't expect they get many good teachers there. I'll be able to teach them all a thing or two!'

'Oh really, there's no talking to you.' Ruth began to walk away. 'You'll live to regret it – and don't be surprised if Edwin doesn't think again about who he's marrying. He's not going to want a wife who just takes off without any warning. He's quite a catch, don't forget. There are plenty of others who'd jump at him, and it'd serve you right!' She stalked back to the sitting room, closing the door hard.

Gwen put her hands over her face, opened her mouth and let out a silent scream which came out as a prolonged hiss of breath. She sank down on the top step.

Whatever happens, she vowed, *I'm going. She's not going to stop me.*

They'd all be there by the fire – her mother, two brothers and Johnny's wife, Isabel. They had little James, and already another on the way. And now she'd broken her news they'd all be discussing her in that sober, let's not really say what we're thinking, oh-dear-what-a-shame sort of way, pretending that her mother's cry of horror and her outburst at Gwen had not really happened, like a bad smell in the room which everyone would ignore out of politeness. Especially her sister-in-law, 'dutiful, beautiful Isabel', as Gwen secretly called her. She was dark-haired and endlessly serene like the Mona Lisa and she was another reason Gwen wanted to scream.

Gwen crept into her room and sat on the bed looking out at the apple tree. On the bedside table was a small picture in a frame. She picked it up, smiling ruefully. She really ought to have a picture of Edwin by her bed, with his thick blond hair combed back and his ever-optimistic smile. Edwin looked almost permanently like someone who'd just enjoyed a good cricket match. Instead she was looking at a picture of Amy Johnson, her heroine. She thought Amelia Earhart was wonderful too, though her being American made her seem more distant. Amy was her favourite. Gwen had clippings about all her famous flights: to Australia in her Gypsy Moth in 1930, then later to Japan, Cape Town, the USA. This was her favourite picture. It showed Amy in her flying helmet, goggles perched on her forehead, wearing a leather flying jacket, the high astrakhan collar turned up round her chin. Her strong face looked out from the picture, up towards the sky, as if she was seeing all the places she would soar away to. Gwen stared longingly. How must it feel to fly a plane by yourself? To climb into the cockpit and take off, away from everyone, knowing your life was in your hands alone?

She put the picture down and sighed. Lately she had felt so odd, thoughts and impulses bubbling up in her that she'd never known before. And the way she'd spoken to Mummy! Gwen wasn't used to disapproval. She'd always tried to be good. She thought of Edwin: tall, good-looking Edwin, who was always so sure he knew right from wrong.

My fiancé, she thought. Dear old Edwin, so good and solid. Her rescuer. She just needed to get this great restlessness out of her system, then she could settle down and marry him.

She sat staring out of the window as the winter sky darkened smokily outside.

SPRING TERM

1936

One

'Miss Purdy!'

Knuckles rapped hard on the door. 'I don't seem to see you downstairs. I did say breakfast would be at seven forty-five sharp!'

Gwen sat up, heart pounding. Where on earth was she? She took in the dressing table next to her bed, the colourless light filtering in between the curtains. Heavens, the new job! Birmingham! And that voice was her chain-smoking landlady's. She was out of bed and peeling off her nightdress all in one move.

'Coming! I'm coming, really I am!'

'Mr Purvis and I are waiting,' the voice complained. 'And your kipper's spoiling.'

Mrs Black's tread departed mincingly – Gwen knew it was mincingly because it was the only way she could walk in those heels.

Gwen pulled her clothes on: brassière, camisole – a squeeze to pull it over her generous breasts – stockings, cursing as a splinter from the bare boards snagged into the ball of her foot. Normally she liked dressing: she enjoyed bright colours, hair ribbons, scarves, but there was no time now. Washing herself would have to wait too.

'Oh, damn you, you wretched things!' She pulled savagely at her suspenders with trembling fingers. How could she have overslept when she'd spent the night wide-eyed as an owl, staring at those limp curtains which didn't quite meet in the middle? The last thing she could remember was hearing a tram rumble past outside and dimly, as she faded into sleep, a rising groan of sound which Mrs Black had told her she'd have to get used to when several went off at once the afternoon before. They were the factory 'bulls', the sirens indicating the beginning or end of a shift. She must have fallen into a deep sleep only minutes before it was time to get up. What a dreadful start to her first day!

She pushed her feet into her shoes without unfastening the straps, hastily coiled her thick hair up at the back, skewering it into place with a hairslide and tore out of her room along the brown lino of the landing and down the sludge-coloured runner of stair carpet. Dear God, this house was awful! But it was an adventure, she told herself, and adventure was what she needed.

'Do I hear you coming, Miss Purdy?' Mrs Black's plaintive voice came to her. 'Your kipper's almost on its last legs.'

Meals, Mrs Black had informed her the evening before, were to be taken in the back room, a fussy place crammed full of pictures and ornaments. A row of dolls with china heads and big sad eyes sat along the dresser. They had sat together, a most meagre fire struggling for life in the grate, for a meal of Welsh rarebit edged with crinkly slices of pickled beetroot, topped off with cherry Madeira cake and a cup of tea. Gwen's fellow lodger, a Mr Harold Purvis, had only arrived two days earlier himself, to take up work in the accounts department of a local machine-tool firm.

'So nice,' their landlady had said fawningly as she introduced them, 'to begin the new year with new faces in the house.' She gave a sigh. 'I'm reduced to lodgers since I lost my George.'

Mr Purvis blushed and murmured a greeting. He was well into his thirties, with a doleful face and a bald pate, around which clung a ring of black, neatly trimmed and rather oily hair.

The Welsh rarebit had had a strangely lumpy consistency which made Gwen grateful for the sharp vinegar in the beetroot.

'It's hard to go wrong with pickles, isn't it?' Mr Purvis remarked gloomily. He was evidently cursed with adenoids.

Gwen smiled and agreed, thinking: *Oh my goodness, are we going to have to sit here making polite conversation every night?* They had asked one another a few questions – yes, he was new to the area, had moved across from Oldbury. Oh, she was a teacher, was she? That was nice. From Worcester? Gracious. Bit different here, eh?

Mrs Black's voice sounded as if she gargled with tin tacks. All the time they were eating, she raided her packet of Player's for one cigarette after another and the air had a blue tinge. She kept calling Mr Purvis 'Harold'.

'Harold is a musical man, he tells me,' she informed Gwen. 'He plays the trumpet. I hope you don't mind me calling you Harold?' She told them her own name was Ariadne.

'I like people to know.' She held a little piece of cherry Madeira between her stubby finger and thumb, little finger crooked. 'The name Black is so very ordinary, isn't it? I like to feel my Christian name is something rather *out of the way.*'

'It's certainly that,' Gwen agreed.

'Latin, isn't it?' Mr Purvis ventured, wiping his chin. 'Wasn't she the er ... lady with the hair made of snakes?'

'Oh, aren't you *clever*?' Mrs Black cried, leaning towards him.

Gwen, from reading books of myths to school-children, knew perfectly well that Ariadne was the one who helped Theseus escape from the Minotaur in the Cretan labyrinth using a ball of string, but this didn't seem the moment to mention the fact. She eyed Ariadne Black, trying to decide how old she was. Anywhere, she decided, between forty-five and sixty. Mrs Black favoured floaty, diaphanous clothes and wore her hair shingled and shaded a gingery blonde that could only come out of a bottle. She looked, Gwen decided, as if she'd just stepped off the stage of a variety perform-ance. And her affected Brummy accent made Gwen want to giggle.

This morning, as Gwen dashed in, mouthing apolo-gies, she found Mrs Black standing behind Mr Purvis's chair, slightly to the side of it, one hand resting on the back almost as if she was expecting someone to come and paint a portrait of the pair of them. Her eyebrows were brown lines pencilled in at an enquiring angle and even this early in the morning she had applied a ful-some coating of scarlet lipstick.

'Oh!' she cried. 'At last! Mr Purvis has been *ever* so patient, haven't you?' She leaned down and patted his arm before taking her seat.

Harold Purvis said, 'Good morning,' and stared so hard at Gwen's chest that she felt compelled to glance down and check whether the buttons of her dress had come undone. She hurried to her seat, bracing herself for the food.

12

They sat in morning light strained through net curtains. The one window faced over the side alley, but Mrs Black still kept it well shrouded. There was no fire in the grate and the room was cold. On plates in front of them, the kippers lay like a pair of moccasins left too long in the sun. Ariadne Black seemed to be breakfasting on cigarettes and tea. Beside her plate lay a copy of the *Birmingham Gazette*.

'I hope you won't mind.' She pursed her lips coyly at them both. 'Mr Purvis already knows I like to have my little read of the paper at breakfast time.'

'Not at all,' Gwen said, picking up her knife and fork.

'You do *like* kipper?' Ariadne Black leaned towards her and Gwen saw swirls of powder across her cheeks.

'Oh yes, thank you,' she lied, wondering how, this morning of all mornings, she was ever going to swallow it down.

In the homes around Canal Street School, the children were getting ready for the first day of term after the Christmas holidays.

Two boys burst out from the front door of a shop, setting the bell clanging madly. Parks's Sweet Shop was situated almost under the railway bridge, so on sunny mornings the colourful array of goodies in the windows blazed in the light, but by the afternoon it was so dark and shaded it was, as Mrs Parks often remarked, 'like living buried in a plot in the bleeding cemetery'. This morning, as it was the first day back at school, she followed her two youngest offspring to the door, pulling her cardi round her in the freezing morning. The two lads were off along the street, hands going to their mouths pretending they were smoking and puffing out warm breath to condense in white clouds in front of them.

''Ere, Ron, Billy!' she called after them. 'You come back 'ere dinner time. I don't want you going down the cut!'

'Awright, Mom!' Ron, the younger of the two, shouted back.

'And go straight to school – it looks like rain!'

They waved in a token fashion.

Not listening to a flaming word as usual. Mrs Parks sighed, watching them with fierce pride. Her lads, bless 'em! Those jerseys she'd knitted them for Christmas had come out a treat. Just right for this weather. She lit a Woodbine and stood, half in, half out of the door, enjoying the warm smoke in her lungs. Cold enough to freeze your entrails out there. She blew a mouthful of smoke out of the door and turned to her husband.

'Reckon I'll have some of them down today, Bert. Give 'em a bit of a spring clean.' She felt wide awake and suddenly enthusiastic about washing the jars of bonbons and cough candy, the bowl of warm, soapy water.

One child, a girl of eight with long blonde plaits, came along from her house in Franklin Street with a slow, dreamy-looking gait. Clasped tightly in her hand was the halfpenny her mother had scrimped to give her for her milk. She was terrified she would drop it and it would roll off down the drain. Mummy would know somehow if she did, she was sure!

'We can't afford it,' her mother had said, the tears coming again. 'God knows – a halfpenny a day! But I'm not having anyone knowing. Don't you go losing it, Alice. And don't say a word to anyone . . .'

With her other hand Alice teased and rubbed at her hair, trying to make it look more untidy. She pushed one of her socks down a bit and tried to walk with a slouch. That was the trouble at the last school. Mummy just didn't understand. It was all right looking neat as a pin when they lived in Solihull. In that other life when they weren't poor. Everything was different now.

'Alice, Alice, lives in a palace!' The girls at Foundry Road School had circled round in the playground, chanting. A palace! If only they knew!

She'd begged to leave and start again at a new school. If it could only be different this time! Would she be able to fit in? Just to be invisible – that was her dream. She left home early so as not to meet too many other children in the street. As she drew nearer the gates of Canal Street School, the butterflies in her stomach got worse. She swallowed hard. She mustn't be sick – she just mustn't! In front of her she could make out the blurry mass of the school building. Squinting, she found her way to the gate. Alice didn't know that not everyone saw the world in this soft-focused way, with people looming up close to her alarmingly, as if she was underwater. All she knew was that it was frightening.

'Please,' she prayed, even more nervous when she could see the blur of other children moving in the distance. 'Please let it be all right this time.'

'You're going to school, Joey, so shut your gob.'

His mother was almost too breathless to speak, but there was no mistaking the iron in her tone. Joey swelled inside. If he felt anything these days, it was always anger, blasting up inside him.

'I ain't – I ain't going! You can't make me!'

'I said shurrup! You're going – d'you hear me?' Her voice rasped at him. 'And for fuck's sake do summat to shut *'im* up an' all or I swear to God I'll finish 'im!' The sentence ended with a long bout of coughing.

The babby, two-year-old Kenny, was crying, nose plugged with green snot. Joey looked at him in disgust, then pushed a scrap of stale bread at him.

'Shurrup, Kenny, will you?' he roared. Then seeing the futility of this, softened his voice. 'Come on – eat the bread, Kenny. Oh, pwor! Mom – he's shat on the chair!'

'Well, clean it up then! No good blarting to me about it.'

Joey carried the chair to the tap in the yard. He turned the tap on, waiting for the icy trickle to sweep the excrement off the seat. It wouldn't budge. He picked up a soggy cigarette packet and poked at it, scowling furiously.

His sisters Lena, six, and Polly, four, chewed their scraps of bread like frightened rabbits. What use were they? Joey looked at them in fury as he put the chair down with a crash which made his mother curse. He'd have to wipe Kenny's arse now. It was he who had to do everything, take it all on. He was the man of the house. Inside it was so cold they could see their breath on the air and there was no food – yet here she was trying to push him off to school like a fucking babby!

'Send Lena to school. I ain't going.'

'Joseph – I've told you, today you're going to that effing school if I have to carry you myself.' The look on his mother's face then frightened him. She frightened him when she yelled and carried on, but even more he hated her crying and now there were tears in her eyes.

Joey felt like crying himself, but he forced the feeling down inside him and crammed his piece of bread into his mouth. It had blue spots on it and was hard work to chew. He tried not to look at his mother, struggling for breath by the dead ashes of the fire. The sight of her gaunt, sick face frightened him too much for him to let himself think about it. Two red patches burned on her cheeks. Her belly stuck out like a growth from her stick body. She stayed most of her day on the bed now. Since his Dad left everything was getting worse, all hope running out of him like water down a drain. He had to fight to stop it with every ounce of his strength.

'The bread's all mouldy, Mom,' Lena whined.

'Shurrup, will you!' Joey yelled at her. 'Just get it down you!'

'Sssh, Joey,' their mother protested faintly. A sob came from her, which made her cough until she retched.

'You gunna be better soon, Mom?' Polly said, frightened.

Still coughing, she tried to nod her head. The tears she had been trying to hold back began to pour out. She sat on the bed, rocking in anguish.

Joey stood up, bracing himself, and frowning fiercely.

'It's all right, Mom. I'll get us our tea. Don't you worry.'

'Joseph,' she snarled. 'Take Lena to school. Go on, clear off!'

Joey jerked his head at his sister. 'C'mon.'

The door rattled on its hinges as it slammed shut behind Joey and Lena, letting in a blast of even colder air.

Dora sank her head into her hands.

The day had come – the first day of school. It was what she had willed herself to reach. What choice did she have? Her cheeks burned against her cold, bony hands. Christ, if only she had a few bob for a drop of summat to knock herself out! She couldn't let herself feel. Not now. It was too late for that. As soon as her eldest left, she'd have to call Mrs Simmons in. She was the only one of the so-called neighbours who'd have anything to do with them now.

Her two young children sat lifelessly. Dora stared between her fingers at the filthy brick floor. A drop of sweat trickled down her back, though her hands were frozen. All she wanted now was to lie down and sleep and not have to wake. God, she and Wally had had dreams. And it had come to this, a slum house up an alley, backing onto the wharf with its dank, stinking air. She thought of her elder son's pinched face and the pain she tried to keep pushed away in her twisted inside her. The lad was already like an old man. Man of the house, protecting her, going out raking in coppers by selling orange crates as firewood or buckets of horse shite. Christ Almighty. She had thought when Wally took her away from her father's gross clutches everything would be a dream. And now . . .

Desperately Dora looked at her younger children.

'Polly, Kenny – come 'ere.'

Warily, they came to her and she pressed their heads to her bony chest, sobbing. She couldn't stop the pain now, had no way of numbing it. It felt as if her heart was cracking apart.

*

18

Joey and Lena went along the entry and out into Canal Street. Both children wore thick, scratchy socks and heavy boots from the *Daily Mail* charity. Joey's were too big and his feet slopped about in them.

'Why's our Mom always crying?' Lena's long brown hair was a mass of tangles. The last teeth had fallen out of the old comb days ago. She tried combing it with her fingers, but it didn't work.

Joey walked with the tough swagger of a much older boy, hands shoved defiantly into his trouser pockets. 'She's poorly, stupid. You know that by now.' They passed the Golden Crown on the corner. Joey was trying not to look at it: his Dad's watering hole. Many's the time he'd waited outside for him, been handed a packet of crisps odd times when Wally was in a good humour.

'I wish she'd stop crying,' Lena said miserably. 'Why can't she get better? My feet hurt.' She was hobbling. Her boots were too tight, her toes a mass of chilblains.

'Oh, shurrup moaning,' Joey said savagely.

The school was halfway along on the right, a red-brick, soot-encrusted building which announced, in figures carved into a stone plaque that it had been built in 1888. The middle of the building was topped by a low spire. Children of infant and junior age were moving towards it in gaggles of three or four, some family groups, some friends, and all from the neighbouring streets, separating into the entrances marked 'Boys' and 'Girls'.

Gwen's morning had not got any better.

'Come on, come on . . .' She found her lips moving.

She was going to be late on her first day! The tram seemed to be forever stopping. The pungent smell of sweat was overpowering, with everyone crushed in there together, and she was all in a lather herself despite the cold. Her neat navy coat and hat felt too hot in here. And she was a bag of nerves. There hadn't even been time to get the splinter out of her foot and she was conscious of its nagging little pain as she stood on the swaying tram.

As they lurched along, bell tinging, the glimpses she saw out of the window did nothing to cheer her up. Birmingham looked even more drab and cheerless than everyone had assured her it would be. All those factories and chimneys smoking – no wonder the buildings looked so grimy and the houses so mean and depressing. Everything seemed to be coated in black!

What am I doing here? she thought glumly. *Mummy was right – this is horrible!*

Edwin, however, had been rather in favour.

'I must say, I think you're jolly brave,' he'd said. Edwin was nearly always enthusiastic. He seemed conditioned to be. 'It's splendid. You'll be a great asset to me in the parish – used to mixing with anyone and everyone.'

'That's true,' Gwen agreed. It was not a thought that had occurred to her, but she was glad he was pleased. It made everything easier.

The tram moved along the high wall of the prison and stopped near to the end of Canal Street.

'Anyone for the nick?' the driver shouted.

As she crossed over the road and hurried towards the school it began to rain. For a moment she felt a powerful desire to be back in her old school in Worcester. She could sleep in her own bed instead of Ariadne's, and not have her clothes stinking of smoke or Harold Purvis staring at her chest over the kippers. For a moment she thought of getting back on a train and admitting to them all that she'd been a fool. All she'd have to do then was carry on as before and wait for her wedding. Simple. Predictable. But no. She didn't really know why she was here, doing something her family kept saying wasn't 'her', but she burned with the conviction that she just had to be. And she'd show them she was right. She pushed her chin out and looked ahead of her along the street, freezing rain stinging her cheeks.

Two

The child had an iron caliper on her leg.

She was among a group blocking the gate into the school. There were four of them, dark haired, dark eyed and Gwen guessed they were all from one family. In the middle of the knot they made, the little girl was crying miserably.

'You'll be all right,' the tallest boy was saying as Gwen reached them. He had a sing-song accent that Gwen couldn't place. The older girl took the hand of the crying one and started to pull her into the school playground. She seemed in a panic.

'Come on, Lucy, you've got to go in. We're gonna be late, else. You're all right, you're near our mam now. See you later!'

The clock in the school tower said five to nine. *Oh Lord, I'm horribly late!* Gwen realized. But hearing the girl's cries, her distress tore at Gwen. Poor little mite.

'I don't want to go in here,' she was sobbing. 'Don't make me, Rosa. Let me come with you!'

Two other children pushed past them to get through the gate. Gwen hesitated. She couldn't just walk by, so she went up to the children.

'What's the matter?'

'She doesn't want to go in, Miss,' the older girl said. She must have been eleven or twelve and had a strikingly pretty face. The four of them drew back, fearful at being challenged by a teacher. 'She can't go with us no more – she's got to go to this school. Only she won't go in.'

'You all go to a different school?'

'St Joseph's, Miss,' the girl said.

'Well, you get along. I'll see to her.'

They obeyed, glancing back at their distraught sister. Rosa called, 'See you later, Luce!' and they departed briskly along Canal Street. The remaining sister was sobbing more quietly now.

'What's your name, dear?'

The girl looked fearfully up at her, and seemed slightly reassured by seeing a pretty, smiling face.

'Lucy Fernandez,' she whispered.

'Well, Lucy, I'm Miss Purdy, and this is my first day too. Shall we find out where you are supposed to go?'

The girl nodded, still wary. She sniffed and reached up to smear the tears across her face. Head down, she limped along beside Gwen dragging her calipered leg. In the playground a number of mothers were standing talking. One of them was a huge prizefighter of a woman with a red, beefy face. Gwen quailed. They all looked terrifying and very rough. And how dark and drab their clothes were! Her spirits sank even further.

As they reached the girls' entrance, a teacher came out and rang a big brass bell, shouting, 'Into your classes!'

'Ah, there you are at last,' a voice said as soon as Gwen set foot inside. She realized this must be Mr Lowry, the headmaster. He seemed to have been waiting for her and stood peering through his spectacles at a brass pocket watch, evidently most displeased. He was tall, thin and balding. Lucy Fernandez immediately

23

slipped away from her side and disappeared from view round a corner.

'I hope this isn't going to set the standard, Miss ... er ... Purdy.' He snapped the watch shut and slipped it into his tweedy pocket. 'The very least I expect is that you will be punctual; you should have been here at least fifteen minutes ago. We've a couple of minutes before assembly. Let's proceed to your classroom now. Meeting the other staff will have to wait.'

'I'm ever so sorry, Mr Lowry,' Gwen babbled as they moved along a corridor at high speed. 'Only I wasn't sure how long it would take, and I missed the tram . . .'

'Nothing like a practice run if you're not sure,' Mr Lowry corrected her. Gwen felt flustered and unprepared to meet a new class. In the distance she could hear someone thumping out a marching tune.

The pianist, a middle-aged lady, was playing at the far end of the school hall beside the stage. A dark red cloth covered the back of the piano. There were high windows to the left and the floorboards were waxed and shiny. To the right were three classrooms, partitioned off from the hall by a wall which was solid up to waist height, but with glass windows above. A low rumble of footsteps approached and the classes began filing in one by one, filling up the hall in rows along the floor. Gwen saw a young teacher with red hair tied back leading a class in and showing them where to sit. She turned and gave Gwen a friendly smile.

'You'll take Form Four,' Mr Lowry said. 'Ah – and here come your charges.'

Gwen turned to watch her class file in. All between eight and nine years old, they moved in a restless, fidgeting caterpillar, staring and muttering, some of the more cheeky-faced boys chattering and poking each other. The line seemed to go on and on, a pale, skinny-legged, motley group of children in an assortment of ragged, ill-fitting clothes. Last in the line came the hobbling figure of the little girl with the caliper on her leg, her face still blotchy from crying. Somehow, Gwen felt pleased to see her.

Once all the school was gathered, they sang 'Praise my soul the King of Heaven' to the tinny piano. Mr Lowry was on the stage. He looked austere in his tweed trousers and jacket, peering at the children through his little spectacles. Gwen saw that now he had something in his hand which looked like an old riding crop. He only put it down when he picked up a book to read some prayers, after which the whole school parroted 'Amen'.

'Today finds us at the beginning of another new term,' Mr Lowry said, picking up the crop again and fingering it. 'And I want to begin by saying a few words about discipline in this school . . .'

Seated on a chair beside her class, Gwen felt her heart sink. There was no welcoming smile for the children from this headmaster, unlike at her old school. She had disliked Mr Lowry instantly and had already put him down as petty and probably a bully. She stopped listening to him and stared round her, trying to acclimatize herself. In front of her was the woman with red hair, who couldn't have been much older than her. The other teachers looked as much of a hotchpotch collection of humanity as the children. Opposite her, across the hall, was a soft, rounded-looking lady with grey hair in a bun and a pink milkmaid's complexion. She wore a full grey skirt and a blouse covered in striking blue and green swirls. Gwen thought she looked rather comforting. She wished assembly could go on for ever as she felt nervous and ill-prepared for what was to come.

When the children filed into their classrooms, Mr Lowry accompanied her. They stood at the door as the children came in, staring curiously at her and eventually organizing themselves behind the rows of desks.

'Quiet!' Mr Lowry bawled, although it already was quiet. The children seemed overawed by him. He glowered at them. 'What is this pandemonium? That's better – I should think so. This is your new class teacher, Miss Purdy. You will behave yourselves properly and you will work *hard* and be *polite*. Any trouble from any of you, and you'll be in my office, and you know what that means, don't you?'

There was silence. A few heads nodded.

'What does it mean?'

'The cane, sir,' a boy said.

'Quite right. So bear that in mind.' And he turned on his heel, looked as if he might salute, then left the room.

Gwen was confronted by a sea of young faces all peering curiously at her. She felt suddenly overwhelmed and full of panic. She had never felt this nervous about teaching before. There were so many of them! Mr Lowry had said fifty-two – twice the size of her form in Worcester. She realized she had not even taken off her coat yet and summoning all her dignity she removed it and laid it on the tall teacher's chair. She could feel the children's eyes on her. Her crimson paisley dress had a full skirt which hugged her hips and she had fastened her hair with a matching crimson ribbon. Some advice came back to her that she had been given during her teacher-training course. *Start off tough with them ... Then they'll know where they stand with you.*

'Right,' she said, stepping forward commandingly and wiping any trace of a smile from her lips. 'We're going to start off in this class as we mean to go on. Like Mr Lowry said, I expect you to be polite and hardworking. Now –' she reached under the desk lid. To her relief, what she needed came to hand – 'I'm going to take the register.'

A little girl at the front leaned towards her. 'Miss?' she lisped. 'We've got no monitors yet. For the milk and biscuits, and the dinner tickets.'

'Of course,' Gwen snapped, as if she'd known this all the time. How was she to choose monitors when she didn't know the children?

'Who were your monitors last term?'

A boy and girl raised their hands.

'You'd better come and help me today as well. I shall select new monitors later in the week.'

The two children went round the room collecting halfpennies from those who paid for milk. Gwen stood watching. Some children shook their heads or lowered them as the monitors passed. Gwen was opening the register in preparation when she heard a low voice say, 'I don't need no milk.' The words were almost snarled. She looked up to see the milk monitor standing beside a boy with a gaunt, frowning face and large, deepset eyes. She was struck by the intensity of his expression.

'All right, I only asked,' the monitor replied.

Gwen picked up the register.

'Donald Andrews?'

'Yes, Miss.'

'Joan Billings?'

27

'Yes, Miss.'

As she went down the long register, Gwen gradually became aware of the smell in the classroom. It was cold in there, but with all those little bodies breathing and giving off warmth there was already a frowsty, unwashed aroma which made her want to wrinkle her nose. In her last school most of the children had come from comfortable homes, and there had only been one child who smelt regularly: Eric Hutchings, the son of poor farmers on the edge of the town. He was out milking cows before school and there was no telling what he might come in smelling of. Here, though, the smell seemed to get stronger by the moment, as if emanating from every corner of the room. And one of the boys to her left couldn't seem to stop scratching himself. His skin was dotted with spots of gentian violet.

The names went on. Suddenly, there was one she recognized.

'Lucy Fernandez?'

'Yes, Miss,' came the miserable reply. Gwen followed the direction of the voice to see a head bent over the desk, hidden behind a curtain of dark hair.

'Ron Parks?'

'Yes, Miss.' She caught Ron in mid-grin towards one of his pals. His teeth – surely she'd been mistaken? They looked black – the whole lot of them! It must be the light, she decided.

'Joseph Phillips?'

A sullen, tight voice. 'Yes, Miss.' She looked up to see the boy with the pinched features who looked angry with the whole world.

Towards the end, when she read out 'Alice Wilson' and received a timid 'Yes, Miss,' the reply came from a girl on the far right, under the window, staring across at her in a slightly vacant manner. She had long blonde plaits and looked startlingly clean and well dressed compared with many of the others, almost like little Heidi off the alp. Taking in the sight of her charges, Gwen saw what a pale-faced, poorly dressed group of children they were. She was just starting to feel tender towards them when a ragged sound burst into the room and most of the children erupted into laughter, all watching their new teacher to see how she would react.

'Jack's farted, Miss!' one of them informed her.

'Where e'er you be, let wind go free!' Ron cried, beaming. Startled, Gwen realized she hadn't been mistaken. The boy had the blackest, most rotten set of teeth she had ever seen.

She stood composed, not a hint of amusement on her face, waiting for the laughter to run its course.

'Have you quite finished?' They stared back at her, some nodding. The boy in the back row was scratching himself frantically. 'Good. I should think so. Now let's get on with our lesson.'

She handed out exercise books and got the children to write their names on them, appointed someone to recharge the inkwells and got every child to check the nib on the cheap wooden pens which were lodged in the groove at the front of the double desks. These desks, each attached by an iron runner to a hard-backed bench, were crammed into the room in tight rows. There were a couple of framed pictures on the walls, one of a road with trees on either side, and one of the king.

We'll need to get this brightened up a bit, Gwen thought, remembering the church schoolroom she had taught in before with her children's paintings stuck up all round the room. 'Her children' was how she had thought of them. And there had only been half as many!

All morning she was taut with nerves, on the verge of thinking she couldn't manage, would never be able to teach these children anything. She couldn't even understand what half of them were *saying*, when the Birmingham accent was combined with lisps or missing teeth or adenoidal pronunciation. By the time the dinner hour came and the green and white tickets were handed out, she had struggled through arithmetic, a spelling test and getting them to write a letter. She wanted to get the measure of them, who was able and who not. But her head was throbbing and she wondered how she was going to make it through the rest of the day.

'So – you're the new girl are you?'

Gwen saw the smiling face of the ginger-haired teacher waiting for her as she followed the last of the children out of the class at midday, some to run home, others to stay for the school dinners.

'I'm Miss Dawson,' she said in a soft Birmingham accent. 'Millie. Nice to see someone else who doesn't look as if they've come out of the ark!' She giggled, and Gwen could only join in, feeling cheered already. 'I gather you were late in. Did Glowery-Lowery whip you by any chance? He rather enjoys whipping people, I'm afraid. D'you want to come to the staffroom for dinner? You can meet the gargoyles in there.'

'Yes . . .' Gwen hesitated. She already liked Millie,

with her friendly, freckly face. 'Only I didn't think to bring any food.'

'Oh, never mind. My mother sends me off with enough for six every day. Come and have some of mine. So – how were the little demons this morning?'

'It's not what I'm used to,' Gwen said. She was feeling overwhelmed by the newness of the experience, the state of some of the children. 'I suppose they weren't too bad – I just feel rather at sea. How I'll even remember their names I don't know.'

'Oh, it'll come to you. They're not bad children, most of them. And when you consider what some of them are coming from ... It's been an eye-opener to me, I can tell you. If you live in a different part of Birmingham it's like another world. I grew up in Edgbaston. The way some people live – it beggars belief.'

'There's one boy who's forever scratching and he seems to have scabs all over his skin ... Is that impetigo?'

'Umm – I should think so. Nasty. Sounds as if he's over the worst, though.' Millie rolled her eyes. 'If you want infestations you've come to the right place!'

She pushed the staffroom door open and Gwen saw a dingy space with a few old chairs scattered round and a table to one side with cups and saucers on it. No one else was in there yet.

'You'll want to wash your hands, and then you sit down and I'll get us a cup of tea before you meet everyone properly.' Millie disappeared into the little scullery at the back. Gwen felt tears of gratitude come to her eyes. The children had been testing her all morning to see what they could get away with and she had had to work hard to maintain authority over them. It was nice to feel taken care of now.

As she was waiting, the door swung open and a woman marched in. Her hair was a lifeless brown, pinned up in a bun, and her expression severe. Her lips were moving as she came through the door as if she was completing an angry outburst at some absent culprit. She caught sight of Gwen sitting near the table, so Gwen smiled and stood up, holding out her hand. The woman stopped. Close up, she was younger than she at first appeared. She could barely have been forty, but she was dressed in shapeless brown clothes and flat shoes which made her look much older.

'Oh! My, my . . .' She laid her hand over her heart as if Gwen's presence had endangered its welfare. Her voice was high and whining. 'Who are you? The new one?'

'Yes – I'm Gwen Purdy.' Gwen's smile faltered. *How very rude*, she thought.

The woman stared at her. 'I'm Miss Monk. How old are you?'

'Actually, I'm twenty-one.'

The woman gave her an unwaveringly hostile stare. '*Twenty-one?* God in heaven.' She tutted, apparently in outraged disapproval and went to the scullery. 'Oh, for goodness sake, let me light it,' Gwen heard her say impatiently to Millie.

Gradually the other staff trickled in from their classes. Millie brought tea over, shared her sandwiches with Gwen and whispered, 'Don't worry about old Monk-face. She's like that with everyone. Goodness knows why she's a teacher. She loathes children.' Millie rolled her eyes and moved even closer to Gwen. 'I think she's really the limit, to tell you the truth – but no one dares gainsay her. Not even Mr Lowry. Actually, Lowry's the root of the problem.'

Gwen frowned.

'She's mad for him,' Millie hissed, with delicious glee. 'And he never takes the blindest bit of notice of her.'

Millie was the most cheerful part of Gwen's day so far. She added her own comments to the introductions after the other teachers had said hello and sat back to drink their cups of tea. Gwen's headache started to ease.

She met Mr Gaffney, the teacher who had rung the bell outside as she first arrived. He was a gentle, middle-aged man with receding hair and trembling hands. 'Something happened to him in the war. He's very nervous. And he is one of the ones who's never actually trained as a teacher,' Millie said. And Mr Lowry was all right as long as you did everything to the letter. He was a Scout leader in his spare time. Very 'pip-pip'. The dumpy-looking lady, Miss Pringle, who wore square-toed shoes, had been the one playing the piano during assembly.

'She makes the children count whenever she gets lost,' Millie whispered. 'They only ever give her Form One and they spend half the day counting out loud. She writes where they've got to on the board and when she loses her thread they start again from there.'

'Well, at least when they go into Form Two they'll be able to count!' Gwen grinned.

A little later the rounded lady in the blue and green blouse whom Gwen had noticed during assembly came in and shook Gwen's hand warmly.

'Welcome to the school.' Gwen felt the plump hand in hers. She couldn't help noticing that the woman's nails were green underneath. She must have been doing painting with the children, Gwen thought. She looked up into a round, rather plain face, which was full of life.

'I'm Lily Drysdale.' The woman's eyes shone. 'I hope you'll be happy here, dear.'

'She looks a bit dotty,' Millie said, when the woman had moved on, 'but she's completely on the ball. And she's a real poppet. Nothing she wouldn't do for the children – especially the ones most in need.' Millie leaned closer and whispered behind her hand. 'And things aren't quite what you might think. I've heard she lives with a man – a *lover*!'

'What – you mean they're not married?' Gwen giggled. The woman was so *old* and so odd looking!

'*Miss* Drysdale!' Millie whispered. 'Hard to believe, isn't it? I think she's one of these arty types. I admire her really – the way she is with the children. I could never be like that. I wish I could. I always wanted to be a teacher, from when I was little.' She looked curiously at Gwen. 'Did you?'

'Not really,' Gwen admitted. 'I thought I'd better do *something*. Couldn't stomach nursing and I thought secretarial work sounded so dull. Oh dear –' she laughed – 'that doesn't make me sound very dedicated, does it?'

'Oh, I don't know,' Millie said. 'By the way, I do like your frock. What a lovely colour! It won't stay clean for long here!'

Millie told Gwen that her 'friend' Lance was a teacher as well. 'I met him at the Martineau Club – on the Bristol Road. Oh, you must come some time. It's the teacher's club – Lance teaches at a secondary school. He's a dream. Oh!' Millie caught sight of the ring on Gwen's finger. 'You're *engaged*?'

'We're marrying in August.' Gwen smiled at her enthusiasm. 'Edwin's a clergyman.'

'Oh.' Millie sounded less enthusiastic. Gwen wondered whether to her a man of the cloth would seem the height of dullness.

'But he's very . . . well –' she searched for a word to sum up Edwin – '*jolly* really.'

When Gwen went in to take the afternoon register, she was struck afresh by the pallid, undernourished look of many of her charges. The class that looked back at her in Worcester had been mostly bright-eyed, rosy-cheeked children, who after dinner would have come in fresh from playing in the field behind the school. She felt a pang of pity for these urban juniors, cooped up between grimy rows of houses. Already, in the afternoon register, she noticed one absence.

'Lucy Fernandez?'

Silence.

'The cripple's got lost on the way,' Jack Ellis jeered.

There were sniggers round the class.

'Enough!' Gwen reprimanded sharply. 'Has anyone seen her?'

'No, Miss,' the class droned.

The afternoon seemed to go on and on. There was no hint of brightness in the day; cloud and smoke lay in a pall over the city. They sat in dreary greyness until Gwen was forced to turn the lights on. She stood in front of the rows of desks and tried to hold the class's attention by reading them a book about the Romans in Britain. Often, when she looked up, Ron Parks was picking at his thumbs or grinning at the boy next door. Joseph Phillips, who was right in the middle, stared down at his desk top, his eyebrows pulled into a stormy frown.

'Ron, Joseph, are you listening?'

Ron, chastened, stared innocently at her. Joey Phillips glanced up for a second as if she was summoning him from another world, then looked down again. There was something about him that disquieted her.

She struggled on, and when the bell rang at four o'clock she almost cheered with relief.

Walking back in the freezing afternoon to the tram stop opposite Winson Green prison, she felt as if her whole body was full of an urgent, heavy ache. It was some time, sitting on the tram, before she knew it for what it was: homesickness. The day hadn't been so very terrible, she reasoned with herself. She'd managed the children, just about, and Millie Dawson looked as if she'd be a good friend. And she didn't want to go home, did she? But it *felt* terrible, and the thought of going back to Ariadne Black's house did nothing to cheer her. It was the first time she'd been properly away from home. Birmingham felt big and cheerless and she longed to see a familiar face. If only good old Edwin was here with his buoyant approach to life to put his arms round her!

She let the tears roll down her cheeks. Her mother was right. She had been mad to come away and do this. She could have just stayed where she was, where she was comfortable, the children loved her and it would have been easy to work out the last months before she married Edwin and they settled down together to a life of village parishes, church fetes and a family of their own.

But this thought made the feeling of panic which she could never fully explain rise up in her. Why did it all feel so inevitable, so stifling, when it was so obviously the right thing to do? No – she had been right to come here! She had to get out. Spread her wings. Then she'd be able to settle down and be the kind of wife Edwin needed and expected.

Three

'Come *on*, will you?'

Joey Phillips strode out of the school gates, hands pushed fiercely into the pockets of his shorts.

Lena trotted behind him.

'Wait for me!' she wailed.

'Can't,' Joey snapped in his gruff voice. 'Things to do.'

He elbowed past a knot of boys from the form above who were peering at cigarette cards in the gloom.

'Oi!' one of them shouted after him. 'Stop shoving! Who d'you think you are?'

'Well, get your bleedin' arses out the road then.' Joey squared his shoulders as if waiting for them to come for him, striding along with his eight-year-old swagger. Insults followed him along the road.

'Got more important things to do.' He put his head down, clamping his jaws tightly so they didn't chatter in the cold. This was money-making weather all right. Fetching coal from the wharf for the people in the bigger houses up the street was one trick. Sometimes he hired a barrow for a penny to carry it. And selling firewood. He could beg a few boxes from a greengrocer he knew among the shops along the Flat and sell them broken up for a penny a bundle. However long it took, he was going to get enough to buy a bowl of hot faggots and peas for Mom tonight. That'd help make her better.

'Good food – that's what you need, Dora,' Mrs Simmons was always saying. And she did her best helping out, bringing round broth or leftover pease pudding when she could. 'You want to get some flesh on those bones.'

Joey wrenched his mind away from the rumbling of his own stomach. The watery scrag end he'd had for dinner seemed a long time ago, but it was more than Mom would have eaten all day.

'You gorra penny, Joey?' Lena said longingly, slowing as they passed the huckster's shop on the corner of Mary Street. There was nothing Lena loved more than the boxes of cheapest sweeties at the back of the shop behind the shelves of matches, gas mantles, needles and string: sweets two for a halfpenny, liquorice laces and imps and gobstoppers.

'*No*,' Joey roared. 'Where would I've get a penny from? And if I had I wouldn't give it *you*, would I?'

It felt as if night had arrived in the entry, between the black walls of houses. In the yard the drain was blocked and a scummy puddle of water lay round it. Lena tiptoed along the edge, watching the water lap at her boots. Impatient with her, Joey strode across to the house.

'Mom?' He thrust open the door, full of his plan to go straight out, earn the coppers to get them their tea.

He recoiled, hurling himself out into the yard, slamming the door with all his strength.

'Fuck! Fuck it!' Frantically scanning the blue bricks at his feet he reached down and found a lump of something and hurled it at the door. It turned out to be a soggy cabbage stump and the impotent thud it made only enraged him further. Lena was coming across the yard and he went over to her and yanked her hand.

'Ow, Joey – that hurts, you pig! Stop it!'

'You're not going in the house! Go to Mrs Simmons's and stay there till I get back.'

'But Joey!' Lena's eyes widened under her scruffy thatch of hair. His tone made her obey. Mouth trembling, she went along to number five.

Joey tore along the yard, his body taut with an electric energy, so highly wired that it was almost out of his control. He wanted to run and run for ever, spend himself, do anything to wipe out the sight in his mind of the bed, the dark bulk of a man jerking up and down on top of his mother.

Gwen sank down on her bed after tea with a long, miserable sigh. What a day! She lay back for a moment across the rough sheen of the eiderdown and closed her eyes under the light with its tasselled shade. Her head throbbed. Faces swirled behind her eyelids: the rows of new children she had met today, the teachers ... Her mind was a mass of names which she could barely attach to faces. The one face that stood out was that of Lily Drysdale. There was something so alive about her eyes.

She groaned and sat up. Don't think about school! Kicking her shoes off, she rolled her stockings down, wriggling her toes. She peered at her legs. She was filthy! The Birmingham air was impregnated with soot. What she would have liked more than anything was a good hot bath, but Ariadne ('the spider' as Gwen had begun to nickname her since she always seemed to be lurking about in the hall) was very strict about all that.

'I really favour the male lodger,' she had said when Gwen first arrived. 'They don't indulge in so much electricity.' Baths were strictly rationed to two a week, and there was a piece of wood in the bathroom with a line marked on it to measure how much water they were allowed.

That evening there had been a fire burning in the back room as they ate. Ariadne had a woman come in to do a bit of cleaning. It was all she could afford, she said, now she'd 'lost George'. George observed them eating from his frame on the mantelpiece. He had a military bearing and a grand moustache. With the blue velvet curtains closed and the fire burning, the room should have felt cosy. Instead, Gwen felt trapped, like a bluebottle stuck in a jar. The food didn't help: chops tonight, with lumpy gravy and tired-looking cabbage.

Ariadne Black positioned her chair close to Mr Purvis's. The night before Gwen had thought this was by chance. Ariadne was wearing rouge and a black lacy shawl over her dress. Her heels were so thin that she wobbled as she walked.

'Did you have a satisfactory day, Harold?' She tipped the gravy jug over his plate as if dispensing nectar from the gods. The dark liquid bulged forward under its skin, then broke through and glooped out in a rush. Mr Purvis murmured that yes, his day had gone very nicely, thank you.

'I'm sure we're both looking forward to hearing you play you music.' Ariadne glanced at Gwen, as if grudgingly including her. As they got up at the end of the meal, Gwen saw her stroke Mr Purvis's arm.

Oh Lord! Gwen thought. *What have I got myself into here?*

It was a relief to be away upstairs, although now she

was on her own she felt restless and lonely. She had tried to make the drab white room as pretty as she could. Her picture of Amy Johnson was arranged on the dressing table. She had draped a scarf over the mirror and arranged a colourful crocheted blanket on the chair, but the room still seemed bleak.

She took her writing case from the chest of drawers and sat under the eiderdown with her legs folded beneath her to keep her toes warm.

I must drop a line to mother, she thought. *And Edwin, of course.* Unzipping the worn leather, she took out two plain postcards and wrote the addresses on each of them: to Mr and Mrs Purdy and the Rev. Edwin Shackleton.

She sat chewing on the end of her fountain pen and twiddling the ends of her hair. It all seemed such a bother. She felt gloomy tonight but she certainly wasn't going to tell them that. She sighed. Amy seemed to be watching her.

'Not terribly brave or glamorous coming here, is it?' she said to her. 'Hardly in the same league.'

Her stomach turned with dread at the thought of going back to Canal Street School in the morning, to those drab, alien streets and to the smell of unwashed clothes, to those pale, scratching children who looked as if they came from some of the poorest human stock. But that's what she'd said she was going to do and she was going to have to stick it out.

She was about to begin writing when a melancholy tune drifted along the passage. Of course – Mr Purvis's trumpet! He was playing a twiddly melody that she half recognized, but could not place. He played it, haltingly, several times through, then stopped.

She picked up one of the cards and turned it over. In her shapely copperplate handwriting she began.

Dear Edwin,
    First day in my city school – finding my feet, but a simply marvellous experience so far. You would find it very interesting. And you should meet my landlady . . .! Will write properly soon.
    Love to all, Gwen x

Night had fallen by the time Joey got back to the yard in Canal Street. The house was dark. His pockets full of coal and a dish of hot food in his hands, he pushed the door open.

'Mom?' Though he didn't know it, his voice was high, little boyish.

There was no reply. The room was deadly cold. Joey put the bowl down on the table and groped to find matches and a candle. He saw his mother lying curled on her side in the bed. He frowned. He often saw her sleeping – she seldom had the energy for anything but lying down these days – but she looked different. In the dim light he could see the blanket pulled up, almost covering her, only the top of her head with its lank hair visible above, and she was curled round, her knees pulled right up as if she was in pain.

'Mom?' His breath condensed in the air. He moved closer with the candle. Slowly, reluctantly, Dora unfolded herself and pulled the cover away from her face. Her expression was terrible, her eyes blotchy from hours of weeping. The sight of her son set her off again. At the sound of her weak, defeated sobbing, Joey's face darkened. His fists clenched in his pockets.

'What's up?' He meant to speak gently but couldn't.

Dora Phillips sobbed all the more, setting off her cough, which racked through her, stealing her breath. She clamped a rag over her mouth, then drew it away carefully, folding it to conceal the bloodstained phlegm. He could hear the crackle of her lungs. With a struggle she pushed herself up in the bed.

'Come here, bab – sit down. Mrs Simmons brought our Lena back. 'Er's asleep.'

Joey perched on the side of the bed, folding his arms, elbows jutting out as if to protect himself.

Dora's face was sunken. Although not yet thirty, the sickness and suffering of her life had worn her and she appeared twenty years older. In the gloom her eyes looked huge and dark in her face and, hard as she tried, she couldn't stop them filling with tears.

'I'm poorly, you know that don't you, Son?'

Joey gave a fierce nod, his face a scowl. 'I'll look after you. I can help you get better. Look.' He showed her his bulging pockets. 'I've got coal. And there's faggots and peas for you . . .'

'Whose bowl is that?'

'Someone borrowed it me.' He wasn't going to tell her the truth, that he'd whipped it from the pawn shop when the man's back was turned.

Dora was overwhelmed with emotion, hearing the intense determination in his voice, pride covering up the fear and grief of a small boy. She reached out her hand to try and pull him nearer to her, but he didn't budge. Slowly she shook her head.

'Joey.' She spoke softly. 'Your mom might not be able to get better. It's the consumption. You know that's bad, don't you, bab? I can't hide it from you any longer. My boy's too grown up for me to hide things from him.'

Joey's frown deepened and he stared down at his boots, his jaw clenched.

Dora was taken by another fit of coughing. Once she had recovered, she went on. 'I'm not much of a mom to you in this state.' Her face puckered. 'Never have been.' She fought to control herself. 'Mrs Simmons'll help us all she can, but she's got so much on her plate already. I can't even manage to get a fire lit for you, let alone feed you right . . .' Her voice cracked again.

'I can feed us, Mom!' Joey burst out. 'You know I can! If I daint have to go to school, I could feed us easy. I don't do nothing at school!'

'You've got to go to school.' Dora raised her hand to stop him. 'Learn to read and write and do your sums, or you won't get nowhere.' She took his hand in hers. 'Listen to me, Joey. Listen carefully. You know that's why your dad left us, don't you? Because I was poorly and he said he couldn't stand to see me getting worse by the day . . .' She had to believe that. Wanted Joey to believe it, in spite of all he'd seen. The truth was too cruel. How could she say it to her son? *I ruined a good man because I can't help myself. I'm carrying another man's child, spawned for the comfort of it . . . And now I've done the worst thing a mother can do . . .*

'Now he's gone I've got no one in the world to help me except for Mrs Simmons and God knows why she bothers with me when the rest don't. So –' she choked over the words – 'I've had to let Polly and Kenny go to be looked after for a bit.' Tears running down her cheeks, she looked into her son's uncomprehending face. 'The lady came for them today to take them to the home. She'll be a sort of ... auntie to them. Just until things get better. Only I couldn't manage – not with all of you ...'

Her head sank to her chest, her whole body shuddering.

'She ain't coming for me!' Joey leapt to his feet.

Dora looked up quickly. '*No*, not you. Course not. Nor Lena. Not unless ...' She shook her head, her face creasing with pain. 'No – you're staying with me. And she said we can see them, sometimes.' She was weeping again. 'Now and then.'

Joey scarcely seemed to hear her. Staring at the flickering candle, he made no movement. On the table the faggots and peas went cold.

Four

'Well, I never!'

Ariadne Black peered long-sightedly at her news-paper, moving a finger along the line of print as she read.

'The ferrets and dogs of Henley-in-Arden Rat Club killed 435 rats this week – on one farm! What a *thing*!'

Gwen, distracted from wondering how Ariadne could make such an incredible burnt offering out of a rasher of bacon, looked up, unsure how to react to this latest piece of information. Ariadne often regaled them with snippets from the newspaper. Gwen exchanged a glance with Harold Purvis, who gazed back at her so soulfully from above his tightly buttoned collar that she wished she hadn't.

'Don't you think, Harold' – Ariadne leant towards him and laid a hand on his arm – 'that rats are, well . . . *vermin*?'

'Er, yes, I suppose they are,' Mr Purvis agreed, his plump face colouring. He edged his arm away and picked up a slice of limp toast.

Gwen sighed and downed the last of her tea. Meals at the table with Ariadne made her sympathize with how a fly must feel caught in a cobweb, though in fact Ariadne more or less ignored her: it was Mr Purvis she was spinning her thread round and round. But Gwen felt more uncomfortable than ever after what happened last night. Or at least, what she *thought* happened.

Ariadne served tea at six-thirty sharp. Gwen left her room and started off down the murkily lit stairs, assaulted by the depressing smell of boiled swede. Mr Purvis appeared at the bottom and started up the stairs with surprising energy. She saw his bald pate moving towards her through the gloom. He looked up, suddenly noticing her, murmured, 'Oh! Sorry!' and flattened himself to one side to let her go by, but as she passed him he began to turn again, too quickly, to continue up the stairs. They all but collided and as they did his hand closed over her left breast, just for a second, so that afterwards she was left wondering if she had imagined it. Yet she knew she hadn't. She kept her eyes on her plate and ate up her singed bacon as fast as possible. Ariadne wiped her full lips with her hanky and complained about the cold.

Gwen prepared herself hurriedly for school – a deep blue ribbon in her hair today – and rushed out, screwing up her eyes against the sudden bright sunlight. She knew now exactly the right time to catch the tram and could get to Canal Street on time in order not to incur Mr Lowry's fury.

Two weeks had passed in a blur. Each night she came home to the house in Soho Road exhausted, washing herself in a basin of water and sinking into bed early, not even kept awake by the sound of Mr Purvis's trumpet. After a time it had become clear that Mr Purvis's repertoire consisted only of one tune, which he told her was 'I Dreamt I Dwelt in Marble Halls', a piece of information which just about helped her to recognize the trumpet's wandering vagaries. At least it didn't stop her sleeping. It was a struggle even to stay awake long enough to write to Edwin, though she did manage it twice a week, sending him cheerful letters full of the doings of school, and receiving equally jolly ones from him about his life in the parish. He always signed off his letters, 'Look after yourself, old girl. Much love, E.'

She was getting used to Canal Street School's routines, and the sheer size of it compared with the tiny church school in Worcester – the high ceilings and windows, the ominous groans of the plumbing, the smell of disinfectant and the ragged, grubby state of the children. As the days passed the mass of faces began to settle into individuals, and she learned their names and, gradually, their characters: the naughty ones; the ones like Joey Phillips and Ernie Toms, who always had the elbows of their jumpers out and holes in the seat of their pants; the little boy who scratched and scratched all day, his skin encrusted with the last stages of impetigo; the tooth-decayed grin of Ron Parks; and the vague, slow-witted look of the blonde girl, Alice Wilson.

And there was Lucy Fernandez. Lucy stood out, with her long, dark-eyed face and thick hair, and her lurching gait, hampered by the caliper on her leg. She was a timid child in class, and during Gwen's turns on dinner duty, she watched Lucy hugging the edges of the playground, obviously trying not to attract attention to herself, keeping out of the way of the able-bodied girls as they flung themselves about with their hoops and skipping ropes. The others called her the 'cripple girl'. This was not usually meant unkindly, just as a statement of fact. The only one who started to hang about at Lucy's side was Alice Wilson. Gwen found this strange to begin with as

Lucy was clearly a very intelligent child who picked up everything straight away, whereas Alice, though having neat handwriting, hardly seemed to be able to follow the work or complete anything properly in her exercise book.

That morning, though, the class were all to discover something else which made Lucy Fernanadez different. Gwen was standing by the blackboard, writing up long multiplication sums. 643, she wrote, adding x 46 underneath it. Light poured in through the long windows, sunbeams dancing with dust. The class fidgeted, longing to be out playing.

'Now.' Gwen pointed at the chalky numbers with a ruler. 'Who can tell me the first thing we have to do?' She moved the ruler between the six and the three. 'Alice?'

Alice Wilson squinted at the blackboard. A desperate expression came over her face and she blushed in confusion. Some of the others had their hands up and a couple sniggered at Alice's discomfort, but Gwen persevered.

'Quiet, the rest of you! Come on now, Alice – six times three? Surely you know that by now?'

A light dawned in her face. 'Eighteen, Miss,' the child whispered.

'Yes. Good. Now – what do we do next?'

Before anyone could answer there came a little clattering noise from the middle of the room. The children all craned round to see what was going on, then started giggling, staring at the floor. In the last fortnight Gwen had established her authority over them, but they knew she was not so fearsome that they couldn't afford the occasional laugh in class.

'What's the matter?' Gwen asked sharply.

'It's Ron, Miss,' one of the girls volunteered. 'His pocket's got an 'ole in and his sweets 've fallen out.'

Ron Parks's face was split in a black-toothed grin.

'Ron, come up here.'

The boy got up. As usual he was wearing a thick wool jumper, which covered his shorts reaching almost to his knees, and was trying to clutch at the hole in his pocket, but as he came up to the front a trail of several more sugar-coated pellets dropped to the floor, red, yellow and green, rolling away under the benches.

'What are those?' Gwen asked.

'Liquorice comfits, Miss.'

'And what are they doing in your pocket?'

'I was going to eat 'em after school, like.'

Gwen stared at Ron, trying to suppress at smile at the artless cheekiness of his face.

'No wonder your teeth are the colour they are, Ron,' she said severely. 'Do you want to spend the rest of your life sucking soup off a spoon because you've got no teeth?'

'Dunno, Miss Purdy.'

'Why do you eat so many sweets?'

Ron looked bemused. 'That's what there is. I live in a sweet shop, like.'

'Oh, I see.' At this, Gwen could no longer prevent herself smiling. An image came into her mind of Ron's entire family settling down in the evening with their knives and forks poised over platefuls of liquorice comfits, dolly mixtures and coloured marzipan. 'You do know sugar rots your teeth, don't you?'

'No, Miss.'

'Well, it does . . .' She was about to enlarge on this when there came another crash to her left. Lucy Fernandez had toppled off her chair and into the space between the desks. Gwen rushed over to find the child lying rigid on her side, hands clawlike, her body convulsing.

'Oh my goodness!' Gwen cried. The child's face was tinged with blue. Her eyes were half closed. She saw immediately that Lucy was suffering from some kind of fit, but she had no idea what to do.

'Stay in your places!' she cried, and ran next door. She was about to hiss 'Miss Dawson' to get Millie's help, when to her horror, instead of Millie's friendly face, she saw the severe features of Miss Monk. The woman's head whipped round.

'Yes?' It was almost a snarl.

Gwen went up close. 'Could you please come and help me a moment? One of my girls seems to be having a fit.'

Miss Monk turned to the class. 'If any of you move or speak it'll be straight to the headmaster's office.'

'Looking for attention, I expect,' she said to Gwen. 'Soon sort her out.'

To Gwen's relief most of her class were still seated at their desks. One or two were in a huddle round Lucy Fernandez, but the others all looked frightened.

'Out of the way! Sit down! How dare you block the aisle?' Miss Monk roared at them. She cuffed one of the boys round the ear as he moved away, then stood looking down at Lucy. Peering over her shoulder, Gwen saw that the child's face had returned to a more normal colour, but she was still convulsed, her body in spasm.

'Hmm. Seems genuine,' Miss Monk acknowledged grudgingly. 'Need to get something in their mouths, stop them swallowing their tongues. Give me that rule.'

Taking the ruler which Gwen used to point at the

blackboard, Miss Monk squatted down, flustered, a lock of hair working itself loose from her bun and hanging over one ear. She rammed the edge of the ruler between Lucy Fernandez's lips, forcing it back as if she was taming a horse to accept a bit. Gwen winced.

'Is that really necessary?'

Miss Monk's brawny complexion turned even redder. 'Are you questioning my judgement, Miss Purdy?'

'No, but . . .'

'Did you, or did you not, ask for my help?'

'Yes,' Gwen agreed. She clenched her hands to stop herself pulling Miss Monk away. To her relief she saw that Lucy Fernandez was beginning to lie still, her muscles more relaxed, but then she saw a pool of liquid spreading out from under her. Miss Monk noticed it a few seconds after and recoiled in disgust, backing away from Lucy's prone body.

'She's wee'd herself,' Gwen heard one of the children whisper.

'Oh, *really*,' Miss Monk exclaimed. 'Filthy little beggar!' She stood up, and to Gwen's horror swung her leg, and with her flat, brown shoe delivered a hard kick into the small of Lucy Fernandez's back. The child let out a grunt, as if air had been expelled from her lungs. Gwen gasped.

'What on earth do you think you're *doing*?' she burst out. 'I don't think that was necessary, was it?'

Miss Monk looked as if she was going to explode. She seized Gwen's wrist.

'Come with me, Miss Purdy.'

She forced Gwen out into the hall.

'I'll thank you not to question my judgement, *Miss Purdy*. Especially in front of a class of children. What do you know? Coming in here all dressed up like a fourpenny rabbit! You've only been a teacher for five minutes and don't you forget it. It was no more than she deserved.' Her face twisted with disgust. 'Trying it on like that. Messing on the floor.' She went to go back into the class, but turned for a second. 'You needn't go running to Mr Lowry. He'd never believe you.'

She marched back into the room.

'Go and fetch a mop,' she ordered a plump boy, Kenny Campbell. 'And hurry up about it! Miss Purdy, make that girl get up now and stop malingering. That's quite enough!'

Gwen was trembling with shock and rage, though she tried not to let the class see. Once Miss Monk had swept out of the room, she took a deep, emotional breath. She was appalled by what she had just witnessed. She had never before seen a teacher treat a child with uncontrolled viciousness. For a second she felt violently homesick for her old school, with its homely ways, and Edwin popping in from the church to help with assemblies. But she became aware of her class watching all this in cowed silence and tried to compose herself.

'We must look after Lucy,' she said, and was surprised she could sound so calm. Avoiding the pool of urine, she went to kneel beside the girl, laying a hand on her head. Lucy's hair felt thick and wiry. She was lying still and appeared to be asleep, her pale face composed. She was not as strikingly pretty as Rosa, the sister who had brought her to school, but the slender line of her cheeks, her almost translucent skin and, when they were open, large dark eyes, combined to give her face an overall sweetness, and Gwen felt tender towards her, especially in the light of all the physical burdens she had to bear. She looked up at her silent class, sensing that in some way they had drawn closer together through sympathy with what had happened.

'Jack – go and find Mr Gaffney for me, please.' She knew the gentle assistant headmaster would help arrange to get Lucy home.

She would have liked to pour out all that had happened to Millie Dawson, but Millie had apparently been taken ill, which was why Miss Monk had taken her place. The staffroom felt lonely without Millie to chat to. Gwen went in at dinner time, dreading having to see Miss Monk again. The woman's cruelty and bitterness horrified her. *She must be unhinged*, Gwen thought. Of course the children were aggravating and a trial at times, but there was no need for that!

Miss Monk was in the staffroom, but had settled herself in the corner with her back to the world and was reading a book in a manner that forbade anyone to come near her. For a moment Gwen felt like doing something childish to release her feelings – sticking her tongue out or thumbing her nose at the woman's forbidding shape.

'Would you like to give me a hand, dear?'

Lily Drysdale was in the corner near the scullery, kneeling in front of what looked like a pile of old rags, sorting through them. Seeing Gwen, her face lit up under its frame of soft, white hair. Looking at her, though, Gwen realized that despite her white hair and spectacles, Miss Drysdale was not as old as she had supposed. She was wearing an unusual dress with a large-buckled belt at the front, in a fabric of a thick, loose weave in a rich green, a colour she seemed to favour. She shifted back on her knees a little with a grimace, then gave a rueful smile.

'Legs aren't what they used to be!'

Drawn in by her, Gwen knelt down. 'What are you doing?'

Lily spoke quietly. 'I do what I can to give a bit of extra to some of the little ones. You'll have seen the state of their clothes. Some of these families are living under such terrible strain. I ask around for contributions, you see. People have got to know – my neighbours and so on.'

'How kind,' Gwen said, touched. 'There are certainly a few in my class whose clothes are in shreds.' She thought of Joey Phillips. His filthy, ragged state was not the only thing that had struck her. She found her gaze often drawn back to Joey's intense, frowning features. Just occasionally, when he was playing with Ron, or when his face relaxed, she saw that his pinched, wide-eyed face had a real beauty.

'Well, that's what they're for, dear. Have a fudge through and see if you can find anything that fits, and take it to them. I'm just trying to sort them into different piles for size.'

Dinner time flew past. Gwen had found a bakery near the tram stop, from where she bought her lunch every day. She munched on one of her cheese and onion cobs, and when Lily Drysdale said she had forgotten about bringing in food, Gwen gave her the second one.

'That's so kind,' the other teacher said, holding the bread with one hand and continuing to sort through clothes with the other. 'I'm really so disorganized about food . . .'

Gwen stored Lily Drysdale up as another thing to tell Edwin. To her Lily seemed more alive than most people she met, but then she wondered if Edwin would really appreciate Lily. He could be quite dismissive about some of the older ladies of the parish, as if in the nervous fussiness of widowhood or spinsterhood they didn't quite count as people. She decided to keep Lily to herself.

Some of the clothes were threadbare, but among them she found a pair of short trousers and a slate grey jersey with patched elbows which she thought might fit Joey Phillips. She wouldn't humiliate him in front of the class. She'd call him aside to wait until after the others had gone. She imagined the austere face of the withdrawn little boy lighting up at the sight of some new warm clothes.

Folding them into a small bundle, she put them away in the teacher's high desk as the children came in chattering from their dinner break.

'Quiet now!' she commanded. 'Time for register.'

Down the list of names she went again, to the mumbles and whispers of 'Here, Miss.'

'Speak up a bit, do,' she urged them. 'Joseph Phillips?'

There was silence. His place was empty.

'Does anyone know where Joey is?'

She saw a couple of the boys exchange glances.

'Jack? Eric?'

'No, Miss. Dunno where he is.'

Gwen frowned and continued calling out the names. It wasn't the first time Joey Phillips had gone missing from afternoon school. In fact it was happening with increasing frequency. She found herself feeling disappointed at not being able to give him the clothes. But where was he? Why had he not returned to school?

*

His hands were warm and sticky from the gravy seeping through the rag. Joey had tipped his school dinner into it in his lap, and the moment he was free to go outside he tore home along the street, cradling it in his hands.

Dora was hunched up close to the dying coals of the fire Joey had built that morning, hugging the blanket round her with her thin arms. Joey had replaced the soggy cardboard over the broken window with a piece of orange box, propped up inside.

'Here y'are, Mom. Brought you some dinner!'

He tipped the cooling stew and potatoes onto a plate. His mother struggled for breath. Her cheeks were red and she was obviously feverish.

'What've you got there?' she whispered once she could speak. 'Oh, Joey – that's not your dinner, is it?'

'Eat it, Mom,' he ordered, feverish himself in his feelings. He handed her the plate and a fork. 'It'll make you better.'

Dora's features twisted. 'No, Joey. It's for you.' *It won't make me better*, she could have said. *Nothing will now.* The sickness and the baby inside her were taking every last ounce of her energy. How would she ever find the strength to bring the child into the world? She had nothing left, no courage, no feeling, only instinct seemed to keep her alive. A force which drove her to survive for this unborn child, no matter how hopeless it was. She'd given up her two babies to the home. Loss and shame were eating away at her from the inside. Shame had been her life's companion, but now it was worse than ever. Joey and Lena would have to go to Barnardo's too when her time came, and it couldn't be long now. When she was alone, she slipped down into complete despair, lying for hours with her eyes closed or rocking back and forth in distress. But now Joey stood mute before her, holding out the plate. She sighed, ashamed, and took it, picking at the tepid stew.

'That fire needs seeing to,' he said gruffly.

No, don't go, she wanted to beg him. *Don't leave me.*

But he'd gone, ignoring the harsh comments of the women he passed in the yard, along towards the coal wharf to stuff his pockets. Once he'd built the fire, he was off again to beg some orange boxes. He walked tall, swaggering. School be damned. That was for babies. He was a man. And he had work to do.

Five

The School Board man turned down the entry off Canal Street. There were two women in the yard, busy with a maiding tub full of washing and a mangle. They looked up and stopped work, arms self-righteously akimbo, and as he went to number three and knocked, they rolled their eyes at each other.

'Huh. Might've known it'd be that whore's lad.'

'You don't want to go near 'er,' the other one called to him raucously. 'You never know what you might catch!'

The man waited, tapping his pencil on his notebook, taking in the state of the house. The door looked about to fall off its hinges, the window frames were all rotten and half the downstairs window was smashed and blocked off with a flimsy bit of wood. *What a bloody awful state to live in*, he thought. And why was no one answering? He peered through the top part of the filthy pane and saw a shadowy movement inside. A second later the door squeaked open a few inches. The man felt the shock of what he saw register on his face. Flaming hell, the woman was no more than a living skeleton!

She was stooped, as if very old, though he could see that in truth she could not be more than a young woman. Between matted strands of hair her face was a yellowish colour except for two burning spots high on her cheekbones. Her eyes, which bulged unnaturally in her gaunt face, held complete hopelessness. She stared at him without speaking.

'I've come about your lad. He's not been to school when he should. Keeps running off of an afternoon.'

There was no reaction, as if she couldn't hear or make sense of his words. A sickening stench came from the house.

'Joseph Phillips? He is your lad?'

She nodded, opening the door a little further. The man's sense of horror increased. The woman was wearing an off-white, soiled garment which looked as if it had been stitched out of an old sheet, and made her look as if she was already clad in a shroud. She was obviously heavily pregnant and the bulge of the child looked grotesque against her wasted body. For a second he caught a glimpse in her features of someone who might once have been pretty, but then her face took on a sly, aggressive look.

'My Joey goes to school. I seen him go off every morning, like.' Talking made her cough alarmingly and she pressed a rag to her lips. The man looked at the ground until the fit passed. The cough looked as if it might split her body apart. In his revulsion he found some pity.

'You might think so, but the school says he hasn't. Goes some days, half the day. Some days he stays away all day. You need to make sure he attends. It's the law.' For some reason he found himself adding, 'I'm only doing my job, Missis.'

He felt the eyes of the two neighbours boring into him as he left.

'You won't get nowt out of her!' one of them called to him. 'Too busy whoring for the rent money to care about her kids.'

'She hands 'em over to Barnardo's when she can't be bothered with 'em no more! Bloody disgrace, that woman.'

The man didn't turn his head. Christ, he'd seen everything now. This job was the limit at times – the way some folk lived! It was a relief to hurry past the slimy bricks of the entry and out into the street again.

Joey's name was read out in assembly. The first time, Mr Lowry stood on the little stage at the far end of the hall, looming over them all, tall and forbidding in his tweeds, and read out a short list of names, among them Joseph Phillips. Heads turned. Form Four whispered to each other. Joey wasn't there. But the next day he was.

Mr Lowry's office was a small, austere room upstairs with a desk and chair and a bookshelf behind them. On the desk lay his two canes. The small, thin boy kept his eyes on them as he stood before the head-master. They were all he was aware of, mixed with the smell of Mr Lowry's shoe polish. You could almost see your face in his black shoes every day.

'Joseph?' Mr Lowry stood up and came round the desk. Joey didn't look up at him, but he knew that, as usual, the headmaster was holding the riding crop, fingering it. He could see the bottom edge of the man's jacket, his legs. 'You haven't been attending school.'

Joey didn't answer. He was numbed by exhaustion. His mind floated off elsewhere. School, Mr Lowry, all of it, was as nothing.

'Have you gone deaf, boy?' Mr Lowry spoke in his commanding, Scoutmaster tone. 'If I ask a question, I expect the courtesy of a reply.' He bent lower and looked into Joey's face. Joey felt forced to look back into Mr Lowry's large, pebbly eyes. They were cold and frightening. He had hairy nostrils and his breath smelt of stale tea.

'No.'

'*No?*' He was working himself up now.

'No, Mr Lowry.'

Stung by the boy's sullen tone, the headmaster straightened up, laid the riding crop very deliberately on the desk and took up the cane.

'You must be punished.' There was exaltation in his voice. 'Give me your hand, boy. You're a disgrace!'

Mr Lowry took a deep breath through his nose with each hard swipe of the cane on Joey's hand. Six times he raised it and whacked it down. The boy flinched physically each time but his expression didn't alter. There were no tears. Joey stood picturing that man he'd seen on top of his mother. One man, a stranger, who could have been any of the others whom she'd let use her. Pain went through him. He stuck his chin out and clenched his teeth. Mr Lowry stopped for a moment and Joey looked up at him. At the sight of Joey's hard eyes something seemed to snap in Mr Lowry. He seized the boy by the shoulder and spun him round.

'Bend over. You will be affected by me, boy. You *will* be.'

Joey heard the cane as it came through the air. He screwed his eyes shut. Mr Lowry thrashed him again and again. Joey couldn't count. He was lost in the pain. It cut through his buttocks, travelled in shock waves down the backs of his legs, but he didn't cry out. Mr Lowry was grunting. At last he stopped and there was silence for a moment in which all Joey could hear was Mr Lowry's panting breaths. The boy clenched his jaw and forced himself to stand straight, steeling himself against the pain, forcing it away in his mind as he had done with his feelings so many times in his life.

Mr Lowry's face was flushed. He ran a hand over his sparse salt and pepper hair.

'Now.' He laid the cane methodically back on his desk and adjusted the shoulders of his jacket. 'I shall be checking with Miss Purdy, and I want to see an end to this truancy, Joseph. You will be in school every day from now on. If your record deteriorates again I may have to think about expelling you. Do you understand me?'

'Yes, Mr Lowry.'

Joey left the room, his face blank of expression.

'Joey – stay behind at the end of the morning, please.'

Gwen knew Joey Phillips had had a caning that morning. But he had come in after his punishment, not wearing the defiant grin boys usually put on to show how little they minded. Nor were there any tears. He just looked as he always did: closed and indifferent.

He stood beside her desk once the others had filed out.

'You have school dinner, don't you, Joey?'

He nodded, glancing at her, then away. Gwen sensed that he was somehow overwhelmed by the sight of her. She was wearing her pretty crimson dress again with a matching ribbon, which made her more colourful than anyone else around, except for Lily Drysdale. Gwen was darned if she was going to give in to the grime and just wear black and grey! She climbed down from her chair so as not to tower above the boy. He was still wearing the clothes she had given him a couple of weeks ago. They had not reached the rotten state of his last set of garments, but she wondered if they had parted company with his body at any time since she had handed them to him. Their state was of general, all-over grime. He had no shirt on, but seemed to have some sort of vest under the grey jersey and his neck and face were uniformly grubby. He was such a poor little thing! Up close this was even more obvious. His limbs were very thin, his pallor evident despite the grime. He stank of poverty. Yet, in his expression, beneath the puckered brows, was something that both puzzled and affected Gwen. In this pathetic, dirty child's eyes was a mysterious strength. Over the past month, after she had offered him the clothes and he had accepted them with silent dignity – if not a word of gratitude – she had found herself paying more attention to him, watching him sometimes when he was bent over his sums or geography. His work was poor. His mind never seemed to be on his lessons. He didn't make many friends. The only boy she saw him have anything much to do with was Ron Parks, who gave him sweets and asked him to play sometimes. He appeared indifferent to the other children, though sometimes he got into fights and usually came off best in them. She had once seen him leave the school with his little sister Lena trotting behind him, striding off like a man with a mission, and the sight had moved her. There was something about him, small and pathetic as he appeared, that was intimidating. In looking into Joseph Phillips's eyes, Gwen felt she had struck up against rock.

'Mr Lowry is very concerned and angry about you playing truant, Joey. You know that, don't you?'

'Yes, Miss.' He spoke woodenly, looking at her only at waist level.

She sat down on one of the little desks. 'Can you not look me in the eye, Joey?'

He looked up, just for a second, then dropped his gaze again, taking a step backwards and Gwen realized her mistake. Teachers were distant, foreign people to him, who often exercised control by fear and violence. Faced by her friendly, smiling eyes he didn't know how to react.

But she had begun so she persevered. 'Where do you go to – when you skip school?'

A shadow seemed to fall across the boy's face. 'Nowhere, Miss.'

'Nowhere?' she spoke teasingly. 'Well, that can't be a very interesting place to be.' She wanted him to laugh, to show some sign of being a child. 'Where's nowhere?'

'Just . . . about, like.' He looked up, but not at her. He stared at the blackboard. That morning she had drawn the parts of a flower on it, with a bee drinking the nectar. *Proboscis* she had written, with an arrow pointing to the bee's long tongue.

'I see.' She stood up. There was no getting to the bottom of it, that was clear. 'Well, don't do it again, that's all. You don't enjoy getting caned, do you?'

'No, Miss.' She couldn't help noticing the utter indifference in his voice.

'Let me see your hands.'

He held out his wizened hands, in a way which reminded her of an organ grinder's monkey. They were grubby, of course, and the left palm was red and sore.

'Bathe it in some salty water when you get home,' she advised him. 'All right, Joey. You'd better go and get your dinner.'

She watched him go to the door with an awkward, stiff gait. Gwen frowned.

'Joey, are you in pain?'

Over his shoulder he replied, 'No, Miss.'

Six

'Cripple, cripple!'

Gwen heard the shouts across the girls' playground. A group of them, including Dora Evan, the class bully, had surrounded Lucy Fernandez. They had a long skipping rope and were swinging it, faster and faster.

'Go on, cripple – get in and jump!'

Gwen hurried over, saw Lucy standing, arms by her sides, her head down. Close to her was Alice Wilson, her eyes screwed up tight as usual, looking frightened and upset. The rope was a blur of movement.

'What d'you think you're doing?' Gwen demanded. They stopped abruptly and the rope hung still in the air for a second then sagged to the ground. No one answered. She saw Dora Evans sniggering behind her hand.

'You think it's funny, do you, you wretched girl!'

She was infuriated by the ignorant look Dora gave her through her slitty eyes and had to hold tightly onto herself not to lose her temper. 'You think it's amusing to bully someone who can't do the things you can! How would you like to wear a caliper on your leg? Go on – away with you. Leave the poor girl alone!'

She chased them away and they went up the other end with the rope.

'Just try and keep out of their way, Lucy,' she said.

The two little girls linked hands and slunk off to

stand by the blackened wall away from the bullies. Gwen watched them for a moment. What was it about Alice Wilson? The girl was obviously not as stupid as she appeared. Sometimes when Gwen asked her a question she was very quick off the mark. At other times she looked completely vacant.

Late that afternoon it began to rain hard. The sky turned deep smoky grey, and rain drummed on the roof and ran in streams down the long classroom windows. The last lesson was arithmetic. Gwen set the children to measure various objects in the room with the spans of their hands, so they were busy sizing up the desks and benches, the size of their friends from knees to the floor and writing the results in their exercise books. Joey Phillips had once again gone missing from school. Gwen was uneasy. He had been there for the afternoon register. During the first period he had asked to be excused to go to the toilets out across the playground. He never came back. Well, the boy would have to be taken in hand. But if only she could deal with it without Mr Lowry having to know.

Gwen looked out at the rain and wondered if it was raining at home. Edwin might be out on his bicycle. She thought of him with a sudden pang. He was so safe, so kind. She'd be able to see him again as soon as the half-term holiday came. *And I'm going to spend the rest of my life with him.* The idea came to her as strange and unreal. Her mind wandered back to Joey Phillips. Was he out in this? He'd be drenched. She felt very uneasy. Why did she feel so worried about this particular child?

'Have you recorded all your results?' She collected herself and spoke to the class. 'All right, finish up now!'

There was a scurry of activity as final figures were written down. They were all finding their way back to their desks when Lucy Fernandez went down again.

'Miss Purdy – Lucy's having a fit!'

Gwen rushed between the desks to the child's side, panic rising in her. Miss Monk had said something should be put in her mouth to stop her biting her tongue. Was that right? It had looked so harsh and cruel the way the other teacher did it. Gwen knelt by Lucy and held her hand under the girl's head as she began to go into spasm, surprised by the wiry force of her body.

'Our Mom says you have to put a spoon in their mouth,' a voice said. 'D'you want me to go and ask for one in the staffroom?'

Gwen tried to sound calm. 'I don't think that will be necessary. Just sit down all of you.'

The bell rang out across the assembly hall then, signalling the end of school.

'Go along all of you,' Gwen said. 'Go home. I'll see to Lucy.'

The children all hurried out, except little Alice Wilson, who hung behind. She peered down at Lucy.

'Will she be all right, Miss?'

The worst of the fit was passing and Lucy was growing still again and sleepy.

'Yes, she will, Alice, don't you worry,' Gwen said, intensely relieved. Thank heavens, she didn't seem to have swallowed her tongue! Once again, though, the pool of urine was seeping from under her on the floor. Alice didn't seem to notice this.

'How's Lucy going to get home, Miss Purdy?'

'D'you know where she lives?'

'Number fifteen, Alma Street.'

'Thank you, Alice. That's not far. You run along home now. I'll look after Lucy.'

'Yes, Miss,' Alice said, though with apparent reluctance. Once she had gone there was silence, except for the wind and spattering rain outside, the classroom clock's ticking and the quiet breathing of the skinny, dark-haired child. Then Mr Lowry put his head round the door.

'What *are* you doing, Miss Purdy?'

When Gwen explained, Mr Lowry came closer and frowned at the child, prone on the floor. He tutted impatiently. 'Oh goodness, what a nuisance. There's not a child left in the building we can send for the mother.'

Gwen felt her hackles rise. Anyone would think the child had fits on purpose! 'Don't worry, Mr Lowry. She lives very close by. And she's only a little scrap of a thing. I'll take her home myself.'

Mr Lowry raised his eyebrows. He seemed to disapprove of any act of kindness. He and Miss Monk deserved each other, Gwen thought sourly. They'd be a perfect match, those two. After a moment's thought he said grudgingly, 'Well, I suppose that might be a solution.'

'Yes,' she muttered in the direction of his departing back, 'and thank you for taking the trouble, Miss Purdy.'

She put her coat on and scooped up the child into her arms. Lucy's back and legs were wet with urine. Gwen wondered if she had a coat, but guessed that she probably didn't. Hardly any of the children had top coats to wear, but ran along to school in the same clothes, rain or shine.

It was pouring again. She hesitated by the door, but

realized she could wait for ages and it didn't seem about to let up. She stepped out, cursing that she hadn't brought a hat, the rain seeping through her hair, cold on her scalp. It was raining so hard that when she turned out of the school gate she could hardly see her way along the road. A cyclist loomed out of the murk, head down, battling against the wind.

Gwen's hair was soon drenched, the cold water running down her face, dripping from her nose. A few people passed her, hurrying home. The splash of water from roofs and gutters was all around. Gwen leant forwards as far as she could, holding Lucy close to her, trying to protect her, and staggered along. Lucy slept on, undisturbed by the wet. Although she was a skinny child, her weight was still enough to be an effort and Gwen's arms soon began to ache. She was glad to see the turning into Alma Street and the Alma Arms looking like a warm haven on the corner.

The houses at that end of the street were small terraced ones. Some of them appeared quite cosy, though in others the windows were dark and desolate looking. She passed a few, then crossed a side street, realizing that number fifteen must be the shop on the opposite corner. The windows were lit up but with advertisements stuck all over them and so full of shelves of tins and packets that she could not see in. She also couldn't manage the handle without putting Lucy down, though she managed to hoist Lucy up in such a way that she could knock.

There was a pause, then she saw someone coming and the door opened with a 'ting!' To her surprise, a man opened the door. For some reason she had automatically assumed the shop would be run by a woman.

In the dim light, the two things she took in about the man were his head of dark, curling hair and the fact that he was walking with a crutch and had a plaster cast on his left leg, the trouser leg rolled to the top of it. She also had the impression of someone solid and immensely strong. Gwen assumed this must be Lucy's father. She could hear other children in the background and became aware of faces watching from the back of the shop. What a sodden spectacle she must look standing there!

'How d'you do. I'm Miss Purdy – Lucy's class teacher. I'm afraid she's just had another fit.'

'Mam!' one of the boys shouted in the background. 'It's Lucy – she's bad again!'

'I see,' the man said, and she heard that he was not local. He spoke differently from Lucy. 'You'd better come in, then.'

Gwen manoeuvred Lucy carefully inside, along a narrow way between two rows of shelves. Lucy's feet caught the handle of a broom and knocked it over. They passed into the back room, which seemed crammed full of people, boys mainly. Rosa, the pretty elder sister, easily stood out among them. The man indicated that Gwen should lay Lucy in the chair by the fire, and as she put the child down, Lucy began to come round. Dazed, she looked round the room as if she couldn't think where she was, especially when she saw her teacher standing there.

'You all right now, Lucy *fach*?' the man asked, bending over her, and she nodded. She seemed happy to see him. In the light, Gwen saw that he was much younger than she had imagined. His hair was black, wavy, the face strong, dark-eyed and weathered looking and she saw a kind warmth towards the child. His voice was deep but soft. She was still trying to place the accent.

'Miss Purdy?' Lucy whispered.

'Yes, dear?'

'Was it you brought me home?'

Gwen nodded and saw the girl smile sleepily and her face was suddenly pretty. She could sense the man appraising her. Though he was standing slightly behind her, his presence was very powerful. She felt something coming from him that was abrasive, close to hostility, but it was not blatant enough for her to be sure and was belied by the teasing light in his eyes.

'So you're Miss Purdy,' he said. 'We've heard a fair bit about you.'

'All good, I hope? Gwen Purdy.' She turned and held out her hand, though she immediately felt somehow foolish for doing so.

The man hesitated, then a strong, rough hand took hers and shook it. 'I'm Daniel, Lucy's brother.'

'I see.' Gwen smiled, surprised. 'I took you for the man of the house.'

Daniel Fernandez did not return the smile. 'That I am when I'm here. There's no one else.'

Gwen felt very awkward because of the serious, unwavering way he was looking at her. The crutch somehow added to his dignity rather than undermining it.

'Thank you for bringing our Lucy home.'

'Not at all.' To herself she sounded posh now and prim, and she was conscious of her bedraggled appearance. All this seemed to put her at a disadvantage. She felt like a foreigner in what was obviously a house of limited means. This room was evidently the family's only living room behind the shop, so that although it was sparsely furnished – other than the armchair by the fireplace there was a table and three chairs, and a dilapidated dresser stacked with crocks – it also contained the gas cooker and shelves, with a small scullery beyond, and everyone seemed to be squeezed inside. The room was lit by gaslight and the mantles 'pop-popped' in the background. The Fernandez children stood round, silenced by the momentous, unheard-of event of a teacher calling at their house. Once more, the man did not smile. He sank down, balancing on the arm of Lucy's chair.

'So – you've come to see how the other half live then, is it? See how the world's workers get by?' His tone was jaunty, but somehow provocative as well. 'You don't sound as if you come from round here.'

'My family live in Worcester.'

'Nice town, Worcester. Been through there myself. Comfortable place, I'd say.'

There was nothing in his words that was actually rude, but they were spoken as a challenge. Gwen saw he had decided to tease her. Despite the laughter in his eyes, it got under her skin.

'You don't sound local yourself.' She met his stare defiantly. His eyes looked black in the poor light and to her bewilderment, as they faced each other, she felt the most peculiar sensation, as if all the hairs on her body were suddenly standing on end. She gave a shiver, then blushed, confused, feeling somehow that the man would sense the odd, electric sensation that had come over her. She was distracted by the sound of someone coming down the stairs, and then the door opened.

'Daniel? What's going on?'

'It's all right, Ma – it's our Lucy, had another fit at

school. This is her teacher, brought her home. Miss Purdy.'

Mrs Fernandez was small in stature but wide and large breasted. She seemed like a larger person than she was. She had round, rosy cheeks and striking blue eyes, which Rosa had evidently inherited. She nodded at Gwen, looked across at Lucy and saw she was all right, then turned back to Gwen.

'Miss Purdy?' Her accent was as strong as her son's and it only then dawned on Gwen that they were Welsh. Lucy, however, spoke with a Birmingham accent like nearly all the other children in the class. 'Brought our Lucy back, is it? Very good of you. Very good. And you're soaked to the skin. *Duw*, Daniel, what're you thinking, not offering Miss Purdy a cup of tea for her trouble? Kettle's nearly boiled – come on now. Where your manners? Rosa, bring Miss Purdy a chair.'

Mrs Fernandez moved with a stately gait across the room to the scullery. She was dark haired, though not swarthy like Daniel. Her hair was taken back softly in a bun and she wore a deep blue dress and black crocheted shawl. She seemed friendly and down to earth, more welcoming than her son, and Gwen warmed to her immediately. Perched on a chair by the fire, Gwen felt more at ease now she was not in conversation with Daniel alone and able to take in more of the room. The walls were painted a rich blue, which made the place dark and cosy in the firelight. Looking up at the mantelpiece, which was draped with a deep rust-coloured strip of material, she noticed a photograph of a dark-haired man, though it was faded and she could not make out much except that he looked too old to be Daniel. Was he Daniel's absent father?

Beside it, flanked by brass candlesticks, stood a small, blue-robed statue of the Virgin Mary. She heard Mrs Fernandez lighting the gas and the kettle hissing and realized she was being watched closely by all the children.

'So I don't suppose you're living round here are you?' Mrs Fernandez asked. Steam curled into the air as she poured water into a huge brown teapot.

Gwen turned to her. 'No – I come in from Handsworth. Soho Road.'

'Oh yes.' The lid clinked into the teapot. 'Vincent *bach* – fetch me the milk. And Paul – go and get the chair from upstairs.'

Both the boys, a good deal older than Lucy, jumped to do as they were bidden. The younger one disappeared into the scullery and came back with a bottle of sterilized milk. Their instant response made Gwen realize that Mrs Fernandez was more steely than her soft appearance indicated. Gwen watched her, trying to guess her age, and thought she must be in her mid-forties. Mrs Fernandez brought the pot and willow-pattern cups and saucers to the table, then poured the strong, orange tea. Gwen moved her chair over to sit nearer. Vincent, who told Gwen he was fourteen and would soon start work, sat across from her. Paul sat on the chair he had brought down and another boy and Rosa sat by the hearth. Gwen could feel Daniel observing her from his perch on the arm of Lucy's chair.

'You don't sound local either,' Gwen said shyly. She couldn't work this family out at all – Welsh accents, Birmingham accents, Spanish name. 'Are you Welsh?'

'Me?' Mrs Fernandez sat down and handed Gwen a cup of tea. She stirred three spoonfuls of sugar into her own cup. 'Not originally, no. I'm Irish, I am – from County Wexford. My mother and father brought us over the water for a better life when I was seven years of age. Met my husband Arturo there – course they'd all come over from Spain to the steel works down in Dowlais – that was before he left to go down the pit.' She stopped and sipped her tea. She seemed quite happy to keep talking. What she was describing though was an unknown world to Gwen, who nodded, hoping her ignorance was not too obvious.

'Arturo died eight years ago, God rest him – after the strikes and that. We didn't want to leave the valleys, but there was no work, see, not down there. My sister Annie's in Birmingham, and her husband Pat, and they wrote and said there's jobs to be had here ... Well, none of us wanted to go, and Daniel here wouldn't come, not straight away. His home was the valley, was all he wanted. He stayed on with my brother in Aberglyn ...'

'Ma, d'you think Miss Purdy wants to hear all our family history? I expect she'd find it very dull, an educated young lady like her.' Again, the tone was ironic, a challenge.

'But I do,' Gwen said sharply, wondering why Daniel Fernandez seemed determined to despise her on sight. She resented this – after all, she'd brought his sister home, hadn't she? 'It's very interesting.' She could barely imagine what Mrs Fernandez's experiences could have been. In fact she realized she knew nothing about anything. The inside of this house was very different from and much poorer than any other she had ever been in. She'd barely ever met a Roman Catholic before. Her mother talked about them as if they were sinister. Even drinking tea with sterilized milk was new to her. She was having to get used to the taste of it. She sensed that this family had come through enormous hardship, while her own life had been so sheltered, so comfortable! It made her feel almost ashamed. She sat forward, elbows on the table.

'I'm so sorry about your husband. What a terrible thing. And you were left with so many children.'

'Eight to bring up. Oh yes. Lucy was born after he died.' She shook her head, took another sip of tea in the silence. 'Course, Daniel stayed in the valley, and our Ann was the only one out at work. But at least there was work to be had over here . . .' She gave a long sigh. 'Oh yes, hard times.' Suddenly Mrs Fernandez seemed to brush the memories aside. 'Would you like a hot drop in there before you go?'

'Yes please.' Gwen held out her cup. 'It's thawing me out nicely!' She was feeling wet and uncomfortable but she was too interested in the family to want to rush away. She turned to Daniel.

'Birmingham isn't your home then?'

His mother replied before he could. 'Our Daniel's a valley boy. Down the pit at Aberglyn when he was fourteen. Now he's up to his eyes in politics and books – a proper red, he is, just like his da – there's no talking to him sometimes.'

There was a bitter note in her voice. Daniel made no reply but she saw that the twinkling, teasing light had gone from his eyes and his face was moving as if he was clamping his jaw in the effort not to retort. Gwen saw there was tension between mother and son that she had no understanding of. She had never taken any interest in politics, never heard much about it except when Edwin talked about pacifism and the League of Nations. Her family were quietly conservative. Politics

had always seemed a dull, provincial affair. Its importance had never touched her, and she certainly knew
nothing about Wales. She could tell the other children
had heard all this before and weren't interested, two of
the boys poking each other and giggling. Only Lucy
was really listening.

Mrs Fernandez changed the subject. 'You being a
schoolteacher – marvellous, that is. I'd like to have
done that if I'd had a better education.'

'Yes,' Gwen said. 'It is quite nice.'

'It's the seedbed of revolution, that's what it is.'
Daniel's voice cut through from behind her. Though
he was talking quietly, his voice carried round the
room. 'Give people an education and you give them
power to change their lives.'

'Yes.' Gwen turned to him. Once again, something
about Daniel Fernandez seemed overwhelming; she had
that odd sensation of electricity sweeping over her,
though she spoke coolly. 'I suppose you're right. I've
never thought about it before.'

He looked steadily back. 'Perhaps it's time you did.'

There was a knocking at the front and a voice called
cheerfully, 'Theresa? It's only me!'

'That's my sister. Come in, Annie!' she called.
'There's tea in the pot!'

'I must go.' Gwen got up as the woman came in, a
thinner Theresa Fernandez, older and a little more
faded, but with the same candid blue eyes. 'I've disturbed you long enough.'

'You're no disturbance. Annie, this is Miss Purdy,
Lucy's class teacher. Lucy had a turn today and she
brought her home. Wasn't that kind now?'

The woman smiled warily. 'You're from St
Patrick's?'

'No – I told you, we've put her in the Protestant school to have her nearer by. It's just along the way.'

Daniel stood up as Gwen thanked Mrs Fernandez for the tea. 'I'd offer to walk you home, but I think I'd hold you up.'

For the first time there was a touch of warmth in his tone.

'There's no need. The tram stop's just at the end of the road.' She glanced down at his leg. 'What have you done?'

Daniel's mouth went up at one side. 'Let's just say I had a little disagreement with a policeman.'

'Oh.' Gwen smiled. 'I see. Well, I don't, but I hope it gets better quickly. Bye-bye, Lucy. I'll see you in the morning.'

A delighted smile met her from the chair.

'Bye-bye, Miss Purdy.'

Seven

The nit nurse was in school.

About once a month she turned up to check the children's heads and this time she arrived the week before the half-term holiday. They lined up in the hall, class by class. Form Four waited for Form Three to finish.

Alice Wilson was sick with nerves.

'Line up now!' Miss Purdy called to them. 'Ron, put those away. I don't want to see those out in school again. Why is it that you always seem to *rattle*, one way or another?'

Ron Parks sheepishly pushed a handful of marbles back into his pocket.

Alice followed the others as they lined up. Squinting anxiously, she managed to get behind Lucy Fernandez.

'I hope I haven't got nits!' she whispered to Lucy.

Lucy turned and peered at her, puzzled by the desperation in her voice. 'You won't have. Your hair's lovely and clean.'

'I know, but my head's itching something terrible.' Alice started scratching at the very thought. Several of the others were doing the same and giggling nervously.

'Ooh – nits're horrible!' Lucy said, quivering, but trying to make a joke of it. But there was no answering smile on Alice's face.

'My Mom'll go mad if I've got nits.'

They filed into the hall and stood on the scuffed floor, which had lost its beginning-of-term sheen. Form Three were going back into their classroom with Miss Dawson. Alice could see their blurry shapes moving through the bright oblong of the classroom door, but she couldn't make out who any of them were without screwing up her eyes so tightly that her face ached. She already had toothache, a nagging pain at the top left of her mouth. She hadn't told her mother. Mummy kept saying she couldn't stand any more bad news and toothache seemed like bad news to Alice. What was she going to do if she had nits? She knew what it would be like.

'Those dirty, dirty children!' Her mother would be shouting, crying. 'How can we go on in this place? I can't stand it, can't stand living any more...' It was frightening when she talked like that.

Up near the stage Alice could make out the stout figure of the nurse. She was wearing a white overall and the tops of her arms seemed squeezed into it because they were so plump. She started to move along the back of the line from child to child. It was the same nurse who always came and she was brisk but kind. Miss Purdy walked along in front of them all, in her soft green dress and neat shoes.

Alice felt a pressure inside her as the ordeal moved closer. She needed the lavatory, urgently. *I should've asked to go before.* Panic was rising in her. *It's too late now. Miss Purdy'll be cross with me if I ask now.* She liked Miss Purdy, with her sweet, pretty face and the the way her hair hung in little waves round her cheeks. And she spoke softly and had lovely curly handwriting. She was the nicest teacher Alice had ever had, but she could still be quite strict and Alice was frightened of being told off by anyone. Everything was frightening, the way it seemed to be for her mother since her daddy had disappeared and they'd become poor. Mummy didn't like being poor. She sat in the house and cried and wouldn't go out because everyone was rough and she was afraid. She hadn't wanted to send Alice to school, but she knew she had to, she said it was the law.

From Miss Dawson's classroom came the sound of voices reciting the three times table. 'Three nines are twenty-seven,' they droned.

The nurse worked her way along. Jack Ellis had nits.

'There's one here,' the nurse told Miss Purdy, who wrote down his name. When you had nits the teachers sent a note home to your parents.

Alice felt a surge of pressure in her bladder and she crossed her legs, looking down at her scuffed brown shoes. Daddy used to make her polish her shoes every evening but now they didn't even have money for polish. She couldn't keep still because she needed to wee so badly. Only nasty, dirty people had nits, that was what Mummy said.

The nurse reached Lucy. She brought with her a smell of disinfectant. Alice thought her heart was going to break out of her chest. Her palms were wet with sweat and she fought a desperate need to scratch her head. If she didn't move, maybe they wouldn't notice!

Miss Purdy moved in front of her and she could sense the nurse behind her.

'Nice head of hair, you've got, dear,' Alice heard the nurse say. She felt the nurse's fingers on her scalp, separating the hairs. The nurse lifted her plaits and Alice could feel her staring, first at one side, then the other. Her cheeks burned and she held her breath. She looked up at Miss Purdy, who did not see the desperation crying out from her eyes. A second later the worst thing of all happened. She couldn't hold her urine any more and she felt it start to trickle down her legs, then come in a rush. She let out a whimper of distress. Miss Purdy's eyes met those of the nurse for a second.

'It's all right, Alice.' She spoke gently. 'Let's take you out to the toilet, shall we?'

But the damage was already done. There was a puddle on the hall floor. Weeping with humiliation and fright, Alice followed Miss Purdy out and across the playground to the toilets. The wind blew freezing cold on her wet skin and she could feel the soaked elastic chafing her legs.

'You go and take your knickers off,' Miss Purdy said kindly. 'I'll be back to you in a moment.'

Alice sat sobbing in the toilet cubicle. She had to blow her nose on a sheet of the hard toilet paper. She felt so ashamed, but how she loved her teacher for being so kind! A few minutes later Miss Purdy came back.

'Alice, I've got something you can put on for the time being.' An old pair of knickers was passed under the door. They were going to holes, but anything was better than the humiliation of staying in wet ones all day.

'Thank you,' she whispered.

Miss Purdy was waiting for her by the roller towel when she came out, feeling a little more comfortable.

'I've rinsed your others through and I'll put them on the radiator in the staffroom. Don't you worry – they'll be dry by home time.' Miss Purdy leaned closer to her and Alice could smell the sweet scent of rose-water. 'Now look, Alice. I could see you were very worried about something in there. Was it about having nits?'

Alice nodded.

'You know you've got some nits in your hair, don't you? I'll have to send a note home to your mother so she can help you get rid of them. But the rest of the class don't need to know. All right?'

Alice's heart sank. It didn't matter about the other children. Whatever would Mummy say!

'You know, Alice – you can check your own hair for nits. Either get your mother to look, or you can sometimes see in the mirror if you look carefully.'

Alice shook her head dejectedly. 'No – I can't.'

Miss Purdy smiled into her face.

'Why can't you?'

Desperately she looked into her teacher's eyes.

'I can't see. I can't see anything, hardly.'

'Would you believe it?'

Gwen threw herself down in a chair beside Millie at dinner time. 'Some of these poor children. I've just discovered that Alice Wilson in my class is practically blind and nobody seems to have noticed – including me, come to think of it! I thought she was just slow, but no wonder the poor girl can never answer any of the arithmetic sums when she can't see the blackboard.' She pulled a ham cob out of a paper bag. 'I'm *ravenous*. Heavens, what a morning. It feels as if the day ought to be over by now. Is there any tea in the pot?'

'Think so,' Millie said quietly.

Gwen got up and fetched them each a cup. She and

Millie had become good, comfortable friends during these weeks of teaching. They always spent their dinner times together sharing groans and jokes about the day. Millie had invited Gwen to her home a few times, where her mother and younger sister Joanna had made Gwen welcome.

'Here you go.' Gwen handed Millie her tea and sat down. 'Have you had your dinner already?'

Millie shook her head and it was only then that Gwen saw what a state she was in. She sat with her hands clenched in her lap, fighting tears.

Gwen put the cup down on the floor. 'Millie? Whatever's wrong?'

Millie shook her head. 'I can't tell you. Not here,' she whispered. The tears began to run down her pale cheeks.

'Come on – finish your tea and we'll go out,' Gwen suggested. She fetched both their coats.

'Off for a walk, dear?' Lily Drysdale said to her. 'Good idea – it's a lovely day.'

They walked through the watery February sunshine, all along Canal Street past the end of the prison wall, to the bridge which crossed the canal, and stood looking down into the long line of murky water. A pair of boats slid away from them in the distance, their bright colours cheerful against the sombre banks and trees.

Millie could hold back no longer. She burst into tears.

'Oh dear – do tell me what's the matter,' Gwen said, worried. Millie was usually such a jolly soul.

'Oh, what am I going to do?' Millie cried desperately. 'I'm so ashamed.'

It took her some time even to begin.

'I feel so ill. I keep being sick.'

Gwen frowned. She was ignorant enough not to put two and two together.

'Perhaps you'd better go and see a doctor.'

'I've *been* to the doctor,' Millie sobbed. 'And he said ... I'm ...' It came out in a great rush of emotion. 'I'm going to have a baby!'

Gwen struggled to know what to say. She had only the haziest idea of how babies came about. 'Well, *how*? Whose is it?'

'Lance's of course! What d'you take me for?' Millie turned to her passionately. Her freckly face was blotchy from crying.

'Does he know about it?'

'No – I only found out yesterday. Oh, what *am* I going to do?'

Gwen was almost speechless. Once again she realized what a sheltered life she had led. 'Well ... surely he'll marry you, won't he?'

'He's going to have to, isn't he?' Millie sounded angry now. 'I never meant for it to happen, Gwen. I didn't even know what he was doing until it was too late. It was one afternoon when Mummy and Joanna were out. Lance came round and we were talking and having a cuddle and gradually ... well, we got carried away. Or at least he did. I mean it was ... it was quite peculiar to begin with. I never knew it would be quite like that. Lance got so excited and I couldn't really stop him ...' She spoke haltingly. 'I felt ... afterwards I felt almost, sort of *dirty* ... And now this.'

Gwen tried to digest this information. She thought of Edwin's embraces.

'Don't you want to marry him, Millie? I thought you were mad about him.'

'I thought I was.' Millie stared along the cut with a desolate expression. 'I don't suppose I really have a choice now, do I? That's if he'll do the right thing. It's just . . . oh, Gwen!' Her tears began to flow again. 'I'm such a silly fool. I've been in love with the idea of love but I don't really want to marry Lance – not yet anyway. I've always wanted to be a teacher so much, and I shan't be able to now. Lance can carry on being a teacher for his whole life if he wants to, but I can't, can I? My life'll be all babies and housework. Oh, I wish I'd never let him come anywhere near me!'

Eight

'Gwen, darling!'

Edwin was waiting on the platform as the train chugged slowly into Worcester Foregate Street. Even in the gloom, under the dim lights, she easily spotted his pale hair. Seeing her through the window, he strode alongside her carriage beaming with delight. Gwen felt as if she had returned suddenly to another, childhood existence.

She stepped down into his arms, his cold cheek pressing against her warm one.

He drew back and looked down at her, full of merriment.

'At last! How's my brave little woman? It feels as if you've been away for months!'

'It does to me too,' Gwen said. 'It's another world.'

'Well, I think it's *marvellous*. Well – except that I have to do without you, of course. Come along, let's get you home.' Edwin picked up her case with his left hand and kept his other arm round her as they moved through the crowds on the platform. She could feel his hand between her shoulder blades, steering her. Gwen looked round. It did feel good to be home! Birmingham had already receded like a dream and now here she was back in her real life again, or at least for the half-term holiday.

'Your father let me bring the Austin,' Edwin told her.

'Thank goodness,' Gwen said, surveying the rainy dark outside the station.

'You wait here – I'll bring her up.' Edwin ran zestfully out into the rain. Gwen smiled at the sight of his eager form, wrapped in his huge black coat, a trilby perched on his thick hair. There was something about Edwin that was somehow inevitable.

They drove from the middle of Worcester to her parents' house, right on the edge. It felt cosy in the car, spots of rain on her coat, Edwin's large, capable hands steering them along as they chatted. She gave him a fond sideways glance. She waited for her heart to leap in some way, to feel excited. It didn't happen, but she felt safe, and at least affectionate. Surely even those two things were more than most people had in marriage?

'How's your mother?'

Edwin's mother was in a wheelchair. Year by year her state degenerated and Mr Shackleton, a retired clergyman himself, battled on, looking after her as his own health faded. Edwin's one sister, Judy, lived nearby with her family, and Edwin tried to visit as often as he could since they lived in a village a few miles away. Gwen knew they would visit sometime over the next few days. Edwin was a very dutiful son.

'Well . . .' He sounded gloomy and she felt for him. They paused at a junction, then pulled out, turning right. She could see the rain falling slantingly in the light from the headlamps. 'I managed to get up there in the week. Dad's arthritis is getting worse and his chest is bad. The nurse comes in, but of course he's lifting Mum far more than he should be.' He paused again. 'It's hard to watch. I feel pretty helpless.'

Gwen reached over and squeezed his arm. 'They

know you do all you can. And they're so proud of you.'

'I know. Almost makes it worse.'

In a moment he was cheerful again – Edwin was never cast down for long – and he was asking her more about things she'd told him in her letters, laughing at her description of Ariadne.

' "Come into my parlour," said the spider to the fly!'

'Yes – just like that! And creepy Mr Purvis looks as if he's going to explode with nerves every time she goes near him!'

'What a pair!'

'He scoots off to his room and plays the trumpet – same tune, over and over again.' She was giggling now. 'I think if I hear it again I'll go mad. And he never gets any better at it!'

They both laughed. Gwen had decided not to tell Edwin much more about Harold Purvis. She tried to avoid any encounter now which could involve being alone with him. One evening, when Ariadne had left the room to fetch something from the kitchen, Mr Purvis had leaned over and placed his plump white hand over hers, gazing soulfully into her eyes.

'Please,' Gwen reprimanded him sharply, 'don't do that. I don't like it and, as a matter of fact, I'm sure I've mentioned that I'm engaged to be married.'

She almost had to laugh at herself, at how prim she had sounded. But she knew she hadn't imagined him fondling her on the stairs, and what with Ariadne drooling over him and the endless renditions of 'I Dreamt I Dwelt in Marble Halls', she was finding the household a trial. This was not, however, something she needed Edwin to know.

Gwen's mother was listening for the car, and had

the door open, waiting as they ran in through the rain in her usual tense stance.

'Come on in, dears! That's it. Thanks so much, Edwin.'

Gwen's mother was always terrifically nice to Edwin. She stood back to let them in, holding her thick cardigan round her. Mrs Purdy was a slim, neat woman in her late forties. Mr Purdy, a few years older than his wife and with a permanent air of anxiety, was also hovering in the hall.

'Hello, Gwen dear,' he said.

'Hello, Mummy, Daddy.' Gwen kissed each of them briefly, struck by the fact that even after an absence of a few weeks they seemed different. Didn't the remaining hair round her father's bald head look greyer? And her mother seemed smaller, somehow, and more compact.

'Come along.' Ruth Purdy hurried down the hall. 'The kettle's boiled. I'm sure you must need a good cup of tea. Morris – take Gwen's case up will you, dear? It's cluttering up the hall.' Her tone managed to imply that he was cluttering up the hall as well.

They sat by the fire in the back room with tea and biscuits. The table at the far end had a huge jigsaw puzzle on it, partially complete, and on the mantelpiece were pictures of the three children: Gwen's two brothers in a rowing boat off the Welsh coast as children, and one of Gwen when she was nine, a rounded, healthy-looking child with a wide smile, standing by the apple tree they had planted in the garden.

Though they didn't say so, Gwen sensed, rather to her surprise, that her parents were pleased to have her home. As the youngest, she had left them with an empty nest, as Johnny was married and Crispin off in the RAF. Poor old Crispin, Gwen thought, looking at the younger of the boys in the rowing-boat picture. Never could do anything right compared with Johnny. No wonder he left home as fast as possible.

They exchanged news about the past few weeks. A neighbour had died a few days ago, a school friend of Gwen's was moving away. Gwen asked her father whether everything was all right at the pharmacy.

'Oh, yes.' He nodded. 'Everything's going along nicely. Yes – ticking along.' She could see him struggling to think of something else to tell her. 'I, er –'

'So,' Ruth Purdy cut him short, staring appraisingly at Gwen, who thanked heaven that Edwin was there – he acted as an excellent buffer against her mother. 'Your manners don't seem to have deteriorated too much.'

She made a great joke out of this, eyeing Edwin to encourage him to join in and Edwin laughed with her, oblivious as ever to the undercurrents in the room.

'Oh, I think I can still remember how to eat with a knife and fork,' Gwen said. She suppressed a smile at the thought of meals in the smoky Soho Road house.

'Well –' Ruth Purdy gave another light laugh – 'I'd think by now you'd have had enough of this silly little experiment of yours. You've proved your point, and Mr Jenkins said they're missing you.' Mr Jenkins was the head of the parish school where Gwen had met Edwin. 'He's very keen for you to come back. I don't know if you realize how disappointed they were when you left.'

Despite her mother's antagonism, Gwen felt temptation tug at her. In a way it was nice to be home, and it would be so easy to stay, to slip into the old routine, comfortably surrounded by the familiar, then slip easily into marriage. She thought of Millie Dawson, who wasn't coming back to school any more. But already Gwen could feel the old claustrophobia coming over her. There was something about this house, about her parents' marriage, that was so static, so *dead*.

'Actually, I'm rather enjoying it where I am,' Gwen replied evenly. She felt very tired suddenly. Her mother was keeping her criticism mild while Edwin was present, but was she going to carry on like this for four days? 'Can we drop the subject now – *please?*'

'It's only that we're missing you,' her mother said tetchily. 'That's all. And Birmingham sounds so *grim.*'

Gwen watched her parents as her mother asked after Edwin's family. Her father sat silent as ever, in his slippers. He leaned forward to poke the remains of the fire. She could sense him longing to be able to settle down with the newspaper. Her mother had evidently had a cold, which had left her nose pink and sore, and she looked tired. She was such a *good* woman, Gwen thought guiltily. At least as far as everyone else was concerned. She had a strict sense of propriety, and always did the right thing for her children with little thought for herself. That was how a virtuous woman was supposed to be, wasn't it? Mummy must love her and Crispin because of all she did for them. So why didn't it *feel* as if she did? And why did this kind of virtue feel so tyrannical?

They chatted about local events and Edwin's work. Edwin had a go at fitting in some of the jigsaw pieces. Later, they all had cups of cocoa and everyone was yawning. Edwin got up.

'Best be getting back.' Gwen saw the warmth and approval in her parents' eyes as they looked up at their son-in-law to be. Edwin, she thought, was the one thing she had ever really done right. She felt very low suddenly. The only way she ever seemed able to get along with her parents was to act as a version of herself that they had decided upon – pretty, biddable and conventional.

Mr and Mrs Purdy stayed tactfully in the back room as she went to see Edwin out. He put his coat on, and as soon as the sitting-room door was closed and they were alone he took Gwen in his arms.

'Oh, I've been waiting for this!' His good-natured face beamed down at her. It was a thoroughly English sporty face with a pink complexion and kindly blue eyes. 'I miss you dreadfully, you know that, don't you?'

'I miss you too,' she said, smiling up at him. 'But it's fun being able to write. And it's not for long.'

Edwin pulled her close and held his face against hers with a sound of pleasure. 'It's still far *too* long! It feels pretty bleak around here without you. I'm counting the days.'

She drew back and looked up at him. 'Me too.'

He put his mouth close to her ear. 'How about coming out into the porch for a moment?'

Sheltered from the rain, they kissed, holding each other close. 'That's my girl,' Edwin murmured, his hands stroking her sides. 'Those lovely curves!' Then, very self-controlled, he drew back. 'Must go.' He kissed her cheek. 'But we've got tomorrow. I'll see you in the morning, darling.'

He stooped to put on his bicycle clips on, then went round to retrieve his bike. She waved as he swerved off along the road, then stood for a moment thoughtfully, looking at the empty path. Was she counting the days?

she asked herself. She turned back into her parents'
warm, orderly house, preferring not to answer that
question.

They walked out to the hills the next day. The rain had
stopped, the air was damp and mild and ragged clouds
moved swiftly across the sky. As soon as they set out,
Edwin took Gwen's hand, smiling down at her. They
were both well wrapped up, Edwin in plus fours and
thick socks, Gwen in slacks and both in layers of winter
woollies under their coats. Edwin wore a little knap-
sack with a Thermos and their sandwiches in it.

'Got you to myself at last!' he said.

Gwen laughed. She felt rested and more optimistic
this morning, setting out with Edwin's big hand
wrapped round hers. They squelched uphill through
the mud, dark trees to one side of them. Edwin told
her news about his work, the latest on some of his
parishioners. There were people he was worried about:
he had misgivings about his preaching. Was it relevant
to anything? Once Edwin got talking there was no
stopping him. She had always been his audience.

'Tell you what I have done.' He reached for his
wallet. 'I've been doing a lot of thinking. About war
and so on. There was a little meeting here last week –
look – I'm going to send this off.'

He held out a little buff-coloured card. Printed along
the top were the words, 'I renounce war and will never
support or sanction another.'

Gwen frowned. 'Is this the white poppy people?'

'It's Dick Sheppard's Peace Movement. Now there's
a priest setting a real example. He's quite right,' Edwin
was becoming emphatic. 'The whole thing *is* lunacy.

The way things are going we'll be into another war soon. And it's utterly un-Christian! How can we ever justify such violence against other human beings? It says very clearly in Micah that we must beat our swords into ploughshares. Look at the Great War – do we want that again?'

'No, of course not.'

Edwin put the card away. 'Sorry, darling.' He smiled ruefully. 'Am I keeping on?'

'No – it's quite all right. I entirely agree with you. But you can step out of the pulpit now.'

He laughed, helping her over a stile. They climbed, chatting, to the top of the hill, where they rested, looking over towards the dark peaks of the Malverns. Edwin hugged her from behind, arms wrapped round her shoulders.

'Beautiful, isn't it?' His mouth was close to her ear.

'Umm,' Gwen agreed. For some reason, she found herself thinking about Lily Drysdale, wondering what she did at the weekend. She imagined her moving briskly from house to house, asking for clothes for her charges. At the thought of returning to Birmingham on Tuesday evening she felt a pang of dread and excitement mixed.

'We'll be able to come up here every week, if we want to,' Edwin was saying. He turned her round, looking deeply into her eyes and she could see the longing in his. 'When we're Mr and Mrs Shackleton.'

'Reverend and Mrs,' she corrected him, teasingly.

'I'm so lucky, my love.' He looked down at her and she could see he was moved. She smiled back, touched by the look in his eyes. Edwin was so good, so true and lovely to her. She loved him, she was sure ... wasn't she? How was anyone supposed to be sure about love? In church they sometimes said love was more about actions than just emotions. About caring for people: doing the right thing. But wasn't it possible to feel more than this? Edwin took her smile as encouragement and leaned down, gently fastening his lips on hers. His tongue searched her mouth longingly and Gwen kissed him back, feeling excitement rising in her, and a great surge of relief that she could feel this way. Edwin's desire, the constant conflict between it and his sense of duty to restrain himself until they were married, could move her more than anything. His hands pressed her close and she shut her eyes and ran her hands up Edwin's strong back. *It's all right*, she thought, with a sense of peace. *It's going to be all right.* Then, abruptly, he pulled away, shamefaced.

'Oh God, darling. I'm sorry. I mustn't.' He was blushing. 'I don't want you to feel that I'm – well, I don't know. Taking advantage – or anything like that.'

'It's all right. I don't. I know you wouldn't dream of it.' Released from his embrace, she felt suddenly cold.

Nine

They were kissing. She had never, ever felt like this before. Even as she saw his lips moving closer, her body seemed to shiver into life as if all her skin had been scraped raw. She was trembling, the touch of his hands throbbing through her, leaving her helpless, only able to surrender to sensation, the hard press of his lips and body against hers as their touching became more intimate. What had come over Edwin? was all she could think. Over herself, for that matter! The feelings became mingled gradually with a sound, a siren, and as sleep slid away and she surfaced into the day, she realized it was the 'bull' from a nearby factory. Desolate, she tried to hold on to the images, the pleasure of it. But it was fading and he withdrew from her, leaving her bereft. As she glimpsed the face receding away in the dream, her heartbeat quickened even further with shock.

She sat up in bed hugging her knees, a burning blush spreading all over her.

'What on earth is the matter with me?' Imagine if anyone else could see inside her head!

As he withdrew, she had seen a tough, dark-eyed face, black curls. Not Edwin at all! She had been making love with Daniel Fernandez.

The dream was so vivid it was hard to shake off. Glimpses of it kept coming back to her through the day, disturbingly real. It happened in the middle of a spelling test. The children were bent over their books, Ron Parks with his tongue stuck out in concentration as usual. Gwen looked at Lucy Fernandez, her neat, intelligent demeanour. Her spellings were almost always all right.

'The next word is "ashamed",' she instructed them. 'That can be a tricky one.'

Lucy's dark hair made her think immediately of her brother and again a hot flush went through her. *For heaven's sake!* her thoughts protested. *This is awful!* There must be something wrong with her, having these depraved thoughts about a man she had only met once in her life.

Dinner time was dismal now, without Millie. She had left because she felt so unwell, and she also knew that it would not be long before her pregnancy began to show and she didn't want to have to face the disgrace. But with no Millie to grumble to and share her lunch with, the staffroom felt a lonely place. Mr Gaffney was always kind and would stop for a little chat, and some of the others were reasonably friendly. But today it was Lily Drysdale who came and sat beside her, a worried expression on her face.

'Hello, dear . . .' Lily paused, frowning, stirring her tea. What was she wearing? Gwen thought, trying not to smile. She looked quite unlike everyone else, who seemed to wear the drabbest possible clothes to school. Lily had on a neat frock which gently swathed her rounded body, but it had unusually wide sleeves, and it was a rich blood red with purple binding round the neck and sleeves and a purple belt at the waist. Gwen was about to mention that she liked the colour but Lily plunged straight in.

'I'm very worried – about one of your boys.'

'My form?'

Lily nodded, swallowing a mouthful of tea. One of the particular things about Lily Drysdale was that, although she was in charge of Form Two, she seemed to know every child in the school and take an interest in them. She also seemed to find out things about them that Gwen had no idea of.

'Joseph Phillips,' Lily said. 'Has he come to school today? I haven't seen him.'

'Yes – he was here when I took the morning register. It's the afternoons when he often seems to disappear. The School Board man has been round but . . .'

Lily was shaking her head. As she held her cup Gwen saw that her fingernails were all blue underneath today. 'There's something wrong there. Have you seen the state of the child? And his sister – Lena. She's in my form, of course. The girl doesn't look as if her hair's been touched for weeks. She's filthy and I don't like the sound of that cough. She's in a bad state. And the boy – they look half starved.'

'Oh dear,' Gwen said helplessly. She felt put to shame by Lily's vigilance. Now she mentioned it, Lena Phillips did look ill, poor little waif. And Joey's attendance had been patchy. There had been several days before the half-term break when he had not come in at all. He always looked thin and pale. 'I feel a bit unsure how to judge what's normal,' she said.

'A child who looks as if they're wasting away is something to be looked into in my book.' Lily spoke robustly and Gwen felt even more foolish.

'See if Joseph comes in this afternoon. If not, tell me. I think I'll pay the Phillipses a visit.'

*

Joey was absent when Gwen took the second register.

She felt uneasy as she took the afternoon classes, and when they broke for a cup of tea at three o'clock she told Lily Drysdale that Joey had disappeared again.

'Lena's still here,' Lily said. 'I'll take her home at the end of the day and see if I can find out what the situation is. They live on one of the yards at the far end of the street.' She looked very directly at Gwen. 'My dear, you may not appreciate quite what a struggle life is for some people in this area. Perhaps you should come with me.'

Gwen thought of Daniel Fernandez's challenging eyes. *Perhaps it's time you did . . .* he had said. *You don't know anything about life*, the words implied. And it was true. What did she know about the way people really lived around here? She felt put on her mettle.

'I'd be glad to,' she told Lily.

An hour later Form Four put away their drawings of Roman soldiers and hurried out of the classroom. Only two children remained: Lucy Fernandez always waited until last so as not to get pushed over in the rush, and with her was Alice Wilson. Lily had told Gwen she would meet her by the gate. Gwen was nervous. She put her coat on, glad of the two girls' presence to distract her. They all walked out at Lucy's slow dot-and-carry-one pace.

'Are you feeling all right today, Lucy?'

'Yes, Miss.' Lucy glanced up at her with a shy smile.

Outside it was bitterly cold, the sky an iron grey. Gwen saw that there was no sign of Lily at the gate and she stopped the children just outside the door. 'Alice? You did give my note to your mother, didn't you?'

'Yes, Miss Purdy,' she whispered.

As well as informing Mrs Wilson that Alice had nits, Gwen's note told her that her daughter was evidently very short-sighted and needed to have her eyes tested.

'And what did she say?' Gwen asked gently.

Alice's face seemed to close over. 'She did my hair. I don't think I've got nits any more.'

'Well, that's very good.' Gwen smiled. 'And what about your eyes?'

Alice's gaze dropped to the ground again.

Gwen was puzzled. Alice was a clean, well-dressed child. She looked as if she came from the sort of home where she was being well looked after.

'Alice?' she prompted.

'I don't know, Miss.'

'Well, you ask your mother to go to the doctor and get your eyes tested. Once you've got some specs you'll be able to see the blackboard – you'll be amazed how different life will be!'

Though Alice tried to hide it, her eyes filled with tears.

'Has no one suggested you see about your eyes before?'

'No, Miss.'

Lucy Fernandez stood beside Alice, watching with sympathetic eyes. Gwen felt perturbed and wondered if Lucy knew what was behind the sense of melancholy that seemed to come from Alice. *It's not my job to get involved, I'm only their teacher!* she told herself. But somehow she couldn't help feeling for them.

They had walked across the playground to the gate and were saying a shy goodbye.

'Miss Purdy! Good afternoon.'

The voice was unmistakable: Daniel Fernandez.

He came to the school gate, limping on his crutch, his leg still in plaster. Once again his expression was amiable but with the smile she could sense challenge, something close to mockery. Was it because she was fair-haired and blue-eyed, Gwen thought irritably to herself. Everyone seemed to assume she had no sense and couldn't think seriously about anything!

'Oh! Good afternoon.' Gwen hoped her voice sounded calmer than she was feeling. Her heart was beating ridiculously hard. This was awful! How could someone she had had such a dream about just appear like this, as if she had summoned him?

'I see your leg isn't better yet.'

'Oh, I wouldn't say that.' His tone was calm, relaxed. 'I'm not quite so lame. It'll be back to normal soon.' Lucy stood looking adoringly up at him, very proud that her big brother had come to walk her home. 'All set, Lucy *fach*?'

She nodded and smiled, and once again Gwen saw how pretty she looked when she was happy. But Gwen's eyes were drawn quickly back to Daniel Fernandez. In the daylight he looked younger. He was bareheaded, dark curls falling over his forehead, and dressed in working clothes, old black trousers and waistcoat, the sleeves of his shirt rolled to the elbow to show his swarthy arms. How could he go out in this cold dressed like that?

'Are you getting on all right here then? Hammering some learning into them, are you?'

'Yes, I'm doing my best, thank you.'

Again, to her own ears she sounded prim. And she was amazed that she sounded so calm when she felt such confusion. She tried to detect the mocking tone that he had used to her before. There was a twinkle in his eye and she struggled to work out if he was teasing her or whether he was simply being friendly. It was hard to tell and this was discomforting.

'How are your family?' she asked.

'Well enough,' Daniel said. 'Yes, they're all right. Best get you home, Lucy, eh?'

As he spoke, Lily Drysdale appeared, moving across the playground with Lena Phillips at her side, and Gwen saw Daniel glance at them. It would have been hard not to notice Lily. Over the dress and flat brown shoes she had put on a worn-looking pigeon-grey cape with a ring of white fur round the hem. She was scurrying along with a basket over one arm.

'Are you ready, Miss Purdy?' she called.

Gwen said she was, then saw Daniel's look of enquiry.

'Miss Drysdale is worried about one of the children,' she told him. 'We're going to see the family – to find out if everything is all right.'

'Very good of you,' Daniel said. Both his tone and look were steady, but she felt very aware of being appraised, that he was still trying to form an opinion about her. Her skin prickled. Why should she care what he thought? Yet she did – she desperately wanted him to think well of her.

Lena Phillips's hair was a matted mess. She was coughing and looked feverish. Gwen saw Daniel watching the girl. Something flickered in his eyes, an emotion she could not read. Then he looked back at Gwen.

'Well, we'll be going. Come on, Lucy. Bye, now.'

'Goodbye,' Gwen said.

For a moment she watched the three of them go off along Canal Street, Alice Wilson walking alongside the brother and sister, both of whom were limping.

Ten

'Not far,' Lily Drysdale said, turning off to the left. 'Just along here.'

Gwen pulled up her coat collar against the wind, which suddenly felt very cold. She realized that she had not even been aware of it while she was talking to Daniel Fernandez.

The little girl, Lena, looked very intimidated at having to walk along her street between two teachers.

'It's all right, dear,' Miss Drysdale told her. 'We're just coming to see your mother. You're not in trouble. Is your mother poorly?'

Lena nodded, wide-eyed. She coughed. Gwen thought the child looked most unwell. She noticed that Lily Drysdale did not bring up the subject of Joey Phillips's absence.

Outside the grimy frontage of the Golden Crown, Lily tutted. Her shoelace had come undone. 'Hold this a moment will you, please?'

She handed Gwen the basket. There was a cloth over it so Gwen could not see what was inside, but it was surprisingly heavy. Lily had been carrying it apparently as effortlessly as if it contained feathers.

'Let me take it,' she offered, when Lily straightened up. 'It's quite a weight.'

'Just a few groceries,' Lily said. 'But thank you. Now, Lena – court five did you say?'

Ahead of them they could see the dark, high prison wall, and the bridge over the canal at the bend in the road. But Lena was leading them into an entry at one end of a row of houses. Gwen had passed the rundown back-to-back houses every day on her way to the tram stop and barely given them a glance. Now she found herself in a dark alley, which looked as if it never saw sunlight. The walls were black and slimy looking. Following Lena and Lily Drysdale, she saw that the alley opened up into a long yard, with houses along the right-hand side. Never had she seen a more dismal place. The yard was dark, filthy underfoot and the only things to be seen were a lamp, unlit as yet, in the middle and two lines of washing strung across from wall to wall. Some boys were in the gloom at the far end, kicking something between them which looked like a soggy ball of newspaper. Seeing strangers, they stopped and stared.

Lena led the two teachers along to her house and went inside. Lily Drysdale paused on the threshold, listening, then she knocked. Even a gentle knock made the door look as if it might collapse inwards off its hinges. Gwen was full of misgivings. Fancy having to live in this horrifying place! This house was the worst one of the lot. At least the others had curtains, but the windows of this one were bare and it was in a terrible state of repair, with one window broken and the other filthy, its walls caked in soot. And how small the rooms must be. She looked along the yard and realized that someone in the next-door house was watching. A round moon-face was looking out at them.

'Hello – is there anyone there?' Lily called. There was no reply.

Lena came back to the door and beckoned them in. Her eyes were wide and troubled.

It was dark inside. Daylight could get in only through the top part of the window and there was no other light. Otherwise, the first thing Gwen noticed was the smell. She did not know enough about life to recognize the stench of human sickness and of imminent death, but the room made her feel instinctively full of dread. As her eyes grew used to the gloom, she took in the spartan poverty, the empty grate, the broken floorboards. For a moment Gwen thought the bed, to their left, was unoccupied, that the pathetic shape lying there was simply a twist of bedding. It took seconds for her to realize that it was the figure of a woman.

'Oh, my dear!' Lily immediately moved closer and leant over the silent form. As Gwen followed and took in what was before her, her heart began to pound with shock and pity. The woman on the bed – and she was identifiable as a woman only because of her long hair – was a living skeleton. Her features were pinched and hollow and, even in this light, could be seen to have a sickly yellow tinge. But where the thin blanket covered her body, her stomach was a disturbing mound. Gwen put her hand to her heart. She was beginning to feel sick and faint. Surely the woman could not still be alive!

But the next shock was the sound of her quick, shallow breathing. Lily Drysdale searched under the cover for the woman's hand. Gwen had never seen such emaciation. Lily felt for a pulse and there were seconds as they all stood, waiting. The woman did not move or open her eyes. Lily shook her head.

'Lord above,' she whispered, 'the poor young thing. She's not long for this world.'

Only then did it occur to Gwen that the woman wasn't old. 'Shouldn't she be in hospital?' she said, trying to compose herself, not to show how deeply she was affected by the sight.

'Too late for that,' Lily said. Carefully she laid Mrs Phillips's hand back at her side and turned to the little girl, who sat shivering behind them.

'Lena – where's your brother?'

'He'll've gone to get coal,' she said. Her cheeks were flushed with fever. 'From down the wharf. Before he goes out to get us some dinner.'

Gwen and Lily Drysdale exchanged glances.

'Where does he go for your dinner?' Lily asked.

Lena looked vague. 'I dunno. He goes out to get firewood and that. Tells me to stay here with our mom. And then he comes back with summat to eat. Most nights he does.'

'Is that what Joey does in the afternoons?' Gwen asked. Her heart was wrung with pity. The solemn nod Lena gave brought tears to Gwen's eyes.

'Mom can't get us our dinner no more,' the young girl said.

There was a tap on the door then and a voice said, 'Dora? Can I come in?'

A very fat woman appeared, dressed all in black, with loose tresses of greasy brown hair. Gwen was sure hers had been the face peering at them through the window from next door. Just walking a few steps here seemed to have exhausted her and she was wheezing and struggling for breath.

'I know she can't answer me, like,' she panted, 'but

I don't like to come in without asking. Are you from the Welfare?'

'No.' Lily spoke with a gentle courtesy which impressed Gwen. 'Miss Purdy and I are from the school. We've been concerned about Joseph and Lena.'

'Well, it's terrible. I'm Mrs Simmons and I live next door. I do what I can but no one else on the yard'll raise a finger and I can only do so much. She's sinking fast.'

'Has she seen a doctor?' Gwen asked.

'Oh ar – the doctor. Oh yes. But it's the consumption ... Galloping, it is. Ain't got nothing they can do for her ... and she daint want no one taking her away. She weren't even this bad yesterday. Still got the two here, of course ... I mean the orphanage had the others.' Mrs Simmons sank down on another of the decrepit chairs. Gwen watched, expecting it to give way under the weight. The woman was forced to pause between each phrase of her speech. 'I said to her ... don't do it, Dora, not to your own flesh and blood ... but what can you do? ... I've seven of my own, so I bring her a bowl of summat ... when I can, but my old man's been laid off, and now ... by the look of her she's past it, bless her ... And a babby coming ... Six month gone 'er is.'

'What about Mr Phillips?' Lily asked.

'Oh, he upped and left – Christmastime ... Never seen a hair of him since. Couldn't cope with her no more, he said ... Had a basinful with her ... She weren't much of a wife to him, it's true. Not much of a man though, neither, Wally weren't, in my opinion.'

As she was speaking, there came the sound of boots hurrying along the yard. They all became aware that a small figure was standing listening at the door, holding a newspaper pressed to his chest.

'Joey.' Gwen moved closer, moved by the sight of his tense little figure. Joey's face was furrowed by a deep scowl at Mrs Simmons's words, but he didn't say anything. He looked unnerved at seeing two teachers in the house, and stood poised to run away again. 'It's all right. We were worried about you – Miss Drysdale and myself. We've come to help you and your mother.'

'Let me know if I can do anything,' Mrs Simmons said, getting up and lumbering to the door. She was evidently relieved that someone else had come to take over.

Joey came in warily. Gwen saw that his pockets were bulging and he went to the hearth and turned them out, depositing coal in a pile and getting ready to light the fire.

'Joseph, could you please show me where the gas meter is?' Lily asked. 'I can get the gas on again and make you all something to eat.'

He did as he was bidden, and when Lily had fed the meter she said to Gwen, 'Come along – I've some soup in the basket, and bacon. Let's get these children fed.'

As Gwen carried the basket to the tiny scullery, Lena looked up at her with feverish eyes.

'Will you give our mom some soup? Joey says if she has some hot food she'll get better.'

A lump came up in Gwen's throat. The poor woman on the bed was a death's head with barely any breath left in her body. Soon she wouldn't be anyone's mother any more.

'We'll see if she wants any,' she said to Lena. 'And

we'll get you lying down. You look a very poorly little girl to me.'

'And you've been a really good boy,' Lily said to Joey. 'You've done everything you could for your mother.'

Gwen watched him for some kind of reaction, of softness even, but Lily Drysdale might as well have been speaking to a block of wood. With his head bent over the grate, he was working desperately to kindle some smoky life into the fire.

Chicken soup bubbled gently in a pan. Gwen stood stirring it by the light of a candle and the kettle was heating up gently over the other flame on the stove. She couldn't get over the bleakness of the house. Half the ceiling in this grim little scullery was bulging with damp and within the small space were the little gas stove, an old stone sink with a pail underneath to catch the slops and a rickety shelf on which stood Dora Phillips's few humble cooking implements. Apart from the remains of a packet of tea, there seemed to be no food in the house.

Lily had packed into her basket two tins of soup, a loaf of bread and pat of butter, bacon, tea and a tin of condensed milk, a packet of porridge oats and half a dozen eggs. She had also included two gas mantles, a box of matches and a bar of coal-tar soap.

'I popped out during the dinner hour,' she told Gwen. 'I had a feeling they'd come in handy.' Gwen didn't have to ask whether she had spent her own money on the food.

Every so often Gwen heard Lena coughing. She looked out into the room. One of the gas lights was going and Joey had built a fire. He and Lena were sitting close to it, staring at the flames. Lena was slumped against her brother, hugging herself, and Gwen was surprised to see that Joey let her lean against him like that. Every so often he looked longingly at the stove towards the smells coming from it. Gwen could see he was ravenous. He reminded her of a hungry little wolf cub. In all those absences from school he had been struggling to be grown up and look after his mother, yet now he didn't seem to want to look at her or sit near her. He seemed unaware that he would shortly lose her for ever.

'Won't be a minute now.' She smiled at him, but Joey merely gave her a blank, almost hostile look and turned back to stare into the fire.

There was only one bowl in the scullery. Gwen poured some of the soup into it and the rest she shared between two cups and a jam jar. She cut good thick slices of bread and set the children to eat at the table. Lily was sitting on the edge of Dora Phillips's bed, trying with a cup and a teaspoon to encourage the woman to drink. She tilted the spoon to Dora's thin lips, saying, 'Come on now, dear, just a sip.' But they saw the water trickle from her insensible mouth. Lily turned and shook her head sadly.

'She won't last the night, I don't think,' she whispered, eyeing the children.

'What shall we do? Lena's not right either.'

'I know. We can't leave them. I'll stay here the night. I don't think the end can be far off, looking at her now. But if you need to go, dear, I'm sure I can manage.'

Gwen thought about Ariadne and Harold Purvis sitting over the latest sample of Ariadne's cooking and speculating about why she was missing. She had no way of letting them know, but how could she leave? She felt somehow bound to Joey Phillips, awed and moved by what he had already endured.

'I'll stay,' she told Lily Drysdale. 'Of course I will.'

'That's very good of you, dear.'

'Not at all. Shall I cook up some of that bacon?'

'Oh yes – that's why I brought it,' Lily said and moved over to sit at the table with the children, sipping carefully at her soup. The bacon was soon ready and Gwen cut more bread and butter to go with it. Joey ate ravenously, though Lena only managed a little of the soup.

'Now,' Lily said, 'when we've eaten our tea, how would you two like a nice scrub in the bath?'

Lena's eyelids looked heavy, as if she was ready to fade out, but she beamed with delight. Joey nodded grudgingly.

'And Miss Purdy and I will give your clothes a wash and put them by the fire to dry. Miss Purdy, let's get some water on the boil now, so it's ready.'

Gwen went out to the tap in the yard and filled the kettle and a pan. The lamp was lit now and she could hear voices from the other houses along the yard. It was a cold night and all the doors were closed. Inside, she settled the pans on the gas and wondered how the fire was doing for drying clothes. When she went to look, she saw that Joey had accumulated quite a little pile of coal.

'Where d'you get all that from?' she asked, joining them at the table again.

He gave a backward jerk of his head. 'Over the wharf.'

'There's a coal wharf just behind here,' Lily said. 'Lumps of it lying about for anyone who'll take the trouble to fetch it – and get away with it. This young man is obviously an expert.'

Once the food was finished Lily went out into the yard and came back dragging a tin bath. She set it by the fire and they poured hot and cold water into it, refilling the kettle to heat up again. Gwen found tears in her eyes at the sight of the children's bony little bodies. Their skin had an unhealthy greyish tinge and they were dotted with bites. Joey's head looked too big for his body and the bones stuck out down his back, pathetically incongruous when set against his tough, manly way of carrying himself. He was a beautiful child, Gwen observed, as Lily set about him with the coal-tar soap, with those big eyes, strong brows and prominent cheekbones. But what sadness he had in him! She wanted to wrap him in something soft and warm, take him to her and cuddle him, but she knew he wouldn't let her. They dried the children on the cloth with which Lily had covered the food, then Gwen put all their clothes in the bath water and scrubbed and pounded at them.

By this time Lena was almost unable to keep her eyes open.

'She's running a high temperature I'd say.' Lily laid her hand on the child's forehead. 'Poor little lamb. We must get her into bed.'

Gwen had her first sight of the upstairs floor. Lily went ahead with a candle, led by Joey, who was wrapped in her coat, and Gwen carried Lena, swathed in hers.

'Watch it,' Joey said when they neared the top of the twisting staircase. To her horror Gwen saw that the third tread down was missing altogether. How easy it would be for a small child to fall right through, she thought.

There were two rooms upstairs and Joey led them into the back one, a small space in which there were two single iron bedsteads each pushed to a wall. There was nothing else. The candle threw their shadows huge on the bare walls. Joey climbed onto one bed and pulled the cover over him. Gwen went to lay Lena down on the other.

'No!' Joey's head shot up. He was all scowls again. 'That ent her bed, it's Polly and Kev's! Lena sleeps here with me.'

Gwen put the little girl down at the other end from her brother. This was what they were used to, of course, and they would help keep each other warm. She and Lily left their coats on the bed for extra warmth.

'Goodnight, dears,' Lily said, face shadowy in the candlelight.

'Goodnight, Joey,' Gwen said tenderly. She knew Lena couldn't hear her. She was already asleep.

Joey didn't reply.

Eleven

Downstairs, Gwen and Lily cleared away the bath, bailing out panfuls of water until it was light enough to carry outside to the drain. The exertion kept them warm, but freezing air poured into the house as they went in and out and they were thankful to come in finally and close the door. Steam rose from the children's clothes. Gwen put the last of Joey's coal on the fire. As soon as it died the room was going to be very cold.

They moved quietly, respectfully tidying the room, always conscious of the sick woman on the bed close by. Every so often they went to check on her, holding their breath until they were certain that hers was still fluttering in and out of her lungs. She was very quiet, as if she had already surrendered.

'It's terrible,' Gwen said, as the two of them stood looking down at her shrunken face. The woman's swollen stomach looked terrible against her body. Gwen was deeply shocked by all she had seen. She had had no idea that people had to live like this! The evening had opened up a world of poverty and suffering that she had never known to exist.

'What a terrible, terrible life. And those poor children!'

'I only wish I'd cottoned on sooner,' Lily Drysdale said. Her pale eyes were full of pity as she stared down at the dying woman. 'Poor thing. All we can do now is try and keep her comfortable until her end comes.'

'It's so cold.' Gwen shivered. Their coats were upstairs keeping the children warm.

'Yes.' Lily looked round the room. 'It's no good. We've got to keep the fire going somehow. Look – this is fit for nothing. We'll burn it.' She was sizing up the most decrepit of the wooden chairs. The back was already coming loose from the seat. 'They won't be needing it for much longer. Poor little mites'll be off to the orphanage by the sound of it. There's no family around them.'

Between them they dismantled the chair and fed the fire. The dry, worm-ridden wood burned well. They sat and drank a cup of tea and after a time, Gwen, rather embarrassed, had to ask, 'Er, Miss Drysdale – where do we go to spend a penny here?'

'Oh, you have to go along the yard.' Lily got up stiffly. 'There'll be a key.' Sure enough, on the mantelpiece there was a key attached to a cotton reel. 'You'll have to take a candle, dear.'

Gwen stepped outside, a stub of candle burning on a saucer. It was bitter. The wind had dropped and the night felt still and deadly cold. The dim light from the lamp barely reached the end of the yard, where there were a couple of dustbins and then the toilets. The stench from each mingled together. There were three cubicles and from the middle one, she could hear someone urinating vigorously and a man humming to himself. She was unlocking the one next to it when the middle toilet door opened and he lurched out and started at the sight of her.

'Christ alive – you made me jump!' he said cheerfully and made off whistling along the yard.

Gwen stepped cautiously inside. Her shadow squirmed ominously on the rough brick walls. A few squares of newspaper hung from a nail. Closing the door, the full impact of the smell hit her. She grimaced and breathed as shallowly as she could, trying to keep the stench at bay. She put the candle down on the floor and, as she straightened up, saw something horrifying moving along the wall above her head. A gigantic spider! She gasped, feeling her skin all come up in goose pimples, before realizing it was really quite a small spider, its shadow stretched monstrously by the candlelight. Giggles of tension rose in her. Standing over the toilet she realized it wasn't a flush toilet at all, but a dry pan, everything dropping down into a hole beneath. She shuddered at the thought of it. What would her mother say? This thought tickled her even more, her nervousness came close to hysteria and she burst into unstoppable fits of giggles. She was in such a hurry to get out of there, fumbling at her clothes and almost knocking over the candle as she tried to push the door open. Fresh air at last!

A hard-faced woman was standing outside, an oil lamp in her hand.

'Something amusing is there?' she asked snootily.

Gwen sobered up as she went back across the yard. What was the matter with her? Joey and Lena's mother was dying and here she was tittering like a nine-year-old. Her spirits sank and she felt almost tearful. It was only then she realized how tired and overwrought she was.

'Let's have a cup of tea,' Lily said. 'We'll need to keep going somehow. I think we could take it in turns to have a doze, though. After all, we've both got to stand in front of our classes tomorrow.'

'All right,' Gwen agreed, though the thought depressed her even more. She didn't want to sit up alone in the small hours of the night with a dying woman. The thought frightened her, and she craved company and conversation, had hoped to spend more time getting to know her fellow teacher. Lily had volunteered a few pieces of information about herself. She had never trained as a teacher but just 'picked it up', starting, aged fifteen, in the school she had attended in Minworth.

Gwen went out to the icy yard again to fill the kettle, and when the tea was ready they both sat close to the fire.

'Goodness me, what a cold house,' Lily Drysdale said.

'No wonder the poor woman's so ill,' Gwen agreed. 'I don't know how they've survived at all.'

Lily put her head on one side. 'Are you all right, dear? A shock, all this, isn't it?'

'It is rather.' Gwen sipped her tea, glad it was sweet and warm. 'Those poor children. There's something about Joey, isn't there?'

'Pathetic. And rather striking somehow, I agree.'

Lily asked Gwen a few questions about herself, and her family, things they hadn't had time to talk about in the staffroom. Gwen wasn't sure whether to ask questions back. It seemed nosy. But Lily was happy to talk. She told Gwen that she spent all her spare time painting.

'I've a little studio in the attic, you see. We go on trips every summer – somewhere glorious like Assisi or the south of France and I paint there and store up all the images in my mind for the winter. Not the most accurate method of reproduction, but it's my way.'

'How lovely,' Gwen said. It explained why Lily's nails were so often stained with colour. She wondered if the 'we' who went on these journeys was the lover Millie had talked about. Or had Millie been spinning fantasies and Lily really lived with a spinster sister?

'Do you have any artistic interests?' Lily was asking.

'Er – no, not really.' She wondered what her interests were, apart from daydreaming about aeroplanes and other means of escape. As hobbies went, this felt a little inadequate.

'Never mind – there's time yet,' Lily was saying. 'I suddenly discovered painting when I was nearly thirty. It's been a great pleasure.'

Later, once they had finished their tea, Lily told Gwen to sleep first, in the old horsehair chair by the fire.

'I'll keep an eye on Mrs Phillips for now.'

Gwen watched as Lily settled herself on one of the remaining two wooden chairs by the bed. Her rounded presence was comforting. Gwen was quite keyed up and she thought she would not sleep, but after a time staring into the red glow, she felt drowsy and dozed off, head resting on the arm of the chair. It felt quite a while later when a hand shook her shoulder.

'Miss Purdy? I think I should like a rest now.'

Gwen was immediately wide awake, heart pounding. 'How is she?'

'No change I think, dear. It could just go on like that, but if anything happens come and wake me.'

Gwen sat on the chair by the bed with her arms folded, shivering. What time was it? There was no clock in the room. The still watches of the night, she thought, glad of the one gas mantle still alight. It was so cold. She eyed up the other chair. That would have to be turned into firewood soon.

Dora Phillips's face seemed to Gwen to be even more sunken than when they had first arrived, as if she was being pulled down towards the earth. Gwen tried to imagine her looking young and well, or to make out some resemblance between her features and those of her children, but found it impossible. The woman's face was too ravaged. She wondered what her life had been, but only knew that it had been so different from her own as to make it impossible to guess.

In the stillness, and the dim light, it was hard not to imagine things. For a second she thought she saw the woman's eyes flicker open and she jumped violently, her heart racing. But there was nothing. How would Dora look if she opened her eyes? What would she say if she could speak? She seemed scarcely human now and Gwen found her frightening. She felt ashamed. What was there to be afraid of in this pitiful wreck of a person? She leaned towards her, wanting to make some contact with her.

'I hope you rest in peace,' she found herself whispering. 'After all you've suffered.' She almost hoped there would be a reply, but there was nothing and she sat back again.

The night seemed endless. After a time Gwen's eyelids grew heavy and she was fighting sleep. She could not tell whether a minute or half an hour had gone by. Lily Drysdale was breathing heavily across the room. Gwen clenched her hands in her lap, feeling the soft wool of her skirt. She was really beginning to shiver. It was too cold to fall asleep: she ought to get up, make tea and see to the fire.

Some sounds broke the quiet. Gwen jumped and held her breath. A wheeze followed by a tiny grating noise which it took her a couple of seconds to understand was coming from Dora Phillips's throat. Her body lifted slightly from the bed, went rigid for a moment, then fell back. The sound stopped. The silence grew deeper, became an absence. Gwen leapt up and pulled the cover back, reaching for Dora's hand. It was ice cold. She could not find a pulse. Leaning down she listened to hear her breathe, felt for her heartbeat.

'Miss Drysdale!' She ran to her fellow teacher, but didn't like to shake her awake. 'You'd better come! I think she's . . . I think she's gone.'

Lily got to her feet immediately, seeing Gwen's stricken face. Going to Dora Phillips, she repeated Gwen's search for a pulse, then looked round, shaking her head. 'Bless her. She's not with us any more.'

She was pulling the blanket up to cover Dora's face, when they became aware of soft footsteps padding down the dark stairs. Joey, his face heavy with sleep, stopped halfway down. Wrapped in Lily's grey cloak, he looked like something out of a pantomime. He stood staring at them and for a moment Gwen wondered if he was sleepwalking. But then, she made out his alert dark eyes. He knew, Gwen saw immediately. What instinct had roused the little boy from his bed at that moment?

His eyes met hers. 'Come down here, Joey,' she said softly.

Slowly, he climbed down, placing one foot then the other on each step before he moved onto the next in a way that twisted Gwen's emotions. It was the first truly childlike characteristic she had ever seen in him. He climbed down until he was standing in front of her, his eyes fixed on the bed across the room, where Lily was still standing over Dora.

'Mom?'

'Joey dear.' Gwen knelt down in front of him. 'Your mummy's not here any more. She's gone to heaven.'

He didn't move, barely blinked, but nor did he resist as she reached out and gently took his thin body in her arms. For just a second, as she held him, she felt him rest his head on her shoulder.

The children sat by the hearth, mute, staring into the fire. They were dressed in their dry clothes, but Gwen had had to dress Lena, who was barely well enough to move. She sat propped against the wall, seemingly unaware of what was going on around her. They had told her gently that her mother was dead, but it seemed unlikely that she could take it in. There was a busyness in the house of people coming and going.

Once dawn had broken, Lily went next door to fetch Mrs Simmons. Gwen had not formed a very good impression of the next-door neighbour, who seemed to her of low intelligence and anxious to pass responsibility for Dora Phillips on to anyone else who appeared. But she had to rethink her opinion. For a start it became clear that none of the other neighbours was prepared to lift a finger, even though the news spread fast and a cluster of women stood in the yard staring at the house. Among them, Gwen recognized the hard-faced woman whom she'd met outside the toilets. But Mrs Simmons waddled round with a pail of coal for the fire and sent one of her daughters to summon the doctor and the midwife, a woman who also laid out the dead for a small fee.

'The poor thing. She looks peaceful now, don't she?'

Standing behind her, as she looked down at Dora Phillips's waxen face, Gwen could hear the heave of Mrs Simmons's lungs. She stank of grease and sweat. 'She weren't no saint, that's for sure – but she were all right if you took your time and got to know 'er ... She had a good heart – always stood by her kids. She'd've done anything for 'em ... There's always them that'll judge.'

Gwen wondered what Dora had done to make the neighbours hostile, but she didn't like to ask.

'Would you like a cup of tea?' she offered.

'Yes, ta.' Mrs Simmons nodded and sank onto the one remaining upright chair, which squeaked in protest.

Lily looked quite fresh and composed, considering the night they'd had. Gwen felt exhausted and over-wrought.

'The children,' Lily Drysdale said gently. It seemed awful to discuss them with them sitting there, but what choice did they have? 'What's going to happen to them?'

Mrs Simmons considered for a moment. 'Well, there's no family. *He* –' she gave a jerk of her head – 'hopped it a few months back. No sign of him since. They'll have to go with the others – no two ways about it.' She lowered her voice for a moment to a whisper. '*Barnardo's* – they came and took the two little 'uns, couple of months ago. But for the moment –' she shifted on her seat, her huge belly shuddering as if with a life of its own under her voluminous black skirt – 'they'll have to come and stop with us.'

'Well, isn't that kind – how good of you!' Lily cried. 'You've been a good neighbour to her, I can see that.'

126

'Someone had to be,' Mrs Simmons said. 'Anyroad – it'll likely only be for a day or two.'

Gwen, standing beside Mrs Simmons, looked across at Joey and Lena. They sat by the fire, not moving, as if they had been turned to stone.

Twelve

'Get your books out, children – this morning we're going to learn something about the roads the Romans built here in Britain.'

Gwen forced herself to concentrate. Everything felt wrong today. She had had one night's sleep to recover since the night up with Dora Phillips, but she was still tired. And Millie had gone and Joey Phillips wasn't here either. The sight of his empty place in the classroom whenever she looked up made her feel desolate. Of course it had often been empty before, but having seen the heroic struggle which explained his school absences, the little boy had touched her heart. The thought of him and his little sister being sent off to an orphanage was terrible. But what else could be done?

The day before, once the doctor had issued a death certificate, Mrs Simmons waited while the midwife laid out Dora's body, then took Joey and Lena home with her. Gwen and Lily Drysdale hurried back to school to begin another day's work.

'I could do with a nice hot bath,' Gwen had groaned as they went out into Canal Street and the cold morning. She was so bleary from lack of sleep that she almost walked into the path of a dray from Davenport's brewery.

Lily seemed quite unperturbed. 'We just need to get

ourselves going and keep busy,' she said cheerfully. 'The day'll soon go by.'

Gwen never understood how, since she never said a word about it, but by the end of the day the entire school seemed to know that Miss Purdy and Miss Drysdale had spent the night with Joey and Lena Phillips and their dying mother. She heard some of her class talking about it in the playground, looking at her and murmuring to each other. Ron Parks came up to her at dinner time.

'Is Joey coming back to school, Miss Purdy?'

'I don't know, Ron.' Gwen felt glad he'd asked. 'He doesn't have a mother or a father now, you see. So I'm not sure who's going to look after him.'

'Only, he was a pal. He was all right, Joey was.'

Gwen looked at Ron's simple, cheerful face. 'Yes, he was. He *is*. It's just that I don't know where he'll be living, so he may not be able to come to this school.'

The whole day she had been affected by melancholy, and a strange feeling that life could now never be the same. When she had arrived back at Ariadne Black's house she had been so weary and downcast that she had forgotten completely that Ariadne did not know where she had been for the past twenty-four hours. Ariadne, clad in a shimmering, pale green dress, opened the door and, seeing Gwen, gasped theatrically.

'Oh! Miss *Purdy*! How could you do this to me? I've been on the point of going to the police. All night! All day! Waiting here in uncertainty! I've been through everything in my mind – right down to the white slave trade. I said to Mr Purvis – will we ever see her again, d'you think? Oh, we passed a terrible evening. And did I sleep a wink? I can assure you I didn't! Where have you *been*?'

To Gwen's surprise, mixed in with the dramatics, she detected genuine pleasure to see her back.

'I'm so sorry, Mrs Black . . .'

'Ariadne, *please* . . . I must put the kettle on . . . Oh, I'm ever so relieved, you've no idea . . . I don't like my lodgers to go missing . . .'

She listened, one hand clasped over her heart as Gwen explained.

'The poor little mites. To an *orphanage*. What a wicked world we live in! Of course, George and I were never fortunate enough to produce children so I can't speak with the feelings of a mother. But to see a child deserted in the world with nowhere to call home – it's wicked, that's what it is. I'm sure Mr Purvis would think it was terrible. He's a very sensitive man, Harold is.'

'May I have a bath tonight do you think?' Gwen asked while the going was good.

'Oh, *yes*. I'm sure we could move you forward a day, dear. I'll strike you off for Friday.'

Over the evening meal, for which Ariadne had done something unique with a fillet of hake, she insisted that Gwen tell them all about the adventures of the night. Harold Purvis ate his meal in silence, listening. He gave off an odd, metallic smell. Every so often Gwen felt him giving her a sideways look. She tried these days to keep out of his way, but later, when she went out of her room to have a bath, she found him standing on the landing, blocking her way. She moved towards the bathroom, expecting him to stand back, but instead he waited. He was standing in the darkest place, away from the light.

'Could you let me through to the bathroom, please?' she said sharply.

Mr Purvis took a step towards her. He was in his shirtsleeves now and he smelled more strongly than ever.

'Who were you really with last night, eh?' She could see his face now, smiling strangely at her.

'What *are* you talking about?' She gripped her towel with a sense of panic. Something about Mr Purvis's manner made her feel deeply uneasy.

'You don't think I was taken in, do you? A young lady like you playing Florence Nightingale in some slum yard. Who were you really with?' He was standing even closer to her now. Gwen felt herself begin to tremble, but at the same time she became furiously angry.

'Get away from me!' she commanded. 'I don't know what you think you're doing, but you come any closer and I'll shout for Mrs Black.'

'Go on then – call her,' Harold Purvis mocked, but he did take a step back.

'Just keep away from me,' Gwen said, trying to maintain her dignity. She passed him to get to the bathroom and, as she did so, felt his hand squeeze her left buttock.

'How dare you!' she cried, but he was walking away, laughing. Gwen locked the bathroom door, shaking. What on earth was she going to do about him? Suppose he was waiting out there when she came out?

After all this, it was a struggle to keep her mind on Form Four and the Romans the next morning. She told them about the Fosse Way and Watling Street.

'The roads were built a little bit higher than the land around them so the water could drain off,' she said. 'And they built them in layers with materials they could get hold of nearby.' She drew a little diagram on the blackboard.

Mr Purvis had not been outside the bathroom. While she was soaking in the bath she could hear him playing his blasted trumpet. Marble halls again. The incident had really unsettled her, though she told herself not to be so stupid. In her bedroom she had sat looking at her picture of Amy for courage. Would Amy Johnson let a creep like Harold Purvis get under her skin? Of course not! If anything else happened she would tell Ariadne what was going on.

As the children copied her diagram of a Roman road, Gwen's eyes were drawn back to the the empty space left by Joey Phillips. Seeing where Joey lived, what he and his family had to endure, had come as a profound shock to her. She had had no idea that such extreme poverty existed and the fact shamed her. How comfortable and easy her life had been. What other children in her form might be suffering terrible things as well? There was Alice, still squinting, half blind with no glasses to help her. But the thought of Joey tore at her especially. She'd go back and see him, she decided. At the end of school.

I'll get some groceries on the way, she thought, putting her coat on, once the last lesson was over. And a few sweets for the children. She thought of Miss Drysdale's generosity the day before. She had told her that she was going to see the Phillips children.

'Well, that's very kind of you,' Lily said. 'I've got a couple of garments I can send along with you if you'd be so good. I suppose the two of them will be gone in a couple of days.'

It was a little milder outside today, threatening rain. The playground was full of children streaming towards the gate. Suddenly nervous, Gwen walked among them, trying to decide what to buy. There were only a couple of small shops in this street – she'd just have to see what they had.

'Afternoon, Miss Purdy.'

Daniel Fernandez was standing just outside the gate.

'Oh!' She had been completely preoccupied and she was startled by the way the sight of him set her heart thudding. Once more he was only in shirtsleeves, white cuffs rolled. Against them his forearms looked very dark. 'Good afternoon. Have you come to meet Lucy?'

'Yes – thought I'd come down as it's not so cold.'

She smiled, and for the first time saw him smile back. A genuine warmth lit his eyes. For a few seconds she held her breath, then remembered to release it again, aware that gaggles of children were coming out of the playground, all staring at them.

'Looks as if spring's on its way today.'

'Takes a while to feel it here.' Daniel shifted his weight, manoeuvring the crutch. 'In the Welsh valleys you can see the work of the seasons more directly.'

'Yes,' Gwen agreed. She felt suddenly more relaxed, that he was not testing her as he had been before. 'That's true where I grew up as well. There's so much smoke in the air here it's hard to pick up anything else.'

There was silence for a moment. Gwen realized she ought to move on, but found she didn't want to.

'Takes our Lucy a bit longer than the others,' Daniel said, looking into the playground.

'Yes, but she does very well. She's settled in now.'

'She likes you.'

This directness threw her off guard.

'Well.' She laughed. 'That's good – I suppose! She's a good girl.'

Daniel was looking at her searchingly, as if trying to work her out.

'I hear you stayed all night with that boy's mother. The one who died.'

'Gracious!' Gwen said. 'News travels fast around here, doesn't it? Who told you that?'

'Lucy. It was good of you.'

'Not really. I went with Miss Drysdale and there was really no choice. Those poor children had been struggling on for I hate to think how long, trying to look after her. It was consumption. And the house . . . honestly, I've never seen anything like it.' Her indignation grew as she spoke. 'The place is practically falling down with damp and neglect and there was no fire, no food. I don't know how she survived for as long as she did. She was expecting a child as well. It's awful – just *terrible*.'

She had not noticed the passion in her voice until she saw it register in Daniel's eyes and she blushed, feeling as if she had somehow given herself away.

Just then, though, Miss Monk stepped out through the gate and, seeing Gwen standing there with Daniel, gave her a poisonous, disapproving look as she passed.

'Looks as if you're in trouble with her!' Daniel said. 'Goodness, that was a killing look.'

'Yes,' Gwen stared after her. 'She's not the sweetest of women. I'm not sure what I've done to deserve that though.'

Daniel laughed then, deep and wholeheartedly, and she found herself laughing with him.

'Ah, here comes Lucy!' He leaned slightly to see through the gate and almost overbalanced.

'Careful!' Gwen reached out and caught his hand,

helping him to keep his balance. As he pulled against her she felt his immense strength.

'Thanks!' Daniel laughed at himself. 'I'll get this blasted thing off in a week or two.'

'Daniel!' Lucy hurried to him as fast as she could. She looked pleased to see them out there talking together.

'Hello, Lucy.' Gwen smiled at her. 'You've done some good work today.'

There was a pause while no one was sure whether to move away. Then, to her surprise, Daniel said, 'If you're not in a rush, would you like to come back with us – have a cup of tea?'

Everything else left her mind then. She was surprised to hear an almost bashful note in his voice, and she found that there was nothing she wanted more at that moment than to go with Daniel Fernandez and spend time in his company.

Joey sat in the very corner of the hearth.

Mrs Simmons's house was full of people. Four of her seven children were home from school, and on and off all day there had been a stream of people in and out, all keen to learn from the horse's mouth about Dora Phillips's death and who those women were who had been in the house for the night. The room was full of steam as the kettle boiled again and again. Mrs Simmons lorded it over the proceedings, dispensing titbits of information. Joey and Lena, the subjects under discussion, were gradually being dismissed as minor characters in a story in which Mrs Simmons had somehow become the main part.

Lena was upstairs on one of the beds. She had grown more and more unwell and her fever was running high. This morning, when she had got up to go out to the toilet she fainted, collapsing on the floor.

'We'll make her a cup of Bovril,' Mrs Simmonds had said. 'That'll help her along.'

Lena had sipped a few mouthfuls of the dark broth, then been sick over the bed. After that, she lapsed into delirium. Mrs Simmons was far too fat to keep going up and downstairs so Lena was left alone.

Joey sat on the hard floor near the fire, skinny knees pulled up close to his chest. He stared at the flames as the people swirled round him, talking about his mother and all that had happened. He tried not to listen. He couldn't feel anything. Although he was quite warm, he was cold and numb inside, as if someone had filled him up with ice. He barely knew where he was, was unaware of time passing. He spent the day sitting in a dream. At dinner time Mrs Simmons had given him a plate of mashed potato awash with thin gravy and he must have eaten it, although he could not remember anything until he handed the plate back empty.

Sounds roused him: the tearing noise of paper – Mrs Simmons's kids were playing at something – then another knock at the door. More voices.

'I've told them.' It was a man's voice. 'I've just been to Barnardo's and the other place – they said they were full. Too many already. Barnardo's said they couldn't be sure they'd all be kept together. But there'll be someone round in the morning, sharp.'

Barnardo's. The word reached Joey, hammered into his stunned mind. The people who took Polly and Kenny were coming for him and Lena! The ice in him melted to be replaced by a tight sensation, as if he was going to explode. He strained his ears, listening to every word.

'It's for the best,' Mrs Simmons said. She coughed convulsively, her whole body quivering. Joey thought he would burst, waiting for her to recover, to hear what she had to say next. 'Still – what else can I do? Sooner the better – get it over with. They'll be best off in a home. Poor little buggers.'

Thirteen

There were two women in the shop when they reached 15 Alma Street and they stood back to let Gwen and Daniel through with Lucy. Theresa Fernandez was behind the counter. Gwen saw she was wearing a navy blue blouse buttoned to her throat and her dark hair was taken back more tightly than last time they met. The overall effect was to make her look neater and younger.

'Afternoon, Miss Purdy,' she said, sounding a little startled. Her eyes were anxious. 'Everything all right with Lucy?'

Gwen could feel the two ladies' eyes examining her coat, hair, shoes.

'Oh yes, she's perfectly all right,' Daniel said, nodding at the customers. 'I just asked Miss Purdy back for a cup of tea.'

'Hello.' Gwen smiled. 'I hope you don't mind.'

'Oh, no!' Theresa lifted the hatch in the counter to let them through. 'It was just, seeing you, I thought the worst for a minute.'

As they went out, she heard one of the women in the shop say, 'Pretty little thing, ent she? She really a teacher? She don't look old enough!'

Daniel led her into the blue back room, then seemed at a loss.

'Won't you sit down?' he said awkwardly, nodding

towards the table. Resting on it was a block of salt, obviously newly delivered. The end where it had been cut was a gleaming white. The chairs were all tucked neatly under the table. Gwen pulled one out and sat down. She felt nervous too.

Next to the salt was a newspaper. The *Daily Worker*, Gwen read. She felt Daniel watching her as she looked at it. She was acutely conscious again of being in a household utterly foreign to her: people who were Catholic, spoke differently, read newspapers she had never heard of before. The thought was both unsettling and exciting.

In the sudden silence she became aware of Lucy making faces at her brother and looking meaningfully at the stove. When he still didn't get the message, she hissed, 'Daniel, aren't you going to make Miss Purdy some tea?'

'Oh yes – sorry!' Daniel looked enquiringly at Gwen.

'Tea would be very nice,' Gwen said, smiling at their awkwardness. But she too felt flustered and self-conscious.

'Right then.' Daniel hobbled over to the stove and stared at it as if he'd never seen it before. He leaned down to turn on the gas.

'Is there any water in the kettle?' Lucy prompted.

'Ah well – no, probably not . . .' He turned suddenly, gave a disarming grin and went to lean his crutch against the wall.

'Let me do it.' Gwen got up and swiftly took the kettle to the stone sink in the scullery in a fraction of the time it would have taken either Daniel or Lucy with their bad legs. It was a big kettle and she had to lift it with both hands once it was full.

139

'There – you must need a big one like this with a family this size,' she said, putting it down over the lit flame. Lucy was smiling, appearing thrilled at having her beloved teacher making tea in her house.

There was a clamour at the door and Rosa came in, followed by Vincent and Dominic.

'I'm hungry!' Dominic cried. He was eleven or so, Gwen calculated – older than Rosa and younger than Vincent, who was soon to leave school, and a handsome, dark-eyed boy with an intense expression, more like Daniel than any of the others.

'You're forever hungry, Dom,' Daniel said, cutting slices from a loaf for them all. 'I think you've got a worm inside you.'

'Sister Bridget took my dinner away when I'd hardly started it – she said I had bad manners,' Dominic said resentfully.

'Why – what were you doing?' Daniel teased.

Gwen watched his face. *He's lovely*, she found herself thinking. For a moment she remembered her dream and a blush flooded across her cheeks. She hoped none of the children had noticed.

'He put his knife in his mouth,' Rosa sounded disparaging. She seemed old for her eleven years. 'You're stupid, Dom – you know Sister Bridget's mad on manners and all that sort of thing.'

'Just mad, more like,' Dominic said sulkily.

'Now, now,' Daniel said. 'We have a teacher here, remember.'

'It's all right.' Gwen laughed and stood up to slip off her coat.

'Take the salt, Dom, will you?' Daniel nodded towards the scullery and Dominic came and lifted the block off the table.

The Fernandez children each wolfed down a slice of bread and margarine, all talking at once, then the room went quiet as they disappeared out through the shop again, Rosa taking charge of Lucy.

'She's very beautiful,' Gwen said, watching the older girl lead her sister out of the front door.

'Rosa? Yes, I s'pose she is,' Daniel said. Clearly he'd never thought about it before. 'She's a good girl. Helps our ma a lot.'

'It sounds as if you all do.' She had been struck by how close the family were.

Daniel nodded, limping to the table with the brown teapot. For a moment his expression was serious. 'Needs must.'

He sat opposite her, the tea brewing between them. There was an oilcloth on the table today, and Daniel had brought over three thick white cups. She looked shyly across at him.

'So – do you have a job? Yourself, I mean, apart from the shop?'

Daniel nodded, jiggling the handle of the teapot. 'Off and on. What I can get. I do a bit of house painting, repairs and that. Can't do any of that with this though –' He looked down ruefully at his leg with the plaster cast on it. 'And I'm not always here, see.'

Gwen was confused. 'How can you keep a job if you keep moving about?'

'I work when I can. But my real work is with the movement and the party.'

She could hear the passion in his voice, but she had no idea what he was talking about and just stared at him, feeling foolish.

'The NUWM – National Unemployed Workers' Movement,' Daniel explained. He leaned forward, elbows on the table. His tone was patient but she could sense his disbelief at her ignorance. 'The valleys are full of unemployed men who've been locked out of the mines or forced out by scab labour. They're expected to let their families starve while the bosses rake in the profits. The princes of capitalism have all the power to decide the fate of the working man. They can cast him aside when he can't or won't produce the profits they want to wring out of him by the sweat of his labour. And even when he's unemployed they beat him down with the means test, take away the last of his dignity and make him live like a beggar, a pauper on the parish. The movement is getting unemployed men together as a body to say – enough!'

All this came pouring out fluently. The intensity of his words thrilled through her. He spoke without looking away from her, eyes ablaze under the thick black curls. In those moments, Gwen knew for certain that she was with someone quite unlike anyone she had ever met before.

'Only when we're together can we be strong, can we stand up to them. We will not be the slaves of capitalist dictators!'

Daniel seemed about to thump his fist on the table, but instead he poured the tea. He got up to take a cup to his mother in the shop and was talking on the way back before he had even sat down.

'Look what happened at Mardy – 1931, when the means test was biting into mining families who'd had no work in months or years. That's what they do, see?' He sat down, leaning forward to impress the words on her, knowing she came from another world, did not understand. She could feel the force of his need to *make* her understand, and she wanted to know, but already she was floundering. Where was Mardy?

'They steal their jobs, then steal their homes. The movement stood with a household where they'd come to take away the furniture before they'd pay them a penny to feed their bellies. Well, they got them for unlawful assembly, didn't they? Called them "conspirators – little Moscow". When they went to the assizes in Cardiff, twenty-nine of them were sent to prison – seven years' hard labour for the lot of them.' Daniel sat back, his lip curling. 'Police courts – that's what they are, lock, stock and barrel. No one else's word counts.'

He took a gulp of tea and there was silence for a moment. Gwen could just hear the distant sounds of children playing out at the front.

She didn't know what to say, where to begin. There had been marches in protest against the means test, that she remembered. Grainy newspaper pictures of groups with banners. But the test had been something far away, had not come near to touching her. Had it touched any of her pupils in Worcester? She didn't know, hadn't thought. One or two, perhaps. She felt ashamed that she didn't know. Everything Daniel was saying seemed so new, so different from the life she had known.

'And the party? You said you worked for the party?'

Daniel reached to take something out of his back pocket.

'My party card,' he said, showing it to her proudly, before replacing it. 'Communist Party of Great Britain.' His voice contained a swell of pride. He was watching for her reaction, but she didn't understand what sort of reaction he expected. Russia, she thought. The Soviet Union. Revolution. Lenin. What else should she know about Communists? She just thought of them as foreign and even more distant from her life than the means test. And she'd never been interested in politics. Edwin talked about it sometimes – about Hitler and Mussolini, how they had to be stopped. But it never felt real and Edwin did tend to go on a bit. Usually she just waited until he'd finished. Her parents never said who they voted for, but she knew they voted Conservative. She wasn't sure how she knew: it seemed to be taken for granted in the circles they moved in.

Blushing, she said, 'I'm dreadfully ignorant, I'm afraid.'

Daniel watched her in silence for a moment, as if trying to decide something. Then he got up. 'Just a moment. Let me show you.'

Taking his crutch, he went to the tiny cupboard under the stairs. Gwen heard a sound like a tin box opening. A moment later he came limping back with a big leatherbound book. She was startled. Of course Catholics had statues of Mary and Jesus, but somehow she hadn't imagined Daniel to be religious. Religion was another thing her family didn't talk about at home. They simply went to church on Sundays and that was that. Even Edwin, in a funny way, didn't actually say much about what he believed. It was taken for granted that it went with his calling, with the dog collar.

'Are we going to do a bible study?' she asked, flippant in her uncertainty.

Daniel stared at her, then burst out laughing as he put the heavy book down on the table. The sound of his laughter passed right through her.

'Well, it's my Bible,' he said, moving his chair closer

to hers. 'And I dare say Jesus Christ would find a lot in here to agree about. Though Mam might have a go at me for saying that!'

Gwen leaned down to read the gold lettering on the spine. 'CAPITAL. KARL MARX.'

'This,' Daniel said solemnly, his hand stroking the worn maroon leather, 'is the message of justice and liberation for mankind.'

She was struck by his certainty, felt in herself immediately a hunger to understand what gave him such passionate conviction. Daniel sat down next to her and in those moments she became aware of an over-whelming combination of feelings, as if her whole being, mind and body, was subject to an electric current stimulated by his physical proximity, by his words, the fact that he was about to tell her his thoughts. Once again all the hairs on her body were standing on end, as if raised by a magnet. She gave a small shudder, as if something had stroked her all over.

'You cold?'

'No! I'm perfectly all right,' she said, smiling.

Daniel opened the book. Its flyleaf was covered in tiny writing in a neat, copperplate hand. Gwen saw a note. 'Read page 786. This chapter is one of the classics of Socialism.' As Daniel turned the pages, she saw that there were footnotes and annotations in the margins, and sheets of paper inserted between pages, again all closely written over. She read various chapter headings, 'Commodities and Money', 'The Labour Process', 'Division of Labour and Manufacture'. Her eyes met Daniel's.

'All that writing – did you do that?'

'Oh yes. I've studied every line of it.'

'But it looks so . . . *dense*.'

'It's not easy. But there were lectures, see. I went to the Labour College down London for a time. Now I study on my own, keep it going like.'

'I've heard of it. But I don't know *anything*,' she said wretchedly.

And Daniel began to talk. He talked about the working classes, about how the only way they would achieve justice for themselves was by uniting together against the enemy, which was the capitalist system. He talked and talked about Marx and his writings, some of which she understood and some she didn't. How, in the course of history, capital had become the basis of commodity production. The workers made something from materials that cost almost nothing, and through giving their labour turned it into something that could be sold for profit.

'Profit is theft from the workers of what is rightfully theirs,' he said.

Gwen nodded, trying to keep up with him.

'The capitalist owners have the power to keep the workers in their place. Capitalism survives on their exploitation. And while we're all divided, our energy sapped, nothing is going to change. Our task in the Communist Party is to unite the workers, that's when we're powerful. I've seen it – I've caught glimpses of it, Miss Purdy, in the valleys, in the coalfields, when the workers unite and speak with one voice.' His voice was low and passionate. 'And it's a vision. A force and a vision of what could be. So yes –' once again he laid his hand on the book. It was a strong, fine hand and she found herself longing to lay her own over it – 'it's my Bible. My vision of the heavenly city if you like. Against oppression and the scourge of fascism.'

She watched him, entranced. For moments, as he

talked, he reminded her of Edwin, talking without pause, eager to voice his ideas. But with Edwin she tended to find her mind wandering, whereas with Daniel she was caught by the earnest force of his words. She felt as if her mind, her life, was expanding as she listened to him, as if a wide window was being flung open onto a way of thinking and seeing that she had never experienced before.

'But . . .' she stammered, 'how?'

'By making them wake up! By education, by speaking and showing people that they don't have to lie down under oppression! By showing them that unity is our strength. That's what I do, you see. That's my life's work.'

This last statement resulted in a pause, during which Paul Fernandez came in from work. Gwen felt as if she had been woken from a dream.

'Afternoon, Miss Purdy,' he said shyly. He was the fairest of the Fernandez children and very like his mother. Gwen guessed him to be about sixteen.

She roused herself. It was time to get home! She was going to be late for tea, and there was no telling what Harold Purvis might accuse her of getting up to.

'Goodness,' she said, 'time's getting on – and I had marvellous intentions of going to see that boy, Joey Phillips – the one whose mother died. I'll have to go tomorrow now.'

'I waylaid you,' Daniel said.

'No, I was willingly waylaid. It's been very interesting – thank you.' Her words sounded feeble compared to the way she felt.

They stood up and for a moment were unnervingly close to one another. Gwen stepped back.

'I'll be here a while longer,' Daniel said. 'Will you come and see us again?'

'Lena. Lena!'

Joey whispered urgently to her in the darkness. There was no reply. He could only hear her rasping breaths beside him.

'Wake up – you've got to get up!' He shook her, desperate now. Lena's only response was a little cat-like whimper.

All day Joey had waited, trying not to show the neighbours anything of what was going on inside him. *Barnardo's.* They passed the word around the room with each new visitor, whispered or spoken aloud as if he was deaf or didn't exist. *Tomorrow morning.* Someone would be coming to take them away. In his mind it was always a man, so tall that his head was out of sight up in the sky, and he would have huge hands, gripping chains which he'd wrap round them like the strong man in the Bull Ring then drag them away to the orphanage. *Orphanage.* The word clanged in his mind over and over, like an iron door slamming shut.

All day he said not a word, but the fear twisted and tightened in him. At last the Simmons family had made their rowdy way up to bed and Joey and Lena were put downstairs to sleep on a straw mattress. Lena had hardly opened her eyes all day. In the evening she woke for a short time and sipped some milk, but then she sicked it up again and went back to sleep.

'Poor mite.' Mrs Simmons gave a quivering sigh. 'Let's hope she feels better in the morning.'

The room was very dark. Joey lay back for a moment. He could hear the fire shifting, the tap dripping in the yard. There was a smell of bleach. He could not sleep. His heart was thudding. The thoughts hammered at him again. The man from the orphanage was coming in the morning! He had to get away, out of here. Whatever he had to do, they were not taking him away. But what was he going to do about his little sister?

'Lena!' He tried again. For the first time since his mother died, tears came into his eyes. He thought of Miss Purdy. Maybe she'd help, but she wasn't here. He tried not to let himself think of her because it gave him an ache inside. No one was here – not even Lena. Who did he have in the world? Dad – where was he? That was another thought he tried never to have.

The memory of his father's back disappearing down the entry that day made him cry in earnest. He lay curled tightly on his side. The night pressed round him. He thought of the dark roofs outside, the streets, endless streets beyond them, and he sobbed. Afterwards, without meaning to, he slept.

He woke with a jolt, heart banging hard. He could see the dim shape of the window, the table across the room. Dawn! And they were coming to get him!

'Lena!' Frantically, he made a last attempt to rouse her. She did not move.

'Lena – come on!' He shoved her. There was no reaction. He'd have to leave her! They'd have to take Lena, but they were never taking him. He'd rather die.

He was seized with the urgent need to relieve himself and he went into the scullery and peed in the bucket under the sink. Then he helped himself to half a loaf of bread. Without a backward glance he went to the door. As he was feeling for the latch, his hand met a garment hanging from the hook on the back. Mr

Simmons's coat. He hesitated. It felt threadbare and soft. It would be far too big, but it would keep him warm. He had nothing of his own. With a jump he managed to get it off the hook and wrap it round him. He tore the loaf in halves and put a piece in each pocket. Then he let himself out into the silent yard.

Fourteen

After the last bell the next afternoon, Gwen walked to the gate among the crowds of children, trying to convince herself that she was not excited, not hoping that Daniel Fernandez would be waiting outside. When she made her way out to the street, Lucy was standing there and smiling shyly up at her.

'Walking home on your own today?' Gwen asked.

'I think so.' Lucy nodded.

There was no Daniel, but instead, waiting a little way along the road, was Millie Dawson. Some of the younger children were gathered round her and a few others called, 'Hello, Miss Dawson!' to her in daring voices.

Gwen waited, smiling, until the children had moved on. 'Hello! 'What're you doing here? It's lovely to see you!'

Millie smiled wanly from under the brim of her hat. 'I'm on my way into town.' She looked towards the school. 'Everything much as usual, is it? How's old Monk-face?'

Gwen rolled her eyes. 'Crabby as ever. I bet you're not missing her!'

'No.' Millie's eyes filled. 'I don't half miss the rest of it, though. Look, Gwen, will you come and see us at the weekend? It'd be good to have a chinwag.'

'Oh, Millie!' Gwen saw the tears roll down her

friend's face. 'Of course I'll come – I'd love to! I'm
sorry you're feeling so miserable.'

'I'll get by.' Millie tried to smile, wiping her eyes
determinedly. 'I seem to be forever crying these days. I
think I'll go mad if I can't have a proper talk to
someone! Look, I'll have to go. See you Saturday –
about three?'

Poor Millie! Gwen walked along Canal Street
towards Joey's yard with a heavy heart. She was going
to Mrs Simmons and felt nervous about what was
to come. In her hand was a big bag of sweets. She'd
gone out in the lunch hour to find Parks's Sweet Shop,
which was tucked in the lee of the railway bridge where
it passed over the junction of Canal Street and Wellington Street. During the school day they heard trains
go by, steaming over the bridge. The windows were
crammed with jars and bars of chocolate and toffee.
Gwen thought of Ron's terrible teeth and smiled to
herself.

'Yes, bab?' the woman behind the counter had said.
She was very plump, with thick brown hair, and wore
spectacles and a big brown cardigan.

'Hello,' Gwen said. 'Are you Ron's mother?'

'Yes.' The woman immediately looked guarded and
folded her arms beneath her large breasts. 'Why?'

'Oh, nothing to worry about.' Gwen smiled. 'I'm
his teacher, that's all.'

'Oh ar . . .' Mrs Parks still looked wary. 'Miss
er . . .?'

'Purdy,' Gwen said brightly.

'Oh yes – he's mentioned you.'

'Nothing bad, I hope?'

Mrs Parks just looked at her.

'He's a good boy, your Ron.'

At this, the woman's eyes lit up behind her spectacles and she nodded enthusiastically. 'Oh, he *is*. They're good 'uns, my boys. Golden, they are.'

Gwen had been taken aback and rather moved by this declaration. Imagine her mother saying that about her!

Now, as she came in through the entry to the yard in Canal Street, Gwen thought the back-to-back houses looked even more mean and dreary than she remembered. Immediately, though, her attention was taken by the two men standing outside Mrs Simmons's house. They wore long, dark coats and one of them had, tucked under his arm, a child-sized white coffin.

She hovered at a respectful distance until Mrs Simmons came to the door and showed the men in. She spotted Gwen behind them.

'Oh dear, what a carry on! You're too late, I'm afraid, if it's about the children.'

'Whatever's happened?'Gwen was appalled. 'What d'you mean, too late? Is Joey – has one of them passed away?'

'The girl. When we got up this morning she was laid down there, stiff as a plank . . .' Mrs Simmons's voice thickened. She groped in her extensive cleavage and pulled out a rag to wipe her nose. 'And no sign of the boy. The people from the orphanage came this morning and I had to tell 'em the bird had flown! What they must've thought . . . He must've scarpered in the night . . .' She stood back to let the men out again, thanking them. 'I don't know if he saw his sister'd passed on and it frightened him, or what. And my husband's coat's gone . . .'

Gwen stood, nonplussed, the bags of sweets in her hand.

'Come in a minute – oh, my word – they've put her in . . .'

The coffin was on the table and Gwen looked in at the terrible sight of Lena's little figure laid in it in her ragged dress, eyes closed, hands laid to rest on her stomach. Dora Phillips had been the first dead person she had ever seen. It was awful for this to be so quickly followed by another, especially a child. She could hardly take it in.

'Oh God, how awful!' she breathed. 'Poor little thing. How could she have died?'

'Well, she was bad last night,' Mrs Simmons said. 'You know, feverish, but I daint think she was that poorly. Ooh – I feel quite peculiar myself.' She sank down on a chair and mopped her face with her apron. 'There's been that much upset . . . My Dolly was beside herself . . . And with the boy going off like that. It's not good for me, all this – that it isn't.'

Gwen could see that Mrs Simmons was genuinely in a state.

'I'm ever so sorry.' She felt tearful herself. 'You've been a good neighbour and ever so kind to these children. You couldn't have done any more than you have.'

'I've done my best.' Mrs Simmons mopped her eyes. 'Only I never expected this.'

'Do you have any idea where Joseph might have gone?'

The woman shook her head. 'No. Not unless he's gone off to look for Wally, that good-for-nothing father of his. He's not been about here for months now. Be like looking for a needle in a haystack.'

Gwen took her leave and walked back slowly down the entry, full of misgiving at the thought of Joey Phillips roaming the streets. He was so small, so ill-fed and fragile. Whatever would become of him? Should she try to look for him? But Mrs Simmons said he had gone very early in the morning. He could be anywhere by now.

She found herself standing out in Canal Street, lost in thought, holding the bags of jelly babies, sherbet lemons and toffees. *What am I going to do with these?* she wondered. *I don't want to eat them all.* She thought about taking them in to school to treat her class. Then another idea came to her. Where was the one place she really wanted to go, to be able to sit in a homely room and where she would find a large collection of children?

Hardly knowing she had decided to go there, almost daring herself, she found her feet straying past the school and pub and into Alma Street. She didn't give herself time to think about whether she would feel embarrassed turning up at the Fernandezs' house again so soon. The desire simply to go there was too over-whelming.

'Afternoon, Miss Purdy,' Theresa Fernandez greeted her as soon as she walked into the shop. She had a good view of the door, between the two rows of shelves and Gwen could see her, surrounded by tins and packets. At one end of the counter were all the cigar-ettes. 'I don't know if you've come to find Daniel, but he's not in, I'm afraid.'

Gwen felt a pang of disappointment, but then she was almost relieved. She would have felt a bit foolish at him seeing her arrive here again. She could explain about the sweets and just leave them without embar-rassing herself.

'Will you have a cup of tea?' Theresa asked. 'Shop's quiet, and I can hear if anyone comes in.'

'Well, that would be lovely,' Gwen said. She enjoyed the woman's Welsh accent and her homely presence. She was wearing her black shawl today over a white blouse. There was something about Theresa Fernandez that felt solid, rock-like, as if you could rely on her for anything. And there was a great warmth about her. To her surprise, Gwen found herself saying, 'To tell you the truth, I could do with someone to talk to.'

'Could you, lovey?'

Once they were through in the back room, Gwen explained, 'I really came to give you these sweets for the children.' She put the bags on the table and explained about Joey and Lena Phillips.

Theresa was distracted from pouring the tea by Gwen's story. She stood at the stove, her hand on the handle of the kettle as it warmed.

'*Duw, duw* – there's terrible, isn't it? The little girl passing on like that! And you think that young lad's out roaming the streets on his own?'

'Well, I suppose he must be – unless he's found somewhere else to go.'

'P'raps it's an auntie or uncle somewhere he's gone to?'

Gwen sighed. 'I hope so. He's such a poor little thing. I hate to think of him out – it's still cold, especially at night.'

Theresa sat down. Gwen wanted to ask where Daniel had gone, but it seemed so forward and she felt self-conscious. But his mother immediately said, 'Daniel's out at one of his meetings – least, getting ready for one.' Gwen was taken aback by the impatience in her voice. 'Just like his father was, only Daniel's even redder than red. 'Twas politics killed my husband. Ate away at him till his heart gave up the struggle and now my Daniel *bach*'s going the same way.'

Gwen wasn't quite sure what to say. 'Don't you agree with his work in the Communist Party?'

Theresa put her cup down and gave out a great sigh. 'I have to struggle with myself, Miss Purdy. The priests say Communism's an ungodly creed which we should never put in place of our faith and the Church. Our Daniel tries to keep the two side by side. He says you can be a Catholic and Communist. I don't know.' Another sigh. She got up and spooned tea into the pot while she continued chatting. She seemed glad to talk.

'I'm a selfish woman, I suppose. All my life it's been going on, all my marriage, lockouts and strikes at the mines, never any work ... I lived through it, like we all did. They were bitter times, Miss Purdy – still are for a lot of them. There was no choice. Then the means test. All the meetings, the protests. Arturo was in the thick of it, you see – never a moment's rest, what with the miners' lodges, the party, the unemployed. Meetings, leaflets, making speeches. Hardly ate or slept sometimes – and I told him, "You won't do yourself any good, Arturo – you'll kill yourself with overwork." And that's how it was.' She paused, steam rising round her as she poured from the kettle.

'One of the meetings, the first protest in Aberglyn, they were marching to the Public Assistance people, police all round, of course. Arturo was one of the ones speaking. He got up and gave it to them – oh, he had a voice on him! So loud and strong. He could have spoken to the whole valley and they'd have heard him!' For a moment she smiled, and Gwen saw the love in her eyes. 'Got to the end, just, and he collapsed. His heart. Never came back home alive.' She carried the last things to the table and sat down.

'That's what's made me selfish now. I suppose it knocked the fight out of me. Once we came up here I just wanted an end to it. There's work here – something you can do, not just the colliery. I want my children fed and schooled, not picking cinders off the heaps in the winter just to survive. I want to forget it all . . . go to Mass Sundays . . .' She shook her head. 'But not Daniel. He can't forget what he's seen. He's ablaze with it. Whatever I say to him falls on deaf ears. It was a police horse broke his leg – doesn't stop him. Back for more! It's no good me saying anything, any more than it was to Arturo. "I'm doing it for you, Ma," he says. "For all of us – for the revolution." ' Gwen could hear the mingled pride and anxiety in her voice. 'And I say to him, "All I've learned about revolutions is that they end up with people losing their heads." But will he take heed of me?' She poured the tea. 'I've seen politics tearing families apart and I don't want it breaking up mine. So I hold my peace most of the time.'

'Thank you,' Gwen said, taking her cup. 'I learned a lot from listening to Daniel yesterday.' She felt like defending him. All his passion for people, for the workers of the valleys. Surely his mother shouldn't be trying to dampen that down!

'Oh, I dare say. He's a one for book learning all right. And a proper firebrand with it.' Theresa smiled ruefully, stirring her tea. 'I suppose I'm just getting old. And there's no stopping him, that I do know. Let's put it away, love. Talk about something else. Tell me about yourself, now.'

*

'Late again, Miss Purdy?' Ariadne Black purred reproachfully as Gwen tore in, barely in time for tea.

One of Ariadne's quirks was that although she insisted on being called by her own first name she never called Gwen anything except Miss Purdy. Gwen thought perhaps it was because she was a teacher. When it came to Mr Purvis, though, he was very definitely 'Harold'. Tonight Ariadne was wearing a floaty dress in a pale coffee colour edged with chocolate brown, and smelled strongly of perfume.

Gwen stared at the plate Ariadne plonked down before her. Shrivelled chops with potatoes and cabbage, boiled to death as ever, and the house stank of it.

'Thank you,' she said with an effort. Thank goodness it was almost the holidays and she could get out of here for a bit! When she looked up, Harold Purvis was watching her with quiet insolence. Gwen put her head down and ate as fast as she could to get away from the pair of them.

That night, she was just falling asleep, when she heard the boards on the landing creak, then a soft, furtive knocking on a door at the back of the house.

'Harold? Harold, darling?'

Gwen sat up, hugging her knees, barely able to believe what she was hearing.

'It's all right, darling. You can let me in,' Ariadne pleaded in a purring voice.

Gwen put her hand over her mouth. She wasn't sure if she felt more appalled or amused. Explosive giggles rose in her chest.

There was a pause, then the knocking again.

'Harold, my beautiful great big panther ... Come on, let your little pussycat in ...'

Snorting, Gwen stuffed the end of the sheet in her

mouth. What kind of household was she living in? Once more she thought of what her mother would say and the laughter began to erupt from her. She lay down, shaking with giggles so much that she didn't hear the door along the landing open to admit Ariadne, then close again.

EASTER HOLIDAYS

Fifteen

'Here we are – eat it while it's hot.'

Gwen's mother dropped a boiled egg into the egg-cup in front of her and sat down, opening out her table napkin.

Gwen obediently removed the top from her egg and dipped in a finger of toast. The yolk overflowed, rich yellow, down the side.

'Really,' Ruth Purdy commented. 'You're no more tidy an eater than when you were four years old.'

Gwen said nothing. She tipped a helping of salt onto the edge of her pretty floral plate. Ruth Purdy liked everything to be dainty: bone-china plates and little tea knives. Gwen thought of the thick white cups in the Fernandez household and wished she was there instead. The clock ticked on the mantelpiece and her father coughed and tried to pretend he wasn't eyeing the newspaper because his wife said it was rude to read at the table. Had her parents ever liked one another? Gwen wondered. It was her third day at home and already she was fit to scream.

'So,' her mother said, 'today's the ideal day for us to go to Mrs Twining and then Russell & Dorrell. We'll start early and that'll give us plenty of time . . .'

Ruth Purdy had been mentioning Russell & Dorrell, the large draper's at the end of the High Street ever since Gwen arrived home.

'It's going to be hard enough for Mrs Twining making your dress with you away so much. We'll have to squeeze in fittings. So we mustn't leave it too late. It would be most unfair on her. And there are so many other things to think about!'

'Edwin and I want to keep the wedding as simple as possible,' Gwen reminded her. She pushed her teaspoon into the bottom of the egg with such force it smashed through the shell.

'I know – but even so. Everything must be done properly. It's *so* important to get it right!'

Important to whom? Gwen wondered.

'And your father has his business to think of – haven't you, Morris?'

'Umm?' Mr Purdy dragged his gaze away from the front page of the *Telegraph*. 'Er . . . of course. Yes.' He obviously hadn't heard the question.

'So you mean the purpose of our wedding is to enhance Daddy's business reputation?'

'No of course not – don't be so silly, dear. I just mean there are standards. People in the town would expect us to put on a good show. That's all.'

Gwen hurriedly drank down her tea and left the table before she said something she'd regret. Up in her room she stood at the window. There were tiny buds on the apple tree just waiting to burst into flower. The grass was sodden underneath, the sky a pale arc above. *How did I stand living here all this time?* she asked herself. She tried to imagine Daniel sitting at the breakfast table with her parents. She found herself setting the idea of him, his dancing eyes, that restless muscular body, his burning ideals, against the nervous respectability of her family. It was as if they were asleep, she saw. And until now she'd been asleep also. She ached to see Daniel. She had to be away from Birmingham for two weeks and how unbearable that felt!

She tried to force her emotions back to where they should be. Daniel was from another world. He wasn't a true part of her life! Perhaps these feelings were just a reaction to the idea of marriage – to the closing down of the possibility that she should ever feel anything for anyone else. She shook her head. What did she really know about Daniel Fernandez? She had known Edwin for three years now and he was kind and true and had never let her down. How could she be so disloyal to him?

'Well, you *have* grown up into a lovely girl, I must say!'

Mrs Twining was a small, plump lady with a tight little voice, several chins and bright red lipstick. For years she had run her tailoring business in a cramped upstairs room and had made a little dance dress for Gwen when she was only six years old. She ran her busy hands up and down Gwen's body as if she was sizing up a cow for auction.

'Lovely curves. Oh yes.' She eyed Gwen's breasts so intently that Gwen found herself blushing. 'You're very *full*, aren't you? Oh I can make a lovely job – something pretty you'll be after? Satin and tulle perhaps?'

'Something quite simple,' Gwen said.

At exactly the same moment, her mother said, 'Silk, perhaps?'

Mrs Twining approached with her tape measure. Gwen quickly felt any control she might have over the situation slipping away.

'Now,' Mrs Twining said, when she'd taken the measurements, 'come here a minute.' She took Gwen's arm and pulled her over to a long mirror on a stand near the window. 'You take a look in there. You're a lovely shape, dear – a real hourglass. I can do something really pretty with a full skirt and perhaps some lace across here.' She ran a finger across Gwen's chest. 'Can't display cleavage on our wedding day, can we?'

Gwen looked at herself, trying to concentrate on the matter of a wedding dress. Her oval, blue-eyed face looked back at her, her full lips, wavy hair tied back from her face, the same green tartan skirt and cream sweater, everything just as ever, and yet suddenly she was a stranger to herself, as if the outer Gwen, who looked the same as she had always been, suddenly did not match the person she felt herself to be inside in the least. Panic rose in her.

Her mother was saying something about seed pearls. Gwen dragged her attention away from the stranger in the mirror. She felt distant from it all suddenly. What did any of this matter really? How selfish she was being, she told herself. Her mother, Edwin, everyone was excited about the wedding. It was every bit as much their occasion. She must stop all these silly thoughts she was having and try to get into the spirit of it.

'That sounds a lovely idea,' she said to Mrs Twining, though she had scarcely any idea what the woman had said.

In the mirror she saw her mother's tense face light up with relief.

'Do you really think so? Oh, I am pleased, dear. And I thought you were going to be so difficult about it all!'

Gwen did not see very much of Edwin. It was Holy Week, one of his busiest times of the year. She spent most of the time with her mother, surrounded by scraps of silk and lace, discussing sleeves and bodices and what colour dress her cousin Jane's little daughter Patricia should wear as a bridesmaid. She tried to be as agreeable as she could to her mother. After all, it was her wedding, she must be enthusiastic, and her mother was doing her best!

On Easter Sunday they all went to the morning Communion service. Gwen stood between her parents. Her father hummed the hymns in a vague sort of way, her mother wore a green hat with a colourful peacock feather tucked in the band and held the book a long way from her to read the print.

'*Christ the Lord is risen today, alleluia!*' they sang as Edwin processed in behind the vicar, Bernard Thompson, looking very upright and solemn, his hands clasped. Gwen watched Edwin's long back in his white surplice move along the aisle. And once again, just for a moment, the strangest feeling came over her. A sense of distance, of tiredness with everything, with the idea of watching Edwin parade about for the rest of her life.

As the service went on, her mind wandered. Sunlight slanted in through the windows and she found herself wondering about Joey Phillips. No one knew where he had gone and there was really no one to ask. Where did a small child just disappear to on the streets?

Just a couple of days before the end of term she had

thought she had seen him when she was outside on playground duty. Standing in the spring sunshine, she she looked along towards the boys' end of the school-yard and caught sight of a small figure outside, pressed against the railings near the gate. Her heart beat faster. Putting her hand up to shade her face she stared, screwing her eyes up to see better. Was that Joey? Something about the size of the child, his slightness, made her think it might be. By the time she had hurried to the end to see, there was no one there. She had opened the gate and looked along the road. Nothing. She was taken aback by how bereft she felt, staring along the empty street.

'Did you see anyone looking through the railings?' she asked the children who were playing nearer that end.

'No, Miss,' they chorused. They were all caught up in their games.

She still wondered now, unsure whether it had been him. Keeping her eyes turned towards the pulpit where Bernard Thompson was preaching, she pictured all sorts of terrible misfortune coming over Joey. Perhaps someone had already picked him up and he was in a home somewhere. That thought didn't cheer her at all. The little she had heard about orphanages was grim and she couldn't imagine Joey in an institution. But to be eight years old, a little scrap like that, and alone on the streets. Her eyes filled at the thought, and she lowered her head, pulling her hanky out from up her sleeve. She felt her mother eyeing her. Why had this one child got so much under her skin?

After the service they were all greeted by the Rever-end Thompson.

'Happy Easter to you!' He shook Gwen's hand outside the church door and added with smile, 'I shall let Edwin off the lead a little after today!'

Edwin was waiting outside. He didn't kiss her in greeting – it didn't seem right to him when he was 'on duty' – but came up to her immediately.

'Hello, darling,' he said fervently. 'I'm longing to see you properly. *Sorry* about this week. It's been non-stop.'

'Not to worry,' she said brightly. 'I can hardly complain when I'm hardly ever here anyway. And Mummy's had me on wedding duty all week. I think I'm the one who needs letting off the lead, not you!'

Edwin appeared slightly wounded. 'I thought you'd enjoy all that.'

'Oh, I do!' She smiled. 'Look, I'll see you for lunch. You'd better go and meet and greet a bit more.'

They were able to spend some of Easter week together, going for walks, visiting each other. On the Monday they went to see Mr and Mrs Shackleton out in Callow Hill. Gwen's father once again lent Edwin the motorcar.

'Mummy's in bed pretty much all the time now,' Edwin said as they drove between spring-green fields. 'She's happiest there really. It's such an effort to move her, and her speech is going as well.'

Knowing that they were expecting visitors, the Shackletons were well prepared, or rather James, Edwin's father, was.

'Well, hello-o, both!' he greeted them, beaming. Rufus, their old red setter limped at his side.

Despite his brave cheerfulness, Gwen was shocked by the sight of him. He was a slightly smaller man than

Edwin, but now in his mid-seventies he had become very stooped and his kindly face seemed more wrinkled and worn than when Gwen had seen him at Christmas.

'Joan has been worth her weight in gold today,' Mr Shackleton said, leading them through the hall. Joan was the woman who gave them extra domestic help. 'There's a leg of pork in the oven – and I'm sure I saw signs of an apple pie. Now, how about a spot of sherry before lunch?'

'Is Mummy up to having one?' Edwin asked.

'Oh, I think so, with a bit of help,' Mr Shackleton said, pouring amber sherry into a row of little glasses. He handed one to Gwen with a smile. 'There – and how is life in old Brum treating you?'

'Very well, thank you. Full of interest – just as you said it would be.' Mr Shackleton had been an ally in her decision to work in Birmingham.

'One of my early parishes was up there,' he had told her when she announced her decision. 'Yes – in King's Heath. I had a marvellous time – splendid place, Birmingham. Jolly good idea.'

Now he picked up two glasses. 'Come on through. We'll go and have a drink with Edwina. She'd like that. Best thing is if I help her with her lunch and then we three can come through and eat here. Easiest that way.' He lowered his voice. 'She's not keen on having an audience – not with eating.'

Gwen felt a plunge of dread as he spoke, despite his considerateness in trying to smooth over the distress of what was happening. Edwina Shackleton's decline over the past three years had been terrible to witness.

Edwina's bed was downstairs now, in a back room overlooking the garden. When Gwen first met Edwin's mother she had been in the very early stages of her illness and was still a tall, hearty woman with a thick head of gingerish blonde hair, frizzy, cut to shoulder length, and a healthy, freckled face. She strode about in slacks, working hard in the garden, and in the summer she put on big, loose sandals. She had a loud, ringing laugh and she had laughed often.

They all filed into the room.

'Darling? Edwin and Gwen are here,' James Shackleton announced. 'And I've brought you your little tipple.' His tone was very loving. Gwen felt a pang go through her. Everything here was good and kind, had been settled for her until now. It *had* to be right. And yet, and yet . . .

Edwina's bed was arranged to face the sunny garden, where she had spent so many hours. There was a paddock at the far end, owned by the neighbours, with a piebald pony grazing in it. Edwina was propped up on pillows, her head inclined to one side. She tried to move and say hello, but her neck went into spasm and her words of greeting came out as an indistinct groan. She did manage a smile. Rufus came and laid himself in a patch of sunlight close to her.

'Hello, Mummy.' Edwin leaned over and kissed her. They were strikingly alike and Gwen had often smiled at the sight of them together.

'Hello, Edwina.' She had always insisted, in her hearty way, on Gwen calling her by her Christian name. Gwen kissed her pale cheek and took her hand for a moment. She smelled sourly of sickness, mingled with rose-scented talcum powder. Gwen felt her hand give an answering squeeze.

'Here we are – take a pew,' James said. 'You can both tell us all about everything.'

With loving carefulness, he helped his wife to tiny

sips from her sherry glass. She no longer had reliable use of her arms, so he had to tilt the glass delicately to her lips. At the same time both of them listened as Gwen tried to think of things they would be interested in: Ariadne's dreadful cooking and about the school and her class. She told them about Joey Phillips. She could see that Edwina was listening intently although she could make little comment, and she made sure she spoke to her as much as to anyone. She had always been very fond of Edwina, who was the free spirit of the family. Edwin was much more proper by comparison.

James Shackleton shook his head sadly. 'Yes – what a terrible thing. Life is so very harsh for so many people.'

'Gwen's certainly seeing how the other half live,' Edwin said. She wondered if she imagined the terse note of disapproval – or was it envy? – in his voice. Hadn't he thought that that was the value in her going to Birmingham? She had always talked about school and her pupils before. Now Edwin seemed put out by it. She stopped talking and asked after affairs in the parish instead.

'Well.' James Shackleton stood up finally. 'Our lunch is all ready for us.'

While he gave Edwina her food, Gwen and Edwin walked to the end of the garden. The air felt clean and fresh and a brisk breeze riffled the daffodils. The pony strolled over to join them at the fence and Gwen stroked its soft nose.

'How lovely to see animals again!' She smiled at Edwin, but he was preoccupied.

'She's not looking too good is she?'

'No,' Gwen agreed sadly. There was no point in

pretending otherwise. His mother's decline was painfully obvious.

There was a long pause while she patted the pony's smooth coat, then Edwin said in a tight voice, 'Not getting too involved up there are you?'

Gwen turned, her hand still on the animal's neck. 'What – in Birmingham?'

'You seem very steeped in it all of a sudden.'

'Well.' She laughed. 'I suppose I'm living there all the time at the moment. I get involved in the things I'm doing, you know that. I always have.'

'It's not for much longer, though. You've got duties and obligations here, don't forget.' He wasn't looking at her. He spoke staring across the paddock, which made his pomposity worse. His hands were pushed into his jacket pockets. She wondered if he was still hurt that she had shown less than his expected enthusiasm for the wedding arrangements.

'I know,' she said, baffled. 'But that's where I am at the moment. And I'm learning so much! Understanding things for the first time.' Her enthusiasm spilled out. 'I mean about the way things work. You know – about capitalism, and the way the workers, who are kept poor, are exploited by the capitalist bosses. There's no justice for the poor in the way things are organized – I've seen it, the way people have to struggle to survive. The way some of the people live round our school – you'd hardly believe it!' Her uneducated impressions tumbled out clumsily. She could have told Edwin about who she had begun to learn from, about Daniel Fernandez, but she didn't want to. Daniel felt like her precious secret.

Edwin looked startled. 'Where on earth did you get all these ideas from?'

Gwen brushed her skirt. 'Karl Marx,' she said rather haughtily. She didn't like Edwin's implication that she should not have any ideas.

'Oh, I *see* . . .' Edwin turned back towards the house, laughing in a dismissive way which enraged her. She found herself clenching her teeth. 'I hope you realize that Communism is an atheist philosophy?'

'It may be.' She folded her arms, not automatically following him. If only she knew more, could express what she wanted to say better, the way Daniel could! 'But what if it's *right*?'

'Darling Gwen –' Edwin beamed indulgently, coming towards her with his arms open – 'you've always had your heart in the right place. But you don't want to tangle with big political ideas and such like. Best leave those to the politicians. And they don't have much bearing on our life here, do they? It may be all very well in the Soviet Union.'

She didn't return his embrace. 'What about the poor?' she demanded. 'And the miners in Wales? It has some bearing on *them*. Surely there's more to things than our life here – the parish?' She could hear the sarcasm in her voice.

Edwin chuckled and insisted on embracing her anyway, although she was stiff in his arms.

'Yes, yes – of course. And you know what I think about the fascists. But we can all only do so much, darling. We belong *here*. And your job is going to be to work at my side. Communists or no Communists.' He looked down into her eyes. 'Isn't it?'

Until now she'd always thought of him as knowing best. Kind, stolid old Edwin, her husband to be. She was destined to marry him and be here, in the place she knew. Why was she even thinking otherwise? She felt completely deflated. Everything would be all right as long as she toed the line. She looked back at him and said neutrally, 'Yes. I suppose so.'

On the Friday Gwen went for a fitting with Mrs Twining, who had hurried to stitch together the beginnings of her wedding dress. As usual she had done an excellent job and the white silk hugged Gwen's curves like a second skin. Gwen stood in her stockings, suspenders and brassière as Mrs Twining prodded and pinned and tucked fabric round her abdomen.

'Very nice,' she mumbled, pins nipped between her lips. 'Oh yes – we'll need to bring that in a shade . . .'

To Gwen the whole idea that she would process along the aisle in this silk creation seemed more and more unreal. But her cooperation and attempts at enthusiasm had done a good deal to appease her mother. They had chosen a pretty fabric for the bridesmaid and agreed on how they would wear their hair, so Ruth Purdy had relaxed and become quite excited. Gwen was glad she had managed to keep her happy.

With Edwin, she kept off the subject of politics. It was a mistake to let Daniel and his thoughts anywhere near life here. Daniel was part of somewhere else, a temporary kind of dream life, and the two should not be brought into contact. She did her best to make it up to Edwin and he was easily appeased, as soon as she settled back into being her old biddable self. She had spent an afternoon putting together the parish magazine with him and he had been very pleased and grateful.

She said her goodbyes to him on the Saturday night

before she was due to return to Birmingham for the summer term, although she would see him at church the next morning. Edwin, ever proper, embraced her outside her parents' house.

'It's the downhill run now!' Edwin looked very pleased with himself. 'Another four months and we'll be married!'

'I can't really take it in,' Gwen said. An odd, physical sensation accompanied the thought, a kind of twist inside her.

Edwin stroked her hair. Longingly, he said, 'Heavens, I wish it was tomorrow.'

Gwen smiled.

'Darling,' he went on miserably, 'I know it was what you wanted, but I do wish you were here. It's miserable without you. It's seemed such a long time.'

'I know, but it'll soon pass. It's only a term, after all.' Teasingly she tapped his nose. 'The best things come to those who wait.'

He kissed her then, in his ardent yet restrained way, hands pressing on her back while managing not to let her body come any closer to his.

'Oh.' He pulled back regretfully. 'Look, I'd better go, darling.' He was wide-eyed, suddenly boyish, hoping that she would try to prevent him.

Gwen stood on tiptoe and kissed his cheek.

'See you *soon*,' she said. 'It'll be the half-term holiday in no time.'

'Yes.' Edwin sighed. 'I suppose you're right. That's if your landlady doesn't finish you off with her cooking first!' He went to fetch his bicycle.

'I love you!' he called, weaving off along the road.

She opened her mouth to reply, but he was already a good distance away.

The next afternoon she caught her train back to Birmingham. It was raining and water ran down the windows, which were steamed up inside. She sat with her coat still on and rubbed the wet window, trying to see out, excitement rising inside her.

Joey's hand slid along the bottom edge of the large windowpane above the frame, which was covered in flaking sky-blue paint. He liked the smooth feel of the glass, as if it was water and he might sink into it, cool and soothing on his body. He pressed his forehead against it. On the other side of the pane were shelves arranged with jars and packets: bottles of HP Sauce, packets of Tetley Tea and Bournville Cocoa and Bird's custard powder. He pressed his burning cheek against the glass. For a moment all the colours blurred. Then his eyes focused. Pan Yan Pickle, he read on the label of a bottle.

''Ere – you still hanging about? I thought I told you to clear off!' A plump woman stood on the doorstep. Her voice seemed to boom out from somewhere very high up. 'Look what you've done! I only polished that window this morning and you're making it all smeary. Go on with you! You should be at school!'

'Oh, Mom,' another voice said. 'The poor little thing. He don't look very well to me.' Through his hazy senses, Joey felt her come closer, battering him with questions. 'Are you poorly? What's your name? Where d'you live? Does your mother know you're here?'

He didn't know what else to do except nod his head, which felt too big for his body. But it hurt his neck when he did and he screwed his face up in pain.

A cool hand touched his forehead. 'He's burning! You been sent home from school have you?'

He nodded.

'You hungry?'

Another nod.

'What's that round your neck?' No answer. 'What's that, Mom? Looks like an old sheet. 'Ere, I'll find you summat to eat. Then you'd best get home to your Mom.'

'You're a soft 'a'p'orth, you are,' the older woman scolded, disappearing into the shop. 'He'll be off round the corner right as rain once you've given 'im summat.'

Joey propped himself against the window frame. Time passed. Then he opened his eyes to see a greasy brown paper bag being dangled in front of his nose.

'Go on, then – take them and away with you,' she said, though not harshly. 'Mom don't like you hanging about.'

Round the corner, in a quiet street, he came upon a pair of big green doors. He sank down on the step and looked in the bag. She'd given him a handful of broken biscuits. He shoved one in his mouth. It was soft and stale and, as he chewed, it turned into a thick lump in his mouth which he only managed to swallow with an effort. He closed the bag. The cold of the step crept up into him, making him shiver violently. He hugged his arms across his chest. Something had happened to his head. It was so heavy he had to lean it against the door, and his eyes wouldn't stay open. Darkness sank over him.

Most of the time now, he didn't know where he was. The first days, after he ran away from Mrs Simmons's house, he'd stayed round Winson Green. Mr Simmons's old trenchcoat was long and heavy and he draped it round his neck, the top half of it hanging down the left side of his chest, the tails on the right side. If it wasn't for the night-time he would have ditched the thing. It stank of snuff and Mr Simmons's stale sweat, and it weighed him down. He felt stupid carting it about. But there was also something comforting about the feel of it, the way it hugged warmly around his neck, and when the light began to fade he was glad he'd carried it all day.

The bread had lasted him until the next day. He had no idea what to do with himself, and he walked the streets, up and down, watching out carefully for anyone who might know him. He was frightened they'd be looking for him – the Barnardo's man with his long chains or a van to push him into and lock him in. He walked along the wall of the prison as fast as he could, looking over his shoulder. There was nowhere to duck into here and hide! What if the orphanage man came now and tried to get him?

He went down to the cut, where he and Lena used to go and play. He didn't want to think about Lena, or Polly or Kenny. He wandered back and forth along the towpath. There were warehouses opposite and he kept hearing the trains going by on the railway behind. At the back of one factory a pipe let out hissing clouds of steam just above the murky water. Joey stood and watched. The canal was busy with boats, the motors put-putting by, the narrowboats passing each other on the thin channel. He liked it down there. There were people about but they didn't bother him. He spent a long while throwing things into the water, stones, twigs and cinders. The coat annoyed him, swinging in his face every time he bent down. Stones were the best, the 'plop' they made, then the little rings of ripples. He had to stand back to let a man go by who was leading a big black and white horse, hauling a boat, its hold heaped high with gleaming coal. The man winked at him as he went past.

Soon after he felt gripes in his stomach and suddenly, urgently needed to relieve himself. He just made it up behind a bush and yanked his short trousers down, grunting at the pain in his stomach. Afterwards he had to wipe himself with leaves and his hand stank. He went and leaned over the bank to wash and found tears running down his face. Those he wiped away on the coat.

He kept away from Canal Street, from the house. In his mind they were all still there for him, those giants from the orphanage outside the house, prepared to wait for ever.

In the afternoon he stole a bottle of sterilized milk from a crate at the back of a shop. If he ran off down the road with it, he knew, someone would be suspicious. He was already quite skilled at pilfering. He held the bottle inside the folds of the coat and slipped quietly out of the entry to the street, walking as if he had every right to be there. In Blackpatch Park he ate some of the hard bread and drank all the milk he could.

As evening came, it grew bitter. The air stung his bare legs and he was too cold to stay still. Joey walked the streets, draping the coat round him, along the Flat, the shops all closed now, past the Railway Inn, the baths in Bacchus Road. Smells filled the air: beer from the pubs, the hot whiff of chips and vinegar and smoke from chimneys. He walked along streets, seeing the lights through the windows, hearing voices as doors opened and slammed shut. He carried with him the remainder of the bottle of stera. His feet were tired and sore, but he didn't think about anything. That night he slept in Blackpatch Park rolled up in the coat, pulling it right over his head. He found a spot under some bushes. He heard little rustling noises in the leaves around him, but he kept his head down, exhausted. The next morning he was woken by a magpie's croaking call on the grass nearby.

Over the next few days he walked further out of town. He found other ways of getting food. In Handsworth, he discovered, there were people in the big houses who were rich enough to throw away food. There were the pig bins – usually full of a reeking mulch of leftovers – but in the misken at one house he found a cooked lamb chop and a lump of stale cake. He gnawed for ages at the chop bone. Later, over the side wall of another house, he saw that someone had left a basin of something to cool on the step by the back door. He couldn't see what it was, only the steam rising. He had been walking the streets for three days now and the temptation of warm food possessed him so much he was trembling. Gritting his teeth, he climbed the wall, seized hold of the basin and tried to get back over with it, but it slipped from under his arm and as he leapt to the ground he heard it smash on the path behind. Heart hammering, he ducked down behind the wall. But no one came.

Slowly, still driven by desperation, he inched himself up, pulled up on his arms and looked down over the wall. Amid the smashed shell of the bowl lay soft lumps of egg custard. Saliva poured into his mouth. He *had* to have some! At that moment he didn't care about anything else, would have risked everything for the comfort of that warm, sweet pudding sliding down his throat. In a second he had scrambled over and was scooping the stuff into him in handfuls, separating it from the bits of broken crock. He crammed in as much as his mouth would take, cheeks ballooning, swallowing convulsively.

He heard footsteps in the house and was on the wall in a second, hands smeared with custard.

'Oi – get back 'ere, you little bugger! Look what you've gone and done!'

But he was over, running and running, the coat weighing him down. He ran until he was well away, gasping with exhaustion. He felt terrible. His innards heaved, splatting custard along the Hamstead Road.

That night he slept in Handsworth Park and it rained. He thought about sleeping on the bandstand, but it felt too exposed. Instead, he burrowed himself as far under some bushes as he could, near the churchyard at the side of the park, wrapping himself right up in the coat. In the night he was woken by something tugging at him. Then he was being dragged and he tried to put out his hands, but he was tangled in the coat. Suddenly he felt himself flipped over, banging his back on something sharp and the coat was yanked away from him.

'Oi!' He leapt up. 'That's mine!'

'Not any more it ain't,' a gruff voice said. He barely even got a glimpse of the man as he ran off across the park.

'Give it back!' Joey wailed. 'It's mine! It's my dad's!' In his mind it felt as if it was his father's. He pushed back into his spot under the bushes and hugged his cold legs. Without the coat, he felt naked. It had been like a companion.

Hungering for the sight of something familiar, he

wandered back towards Winson Green the next morning. The day brightened, but it took his damp clothes a long time to dry out. He went to Canal Street under the railway bridge, all his senses alert for meeting anyone he recognized. Near the school he could hear the shouts and screams of children playing. He couldn't help it: he was drawn closer, just wanting to be near, to see. The school playground was lit up with sunshine at the far end. He stood at the corner in the shade, pressed against the railings, peering through. There was a group playing hopscotch. He saw Lucy Fernandez with her long dark hair, limping in the heavy caliper. And Ron – wasn't that Ron? But then his attention was snatched away. Miss Purdy was on dinner duty! At the sight of her in her neat blue coat, with her pretty hair and pink ribbon, something seemed to expand inside him, right up to the back of his throat, an ache that made him swallow to try and make it go away. But then he saw her shade her eyes and he thought she was looking at him. She began to move towards him. He tore himself away, running fast along the street and round the corner.

The nights were the worst now. All he had to wear were his short trousers, his ragged vest, the grey jersey that Miss Purdy had given him and his boots and socks. In the daytime all he thought about was finding food and keeping out of trouble. He wandered from neighbourhood to neighbourhood, begging and stealing food from shops and houses, drinking stolen milk and water from water butts and taps. He went for several days without speaking to anyone, or them speaking to him. Sometimes he felt as if he was invisible.

At night he always found a park to sleep in. Once he slept in a shed at the bottom of a big garden, and was very glad he had as it rained hard that night. In the shed he found a soft old sheet, which was full of dust and made him sneeze. He rolled it up to take with him in the morning and found it was a dirty cream colour and encrusted with stains of deep green paint. It was not much against the night-time cold but he found it a comfort. In the daytime he slung it round his neck, as he had the coat.

By the time darkness fell he was usually exhausted from moving round all day and fending for himself. He wrapped himself round in the sheet and pushed himself under a bush where no one could see him. He had grown used to the rustlings of the night. One night, as he lay curled up in the sheet, he heard miaowing close by. He could sense the cat looking at him and he uncovered his head.

'Here, puss,' he whispered, reaching out his hand. His own voice felt strange to him. The cat allowed him to touch it and began to purr.

'Come on – come in here with me.'

Curled up beside the warm, purring body he slept, comforted. Sometime before dawn the cat woke with a commotion and scrabbled about, frantic to be released from the sheet.

'Don't go!' he heard himself say, but as he lifted his head the cat shot past him. He lay down, feeling how sore his throat was. His head ached and his neck felt stiff. He didn't feel well all day and he didn't move far. That night he slept in the same spot, hoping the cat would come back, but there was no sign of it. He lay on the hard ground, cheeks burning, yet his body was shaking and the cold seemed to bite right into him. He barely slept and when he did his dreams were frightening. When he woke in the morning he could hardly tell who he was, and it was later that day that he found himself waking on a doorstep, propped up next to two big green doors, with a greasy bag of broken biscuits in his hand.

He leaned his head against the rough bricks. His breathing was too quick, his body pulsing like a chick he once saw hatch from an egg in the brewhouse when his father kept hens. Everything about the baby bird had seemed too fast, as if it must burn itself out with living within minutes of being born. Joey's vision blurred, then corrected itself. He could hear his pulse banging in his ears. It was a quiet street and only a couple of people passed, who gave him no more than a glance. Joey didn't move. He sat still, his eyes half open.

A figure was approaching briskly along the street. Joey watched dully, then his eyes snapped open. That uniform! It was the School Board man, whistling as he came along the road! He'd come to get him, to take him away and lock him up behind the walls of the orphanage! Joey wanted to get up and run away, but his body wouldn't obey. He managed to turn himself sideways and cringe back into the darkest corner of the doorway, pulling his knees up tightly to his chest and turning his face away. The whistling came closer. Joey pushed his head down against his knees, eyes squeezed shut. His kneecaps felt huge and hard. He held his breath. The whistling passed without a pause and he uncurled, trembling.

He couldn't bear the thought of sleeping out again that night. He would have liked to go and find the shed from where he'd taken his sheet, but he didn't have any idea where it was, or where he was now. By the time darkness was falling he found himself in a street of high houses with roofs like triangles and front gardens and gates. There were curtains and lights on inside – electric lights like the ones in school. He had eaten nothing all day except that one mouthful of biscuit and his legs were shaky. A road intersected with the one along which he was walking, and at the end the last two houses were dark with no curtains in the windows.

Hardly knowing what he was doing, Joey pushed open the gate of the end house. The path was over-grown and plants brushed against his legs, scratching him. Joey wondered if anyone lived there. He went round to the back. There might be a shed down the garden. He was desperate to lie down anywhere under cover and rest his pounding head and shivering bones. Even the weight of the sheet he was carrying felt almost too much to bear.

The path took him round to the back door. To his surprise, when he went up close, he saw it was slightly ajar and he pushed his way in. It was dark and he noticed that the floor felt uneven underfoot. There was a sound like running water somewhere near him. If he could just lie down anywhere – he didn't care now if someone lived there, if he got caught. He had to lie down, to sleep . . .

In the hall he felt his way along the wall and came to a doorway on his left. He fumbled for the handle and stumbled inside. Here – he'd sleep here. It was the last thing he would remember for some time after that: taking his sheet from round his neck and sinking onto it on the hard floor, as he pulled it round him. Later he remembered that, as he drifted quickly into uncon-sciousness, he heard the sound of someone snoring.

SUMMER TERM

1936

Sixteen

'Donald Andrews? Joan Billings?'

'Yes, Miss.'

'Here, Miss!'

'Ernie Davis?'

'Yes, Miss.'

Gwen smiled at her class as she took the register. It was a bright spring morning and she felt full of energy and enthusiasm. The classroom looked colourful now, with all the Easter pictures they'd painted pinned up round the walls, and the sun was pouring in through the long windows. It occurred to Gwen just how much she liked being a teacher.

'Lucy Fernandez?'

'Yes, Miss.'

She glanced up to see Lucy's intense dark eyes fixed on her face.

'Ron Parks?'

As usual, there was some sort of kerfuffle going on round Ron. His hands were stuffed into his pockets and the boys round him were grinning from ear to ear.

'Oh – yes, Miss!' he said distractedly.

'Ron –' Gwen looked sternly at him – 'if you're going to be our milk monitor this term, you're going to have to behave much better and learn to be sensible.' She moved closer to Ron's place in the third row. 'Aren't you?'

'Yes, Miss.' Ron clamped his mouth shut, looking as if he was going to burst with the need to laugh.

'Well, take your hands out of your pockets and sit up straight. What *is* the matter with you today?'

Ron carefully extracted his hands from his pockets. Puzzled, Gwen could see the other children watching intently. Freddie Peters's mouth gaped open. Doreen Smith had a hand clasped over hers. Gwen was just about to ask whether the sight of Ron Parks taking his hands out of his pockets was really so fascinating when she saw Ron give a great squirm and his expression turn to one of horror. Suddenly everyone was staring at the floor by his chair. Sitting in a confused heap, after its escape into the light, was a sizeable toad. The children erupted with equal delight and revulsion, the boys roaring, some of the girls squealing.

Then everything went quiet for just a second. They all looked at Miss Purdy, waiting for her reaction. Ron had gone very red.

'Sorry, Miss,' he said.

'Sit still, all of you!' Gwen dashed across to the corner, seized the empty wastepaper basket and stalked along the aisle towards the toad. Even in the midst of everything, her capacity to view the situation from the outside and see its funny side was bringing her danger-ously close to giggles herself. The terrible thought that Mr Lowry might be patrolling in the hall outside and peering in through the windows somehow made it even funnier. He'd probably give her the sack!

The toad saw her coming and began to hop frantic-ally towards the back of the classroom.

'Don't let it get under the desks or we'll never catch it!' Gwen cried. 'Hold your hands out – fend it off!'

The toad reached the skirting board at the back of

the room. On each side children's hands were flapping at it and a strange creature was homing in on it with a waste bin. Caught in this impasse, the toad looked understandably gloomy. Gwen dropped the bin over the top of it and held it down with her foot. The children all started to clap. Gwen couldn't help a grin spreading over her own face.

'There!' she laughed. 'Got him!' She attempted to look more sober. 'Well, Ron has given us an interesting natural history lesson this morning – before I've even finished taking the register. Unfortunately, though, we're supposed to be having a geography lesson. Ron, come and remove this toad, please, and take it outside. Preferably without running into Mr Lowry.'

She finished the register.

'Alice Wilson?'

'Here, Miss.'

Gwen was reassured. Alice had been absent the day before.

'Were you poorly yesterday, Alice?'

'Yes, Miss.' The child barely spoke above a whisper.

Gwen frowned. She was growing increasingly concerned about Alice. Even though she had suggested such a time ago now that Alice should be provided with some spectacles, she still had none and sat through the classes squinting hopelessly, unable to see the blackboard, even though Gwen had seated her at the front. And, having begun the year neat as a pin, she was looking more and more down at heel.

'Now – books out, children. We're going to learn some more about Australia. But first of all – can anyone tell me the name of a famous lady pilot who flew to Australia all on her own?'

Alice Wilson's hand flew up.

'Alice?'

'Amy Johnson,' the girl said enthusiastically. 'And her aeroplane was called Gypsy Moth.'

'Very good.' Gwen smiled. 'Amy Johnson landed in Darwin on May 24th, 1930. That's *eleven thousand* miles away. Now, I'm going to show you where Darwin is.'

At the end of the morning, she told Ron Parks to stay behind. He came to her as she sat at her desk.

'What I should do by rights is send you to Mr Lowry.'

'Yes, Miss.' Ron lowered his head.

She paused, thinking with distaste of Mr Lowry and his collection of canes. 'I don't think it will be necessary this time. But, Ron, do you think you could try to come to school with *nothing* in your pockets – just for once? No gobstoppers, marbles, toads . . . Nothing except a handkerchief, perhaps?'

The corners of Ron's mouth twitched.

'Yes, Miss Purdy.'

Fondly she looked at his round face, the rumpled brown hair. Ron seemed to her to be a boy without a streak of malice in him.

'Ron, have you seen anything of Joey Phillips since he left?'

Ron's face creased in a worried sort of way. 'No, I ain't seen him. Don't know where he can've gone to. I s'pose they took him to the home. That's what they said.'

'Who said?'

Ron shrugged. 'I dunno. Just, you know, our Mom. I ain't seen him.'

'All right. Well, if you do, will you tell me?'

Ron nodded.

'All right – go and get your dinner or your mother'll be cross. And . . .'

'Yes, Miss?' he said, from the doorway.

'Where exactly did you put the toad?'

'I put him down over by the wall of the pub, like, so he daint have to cross the road by himself. I thought he might be able to get back down to the cut.'

'Well, let's hope so,' Gwen smiled. 'Go on. Off you go.'

They'd been back at school for a couple of weeks. Millie Dawson had been replaced by a young woman called Miss Rowley, who was now teaching in the room next to Gwen, and she was civil enough, though Gwen didn't find the immediate warmth of friendship that she had with Millie. Charlotte Rowley was a tiny, doll-like person with brown eyes, a sallow complexion and black hair cut short and very neatly round her collar. She was always immaculately dressed and, despite her shrill, childlike voice, seemed to wield absolute control over her class. At the same time, the fact that she was young and had a slightly sultry air about her provoked the immediate and bitter suspicion of Miss Monk, who couldn't find a polite word to say to her.

'What is the matter with *her*?' Miss Rowley asked Gwen on her second day, when Miss Monk had been blatantly rude to her. 'Have I done something to upset her?'

'Only being young and pretty,' Gwen said. 'She thinks anyone younger than her is a threat to her chances with old Lowry.'

'Lowry?' Charlotte Rowley's brow wrinkled.

'She keeps waiting for him to notice her. It'd be sad if she wasn't so incredibly unpleasant to everyone else.'

Miss Rowley said nothing in reply. She just stared back at Gwen, who decided she was rather strange.

The first weeks of term had been a period of calm. Gwen returned to school full of common-sense resolve. She had been measured for her wedding dress, she had managed to get on amicably enough with her mother and she was going back to marry Edwin in August. Edwin was right: that was where she belonged, not trying to concern herself with the woes of the poor of Birmingham or anywhere else. Something about her marriage to Edwin felt inevitable. Anything else would be unthinkable now. And this was not just because of herself and Edwin – it involved her parents, and James and Edwina Shackleton. She was almost like one of their family already. There was something reassuring and safe about this, but at the same time it was frightening, as if she had no say in deciding her own fate.

All brides are nervous and worried, she'd told herself as her train chugged its way closer to Birmingham at the end of the holidays. *This is just normal.* And on the first day of school, as soon as she reached the prison and got off to walk along Canal Street, her whole being seemed to tingle with anticipation and she worked hard to persuade herself that this was not because she was in the neighbourhood where *he* lived, that she was not hoping with every fibre of her body that round every corner might appear Daniel Fernandez.

The first afternoon, as the children left at the end of school, Lucy was the last one out as usual.

'Lucy.' Gwen called her to her desk. Surely it would not be out of place to ask after the family now?

'How are you all?' She tried to sound casual, fiddling

with the top of her fountain pen. 'Everyone well at home?'

Lucy nodded with a shy smile. 'Daniel's not here.'

Gwen felt the blood rise in her cheeks. It was as if the child could read her mind! Was it written all over her face that this was the one thing she was really longing to know? But she soon realized this was not the reason.

'He's gone to Cardiff,' Lucy announced proudly. 'He's going to speak to people outside the assizes and tell them not to send all the miners to prison.'

'Is he?' Gwen replied, startled. She hadn't the least notion of what the child was talking about. 'Why should the miners be sent to prison?'

'Because of the strikes. They stayed down the mine at Taff Merthyr.' As Lucy spoke, Gwen could see in her the same fire that she saw in her brother. 'Daniel says they were on strike against the company's union – last year. They stayed down the pit for days and wouldn't come out. And now the bosses want to send them to prison.'

'And Daniel?'

'Daniel goes all over the place, speaking and that.'

Ashamed of her own ignorance once again, Gwen bought a newspaper on the way home. Why was she so unaware of everything going on in the world? It was as if she had been living in a dream all these years. Waiting for her tram, she scanned through the paper. In a column inside she read that the trial at Cardiff Assizes was to be the biggest mass trial of industrial workers ever held in Britain and she sat on the tram burning with pride that Daniel was there, would be speaking out against injustice. She wasn't even sure why it was unjust, but Daniel would know. She imagined him standing in front of a crowd, shouting out with the passion she had seen when he talked to her.

She had found the courage to ask Lucy whether he was coming back to Birmingham. 'He'll be back,' Lucy said assuredly. 'He always comes home to our mam – we just never know when, that's all.'

But the days had gone past and there was no sign of Daniel's return. She read that the court had sentenced fifty-three men and three women to terms of hard labour, ranging from three to fifteen months. How could this be? she wondered. If all they were trying to do was to defend their livelihood? Surely they must have done something terrible to be sent to prison to do hard labour. For a time she doubted Daniel. What was he really involved with? After all, she barely knew him. She wasn't used to being associated with people who went to prison.

When he didn't return she calmed down a little and tried to persuade herself that it couldn't possibly matter if she ever saw him again. After all, he was just the brother of one of her pupils: he was nothing to her, nor she to him. It was true that she found his company a novelty. It was exciting. But Daniel must see her as an ignorant little miss, with her comfortable middle-class home. He probably despised her. And she was engaged to be married, for goodness sake! Even if she hadn't been, Daniel was certainly not the class or type of person her parents could ever conceivably approve of. The very thought was absurd! So she kept herself in a calm, sensible mood and wrote jolly letters to Edwin, telling him the details of her daily life that she thought he would want to hear. And they certainly did not include Daniel. Nor, for that matter, did she describe just what it was like living, these days, in the Soho Road house.

Seventeen

Ariadne shuffled into the breakfast room, bearing a rack of toast which left a trail of blue smoke in the air behind it.

'I've overdone it again just a little bit, haven't I?' she said with a playful glance at Harold Purvis. She deposited on the table the charred remnants of what had been a reasonable loaf of bread, shedding a miniature cascade of black crumbs onto the embroidered cloth. Harold Purvis stared gloomily at it. Gwen tackled her egg with the vigour it demanded after fifteen minutes fast boiling and managed to prise the top off to reveal a pale yoke, ruffled and dry as old velvet. She tried not to think about who had slept in whose bedroom last night, or feel Harold's little sideways glances at her. Every morning was like this now. It might have been amusing to begin with but it certainly wasn't any more.

While she had been away, things had developed. Almost every night now Ariadne crept along the landing and begged to be let in at Harold's door. Or Gwen might hear her saying, through the door, 'You come to me, Harold, darling. Why don't you come along to me? I'll be waiting for you.' And once or twice she had heard him go. She lay in bed picturing Harold plodding along the landing in his striped pyjamas, his white hands hanging below the sleeves. Every time he passed her door she tensed, her heart pounding. He had never tried to come in, but she still had the feeling that he might. She had started pushing her chair up against the door just in case. What with that and Harold's trumpet dreaming of marble halls every evening, living in Soho Road was becoming a horrible strain.

Ariadne had lately got into the habit of coming down to breakfast in her dressing gown. It was pale green cotton, reaching almost to her ankles and she fastened it very tightly at the waist. Her bright pink slippers had ribbons at the front and made little slip-slap noises as she walked. Her hair was bagged up in a brown net, under which were rollers, and pins securing kiss curls round her forehead. She invariably had lipstick on and had pencilled in her eyebrows.

'I put my face on after,' she once confided to Gwen. 'But I can't come down completely *naked*, can I?'

Ariadne breakfasted on her usual diet of tea, cigarettes and whichever newspaper came to hand, which this morning was the *Birmingham Gazette*.

Gwen smeared margarine over the raven-coloured toast.

'Oh, my word,' Ariadne said, 'look at this – "Man Chased to His Death by a Dog..."' She took a long drag on her cigarette and blew smoke across the table.

Gwen frowned. 'So how did he die?'

There was a pause as Ariadne ran her finger along the lines of print.

'Says here he drowned – jumped off a pier ... And oh, look – that Nurse Waddingham's going to be hanged – day after tomorrow.'

Nurse Waddingham had been sentenced in February, but now the hanging was about to happen, on 16 April, and it was the talk of Birmingham. Ariadne was full of it and the teachers at Canal Street School debated the pros and cons in the dinner hour, sitting round on the battered old chairs with their sandwiches.

'There's no smoke without fire,' Miss Monk declared, crossing one hefty brown stockinged leg over the other. 'She's benefited from the woman's will – seems obvious she had a hand in hurrying the old girl's end. Good riddance to her, the scheming shrew.' She cast a bitter glance at Charlotte Rowley, as if bracketing her in the insult as well.

Gwen had learned from Ariadne that Nurse Waddingham was a thirty-four-year-old mother of five children, who had been nursing eighty-nine-year-old Louisa Baguley in a home in Nottingham. Both Louisa Baguley and her daughter Ada, who was fifty-five, had died in mysterious circumstances, having willed money to 'Nurse' Waddingham.

'I think it's a scandal,' Miss Drysdale declared, with an emphatic gesture which caused tea to spill from her cup onto the brown linoleum. 'Imagine, that we're still hanging people in this country. Taking a life for a life – it's most un-Christian!'

'Huh – calling *yourself* a Christian!' Miss Monk scoffed half to herself, and Gwen wondered what on earth she meant. How vile the woman was! Otherwise, though, there was a general murmur of agreement. Mr Gaffney was nodding.

'You're right,' he kept repeating. 'It's a terrible thing. Terrible.' Gwen saw that he was quivering, as he did from time to time, seemingly overcome by his nerves. He had wispy remnants of hair round his bald pate and kind, watery eyes. She wondered what had happened to him in the war.

'Well, I agree with Mr Lowry,' Miss Monk pronounced.

'Of course you do,' Gwen said, managing to keep her tone so neutral that Agnes Monk wasn't sure whether she was being insulted or not. Gwen looked back innocently at her, and pulled a cheese and onion cob out of a paper bag. From the corner of her eye she saw the corner of Charlotte Rowley's mouth twitch with amusement.

Miss Monk glowered suspiciously at Gwen. 'You may be aware, Miss Purdy, that Mr Lowry is a strong believer in discipline and I have respect for his views.'

'There's discipline, and there's barbarity,' Lily Drysdale said. 'The woman has five children – the baby's only a few months old! Who's going to bring them up? I shall protest with the others who'll stand against this, in the strongest terms.'

'Huh,' Miss Monk said contemptuously. 'A lot of good that'll do you. They're set to hang her, whatever you say, or that red, Violet Van der Elst, and all her campaigning. Good riddance to her.'

Gwen listened to the arguments, feeling immediately opposed to the hanging because Agnes Monk was for it. Her whole being rebelled against the idea – she thought of the woman waiting in her cell, imagining the rope tightening round her neck, her last gasp of life followed by everlasting darkness. Frightful even if she was guilty. But what if she wasn't?

'It *is* barbaric, isn't it?' she said to Miss Rowley.

'Oh, I don't know,' Miss Rowley said. She sat very straight and neatly, her feet lined up side by side in little blue shoes with straps. 'She took someone else's life, after all. She showed no pity.'

There was a coldness in the way she spoke that made Gwen like her even less.

The day before the hanging Mr Lowry announced in assembly that school would be starting late the next morning. The streets would be cordoned off round the prison to keep the crowds away until the hanging was over.

Gwen did not sleep at all well that Wednesday night. First of all, when she came back from the bathroom before bed, she found Harold Purvis on the landing, blocking the way to her room. Gwen felt her pulse begin to speed up with alarm. She told herself not to be so silly. What could Harold Purvis do to her, with Ariadne just along the corridor? But he loomed over her, standing there in his suit, shiny with wear and his big black shoes. And she was already in her nightdress, dressing gown over the top with no underwear on and felt naked and very much at a disadvantage.

She folded her arms tightly, and in a sharp tone said, 'Excuse me – could you please let me get to my room?'

Harold leaned against the wall, facing her, a half smile on his face. Gwen realized instinctively that he wasn't actually going to do anything, but that he enjoyed the feeling of power he gained from tormenting her.

'You look very nice,' he said, in a snaky, repellent voice. 'Very nice indeed.'

'I'm waiting to get to bed,' she said, more annoyed now than alarmed. 'And I don't like personal comments, thank you.'

'Not even nice ones?' He smiled suggestively.

Not from you, she wanted to say, but sensed that getting into that kind of banter with him would be to play his game. Instead, she stood her ground, staring back at him.

'A man can't resist the sight of a beautiful woman,' he said softly.

'No. Well, that's obvious,' she snapped, then lurched inwardly with alarm as Harold moved suddenly closer.

'D'you think *she's* really what I want?' His breath stank of onions. 'An old thing like her, when I can see you in front of me, day after day?'

Gwen froze. To her horror, she felt Harold Purvis's hand slide round her left buttock, over the silky, peach-coloured dressing gown.

'You're *much* more my type,' he whispered, dealing her another blast of onions.

'Get *off*!'

She gave him a hard push, and Harold staggered backwards against the opposite wall.

'Stuck-up little cow!' she heard as she fled into her room and pushed the chair up against the door.

'I've got to get out of here,' she thought, sitting up shakily in bed. She didn't want to turn off the light. She knew she wouldn't be able to sleep. All her senses were alert to what was going on outside her door. Once she was sure things had quietened down outside, she lay in the dark and tried to settle. But she felt humiliated and one nasty thought followed another. Once she'd managed to get her mind off Harold Purvis, the thought of Nurse Waddingham came to her, living through her last night. However must she feel? She imagined her with long, dark hair, sitting with her head lowered, tortured by the thought of her children, soon to be motherless, and of her own remaining hours before her thirty-six-year-old life was snuffed out.

The next morning Gwen picked at her breakfast, which was Ariadne's porridge – not burnt for once, but still a strangely unpleasant consistency – and avoided looking at Harold Purvis. Ariadne smoked and avidly read bits of yesterday's paper.

'"Fiancé's Suicide on Wedding Eve" – oh, what a *shame*. Found with his head in the gas oven . . . That'll be money, won't it?' She lit another cigarette and turned the page.

'Here we are . . . Protests outside the prison. That Mrs Van der Elst says she wants aeroplanes flying over, dropping leaflets protesting against capital punishment . . . First woman this century to be executed at Winson Green Prison.'

Gwen swallowed her last mouthful of porridge and fled. It was a relief to be out of the house. She got off the tram a stop early, making her way through the grey morning. There were a lot of people about, milling through the streets as she got closer to the prison, and an atmosphere of anticlimax. The hanging was already over. Following the crowds, she walked to the end of Villiers Street, where the main entrance to the prison loomed forbiddingly, like a dark castle. A row of policemen stood across the entrance and a large number of people were gathered round the gates. Gwen found herself being herded towards them, carried along by the press of people.

'Why's everyone going over there?' she asked a woman whose face was alight with an eager expression.

'We want to read the death notice!' the woman said avidly. Gwen found her excitement repugnant. The crowd was under control, but the force of it was still alarming. Gwen was knocked from behind so that her hat was pushed right down over her eyes.

Oh, I've had enough of this, she thought, shoving it back so she could see and trying to push her way towards the edge. There was a lamp post out to the right of the entrance and she headed for that.

'Here you go.' A policeman stood aside to let her through as she forced her way out, and stood beside the lamp post to get her breath back, looking back at the prison.

'Come to join the baying crowd, have you?'

She turned, thinking for a split second that she had mistaken that voice, or dreamt it, but found herself staring up into Daniel's challenging smile. He looked exactly as he always did: shirtsleeves, no collar and bareheaded today, a cigarette at the corner of his mouth. He was holding in front of him several copies of the *Daily Worker*. Immediately she was aware of a new sense of life, as if a light had gone on.

'You're back!'

She felt foolish then, as if she had let him know she had been waiting, and it was only in that moment she realized how much she had been doing just that and the realization made her blush.

'I'm back,' Daniel agreed. He took a last drag on his cigarette and threw it down. She wasn't aware of having seen him smoke before. Edwin didn't approve of tobacco, she thought, seeing Daniel crush the stub on the cobbles with his heel. 'Who told you I was away? You been round to find me?'

'No!' she said quickly, resenting his assumption that she would come trotting round to find him. But then she saw from his eyes that he was teasing. 'Lucy told me. She said you were at the trial in Cardiff.'

Daniel's face darkened. 'Trial's not the word,' he said contemptuously. 'But yes – I was there.' He glanced round. 'Let's get away from here. Too late now. The woman's dead. We can't bring her back. And no one's buying these.' He rolled up the *Daily Workers* and put them in the bag, slung over his shoulder. 'All too keen on baying for blood.'

She felt him take her arm and let him steer her through the edge of the crowd, which was thinning and dispersing now, along the surrounding streets. She was filled with a prickly awareness of his closeness.

'Were you part of the protest?' she asked.

Daniel nodded curtly. 'Fat lot of notice anyone takes. Even that Labour woman, Van der Elst . . .'

'Who *is* Mrs Van der Elst?' Gwen asked. They reached a quieter part of the street and Daniel let go of her arm. The warmth of his grip faded from her skin.

'Oh, she's a toff who's got ideas about standing for the Labour Party – round here first thing, she was, with her car and her furs on. Giving out leaflets.'

'Against the hanging?'

'Against *all* hanging. Barbarism, that's what it is. They wouldn't listen. If they won't listen to someone like that, what chance does the ordinary working man have to be heard?'

'Well, yes,' Gwen agreed. 'I suppose that's how things are.'

'Things are as they are because we let them stay like it!' he exploded. Apparently she had just said the one thing that was a red rag to Daniel. 'We make the world – every one of us – by choosing to act or not act on what we see. It doesn't just happen. We're not puppets!'

'I wasn't saying I thought things *should* be like that,' Gwen flared, annoyed at being misunderstood, at always being seen as someone who didn't know anything. 'I just meant that's how they *are*. Exactly like you just said – with no justice for the right people. I don't believe they should have hanged that nurse. It was wrong and terrible.'

Daniel was walking fast, hands thrust into his pockets. It suddenly occurred to Gwen that she had never seen him without the plaster cast on before. He moved so fast she had to trot sometimes to keep up.

'Your leg's better,' she remarked.

'Oh yes,' he said carelessly. 'Sound as a bell. I can get a bit of work now here and there.'

'I still don't understand what it is you do,' she said, as they turned into the end of Canal Street. 'Are you some sort of roving speaker?'

'I work for the party and the movement, like I told you. I work as much as I can, in between, but I go wherever I'm needed. They say I'm a good speaker. I rally people, see – not just in the valleys – here, and wherever the work takes me. But I don't like to stay away from Mam for too long. Her life's been hard.'

Gwen was puzzled. Theresa Fernandez had sounded hard, bitter even about Daniel's activities. Yet here was he speaking about her with such care, tenderness even.

'Has it?' she said.

Daniel stopped. They were only yards from the school gates and he looked down into her eyes.

'You've no idea, have you? What it's like?'

'No,' she agreed quietly, 'but I want to learn.'

The look on his face dizzied her. His brown eyes stared hard into hers, not teasing now, but examining, challenging. She held his gaze, feeling it go right through her. Then he looked away. There were children coming in groups along the road. Gwen caught a glimpse of Alice Wilson moving along in her dreamy way. Why did she feel responsible now for these people? Really they were nothing to do with her.

'Sunday,' Daniel said abruptly. 'We could go up to the hills. If you want to, that is.'

'Yes,' she said. 'Yes, I do.'

Eighteen

'How old are you, then?' Daniel asked as they sat squeezed close together on the tram. Daniel was seated to Gwen's right.

She laughed, taken aback by his directness. He was in a jaunty mood. She had already seen that when he wasn't talking about politics he could be full of cheek and banter.

'Twenty-one last October. And you?'

'I'm twenty-six.' He grinned and lit a cigarette, eyes full of laughter. 'An old man compared to you.'

'Oh, ancient!' Gwen agreed.

They were squeezed onto the tram seat. Gwen had been excited and nervous all at once about spending the day with him. She thought it might be very awkward, conscious as she was of the contrast in their backgrounds, how different her life had been from his. But now they were together she found they talked more easily than she had expected. And to be going anywhere with Daniel felt like embarking on an adventure, as if his very presence made life exciting.

They met at the tram stop where she usually got off for school. She arrived at the stop first, and saw him walking up the road towards her with his muscular stride, his jacket over his shoulder in the sunshine, looking quite leisurely and different from how she had ever seen him before.

'Morning, Miss Purdy!' He smiled mischievously.

She tutted, but returned the smile. 'I'm never called Miss Purdy on Sundays. It's the rule.'

'Ah well – I like breaking rules, see. Gwen though, isn't it?'

Of course Lucy would always call her Miss Purdy, she realized, so Daniel barely even knew her name!

'I think I can let you call me Gwen,' she said, with a mock primness that seemed to amuse him.

They had a brief discussion about where to go. Sutton Park would have been nearer, but Daniel was determined to find hills.

'Let's get up high somewhere – have a good walk. You can't breathe, sometimes, walled up in this place.'

'You'd like it where I come from,' she told him as they waited for the tram. 'It's at the edge of town and then you get out and there are beautiful hills and views. And the Malverns not far away – it's lovely.'

'Nothing like it.' Standing beside him, she could sense once again the power which seemed to emanate from him. He looked at the sky. 'Don't think this is going to last, though.'

It was sunny, but clouds were piling up ahead of them. Gwen was glad she had put on practical clothes – slacks and flat walking shoes. By the time they were halfway down the Bristol Road, rain was spattering against the tram windows.

'Soon be over,' Daniel said, twisting round to wipe the steamy window. 'It's bright over there.'

Gwen didn't care two hoots whether it rained or not. They'd make the best of it, whatever. It was being here that mattered. Being with him. A wave of panic went through her when she realized how strong this feeling was, but she pushed it away. Now was what was important. These moments and the day ahead of them. She would not think of anything else.

Each of them had a coat lying on their lap – Gwen's blue macintosh and Daniel's old jacket. She looked down at them, at Daniel's right hand resting on the faded black serge. His fingers were strong and slender. She could feel the warmth of his leg beside hers, the press of his shoulder and arm. It was strange, she thought, what an incongruous-looking pair they were. Yet it felt right. It felt as if there was nowhere else she wanted to be ... She pulled her thoughts together. Daniel might become a friend, that was all, and to him she was ... What was she? A bit of female company to while away a Sunday afternoon with? Perhaps someone he could educate with his political views?

She had thought they might find conversation difficult, but instead it flowed easily. Surrounded by other passengers, they talked softly. Before they had got off the tram Daniel asked about her family and she told him, with a frankness that took her by surprise, about her parents and brothers and about her mother's horror at the idea of her coming to teach in Birmingham. Daniel laughed at her descriptions.

'She doesn't want you mixing with the riff-raff then, is it?'

'Mummy's never been anywhere very much all her life. She was born in Hereford, hardly left there until they moved to Worcester, when she married Daddy. She never even seems to *want* to go anywhere.'

Daniel watched her face. 'But you do?'

'Oh yes. I mean, I've never been anywhere much, either. Not even to London or anything. I'd like to go *everywhere*!'

Daniel smiled at her fervour.

'You seem to have been to so many more places than me,' she said. 'Wales, and here and . . .'

'London,' Daniel added. The tram slammed to a halt suddenly, making them all lurch to one side. Gwen was thrown against Daniel for a second.

'Steady!' he grasped her forearm for a moment, then released it.

'You've been to London?' She was talking quickly to cover how much his touch affected her. 'Of course – you were at the college there!'

Daniel nodded. 'I was – a few years back, for a while. Last time I went was on foot. Two years ago. Marched from the valleys. You've heard of the Hunger Marches, surely you have?'

He looked at her quizzically. While her ignorance of political matters had seemed at first to aggravate him, now he seemed to find her other-worldliness amusing.

'I have heard of them!' she protested. 'And you were on them?'

'On that one, I was.'

'So you were all marching because . . .' She dredged her memory. 'Because there was no work?'

'No work for some. And the Unemployment Bill – Slave Bill we call it – that the government saw fit to pass to starve and bully the miners who've already had their jobs stolen from them by fascist bosses and blacklegs. But it brought the people together.' His voice began to rise with excitement. 'They're turning to the party now. They can see that the only way to victory is for the working class to unite, to overthrow the tyrannies of capitalism and fascism!'

A pale, middle-aged man turned his head and stared at Daniel in disgust. 'Why don't you shurrup, you silly bugger? Carrying on as if you're on a bleeding soap-box.'

For a split second Gwen thought Daniel was going to get up and punch the man, but instead he lowered his head, hands clenched into fists. She could feel the tension in him, his whole being seemed to throb with feeling beside her.

'They're all blind,' he said, through his teeth. 'Been duped, all of them. But they'll see. One day they'll all see.'

By the time the tram reached the terminus at Rednal, the sun was out again and the grass sparkled with raindrops. They climbed down and Daniel turned, with sudden gallantry, which took her by surprise, and took her hand. But then he said, 'Right – let's go!' Seeming released, he set off at such a pace that Gwen had to run after him.

'I can't keep up, not this fast!' she panted.

'Sorry.' He was relaxed again now and gave an easy grin, slowing his stride.

They climbed to the spot where they could look across the vista of the surrounding counties.

'Home's over there somewhere.' Gwen pointed.

'And mine's over there . . .' He turned further west.

'Is Wales still home then?'

'Oh yes. It is really. Even though Ma's here. She wanted to be away and I don't blame her. Not after everything she was put through there. But my heart's in the valleys. That's where my people are.'

As they began to walk the paths, between trees and bracken awakening from its winter brown, she asked Daniel to tell her about his home, hoping it would shed some light on him and on his mother's past. She was intrigued by Theresa Fernandez, by the gentle, almost passive exterior, which seemed to conceal something steely underneath that she was at pains not to show.

He described Aberglyn, the narrow, sloping streets following the contours of the valley, the houses shoulder to shoulder and the colours of the hills behind as the seasons passed and as he spoke she could see what he was describing, how in childhood he woke often to the sound of men's boots clumping along the morning streets when it was still dark, all moving quietly to the pit train, which took them to the colliery at the head of the valley, and how he knew that soon it would be his life also, like his father's.

'Except it hasn't turned out like that.' It was sunny again now, and they were walking along a shining sward of green. Gwen unbuttoned her cardigan.

'But your father was Spanish – he didn't grow up in the valleys.'

'No – he started off in the steelworks. 1907 they were brought over – he was twenty. Came over on a ship to Cardiff and then they sent them to Dowlais . . .'

Gwen frowned. 'But why did they come from Spain?'

'Dowlais Iron Company owned one of the Spanish iron ore companies from some way back. So –' his tone became hard – 'true capitalists, they thought they could bring cheap Spanish labour into Wales and undercut wage rates, and that Spanish workers would toe the line . . . Our da worked there for a time. The heat in there – phew! It was terrible! So bad their clothes were smouldering. Had to throw buckets of water over each other. He left after a bit and went to Aberglyn down the pit, became a collier. That's where he met Ma.'

They walked, staring at their feet, the worn path edged with sodden grass. To Gwen's surprise, Daniel chuckled suddenly.

'They made a street in Dowlais for the Spaniards – Alphonso Street. Da said it gave them the shock of their lives – a quiet Welsh town and suddenly there's him and the others with their garlic, playing music on a Sunday and being Catholics with their strange ways and that. I s'pose they didn't know what'd hit them to begin with! Course, there were Italians in the towns too – same with them really. Our da played the accordion – it was the one thing he brought over with him.'

'Can you play it?'

'No, I never got the hang of it. Our Paul's the one – he can squeeze some tunes out of it when he puts his mind to it. He's got the touch with it, and Ma likes to hear it.'

'So . . .' she asked hesitantly, 'your father died young, didn't he?' Theresa had told her this, but she wanted to hear Daniel's account of what had happened.

'Dead at forty-three. Heart gave out. He was a strong man, you could see that to look at him. But he was working every spare moment for the federation, the movement, the action committees. Some weeks he hardly slept, barely ate. Ma was forever keeping on, but he wouldn't listen. "What choice is there?" he'd say. "Our energy and determination is the only thing we have left." Everyone came to him – knocked on the door with all their troubles. It was the big strike, did it, made him see what the bosses were capable of. Changed him. He was never the same after . . .'

Gwen was only dimly aware, as they walked on, of heavy grey clouds covering the sky again and in a few moments the rain started to come down, slanting across the side of the hill.

'Oh, here we go!' Daniel said, starting to run towards the trees. 'Come on – let's get under here!'

She ran after him and they huddled together under the branches as the rain poured down. Daniel arranged his jacket over their heads and Gwen felt it rest on her hair, scratchy against her ear. She peered out from under it at the tippling rain. Her left side was pressed close against Daniel.

'It goes hot and cold so quickly!' She shivered, buttoning her cardigan again. She would have liked to put her coat on as well, but it was too difficult to move.

'Come on, I'll keep you warm.' Almost with a sense of panic she felt his arm round her, pulling her closer. Once again it was as if every hair on her body was standing on end, her heart thudding, while she tried to show nothing, to be light and careless about this closeness.

'That better?' Daniel said.

She could feel his gaze on her and did not dare turn her head to look into his eyes.

'Yes, thank you,' she murmured.

The rain fell more and more heavily, so that for a few moments they could barely see the other side of the path. Its force exhilarated her, making her want to run and jump, but Daniel's arm burned into her back so she hardly dared to move.

He moved his arm further down until it was curved round her waist and then, as the rain gradually let up and the sky lightened, they were left with the sound of the dripping trees and the sun came out. They both knew they had to move. For a second Gwen turned and their eyes met. His gaze was deep and serious. Emotions twisted in her and she looked quickly away again. Daniel released her and removed the sodden coat from their heads, tossed what water he could off it then laid it over his arm. Shaken, Gwen followed him back to the path, her shoes shiny with water. The silence between them was so electric that she had to do something to dispel it. She knew what she had seen in Daniel's eyes, and wondered if her own had spoken in the same way. The strength of it was frightening. She had to keep it at bay.

'Your family are so different from mine,' she said brightly. 'Will you tell me about growing up there, about the politics and everything. And why it was all so hard for your mother? You know me – proper old ignoramus.'

Daniel was silent for a moment.

'Ma doesn't like to think about any of it,' he said at last. 'She's put it away, in the past. She prays – offers it up. The Church comes first for her always.'

'What about you?'

He looked ahead along the path.

'Oh, I think about it, all right.'

Nineteen

They walked on, along the paths of the Lickey Hills, paying no attention to where they were going or the other Sunday afternoon walkers and kissing couples they passed on the way. The heavy clouds stayed away for a time and, bright sunlight brought out the vivid spring greens of the grass and trees. But Gwen paid attention to nothing but Daniel's face, heard nothing except his deep lilting voice. Though she had never seen him in action, addressing political meetings, she realized as she listened that he must be good at what he did, that his fluency and passion would convince people and carry them with him.

'It was the big strike, the General Strike – that's what set me off. You couldn't do anything else, see, once you'd lived through all that. That's what it did for our da as well. Course, there were other strikes before – plenty. The year before, over in the west at Ammanford – there was all sorts of trouble there. It wasn't the same over our way, on the east side, but there were all the politicos – Bolshies, some would say. Opinions were divided. But we weren't paying much attention – not then. I left school, started down the pit soon as I got to fourteen – 1925, the year before the strike. I went down with Da and my pal Gomer, who lived along the street. We left school together. Rosa had been born just at the turn of that year.' He paused for a moment and she saw he was smiling.

'Ma stood at the door with her in her arms the day I left for the pit the first time. Dark, it was, light coming out of the house and she was telling us both to hurry, the train'd leave us behind. She used to talk to Da as if he was a child at times.' His face had quickly grown serious again. 'Things were hard enough then for her already, keeping food in all our bellies and that. Thin as a pole, she was.

'So I started off with all the other old butties who'd been working the pit for years, coming up for their tobacco and beer in the evening. Got my lamp, caught the colliers' train: my life was dictated by the pit hooters – I didn't think of any other way. That's what my da did and there was nothing else I could see. You soon pick up the ways of the pit: keep the ventilation doors shut whatever, all the gases down there that could send the place up in a flash – methane, carbon monoxide, black damp. Keep out of the way of the drams – those are the coal trucks. That's what did for my cousin, Billy. Hit by a dram, fifteen years of age. He'll never walk again.' He looked down at his feet. Bread and butter to colliers, all that. And the pit ponies – I knew all their names. You learn fast.

'Then came the strike. Course it was brewing the year before, but the government held the miners off by subsidizing the pits – Red Friday they called it, when Mr Baldwin paid out to the coal owners. I don't s'pose you remember any of this.' His tone was teasing again.

'I was only ten at the time,' she retorted.

'Ten? So you were! Well, they said the pits were losing money. None of us could work fast enough for them so they put some money in for a time, but it had run out by the 26th of May. So the crisis started off again, just as the Communist Party said it would. They were losing markets for the coal, see. The United States were taking markets, that was part of it. So, they said – we'll cut your wages, and you work longer hours. That's how we'll do it. Bleed the workers while the owners milk the profits. Anyone with a grain of sense could see it was downright pillage of the rights of the working man.' He paused as they reached a fork in the path and steered her to the left.

'When the strike started, I didn't realize at first how big it was, what it meant. That all over the country the unions were coming out on strike in solidarity with the miners – railwaymen, dockers, builders – hordes of them, all because they stood together against exploitation and injustice. The working class had unified and raised its voice as one!' Once again, Daniel was becoming heated, his voice rising.

'For those days, the pit was silent. Ghostly, like. But the town streets were full of people, police right up to the isolation hospital, just waiting for any hint of trouble. They'd brought them in from all over – Birmingham, you name it. Everyone was excited, see, on the streets every day reading leaflets, and the *Labour Bulletin*, wanting to know what was going on with the strike all round the country, what Parliament was saying. There were couriers on motorcycles carrying news over the mountains, town to town. The atmosphere was electric. Everyone pulling together, no choice, and the more it went on the more united everyone was. We thought we were going to win against the pit owners. We were all in it together, see, with food and everything – corned beef stew from the soup kitchens every day. The Council of Action met across the road from our house. Da was there nearly every moment, with meetings and speeches and that, and they were making sure the blacklegs couldn't get their coal transported out from the Aberglyn pits, by blocking off the roads. Course, some of them wanted to get going and hound the police out of the town. Why should we have them there? Why should we put up with being victimized for asking for a living wage? Da wanted to stop a fight. "You're playing into the hands of the government if you start on them," he kept saying. "That's what they're waiting for – an excuse to go for us, baton us and shoot us. We've got to keep the peace." They found out that some of the ones calling for riots weren't from the valley at all – they'd been planted to cause trouble. Da was having none of it.'

Gwen was struggling to follow everything he was saying, but she didn't like to interrupt.

'And then . . .' Daniel kicked hard at a clump of grass, shaking his head as if even now he couldn't believe what had happened. 'Next thing is, they're calling us all back to work. Strike's over. The *Labour Party*' – Gwen heard the bitter contempt in his voice – 'and the trade unions sold out on us. Called it off. Ten days, that's all they managed, and then everyone else was back at work. That was the first time . . .' He stopped speaking so abruptly that she looked round and saw he was struggling with his emotions. '. . . I ever saw my da with tears running down his face.' She could hear the thickness in his voice and was moved by it. 'Wasn't the last time that year either. Labour was supposed to be the party of the working man and it sold us down the river in a leaking boat. We miners were left on our own.'

Daniel fell silent for a moment. The sun was still hot

and bright. Gwen wasn't sure whether to speak, to acknowledge his emotion, but she didn't want to interrupt the flow of his thoughts. She could feel the force of the strike, the effect it had had on him at fifteen years to watch his father weep helplessly at the betrayal of everything he cared about.

'It was seven months the strike went on, then, and we were locked out of the pits. There was nothing else, see. The foundry in Aberglyn was closed. It's just a rusting heap, no work for anyone. There was no strike pay: all the Federation funds had been drunk dry. Only thing keeping the soup kitchens going was the subsidy from the Co-op. We used to go to the school and they'd give us stew and a bit of bread. Cocoa, when they could. There was Ma with seven children and another on the way and not a penny for food.'

He smiled, suddenly. 'It wasn't all gloom. There was always singing, choirs and that, and the men got up bands – kazoos, tin whistles, anything they could find – banging on a tin chest for a drum, dressing up and making a show. There was a great spirit in the town, but as the strike went on it bit deep. You could see it all round – the children's clothes. There were plenty without shoes through the cold months. Ma hardly had a stitch to put on Vincent and Dominic and they were poorly and pinched.'

He glanced at her, as if to check she was still listening and their eyes met for a second.

'And there was always trouble with the police. They were vicious bastards – 'scuse me, but they were – tried every trick to make you go over to the scab union in Aberglyn, to work for them. The police round us had been drafted in from the West Country somewhere – in England, I mean. Anyway, a couple of them came round to the house one day with the colliery manager. Da wasn't in at the time and nor was I, but they said to Ma, your husband's known as a good worker (which he was, one of the best). Course, they knew he was one of the best organizers in the town as well. Any group meeting, they'd stamp it out – charge you with unlawful assembly and you'd be straight to the assizes in Swansea or Cardiff. So, they said, we want him at work – he's needed. If he goes back, he'll be given protection. They didn't say much more but they left a florin on the mantelpiece. Well, Da wasn't having that. He sent our Ann to take it back to the manager's office. He knew she was a good one to ask – better to send a girl, he thought, and Ann was full of fire then, even though she was only thirteen. Made her who she is, that strike did.

'Anyway, that was that for a day or two, then two policemen started standing outside our house. They'd follow Ma home if she'd been out and that. Well, my da asked what they were doing and he was told to shut up. But we knew all right. They were trying to make it look as if they were protecting us – turn everyone against us. It made it look as if Da was up to something, as if he was a blackleg.

'"You get away from my door," Da said to them. "I've never worked for a scab union and I'm not going to start now." They went for us then – pushed us in through the door, right in front of Ma and the others, out the back, and they gave us both a beating. Broke Da's nose. He was a strong man but they were about twice the size of him. Both of us were all blood by the time they left. They went for him another time too, when he'd gone out digging a seam out on the mountain. The valley's full of coal, but only the owners think

222

they have the right to dig it up! Sometimes we'd be that desperate we'd be picking cokes out of the ash paths as they were laying them. Anyway, they caught him and beat him about the face.'

Daniel laughed suddenly. 'Didn't get him when he went up and got that sheep off the mountain, though. Best feast we had all year that was! Kiddies on the farms round about, see, they were better off. The miners had almost nothing. We were under the Poor Law. Ma was in a terrible state come the autumn. Starvation levels we were at. Bread and taters and not much of them. The baby came weeks early and it was born dead. She hardly had the strength to birth it.'

He stopped for a moment.

'How awful,' Gwen said gently. It was as if she could feel his pain inside her.

'Da made a little box to bury him. We thought Ma was going to die. There was nothing to her. She was ill for weeks after. Pernicious anaemia, the doctor told her. You'd never think it to look at her now. She was skin and bone. Frightened you to look at her.' He paused. Gwen looked up at him, his set, serious expression. He glanced at her.

'We were all trapped like animals. Nothing we could do, that was how it felt. She's strong, though, Ma. Stronger than she knows. Father O'Connor used to come to the house and see her. She's never forgotten his kindness to her. She pulled through.

'The strike went on to the close of the year. All through, and after, Da still wanted to believe in the Labour movement, the Labour Party. Couldn't let go of the idea that Parliament was where the power lay, that that was where change would come from. We had a branch of the NUWM in Aberglyn and he gave it everything he had. But I was learning other things then, see. I used to walk over to Tredegar – there's a library there full of political books. Best for miles. There were talks and discussions and I joined the Socialist League – me and Gomer set up a branch in Aberglyn, in a room behind the chapel. We had a big poster of Lenin in front of a red flag. That was the first time I began to read Marx.'

'And you joined the Communist Party?'

'Not straight away. But yes – when I became sure that the only way was the revolution. And Da joined soon after. He was . . .' His voice thickened again. 'He was so proud when I got into the college, down London. And then, while I was there, he died. Ma was left with no breadwinner in the family. Ann was working in the bakery up the road and did what she could. I came home and tried to go down the pit but there was hardly any work to be had. Ma was in a bad state. Lucy was born after Da passed on and she was sickly, what with her gammy leg and being small. The fits didn't start till later, but she was a sickly baby and Ma was poorly herself after. That's when Auntie Annie said we had to come to Birmingham.'

'But your mother had so many young children! How on earth did you all manage?'

'Annie and Pat were good to us, but they had their own troubles. There was only Ann and I who were old enough to work. Our Mary was a year off leaving school. Ann got a job first – in a shop. But then they hit us with the means test. You got your twenty-six weeks unemployment benefit and then they transferred you to Public Assistance. They come nosing round to see if you've anything in the house to sell, or if anyone's working, because then they say you don't need assistance and take it away! They'd be asking questions of the neighbours, expecting people to spy on one another, the lot! Ma had a struggle on her hands, even though there was more work over here. In the end, best thing was for Ann to go and live with Auntie Annie and I went back home. Pat had a job and they weren't claiming assistance so Ann was working, giving Ma the money. And me, later – even after she was married she put money my way where she could. Ann was always totally committed to the party and the cause. She's solid gold, my sister. And I was up and down to the valleys, keeping up the politics, working if I could . . .'

'Things seem a bit better now?' Gwen ventured to suggest.

Daniel nodded. 'Oh yes. Annie and Pat helped us get the shop, and Mary and Paul went out to work. Vincent'll be out looking for a job soon. Never feel I do enough for her myself, though.'

They were silent for a moment, walking a spongy path cut through a patch of woodland area.

'She worries about you. What all the politics will lead to.'

'I know.' There was wretchedness in his tone. 'I wouldn't upset her for anything, but I can't do anything else. It's my life.'

'I think it's . . . it's amazing what you do,' Gwen said fervently. She could barely find words for her thoughts, she was so full of emotion after what she had heard. 'It's brave and important and standing up for what you believe in!'

Daniel stopped suddenly. 'Not many people see it that way – that the world's got to change. There's got to be a revolution, to do away with the order of things as they are. Can you imagine living on, knowing things were going to stay as they are, with the tide of fascism sweeping towards us, a world where the jackboot rules, and the honest workers are trampled on?'

'No!' In her mind's eye, Gwen saw a faceless line of soldiers tramping across the country, stamping on everything in their path. 'No I can't!'

Daniel turned fully towards her, his eyes still fixed on hers. 'God, you are a captivating woman, d'you know that?'

Her body felt weightless, fluttery under his gaze, and deeper inside she felt a taut longing, a sense that she could not bear it if he did not touch her.

'And you . . .' She tried to say something but could not finish.

He turned away and walked on along the path. Gwen took a deep breath, watching him in front of her, the wet jacket over his arm. A moment later he stopped. A little branching way led off under the trees, away from the main path.

'Come on in here.' He pushed through the wet grass and weeds, and she could never have not followed him, the white shirt, his striding legs. The warnings in her head were silenced, and it was as if she was tied to him, body and soul, could simply not be anywhere else.

They were moving between young, spindly trees. The green woodland was lovely, their footsteps silenced by the sodden ground. A few yards on Daniel stopped between the trees and turning, dropped his jacket to the ground. Gwen did the same. Once more their eyes met and in a second they were clutching each other in an embrace such as Gwen had never experienced before. The strength of Daniel's arms drew her to him, his hands moving on her back, hard body against hers, not holding back in the gentlemanly way that Edwin held her, but urgently, unabashedly wanting her pressed close.

'I can't keep my mind off you.' He ran his hands down her sides, over her curving hips. 'You're such a beauty – God you're lovely, you are!'

His voice, his touch melted her. 'Daniel,' was all she could manage to say. 'Daniel, Daniel . . .'

She was lost to him, helpless with feeling as his face moved slowly closer to hers and she felt his lips exploring hers.

Twenty

Joey lay in a fever for four days. That was what they told him later. It was all a confusion of sounds, the blood banging in his ears, boots crossing the floor, clattering and coughing. At times he was aware of other people, and voices, a woman's voice in particular which he thought was his mother's, though she was talking in a strange way.

'Ah, will you look at him now, Christie? He's as thin as a sparrow.' A cool hand touched his head and someone lifted him and dribbled water between his dry lips.

'There y'are, darlin',' the voice said. 'Come on, now – drink a bit of this, will ye?' And he could remember trying to swallow and the feel of water running coolly down his throat and chin. He was half certain he remembered being held and rocked, but he knew that must have been a dream. In a blissful part of his dream he knew the arms around him were those of his teacher Miss Purdy, and he saw her pretty face smiling down at him.

Dots of light wavered in the darkness. Sometimes the room seemed a fraction less dark, and a quiet stillness fell around him. The first time he could open his eyes properly and focus it was evening and dark outside, but he could make out an elfin face looking down at him, with a pointed chin and straggly black hair hanging loose over her shoulders. Seeing him look up at her, the young woman smiled. A tooth was missing at the side of her mouth.

'Well, so you're looking at me! Back in the land of the living now, are ye?'

'Is the little fella coming round?' A light appeared in the gloom, a candle held by a dark-haired man with kind, dancing eyes. There was an orange glow of firelight coming from one side of the room. 'Well, here's our little Lazarus – you'll surely be wanting a hot drop of tea now then.' The man moved away again.

Joey tried to sit up, but his body wouldn't obey him. He felt himself to be all bones.

'Don't go thinking you can get up and dance a jig now.' The woman laid her hand soothingly on his. The sound of terrible coughing came from nearby and Joey sensed there were several people in the room. He felt bewildered, but somehow safe and reassured.

'What's your name, sweetheart?' the woman asked. Her face was so pale and thin.

Joey opened his mouth. He could barely remember how to speak. His throat felt closed up, but he noticed that it no longer hurt.

'Joey,' he rasped.

'Joey? You're a Joseph, are ye? Did you get yourself lost, coming in here?' The man was back again now, behind the woman, holding a jam jar of milky tea. He squatted down and Joey felt his strong arms go round him to hoist him up into a sitting position.

'There you go now – nice and sweet. It won't scald you – I put a drop of cold in.'

The tea was delicious: strong and syrupy with sugar and seemed to stroke its way down into his stomach, warming him inside. He drank, then stopped, closing his eyes for a rest. He was so weak that everything felt hazy and distant.

'He's had enough, Christie,' the woman said. 'Don't go forcing him.'

'No!' Joey's eyes snapped open and he clasped his hands round the warm glass, pulling it to his lips.

'Sure, he's like a little suckling lamb!' the man chuckled. 'Go on there now, little fella – you drink as much as you want!'

At last he was satisfied and Christie gently laid him back down. It was only then Joey noticed that he was no longer lying on the bare boards, but on a mattress. He felt warm and comfortable and suddenly happy.

Christie moved away, but the woman stayed at his side.

'Where's your mammy, Joey?' she asked softly.

Once again, he shook his head.

'Is she gone to Jesus?'

Joey wasn't sure about this. He just stared at her.

'Did your mammy pass away?'

She could see by his eyes that this was so.

'Poor little lamb,' she crooned. 'And what about your daddy? Won't he be looking for ye?' When she asked whether his daddy had passed away too, he shook his head.

'D'you have a home to go to, Joey? No? Oh, poor little darlin'!'

He found himself lifted and cradled against her soft breasts, then she rocked him gently.

'You're all skin and bone, so you are.'

Joey heard the door open then and the sound of boots. Another face appeared, but all he could see in the gloom was a squashed-looking hat and a huge black beard.

'All right there, John?' the woman asked.

The man made shy little nodding movements with his head.

'Is he getting better?' He had a high voice which seemed to come through his nose.

'He'll be grand.' A sudden sly look came to her face and she whispered, 'Did you get it for me?'

The man nodded.

'Thank Christ.'

He pulled something from under his coat and a furious cry came from Christie across the room.

'Oh, God Almighty, John. How could you bring it to her?' He stood up and rushed over to them. 'No, Siobhan – for God's sake don't start!'

But she had lain Joey down in a trice and scrambled to her feet, snatching the bottle from John's hand. She took a long swig, shuddering as the liquid went through her, then stopped and wiped her mouth. Christie was at her, trying to pull the bottle from her hand. In a moment, he succeeded.

'Don't let Micky drink all the rest!' Siobhan shrieked. 'He always takes more than his fecking share. I want it – I need it, for the love of God I do!'

Her tone was aggressive, out of control, and Joey felt a chill go through him. Now she really did sound like his mother. He curled up on his side and put his hands over his ears. He couldn't block out the voices, though. Siobhan slid down beside him again and when she lifted him into her arms, the smell on her breath was strong and familiar. It stank of danger. He turned his head to one side, screwing his eyes tight shut. He had the strength for nothing else.

'I want more!' she demanded.

'For God's sake, Shiv!' Christie's gentle voice was hoarse.

'Give it to me!'

'John – will you leave her?' There was scuffling the other side of the room. 'You know what it'll do to her!'

'Just a little bit,' John said. 'Let her have a bit. She wants it.'

In a moment John was back with the bottle and she drank again. The smell wafted over Joey. It made him want to cry and shout. He pushed the feeling down inside him.

'That's Christie over there.' She nodded her head, though Joey wasn't looking at Christie, couldn't see what he was doing. 'He's my brother – my *little* brother, though you'd not know it the way he bosses me. And there's John, who'd do anything I ask, wouldn't you, John darlin'? Like a child he is ... And then there's Micky over there. You'll hear him coughing. He's none too good, is Micky. Are you hungry, darlin'?'

Joey felt as if he was floating, couldn't move. He did not want food. He felt sick now, instead of happy. He could smell the liquor and the woman's body close to him.

'Joey – little Joey ...' Siobhan was stroking his head, rocking. 'You make me forget, little Joey, my baby,' she whispered.

She began to sing then, a sweet, lilting tune that he had never heard before and he closed his eyes to shut her out. A few moments later the singing stopped and her body began to jerk next to him.

'I was going to have a baby of my own, Joey. He died, my little baby ... They killed him inside me and I'm going to go to hell, saints preserve me.' Deep, terrible sobs came from her and she was leaning over and clutching him close.

'"The Angel of the lord declared to Mary..." Oh, John, give me a little drop more for pity's sake!' She drank again in long, greedy gulps. '"... And she conceived of the Holy Spirit ... Hail Mary, full of grace, blessed art thou among women..." Oh, Lord God!' Her hair fell over Joey, blocking out the firelight and her tears fell on his face. Her crying sounded very loud to him and he swelled inside with bad feelings. He wanted desperately to push her away, to run and run from these people but he hadn't the strength.

'Come on, Siobhan – come away now.' Christie's voice was gentle. 'Put the lad down – let him sleep.'

Joey was replaced abruptly on the mattress and he saw Christie trying to calm his sister. She was distraught, crying and fighting him as he struggled to keep hold of her wrists.

'Let me go! Just feck off and stop bossing me, Christie. You're not our daddy! I'm going – I can bring in the money as well – that's what I'm good for, isn't it? You know I am! Sister Assumpta always said I'd go straight to hell to sup with the devil ... I'm already in hell, so what difference will it make? Go on, tell me that, oh so perfect Father Christie Cody ...'

'For God's sake, Shiv, just keep quiet!' Christie sounded distraught. 'D'you want us thrown out of here? Don't be like this. It kills me when you're like this.'

'For God's sake, Shiv!' She mimicked him in a spiteful tone. 'Tell you what – I'll do it with John. I'll do the one thing I'm good for, eh Christie? John loves me, don't you, darlin' ... No, don't you come taking his side! You're on my side.' Her voice rose to a screech as John attempted to come to Christie's aid.

'What's all the feckin' racket . . .' Micky's confused voice protested from across the room, but then lapsed into coughing and incoherent mumbling.

Siobhan pulled away from her brother and Joey heard her go out of the room.

'Siobhan!' John's nasal voice called.

'It's no good – you'll not stop her.' Christie spoke softly, and his tone was despairing. 'Not when she's like that.'

Hands still over his ears, Joey drifted gratefully into sleep.

Over the following days as Joey recovered his strength, he began to make sense of where he was. There was never full daylight inside because all the windows were boarded up and only fragments of light crept in between the boards. The room seemed very big and he wondered if he was in a school, as he'd never seen such a large room anywhere else. Houses, so far as he knew, were tiny and cramped, though apart from the size this one felt familiar: boarded windows, the walls reduced to bare, crumbling plaster, bare, rotten floorboards and the stink of damp and smoke.

'Whose house're we in?' he asked Christie, that first morning when he was truly conscious.

'It's no one's.' Christie turned to him from the fire, into which he was poking sticks. 'We're just borrowing it for a little while – like birds of the air looking for a place to rest. And we want to keep it that way.'

Joey experimented with moving his body. He wanted to get off the prickly mattress. It felt as if he had been lying on it for years. His body felt weak and shaky, but he managed to get to his hands and knees.

'You ready to get up now?' Christie was beside him in the gloom, lifting him over to the fire. 'Come on over here.' Joey found he was sitting on the man's coat. It made him think of Mr Simmons's coat which had been stolen from him. There was a pan of water heating over the flames. Christie squatted beside him. Something about him felt safe.

'You're looking grand now this morning! I'm just making a hot drop of tea. It's Sunday today – did you know that?'

Joey enjoyed sitting looking into the flames. He didn't feel like running away any more, now it was quiet and he was by the fire. His days spent sleeping in cold parks and wandering the streets alone already felt a long way in the past. He peered round the room. The sound of snoring aroused his memory of arriving. It was coming from a big, dark shape lying over to his left.

'That's Micky.' Christie saw him looking. Joey could just make out a bearded face with thick, frightening-looking features. The other man wasn't there and he wondered where the woman called Siobhan had gone, but a moment later saw that she too was asleep across the room. He remembered her crying and dread gripped him for a moment. But she was quiet now.

He watched Christie as he tipped tea leaves into the pan of hot water and stirred them in with a sliver of wood. The man was thin and didn't look very strong. His clothes were black, his hair was dark and curly and he hadn't shaved for days, but his beard was nothing like as bushy as John's or Micky's. Joey noticed that he was hugging himself, shivering as if cold. He thought the man had sad eyes.

'Here now.' Christie handed him tea and a piece of bread torn from a loaf. His face was kind and gentle and Joey felt soothed by his company. 'You get that down you.'

Twenty-One

'Millie – you're looking ever so well!'

Gwen found Millie waiting for her as she came out through the school gate. Millie smiled bravely. It was a day of showers and she was sheltering under an umbrella.

'You're not looking so bad yourself. In fact –' she peered at Gwen – 'you look like a cat that's got the cream! What's come over you?'

Gwen laughed. 'I don't know – must be the spring weather!' How could she possibly say what was making her glow from the inside with love and happiness and excitement? *Daniel*, she thought, hugging the very sound of his name inside herself. *My beautiful Daniel!* He was busy this afternoon, she knew that, or she might have been rather less pleased to see Millie waiting for her.

'Got time for a cuppa?' Millie asked.

'Yes, of course. Come on – let's get away from here. Agnes Monk'll be out in a minute.'

'Oh Lord – I can't say I'm longing to see her!' Millie grimaced.

They went to a little place along Wellington Street and ordered tea and currant buns. Gwen examined Millie as she took off her mac to sit down. She was wearing a green skirt and neat cream blouse with frills on the collar and cuffs.

'You really do look better,' Gwen said, trying to be encouraging. Millie's freckly skin had some of its bloom back and she looked a little healthier, though tired and strained. As Gwen spoke Millie's eyes immediately filled with tears.

'Sorry.' She wiped them with her hanky. 'Keeps happening. I don't know what's come over me.'

'Is everything all right?' Gwen eyed her anxiously.

'As it'll ever be,' Millie said gloomily.

'The wedding's still on and everything?'

Millie rallied. 'Look – sorry. I'm being such an old grouch. Yes, of course it's still on. That's what I've come to tell you about – to invite you. It's going to be the second Saturday in May and I'd love you to come.'

'Oh, how lovely!' Gwen realized as she spoke that she sounded just a little over-enthusiastic, as if she was humouring Millie. 'I mean – how do you feel about it?'

Millie shrugged. 'What choice do I have?' She lowered her voice, leaning across the table. 'I don't exactly want to bring a bastard child into the world, do I?'

Gwen was appalled by the bitterness she saw in her friend's face.

'I just have to be grateful that Lance is prepared to stick by me and do the right thing.' Millie sat back and fiddled with the spoon on her saucer. 'We'll have enough money and the baby'll have a proper family. I'm lucky really when you think what happens to some people. My mother's been ever so kind and reasonable, and stuck by me. I won't be thrown on the streets. What more could I want?'

'Oh, Millie.' Gwen sat back, looking at her. She could scarcely think what to say to be of comfort. 'It'll be all right. You *do* love Lance, don't you? You must've done to . . . to . . .' She had been going to say to get *into this situation*, but she couldn't finish. Immediately the thought of Edwin came to her. Wasn't she supposed to love him? And look how she was behaving! But somehow Edwin and her feelings for Daniel felt like two completely different worlds. Edwin was her fiancé, of course he was! But as for love – heaven knew, she hadn't known what love was until she met Daniel.

As she spoke to Millie, trying to cheer her up, she was all the time guiltily aware of her hands in her lap under the table. With her right hand she kept feeling the third finger of her left. In the chest of drawers in her room at Ariadne's house was a little dark blue box, and in its silky interior nestled her engagement ring with its tiny sapphires. She had slipped it off the morning she went out with Daniel. It had been in the drawer ever since, and her finger felt bare and strange – and guilty.

'The other thing I was going to ask you . . .' Millie hesitated. 'Mum thought we'd live with her, at first anyway. But Lance is dead set against it. Says we need our privacy and all that. He's already found us a flat to rent – just the upstairs rooms of a house in Handsworth. The thing is, it's still quite a lot of rent, what with me not working, and then there'll be the baby. So we thought if there were three of us to share, it would all be easier. I just wondered if you'd think of having the spare room. You seem pretty fed up where you are now.'

'Oh, Millie, that'd be perfect! I keep thinking I ought to look for somewhere else, but I've been so idle about it. I'm sure that woman's going to poison me in the end if I stay there – entirely by accident, but even so. And that Mr Purvis creeping about all the time with

239

his flaming trumpet . . .' She had given Millie a toned-down version of what went on in the Soho Road house. 'Are you sure you can stand having another person around? Married bliss and all that?'

Millie looked earnestly at her. 'Gwen, I think if I don't have other company apart from Lance, I shall go right off my rocker.'

'Come round to ours and see us, any day,' Daniel had said as they parted at the tram stop that Sunday.

She felt dazed, and as if she was dreaming after an afternoon in his arms, with his kisses. They had stood in the woods, wrapped round one another. Daniel was not full of gentlemanly reserve in his embraces, unlike Edwin. He pulled her tightly to him, his tongue feeling its way gently, then more urgently between her lips until both of them were alight with desire, kissing each other's face, neck, lips, breaking away for a few minutes to walk, before they were drawn together again like magnets. By the end of the afternoon her cheeks were tingling after the chafe of his skin against hers, his dark stubble prickling her, and the feel of his strong body was imprinted on her as if she knew him through and through, had somehow always known him. It was a wrench to separate and to say goodbye. But his invitation to come to the house, to see more of him and his family, was compensation.

'Won't your mother mind me dropping by?'

'No, course not.' The serious look he gave her further affected her. 'With the shop there're always people coming in anyway. And she likes you. Lucy talks about you and Ma's liked talking to you when you came. She said you were . . .' He glanced at the sky as if for inspiration. 'What was it now?'

'Stop teasing me.' She poked him and he jumped.

'I'm not! I think she said you were very sympathetic.' He chuckled. 'Oh – and very frightening.'

'Frightening?'

'No, she didn't really say that! But come round.' His face grew serious and he laid his hands on her shoulders. 'Or I'll have to come to the school every day and show all Miss Purdy's class what I feel about their teacher.'

'Don't you dare! Of course I'll come. As long as it's all right.'

'Oh, it's all right.' He held her close and kissed her forehead, just close to the line of her little waves of hair. 'My lovely Gwen.'

That first week, she had left it for a couple of days before visiting, forcing herself to wait, to be measured in her behaviour, even though there was nothing measured in her feelings. Her emotions were in turmoil. Even in two days she had convinced herself that the walk on the hills was, if not a dream – she remembered it too vividly for that – an aberration, and that when she saw Daniel again everything would be different and the love and closeness would all be lost. He had been doing nothing but play with her. These thoughts almost made her afraid to go again because she could not bear to face the loss of him, the expression in his eyes when he looked down at her.

On the third day, when she knew she could stay away no longer, he was waiting for her. She caught a glimpse of him outside the gate as she came out of the school and her heart leapt with excitement. She hurried towards him, attempting to look poised and calm in front of the gaggles of children all trying to push through the gate at once, but a delighted smile broke over her face in spite of herself.

'Hello, Miss Purdy.' Even the sound of his voice brought her up in goose pimples. He was smiling, speaking with teasing formality.

'Good afternoon, Mr Fernandez.' They were surrounded by children. 'Have you come to collect Lucy?'

'That's right. I don't s'pose she'll be first out, though.'

The Canal Street children dispersed quickly, leaving them standing alone. Gwen saw Lucy emerge from the girls' entrance with Alice Wilson beside her.

'I thought you were coming to see us?' Daniel said.

'I am – of course. In fact I was going to come today.' The children were moving closer. 'D'you see this little girl, with Lucy? This is Alice. The poor child can hardly see a thing.'

Daniel looked at Alice's bedraggled figure. Her plaits were roughly tied and her clothes looked unkempt and messy. Nowadays she looked worse than some of the other children in the school. She didn't look like the Alice who had arrived in January.

The girls parted and Lucy walked home with her brother and teacher.

'Miss Purdy's agreed to come and have a cup of tea,' Daniel said.

'Have we got anything to eat?' Lucy asked eagerly.

'Oh, I expect we can find something.'

Theresa was talking and laughing with a woman in the shop as they walked through, but she broke off and said cheerily, 'Afternoon, Miss Purdy!'

On the table in the back, beside the brown teapot

and cups, was a plate of homemade tarts. There was also a jam jar with a little bunch of pink tulips in it.

As Daniel and Lucy were making tea, the bell in the shop rang as the customer went out and Theresa came through to the back, a smile on her face.

'That Mrs Harvey's a character. Always gives me a good laugh, she does.' She sat down at the table. 'Help yourself to a jam tart, won't you?' Gwen, who was hungry, obeyed eagerly. 'I hope those children have been little angels today?'

'Well, yours has!' Gwen laughed. Lucy blushed, carrying a bowl of sugar lumps to the table. 'She's as bright as a button. And you've been helping Alice, haven't you? She can't see what's on the blackboard, you see.'

'She can't see *anything*, hardly at all,' Lucy said.

'I wrote to her mother weeks ago, suggesting she get the girl's eyes tested,' Gwen said indignantly. 'She doesn't seem to have done a thing about it.'

'Can't afford it, most likely,' Daniel said.

'But she's one of the best-dressed children in the school. Well, she *was*.' There was something about Alice that really perplexed Gwen. 'I'm not sure what else to do.'

She finished her jam tart. 'That was *so* nice. My landlady's cooking is very peculiar. I hate to think what she'd manage to do to jam tarts.'

Theresa chuckled. 'Have another one then, my love. I've made plenty.'

'No, it was delicious, but I won't. I'm sure they'll soon go with all your family – let the children have them.'

They chatted on about the schools the other Fernandez children attended and Vincent's first job. At fourteen he had just left school and acquired a job with a coffin maker.

'He has to paint RIP on the side of each one!' Daniel said.

'Always was good at drawing.' Theresa smiled.

Gwen felt relaxed and comfortable sitting in the simple room with Daniel and his mother. Lucy eventually grew bored and after her siblings had come home and polished off the rest of the tarts, she went outside with them. Theresa and Daniel took turns to go into the shop and serve people, and in between they talked about things in the news – Herr Hitler was moving troops back into the Rhineland, and there was talk that the Italians had used mustard gas in Abyssinia – but they avoided discussing politics. Gwen had the impression, with Theresa Fernandez, of a woman who was keenly intelligent and interested in the world around her, but who simply wanted an end to politics taking over her home. She wanted some peace and Daniel, at least for the moment, appeared to respect that. The only mention Theresa made of his activities was to ask if he was going out that night.

'For a bit,' Daniel said. 'I'm going chalking up for the meeting on Sunday.' He looked at Gwen's puzzled face. 'Haven't you seen the signs? We chalk them up all over – for the meetings and that.'

'I haven't noticed,' she admitted.

'Obviously not doing a good enough job then, are we?'

When the shop bell rang again, Theresa got up to go into the shop.

'Do you think . . .' Gwen asked quickly, knowing it was time she went home. Alice was still playing on her mind. 'I'm concerned about that girl, Alice. Would it be completely out of place for me to go and see her mother? Perhaps she never even had my letter? It's just that I think Alice is a clever child and she's being badly held back.'

'I think you're very kind to think of it,' Theresa said carefully from the doorway.

'But wouldn't you think it a bit peculiar if one of your children's teachers arrived on your doorstep?'

Daniel chuckled. 'Oh yes – we would!'

Gwen blushed. 'I don't mean – I mean it was different, the night I brought Lucy home. There was no one else.'

'And we were very grateful,' Theresa said. 'Don't take any notice of him. You do what you think's best, Miss Purdy. It's only a rare person would think of it.'

'Thank you ever so much for the tea, Mrs Fernandez.' Gwen got up. 'I think I will go and see them.'

'Can't do any harm, can it?' Theresa said and disappeared into the shop.

'I'd better be off as well.' Daniel stood up. Suddenly she was acutely aware of him, his lean back moving under the white shirt, his hands, the soft edge of his hairline at the back of his neck. As he came towards her, she felt alive in every nerve. He drew her into his arms.

'I've been waiting for this,' he said. She sank against him with relief, as if she had come home, and felt his hand warm on the back of her neck. For a long, taut moment they held apart as if waiting, holding each other's gaze.

'Daniel,' she whispered. 'God, Daniel.'

Then her lips were silenced by his.

Twenty-Two

It was a warm spring morning. Smoke from factory chimneys hung high and still in the air. Gwen had ventured out into the sunshine without a coat, in a pretty floral frock with a soft, swinging skirt, her bag over her arm. That morning, after she had dressed, she leaned down to the mirror, saw her face smile radiantly back. *I look so happy!* she thought. *Have I ever looked like this before?* She startled people in the street with her smile. She could think of nothing but Daniel and his loving eyes, and when she might see him again, so that she was full of bubbling excitement and wanted to dance along the road, skipping and whooping like a child. Yet, in a strange way, it seemed to her she had never felt so grown up. She was away from home, deciding things for herself!

One thing she had decided was that she would get out of the claustrophobic atmosphere of the house in Soho Road and lodge with Millie and Lance. Not that she'd told Ariadne of her plans yet. She didn't think she would be very pleased.

Gwen waited at the tram stop. When she was out on the streets a part of her mind was always on the lookout for Joey Phillips. After the day when she thought she caught a glimpse of him looking into the playground, there had been no sign of him. What happened to children like Joey? she wondered as the tram drew to a stop. She flinched as a shower of sparks fell hissing from the wires above. It was as if Joey had melted away into the streets.

The first lesson was arithmetic and they were starting to learn long division. Though there were a few children like Lucy Fernandez who were very sharp and picked up things straight away, a lot of them were struggling. Gwen watched as the class copied the sums down from the blackboard. Jack Ellis's head was bent, his hand clutching his pen far too tightly. He snapped a nib off almost every week and dug holes in the paper. Gwen sighed. Jack was ever so dense. It would be a long time before he got the hang of this.

She walked along between the desks, noticing that even now some of the children cringed as she passed, used to being cuffed and whacked for getting a sum wrong.

'No, Ron.' She leaned over Ron Parks, whose tongue was out, almost touching his nose in the effort to concentrate. There was a slug of snot on his upper lip and around him hung an aura of grime and sweet stickiness. 'You have to carry that one down. Yes, down there. Then how many times does twelve go into one hundred and fifty?'

Ron's brow furrowed, then his face lit up with inspiration. 'Seven?'

Gwen walked back to the front. 'Let me hear you all say the twelve times table!' she commanded. The children obeyed, droningly. She went through the sum on the blackboard.

'If twelve twelves are one hundred and forty four, how many do we carry over?'

Joan Billings timidly raised her hand. 'Six?'

'Very good. Now try the next bit.'

She went to the desk where Lucy sat beside Alice Wilson.

'Have you got the sums copied down all right, Alice?'

'Yes, Miss.' Alice squinted up at her. Her face was forever screwed up with the effort to see and it made her otherwise sweet face look tense and sly.

'And did you do the sums by yourself?'

'Yes, Miss.'

Gwen looked at Alice's page of numbers. The girl had understood and worked it all out straight away. But if she hadn't had Lucy to help her she would have looked dimwitted and slow.

At breaktime Gwen went into the staffroom, determined to have a word with Lily Drysdale. As soon as she walked in, however, she could sense a strange atmosphere. To her surprise, Mr Lowry was sitting drinking a cup of tea. Usually he hardly ever mingled with his staff, but instead kept himself aloof up in his office. The problem was obvious. Mr Lowry was sitting beside the new teacher, Charlotte Rowley. Across the other side of the room sat Agnes Monk, whose entire body, not just her face, seemed to consist of one gigantic glower.

'I'm delighted to hear you play the piano as well,' Mr Lowry was saying.

Miss Rowley, dark-eyed and inscrutable, stared back with cold politeness and Gwen saw her lean further away from him, drawing her skirt closer round her primly set knees. This only seemed to provoke Mr Lowry to try harder.

'Do you play any other instruments?' Gwen heard

him say as she walked past with her cup of tea. Miss Monk was reading her book, her face and neck an angry red. On the noticeboard above her head was pinned a sheet of paper headed 'Empire Day Pageant'.

Lily Drysdale was sitting to one side of the room, knitting what appeared to be baby clothes. The delicate rows of white stitches looked incongruous in her big hands. Gwen saw that her fingernails were stained with green.

'Hello, dear,' she said as Gwen sat beside her. She gave a wry smile suddenly and leaned in closer, whispering, 'Trying to keep away from the love triangle as well, are you?'

Gwen was so startled she didn't know what to say.

'Er, yes!' She blushed too easily, as ever. 'But I came to ask you something too.'

Lily laid her knitting down on her lap. 'For my niece's baby,' she said with a smile.

'Oh how lovely.' Gwen felt faint surprise that Lily had family and infant relatives like anyone else.

'What is it, dear?'

Gwen poured out her worries about Alice Wilson and how her eyesight was holding her back. 'I just can't understand why her mother doesn't do something about her,' she finished indignantly.

'You have to remember, they're probably living on very slender means,' Lily pointed out. 'I find that paying a call is often the thing.'

'D'you think I should?'

'Best thing. Would you like me to come with you?'

Though she was grateful for the offer, Gwen felt instinctively that she should do this by herself. Two teachers turning up at Alice's house would surely feel far more alarming than one. She thanked Lily, and said she would try and go that afternoon.

'T'ra then – see you tomorrow,' Lucy said, limping to her front door in Alma Street.

'T'ra,' Alice echoed.

Lucy turned on the step and Alice could just make out through the blur that she was smiling before she disappeared through the front door. Alice felt a pang go through her. How she'd have loved Lucy to invite her in! She liked Lucy's mother with her kind blue eyes. She was always in the shop, and the house usually smelt of cakes cooking. There was something comforting about Mrs Fernandez and Alice liked all the hubbub of the family, with Lucy's brothers coming in and out. She thought Rosa was the loveliest person she'd ever met – after Miss Purdy, of course. And sometimes Dominic would give her a ride in the old wheelbarrow up and down the pavement, until she screamed at him to stop. The combination of Dominic's crazy speed and the fact she couldn't see made the rides thrilling and petrifying at the same time.

She always walked home with Lucy, although it took her a little out of her way, because it put off going home for a bit longer. She dawdled now along Alma Street and crossed Wellington Road, squinting hard. She was always afraid of something coming at her that she couldn't see and knocking her down. Bicycles were the worst because you couldn't hear them. When she turned into Franklin Street the rag-and-bone man was calling out from somewhere along the road. She was so busy peering to try and see him with his cart and his supply of goldfish that she didn't notice the boy swinging on a rope tied to the lamp post near her house. One minute she was walking along and the next a body came flying at her and knocked straight into her from the front. Alice fell over backwards, jarring her back and scraping her elbow hard on the kerb.

'You blind or summat?' the boy jeered, skidding to a halt. 'Why don't you watch where you're going?'

Alice got up carefully, rubbing her back. She didn't want to show him how much it hurt, but she couldn't stop the tears running down her face. She hurried to her house, wiping her eyes. As she went to open the door, she noticed the state of her sleeve. Round the elbow her blouse was all muck and blood.

'Oh no, don't let it be torn as well!' she muttered. Frantic, she struggled to see, pulling her elbow up as near to her face as she could. It looked as if the sleeve was intact. She hurried down the entry. Maybe if she sneaked in quietly, she could get it washed without her mother finding out.

She was already used to the scrubby little yard behind the house and the wall with the loose bricks at the top looking ready to topple off. Her mother still couldn't accept that they lived in such a place, instead of their lovely house with the garden and the tubs of flowers outside the front door. No one else in the family knew they lived here, not even her grandma. Mummy said she would die of the shame of it if anyone came and saw . . .

The back door squeaked open. Alice cringed, but no sound came from inside. If she could just get her blouse washed so that Mummy didn't see how dirty it was, she wouldn't get angry and cry.

There was no sign of her mother downstairs. Some-times when Alice came home she was sitting in the back room. This meant today was one of her bad days and she was in bed. Normally that would be a bad sign, but at least it meant she wouldn't see the blouse.

Alice hurried into the scullery and took out the wash pail, managing not to clank it against the basin. While it was filling with water she hurriedly undid the buttons, wincing as she peeled the sleeve from her arm. The pain made her eyes water. She shoved the blouse down into the pail. Standing in her little vest she examined her skinny arm and saw a blur of red. The arm stung, but it was nothing serious. Reminding herself to hurry, she seized the lump of wash soap and scrubbed at the sleeve, bringing it up close so she could see what she was doing. To her enormous relief, with each scrub and dunk in the water the blood washed pinker and lighter till it had almost disappeared. She scrubbed at the dirt. It would show a bit, but maybe not enough to cause trouble. Just as she was trying to wring the blouse out over the sink, she heard her mother's slow tread on the stairs. Quickly! She fled outside in her vest and pegged the blouse, still dripping, on the line.

As she came in again, her mother came down into the back room. At least she was dressed, Alice noticed, in her black skirt and blouse, which always looked nice against her blonde colouring. But she had no stockings on, she was standing in bare feet on the lino and she hadn't combed her hair. Alice couldn't see her face properly, but her voice was dull and expressionless in a way that Alice had come to dread more than her anger.

'What're you doing, Alice?'

'I . . . I got my blouse a bit dirty. But it's all right. I washed it.'

Her mother sank down on the chair, almost as if she hadn't heard.

'Put the kettle on for a cup of tea, will you?'

Alice ran to fill the kettle, feeling her chest unknot a little. Mummy didn't mind. She hadn't even seemed to notice! She peered out at her mother. Poor Mummy on that awful old horsehair chair with the stuffing hanging out! There was a rickety table and chairs and, apart from the two beds, nothing else. Every stick of their lovely furniture had been taken with the other house. Before, there had been armchairs covered with a pretty pale green material and shiny tables with vases of flowers and rugs on the floor. Alice felt tears rise in her eyes again and her throat hurt. She didn't often think about before, about where Daddy was or what had happened to Mummy because she was too busy trying to survive from day to day, but every so often it all welled up and spilled over and she found herself crying as if she'd never stop. But not now, she told herself, digging her nails into her palms. She must be quiet and not make Mummy upset.

When she'd poured the tea, she found her mother lying back in the chair, arms folded tightly across her, as if she was cold, and her eyes closed. She sat like this a lot now. Alice leaned closer, wondering if she was asleep. Her mother had lovely thick pale hair which had been cut in a fashionable pageboy, though it had grown long and straggly now. She had been so pretty, with her sweet, feminine face and laughing blue eyes, when her friends came round to drink tea in the afternoons. And Daddy's parties – Alice always associated them with her mother's perfume, which had smelt of flowers. All she smelt of now was cheap soap. She'd had a pink silk dress which fitted her slim figure beautifully and brushed the carpet as she walked. Alice had seen her hurl it, screaming and crying, onto a pile of things to be sold, before they left the house.

'I won't be needing this any more!' she cried. 'Since I shan't have any life any more!' Then there'd been a great, agonized scream, 'You bastard! You rotten, deceiving bastard!'

'Mummy—'

Alice didn't want to touch her.

The blue eyes opened, with dull, vacant expression.

'I made your tea.'

'Oh. Thank you.' She hauled herself up in the chair as if she had no energy, and took the cup.

'Why're you in your vest?'

'I washed my blouse.'

'Oh.'

Alice stood by the chair. She was always on tenter-hooks with Mummy now, never sure of her mood. Alice was hungry. Should she ask if she should go along to the shops? Was there anything for tea? Mummy didn't leave the house. Not ever. She'd have to put her one other blouse on to go out.

Her mother drank half the tea, then sat back with the cup balanced in her lap. She closed her eyes. Alice didn't know what to do. But then she heard a sound, someone knocking on the front door!

'Go and get rid of them, Alice.' Louise Wilson gave a bitter little laugh. 'We aren't buying anything at the door.'

Alice crept through to the front and went to the window to see who was knocking. Screwing up her eyes, she saw a woman on the doorstep. Her heart gave a jolt before starting to pound madly. It was Miss

Purdy! She could see the blurred blue of her dress. What on earth was Miss Purdy doing here? And whatever was she going to do?

Paralysed, Alice stood very still, praying Miss Purdy couldn't see her and that she'd just think no one was in and go away. Part of her longed to ask Miss Purdy in, to say to her: please help me, just help me, I don't know what to do. But she just couldn't open the door. Mummy would have a fit! Not knowing what else to do, Alice tiptoed away to the back room again.

'Who was it?' her mother asked, indifferently.

'No one,' Alice was saying, when the knocking came again.

'Oh, for goodness sake, go and tell them we don't want anything.'

Alice's body seemed to turn to water. She couldn't argue with Mummy. Full of dread, she went and opened the door.

'Hello, Alice!' She could make out Miss Purdy's lovely smile. 'I've just come to have a word with your mother. May I come in, please?'

Alice had only opened the door wide enough to poke her head round. She squirmed. How could she lie to Miss Purdy and refuse to let her in? Helplessly she stood aside.

'She's in the back,' she whispered.

Alice saw her mother look round as they walked in. At the sight of a stranger in the house she sat bolt upright.

'Who's this?' she demanded sharply.

'Mummy,' Alice pleaded. 'This is Miss Purdy, my teacher.'

'It's very nice to meet you,' Miss Purdy said, with her hand held out. Mrs Wilson automatically responded, and for a second Alice thought it might be all right after all. 'I'm sorry to disturb you. Only I'm a bit worried about Alice. I wrote to you a little while ago about her eyes . . .'

But Alice saw her mother withdraw, fold her arms across her body and lower her head.

'Get out of my house,' she hissed. To Alice's horror she started to rock back and forth. 'Just go away. I never asked you to come here. I don't want anyone here. Leave us alone!'

Miss Purdy turned to Alice, utterly bewildered, but she couldn't look up. She was so mortified she just stared at the floor, tears welling.

'I'm very sorry,' Miss Purdy said wretchedly. 'I didn't mean to . . . to offend you in any way. I'd better go.'

'Yes – go!' Alice's mother screamed suddenly, then broke into sobs.

Alice followed Miss Purdy to the door, her throat closed with emotion.

'I'm sorry, Alice. I didn't want to make things more difficult,' Miss Purdy said, on the step. She looked upset. They could hear Mrs Wilson sobbing in the back room. 'I'll see you at school tomorrow.'

Alice couldn't say anything. Through her tears, she saw the blurred figure of her beloved teacher turn away and walk off along Franklin Street. She got further and further along until she was a small, blue blob, and her disappearing felt like the most desolate thing Alice had ever seen. She couldn't bear to be alone with all this any more. Desperate feelings swelled in her until she could no longer stand it. Her throat unlocked.

'Miss Purdy!' She shouted along the street at the top of her voice. 'Miss Purdy! Don't go – please!'

Twenty-Three

The little girl's cry pierced through Gwen.

Fighting back tears of shock at Mrs Wilson's violent dismissal of her, she turned to see Alice's forlorn figure by the lamp outside her house. Alice's desperate call was the loudest sound she had ever heard from this timid child.

Whatever was wrong with her mother? Gwen had been horrified by the glimpse she had had of the Wilsons' house. The front room was completely bare, not a stick of furniture in it, and the back room hardly better. In its way, it felt even more dismal than the crumbling squalor of Joey Phillips's house because Mrs Wilson was so obviously genteel. Gwen hesitated, unable to think what to do. It would be easiest to run away – Mrs Wilson had made it very clear she didn't want anyone. But the least she could do was to try and comfort Alice.

Seeing her teacher approaching her again, the little girl lowered her head and cried heartbrokenly. It was only then that Gwen noticed that the child was dressed only in a vest with her skirt. Gwen did the only thing she could think of and took the fragile child in her arms, stroking her head.

'It's all right, Alice,' she said softly. The intensity of the child's grief made her want to cry as well, but she fought back her own tears. 'It's all right, dear. It's all right.' The words came instinctively. She held the child and let her cry.

'Is your mummy often upset?' she asked when Alice was a little calmer. She felt Alice nod.

Gwen had no idea what to do next. She could hardly go back into the house when Mrs Wilson had ordered her out so angrily. She was frightened of the way the woman had looked, the hysterical sound of her voice and of her own role as an interfering busybody. She felt completely out of her depth. But how else could she help Alice? The poor child had to live with this day after day, quite apart from not being able to see properly. Surely there was something that could be done.

'Come along, Alice.' She sounded a great deal more decisive than she felt. 'Perhaps I should come in again and see if I can have a word with your mother.'

Alice didn't protest, though Gwen couldn't help wishing she would.

In the house Gwen and Alice could hear weeping. They tiptoed into the room. Mrs Wilson was sitting hunched in the chair, rocking back and forth. The fury seemed to have left her and she appeared smaller, girlish and completely bereft. It was only then that Gwen noticed that although Alice's mother was quite nicely dressed she was not wearing anything on her feet.

Mrs Wilson looked up, her cheeks wet with tears. It was a sweet, blue-eyed face. Gwen realized that she was not a great deal older than herself, barely thirty.

'Oh *no*!' she wailed, her face crumpling again. 'Why can't you just go away and leave me alone? I just want everyone to leave me alone!'

Her voice was light and well spoken, at odds with

the poor, bleak surroundings. Gwen couldn't make any sense of it.

'I'm sorry,' she began, 'only Alice was so upset, and ... well, you're obviously so unhappy too and I wondered if there was anything I can do to help you?'

'No!' Alice's mother began crying afresh then. 'Just go away! Leave me!'

Gwen could see that despite all her protests, the woman desperately needed someone's comfort. Finding all the courage she could, she went and knelt by the chair.

'Please don't worry. I only want to help – you and Alice. She's such a good girl, and you seem so terribly sad ...'

These words of kindness made Mrs Wilson cry all the harder. She put her hands in her lap, kneading them in dreadful agitation.

'Oh!' she burst out eventually, between her sobs. 'Oh, I can't bear it any more. I can't go on struggling on alone like this!'

Gwen dared to reach and take one of her hands and the woman quietened a little and looked into her face, as if trying to decide whether she was worthy of trust. Gwen could see how much Alice resembled her, with her pale hair and eyes.

'It's all right.' Again, it was the only thing Gwen could think of to say.

'You won't tell anyone?'

'Of course not.'

'Alice, dear – I'd like to talk to your teacher. Would you go upstairs for a little while, please?'

Alice obeyed. Her face was blotchy from crying, but Gwen could see she was relieved. They paused, listening to her tread on the stairs. Gwen found herself wondering if they had any furniture up there.

'She's a dear little thing,' she said to break the silence.

'Yes,' Mrs Wilson said miserably. 'Poor Alice.' Her tears fell again and she gripped Gwen's hand. 'Can I trust you? I don't know who I can trust any more. I don't know who I am or what I'm about!'

'It's all right, really it is. I just want to help.' For some reason Gwen added, 'I'm not from round here myself.'

Mrs Wilson's pale eyes searched her face.

'Is it just you and Alice who live here?' Gwen asked.

'Yes. We never had any more children. A blessing as it's turned out. I can hardly manage with Alice.' She seemed to come to herself for a moment. 'I should make you a cup of tea . . .'

'No, please don't bother. I'm quite all right.' Gwen imagined that Alice's father must have died, or deserted her, for her to be left alone like this. The poor woman was obviously finding it very hard to cope with her reduced circumstances. She decided it might be easier to be direct.

'What is it that's troubling you, Mrs Wilson?'

While Gwen stayed kneeling on the floor at her feet, Mrs Wilson's story came pouring out. Until a few months before, she and her husband and Alice had lived a very comfortable life in a respectable part of Solihull. Her husband, Bernard, was a partner in a thriving engineering business in Birmingham. He was almost a decade older than her and Louise Wilson – she told Gwen her name – had married young, had Alice, and settled into being the pretty, sheltered wife of a prosperous businessman. She attended the business functions, ladies' nights at the masonic lodge of which he was a member, always pretty and admired on his arm. Alice went to a good private school, where she had nice little friends. Louise had servants, but she liked to make things to decorate the house, curtain pelmets and flower arrangements. Her home was her pride: her project to make it a pretty, orderly haven for her friends to visit and her busy husband to come home to. She felt he was proud of her and that she was a success as a wife. As she spoke, the tears dried on her cheeks and despite her unkempt hair, Gwen could see glimpses of the pretty, contented person she had been.

'I've asked myself over and over again how I could not have seen . . . whether I could have done something to stop it. I feel almost sorry for Bernard and I wonder if it was my fault.' She turned to Gwen for a moment with an agonized expression on her face. 'That's what he said, you see – that he did it for me. Because he wanted to be a good husband . . . But that's wrong. It's so wrong and stupid . . . Couldn't he *see* that?' Tears rolled down her cheeks again.

'It was the end of the summer – a horrible wet day. Bernard came home in the afternoon. He never did that normally, so I thought he was ill. He was in the most dreadful state. I'd never seen him like it before. He was as white as a sheet but he wouldn't say anything. In fact he was dreadfully rude to me. And then the police came. Alice was at one of her little friends' houses, thank heavens. She didn't see them taking him away . . . Stupid, *stupid* . . .' The words were spat out and she clenched her fists. 'That's what makes me so angry – that he thought I couldn't be strong. That all that mattered to me was . . . was *fripperies*! And he didn't think enough of me as his wife to tell me what was going on!'

'What did he do?' Gwen asked gently.

'He was siphoning off money from the firm. Embezzlement. I didn't even know the word before. All our nice home, our things, were riding on him stealing. Of course the firm wasn't doing nearly as well as he wanted me to believe but he couldn't admit it. Times are hard for everyone, but Bernard always wanted to be the exception who held the biggest parties, drove the best motor car, smoked good cigars, was generous to people. But –' her voice rose higher with emotion – 'it was all appearance and show to make him the big noise in front of everyone. He didn't care about me or about Alice – he just had to show off all the time. And look where it's got him!'

Gwen had seldom heard anyone speak with such bitterness. Louise Wilson looked hard into her face.

'So you see – here I am. As it turns out, I'm only a stone's throw from Bernard, in there behind the prison walls. The bailiffs took everything we owned, except for a little money I had from my father's will in an account of my own. They didn't find that. I took Alice and came here – I hardly knew what I was doing. I just knew I didn't want anyone to know where I was – my mother, my sister, our friends. No one knows we're here. I didn't go to court with Bernard. I thought: *Damn* Bernard, for what he's done to us. I've never been to see him . . .' She crumpled for a moment, unable to speak.

'I should have gone, I know, but I can't face it. Alice has no idea where he is. I suppose she just thinks he ran off and left us. I don't want her to know her own father was a liar and a cheat. A fraud. I was going to do it without him – show him I didn't need him. But the truth is . . .' Louise Wilson began sobbing then, her body shaking, and Gwen held her hands tightly, not sure what else to do. For a time the woman was unable to speak.

'What a terrible time you've had,' Gwen said.

'I can't . . .' Louise Wilson gulped, trying to speak. 'I . . . I never go out. I'm frightened. I don't know how to live any more, and poor Alice has to go and do all the shopping and . . . I'm so useless. We've almost no money left now and I just don't know what I'm going to do!' She broke down completely then. 'We're going to starve if I don't pull myself together! It's bad enough that Alice has to live here in poverty with all these rough children. She looks like a . . . a *slum* child now – she's even starting to talk like one! Look at how we live – I can't even take care of her properly! I don't know how to and I've no one to turn to. I'm so alone and sometimes I feel as if I'm losing my wits!'

'Oh dear!' Gwen said, helplessly. While she was sorry for Mrs Wilson, upset by her distress and the sight of this miserable, spartan house, she also felt stung by her dismissal of all the other children in this snobbish way. Dismissing Lucy Fernandez as nothing but a 'slum child', if you please! But she kept these thoughts to herself. After all, wasn't that just how she used to think when she had first arrived? 'I'm so sorry, Mrs Wilson. Is there anything I can do to help?'

Louise Wilson shook her head. 'I don't see what anyone can do. What's going to become of us both?'

'Well,' Gwen said hesitantly, 'I suppose you'll have to go out and find some work.'

The woman looked at her in horror. 'Work – what,

round here? I'd have to go out and mix with all sorts of people and what work is there round here? In some filthy, dreadful factory with goodness knows who!'

'Well – or a shop, perhaps? Surely that's better than the pair of you starving?'

Gwen began to feel a little irritated. She thought about Theresa Fernandez and all she had been through. Theresa had certainly worked in factories when she came to Birmingham and it hadn't been what she was used to either.

Mrs Wilson stared dismally ahead of her. 'Bernard always used to say, "My wife will never need to work, you can be quite sure of that."' She gave a bitter laugh. 'And now look at me.'

'But I suppose . . .' Gwen felt out of order giving advice to a woman older than herself, but it was common sense surely, wasn't it? '. . . that really is the only thing you can do, isn't it?'

Twenty-Four

'So I offered to buy Alice some spectacles myself,' Gwen said. 'After all, the woman doesn't seem to have two pennies to rub together, and poor Alice can barely see a hand's width in front of her!'

She and Daniel were walking arm in arm in Lightwoods Park. They reached the bandstand and turned to sit perched on the edge of it. It was a Saturday, grey and muggy, but Gwen couldn't have cared less what the weather was like.

'Well, I should say that was a very kind thing to do.' He looked into her eyes. She felt his arm move round her back and she leaned nearer to him. As ever, being anywhere near to Daniel filled her with excitement, and a sense of being fully alive. And she was close to Daniel rather often now when he was at home. Sometimes he disappeared for days at a time – to Wales or to meetings in London – and she never knew when he would be back. When he was away she felt abandoned, but when he was here, he pursued her with an eagerness that made her breathless. It was as if she could not see round him. He blocked out the sight of anything else, of Edwin or her life before. A letter had arrived from Edwin that morning and she had seen his neat, careful writing on the envelope with a surge of guilt. But her feelings for Daniel were something with which she could not argue.

As they walked across the park, Daniel had been

telling her about the meeting he had been to the night before, in a hall in Smethwick. He was excited. There had been much talk about Spain and how the revolutionaries were standing up to the landowners and the Church.

'They're turning the farms into collectives like in Russia. The revolution is starting to take hold there and we'll bring it about here – I know it!' Feeling coursed through him like a ripple of muscle and he gripped her arm more tightly. Suddenly, though, he turned abruptly, looking across the park.

'What's the matter?'

'Just checking. You never know if someone's following you.'

Gwen burst out laughing. '*Following* you! Why on earth would they want to do that?'

Daniel whipped round, angrily. 'You don't understand. We're seen as enemies, party members. Enemies of the state. They want to keep an eye on what we're doing.'

She stared back at him. Was he exaggerating? It seemed both awesome and frightening. If Communism was so good, why were they worried about it?

'You should come to the meetings, Gwen *fach*.' His anger was soon gone. 'Come and join the revolution and make it happen. We need everyone – not just the poor and oppressed. We're all workers and we all need to join the struggle.' He looked deeply into her eyes. 'Come with me. Come and join us.'

At that moment Gwen felt she would go with him anywhere, but she felt very inadequate. 'The trouble is, I don't know anything about politics.'

Daniel's dark eyes seemed to drill through her. 'But you know about justice and about right. It's deep in you – I've seen it. You believe that the poor should have a say in their own lives, don't you? That they should be able to take control of the work they do instead of leaving it in the hands of capitalist owners who rake off all the profits?'

She nodded. Yes, this sounded reasonable and right and true. She tried not to hear Edwin's voice in her head telling her not to tangle with this. Edwin did not believe that women needed to involve themselves in any sort of politics, which he saw as messy and fundamentally vulgar – let alone this sort of politics.

Daniel led her to the bandstand then, and they sat leaning close together.

'I suppose I should come,' she said. 'I've never heard you speak to a meeting.'

'Oh, I don't do all that much speaking. There are plenty of others with things to say. And a lot to organize. Getting the word out, communicating with the workers – there's always so much to do and we always need more people to help. But everyone who works for the party considers it an honour to further the revolution.'

Gwen immediately felt humbled that she was privileged to be asked to join something so momentous. It was a feeling she often had with Daniel when he talked about Russia and Spain, about Rosa Luxemburg organizing the party in Germany and being shot, about revolutionaries all over Europe who were drawn together by the class struggle for justice and equality. She felt for the first time in her life as if she were being asked to be part of something important. And what she had seen in Birmingham, poverty and squalor among working people such as she had never known about before, had brought the injustices right before her eyes and into her heart. She wasn't sure how any of this fitted together or what should be done about it: she just knew it was wrong. But Daniel seemed to know and she wanted to learn from him. She wanted to be with him every possible moment.

'I will come with you,' she told him. 'I want to understand.'

His arms squeezed her tightly. 'My lovely Gwen. My comrade.'

At that moment a black, springy dog bounded across the park towards them and sniffed round their knees. It was so full of life, it made them both laugh.

'Go on, boy – off you go!' Daniel said stroking its head. The dog took off again. It made Gwen think of Edwin's father's dog. A terrible stab of guilt went through her, with the thought: *How can I marry Edwin after this?*

Daniel stroked her back and she felt him looking at her. She knew that as soon as she looked into his dark, challenging eyes, she could only surrender to him, the effect he had on her was so overwhelming. She gazed across the park from under the brim of her hat.

'Gwen.' His deep voice twisted right through her. 'Look at me, girl.'

Turning her head, she looked into his eyes and for a moment they sat quite still, caught in each other's gaze.

He stroked her cheek. 'You're so lovely.'

Once again, they were reaching for each other, and she held him close. There was nowhere else she wanted to be. She had never told Daniel that she was engaged to be married. Her ring, with its tiny sapphires, was still tucked into its little silk-lined box.

*

Alice Wilson came and stood shyly by Gwen's desk. She was wearing the spectacles Gwen had collected for her the day before.

'I can see leaves!' she reported with a huge smile. 'And . . .' She looked wonderingly round the classroom. '. . . everything on the blackboard, and faces and . . . and *ants* outside!'

Gwen laughed, delighted.

'This is from my mother,' Alice said, suddenly sober. She produced a piece of folded paper from her pocket.

'Thank you, Alice. You go to your seat now,' Gwen said.

'Dear Miss Purdy,' the note read in a neat hand. 'I am very grateful for the help you have given to Alice in getting her spectacles. It was very kind of you. Sincerely, Louise Wilson.'

Gwen frowned at the stiff little note. She felt very sorry for Mrs Wilson. She seemed trapped as much by her pride as her sudden poverty.

Alice had been eager as anything in class ever since she could see. And they had offered her a place dancing in the May celebrations, but she said she didn't want to. On a cool but bright day the children celebrated the crowning of the May Queen, a sweet-faced little girl in Form Five who was the envy of most of the other girls. Some of them danced round the Maypole in white dresses. Noticing Alice watching the dance with Lucy Fernandez beside her, Gwen saw that this was obviously why she had refused to join in. If Lucy couldn't dance, obviously Alice wasn't going to either.

Millie's wedding was to be the second weekend in May, and Gwen knew she would have to give notice to

Ariadne that she would be leaving Soho Road. This was not nearly as straightforward as she had hoped. She tackled Ariadne one evening after the three of them had downed an unusual version of Lancashire hotpot, topped with slices of turnip instead of potatoes. Being undercooked, they had the consistency of a damp cardboard carton.

'Could I have a word with you, Mrs Black?' They were standing in the dark hall. Harold Purvis passed them and went up the stairs, belching gently to himself.

'Ariadne, *please*. Is it something of a private nature?' She drew Gwen into the front parlour, which was cold and full of dark, heavy furniture. Ariadne stood waiting with a pained expression as if preparing for bad news. Her lips were painted a hard, dark red.

'I'm afraid I shall be needing to move on,' Gwen said, wondering why she felt so frightened about this encounter. After all, she had every right to move to different lodgings if she wanted to. It was just that Ariadne always seemed to take everything so personally. 'I shall be moving out at the end of the month.'

'Oh dear!' Ariadne's face became such a mask of dismay that Gwen immediately felt horribly guilty. 'Oh no! How very upsetting!' Ariadne clasped her hand over her heart. 'And there was I thinking my little abode here was a satisfactory lodging for a respectable young woman – and things seemed, just for once, to have settled into a harmonious situation. We've all been so happy here, you and I and Mr Purvis, haven't we?'

'Er – yes, haven't we!' Gwen agreed fervently. 'Only it's to do with a friend of mine.' She explained about Millie and her need for a lodger and how it seemed the only thing to do. Ariadne seemed a little appeased.

'Well, as long as it's nothing I've done to offend

you. Nothing you've found lacking here ... My George would have been so disappointed in me if he thought I hadn't provided adequately ...'

'No, not in the least! Staying here has been ...' No words seemed adequate. 'Well – it's been a home from home.'

This seemed to satisfy Ariadne, and all was well. However, the next day she announced to Harold Purvis at the breakfast table that Gwen was leaving. Harold took the news silently, though Gwen felt him eyeing her aggressively across the table. That evening Ariadne did not eat with them. She carried in the food – rissoles and blancmange – in silence, with a tragic face, and sat in an easy chair by the fire as they ate, shrouded in clouds of cigarette smoke. Harold was smirking in a way which made Gwen long to kick him, and the silence was too heavy to break.

'Thank you, Ariadne,' Gwen said as they left the table after this painful meal.

Ariadne did not even turn her head.

'What on earth is the matter with her?' Gwen demanded of Harold on the upstairs landing. She knew it was something to do with him from his snide, smug expression.

Harold stood with his hands pushed in his pockets. 'Told her I'll be moving on.'

'You as well! *Why?*'

Harold leaned closer and Gwen flinched. 'D'you think I want *that*?' His mouth contorted with disgust. 'Old bag of bones pawing at me all the time. When it's you I really want ...' He reached out to her and Gwen stepped backwards.

'Please don't touch me, Mr Purvis. You know I don't like it.'

Harold smirked. 'You might if you gave it a chance.'

Ignoring him, she went back downstairs, to find Ariadne still hunched by the fire. She looked up at Gwen with tragic eyes, which immediately filled with tears.

'I gather Mr Purvis is leaving too,' Gwen said gently. She pulled up a chair from the table to sit beside her.

Ariadne nodded, her lips trembling. She had forgotten to put any more lipstick on and her lips were dull and puckered.

'It's cruel,' she sobbed. 'Him going and leaving me like this. And you – you don't need him. I *love* him. I thought he was mine – my Harold! I thought he cared for me and would stay with me. And now he's going away, casting me off like an old piece of clothing!'

'Oh dear, I am sorry.' Gwen couldn't think what else to say. She suddenly felt great sympathy for Ariadne. She looked so pathetic, poor thing. And fancy imagining that that slimy worm Harold Purvis could truly have feelings for her!

Ariadne was looking at her with bitter reproach. 'You didn't have to take him. You don't feel for him the way I do. I've got no one else and you'll have lots of young men interested in you. It's not fair, it really isn't.'

Gwen stared at her, appalled. 'But it's nothing to do with me, Ariadne! I didn't ask him to leave! I'm not the least interested in Harold Purvis, I can assure you.'

'But I've seen the way he looks at you, dear. And why wouldn't he – you're such a sweet young thing. But it's torture for me! I've never seen him look at me like that ... But sometimes I thought he cared for me. I really thought he did!' Tears rolled down her cheeks. 'I'm so lost and alone. I'll have to have another houseful of strangers!'

'I'm ever so sorry, Ariadne.' Gwen was full of pity for the scrawny, overdressed woman beside her. 'But all I can say is that Harold means nothing to me at all. He really and truly doesn't.'

Ariadne looked up desperately at her. 'Do you have to go and leave me as well?'

'I've promised.' She reached over and touched Ariadne's bony hand with its long, painted nails. 'I'm helping a friend – she's having a baby. But it's not far away. I'll come back and see you.'

'Will you?' Ariadne suddenly clasped Gwen's hand, managing a watery smile. 'Oh you are a sweet girl! None of my lodgers has ever said that before!'

Twenty-Five

'If I wasn't having Lance's baby,' Millie said a week before her wedding, 'I think I would have got over him fairly quickly, really.' Sighing, she looked into the distance and added, 'Well – I'll have to see it through. I've only got myself to blame.'

The ceremony was held in their local parish in Edgbaston. Millie's mother, Mrs Dawson, greeted Gwen with a tense smile as she went into the church. She was a kind woman who had stood by her daughter, despite her embarrassment over Millie's condition, though she had drawn the line at 'any fuss' over the actual wedding.

'She just wants to rush it through,' Millie said. 'I feel as if I'm being *smuggled* into marriage.'

The vicar had kindly suggested that as there were to be fewer than a dozen people present, they hold the ceremony in the Lady Chapel, where Gwen sat two rows behind Millie's mother and sister. She had worn her favourite summer dress, a pretty frock covered in sprigs of sweetpeas, in mauve, pink and white. She sat looking at the back of Lance's head as he waited on the other side of the aisle, and pictured Millie arriving outside. She wondered how she was feeling. In a moment there came a small flurry at the back of the church and there was the bride.

Millie had no father or brothers, so she was escorted

along the aisle on the arm of a family friend, a middle-aged man with a black moustache, who was smiling broadly. Gwen warmed to him for trying to add some joy to an occasion which everyone else seemed to regard as one of gloomy necessity. Millie looked very pretty in a cream dress with a softly gathered skirt which hung just below the knee and disguised any hint of pregnancy, and she was carrying a small bouquet of yellow roses and white carnations. She was well made up, and smiled when everyone turned to look at her, catching Gwen's eye as she passed. Gwen felt a pang, watching her. She could see the strain Millie was under, despite the brave expression. She was delivered to Lance, who was now standing and watching her solemnly. He was a tall, gangling man, an academic sort who, Gwen observed to herself, could not even manage to look smart on his wedding day. He had a long face, with a sagging expression, and his clothes, though not actually crumpled, looked somehow limp. Did he want this wedding any more than Millie?

The thought that Millie was now stuck with the droopy, if kindly, Lance for life seemed dismal. And, Gwen thought, as the two of them both quietly pronounced their vows, in less than three months it was going to be her turn. She would have to make the same vows and become Mrs Edwin Shackleton. That was the reality. Edwin was her fiancé and he was kind and reliable. And where, in fact, was Daniel this week? Once again he had gone off without warning. She tried to pretend she wasn't hurt and angry, but the feelings welled up all the same. When he came back, of course, he would be all over her, but sometimes she felt she was being picked up and put down. No: whatever she felt for Daniel Fernandez, she should be facing the fact that he could have no part in her future.

Within days, however, he was back and she went to her first party meeting with him in a murkily lit room in the centre of town.

'What's it going to be about tonight?' she asked on the way.

'Oh, it's not a speaker or anything like that tonight. More of a business meeting. But it'll give you an idea – it's the centre of all the activity, where we get things done.'

The party offices were over a left-wing bookshop. The room was thick with cigarette smoke, though there were fewer than a dozen people round the table, and on first impressions Gwen thought them disappointing. The great majority were men, though she saw three women, all of them dressed in the most workaday clothes and two looked particularly dowdy. The third had a head of thick, black curly hair which could have looked very pretty but was scraped severely back into a bun, and she had thick eyebrows and strong, intense features. A certain intensity marked the atmosphere in the room. Gwen immediately felt as if her pretty frock and hair ribbon and the smile that she directed at them marked her out as trivial and she shrank back inside herself, wondering what she was doing there.

Daniel's manner was confident, though she felt suddenly as if he was very distant from her.

'This is Gwen Purdy,' he told them. 'She'll likely join the party. She's here to listen in, see how we do things.'

There were nods and looks of approval in her direction and she immediately felt proud to be with Daniel. The man closest to her stood up, holding a cap in his hand and offered her a chair.

'Welcome, comrade,' he said solemnly.

Gwen sat, feeling the intense, unsmiling gaze of the black-haired woman on her from across the table. On the wall to the woman's left she saw a banner on which a muscular man was waving a huge red flag.

Once the meeting began, Gwen struggled to concentrate. There was a good deal of talk about the practical details of printing leaflets and recruiting members.

One of the younger men spoke despondently. 'It's such an uphill struggle. Everyone seems to live with their head stuck in the sand. They can't see that it's getting closer. The fascist tide is sweeping over Europe and all they can think about is the next pint, the next pay packet . . .'

'That's for those who get any pay,' an older man retorted scathingly. 'You don't know what it's like to have a clutch of screaming kiddies with empty bellies, that's your trouble. No wonder the masses can't think for themselves when they're drugged with hunger and want. After the revolution, no one will go hungry. They will be awake!'

A debate ensued about tactics. One minute they were talking about a United Front and a Popular Front and about Italy and the National Government's appeasement of Mussolini. Then the discussion moved on, bitter in tone, to the Labour Party and the ILP and during this Gwen began to feel sleepy and wished there was a clock in the room. The trouble was that the problems of fascism and what was happening in Europe all seemed too big and far away for her or anyone like her to be able to do anything about them, and other things

277

like which parties would let the CP be affiliated with them seemed tedious and nothing to do with reality. With a sinking heart she realized she really wasn't made to be involved with politics. All she really wanted was for the meeting to end so that she and Daniel could be alone. She sat pressing the soft cotton of her skirt into sharp creases and trying to stifle her yawns. It was only when Daniel spoke beside her that she jerked to attention again.

'Comrades, once again we're getting ourselves bogged down in discussions which send us round and round like rats in a trap. That's what they want, our oppressors. They feed on our divisions, on our lack of clarity.'

He spoke quietly, but with such conviction and authority that immediately Gwen saw everyone was listening.

'We must keep in mind our strategy. We know that for many years now – I've seen it over and over again in the Welsh valleys – we've been divided, we're broken into splinters and fought a little battle here, a strike there. That suits them. They can defeat us when we are divided and we divide so easily with our preoccupation with the details, with our squabbles over purity and ideology! We must be practical, comrades! The threat of fascism is real and it is growing, and it is a capitalist threat. Unless we keep our eyes on our strategy of unity, we shall be defeated.'

There was a pause and Gwen glanced at him, to see him looking challengingly round the room. He was sitting bolt upright, hands on his thighs, arms straight, tensed, his eyes alight. It was as if he spoke as the conscience of the meeting and she loved him so much in that moment, which, if she tried to see it through his eyes, transformed a tired-looking collection of working people into the visionary agents of revolution. They waited for him to finish.

'But if we are united in right, if we are disciplined and work as a united force of justice for the oppressed, nothing will be able to stop us!'

'Comrade Fernandez is right.' The dark-haired woman said fervently. She had a powerful, well-spoken voice. 'When we bicker and get diverted into arguments we are behaving like amateurs, like a group of small-minded bourgeois shopkeepers! We are betraying the true spirit of the revolution!'

As she spoke she was looking across at Daniel. Gwen saw him nod in approval. She felt herself wither inside again. What on earth was she doing here? She knew nothing about any of this. She wasn't really part of Daniel's world. He needed someone who shared the same passion and could debate with him, walk side by side with him into the revolution that they so believed in! She felt close to tears as the meeting ended.

As soon as they stood up a number of people came to greet her and she had to compose herself to talk and smile. They seemed so glad that she was there and she knew it was because they wanted to recruit her to the party, but it still felt like an honour to be welcomed and treated in this way. The dark-haired woman had come to them straight away. She wore a long, straight dress in dark blue corduroy, a crimson scarf at the neck and flat brown shoes. The overall effect was at once severe and bohemian and she looked striking.

'So – Gwen, isn't it? Are you going to join the party?'

Though she felt flustered, Gwen looked back coolly at her. She wasn't going to bark because this woman commanded it!

'I'll consider it,' she said. 'This is my first meeting, after all.'

'I'm Esther Lane.' She held out her hand and shook Gwen's with masculine vigour. 'I'm from the BCPL but I've joined the party as well.'

'Pleased to meet you,' Gwen said, which provoked an ironic smile on Esther's face which Gwen took to mean that she had just said something bourgeois or in some other way considered not quite the thing in Communist circles. She had no idea what the BCPL was but she wasn't going to let Esther know that.

After that, the woman spoke only to Daniel. Watching her, Gwen tried to place her age, and guessed that she must be in her late twenties, perhaps older than Daniel. Whatever the case, she knew she was not imagining the woman's attraction to him. She was talking about a leaflet they were about to produce and seemed determined to delay him, actually holding onto his arm as they talked. In fact a number of people were keen to talk to him afterwards, and in the end Gwen went and sat down by the table again to wait, trying to put aside a desolate feeling of being ignored. She told herself not to be so childish. This was Daniel's work, after all.

At last his comrades seemed prepared to leave him alone and he came over to her, his smile cheering her immediately.

'Sorry to make you wait like that,' he said. 'There's always so much to be done . . .' He reached for her. 'Come on now, lovely.'

Gwen felt Esther Lane's eyes on her as she and Daniel left the room and she couldn't help feeling triumphant. Esther might be very clever when it came to politics, but it was her Daniel chose to be with.

'Well, what did you think?' he asked eagerly as they set out along the street.

She was happy now, able to be full of enthusiasm.

'It was ever so interesting. But I've got so much to learn!'

'Oh, you'll learn, my girl.' He flung his arm round her shoulder and she revelled in his closeness. 'It's not difficult – not the basic principles, least. What Marx and Lenin and Engels – all of them – were teaching us was justice and common sense. What we have to do is put it into practice – bring it about!'

As they walked home, Gwen asked him what the BCPL was. Daniel told her that the Birmingham Council for Peace and Liberty were a group who were against fascism. Then he set off to explain at length about the discussion the meeting had had about the Labour Party, that it had not wanted Communists in its ranks after the CP was formed in 1920.

'What we're asking for is a Popular Front of all the groups opposed to fascism, but to do that we have to unite all the socialist parties. The Labour Party still won't have us.' His voice was bitter. 'They're not worthy of the name socialist! They've no vision – they've betrayed the working man right down the line!'

He talked on and on and she started to feel glum. Was he going to talk like this all the way home? She was interested, it was true, but she didn't want to hear about politics, politics all the time. Couldn't he give a little bit of time just to her? Suddenly, though, he broke off.

'Here's a good patch!' Taking a piece of chalk from his pocket, he began to write on a smooth piece of wall

281

next to them. He wrote the time and place of their next meeting and stood back to look. 'There – another brick in the wall!'

'That woman at the meeting,' Gwen said as he flung his arm round her shoulders again. 'Esther . . .'

'Oh yes – our Esther.' There was amusement in his voice.

'She seems – interesting.'

'She's all right. Very academic. She's from the university.' He chuckled. 'Quite formidable, isn't she? The sort who won't stop until she gets what she wants. The revolution needs people like her, full of passion.'

She wants Daniel, Gwen thought, going cold inside. Did he know? Did he want her in return? She was horrified by her jealousy, by the sense that she wanted to know about every encounter, every word that had been spoken between them ever. She told herself not to be so ridiculous. Daniel sounded quite offhand about Esther and he'd known her for some time. If he was interested in her, surely he'd had his chance?

She said nothing more, and a moment later Daniel stopped. 'Oh, I forgot! I've got something for you.'

He released her for a moment to pull a little book out of his jacket pocket.

Gwen took it, but could seen nothing in the dark street.

'What is it?'

'*Ten Days that Shook the World.* It's all about Leningrad in 1917, when the Bolsheviks seized power. The man who wrote it was there! Now – you read that and you'll touch the heart of the revolution! I promise you will. You can keep it.'

'Oh, thank you – I will!' She was delighted with the

book, more because he had given her a gift than because of its contents. She felt him watching her as she turned it over in her hands and she looked up at him. He held out his arms and drew her to him.

She wrapped her arms round him with a sense of relief. 'I've been longing to do this all evening.'

Twenty-Six

'Come on now – eat up, little sparrow!'

Siobhan sat beside Joey on the mattress, as he spooned sweet porridge into his mouth. He could feed himself now, but it was one of her good mornings. There were days when she wasn't well after drinking and lay on the floor until the afternoon. Sometimes she got sick and would retch over the old tin can, then ask him to bring her water from the broken pipe in the kitchen. But at the beginning, when he was still too weak to move, she or Christie sat and fed him and every day he grew stronger.

Every day, except on Sundays, Christie was gone by the time Joey woke. He went out, and waited to be picked up at dawn to work on the building sites, coming back like a ghost, sagging with exhaustion and coated in brickdust and plaster. However early he got up, he almost always built a fire and made a pot of porridge. Siobhan told Joey that they had taught Christie regular habits when he was in the seminary in Ireland. Joey didn't know what a seminary was, but Christie made the best porridge over that fire in the grate that Joey'd ever had.

John was out all day too, 'bringing in the taters' as Siobhan put it. Joey didn't know where John went, but there never seemed to be a day when he didn't come back without some money or food, at least, and sometimes the bottles for Siobhan that got Christie angry. Joey dreaded John bringing the bottles too because they made Siobhan bad and she cried and moaned and then often just ran off, out of the house and sometimes Christie tried to go after her. He couldn't stop her, and he'd come back in and sit by the fire so silently, so far away he might not have been there at all. Sometimes, long after he'd settled to sleep, he heard Siobhan come stumbling back in and Christie always seemed to be awake. Joey wondered if Christie ever slept. He hated it when they were both like that and tried to shut his mind to Siobhan's broken weeping. Worst of all, to Christie's. He made himself think about other things. Often he thought about Miss Purdy, remembering how she had put her arms round him and how she smelled lovely, of flowers.

Micky hardly ever moved from his position in the corner.

'He's not a well man,' Siobhan told him as they sat together in the dusky light of the room that morning. Things felt safe for now. Siobhan was sober, and kind. 'He won't be long for this world by the sound of him.' Micky's cough bubbled up from him and he had to fight for each wheezing breath.

Joey scraped the last bits of porridge from the old pan. The bottom of it was black and knobbly with 'mend-its', bits screwed in to block off holes, and they had one bent metal spoon between them.

'There ye go.' Siobhan took the pan from him and snuggled up closer, putting her arm round him, cradling her to him. It was comforting and warm, but the soft feel of her body filled him with dread. He wanted Siobhan in the same way he longed for his mother, and she was like Mom had been, pretty and sweet with her blue eyes and thin, pointed face and – all his instincts screamed – dangerous. With her would come something terrible. He pushed her away and scrambled to his feet.

'You're a peculiar child if you'll not have a cuddle!' Siobhan leaned over on her elbow and held out her other arm to him, looking up through her long black hair. He could tell he had roused some emotion in her, something which crouched curled up inside. 'Ah, come on – come and be with your Auntie Shiv!' Her voice was wheedling now, and Joey felt panic rise inside him.

'No!' He felt his face harden into a scowl.

'Sure, you're the hard man, aren't ye?' she said, and her voice had a savage edge to it. 'Well, please yourself, though you'd think you'd have some gratitude, you little slum rat. Christie and me – we're from a good family, I'll have you know. You needn't go thinking you're anything so special, you little bastard!' She shouted as he let himself into the hall.

Over those days of recovery he came to discover more about the house. The four of them inhabited the front room, which was boarded up except for the loose plank Christie slid back and forth at the side so they could see better. There was barely any light in the hall and all the floor tiles were loose and clinked underfoot. Joey was still learning to find his way round, avoiding the holes where the tiles had come away altogether. The back room was full of rubble where the floor above had collapsed, and if you stepped just inside there was a place where you could look up through the jagged wreckage and see the sky. Beyond was a dark kitchen and scullery from which came the sound of running water. The tap had been wrenched off the water pipe, leaving a trickle of water running constantly into the stone sink. Something scuttled away into the darkness as he approached. The door to the front room had to be kept shut always – it was Christie's strict rule.

'There's two or three things you've got to remember if you're staying here with us,' Christie had told him once he was well enough to listen. They were squatting by the grate and Joey stared intently into Christie's gaunt face. He had immediate respect for Christie and felt safe with him.

'We don't want anyone knowing we're here, right? So you never, *ever* go out the front. There's a way out the back, I'll show you. We never keep the fire going when it's light outside – even in the cold. We don't want anyone seeing the smoke and getting suspicious. So no building up the fire when I'm gone out. Whatever we earn we share – that's another rule. Micky can't work but that doesn't mean we leave him to starve. And –' he pointed emphatically – 'you keep that door shut at all times. Got that, little fella? This place is like a barnyard there's that many rats. You'll hear them running under the boards. But this room's the one place in not bad repair. I've blocked off a couple of holes in the floor and we're sound enough. We don't want to be inviting them in to share our dinner, now, all right?'

Joey nodded solemnly, and Christie's usually woebegone expression lit with a rare grin.

'C'mere.' He held out a thin arm. Once again Joey was struck by how hard and sore his hands looked. Christie put an arm loosely round him and looked into his face. In a whisper, he said, 'And the other thing is . . . Siobhan, my sister . . .' Joey saw a look of pain cross Christie's face. 'She's not always very well.

You've seen she's not always herself. That's all. That's why we're in England, see. We came to . . . help her.'

Christie's face looked very sad as he spoke. Joey nodded. He couldn't think of anything to say, but deep in himself he knew things about the kind of not very well that affected women like Siobhan, like his mom.

He pushed open the back door, screwing up his eyes in the bright morning. A bird was singing close by. He pushed his hair back. It was longer than he'd ever known it before, hanging over his eyes. He stepped out onto the narrow area behind the house, which was paved with broken blue bricks. The rest of the garden was a chaos of brambles. Using the three fruit trees in the garden as a scaffold, the brambles had grown, spread, interwoven to a height about the same as Joey's so that the whole garden was taken over by them. Except in one part.

'This is how you get out.' Christie had taken him outside to show him. 'I cut a way through – with John, and Micky when he wasn't so bad. Through here, look!'

The men had cut a tunnel through the bramble forest. Christie bent right over to lead him through. Joey only had to bend his knees a bit to follow Christie's dark back between the green walls of hacked brambles, treading down some scrawny nettles trying to grow in the gloom. Christie stopped and cut back more bramble suckers which were trying to advance again.

'They're determined fellows these,' Joey heard him say. 'Come on, watch yourself now – we're nearly there.'

They followed the path down the length of the garden.

'Now – this is our gate,' Christie said, squatting

down by the hedge. He was talking in a low voice. 'We've not had any problem. The road out there's quite quiet, but you have to look carefully before you step out. You don't want to run into the Guard.'

Joey frowned.

'Your police fellows. Sure, you're a solemn little man!' Christie tweaked Joey's ear playfully. He leaned forwards, parting a place in the hedge and looked cautiously about. He stepped outside and Joey joined him. Christie was still looking warily up and down the street. There were houses further along, but down this end they faced the back ends of gardens and a warehouse and it was quiet. Joey found that he felt tired and shaky, just after walking that short distance. Looking up at Christie, he thought he looked smaller out here, and defenceless.

'When you're coming back, the place to go in is just after that drain.' He pointed. 'You'll soon find it – can't go wrong. But you don't need to be going out and about yet, do you now? Unless you've somewhere to go back to. Have you, Joey? Is there someone waiting for you at home?'

The question made Joey's chest ache. He shook his head fiercely.

Christie reached out and ruffled his hair. 'You can go with John, in a day or two, if you've nowhere else to go. He can always use a bit of help.'

Standing alone in the garden now, Joey looked at the green tunnel through the brambles. He'd been restless since he felt better, and fed up with staying inside. He thought of just going. He could do what he liked, after all! But he wasn't sure he'd be able to find his way back yet if he left. He sat down, cross-legged and poked at the bricks idly with a dry twig. He didn't want to go back inside. He didn't want evening to come either.

At night they sat round the fire. It was John who brought in the food. Christie seemed to trust him with the money he earned. John knew the place well, all the ins and outs. They cooked up stews in the one pan – always potatoes, boiled in the skins, and anything else John could get, flavoured with Bovril. Sometimes meat, and bread to mop it all up. Christie was so famished sometimes he could barely wait till it was cooked. They took turns with the spoon, out of the pan.

No one talked much. They were all too tired. Joey learned odd scraps about the adults around him as they talked to one another. He didn't understand much of it. He picked up that Christie had been in training to be a priest in Ireland. That he'd run away because of Siobhan. Something bad had happened. Joey didn't know what. He could feel Christie's intense protective-ness towards his sister, though. Once or twice he wondered what had happened to Lena. Did they take her away to the home? And Kenny and Polly? But he pushed those thoughts away.

Micky didn't talk now. Christie tried to feed him but he coughed and spat it out. Joey had been afraid of Micky, with his big, whiskery face. He wasn't like a real person to Joey at first, lying there, the coughing, the stink of him, which hit you every time you stepped in the room, but more like some kind of animal, or monster. But once or twice Micky had sat up in the evening and Joey saw he was a real man, heavy and weary and very sick. Once or twice Micky's bloodshot gaze had swivelled towards him and in his thick, rasping voice, said, 'Who's this little fella then?'

The next time, Micky glowered at him and roared, 'Get out o' here you little bastard!' Another evening, while still lying down, he said in a bewildered tone, 'So, you're all grown up then are ye now, Seamus?'

'He doesn't know you,' Siobhan whispered to him. 'He's muddled in his head. Don't go taking any notice. And our John – he's simple in the head too, but he'll do ye no harm.'

From things John said, Joey knew he had grown up somewhere across town. John had an odd, wooden-sounding voice, so different from the fluid rise and fall Joey heard in Christie's and Siobhan's voices. He seemed to speak all on one note and to keep on talking whether or not his mouth was crammed full of potato. He kept complaining about 'the camp'.

'Don't let them ever put you in one of them camps,' he warned Christie, as he did most evenings.

'I won't, John,' Christie said, rubbing his face wearily. 'I've heard you.' Sometimes Christie's mood seemed very low.

'Whatever they say, you're better off on the dole . . . Take you off to the depths of fucking Wales . . . Sorry for my language . . .' He nodded round at them. 'Sorry, Siobhan – didn't mean it.' He was devoted to Siobhan. Often he sat just staring at her while she slept.

'Ah, you're all right there, John.' She took her turn spooning food out of the pan. Her hair fell forward either side of her face and she shook her head to get it out of the way. Joey thought it was strange the way John was always saying sorry to Siobhan when her language was even worse than his.

'Wales. Brechfa . . .' John spat the word out with loathing. 'Christ, what a hellhole. Nothing there – not even a fucking pub for miles. Slavery, that's what it is. Dawn till dusk they had us slaving with a pick and fucking shovel. And for what? I'll have 'em for it one day – you'll see. Last time I take anything off of anyone. I'm never going back down that Labour Exchange. I'm my own man from now on – no dole, no fucking nothing off of none of 'em . . .'

After a certain point every evening, Christie would say, 'Joey – get to sleep now.'

And as if Christie was his father, Joey, usually tired by then, would settle on the floor and close his eyes while the adult voices murmured on around him and their shadows moved on the walls.

One night Joey woke to the sound of the front door shuddering open and low voices. There was only the barest glow from the fire and he could hear Micky's laboured breathing across the room. Joey lay with his heart pounding. No one came in through the front! They had no way of locking the door but it was so swollen and stiff that it was hard to get open in any case. Whoever had come in was now struggling to shut it again. He heard a bang, followed by a giggle, and whispering outside the door. The tiles in the hall clattered and he heard, 'Ssssh, you're enough to wake the dead so ye are!' in a fierce whisper.

Joey sat up. Inside him a struggle was going on. He should just lie down. He didn't want to know who it was or what was going on. He knew already though, really, that it was Siobhan. She'd been on the booze earlier, had been carrying on, loudly and nastily and

Christie had begged her not to leave the house. 'Don't do it!' he'd pleaded, trying to restrain her. 'Oh God, Siobhan, don't do this to yourself!' Joey knew all right. Like going home. Like Mom. Yet he was drawn up and out of bed and couldn't stop himself, as if he was being pulled by a magnet like the one Miss Purdy showed them at school. He thought no one else was awake.

Barefoot, he felt his way across the room and took the door handle in both hands, hearing the rusty rasp of the catch turning. The door squeaked open. He heard someone stir behind him.

'Siobhan?' Christie's voice was thick with sleep. 'Is that you?'

Without answering, Joey slipped out, closing the door out of habit. It shut with a loud click.

The floor was rough and cold against his feet. He felt his way along the knobbly wallpaper in the hall. Already he could hear sounds he recognized. They drew him, numbed, chill inside, along the hall. He clenched his jaws tightly together in the darkness, barely even feeling the sharp edge of a tile cutting into his foot. They couldn't hear him coming over their own noise. Joey stood at the door of the scullery, forcing himself to listen to the woman's mewling sounds, the man's grunting.

A light appeared behind him. There was a rattle of the tiles. Joey stood holding tightly to the doorframe, aware that someone was beside him, and then the candlelight fell on the pair coupling up against the sink, Siobhan's legs spread each side of the man, her head back against the wall, long hair hanging.

Joey didn't notice Christie moving. He seemed to be upon them in an instant, without a word, banging the candle on the shelf next to the sink, locking his arm round the man's neck and yanking him off. Joey caught a glimpse of a bullish, drunken face.

'What the fuck...?' Three slurred words before Christie punched him with all his force in the face.

'You filthy bastard!' Christie hurled a blow into the great belly. 'You stinking scum – get your hands off my sister!' He delivered another body blow, then another to the head until the man sank with a groan onto his back, flies gaping.

Dazed, Siobhan lowered herself off the edge of the sink.

'Christie ... oh, for the love of God, what've you done?' She was wailing, swaying. Joey could see she was very drunk, her eyelids drooping, voice thick and slurred. 'Why d'you have to come interfering? Why can't you just leave me be?' She sagged to the floor, sobbing. 'He was giving me a baby. They killed my baby, my little baby...' She folded her arms tight to her and rocked back and forth, weeping in agony. 'Oh God, Christie, why did I let them do it? His little soul's hovering round me, in torment ... I'm a murderer ... and I can never make him rest ... I want his soul to be at rest ... I want to die, Christie ... just let me die...'

Christie sank to his knees, gathering her into his arms. 'Oh God, Shiv ... Oh Lord Christ, don't do this...'

Siobhan was crying, but it was the sound of Christie's distraught sobs that drove Joey back, away from them. He flung himself out through the back door, slamming it with every ounce of strength he had in him. The sharp stones on the path bit into his feet as he stormed along, and he didn't care, welcomed the feeling, the hurt. He wanted to do it to himself, for it to hurt more and more. Stamping his feet down, yelping, his body started jerking and he couldn't work out for a moment what was happening to him as his sobs began to release themselves. He limped out through the gate into the street, barely able to see because of the darkness and his tears. He stumbled along the middle of the road with no thought to where he was going or where he would end up. The very air he breathed hurt him. He was lost in it, blind to anything round him.

He didn't know how long the voice had been calling to him. Only when it came close and he heard running feet, did it penetrate through to him.

'Joey, Joey – where're you off to?'

And he was lifted up into Christie's strong arms and held close and tight.

'There now, little fellow ... It's all right now.' Christie's hand stroked his thin back, cradling, soothing him. Joey let out a wail from the depths of himself and for the first time in the years he could remember he cried in someone's arms until he could cry no more.

Twenty-Seven

'Comrades, we know Mosley's thugs are attacking Jews in the East End – attacking innocent working men like ourselves!'

Daniel stood on the platform at the front of the dingy hall, his sleeves rolled up. Behind him was a huge red banner with a black hammer and sickle blazing in the middle.

'We've seen the fascists holding their rallies – even lording it in the Albert Hall! We've seen Oswald Mosley in our own city, in the Bull Ring, spreading his poison to infect the minds of those who know no better ... But we've also seen our people silence their foul fascist rhetoric in Tonypandy last week. What was Mosley's slogan? "Blackshirt Policy Alone Can Save the Coalfields"? And what did our members do? Drowned them out by singing the "Red Flag", that's what!'

There was a brief outbreak of clapping and cheering. As Daniel spoke, he paced back and forth, emphasizing phrases with a clenched fist. His speech was reaching its climax.

'The fascists are capitalists to the core. If anyone knows that, it is the people of my home, the miners of the South Wales valleys! I've seen it, brothers, and I've seen the way we fight it, by the protest of working men. By our dignity and our passion in the struggle!'

Gwen looked round at the people close to her. They were all listening intently. A young man sat along the row from her, his eyes fixed on Daniel, bright with passion.

'Capitalist oppression and despair is bleeding its way across Europe and it is we – us! – you and me, brothers, whose glorious duty it is to stem the tide of this oppression. We've fought against it – we all know that. We've broken up their meetings and rallies. We've stopped them using our halls and meeting places.'

Daniel leaned towards the audience and wagged his finger. 'Oh yes – make no mistake. The capitalists, the police and the fascists are all hand in glove in the valleys, while they destroy our unions and throw anyone who gainsays them in jail to rot! They victimize our workers and slash our wages to starvation levels. But we shall not be beaten! We shall fight it! We shall come together in unity in the struggle. And together, through the strength and solidarity of our party, we'll see a new dawn for our people. We *shall* bring about the revolution!'

Daniel finished with one hand clenched high in the air. The room erupted into clapping and cheering and most of the audience got to their feet. Daniel stood, looking solemn, dignified, nodding in acknowledgement.

Gwen jumped up as well, full of pride. And soon this meeting would be over and she could be alone with him and in his arms! Looking across the hall, she caught sight of Esther Lane standing at the end of the front row and this dented her happiness. Esther was wearing an extraordinary green dress and leading the ovation to Daniel, clapping her hands high in the air. Gwen had noticed that, over the past weeks while she had been going to meetings with Daniel, Esther was almost always there, no matter in what part of the city the meeting was held. Every time she saw Esther she felt a pang of panic, of jealousy. It was so clear that Esther was infatuated with Daniel, and she was such a handsome, stormy-looking woman, strong and passionate like him, and so committed to the party. How could he not be interested in Esther? Daniel always denied it, though, and spoke of Esther with a kind of amused detachment.

'Esther's all right. She's a good party worker – one of the best.' He didn't seem to think of her in any other terms, but Gwen was never comfortable when Esther was around. All she knew was that she wanted to learn to share Daniel's passion, that same commitment to the party. Nothing else now seemed to matter except this life – and Daniel.

Gwen waited patiently, as she always did at these meetings, for Daniel to deal with all the people who wanted to speak to him. She exchanged a few words with people she knew, then sat quietly at the side of the hall with her bag and watched. Though trying not to think about it, she was conscious all the time of where Esther was in the room. The vivid green dress stood out among all the drab clothes of the men as she worked her way over to Daniel. Gwen saw them laughing together.

He may be laughing with you, she thought, *but he's coming home with me.*

She looked down into her lap, at the skirt of her pretty blue frock. *I'm jealous*, she realized. She'd never been jealous before. Never with Edwin. It was a bitter, fearful emotion, which shamed her. She looked up again to see Esther lean forward to say something, then languidly kiss Daniel on the cheek. The sight filled Gwen with outrage. Who did Esther think she was? But Daniel was already trying to move away and, as he did so, his eyes met Gwen's. He raised his eyebrows in acknowledgement that she was waiting.

'I'm going to be off now,' she heard him say. He strode towards her and she got up to meet him ... 'Sorry about all that. The comrades always have a lot they want to say. Did you meet some of them?'

They went out into the street and Daniel immediately put his arm round her shoulder. At last, they could be close, she thought. But his mind was still very much on the meeting.

'I could feel them tonight – feel the energy,' he said excitedly. 'It's not always like that. We recruited two new members as well.'

'That's marvellous,' Gwen enthused. She had yet to join the party herself, and Daniel was working on her. She knew she would, soon, and wasn't sure exactly why she was hesitating. It was something to do with the shift in her life, stepping over a line away from the past. Joining the party seemed to be a symbol of that.

Daniel talked excitedly as they walked across town in the mild evening. His body felt taut and almost explosive with energy beside her. They were the only ones waiting at the tram stop. Daniel gave his habitual look around to see if he was being followed. Then he turned and took her in his arms, but she was still sore over Esther.

'Why does she kiss you?'

'Esther? Oh,' he said dismissively, 'she's just one of those people who carry on like that. Doesn't mean anything – forget it.' Hs gaze was burning into her. 'You're so damn lovely.'

At the feel of his hands on her back, his lips on hers, desire coursed through her. For these past few weeks she and Daniel had spent so much time together – at meetings and afterwards, talking, kissing in the dark. Every time they met felt more charged and when they were apart she struggled to think about anything except him and being with him again.

They sat close together on the tram out to Handsworth. At the end of May Gwen had moved out of the Soho Road house, parting with a genuinely tearful Ariadne, and had moved into the room she was renting from Millie and Lance in Broughton Road. Daniel stayed on beyond his own stop to see her home. As soon as they'd turned into the road with its big, respectable villas, Daniel stopped her again, kissing her hard and hungrily.

He drew back suddenly, his expression taut. 'God, girl – I want to have you.'

She stared at him, longing and frightened at once.

'I've never ... I was brought up to believe it was wrong ... You know – if you're not married.'

Daniel stroked her back. 'I know. We all were. Church and all that. And bourgeois morality. Anything they could do to control the passions in us.' He looked down at her intensely. 'But we can be as free with our bodies as we can with our minds. Truly free. You needn't ... You know – there needn't be a child from it. I've got something to stop it.'

Gwen felt herself blush all over at the intimacy of what he was saying. She had only the haziest notion of what he was talking about.

'I do love you ...' she faltered.

Daniel ran his hands down her sides, then pressed her close to him so that she could not mistake how much he wanted her. He reached round and pulled the bow undone so her hair fell in waves round her cheeks.

'Don't make me wait any longer.'

She looked up at him. 'How can we? Where can we go?'

'The park? It's not far.'

She thought about the dark park gates, the damp grass. It didn't seem right.

Daniel sensed her hesitation.

'What about your room? You said it was at the back.'

Her heart beat faster. How awful, sneaking a man into Millie and Lance's! But she knew she would – she had to. For all her misgivings she ached to lie with Daniel.

'They'll be in bed by now. Millie's so tired with the pregnancy and Lance is so . . .' She gave a wicked giggle. 'Sort of *limp*. He falls asleep almost as soon as he's had his tea. Least it means they can't argue if he's snoring away on the couch! And Mrs Markham's not bothered with us at all so long as we pay the rent. She's too old to be a dragon landlady.'

Gwen felt in her bag for her key, her hands trembling. She opened the door as quietly as possible. Inside, the hall was lit by one faint bulb. All seemed quiet, but Gwen had to stifle giggles from pent-up nerves, especially as Daniel made exaggeratedly frightened faces at her as they crept up the wide staircase, waiting for each tread to creak like a thunderbolt. Once they'd managed to get safely into Gwen's room at the back, they both erupted into laughter, trying to repress the noise.

'Ssssh – for goodness sake!' she hissed at him as he flung himself down on the bed.

The room was basic, with bare wooden boards and shabby curtains, but half the ceiling sloped where the attic stairs ran up above it and it looked out onto the garden at the back. Gwen thought it had atmosphere, especially now she'd arranged her few belongings in it and her pictures.

'Least you don't have to share it!' Daniel whispered. 'Not like at Ma's – all boys together!'

'Well, not until now, anyway!'

Daniel bounced on the edge of the bed. 'Squeaky bedsprings? No – not bad.'

Gwen's heart beat faster. 'She's a bit deaf, anyway – Mrs Markham.' There was something she didn't like about the way he was testing the bed. It felt calculating and for a moment she wanted to draw back, to say she had made a mistake and ask him to go. It had robbed the moment of intimacy. But he leaned forward and picked up the picture on the table near her bed.

'Amy Johnson?'

'Yes – she's a heroine of mine.'

'Remarkable woman, she is.' Daniel stared seriously at the picture for a moment, then put it back. Gwen was appeased by this, and then Daniel got up and came close to her. They stood looking at one another and his eyes grew serious. He put his hands on her shoulders. She knew she was not going to refuse him. She blushed. 'I've never done this before.'

'I know. That makes me want you even more.'

He kissed her gently, easing her lips apart with his tongue, as if they had all the time in the world and in seconds her doubts had gone. She wrapped her arms round him and he kissed her deeply, his body pressing tightly to hers. He drew back and looked at her again.

'Let's see you, my lovely.' His finger played at the neck of her dress and slowly he unfastened the buttons, peeling back the soft cotton. Her dress fell to her waist, leaving her naked at the top except for her bra. She felt vulnerable, being more naked than him.

'Take it off,' he whispered.

She reached round for the fastening. 'Take your shirt off?'

He pulled it off over his head and flung it on the floor, watching hungrily as she removed her bra and dropped it on the chair beside her. His hands cupped her immediately, fondling her, then he reached down to lick and suck her. With sudden abruptness he took her hand and led her to the bed.

'Get undressed.'

His tone was so urgent that she did not feel offended. He was pulling his clothes off, then pulling her to her feet again, helping her remove the rest of hers, so fast that she did not have time to feel embarrassed or afraid. She was carried along, excited by his need. She reached out to hold him and his muscular arms pulled her close.

'Lie back!' Daniel ordered. She lay on the candlewick bedspread and he kneeled over her. For the first time in her life she saw the strange, alien sight of a naked man, smelt his hungry, sweaty smell, and he was stroking her thighs apart, gently but urgently.

'God, girl, I can feel you want me – let me in. Lift your legs!'

She obeyed, moved by his desire, but with a feeling of somehow having been left behind in what was happening as he pushed into her, groaning as he released himself into her. He lay panting, his head next to hers, and she kissed his cheek tenderly and stroked his thick hair, her arms and legs wrapped round his back, holding him close.

'My girl,' he whispered, looking into her eyes. He kissed her nose playfully. Then she saw the loving contentment in his eyes turn to a look of horror.

'Jesus, Mary and Joseph!' He pushed himself up on his arms.

'Sssh!' she warned him. 'What's the matter?'

'I forgot. Christ, I forgot all about the French letter! I got that carried away!'

A sick feeling jolted into her. It hadn't crossed her mind! After all, she had no experience of this – had barely even been able to visualize it before.

'Does that mean...?' Heavens, why was she so ignorant? What did it mean?

'Not always. It doesn't always mean there's a child. Course not. But there's a chance.' Daniel rolled off her, suddenly far away from the closeness of a moment before. He seemed to decide something, and said almost carelessly, 'Chances are it won't happen. Don't you go worrying, pet.'

He dressed hurriedly and she felt a coldness, as if there was something she had lost. She got up, feeling something trickle wet down her thighs and she had to get a hanky out of her drawer to mop herself with. She put her dressing gown on.

'I'll have to come down and let you out,' she told him.

'Right you are.' He smiled at her, but she thought it was a nervous smile.

'Daniel?'

He was moving towards the door, putting his waist-coat on. He turned. 'What?'

She wanted him to be warm to her, to hold her and tell her he loved her, that it would all be all right.

'Was it . . . all right?' She felt pathetic, asking like this.

He stepped back to her and quickly kissed her cheek. 'It was marvellous. Night, night.'

He departed along the street with a brief wave. Once she was back in her room, Gwen lay with the light on for a long time, staring up at the cracks in the sloping ceiling. Her body could still feel his touch and between her legs felt damp and sore.

I'm his now, she thought. That was what it meant if you gave your body to somebody, wasn't it? *I've burned my boats. My life now will be with Daniel Fernandez.*

Twenty-Eight

'How do you know when you're first expecting?'

Gwen slipped the question casually into the conversation when she and Millie were washing up the tea things. The cooker and sink were squeezed into a wide part of the corridor between the bigger bedroom at the front and the living room behind it, where Lance was already sprawled on the couch, his eyes closed. Questions about babies didn't seem out of place, with Millie's on the way.

'Oh, well.' Millie held out a wet, soapy pan for Gwen to dry. Gwen saw that her nails were chewed right down to the quicks. 'The first thing was,' she lowered her voice, 'my, you know – monthly visitor – didn't appear. I didn't think much about it because I've never kept track of that very well. Then I started feeling ropy all the time – not just in the mornings. That was when I went to the doctor.'

Gwen made a mental note of all this. She wasn't exactly worried about it. It all seemed too unreal. Even what had happened last night between her and Daniel felt distant, as if she had dreamed it. A letter had come from Edwin that morning and he seemed unreal too. Gwen smiled into Millie's round face. Millie was starting to put on quite a bit of weight. She looked softer round the edges. 'Are you all right?' Gwen asked.

'Not so bad.' Millie's eye wandered towards the

living room, and Lance, and for a moment Gwen thought she was going to say more. Instead she just sighed and turned back to the sink. 'It'll all be different when the baby's here.'

Gwen eyed her, worried. Millie tried terribly hard with Lance, but he was such a lethargic, moody so-and-so and they squabbled often. It certainly would be different when the baby was there but would it be better? Gwen felt a worm of fear twist in her. What if Daniel had – she struggled to think of the term – impregnated her? But she dismissed the idea again. It seemed too ridiculous. And there were plenty of other things to worry about.

The Whitsun holiday, which had occurred a couple of weeks earlier, should have given her the opportunity to go home to Worcester. But the thought of being at home with her mother and Edwin and trying on wedding dresses seemed out of the question now. Whatever was she going to do? She couldn't face the fact that there were decisions to be made, that she could not just go on writing cheerful notes to Edwin pretending everything was as normal. She was supposed to be marrying him in less than three months. She was Daniel's now. She loved him. She had given herself to him. This meant everything so far as she was concerned. Yet she could not quite face the reality that she was going to have to step right out of that secure life, tell Edwin the truth – jilt him, that was the truth of it!

She had written to tell her mother and Edwin that she could not come home because she was moving her lodgings over the holiday, and in order to salve her conscience she had moved to Millie's then. The two holiday days she had spent with Daniel and the Fernandez family. On the Sunday they had gone back out to the Lickey Hills, spending most of the time wrapped blissfully round one another.

A stern letter arrived from her mother:

I can't imagine what you think you're doing not
coming home for Whitsun. Your father and I are
deeply concerned about your behaviour and your
disgraceful treatment of poor Edwin. It's bad
enough that you are away at all at this time, without
showing any sense of duty. He's your fiancé, for
goodness sake! And Mrs Twining is waiting to work
on the alterations to your dress. I strongly suggest
you come home next weekend and try to make up
for it. I'm appalled at the way you're letting
everybody down. I can't imagine what you're
thinking of.

Gwen didn't go home. How was she ever going to face them? Edwin had done nothing wrong. He was a good man, she knew perfectly well. She had been content to be with him until she found out what it was possible to feel when she met Daniel. Daniel had awoken in her not just passion, but a new sense of herself. That wasn't Edwin's fault and she knew how much she was going to hurt him. She couldn't bring herself to write to him, though, even to apologize. From this distance the situation still all seemed like a dream that might just fade away if she didn't think about it.

'Where're you off to?'

Millie's tone was wistful. It was a warm, humid day and she was on the old couch in the sitting room with her feet up, hair loose, her hands resting on her swollen stomach. She looked hot and tired. The three of them had had some toast for breakfast and Lance had gone out for the day to the Blues match. Gwen felt guilty leaving Millie.

'I'm just going to meet my friend. There're a few things she needs help with.'

Millie frowned. 'You seem to go out such a lot. Who's this friend then?'

Gwen forced a smile. 'Just someone I met. She wants some help printing leaflets – bit of local politics. All rather dull, but never mind.'

'Oh. I didn't know you were interested in that sort of thing.' Millie looked bored by this. 'Why are you dressed like that?'

Gwen had put on her oldest skirt, a very unglamorous, straight navy thing, and a plain black blouse.

'She said we'd get grubby. Anyway' – she picked up her bag – 'have a peaceful afternoon. It'll do you good.'

As soon as Gwen was out of the flat she tore down the stairs, ashamed at her lie to Millie in referring to Daniel as 'she'. Millie had not met Daniel, and as far as she knew Gwen was all set to marry Edwin. It was three weeks since Daniel's secret visit to the flat, but Gwen could not bring herself to confide in her about it all – about her feelings for Daniel. About the party. Daniel seemed like her secret life, yet her real life – the one she hungered for.

There was a yellowed looking-glass in the hall and she paused in front of it. Her hair was pulled back more severely, more carelessly than usual, held by a thick rubber band. She had no ribbons on, no make-up and in the austere clothes and flat shoes she felt serious, more like a proper Communist worker. She had decided now that she was definitely going to join the party, to identify herself with those other passionate, purposeful people who were going to change things for the sake of working people, for the human race. People who got up and did something, instead of just talking about how the world should be a better place! She stared sternly at herself, then, at the thought of Daniel's face if he could see her, an irrepressible smile broke across her face. She let herself out into the street, bouncing with happiness. *I love him!* she sang inside herself. *I love him so much!*

She ran eagerly up the stairs into the offices. Daniel was already there, his dark head bent over the temperamental duplicating machine. He turned and grinned at her.

'Hello – can't come too close like this!' He smiled, holding up his hands, and Gwen saw they were covered in ink. She went to him and kissed him.

'Playing up again, is it?'

'Blasted thing.' Daniel lifted his arm and shoved his hair out of his eyes. 'I've been fighting with it an hour already. Herbert thinks he knows what to do – he'll be back soon.'

Herbert worked as a toolmaker. Gwen was not especially cheered to hear he was coming back. She perched on an old stool and looked out of the back window at the dirty rooftops beyond.

'Isn't anyone else helping?'

Daniel was peering into the machine. 'Esther'll be back soon. She's gone out to buy a couple of things.'

Not anything for lunch though, I'll bet, Gwen thought, deflated by the fact that Esther was going to be there and had arrived long before her. No one in the party seemed to be very practical. They didn't seem to care whether they ate or not. Esther just smoked long, thin cigarettes one after another, and Daniel didn't ever seem to bother about eating. Gwen spent most of her time with the party starving hungry.

'Right – l'm going to give this a go.'

Daniel was just about to try again to get the machine started when Herbert slouched in. He was a sandy-haired man, thin as a greyhound, wearing a seedy black overcoat, even in the heat.

'I shouldn't do that if I was you,' he said gloomily. 'Let me look at it first.'

He gave Gwen the briefest of nods. She wrinkled her nose as he passed her. He didn't smell very nice. The two men busied themselves over the machine. Gwen soon grew bored, so she took out her copy of *Ten Days that Shook the World*. She was almost at the end now, but she'd had to struggle to get to grips with the Bolsheviks and Mensheviks and all the different parties and revolutionary movements. She began a chapter entitled 'The Peasants' Congress'.

It was on November 18th that the snow came. In the morning we woke to window-ledges heaped white, and snowflakes falling so whirling thick that it was impossible to see ten feet ahead . . .

'Well, comrades, how are we doing?'

Esther's booming voice cut jarringly through Gwen's immersion in the Soviet snows.

'I think I know what's up,' Herbert said.

'Oh – hello,' Esther said to Gwen in an offhand way. 'What're you reading?' She bent over to look. She was wearing an extraordinary pair of baggy black trousers and a navy blouse polka-dotted with white tucked into them. Her plump arms protruded out from the short sleeves. 'Ah – *Ten Days*... How sweet! Imagine being able to discover all that afresh again!'

Gwen closed the book and stood up. She was an inch or so taller than Esther Lane. For a moment her eyes met Esther's intense deep blue ones. Esther's stare was provocative and, Gwen thought, rather scornful.

'Well, we all have to begin somewhere,' Esther said, moving away with an amused look. 'I'm sure Daniel's a very good teacher.'

Gwen felt a flush rise in her cheeks, fully aware that Esther had not been referring to revolutionary politics.

Esther joined the men leaning over the machine, deliberately excluding Gwen. Herbert was tugging at something inside the workings.

'There,' he panted. 'If that don't do it, I'm stumped.'

A few minutes later the machine cranked into action and the leaflets came fluttering out. *Bread Not Batons!* it was called. It was about the means test.

'Shall I help pile them?' Gwen asked Daniel eagerly.

'Yes, I can't do a thing till I've been and washed my hands!' Daniel laughed. 'Nor Herbert.'

Glad to have something to do, Gwen arranged the leaflets, which smelt strongly of ink, while the men disappeared outside to the toilet, where there was a tiny handbasin.

Esther rested her cigarette in an ashtray on the desk and carried on with the printing, her dark brows pulled into a frown. After a while, without looking up, she asked, 'So what do you do with your time?'

'I'm a teacher. At Canal Street, Winson Green.'

Gwen saw a hint of surprise on Esther's face. 'I say. That must be a challenge.'

'And what do you do?'

'Oh, I'm doing some research.'

'At the university?'

'Well, I use the library.'

'Gracious,' Gwen said, looking innocently across at Esther. 'However do you support yourself?'

She saw a slight flush rise in Esther's cheeks. 'My father's a lecturer.'

'Oh, I see – *he* supports you?' Gwen felt triumphant. Here was this woman going on about the workers of the world and she was living off her father! 'Well, how very nice! It's so inconvenient having to work for a living.'

'I devote most of my time to the party,' Esther retorted, busying herself with the printing.

The men came back then and for the remainder of the morning they all worked hard. Daniel and Esther discussed a pamphlet that they were working on, but although Daniel sat for some time at the desk with Esther, Gwen knew that his attention kept returning to her. Once he came over to her by the machine and put his arm round her.

'All right, comrade?' He looked deeply into her face. His cheeks were shadowy with stubble.

'Yes, of course.' She smiled, putting her arm round his waist. She felt close to him and as if she belonged, was part of what was going on.

By about two-thirty, Herbert murmured something about having to 'get back to the Missis' and slunk out.

'Thanks, comrade!' Daniel called after him.

Herbert raised a fist in reply, which, given how puny he was, made Gwen want to giggle.

Her stomach was gurgling with hunger by now.

'Shall I go out and get us something to eat?' she suggested, since obviously no one else was going to.

'That'd be nice,' Daniel said, glancing up from the desk where he was writing furiously.

It was good to be out in the sunshine. Gwen felt odd being in the street, amid shoppers leading small children by the hand and messenger boys on bicycles, the ordinary world where people were not interested in the revolution. She bought three cheese and pickle cobs and three iced buns and hurried back to the office with the paper bags in her arms.

As she pushed open the squeaky office door, the sight that met her made her feel as if she'd been punched. Daniel was still sitting at the desk and Esther Lane was standing behind his chair, leaning over him, arms wrapped round his neck. Seeing Gwen at the door she straightened up, unhurriedly, fixing Gwen with a defiant stare. Gwen was too shocked, too hurt to speak. Daniel smiled, apparently oblivious to the shock on Gwen's face.

'Those look a treat. Thanks, Gwen.'

No one, she noticed, offered to pay her for their share. *I suppose I'm the one who's working*, she thought. She couldn't look at Daniel. She was close to tears. Daniel took his food back to the desk and he and Esther continued to work.

'Won't be much longer,' he said, looking over at her. 'Just get this done and we'll go.'

Gwen nodded. The lump in her throat made it impossible to eat.

The hurt sat in her like a stone for the next hour until Daniel pronounced that he'd finished and they could go. They had a brief discussion about which of the party workers had been out chalking up details of the public meeting they were holding on Sunday night.

'Thanks then, Esther,' Daniel said eventually, picking up his jacket. 'Gwen and me'll be off now.'

'All right, Daniel,' Esther said in her smoky voice. She ignored Gwen. 'See you tomorrow night?'

'Right you are.' Daniel took Gwen's arm and they headed out into the balmy afternoon. 'This is nice.' Daniel turned his face up to the light. 'Let's go somewhere different. How about Cannon Hill Park?'

'Daniel.' She couldn't contain herself any longer and pulled at his arm to stop him. 'I don't understand what's going on. Are you in love with Esther?' At last the pent-up tears ran down her cheeks. She felt miserable and stupid.

'Hey, what's the matter?' He pulled her into his arms. They were standing by a shop window in a busy street, but she couldn't have cared less. 'Why're you asking me that? Old Esther – how could you think that?' He pushed her away a fraction to look into her eyes. 'She's got a bit of a thing about me, that's all. Nothing that matters. I think she sees me as a romantic example of the working class – you know, from the valleys and that.'

Gwen looked up at him. 'Romantic – you?' She tried to smile through her tears, then grew solemn again. 'You're not . . . in love with her?'

'No!' Daniel laughed. 'Don't talk daft! She's just one of those Bohemian types – goes draping herself round anyone.' With his thumb he gently wiped her eyes. 'You're my lovely. You know you are – haven't I told you enough times?'

She pouted, more playful now. 'No!'

'Well, you are.' He kissed her nose. 'Come on – let's go somewhere where I can really show you.'

They took a tram down the Pershore Road and walked to Cannon Hill Park. For the remainder of the afternoon they strolled across the green spaces with their arms round each other. They bought ice creams from one of the Italian barrows and tasted the sweetness on each other's lips. There were a lot of other people out enjoying the sunshine, but as the sun sank lower and prams were wheeled back towards the big houses of Moseley and children taken home for their tea, the park became quieter. They found a spot near the top of a gentle slope and sat together. Gwen was glowing with warmth and happiness, her fears about Esther Lane pushed aside. It was her Daniel loved – he could hardly help it if Esther had a crush on him.

Daniel moved closer and put his arm round her back. They kissed, then sat close.

'Did you . . .' Daniel spoke suddenly. 'I mean, I wondered if you'd had your . . . your monthly yet?'

'It's all right.' Her cheeks went red. But she was touched that he was thinking of her in this way. 'It started three days ago.' She hadn't realized herself just how much the worry of it had been needling away at the back of her mind until she knew it was all right. She was not going to have a baby! Look what had happened to Millie, after all. But even despite that, she couldn't fully believe it would ever really happen to her. 'You're very well informed, for a man.'

'I was worried, that's all. My stupid fault – not using something to stop it. I don't want to get you into trouble.'

'Well, we won't forget again,' she said, looking into

his eyes. They had not made love since that first time. There had been no opportunity.

Daniel kissed her and she reached round and stroked his cheek.

'I wish we had somewhere we could call our own,' she said. She found herself full of longing just to lie back, to hold him and feel his weight on her and was caught up by surprise at herself. Was this her, feeling like this all the time, behaving in this way? And would they always have to sneak about and hide like this?

With his lips close to her ear, he said, 'If we wait here long enough, everyone'll go home – except for the other lovers!'

'Daniel! We can't – not here!'

'Can't we? Why not?'

She stared at him, her body aching with need.

His eyes narrowed. 'God, I want you.'

'You'll have to wait –' playfully, she touched his nose – 'till the moon comes up.'

Twenty-Nine

Joey started going out in the day with John. People stared at them. John's height, his black clothes and huge matted beard attracted attention. The others in the house – except Micky – washed under the broken pipe at the back, but Joey had never once seen John wash or change. You could always smell him.

'I do a bit of this – bit of that. Anyone who'll give me a bob or two for a job,' John told him. 'If they won't, then fuck 'em. I get this out.' He reached into the pocket of the long, shabby coat and pulled out a mouth organ. 'That can earn you a few pennies if you can make it sing.' Which John could. His favourite tune was 'Waltzing Matilda'.

Some days John took Joey to the Bull Ring and he'd pick up an odd job around the market, carting potatoes, bringing in ice for the fish market. Joey liked the Bull Ring, the bustle and colour, the birds and animals in the Market Hall, the knife grinder showering sparks from his stone. All the smells, especially the rich aroma of cooked meat from the eating places up Spiceal Street could make his mouth run with saliva.

'Why aren't you at school?' the market traders asked sometimes. 'You'll have the wag man after you!'

'He's helping me,' John would say firmly. 'He's my lad.' Joey knew everyone thought he was John's son and he found he liked this. He had a deep, almost adoring, regard for Christie, but John was all right. You never really knew where you were with him, but when he spoke, to Joey's ears he sounded like his dad.

Joey kept a sharp eye out for the School Board man, and was always ready to duck under the nearest stall or run for it. Some days John went house to house, sometimes he was turned away rudely, at others he was invited in to do odd jobs: to chop a pile of logs, distemper the wall of an outhouse, hoe a vegetable patch. Despite the dole queues winding out of the Labour Exchanges – John wouldn't go near them, or any other official body – he almost always found something to do in a day, even if in the end it was to stand in town and squeeze out some tunes. Sometimes they begged clothes off the rich people in Edgbaston and pawned them. And he would send Joey thieving: nipping into shops, even houses, for food.

One day John stole a butcher's delivery bike, which was propped outside a shop in Edgbaston.

'We're just borrowing it,' he said.

Joey liked that day. John got the hang of the bike after a while and towards the end they had a bit of fun on it, whizzing down Rotton Park Road. The metal was hard and uncomfortable under Joey's thighs, but he lodged himself sideways on the crossbar as John wobbled faster and faster along the streets.

Joey clung on, excited, terrified, feeling an odd, bubbly sensation rising in him, a pressure in his chest. He heard noises coming out of his mouth and it took him a while to realize that he was laughing.

One morning Joey woke in the summer dawn, sensing that something had changed. The room was very quiet.

He lifted his head. The plank had been slid back from the window and he could see Christie squatting in the corner near Micky, his head bowed.

Joey got up and tiptoed over to him. Siobhan was asleep nearby, curled up on her side with her chin tucked in, her face mostly hidden by her hair. She didn't look peaceful: more as if she was hiding.

Christie looked round at him. 'He's very sick, Joey boy. Our Micky's not got long to go.'

Joey looked down at the bloated body. Micky had not moved for days. Joey saw his belly going up and down, but his breathing was wheezy and shallow. Siobhan had kept saying he was sinking. They'd boiled water and tried to clean him up. He had a terrible smell on him. It hit you when you came in the room.

'Poor old fella,' Christie said.

That evening, when Joey came back in with John, the stench was terrible. Joey could taste it, over the smell of stew and cabbage, like fur in his mouth. He went and crouched at the side of the hearth, hugging his knees, near John, who was stirring the pot. Joey's stomach was twisting with hunger. Siobhan and Christie ignored both of them because they were arguing, though for once this was nothing to do with Siobhan's drinking. She was sober, but distraught.

'Don't you dare go fetching one of them here! We don't want them pushing their noses into our business, knowing we're here! Christie, for heaven's sake he'll go running for the Guard and they'll have us out of here – sweet Jesus, they might even send us home!'

Christie was sitting by the fire, hands over his face. Joey could see that he was coiled like a spring. Christie spoke through his fingers.

'I've got to, Shiv. You know I've got to. It's the only thing left.'

'Don't bring one of them!' She was sobbing. 'They'll see into my blackened soul, sure they will! I can't stand it!'

But Christie was not to be budged. 'God knows he's had little comfort in his life. And he was a right enough old fella.'

Siobhan sprang up suddenly. Joey caught a glimpse of her white thighs before her skirt fell over them again.

'I tell you, Christie O'Brien, you bring a priest to this house and I'm parting company with you – for good. I'll not stop here a moment longer.'

Christie snatched his hands from his face and stood up, so toweringly angry that at that moment he seemed to Joey twice his normal height.

'Have you forgotten I'd still be training to be a priest myself had it not been for you? For your carrying on with Sean Flaherty? Did you forget I ran away from the seminary for you? For *you*, you selfish bitch. Don't you think I mightn't rather be back there now than rotting here in this filth and squalor? You never think of anyone but yourself, do you?'

'You *hated* the seminary!' Her voice rose. 'You never wanted the priesthood and you know it – baptizing brats all your life in some God-forsaken country! Don't you bring that down on my head! It wasn't you wanted to go – you had no will of your own when Mammy was at you all the time. Sure, couldn't one of her sons bring blessings on the family – be a priest and join the missions? Well, Paddy and Donal weren't fit for it, were they? Mine wasn't the only bastard baby on the farm, don't forget!'

'Keep your voice down!' Christie shouted. 'Will you have some respect for a dying man?'

'I'll not stay, I tell ye, Christie. I'll go from you!'

'Will you? Will you now?' Joey had never seen Christie so angry. He was quivering, his face pushed right up close to Siobhan's. It was as if she had twisted at something deep inside him. 'And where will you go, Shiv? On the road? Selling yourself along the way? Or back in the spike bedding down with whores and drunks?'

There was a long silence. The two stood with their eyes burning into each other's in the firelight as if neither could let go. At last Siobhan looked down.

'The *rest* of the whores and drunks, you mean, Christie.' Her voice was low, and filled with an ache of shame. 'For that's what I am and in your heart you know it.'

She sank to the floor, as if all her energy had gone.

'Do what you like,' she said pitifully.

Christie went to the door. Before going out he turned and said quietly, 'He deserves to have the Church at the end.'

John went over to Siobhan.

'I've got some biscuits,' he said sweetly to her. They'd bought broken biscuits in the Bull Ring.

'Have you, John?' There was a deadness to her voice. She stared into the fire. John laid the food they had brought beside her like an offering.

'Did you bring me a drop of anything, darlin'?' Her tone was wheedling now. Joey, crouched at the edge of the hearth, felt himself tighten inside. He hadn't seen John buy anything, but he hated it when she even asked. He didn't know why John did it, making trouble. He might offer to go out again, down to the Outdoor to fetch it for her . . .

'No, Shiv. Sorry,' John said abjectly. 'We didn't make very much today.'

'Never mind.' Her voice was sad, but she patted John's arm. 'You're sweet to me, John, so you are. Come here and give me a kiss.'

John didn't move any closer. He froze, kneeling bent over the bag of potatoes they had bought. Instead, Siobhan had to move, leaning over to kiss his cheek. Then she looked into his face. John looked woodenly back.

'Sure, you're a funny one. D'you not want me, John? D'ye not need a woman?'

John stood up. 'I'm going to get some water.'

The potatoes were boiling over on the fire when they heard footsteps in the hall. Siobhan froze.

'In here, Father,' they heard. 'I'll just get us a light.'

'There's a powerful smell on him, all right,' a voice said.

As the door swung open, Joey saw that Christie was accompanied by a thin, dark-haired man in glasses.

'He was very bad when we woke this morning.' Christie spoke in a low voice, as if not wanting to wake Micky up. 'But he's holding on. Pass us a candle, John.' The priest squatted down by Micky's body. Joey saw him react, just a fraction, to the pungent stench.

The priest took a little bottle from his pocket. He tipped it up, then touched Micky's forehead. He hesitated and reached down for Micky's wrist. Then he looked solemnly up at Christie.

'He's gone.'

'Has he?' Christie sounded startled. 'It must have been just in the past few minutes.'

'Well, he's dead, sure enough.' The priest murmured some words which Joey couldn't understand. Christie was standing with his hands clasped. He said, 'Amen', and made the sign of the cross. Joey heard Siobhan say 'Amen' very quietly as well.

The priest stood up and looked round, and Siobhan shrank closer to the wall.

'What is this place? Sure, you're not living here?' His tone was gentle. Joey did not feel afraid of him. 'Have you all nowhere else to go?'

'We haven't,' Christie pleaded. 'We've no other home. When my sister and I came over we were on the road, dossing down in the spikes – we were separated and she was in with all kinds of people ... It's not good for her, Father. We're getting along nicely enough here if we're left alone. Please don't tell anyone we're living here, will you?' Joey almost thought Christie was going to kneel down in front of the man he sounded so desperate.

The priest nodded, seeming to agree. 'Where're you from back home?'

'Tipperary, Father.'

'My grandmother's country. Myself I'm from County Mayo.'

'Are you, Father?' Joey could hear Christie's nervousness in the quick way he spoke, the way he wasn't really listening to what the man was saying. 'I wouldn't have come bothering you if it wasn't for Micky there.'

The priest was silent and seemed to be thinking. After a moment he nodded.

'I can think of a couple of fellas I can get to help move him out of here. They've a handcart – we can keep it quiet. God knows, you'll not be wanting to live with this any longer.'

'Tonight?'

'I'll see what I can do. He's no family that you know of?'

'No, Father. Not over here.'

'Will we move him out of the room? The smell on him's terrible.'

Between them, they lugged Micky's body into the hall. Once the priest had gone, Christie brought a can of water and he and Siobhan scrubbed with a rag at the stain on the floor where Micky had lain.

A couple of hours later, when they'd eaten the thin stew, they heard movements at the back of the house. Everyone tensed. The tiles in the hall clinked and rattled. Christie went to the door.

'Don't trouble – it's only myself.' Joey heard the priest's voice and followed Christie curiously.

Two strapping men were squeezed into the hall by the back door. They touched their caps, saying, 'Evening to you,' and looked round bewildered. 'You can smell the fella, anyway,' one said.

Joey heard the priest say to Christie, 'They won't say anything. We've a handcart out at the front.'

The two men hauled Micky up, taking an arm and leg each.

'God now, he's a weight,' one of them groaned. And they took Micky away. Christie followed them out. Joey went back into the room.

Siobhan seemed to uncurl, as if a great danger had passed. 'God rest him,' she said tenderly. 'That was a hard life he lived.'

Thirty

'Lance? The least you could do is answer me – I said d'you want it boiled or poached?'

Millie's complaining voice drifted to Gwen through her bedroom door, mingled with the smell of toast. Gwen heard a brief, languid reply from Lance. She frequently felt an urge to get hold of Lance and give him a good shaking. Compared with Daniel's burning, physical energy, he was like a soggy dishcloth. No wonder Millie was turning into such a nag!

Turning over onto her stomach in the warm bed, Gwen decided to stay there a while longer. It was Saturday. There was no hurry: Daniel was away. At the thought of him she felt a kind of inner lurch, her whole body seeming to long for him, like a deep hunger. Sometimes she could scarcely believe herself: she had given herself to a man without being married! And her life was caught up in politics which she knew it was wisest on the whole to keep quiet about.

And there was Edwin. For a moment the shimmering bubble of joy and excitement in which she existed was ruptured, leaving her with a terrible sense of doubt. Every week brought a more angry and insistent letter from her mother, ordering her to come home. And, of course, many of the things she said were true. Whatever had Edwin done to deserve this? Even his letters had begun to sound a little put out, but Gwen knew Edwin well enough to realize that he would blithely assume everything was all right.

She made herself think about all the happiest times she could remember with Edwin: walks in the Malverns, moments when he had come smiling into her classroom in Worcester, how pleased she had been to see him. She *had* loved him, surely? But then she thought of Daniel and the effect he had on her. With Daniel she was *alive*: with him she flew instead of merely walking. It was as if he set something free in her, and it was inconceivable that she could forget it and go back to what she had been, even though she felt less safe with Daniel, less sure.

'I'll always be back, you dafty, you know that,' he said, with his easy grin, after returning from a trip away without telling her.

She'd reproached him gently. 'It's not very nice of you – just going off without a word. How do I know where you are or when you're coming back?'

There – she was getting just like Millie! She'd seen it even at the time and stopped immediately. A nagging housewife was not what she wanted to be. It would just have been nice to feel as if he considered her feelings, that was all. But she'd told herself she was being trivial and little-woman-ish. *Bourgeois.* There were such big things to consider – the class struggle, the revolution. Where were her feelings in all that?

There was nothing to hurry for so she took a long bath. Their landlady was less of a tartar about hot water than Ariadne had been, but the chance of a hot bath was still rare because of the temperamental nature of the boiler. The pipes groaned loudly as the water ran in. Lying in the bath, she thought guiltily about Ariadne. She'd promised to go and see her and so far she hadn't. In fact, she rather missed Ariadne hovering about when she came into the house, filled with some emotion or other and fussing over her. That's what she'd do today – go and see Ariadne.

'Oh!' Ariadne gave a great cry on opening the door, as if Gwen was a long-lost relative returned from years in the goldfields. She laid her hand on her heart and closed her eyes for a moment. As usual her eyelashes were laden with mascara.

'My dear, how *very* nice to see you. I thought you'd deserted me for ever, like that *dreadful* Mr Purvis.'

She led Gwen along the hall, tottering on her heels, as ever. She was wearing a deep purple frock, with fussy frills round the neck. The house felt chilly after the warm afternoon outside and held its usual dubious cooking smells, but there was a new, sickly aroma mingled with them. Ariadne was clearly aware of it. She paused, holding up one ring-encrusted finger.

'*That*,' she said accusingly, 'is Miss Hines. Simply *douses* herself in it. I hope you're going to have a cup of tea with me? I can't begin to tell you how much you're missed in this house, Gwen dear.'

'That'd be nice,' Gwen said, remembering that tea was the one reasonably safe item in Ariadne's culinary repertoire.

Ariadne settled Gwen in the back room, where she had so often taken meals with Harold Purvis. As usual, there was a newspaper laid open on the table. Gwen eyed it while she waited. A photograph in the middle showed a truck with a tent-like contraption on the back. 'Travelling gas chambers,' the caption said. 'Training for gas attacks.' The report beside it said that the whole of Spain was cut off from telephonic communication, for what were believed to be 'serious political reasons'.

Ariadne carried in tea and arrowroot biscuits and one cream horn on a plate. 'I was going to treat myself, but you must share it with me.'

'Oh no, Ariadne, you have it. The biscuits will do me very well.'

Ariadne beamed at her. 'You always were such a polite girl. Not like *that* one.' She rolled her eyes ceilingwards. 'Proper little piece she is. Calls herself a secretary, but all she is really is a little typist from the pool. And the way she walks! You've never seen anything like it!'

'Does she have a lot of admirers?' Gwen asked, nibbling one of the musty biscuits.

Ariadne gave a fastidious shudder. 'I don't like to think about it. None that are allowed in here, I know that much.'

Gwen thought of herself and Daniel creeping up the stairs past Millie's landlady. She realized Ariadne was looking at her intently.

'Forgive me for saying so, dear, but you don't look quite as . . . well, *feminine* as you did.' She eyed Gwen's old navy skirt and unadorned hair. 'I don't like to pry, but is everything all right? Your fiancé? And your wedding plans?'

'Yes thanks, Ariadne.' Gwen smiled, but a blush seeped into her cheeks. She had been on the point of talking about Daniel. He was so much a part of her life now that it seemed normal to her. But of course she couldn't! Ariadne still thought she was engaged to Edwin. And, she remembered with another jolt, *Edwin* still thought of her as engaged to Edwin as well.

'I'm doing very well,' she said hurriedly. 'I'm enjoying my job, and I've grown ever so fond of some of the children. Coming here has really made me realize how much I like being a teacher. Anyway,' she added, 'what happened to Mr Purvis in the end? Do you hear from him?'

Ariadne's lips tightened into a hard line and she sat straighter in her chair, on her dignity.

'No, I do not hear from Mr Harold Purvis. And I'm not party to any information about his whereabouts. In fact, Mr Purvis is a subject I'd rather not talk about at all, if you don't mind.'

'Of course not,' Gwen said quickly. She wasn't exactly bursting to talk about him either.

Instead, Ariadne was far more interested in talking about June Hines, the 'little number' upstairs, towards whom she seemed to harbour almost unlimited resentment.

'If I could find someone else, she'd be out on her ear, I can tell you,' Ariadne declared, teasing a fluffy dot of cream from her upper lip. 'She stinks like a polecat! But I haven't even found anyone else to fill the *other* room since that fly-by-night Miss Polensky took off.' She sighed. 'George would be *mortified* if he knew how I was having to get by these days.'

Gwen never got to the bottom of what it was that irked Ariadne so much about Miss Hines, but she left to pleas that she come back and rent a room with her again.

'I'd welcome you with open arms, dear, if you'd consider it.'

'Well, that's very nice of you,' Gwen said as they parted. 'I'm all right where I am at the moment. I'll bear it in mind, though.'

Ariadne waved from the step and Gwen felt a little sad turning away from the house. Perhaps she should move back. Mr Purvis was gone, at least. But would her digestive system stand it? And, anyway, for the moment she was trying to be a good friend to Millie and not spend every single night at party meetings. But her heart sank at the thought of another evening in with Millie and Lance and the wireless.

Oh, Daniel, she thought crossly. *Why aren't you here?*

He was back the next day, full of fervour for the Welsh NUWM protests about the unemployment regulations.

Gwen caught up with him on Sunday afternoon. When she reached the Fernandez's house, everyone was at home, him included.

'Hello there!' Daniel didn't touch her, not in front of his mother and siblings, but his eyes glowed at the sight of her and Gwen felt her spirits rise and swoop with happiness. He had caught the sun and looked even darker and more handsome.

'Sit down and have a cup of tea, Miss Purdy,' Theresa said comfortably. 'We've not seen you in a while. Oh, by the way, I called on Alice's mother, Mrs Wilson. A couple of times I went. I can't say I felt welcome. She's very closed in on herself, isn't she? Very miserable.'

'Thank you ever so much,' Gwen said. 'I'm sure she appreciates it really.'

'Poor soul.' Theresa carried the big teapot to the table. 'Daniel – sit, for the love of God. You're like a dog with fleas today.'

'I can't sit, Mam!' Daniel laughed. 'I'm too worked

up!' Gwen could feel the fire coming from him. His whole body was electric with energy.

Lucy sat by the table smiling, overjoyed to have her brother back and her beloved teacher there too.

'Have you been back home?' Gwen smiled, already infected by his huge enthusiasm.

Daniel nodded. 'Came back last night. I managed to hitch a lift on a truck full of sheep. Bound for slaughter all of them, and I'm sure they knew it – they didn't half make a racket all the way, I can tell you!' He compromised on his mother's request by turning a chair round and straddling it, back to front, arms resting on the rail and rocking it to and fro.

'Daniel, stop that – you'll break it! You're like a great big baby!'

'So, what's the news?' Gwen said.

'Unity's coming.' Daniel spoke urgently. 'You can almost smell it in the valleys. Down there they've got leadership – and real comradeship. You can feel people rising to it as every week goes by. My God, the state of things there!' His voice rose. 'Auntie Shân said they've knocked eight shillings off Billy's disability payment now, what with Uncle Anthony on the dole. They've hardly a farthing between them for food.' He sucked his breath in, hand clenched. 'If it wasn't for us being able to help them . . . Jesus, it makes you want to . . .' The fist hovered over the back of the chair.

'It's a wicked, cruel system,' Theresa agreed quietly. 'But blaspheming won't bring it to an end – nor you getting arrested.' She sipped her tea. 'Nor you breaking up our chairs, Daniel *bach*.'

Daniel unclenched his fist and his gaze burned into Gwen.

'Next weekend's the big demonstration – at Tonypandy. The party is calling on workers from all over the valleys to come together in full strength, show them what we think of the means test! Come with me? Come and see it happen?'

His excitement poured into her. She could feel herself glowing, and beamed back at him. 'In a sheep wagon?'

Daniel's slow grin met hers. 'I was thinking more of a train.'

Throughout that week news gradually trickled out from Spain. There had been coordinated uprisings by the right and the landowning classes against the recently elected left-wing Popular Front government. Franco's garrisons in Morocco joined in the insurrection and Franco himself led the troops who took over Las Palmas.

The party meetings that week were in a ferment with the news. Spain was under threat of fascists overthrowing the government! The republican groupings were struggling to defend a people's government of justice and democracy against the tyranny of military force and capitalist aggression! The party had to respond! What instructions would come from the headquarters in King Street, in London? They must act immediately, get on to the streets and outside factory gates, to raise support and funds for the republican fighters.

Gwen went with Daniel to every meeting that week. The news, as it came in, was at once exhilarating and terrible. Germany, Italy, the Blackshirts at home and now Spain: the urgency to act in the face of fascism was infectious, heady, but at the same time the threat of it seemed to move closer, like an evil cloud.

Another cloud was Esther Lane. The party was working ever closer now with the Birmingham Council for Peace and Liberty. Esther was involved in the council as well, and there she was at every meeting, her face set tightly in concentration as she listened to speakers in halls all round the city as they tried to rally support. And she was close to Daniel at every opportunity, and always, Gwen felt, ready to belittle her. Daniel laughed when she complained, said she was imagining it. He always talked about 'old Esther' as if she was somehow amusing and not to be taken seriously, in her outlandish clothing and with her posh, hooting voice. She wasn't Daniel's type – even Gwen could see that – but she could see what was in Esther's eyes when Esther looked at Daniel and it frightened her.

On Wednesday night Daniel came back to the house with her after the evening's meeting, both of them sneaking in again like thieves, both full of a taut, frantic energy. The second they were inside the room, their hands were under each other's clothing, Daniel pushing the door shut with his foot.

'God, girl.' Daniel pulled his shirt off, then hers, in a fever of impatience.

They made love fast, hungrily, fighting the temptation to forget any worries about babies, longing just to surrender to it, naked and complete. The rubbery smell of the French letter was so horrible, the delay such an intrusion, but Daniel insisted, hurrying to put it on.

'We've got to – don't need any complications, now, do we?' His eyes narrowed with desire and he lay back. 'Come down on me. I want to feel you over me.'

She lay crouched, cuddled close round him, for a

long time after, with him still inside her, their skin slicked together in the muggy night. Gwen nuzzled her nose into his neck, felt his hands hot on her back.

'I don't ever want to be anywhere except with you,' she whispered.

She felt him give a low laugh of pleasure and the pressure of his lips on her cheek.

'That's my girl, my beauty.'

A moment later, he said, 'It's going to happen this weekend. They won't let us down. I can feel it.'

She looked into his dark eyes, stroked his cheek. 'Never off duty you, are you?'

And he laughed again, eyes crinkling at the corners.

Letting him go, to creep out into the night, she felt as though they were being torn apart.

Thirty-One

They didn't go to Wales by train after all. Gwen had been looking forward to a long ride in a secluded railway carriage alone with Daniel, but Esther Lane and two other party workers were to come as well, and Esther announced that they would motor down in her father's Daimler. Dr Lane, it appeared, was also a member of the BCPL.

They gathered outside the party offices at five thirty. Five of them were going: Gwen, Daniel, Esther, Herbert – the thin, red-headed man – and a young, softly spoken social worker with a neat little moustache, called Ernest, whom Gwen recognized from some of the meetings. He wore grey flannel trousers and a red kerchief tucked into the neck of his shirt.

'Good, I'm glad you haven't overdone the luggage,' Esther remarked, eyeing the small holdall Gwen had brought with her. 'It's going to be close quarters as it is.'

Gwen felt immediately patronized and as if she didn't in some way measure up, as she always did in Esther's presence.

Well, at least I'm not colour-blind, she thought pettishly. Esther was wearing her baggy black slacks and an equally voluminous short-sleeved blouse in a sickly shade of turquoise. Her hair was taken up in a bandanna of glaring pea green covered in yellow polka

336

dots. Gwen had also dressed casually, in navy cotton slacks and a blue and white striped shirt. She had a sweater flung over one shoulder for when the evening cooled.

'Get in – do!' Esther stood by the open door beside the driver's seat. 'Daniel, why don't you join me in the front so we can talk tactics?'

It was almost a command. Gwen felt herself stiffen with resentment at Esther's proprietory manner towards Daniel. Who did she think she was?

'No, let Ernest sit up front,' Daniel said easily. 'Gwen and I'll squeeze up with Herbert.'

Esther, having taken it for granted that Daniel would do as she asked, had been about to climb into her seat. She stopped, and frowned across the roof of the car. 'I really do think it would be better if Ernest sat behind. I need you here with me.'

But Daniel was already in the car, seating himself in the middle, Herbert to his right. Gwen got in after him.

Daniel gave Gwen a wink. She grinned back at him and under her navy sweater, which she laid on her lap, they linked hands. They began the journey with a great shuddering lurch, which made them grin all the more. Gwen could just see the side view of Esther's face, scowling with concentration under the green and yellow bandanna and a lock of escaped black hair.

'Sorry – don't drive her very often!' she called.

They left Birmingham as the sun sank low in the sky, passed through Kidderminster and turned towards Hereford. The fields were bright with corn and warm air blew in through the windows. In the bronze light and the warm, muggy air Gwen began to feel drowsy and leaned her head on Daniel's shoulder.

At dusk they stopped south of Hereford and shared

the food they'd brought. Esther handed round potted-meat sandwiches, and they went to a pub and had a half of warm ale before pressing on. Revived by the food and the cool of the evening, Esther led them in singing the 'Internationale', the 'Red Flag' and 'England Arise' several times through. She had a strident, though tuneful voice. Ernest had a reedy tenor, though Herbert came out with a surprisingly strong baritone. Gwen enjoyed singing with Daniel, hearing their voices mingle.

'This was written during the uprising – the Paris Commune,' Daniel told her, between verses of the 'Internationale'. 'In 1871.'

Pale moths batted into the windscreen and the only light came from the beams of the headlamps. Later the road became more twisty and they were going up and down. Daniel leaned forwards to give Esther directions.

'Just a mile or two and we've reached Aberglyn. It's in the next valley.'

He directed her to a narrow side street. All they could see were little windows, some with lights behind them, in a row of tiny cottages.

'I say.' For once, Esther sounded unsure of herself. 'Are you sure this is going to be all right, Daniel? I mean there is rather a gang of us.'

'They're expecting us. We'll manage – just for a night.'

As they climbed out of the car, a dog barked shrilly at the front of a neighbouring house. The cottage door opened, and framed in the soft light Gwen saw a stocky man. In a deep, melodious voice, he called, 'That you, Daniel *bach*?'

'Hello, Uncle! Hope we're not too late for you?'

'You've come a long way, boy.' Gwen saw his eyes linger on the elegant lines of the Daimler.

'This is my uncle, Anthony Sullivan.' Gwen knew that he was Theresa Fernandez's elder brother.

Esther stepped forward, hand outstretched. 'Esther Lane. So pleased to meet you. This is *awfully* good of you.'

The man took her hand and nodded. 'You a party worker?'

'Oh yes!' Esther said. 'Very much so. And Daniel's such an inspiration to us all!' She introduced Ernest and Herbert, who both shook his hand.

'Uncle Anthony, this is Gwen,' Daniel said, ushering her forward.

Again, the man gave a nod, and Gwen thought he smiled faintly at her.

'Anthony? Are they here then? Bring them in!' Daniel's Auntie Shân appeared in the doorway, a shawl round her shoulders.

'I don't know why he's keeping you out on the step. Come in, come in!' Her speech ended in coughing and she was doubled up by it for a moment.

'You still not well, Auntie?'

'Can't shake it off. Been like it since the end of the winter.' Gwen saw that the woman's face was worn by worry and sickness. She couldn't have been more than fifty, but she was gaunt and stooped as if older than her years. 'How's your mother, Daniel?'

'She's well. Sent you over a few things.' He had brought a bundle from the car. Gwen saw his aunt's eyes fix on it for a moment, lighting up hopefully.

Gwen heard Daniel lower his voice and ask, 'How's Billy?'

'Oh, you know.' His aunt's tone was flat. 'Going along. Come and see him. He's been in a lather waiting for you.'

They all piled in, seeming to fill the place right up. In one of the two threadbare old chairs facing the empty grate, Gwen saw a young man with brown hair and a thin, shadowy face. At the sight of Daniel, a grin broke across it. 'Danny boy!'

'Billy!' Daniel rumpled the young man's hair playfully. 'You're a sight for sore eyes.' He looked round. 'Brought some of my comrades to visit. This is Gwen . . .'

Gwen said hello and shook Billy's clammy hand.

'Nice to meet you,' he said shyly. She felt desperate for him. He was her age, Daniel had told her, and had been felled by an accident down the pit when he was fifteen. He'd got in the way of a loaded dram, the trucks pulling coal through the pits, and was paralysed from the waist down. His two brothers and sister had left home for London to find work, but Billy had no choice but to stay at home. He was a Communist, but he couldn't even move out of his chair without assistance, let alone get to meetings.

'Nice to meet you, comrade,' Herbert was saying. Gwen heard Esther and Ernest greet him as well. She looked around her.

The small front room bore all the signs of poverty. The floorboards were bare and scrubbed, there was a wooden chair as well two old armchairs and a china jug and a candlestick set on the mantelpiece, along with a few other knick-knacks. On such a balmy night there was no call for a fire in the grate, but it would have cheered the room. She caught sight of a china po pushed under Billy's seat – somehow that was the saddest sight of all.

'Anthony, go and get that stool from out back!' Shân said. 'Now, you ladies come and sit down.'

Gwen and Esther were united, for once, in protesting that they couldn't possibly sit and deprive the woman of the house of a chair. Gwen was allotted a stool to sit on, and Esther the wooden chair. Herbert and Ernest settled on the floor on each side of the hearth.

Shân reluctantly took the softer chair, pulling her shawl round her thin shoulders. She managed a rueful smile, and Gwen saw that beneath the veil of tiredness and care her heart-shaped face was rather pretty.

'There's hardly a crumb I've in the house to feed you on,' she said ashamedly. 'We've put the kettle on, that's all.'

'Here, Auntie.' Daniel presented her with the bundle. 'Ma put this together for you.'

'*Duw!* Oh, my, what a lot! My lap can't hold it all!' She was so eager, almost like a child, and laid the bundle, tied in part of an old sheet, on the floor and unknotted the ends. 'Oh, God bless Theresa – she always did have a heart of gold. What'd we do without her? Oh, Billy, look at this now!'

Gwen felt a lump come into her throat at the woman's excitement in the face of the simple things in the bundle. Theresa had included a loaf of bread, a few ounces of butter, some tea, a jar of jam, a large knuckle of ham, some soft buns she'd baked, a cake and a bag of carrots. There were also oddments like a bar of washing soap and a little bundle of candles held together with a rubber band.

'Well, we've buns to have with our tea now!' she cried, delighted.

They all tried to protest that the buns were meant for the family, but Shân wouldn't hear of it.

'I haven't even got enough cups to go round!' she laughed, getting up to make the tea. 'Mrs Evans next door has lent us a couple!'

Daniel's Uncle Anthony perched on the arm of Billy's chair and immediately the talk turned to politics. At first the Birmingham group sat listening, riveted. Here they were in South Wales, in the heartland of the party – the place Daniel described to them as the beacon of hope, where there was strong leadership and growing unity! They wanted to hear all about it, to drink it in. Gwen was filled with pride and excitement.

The talk turned first to the latest unemployment regulations, in force for eighteen months now, which were the focus of the next day's protest in Tonypandy. The government's Unemployment Assistance Board had introduced national rates of benefit which in many cases were lower than the previous ones. They heard stories of distress from all over the valleys.

Billy's face lit up with passion. 'I've lost my legs, my livelihood and now I'm sat rotting here, and there's no use I am except to cause my family hunger and worry. It's all wrong. No, Mam –' he flung her arm off as she tried to protest at his harshness – 'that's the truth and you know it. It isn't your fault or mine – it's capitalism does it. Capitalist oppression!'

Gwen realized that Billy did not often allow himself to voice these thoughts. He looked heated, overexcited by all the company and she felt deep sorrow for him. She saw the impact of his words on his mother as well, in the way she clenched her jaw, tightening her lips.

'We need another march like in '34,' Anthony said. He was a dignified man, whose deep, powerful voice held a quiet authority. 'Action – that's the thing. Unified action. We can't sit back and let them starve our people into submission like trapped animals.'

Like Daniel's father, Arturo, Anthony had first been employed at the steel works at Dowlais. The two of them had met there and later moved to work down the pit at Aberglyn. Anthony had been out of work now for over a year and had become a member both of the NUWM and the party.

'Our poverty is what brings us together.' Gwen heard Billy's passionate voice across the room. 'God, I wish I could come to Tonypandy with you tomorrow, Daniel, and hear Lewis Jones. Be there with everyone!'

'I wish we could get you there too, Billy boy.' Daniel frowned, as if he was thinking of a way in which it could be managed. 'Are you coming, Uncle Anthony?'

'We could certainly fit another one in the car, couldn't we?' Esther spoke up.

Anthony Sullivan nodded in a dignified way, as if to say, car or no car he'd get there somehow.

It grew later and later as they moved on to talk about the uprising in Spain, and the limited news reaching them from there, for the need for the party to mobilize in favour of the government, and Gwen, who had heard a lot of this before, found her eyelids beginning to droop. After a time, Shân noticed.

'It's exhausted your pretty friend here is, Daniel!' she reproached him. 'You all talking her to pieces. Let's be getting some sleep now. Boys, you can sleep down with Billy. There's a bed up at the back, if you girls don't mind sharing.'

343

Gwen's eyes met Esther's. She knew they were both thinking the same thing: *I don't want to share with you!* But neither of them would have dreamt of protesting.

'That would be perfectly all right,' Gwen said, getting to her feet. Esther did the same. She seemed humbled by Shân Sullivan and was quieter than usual. Daniel was sitting beside Billy, catching up on news of old pals. Gwen went to him and gave him a peck on the cheek.

'Night then. Goodnight, Billy.'

'Sleep tight.' Daniel smiled up at her.

'Night!' Billy said. As she went to the door, Gwen heard him say to Daniel, 'She's lovely, isn't she?'

'Watch the third step.' Shân turned, holding a candlestick, to warn Gwen and Esther, as they followed carrying the few things they'd brought for the night. The third tread of the bare staircase creaked ominously.

'It's not much, I'm afraid,' Shân said, showing them the tiny back room. Between its whitewashed walls was a three-quarter sized bed, a small chest of drawers and a chair. There wasn't room for anything else.

'It's *perfect*,' Esther said, just a little too enthusiastically.

'Thank you for putting us all up,' Gwen said quietly. She felt a kinship with Shân, could sense all the burden of her life. 'We're an invasion.'

'Oh no – it's nice to have some life about the place. Our young ones slept in here once – all in a row.' Her wan expression lit with a smile for a moment. 'But it's grown up and gone they are now. Except Billy, of course.'

'God, it's so *tragic*,' Esther said once Shân had gone,

wishing them goodnight. 'What life will he ever have now?'

'Umm, I know.' Gwen pulled her nightdress out of her bag. Esther grated on her so much that she felt her usual urge to disagree with her on principle, but there was nothing she could say to contradict her. Billy's situation *was* tragic.

Gwen felt deeply uncomfortable at such close quarters with Esther, whose personality seemed to take up the whole room. Added to that, she gave off a ripe, musky smell. She stripped off with no sign of inhibition, pulling her blouse over her head to reveal dark tufts of hair under her arms and heavy breasts encased in a stout bra, which she then proceeded to unfasten as well. Gwen turned away, though not without wondering, in spite of herself, whether Daniel would find the sight of Esther attractive. She slipped her own pale blue nightdress on and went to get into bed, seeing Esther in a voluminous white garment. Esther unwrapped her hair from the bandanna and brushed it out. It hung on her shoulders, thick and slightly frizzy. Gwen hadn't thought to brush her hair. She was too anxious to lie down and sleep. Neither of them spoke.

At last, Esther climbed in beside her and lumped about, getting comfortable.

'Blow the candle out, do,' she said, as the chest of drawers was on Gwen's side of the bed.

Gwen closed her eyes in the darkness. After a moment she heard Esther's deep voice.

'You're really in love with our Daniel, aren't you?'

Gwen hesitated, wondering whether to pretend to be asleep. What was Esther's tone? Curious? Mocking?

Our Daniel. After a few seconds, she said matter of factly, 'Yes, I am.'

'Ah. Well, you wouldn't be the first.' This time the voice held a knowing sense of regret. 'Poor old you, darling.'

Thirty-Two

Gwen woke to the sound of a train chugging slowly in the distance. There was a high squeal from the engine, releasing steam. The pit train, she thought. Otherwise the house was quiet.

Opening her eyes, she saw daylight on either side of the thin curtain. Beside her, Esther's curvaceous shape lay turned away, and she could hear her breathing heavily. She didn't like lying so close to Esther. That comment she had made last night came stinging back. Gwen had lain awake, furious. The cheek of the woman! What the hell did Esther think she knew about Daniel?

Pleased to be awake before Esther, to get away from her, she slipped off the lumpy mattress, dressed quietly in the gloom and crept down the stairs, wincing as they creaked. But she was not the first up. Shân was already moving about in the kitchen at the back, and Daniel was just rousing himself. Round him the others slept, Billy on his mattress, the others on blankets on the floor beside him. Daniel sat up and waved in greeting.

'Did you sleep?'

'Yes thanks,' she whispered.

He got up and came to her, taking her in his arms. His cheek felt rough against hers and he was warm and soft, somehow, from sleep.

'Big day today.'

'Yes.' She smiled.

They greeted Shân, who was once again wrapped in her shawl though the morning was mild.

'I'll brew us a cup of tea,' she said.

'Just thought I'd take Gwen out for a minute, along the road,' Daniel said. 'Show her the valley.'

'Oh you must show her, Daniel *bach*.' Gwen saw Daniel's aunt looking at her with a new curiosity. 'There's beautiful it is up there for those with the strength to walk. The tea'll still be here when you get back.'

'Here – come and see.' Daniel took her arm and they went out into the sunny morning.

There was no view at first, except for the worn, grey cottages opposite. They were in a little sloping street, and Dr Lane's Daimler looked absurdly large and out of place parked at the kerb.

'Come and have a look this way,' Daniel said, following the upward slope of the road.

The cottages clung along the contour of the incline. They were a poor, unkempt line of dwellings and the sufferings of their occupants seemed to be etched into their facades. The street was quiet except for a woman scrubbing at her step and a man with a stooped, wiry body, walking with a stick, who peered up from under his cap at them.

'Daniel Fernandez? Is that you?' His tone was commanding, and, Gwen thought, not especially friendly.

'Yes, it's me, Hywel.' Daniel sounded tense.

The man squinted at him. 'What're you back here for, mun? Making trouble again, is it?' He shook the stick. 'They ought to round up the whole bloody lot of you and send you to Russia!' He started off up the road again with renewed energy, but Daniel swivelled on one foot and called after him, 'The Labour Movement's dead, Hywel – all over the world. They've given in to capitalism and fascism! When're you going to face reality?'

The man turned, banging his stick on the ground. 'We could have kept our men working! Now there's nothing in the valleys but empty bellies and empty Bolshevik principles to go with them. No one gains any fat from principles!'

'What – keep them working by joining the bosses' Federation, and the blacklegs? That's slavery, Hywel, and you know it. The slavery of ownership and capital. The workers are making the revolution – here today, whether they're in work or not. They'll show their strength in Tonypandy . . .' Gwen could hear a particular desperation in Daniel's voice as he tried to impress his views on the old man. His fists were clenched, body tensed with emotion. She could see that this was a division which went back a long way and went deep. 'There *will* be a new dawn, Hywel, if you'd only put your faith in it.'

'The only place I put my faith is in almighty God, Daniel, and there was a time when you did the same. You've betrayed yourself by putting it anywhere else. Now don't speak to me any more . . .' He waved Daniel away with violent exasperation and continued on down the road.

'God didn't stop them throwing my ma into gaol, did he?'

Gwen was shocked to the core. *Theresa* in gaol? Whatever was Daniel talking about?

The old man strode furiously along the road. Gwen waited behind Daniel and saw he was quivering with emotion. After a moment, he shook his head and let out a sharp sigh, turning to her. 'Hywel Jones and my da were in the Labour Party together. He never forgave Da for becoming a Communist.' He gave Gwen a look, revealing a vulnerability which touched her. 'Why can't he see? Why can't they all see?'

She had no answer for him. She wanted to ask about Theresa, what had happened. Why had he never said anything before?

'Daniel?' But he shook his head and turned away. This was not the right moment. Silently she reached for his hand and they walked on.

They were evidently near the edge of the little town, soon the houses ended and from the road they could see right across the valley. They stopped for a moment and Gwen became aware of the wind in the grass.

'It's lovely, Daniel.' She was slightly breathless from the walk.

'It is.' He nodded, smiling. He seemed to be calmer again. 'Your cheeks have gone pink!'

The valley lay spread out in front of them, a deep summer green dotted with little cottages. Further away, far down to their left, she saw the dark, protruding shapes of the pit, and heaped beyond, black, ugly mounds of slag. In front of them, where they stood, beyond the green swathe of the valley, rose the flank of the mountain on the other side. The breeze blew across, strong and fresh, and there were flowers in the grass at her feet. Further down the bank she saw a shining thread of water and realized there must be a spring running down to the valley.

Daniel went to put his arms round her from behind, but instantly the stance reminded her of Edwin.

'Don't.' She spoke abruptly and to soften it turned round to him. 'I can't see you if you stand behind me.'

They stood side by side and put their arms round one another, breathing in the fresh, clear air.

'Was that the pit you worked in?'

Daniel nodded. 'And my da. And Uncle Anthony and Billy.' He gave a deep sigh. 'Not many of the old butties left working it now, what with them splitting them all up and scab labour, and foreigners being brought in.'

He pointed out things to her, the railway threading along and the stream in the valley.

'Over the mountain there, there's one of the steel works – all deserted. At night-time it used to send up a great glow. It's just a heap of rust now, poking up into the sky.'

They stood in silence for a moment, and then she said, 'Love, why did your mother go to prison?' The emotion behind his outburst had affected her strongly. 'You never said before.'

'No.' Daniel evidently didn't want to expand on it. 'I know.' After more silence, in the sound of the wind, he turned to her.

'We're going to do it today.' There was a catch in his voice. 'Another step towards the revolution for our people. Aren't we?'

He looked searchingly at her, an appeal in his eyes, and she saw that he was still feeling the old man's anger. She looked back and squeezed his waist, wanting to believe that it was true. Russia, the Bolsheviks and collectivization, the idea that things could change so radically still felt distant and unreal. She wondered if he realized how faint her belief was. She wanted to believe it for him because it moved him so much. Because of Auntie Shân, and because it was his life, and now hers too.

'It will be a great day.' She took his hand. 'Come down here.'

She made him follow her down the bank to the trickle of spring water, bubbling out from under a thatch of grass, and she lifted handfuls and washed her face.

'Oh, it's cold! It's lovely!' she laughed, and Daniel doused his face too. He took her in his arms then, and they kissed, hungrily, faces still wet.

'I wish we could stay up here,' she said longingly.

'We'll come back here again,' Daniel said. 'Just you and me.' They walked back to the house, the wind blowing the water dry on their cheeks.

'Auntie, we'll be bringing Uncle Anthony back later!' Daniel told Shân fondly as she fussed about what they were going to eat. 'It's not a week we're going for. We've got to go back tonight.'

'Are you not staying a while with us, Daniel?' Gwen saw Billy looking disappointed too.

'No, Auntie. But we'll come back soon, really we will.'

Billy sat drinking in every word excitedly as they breakfasted on bread and tea. Gwen could see how hard he was trying not to show the bitterness he felt at having to be left behind. In a quiet moment she went to Shân in the tiny kitchen. She found her standing pensively by the stove as the kettle reboiled, her shawl pulled close round her shoulders.

'Mrs Sullivan?' The woman turned, smiling, her grey eyes full of kindness.

Speaking softly, Gwen said, 'I was wondering about Billy. I know how much he'd like to be going with us today. If I was to stay behind, he could have my place in the motorcar. I just don't know if there's a way he could manage at the other end. If they could carry him or something?'

Shân Sullivan's face softened, then shaded with further sadness. Slowly she shook her head.

'It's a kind heart you have, Gwen *fach*. But our Billy can't go anywhere for very long. We've the wheelchair out the back, but you couldn't be taking that. And Billy can't even do his business without a helping hand, see. He'd soil himself and he'd hate that more than anything.'

Gwen blushed, feeling stupid. 'Sorry. Only I thought I'd ask. I would have stayed, if . . .'

Shân touched her hand. 'There's the way it is. There are things that even God can't do anything about.'

Gwen sat on Daniel's lap for the journey, the two of them squeezed in beside Ernest and Herbert, while Uncle Anthony sat in the front with Esther, who had replaced yesterday's green and yellow bandanna with a bright scarlet one. He sat very upright, obviously ill at ease in this unaccustomed luxury. They set off towards Tonypandy, and decided to leave the car outside the town so they could join the others walking in for the demonstration.

As they drew near, they started to see people moving along from quite some distance away along the mountain roads.

'Let's stop here!' Daniel cried as they passed a group of people carrying a red banner between them, struggling with it as it bellied out in front in the wind. 'It's all wrong driving when other comrades are on foot!'

'Quite right.' Uncle Anthony sounded relieved at the suggestion.

They were on a hill, looking over the town with its closely packed, slanting rows of houses. As they got out to join the general camaraderie of the walk into Tonypandy, Gwen began to realize the scale of what was happening. More and more people appeared, from cottages and villages over the mountains, increasing the thick column of people and banners. Herbert and Daniel struck up a conversation on the way with a group of men from the next town carrying an NUWM banner, which read, 'STOP STARVATION IN BRITAIN'. Gwen saw the poor state they were in, their clothes limp with wear and faces gaunt with malnourishment.

One told them about his wife's death. 'They said it was the tuberculosis,' he said, his eyes filling, 'but it all just wore her down. She half-starved herself for the rest of us. Wore herself into her grave, my Myfanwy did, and the little one followed soon after.'

They were all convinced there would be thousands at the demonstration. The only sour note was a woman on the edge of the town, on her step in her bonnet.

'You should all be kneeling before God on this Sabbath day,' she called shrilly. 'Not bowing to the idols of Bolshevism!'

Infuriated, Daniel shouted back at her, 'Does your God want children to starve then?' Scowling, he faced the front again. 'This is politics, not religion. Why can't they see that?'

Light clouds moved across the sun so that every few minutes they were bathed in its warmth. The mountains around them were so close that Gwen almost felt she could touch them. As they moved into Tonypandy, the streets were packed with people, flags and banners rippling around them in the breeze, and there were ragged outbreaks of singing among the crowd. Gwen felt her spirits rise and bubble into euphoria as they turned into De Winton Fields, the site of the demonstration, to the strains of

Then raise the scarlet standard high,
Within its shade we'll live and die . . .

She saw Daniel looking round at the hordes of people and red banners coming from all directions, his face breaking into a wondering smile.

Though cowards flinch and traitors sneer,
We'll keep the red flag flying here!

'Look at them all! That's unity for you, Gwen *fach*! At last the message is getting through. Look at us – there's thousand upon thousand here. We're far stronger than they could ever know!'

'I say.' Esther moved closer. She and Ernest were carrying a BCPL banner between them. Ernest looked quite radiant. Esther took hold of Daniel's arm. 'Let's see if we can get close to where the speakers are going to be.'

Gwen felt herself tense up angrily. Why was Esther grabbing Daniel like that, as if she owned him? Her odd remark from last night about Daniel came back to her. *Poor you!* Gwen seethed. Had Esther been warning her off?

Herbert, his thin, foxy face the most animated Gwen had ever seen it, was nodding enthusiastically. 'We want to make sure we hear Lewis Jones,' he said. His real hero was the NUWM leader Wally Hannington, but he was addressing the big demonstration in London that day. But Lewis Jones, a miner, had been elected as a county councillor in Glamorgan for the Communist Party – one of the only two Communist councillors.

They inched their way through the growing throng of people towards the speakers' platform. The morning seemed to pass quickly as De Winton Fields filled with more people than Gwen had ever seen together on one place before. Round them, people were singing and cheering. In front of her a banner read, 'BREAD NOT BATONS'.

At last, when the space was filled with demonstrators and police patrolling at the edges of the crowd, figures began to appear on the platform and a great cheer went up. A man came to the edge of the platform.

'Comrades!' he shouted. 'Why are we here? We are here to defeat the means test! The iniquitous regulations of the UAB!' Great rippling cheers and clapping followed each phrase, and it was some time before he could move on to the next. 'As we gather here, our comrades in London are marching on Trafalgar Square with the same demands . . .'

The first speaker was a local MP, then, after he'd finished, the strong, distinctive figure of Lewis Jones appeared on the platform. Gwen strained her ears trying to catch every word.

'Comrades!' he roared across the crowd, and they roared back in response. 'Can we, from this vast demonstration, call for five hundred men and women who will march on London and take the fight to the Labour Members of Parliament, both inside and outside the House, against these cuts?'

Lewis Jones was met by a vast swell of sound. He held up his hand until at last the shouting died down around the park.

'We can light the flame,' he cried, 'that will consume these iniquitous regulations, and with them the National Government which gave them birth!'

He was met by a huge, full-throated cry of enthusiasm which went on and on. Daniel was yelling and Esther and the others and Gwen heard herself shouting as she'd never shouted before from somewhere deep inside her, and she felt a power rise in her, as if something was unlocking, being untethered and she might lift off and fly free over all the heads in the park.

They were all exhausted during the long drive back to Birmingham, and Gwen had to give Esther credit for her stamina in keeping going. Ernest offered to take over more than once, but she replied breezily, 'I'm really quite all right, thank you. I'll let you know if I need you.'

Gwen slept for almost the entire journey, leaning alternately against the window and Daniel's shoulder, exhausted by all the newness and excitement and fresh valley air. She woke when Daniel gently shook her arm.

'Esther's going to drop us off,' he said. 'We're nearly there.'

It was dark outside. Daniel gave directions to Millie and Lance's place and soon Gwen was kissing Daniel goodbye and slipping into the dark hall. She switched on the light and looked at the clock. Nearly eleven o'clock. No doubt Millie and Lance would already have turned in. Could she make a cup of tea without disturbing them, she wondered?

The upstairs landing light was on, and when she crept upstairs, she saw that the light was also on in the little sitting room. Bother, she thought. Did that mean

Lance was still up, sitting reading the paper? She was so tired, and she'd hoped to be able just to go to bed without facing anyone else. If he was up, though, it would be better to go and speak to him and get it over with. She put her head round the door, ready to say something brief. Her heart hammered with shock. Sitting in the chair by the reading lamp was Edwin.

There was a silence as he sat looking up at her. At last he got to his feet.

'So – you've come back.'

Thirty-Three

Seconds passed. Edwin didn't move towards her.

Gwen looked at him, trying to adjust to the situation. She could still feel Daniel's goodnight kiss on her lips. Thank heavens he hadn't come up here with her tonight! Edwin's face was in shadow, but she could feel his gaze on her like a physical force.

'I suppose they know you're here?' She jerked her head towards Millie and Lance's room.

'Of course. I've been here half the day. They were charming to me. Even provided me with bedding, as you see.' He indicated the rolled-up eiderdown on a chair. 'Not that they seemed to know where you were either.'

His voice was clipped. She could feel the anger in him waiting to be released and she knew he was expecting her to tell him where she'd been.

'I'm sorry – if I'd known you were coming . . .' she said, taking a step back. 'Look – I'll put the water on. Would you like some tea?' She hurried out of the room, trying to gather her thoughts as she filled the kettle and put it to heat on the two-ring stove. She felt cruel and sinful, yet also certain somewhere inside herself. She pulled her shoulders back and went into the room, closed the door and leaned against it, feeling utterly weary at what was to come. But they had to pass through this, somehow.

'Gwen, for God's sake! How can you be like this? I don't recognize you!' Edwin moved closer. His pale hair was falling over his forehead and there was a terrible, strained expression on his face. To her horror she realized he was close to tears and that she had done this to him. He gave a shrug in which she could see great hurt.

'I've been patient, haven't I? But you never come home, you barely tell me anything of substance in your letters. My mother keeps asking for you, yours keeps making excuses for you! What the hell's going on? Don't you see that makes me feel a proper fool?' His anger subsided for a moment. 'Darling, we're getting married in a month's time and you're never there. I know you'd never be deliberately cruel, but you don't seem interested – in me or in our wedding. I feel as if you're ... you're lost to me.' This last sentence was said with desperation.

Gwen found it impossible to speak. If she told him, she had to make it real: Daniel, all that had happened, how she couldn't possibly go back to her old life. Now she knew starkly, seeing poor Edwin, that she couldn't marry him. Everything had changed. Yet putting it into words would be momentous. She stared back at him, at the open collar of his shirt, his pink neck, unable to look him in the eye.

'Where have you been?' He spoke quietly, but she could hear the swell of emotion underlying the question.

'To Wales. With some friends.' She pushed herself away from the door, picking a white thread off her sleeve.

'So you can go to Wales for a day, but you can't

manage Worcester?' He was barely able to contain his hurt and anger now.

'We went for a special reason.'

'Well, *what* reason?'

'A demonstration – against the UAB and the means test.' She looked into his eyes for a moment. 'It's breaking people, Edwin – it's persecuting the poor, the people who are already barely able to live. It's bad enough here, but in the Welsh valleys...' Her voice rose with excitement for a moment before she remembered that they had to be quiet. 'You should have seen all the people there – thousands and thousands all together! There was another demonstration in London as well.'

Edwin took another step towards her. Every line of his body was tensed.

'What are you getting involved with, Gwen? You're keeping secrets from me: you're like someone else! For God's sake, tell me what's going on!' He looked as if he was going to lay his hands on her shoulders, but he held back, clenching them at his sides. At last he began to lose his hold on his emotions. 'Tell me, Gwen. You're miles away from me. I don't know you any more and I don't know what's happened.'

She opened her mouth, then closed it again. It felt impossible to make the stride, in words, across her changed feelings. She barely knew herself either, she felt as if she'd left herself behind.

'You're not ... a Communist, are you?'

'I am, yes.' She had to seize the moment, to carry this through. Holding herself strong inside, she said, 'Edwin, I'm so very sorry. This is awful. You're a kind, good man and you don't deserve this. But I can't go on pretending. I can't marry you next month. I should have told you before and I . . . I couldn't.'

She saw him start to crumple, but then he held firm. He turned away from her and moved across the room until he could go no further. He stood with his knees pressed against the little coffee table.

'Truth at last, then. May I ask why?'

'I . . . I love someone else. Edwin, I'm sorry.' She knew she was hurting someone who didn't deserve it. She wanted to go to him, to offer comfort, but how would that help?

There was a long silence.

'And when exactly did you think you might get round to telling me, had I not come here?'

'I don't know.' Her weeping, suddenly, took her by surprise. 'I kept putting it off . . . It affects so many people. After term finishes on Tuesday, I was going to come home . . .' She knew she would have had to, but she had not even faced that yet. 'I'll have to tell Mummy . . .'

'And how long have you been *pretending*, as you put it?'

'Don't, Edwin—' She went closer to him, wiping her eyes.

'Don't what?' He turned to her, his face taut with hurt and anger. 'Don't ask for the truth? Don't expect to be treated with a bit of straightforward decency when my fiancée's run off with some blasted Communist agitator! D'you think I like being deceived and made a complete fool of?'

He picked up Lance's glass ashtray from the table and hurled it against the wall behind her. It smashed in halves on impact and clattered to the floorboards. There was nothing else on the table but the day's newspaper, so he threw that as well and it fluttered into a scattered mess. He stared round the room in contempt.

'Look at yourself! You don't belong here with these people. With all this political stuff. God, Gwen, that's what I loved about you when I saw you – when I walked into that schoolroom! You were so sweet and fresh, so unspoilt. I'd never seen anyone quite like you. You're so beautiful, and you belong there – with me – not here. Can't you see that? It's as if someone's put a spell on you!' He sank into a chair.

'I did belong there – but I don't any more.' She spoke gently. 'I feel terrible about this, Edwin. I haven't been able to face it because of how much it would hurt you ... But even when I was there, I felt...' She shrugged. Felt what? Stifled? Hemmed in? It was hardly fair to tell him that. 'I've changed. I needed to branch out. To grow into myself.'

Edwin looked up at her as she spoke. Seeing her determination, he put his head in his hands and let out a long groan.

'Was I holding you back? Can't you come home, grown and changed, and still let me love you?'

She had to hold herself very strongly against his expression as he looked up at her. His boyish face was full of hurt and longing.

'Oh, Edwin—' She knelt beside him. 'I can't. Because of Daniel.'

Steam was pouring out of the kettle. She made tea for them both, but found there was no milk. She could hear Edwin's defeated weeping in the other room. He was sitting back in the chair as she came in, and took the black, sweet tea she handed him, wiping his face. Gwen moved the eiderdown and sat opposite him.

'Why are you here today? It's Sunday.'

'Bernard gave me the day off. Said he was fed up with me mooning about and I should go and get myself sorted out.'

Gwen tensed. The reality of what she was going to have to face at home, everyone knowing, was awful to think about.

'Did you tell him then?'

'Not exactly, though it was pretty obvious. You haven't been near the place for weeks, have you? He's no fool.'

Gwen looked down into her cup. She thought about telling her mother. After a long silence, in which Millie's clock ticked, Edwin said very sadly, 'Don't you think you could come home and, well, give it a try? I mean, if you got away from here. Couldn't we recapture something?'

'Oh, Edwin.' Her eyes filled with tears again. Why was Edwin so decent? It might have been easier if he'd stormed and raged more, made demands on her. 'No. I really don't think we can. Well, I can't, anyway.'

'Tell me something.' Edwin spoke in a hard, distant way, looking into the empty grate. 'When you told me you loved *me* – were you . . . pretending? Lying?'

'*No.* Of course not. I just . . . I mean I do love you, Edwin. And I care very much about what happens to you. I'm thoroughly ashamed of myself for causing you so much pain and trouble. But things change. *I've* changed. Because I've found that you can . . .' She was groping for the words. 'You can expand and discover that you can love more deeply than you ever realized.'

Edwin nodded. 'I see,' he said bleakly.

He left early to catch a train the next morning. Lance was up getting ready for school as well, so they said their goodbyes down in the hall.

'You will have to come home and face up to it all.' Edwin was distant now and on his dignity, not allowing the sadness of the evening before.

'I know.' They stood just inside the front door. 'Edwin, I'm so sorry.'

'Yes,' he said bitterly. 'So am I. You really haven't behaved very well, Gwen.'

'No.' There was nothing else to say.

He leaned down and gave her a quick, impersonal peck on the cheek, and then he was gone. She stood on the step in the mild, wet morning, watching him walk away, his strong, steady walk, the light hair. Every line of him gave off reliability. She knew how good he was, yet even now in her guilt and sorrow for him there was something about the sight of him that made her feel earthbound and restricted. She couldn't go back.

'You be happy,' she whispered after him. Tears ran down her cheeks. 'Someone else'll make you happier than me.' A moment later he turned the corner and was out of sight.

'Settle down now for the afternoon register, please!'

Gwen watched fondly as Form Four settled, wriggling in their chairs, or turned from chattering to face the front. After the emotions of the night before she felt a sudden lightness, a relief that it was over at last. She had done wrong, she had hurt Edwin terribly, and she would have to face the wrath of her parents. But she was free! She didn't have to go home, she was earning her own living, and she could be with Daniel, her beautiful Daniel. Ron Parks's cheek was still bulging with something, even though the dinner hour was over. Gwen looked sternly at him.

'Ron? You're not eating sweets are you?'

'No, Miss Purdy.'

The boy hurriedly swallowed whatever was in his mouth. The whatever-it-was was rather large and Ron gulped. Gwen was reminded of a snake swallowing an egg. She tutted.

'Do you need a drink of water?'

'No, Miss Purdy,' Ron gasped, eyes goggling.

'All right. Well, don't come in here with your mouth full again. You'll choke.'

She opened the register.

'Donald Andrews?'

'Yes, Miss Purdy.'

'Joan Billings?'

'Yes, Miss – Purdy,' Joan said absentmindedly. The thought flashed through Gwen's mind that she would never, now, be Mrs Shackleton.

'Lucy Fernandez?' Mrs Fernandez? Would she be that instead?

'Yes, Miss Purdy.'

Tomorrow they'd be handing out a few prizes for achievement to some of the children. Lucy was outstandingly the top child in Form Four. No one took the rise out of her or called her 'cripple' any more. She could run rings round most of the others in class.

Gwen passed the place in the register where Joey Phillips's name was crossed out. She could still see his ghostly little face looking at her from the empty space where he used to sit. The memory came to her of the half-seen figure pressed against the railings of the play-ground that spring day. Had that been Joey? What on earth could have happened to him?

When she had reached the last name she put the register away.

'Now, all of you, I've got something to tell you.' Her heart beat faster. 'When I came to teach you this year, I thought it was only going to be for a little while. But things have changed. I went to see Mr Lowry this morning and it has been decided that next year, when you come back into Form Five, I shall be your form teacher again.'

She heard a little gasp from Lucy Fernandez and saw the child's face light up with delight.

Thirty-Four

'Joey – come on. Let's get back.'

John's high, wooden-sounding voice came to him over the barrows, all packing up for the night in the Bull Ring, which they were passing through on their way back. Joey dived under one of the stalls, seeing the murky orange of half a dropped carrot no one else had spotted and crunched into its earthy sweetness. There was still a long walk ahead and his belly was gurgling with hunger.

'You again!' the stall owner called after him with mock annoyance. 'You'll put me out of business you will, young nipper!' He watched Joey scurry after John. 'Poor little bleeder,' he remarked.

The Bull Ring was full of late-afternoon activity on this mild summer evening. There was a whiff of ale coming from the pubs in Digbeth, and the faint aroma of meat cooking on the breeze with the smells of rotting fruit and vegetables, cauliflower stalks and crushed apples trampled underfoot. Someone was singing loudly as he shut up shop for the night, shop awnings were being put away and someone was playing a slow, idle tune on the accordion by Nelson's statue. A newspaper seller was shouting about Spain. The working day was over and most of the men were heading off to the pub. They were passing one man when Joey saw a little head pop out of his breast pocket and tiny, bright eyes fixed on him. Joey jumped, startled.

John chuckled. 'That's old Ted with his ferret – he's the rat catcher at the station.'

Fascinated, Joey turned and watched the man go by, and almost collided with a market trader.

'Oi – watch where you're going, will yer!'

Ignoring him, Joey took another bite of the carrot, staring into its orange core.

'We've had a good day today,' John said. They'd spent the day filling boxes with metal brackets at the back of a warehouse. The gaffer had turned a blind eye and let Joey stay and work as well. Now they were well set up with a bag of taters, cabbage and scrag end. 'We'll stop for a drink.'

They went to a pub in Digbeth that Joey remembered going to once before, called the Royal George. John went in while Joey sat on the step outside with a glass of lemonade. It tasted delicious. He listened to the rumble of male conversation inside, amid the wafting smells of beer and cigarette smoke. He still had the little stalk of the carrot in his hand and he threw it under the wheels of a tram as it came up the sloping street. Now and then someone passed him, going in or out. One or two men spoke to him, but the rest ignored him. Sitting down now, he noticed the soreness of his feet. His socks were in tatters and what was left of them had almost grown to be part of his feet. The boots, which had been so big, now almost fitted. He looked down at his grimy legs, bare between his short trousers and the boots. It felt strange seeing them. His body was something he took no notice of normally. His hands came into focus, bony, gnarled, with long nails, dirt scraped under them, cupped round the glass, which although scratched and murky, felt like a jewel in his hands. He held it up to the light and saw blurry shapes through it. Slowly he sipped the lemonade, making it last.

The voices inside grew louder: men shouting, drunken and quarrelsome. At first he took no notice. In a few seconds something in the sound started to vibrate inside him. He began to shake. He didn't know what was happening. The voices came closer, two men brawling in the pub doorway. They were coming out and they passed him, dark trousers and boots. One of them shouted a final oath and stormed off along the road. The other stood swaying, calling after him, slurred and loud. The voice sank into Joey. He looked up at the beaten-looking man standing with his legs braced apart to steady himself, at his pale, pinched, familiar face.

Joey managed to get to his feet. His legs felt rubbery. He stood looking up at the man, whose cheeks were covered in stubble, his eyes glassy with drink.

'Dad?'

Joey didn't need to ask. He knew who it was, that hunched back which had moved away from them all along the entry that cold morning.

'Dad, it's me. Joseph.' He had to struggle almost to remember his name. It felt a long time since he had been Joseph Phillips. 'It's Joey.'

The man's gaze swivelled towards him. At the blankness in his father's eyes, Joey felt something give way inside him.

'Dad!' He grabbed the man's arm, pulling at it in a frenzy. 'Dad, it's Joey! You're my dad – and Lena and Kenny and Pol's! Dad – *Dad*!' Sobs choked out of him. 'There's no one else, Dad – I dunno where they've all gone!'

Wally Phillips jerked his arm violently, sending Joey tripping and stumbling backwards. He landed on the hard step and jarred his back.

'Get off of me, yer little bugger! What're you playing at? Go on – gerroff!'

And Wally staggered off up Digbeth, cursing and shouting.

Joey watched him go, his back disappearing again.

And then he couldn't see. Trying to look out through his tears was like looking through the blur of the murky pub glass.

Summer Holidays

Thirty-Five

Gwen didn't see the *Daily Worker* until Wednesday, the first day of the summer holidays. She read Monday's edition in the party offices, sitting near Daniel as he banged away on a typewriter, scowling with concentration. The room was abuzz with activity. The nationalist uprisings against the republican government in Spain had galvanized the party into action in a way none of them had seen before. New members were joining at an unprecedented rate.

'ANSWER TO THREAT ON SPAIN' read the banner headline. 'THOUSANDS CHEER POLLITT'S CALL TO ACTION.'

Most of the news was about the London demonstrations. Harry Pollitt, General Secretary of the Communist Party, had been speaking in Trafalgar Square.

'You not only have to reckon with the people of Spain,' he had told the huge crowd, thundering a challenge to the fascists and militarists. 'You have to reckon with the people of every land where democracy is in existence. Behind the Spanish people stand millions of men and women of all political parties who are not going to stand idly by, while your gang of parasites, moral perverts and murderers get away with it.'

Gwen read the report about the march on Tonypandy, swelling with pride. They had been part of this great movement, making things happen!

'Sixty thousand of us, it says here!' she exclaimed to Daniel.

He looked round at her, his face intense. 'That's just the beginning. Our time's come. We've got to carry it through now.'

She could never have foreseen how totally their lives were about to be taken over by the party. What had begun as a nationalist uprising in Spain quickly turned into a civil war, and the Communist Party seemed to be the movement responding most promptly and vocally for the republican cause.

Gwen spent almost all her time now with Daniel and the other party workers. Daniel was in constant demand as a speaker.

In the early days of the war in Spain, it looked as if cooperation between the Communist Party, the Labour Party and the Birmingham Council for Peace and Liberty would be possible. 'About time they saw sense,' Daniel said. 'We can't afford divisions now.'

Of course they all had to work together to fight the evil of fascism! There were to be joint meetings and rallies all round the city, public addresses in parks and halls and at factory gates in support of the workers' organizations in republican Spain.

The party offices were in a constant fever of activity: organizing meetings, printing leaflets, organizing speakers and 'chalkers' to announce them. Now the holidays were here, Gwen was free to throw herself into the work, caught up in the emotional intensity of it all. A national committee was formed, the Spanish Medical Aid Committee, especially to support the republic.

All of them were caught up in a cause bigger and more important than their own needs and lives. Gwen found herself feeling ashamed of her petty jealousies about Esther Lane. She didn't much like Esther whose bossy ways grated on her, but she could see her genuine commitment to the cause. And Daniel was far too busy to be paying Esther any attention. The truth was, he was almost too busy to pay any to Gwen either, but she swallowed down her periodic feelings of rejection and neglect. They were working for the party, for the revolution, compared with which individual feelings were as nothing.

One morning when Gwen arrived, the offices were already very busy. Esther was talking on the telephone in a loud voice to someone from a church group supporting Spanish aid, party workers were moving busily to and fro and a collection of cartons was piled just inside the door.

'What are these?' she asked Daniel, who was poring over a paper on a desk with Jim Crump, one of the main party officials.

'Pamphlets. From King Street,' Daniel said, without looking up. 'Can you get some of them out? We're going to the works along Bradford Street today – we'll start with them there. We've asked them to send more for the sixteenth.'

King Street was the party's national HQ. Gwen reached into the top box and pulled out a handful of red pamphlets. They were titled simply, *Spain*. The party was planning a special demonstration in the Bull Ring.

By the late afternoon that day she went out with Daniel and some of the others to Bradford Street in time for the end of the factories' afternoon's shifts, carrying bundles of the *Daily Worker* and the *Spain* pamphlet. Daniel had his big canvas bag slung over his shoulder. Gwen walked beside him, though he felt remote, caught up in his work. And Herbert began needling him again about the Catholic Church and its role in Spain. How could he be a Catholic when the Church was officially backing the nationalist cause?

'Don't start,' she heard Daniel say tersely. He was frowning and she could hear the tension in his voice.

The Fernandez household was full of anguish over this. Theresa read the Catholic paper, the *Universe*, which was full of reports about Catholic neighbours killing one another, churches being burnt, nuns and priests being dragged out and shot by republicans, the very people whom Daniel was ardently supporting and she frequently said so. Gwen knew that Daniel, like many Catholics on the left, was torn in two by the dilemma and she was tempted to tell Herbert to shut up and leave Daniel alone.

They reached Bradford Street just before the factory bulls began to go off at the end of a shift. When the men streamed out of the works they were waiting with their pamphlets and papers. Sometimes a sympathetic factory worker would take a copy of the *Daily Worker* and leave it in the factory toilet, so others could get a look at it. Gwen handed the *Spain* leaflet into dirty, workworn hands. Some men appeared interested, but others said, 'No, ta,' with tired indifference, while others called them 'bloody reds' or walked straight past, ignoring them.

'There's a meeting in the Bull Ring – every Sunday evening,' Daniel kept telling them. 'Come and join us, comrades. Unite the workers. Together we are strong!'

By the evening, Gwen was off with Daniel on the

speaking trail. Some evenings he did several, one after the other, and they had to have a car to get the speakers from one place to the next. Tonight there were only two meetings: Saltley followed by Alum Rock, and for once Esther needed to be elsewhere. Gwen sat in two drab halls, her stomach rumbling with hunger, while Daniel spelled out to his audience with apparently tireless passion the iniquities of the National Government and the means test, the betrayal of the working class by the Labour Movement, the plight of the Welsh mining towns and the Spanish republican causes of justice, collectivization and the power of workers' movements. In the car on the way back he was still full of life.

'I could see it in some of their faces tonight,' he said, on fire with his own oratory. 'They were hearing me. Really hearing. It's no good, see, thinking you can just go out and feed people propaganda. It's like Comrade Lenin said – the people have to have the political experience *for themselves*. They have to be *reborn* politically. They have to feel it in their *blood*.'

Gwen listened, leaning against his chest, tired and hungry. She could feel when he took a breath, the strong muscles of his chest. She leaned round and looked up at him.

'Do we have enough money for fish and chips? I'm ravenous.'

Daniel laughed, though she could sense his impatience with her. He wanted response, debate. 'You don't leave the ground for long, do you?'

'Well.' She was determined not to rise to this. 'An army marches on its stomach – that's what they say. Anyway, aren't you hungry too?'

'Come to think of it, yes.'

She looked solemnly up at him. She was longing to spend some time with him. Although they were so much in each other's company, they were seldom ever alone these days. She put her lips right up to his ear.

'Are you coming back to Millie's?'

Both of them knew what she meant. That they would sneak up the dark stairs, make love in the dip of the old bed. That she would hold him close, longing for a day when he would not have to get up and creep out again, to the dark streets, but that day had not come, nor could she see that it was going to. She would have to be content with being left to sleep alone.

'D'you want me to?'

'I wouldn't have asked otherwise, would I?' She kissed the tip of his nose.

'You're a very forward woman.'

They were both whispering, trying not to laugh and attract the attention of the party worker who was driving them. She *was* forward, she thought. Sometimes she felt like someone different altogether. Who was the person who had lived in Worcester and had been going to marry Edwin Shackleton? Did she miss her? No – scarcely ever. In those moments she was perfectly happy because Daniel had come back to her again, to be close, and that was all that mattered.

Daniel squeezed her. 'I'm coming with you all right.'

Going back to Millie's now felt like retreating into a different and increasingly irrelevant life, and the more caught up she became with the party the more glad Gwen was to stay out, even though it made her feel guilty.

Millie was seven months pregnant and was feeling huge and ungainly. Now the heat of the summer was here she was suffering with swollen ankles. The doctor had told her to rest and keep her feet up as much as possible, so she was no longer able to escape to her mother's as often as she had done. Her face was puffy and her hair hung limp and straggly so that she looked quite altered. She was always complaining about her hair, of which she had been rather proud until now.

'Why don't you go and get it trimmed?' Gwen had asked the day before, trying to be patient as she bustled about, just in from the party offices. There they were, she and Daniel, involved in making the revolution happen and all Millie could think about was her hair. 'It'd make you feel better.'

'Oh, it all feels too much effort.' Millie was sprawled along the couch, sipping a cup of tea. 'And Lance will keep on about me spending money. You know what he's like. There's some tea in the pot if you want it.' Reproachfully, she said, 'Where've you been again? You're never in. I thought now school had broken up you'd keep me company more.'

'Oh, I will – I'll try.' Gwen took her tea and sat on the chair opposite.

'You're always with Daniel, I suppose?'

Gwen felt her face light up at the mention of his name.

'Mostly, yes.' She managed not to make a face at the tea, which was lukewarm and bitter.

Millie sighed and looked at her. 'I don't understand you. I thought that Edwin chap of yours seemed very nice.' After Edwin's arrival and Millie and Lance having to look after him, Gwen had had to explain what was going on.

'He *is* nice. I just don't feel for him the way I do for Daniel.'

Millie almost glared at her. 'You're really *in love*, aren't you?'

'Yes.' Gwen was aglow.

'What does that feel like?' Millie pushed herself up a little on the cushions. Her ankles were mottled and puffy. 'What does being "in love" really feel like?'

All Gwen could feel was a deep stirring inside her. How could you ever put that into words?

'I'm not sure I can tell you. I just know I am.'

Millie sighed, putting her cup and saucer on the table. 'Better you don't tell me, anyway,' she said grumpily. 'I'd better not know what I'm missing. I'm not going to have the chance to find out now, am I?'

On 16 August there was a Communist Party weekend for Spain in Birmingham with a rally in the Bull Ring. Gwen stood out in the sun selling the *Spain* leaflets, looking over the sea of heads at the CP and BCPL banners and straining to hear the speakers as they railed against the neutral stance Baldwin's government had taken on Spain. Between them they sold five hundred pamphlets in the centre alone, and there were other meetings scattered round the city.

As Gwen patrolled Spiceal Street that afternoon with her leaflets, a figure came towards her from the crowd whom she suddenly recognized. Small and urgent looking and dressed in a baggy cream frock patterned with huge blue roses.

'Hello, dear.'

'Oh!' Gwen was startled. It was so strange to see another of the school staff in a different place. Though with Lily Drysdale it seemed less strange. 'Hello, Miss Drysdale . . .' Her mind raced. Lily Drysdale was here at the rally. Had she just come as an interested bystander or could it be that she too was a party member?

'I'm a supporter of the BCPL,' Lily Drysdale announced. Lily's dress had short sleeves and with her soft, rounded arms protruding from them, she looked rather attractive. 'Are you a Communist? A member, I mean?'

Gwen blushed. 'Yes, I am,' she said defiantly.

Lily nodded. 'Well, I can understand it. But if I were you, dear, I'd keep very quiet about it when you're at school. Mr Lowry doesn't hold with that sort of thing. You don't want him finding out.' She squeezed Gwen's arm for a second. 'See you about the place.'

As she walked away, Gwen saw a tall, bearded man join her, at her side. Gwen watched, fascinated. Was that Lily Drysdale's secret lover, whom Millie had told her about? No wonder Lily knew when to keep quiet!

'Letter for you.'

Millie slipped the envelope under Gwen's bedroom door with a slight grünt. It was the following Tuesday and Gwen was getting ready to go out again. The writing was familiar but it took her a moment to recognize, with a horrible jolt, that it was her father's hand.

The reality that she was supposed to have been marrying Edwin this coming Saturday flooded in on her. She had behaved so badly, not going home to face things, to sort it out! When Edwin had left here, the pain of her answer to him written on his face, she had known he would be the one to tell her parents. How shameful that she had left him to face it for her! She sat down on the bed, her heart thudding, telling herself she was lucky to get away with just a letter. Her parents might have arrived on the doorstep to remonstrate with her. At the same time, the fact that they hadn't taken the trouble to was hurtful. She was the one in the wrong and should have gone home. Yet they didn't care enough to come and find her.

She stared at the envelope. Perhaps she'd delay opening it until tonight. But then the dread of it would hang over her all day. Shakily she got up and found her paper knife to slit it open. The letter did not even cover a whole side of the paper:

Gwendoline

Just her name. He couldn't even bring himself to write 'Dear'. He wrote in deep blue ink, with his precise, pharmacist's handwriting.

Your mother and I have waited for you to come
home and explain yourself, the least you could
manage in the circumstances. Instead, it was left up
to poor Edwin, who has been treated atrociously.
You have behaved in a deceitful, cowardly and
selfish manner, bringing shame and acute
embarrassment to your mother. Have you even
given a thought to all our friends and to all the
preparations which were in train? I would never
have expected anything like this from my own child.
A complete disgrace.

It's no good coming back now, thinking you can
make amends. Your mother and I feel that we have
washed our hands of you. She can't bring herself to

communicate. Since you seem to want to live an independent life you'd better consider that you have left home. Don't think you can just come running back when it suits you.

Your Father

Thirty-Six

'Ah, come on – dance with me!'

John was squatting by the grate, trying to rouse a fire to cook on for when Christie came home. The doors were all open and the summer breeze blew along the hall from the garden. They lit the fire even in daylight now, risking it. The evenings stayed light too long to wait that late for food.

Siobhan was worrying at his shoulder, trying to force him.

'What's with you, John? ... John, John, John ...' she chanted in a sing-song voice. 'Will you not come and have a dance with your little Shiv? You're a funny kind of a fella, John ...' She jigged around him like a sprite, dark hair lifting and falling, then prodded him again.

John kept his head down, blowing on the smoking sticks in the grate. Joey was crouched beside him, wrapped in a filthy old curtain that had been left in the house. Underneath, he was naked as a babe, except for his boots. He could feel the heaviness of the curtain's dusty fabric against his back. Inside him was a tight, swelling sensation. *Why* did John bring the stuff for her? *Why* the bottles? *Why* make her be like that? Her voice was sweet now, cajoling, but he knew it wouldn't last, that her mood could turn in a split second. Joey sat with the edges of the curtain gripped tightly in his fists.

Siobhan snatched her hand away from John's shoulder.

'You're not natural!' Her tone was hard, and edged with spite now. 'You're not a real man, are you, John? What's the matter with you – you're a girly, John Cliff, that's what you are!'

Joey got up and ran over the loose tiles out into the garden. He didn't like the feel of being naked. The curtain wafted round him, puffing little breezes against his skin. It made him remember the Christmas play at school, the kings adorned in old curtains. That was before Miss Purdy came, Christmas was. He knew she hadn't been there then. This curtain, under the dust and filth, was a deep red with gold swirling patterns across it.

Earlier Siobhan had been tender with him, and motherly, as she could be sometimes, though that frightened him too because sooner or later her mood would change and you could never tell when. The deep, frightening hunger to be held welled up in him. It had been different when Miss Purdy held him. But Siobhan was dangerous.

'You're a filthy urchin, sure you are,' she said when he and John came back that evening. She had seemed quite well, cheerful even and with sudden energy. 'We're going to wash those clothes of yours, what's left of them, God love you. Will you look at those shorts – there's no arse left on them! John, can we not get hold of something else for the child to wear? These rags are almost dropping from him!'

'S'pose so,' John said in his wooden tones.

'Come on now, fella, get them off – you can give yourself a scrub then cover yourself with this.'

Joey looked down at his little pile of clothes when

he had removed them. They were nothing more than a pile of rags. He gave himself a quick wash with the cold water, feeling strange with the air on his skin.

Siobhan kept going on at him. 'Come on, now – get some soap round that neck. Will you look at the filth on you!' She was strange and overexcited. He didn't like it and escaped as soon as he could, wrapping himself in the curtain while he was still wet. Siobhan pummelled at the clothes in the old sink at the back with a sudden burst of energy. She had wrung them out and now the clothes were laid across the bushes and brambles outside. The vest was worn so thin you could see through it and there were holes all over it. The clothes weren't yet dry, but he put them on anyway and felt safer.

The air was warm and balmy. Now that summer had come and the leaves were all out, the house was completely secluded at the back. They had all relaxed about the worry of being discovered. The house next door was empty and in bad repair and no one further along seemed to want to know. In the spring there had been pink and white blossom on the two apple trees and now they were covered in tiny, unripe fruits. Joey had given himself belly ache by gnawing at them long before they were ripe. He had had to stay in that day, curled up with cramps.

Sitting on the back step, he shivered in the wet clothes. His boots were dry and bleached, the leather moulded to his feet. At least they fitted now. The feet had gone from his socks, just rotted away, so now he wore the boots with nothing inside. He pulled them off, enjoying the feel of air on his feet, and wiggled his toes. His feet were filthy and callused, with rough, discoloured patches. He stared at them indifferently for a time. Then he realized he could hear Siobhan's voice inside, high and aggressive.

Things had got worse since Micky died and that priest came. That's how Joey remembered it. Before, there had been more times when she was peaceful, motherly to him. Those were the worst times. When she wanted to cuddle him and sing him songs like a baby which made him ache inside so that he had to push her away. He saw her as wearing a mask that would split open at any second to show her other face: crazy and frightening. At least when she was drunk and screaming like a witch he knew he was seeing the real thing: there could be nothing worse hidden underneath to leap out and hurt him.

Since that night she had been forever on at John for drink, begging and wheedling. Joey never understood why John bought it for her. It was almost as if he wanted to cause devilment. He bought cheap, harsh liquor, which was all he could afford, and night after night now she drank and sobbed and picked fights. Finally she would slump to the ground and sleep. But sometimes she just went out, slamming the door so that the house shook and returning long after Joey was asleep. She was never awake when he and John left in the morning. And she had money after those nights, which she gave to John for 'another drop' for the next night.

Hearing her again now, Joey got up, carrying his boots, and moved away into the shelter of the tunnel through the brambles, where there was no shouting and the light was green.

Christie stood with his head under the water pipe, washing the plaster dust from his face and hair. His trousers and boots were white with it. He stepped back and flung his head back, showering Joey with water.

'Oh – sorry little fella – didn't see you standing there!'

Christie tried to sound chirpy, but Joey could hear the flat exhaustion in his voice.

'All right, are you?' He pushed back his hair with his hands, trying to flatten it. Water dripped from his chin and rivulets ran down from his hair.

Joey nodded.

'Cat still got that tongue?' Christie's rough fingers chucked his chin.

Joey nodded again. Couldn't seem to find words.

'There's taters over the fire. Come on, now.'

Joey followed him. Things felt safer when Christie was there.

But not for long. Siobhan was swaying in the middle of the room, the bottle in her hand.

'He won't talk to me. He won't dance with me.' She looked down and after some time, managed to take a step forwards. 'He's . . .' She had to take time to think. 'He's a bastard . . . A freak . . . He won't listen to me. Won't take any notice of me . . .'

'Siobhan, for the love of God . . .' Christie's tone was despairing. He seemed past being able to summon anger with her. 'Sit down and we'll get some food into you . . .' He pulled the bottle from her hand, despite her struggle. She was too drunk and weak to be able to fight back and Christie flung it against the far wall. It smashed and Siobhan started to cry.

'You bastard, Christie, taking away my one bit of comfort in this world. I hate you . . . I do . . . you bastard *priest* of a brother!' The word priest held all the contempt she could muster.

She gasped all this out between sobs as Christie seized her arm and pulled her over to the mattress. Joey could sense a new intensity in Christie's mood. Joey stood stock still in the corner by the door. In his head he went back outside to the quiet green peace among the brambles and trees.

'No!' Siobhan shrieked and yanked away from him. 'Don't boss me! I hate you, Christie!'

'Sit down, I'm telling ye!'

In search of shelter from the shouting, Joey sank down in the dark corner, arms round his knees, rocking back and forth, his back slamming against the wall. *Not Christie . . . not Christie . . .* Christie was the one who didn't shout or drink, who was safe . . . He squeezed his eyes closed. *Make it stop . . . make it stop . . .*

Christie pushed his sister down roughly onto the the mattress.

'Why d'you bring it to her?' He turned on John, completely beyond control. 'How many times have I told you? A thousand times I've told you not to bring it to her!'

John stared dumbly at the pan of potatoes over the fire. This time it was Christie who went and shook him violently by the shoulders. 'What is it you're wanting, John, eh? The ruination of us? Can you not see it's like feeding poison to her – that she can't help herself . . .'

'She asks me for it,' John said without looking up. 'She wants it. So I give it to her.'

'You don't give me anything else, though, do you, you freak show?' Siobhan's harsh shriek rang across the room.

'For the love of God!' Christie was still shaking him. 'Can't you see what it's doing to her?'

Peering through his fingers, Joey thought Christie

391

was going to throttle John. 'What is it – are you stupid? You're an idiot, John . . .'

John got to his feet, hurling Christie away from him. He was taller than Christie and, roused to anger, he looked fearsome with his great curling beard. He stood with his legs apart, arms working. In his strange nasal voice, he yelled, 'I'm not an idiot! I'm not . . . Don't call me that!'

'Yes, you fecking well are for giving strong liquor to my sister – just look at the condition of her!'

'Don't call me that! Don't call me that!' John was howling, over and over, springing up on the balls of his feet as he did so, like a crazed jack-in-the-box.

'I'm going from here.' Siobhan dragged herself to her feet and started to make for the door.

'No, you're not – come back here . . .' Christie flung himself over to the door and stood backed up against it.

'Are you going to stand there all night to stop me?' she mocked. She could not stand without swaying.

'You'll not leave this room . . .'

It went quiet for a moment. John stopped shouting. Christie was panting and he and Siobhan stood close, their eyes blazing into each other's.

'There's you, Father Christie,' she goaded him. 'Always the hero, weren't you? Mammy's favourite – the priest, the family saviour . . . Couldn't save me though, could you, Christie boy? Couldn't stop me spoiling myself.'

'Shiv – for God's sake . . .' His anger was gone. He sounded close to weeping.

'I'm going to hell anyway, Christie. It's too late. My sin cries out to heaven for vengeance . . . and yours . . . you helped me and you know it . . .'

'You didn't leave me any choice.' It was barely more than a whisper.

'Move, brother. You'll not be able to stop me.' She seized the door handle and pulled on it impotently. 'Are you going to stand there all night? Just get out of my way, Christie!' It was a harsh shriek. 'You can't save me.'

He did not move immediately, but at last, caught in her burning gaze, released his weight from the door. In a moment, Siobhan was gone.

Christie came and sat by the hearth. He put his face in his hands. When he heard the sobs, Joey crept closer and sat beside him.

Joey sat up, hearing Christie move about, striking matches for the fire. Daylight forced into the room through crevices in the wood. No one was lying on Siobhan's mattress. Joey rubbed his eyes, got up and put his boots on. He had an urgent need to relieve himself so he went out to the garden and pee'd in the bushes. He looked back at the dark bricks of the house. The hour was very early, the sky hazy, and the garden was quiet except for pigeons somewhere in the trees and one on the roof, cooing and puttering. Joey liked the sounds it made. He could see its plump shape perched on the ridge beside the chimney stack.

Inside, John was still asleep. He hadn't taken his hat off to lie down but now it lay displaced by his head. Christie was blowing on smoking twigs.

'Where's . . .?' Joey began to ask.

'How the hell do I know?' Christie snapped.

Joey slunk away and sat in the corner. Normally, when he spoke harshly, Christie would come to him after, in a kinder mood and make peace. But not today. He brewed tea in silence and woke John. He handed Joey a jar of tea and a lump of bread.

'Where's Siobhan?' John said. He stared vacantly at the empty mattress.

'Not back. I don't know. There's nothing I can do just now.' Christie chewed in silence for a moment. 'I expect she's found a spot to sleep it off. She'll be right by tonight.' But his tone was desperate.

Joey spent the day with John shovelling coal for a firm at one of the wharves, and when they got back to the house, black from head to foot, Joey expected Siobhan to be there scolding him about coming home in a state when she had washed his clothes. In an odd way he was almost glad of the thought. It had seemed strange and empty without her there this morning. He noticed that John did not spend any of their earnings at the Outdoor this time, getting drink for her.

When they arrived home, the room was empty. John stood in the doorway as if he couldn't take it in.

'Where's Siobhan?' he kept saying. 'She's not here. Where's she gone?'

Joey thought if John said it again he would explode. How did he know where Siobhan was? Silently he went into the garden and began looking for sticks for the fire to add to the assortment of bits they'd picked up on the way home. He tried not to think about Siobhan. He shut her out of his mind.

But Christie's face, when he got back, cut through him. His gaze sweeping the room, his expression when he saw she was not there.

'Not been back?'

Their silent looks gave the answer. Without another word, Christie left again.

It was hours before he came back and he was alone and so weary he could barely move. John handed him the pan of food and he sank down by the remains of the fire.

'I've walked the streets for hours. I tried the pubs, the priest. Where would she go?' His voice cracked and he put the pan down. 'Oh God, where is she? Is she doing this just to anger me? I can't think she'd do that. She can't manage on her own. She's like a child . . . She needs me with her . . .' Once more he put his face in his hands.

Three days passed. A week. Each night they came home full of hope that she would be there, but each time the room was empty and there was no sign of her. Christie stopped looking for work and spent the days searching.

'I'm not calling the Guard,' he said. 'We don't want them coming here. If anyone can find her, I can.'

In the evenings he told them where he'd been, the streets, parks, pubs, churches. Then one day Christie did not come home either. They kept his food warm in the pan until late at night while they waited.

In the end, John said, 'He ain't coming, is he? We'll eat the rest of this.'

Between them they shovelled down the potatoes and stringy bits of meat.

Thinking of Christie, Joey could barely swallow the food. But then he thought, he should've come back at the right time if he wanted it. Too bad.

Thirty-Seven

The summer weeks were flying past. They lived and breathed the party, the meetings, the debates at the factory gates and in the parks, flags and banners flapping over the scuffed summer grass. Every day in the offices they pored over the newspapers for news about the Spanish campaigns: the nationalists' bloody push on Madrid, the waves of reprisals in the republican zone against the Catholic Church. Gwen watched Daniel as each fresh piece of news arrived. He showed no reaction, especially to his non-Catholic comrades, but she knew the situation hurt him deeply.

Gwen worried about him: the way he constantly drove himself. His face was thin, and sometimes he looked glazed from lack of sleep. She knew his mother was worried about him too. Gwen had grown very fond of Theresa Fernandez, and sometimes popped in to see her even if Daniel was not there. Theresa didn't often talk about her feelings, but one afternoon when Gwen paid her a visit, she said, 'See if you can slow our Daniel down a bit, will you, Gwen? He won't listen to me, course, but he's hardly been in his own bed these last few days. He's starting to look like a ghost.' Since the holidays had begun, she had dropped the formality of calling Gwen 'Miss Purdy', even in front of Lucy and the others.

Gwen avoided her eyes. Theresa was so upright

in her morals, Gwen knew it would never occur to her that the main reason Daniel had been away from his own bed so much in the past week was that he had been in hers. Millie and Lance had gone away for a few days to Gwen's great relief. They had started arguing more openly lately, as Millie got more heavy and uncomfortable and less tolerant about everything, especially her husband. Gwen and Daniel had been able to snatch a few hours together in the flat without anyone else about, before Daniel crept out in the small hours back to his own bed at home.

'He's so like his father,' Theresa sighed over her teacup. She looked tired and strained herself. 'On and on – driving themselves. They just can't seem to stop. I'd thought coming to Birmingham would end all that, but . . .' She shrugged. 'I can see it coming out in Dominic too. Heaven help us when he gets older.'

'Daniel says he wants to go back and see your brother and his wife,' Gwen said hesitantly.

'Our Anthony and Shân? Oh yes!' Theresa's eyes lit up. 'You see if you can persuade him, Gwen! Get him to take a rest for a bit. Knowing our Daniel, though, he'll go down there and be running up and down to Tredegar and along the valleys to every meeting he can get to! I don't know . . .' She looked forlorn. 'I'm proud of him, God love him, I really am. I know he's right and he's trying to do the best for all our people. I just don't want to lose him – have him go the way Arturo did.' She looked up at Gwen as if a light had just dawned.

'Tell you what – perhaps you could go with him? You could try and tie him down a bit!'

Gwen smiled at Theresa's obliviousness to the fact that accompanying Daniel was exactly what she already had in mind.

'Just for a couple of days,' she pleaded with him. 'You can spare a little while away – Esther and the others can take up the slack and you did promise your Auntie Shân . . .'

They were on their way back from a meeting in Small Heath Park, where voices had boomed through megaphones over the ragged crowd, while the ducks glided past on the pond behind. Daniel had not been speaking today: they had both been busy selling pamphlets and the *Daily Worker*. Gwen's few remaining pamphlets were in the bag slung over her shoulder. The two of them caught a tram into town. It was a great relief to sit down; her feet felt sore from standing in the heat all afternoon.

'There's just so much to get done here,' Daniel said, staring ahead of him. He was in one of his distant moods again, somewhere she felt she could not reach him, and he looked very tired.

Gently she touched his back. 'Your mother really wants you to go. We could take all sorts of things over for them – books for Billy as well.' As she spoke, Daniel gave a great exhausted yawn.

'See!' She kept a teasing tone in her voice. 'You're tired out all the time. You'll be no good use to the revolution if you collapse in a heap, will you?'

He came to himself suddenly, was with her again, and took her hand. She was filled with happiness.

'All right. Are you coming too?' He asked so carelessly that she was hurt. She had taken for granted that they would go together. Didn't they do almost every-thing together now?

'D'you want me to?' she asked uncertainly.

'Yes.' He squeezed her hand and forced a smile to his exhausted face. 'Course I do.'

The local train pulled into Tredegar late on the follow-ing Thursday afternoon, and they caught the branch line to Aberglyn. It was a warm, muggy afternoon, and they had both slept for much of the journey. But the air grew a little fresher as they toiled up the hill, along the narrow streets to Anthony and Shân Sullivan's house, Gwen carrying the bag with their clothes in and Daniel his mother's bundle. Smells of cooking came to them on the breeze.

They stopped for a moment, panting, and looking back down the street. Two barefoot, ragged children were tearing down the hill away from them, after a runaway hoop, a small black and white dog barking excitedly at their heels. A couple of people had greeted Daniel on the way up. Everyone here, Gwen thought, looked so worn and weary. So ill fed. The children playing outside had pinched faces.

'You did tell her I was coming with you, didn't you?' it occurred to Gwen to ask.

'I sent a telegram. All I said was, "Coming Thursday p.m. Bringing friend."'

'Honestly! You could have put my name!' She felt genuinely aggrieved. Fancy him sending a telegram about a 'friend' as if she were just anybody.

As they approached the houses higher up, they saw that Billy was sitting outside the front door. He soon spotted them and waved madly with both arms.

'Mam!' they heard him call into the house. 'Our Daniel's here!'

When Shân Sullivan stepped outside, Gwen was momentarily shocked by the sight of her. Her shawl had hidden the true extent of her emaciation the last time they met. Now she came to the door in an old pale pink frock with an apron over the top and Gwen saw the frightening thinness of her arms and neck, from which her faded hair was taken up into a loose bun at the back. But her tired face was full of pleasure at the sight of them.

'Daniel!' She came out through the gate towards them. 'Oh and it's you, Gwen *fach*!' She sounded startled. 'Oh, Daniel, you silly. Why didn't you say it was young Gwen coming with you? I thought you were coming with another of those boys from the party.' She kissed Gwen, a quick peck. Close up, Gwen realized she was probably no thinner than she had been the last time. Her wristbones were very prominent, her hands bony and raw from hard work.

'Billy's been waiting for you all afternoon! Come on, I'll make us a cup of tea. Oh, it's a treat to see you both!'

But as Shân turned towards the house, Gwen wondered if she imagined the momentary combination of worry and puzzlement in the other woman's eyes as they fixed on her.

'Daniel!' Billy was pushing up on the arms of the chair in his excitement.

'All right, Billy!' Daniel cuffed him again in his friendly way. 'Got something for you here. Pass us the bag, Gwen.'

He squatted down by Billy's chair. From the bag he pulled out a book and handed it to his cousin.

'There, that should keep you busy for a bit.'

Billy turned it over, stroking the red-bound cover.

'*World Politics, 1918–36*,' he read in awed tones. 'Rajani Palme Dutt. *Thanks*, Daniel.'

'Gwen's idea,' Daniel admitted. 'It's from this new thing, the Left Book Club.'

Billy shot Gwen a radiant look.

'Don't eat it all at once!' Daniel stood up again and ruffled Billy's hair. Gwen wondered if Billy minded being treated as if he were a child, but he grinned, seeming to enjoy it.

'I'll go and give Auntie a hand.'

Daniel went inside. Not liking to desert Billy, Gwen stayed out, enjoying the warm evening.

'How're you keeping?' she asked shyly, squatting down so that she wasn't towering over him.

'I'm all right.' He spoke guardedly, still fondling the book. Abruptly he looked round and words seemed to burst out of him. 'I say I'm all right. What else can I say when my mam's having to do everything for me like a baby?' He looked down, blushing. 'Don't know how long I can stand it, that's all.'

'Oh, Billy, I'm sorry.' She was surprised by this immediate outburst and somehow honoured by it, as if he had to say it to someone while he had the chance, with Shân out of earshot. 'Not much help to say that, is it?'

He shook his head. 'No. Not really. But at least I could say it to you. Don't know why.' He couldn't meet her eyes but the words kept pouring out. 'I try and keep a diary, see. I'm not much of a writer but it's someone to talk to. I'd've liked more schooling.' He gave a harsh laugh. 'Not much hope of that round here.'

'You like reading.'

'Oh yes. I like Dickens. He's a good long read –
Hard Times, that's my favourite. And *David Copper-
field* ... And Jack London...' Billy seemed to get
excited easily, with the least bit of stimulation and
encouragement. 'I read *People of the Abyss*. It was the
best book I've ever read. It's a proper demolition of
capitalism. Everyone should read it – everyone should
be made to, to understand! Have you read it?'

Gwen was just admitting that, no, she hadn't,
although she'd heard Daniel talk about it, when he and
Shân appeared with a cup of tea in each hand. Shân
handed Gwen her tea and perched on the doorstep,
patting the narrow space beside her.

'Come and sit here, Gwen. There's enough space
beside my old bones.'

Gwen obeyed, and they were so close together they
touched at the hips and shoulders.

'Billy was telling me about the books he likes.'

'Oh, he's a reader, all right,' Shân agreed.

Daniel was squatting beside Billy now, near the
gate. The two women watched them for a moment
in silence, the dark heads close together, Billy apparently asking urgent questions about Daniel's work.
Gwen glanced at Shân Sullivan and saw her watching
them. For a moment her eyes clouded with pain. Billy
looked so like Daniel in some ways that seeing him
must be a walking reminder of all that Billy might have
been.

'He wanted to go to the Labour College, like Daniel
did.' Shân spoke very softly. 'Full of dreams, he was,
right from a boy.' She sighed, hands clasping her cup
as if for warmth, although it was not cold. 'D'you

know, Gwen, if I could do it for him by giving up my own life, I would.'

'I'm sure he wouldn't want that.'

'No. But that's the truth. There's no life here for any of us the way things are. Survival level – that's how we live. Nothing but taters, one day to the next the winter through. Will there be enough for the next meal? How to save enough for anything to wear. Shoes!' She gave a grim laugh. 'When do we ever think we'll be able to afford shoes? Can't even afford the blacking for them!'

'Theresa's put some in for you, I think.'

'She's all kindness. And she sends us a bit when she can. That's more than many ever get. But that's not the point. The truth is, people here are wrung out with it. You go looking for a woman in this town who'll tell you she ever has a night she can sleep without worrying and you'll not find one. They've betrayed the miners' families – all of them. Bosses, government, unions – the lot. We've reached the end of the line. You know, I was never much one for politics. I never joined the party. Not till now. Even when Anthony became a Communist I still thought they were trouble, dividing up our people, dividing our *family*, then, was how it felt. I thought there must be another way. But if there is, I'd like to know what it is.'

Gwen was moved by the gentle woman's bitterness. 'Have you joined?'

'A fortnight back.'

Gwen could feel a smile tugging at her lips. 'Does Daniel know?'

'Not yet. I'll tell him inside.'

There was a pause. They drank their tea and heard

the murmur of the two men's voices. Then, gently, Shân said, 'When you came last time, with the others, I didn't know you and Daniel were . . . well, if you were courting.'

'Oh yes,' Gwen said. 'We are.' In her own voice she heard the effusion of all the love she felt for Daniel.

Shân was examining her closely. There was a strange closure in her expression suddenly that Gwen could not read, and Shân looked away. 'Well, that's nice.'

Gwen was hurt. Did that mean Daniel's aunt didn't like her? Didn't think her suitable for Daniel? It wasn't to do with being a party member. How could it be? The woman had just admitted to joining the party herself. She couldn't bear to talk about something else without clearing the air.

'Is there something wrong?' she asked.

'No, Gwen *fach* . . . What on earth makes you think that?' She stood up. 'And look you – here am I sitting about when that chicken needs the oven straight away!' She swayed, leaning against the door for support.

'Are you all right?' Gwen leapt up to help steady Shân, alarmed by her sudden pallor.

'What's up, Auntie?' Daniel ran to her as well.

'I'm quite all right.' Shân laughed it off, bending over for a moment. 'I just stood up too quick, that's all.'

Thirty-Eight

Shân did seem to be all right, and for the next couple of hours the smell of roasting chicken filled the little house. All the time, Daniel's aunt made conversation, obviously trying to keep things pleasant and cheerful, asking Gwen about her home and the school. Gwen found herself pouring out the story of little Joey Phillips, and as she told Shân what had happened and how he had gone missing, she found herself fighting back tears.

'Oh, the poor little lamb.' Shân stopped slicing the carrots and looked intently at her. 'What a thing. It's really touched your heart, hasn't it?'

'Yes, I suppose it has.' Gwen was surprised by her own emotion. She tried not to think about Joey normally, knowing there was nothing she could do about it.

Shân's eyes clouded. 'There's a harsh, cruel world we're living in, and no mistake. And you've a kind heart, Gwen, I can see that.'

By the time the meal was ready it felt like a celebration. When Anthony came home Daniel went out with his uncle to fetch a jug of ale and the five of them sat round the scrubbed table enjoying the chicken, potatoes and carrots, and a few beans which Gwen had help Shân pick from the tiny garden at the back.

'This is a real feast!' Shân said. Her pale cheeks had

some colour in them from the hot kitchen and she seemed more relaxed and younger suddenly.

'Let's raise a toast to our Theresa!' Anthony said, lifting his cup. He smiled across the table at Gwen. She had always assumed that Daniel was in every way like Arturo, his father, but now she'd met Anthony with his deep, rumbling voice and laughing eyes, she could see how much Daniel resembled him as well.

Shân wanted to hear all about the Fernandez family and Daniel told her all the news of his brothers and sisters.

'They think Dom should try for the grammar school,' he said.

'And will he?' Anthony looked up from his plate.

'I think he should. More education he can get the better. We'd have to pay for uniform and all that.'

'He always was a bright one,' Shân said. Gwen saw that she looked better for a good meal. 'And Rosa too – will she try? The others never wanted to, did they, Daniel – not after you!'

'Well, times were hard.'

There was a silence, in which Gwen again realized that there were so many things she didn't know about Daniel's family.

'What about little Lucy?' Shân asked. 'How's she getting on, now?'

'You'd better ask her teacher!' Daniel looked at Gwen.

'Oh, I was forgetting!' Shân laughed, a bubbling, full-hearted sound. Gwen saw Anthony look at her. She wondered when he had last heard her laugh like that.

'Lucy's a lovely child,' Gwen said. 'And she's easily

the cleverest in my class. If she has the chance to go to the grammar school, I'm sure she'd get a place.'

'Well now, who'd have thought?' Shân looked wonderingly at her. 'I suppose we all thought – you know, what with her leg, and the turns she had and that ... And she must be all grown up now. Oh, I'd so love to see them all.' Shân had not set eyes on most of the family since they left Wales four years earlier. 'Is she ... is her leg ...?'

'She's still wearing a caliper,' Daniel said. 'They think maybe she'll be able to walk without when she's older.'

Shân's eyes clouded. 'And the fits?'

'Still every so often,' Gwen said. 'Although I'd have said a bit less often than before?' She looked at Daniel, who nodded.

'She's full of beans. Mad about school – and her teacher.' His smile warmed Gwen across the table. 'Miss Purdy has done wonders for her.'

'Well, you were always the shining star in school I remember, Daniel,' Shân said.

Gwen looked at Billy. 'I bet you were too.'

'Oh, he was clever enough,' Anthony said brusquely. Billy flushed, and Gwen could tell this counted as high praise.

After that, the men could hold back no longer from talking politics. Billy asked Daniel about his work in Birmingham, and they were soon on to the NUWM in Wales. The government had brought in new unemployment regulations the previous month.

'Now we're two bob worse off that we were before,' Anthony said. He sat with his elbows on the table, rubbing his big, strong hands together. He spoke quietly, his voice deep, controlled, but the anger in it was unmistakable. 'There's got to be this next march. Something's got to be done to make them listen.'

'All the government does is bring out reports to tell us we're starving,' Billy said. ' "A Distressed Area." Not as if we need a report to tell us that, is it?'

'The party's behind another march,' Daniel said.

'It's got to be more than just the party. We need a national march – the Labour Movement, the workers. If it's just the party, they'll dismiss us as a bunch of reds. All in, full unity – that's what we need.'

In the shadow of the men's powerful voices, Gwen said quietly to Shân, 'You look so thin and tired. How are you managing?'

She saw tears rise in the woman's eyes, but Shân quickly wiped them away.

'It's all right – I'm just a silly. I get so tired all the time. There's no end to it, see.' She tried to smile, bravely. 'Every day if I go out all I see is working men standing on corners or going to meetings, when they should have a livelihood and all the while the pit's full of scab labour. And the women . . .' Against her will, her eyes filled again and she shook her head. 'I've seen some terrible things . . . The state of the place, of people . . . Sometimes –' she looked at Gwen and her face was hard suddenly – 'I just loathe all of it. Politics, all the talking and meetings and speeches. All the struggling. I want to be a family – normal, like, without it all . . . Selfish, there's what I am, I s'pose . . .'

'No, you're not selfish,' Gwen said. 'I think Theresa felt the same, didn't she?'

'Oh well, Theresa. After all that happened to her. I'm surprised she's not . . .' Shân cut off abruptly. 'Still – let's not dig it all up again.'

Gwen helped her as they cleared the plates away and made a cup of tea.

'Here, Billy – I can teach you the "Internationale" in Spanish,' Daniel was saying as they filled the teapot.

Shân's eyes met Gwen's over the cups and she gave her an uncertain smile, as if unsure whether to speak. Behind them, under Daniel's instruction, the men all burst into singing, '*Arriba, parias de la tierra...*' and Shân said, very quietly, 'You know how much politics means to Daniel, don't you?'

'Yes,' Gwen said, puzzled. 'He lives and breathes it – I'm used to that, if that's what you mean.'

'How long have you know him?'

'A few months. I only came to Birmingham this year.'

Shân nodded. Gwen felt herself tense inside. What was Daniel's aunt trying to say to her? At the same time, she felt she didn't want to know. She was about to turn away when Shân caught her wrist.

'All I'll say to you is this. Daniel's a good boy – I've known him all his life and you'll never find a more loving son to his mother...'

The men's voices rose for the chorus: '*Agrupémonos todos, en la lucha final. El género humano...*'

'It's just – I've never known Daniel put anything, *anything* before his politics. Not anything. Just remember that, Gwen *fach*.'

Billy was waving his cup as they sang, '*Es la internacional!*'

Gwen understood that this gentle woman was warning her, in the way Esther had tried to warn her too. But of what? She sat at the table with them all and Daniel didn't appear to notice her at all, even though she tried to smile at him. She felt cold inside and full of doubt.

Gwen slept in the little upstairs room again, but alone this time. Without Esther's voluptuous form beside her, she enjoyed lying across the three-quarter sized bed, between threadbare cotton sheets, looking round at the room in the light from the candle on the chest of drawers. To her left was a chair on which lay her blue frock and underclothing from the day, and to the right was the window, open a crack, through which came the occasional sounds of the night: a dog barking in the distance, a low murmur of male voices on the path outside.

She would have liked to stay downstairs and be part of the debate, but Shân had grown sleepy and when she suggested showing Gwen up to her room, it was hard to refuse. And it felt right to leave the men to talk. Anthony's voice was a steady rumble through the floorboards, Billy's chipped in, ardent and excited at times, and she could hear Daniel talking passionately, voice rising and falling. *The voice of the man I love*, she thought. He was there, doing the thing most dear to him. Sadly, she wondered whether the next day he would just go off with his uncle to meeting after meeting, or whether he would save any time for her. She didn't mind the thought of being left with Daniel's aunt: she was growing to like her very much and had a high regard for her. But Daniel had promised . . . 'We'll go up on the mountain when we go back there.' But she was learning with Daniel never to take anything for granted.

What had Shân meant by her warning? And Esther?

Leaning over to the chest of drawers, she blew the candle out and lay longing for Daniel, needing his reassurance. She felt miserable and alone. *It's like being in love with the Scarlet Pimpernel,* she thought. Would she ever be able to be sure of him? With a sigh she turned on her side and hugged herself, falling asleep in the muffled sound of his voice.

'So – are you ready for a walk?'

He was waiting for her when she came down the next day into a golden morning, beams of sunlight pouring through the little windows of the kitchen, motes of dust swimming in the light. Shân was at the stove, stirring a pan of porridge. Daniel stood, loose-limbed by the kitchen table, face dark with stubble, a teacup in his hand. Gwen had dressed in her slacks and a comfortable short-sleeved blouse, in the hope that he would honour his promise to walk out with her. She felt her spirits soar.

'Of course – I'd love to!'

It was a relief to be out of the house. Billy said goodbye to them without displaying any resentment.

'He's so brave, isn't he?' Gwen said as they set off up the hill.

Daniel nodded. 'Could have happened to any of us. I don't think I'd have managed it at all. It appals me to think of not being able to get about, stuck in with his ma all day ... And given a pittance for it – for a life ruined.' She touched his hand, moved by the bitterness in his voice, and he squeezed her fingers for a moment.

'I've never seen the town properly,' Gwen said as they left it behind and headed up to the mountain.

'Well, it's no size. Town hall, chapels, churches and

411

a few shops trying to scrape a living. They have a job surviving when there's no wages for anyone.'

They left the road and climbed the path. Daniel obviously knew the way intimately and she followed his assured stride up and up, as the path became steep and rocky. They stopped for a breather and looked down over the town, a tight scattering of buildings strung along the valley, towards the pithead, the railway passing through like a steel spine, and the enclosing hills around in varying shades of green and grey. The slow-moving clouds passed as shadows over the valley.

'It's so beautiful,' Gwen said. They were both breathing heavily. 'Did you come up here a lot?'

'Oh yes.' Daniel shielded his eyes from the sun. 'With my pals – and Ann sometimes.' He pointed ahead. 'There's a seam over the other side. We came up here, she and I, when the big strike was on – we'd dig out as much as we could carry and bundle it up in a sack for home. Ann was always strong. We never got caught – it was illegal, see. The pit owners thought they owned that as well.' His voice was harsh and he seemed on edge, full of raw emotion. But at last he reached out and put his arm round her shoulders and kissed her, and they walked on further, still climbing.

When they reached the top of the rise the scenery opened out ahead of them, the peaks and shoulders of the hills all bathed in sunshine. It was one of the most beautiful places Gwen had ever seen.

'Daniel.' She had been wanting to ask him since the last time they were here but the right moment had never come. She could not forget the emotion in his voice when he had shouted after Hywel Jones that morning. 'You said that your mother was sent to prison?'

Looking up, she saw Daniel's jaw clench. He reached into his pocket for a cigarette and lit one.

'What on earth happened? Why her?'

'Oh, it was all a mistake,' Daniel said furiously. 'Whyever would our ma go to prison? They treated her like . . . like dirt.'

For a moment they walked in silence. She could feel the hot sun like a pressure on her face.

'It was after our da died. Only a month or so. There was all sorts of trouble. Up until then there'd only been a handful of scab labour here in Aberglyn. But then it started. There are rules in the pit, see, always have been – about seniority, who works where. A pecking order, if you like. The management wouldn't keep to it. This was in the spring of thirty-two. There was a protest and they locked them all out again. I wasn't here then, not just as it started. I was at the college, see. Anyway, they started to bring in scab workers from round the valleys. Course they were starving, needed work like anyone else. You couldn't blame them in a way.'

He paused to take a drag on the cigarette. 'Most days there was a crowd out early, protesting behind the scabs when they came to the pit, shouting and that. This particular morning Lucy was ill with a fever. She wasn't even two years old. Ma had been up half the night with her and she . . . well, she should've got someone else to get the doctor – Mary or Paul. But she wasn't thinking straight. She was in such a state, I s'pose. Da'd died and she didn't have the money to call the doctor out. I suppose she panicked and thought if she went to him ... It was only just getting light and she went out with Lucy wrapped in a shawl. Course the streets were filling up and she got caught up in it. The police were waiting and there was a baton charge – all hell let loose. Ma was just at the edge of it, she said, but this policeman grabbed hold of her – arrested her and another woman who was nothing to do with it.

'Ann and Mary were at home and they didn't know what had happened for a time. It was the neighbours who saved us. The Prisoners' Aid Society tried to take Lucy away from Ma – said she wasn't a fit parent. They wouldn't listen, she said. She tried to tell them her husband had died and all of it, but no one heard a word. She was issued a summons for unlawful assembly and they sent her to prison for two months in Cardiff ...

'Ann sent me a telegram and I came straight home. Everyone had banded together and offered to pay our rent. And they threatened to go and wreck the pit if Lucy was taken away. Mary and Ann got her back off the Prisoners' Aid people and we all managed the best we could. There were enough of us old enough to manage. But we were all worried sick about Ma. She wasn't considered a political prisoner, so they put her in the reception part, dishing out the rags of clothes they had. But she was in a state over Da. She'd lost him so sudden like, no warning. And she was worried about all of us. Pining really, she was, as well as torn apart with the injustice of why they put her there. And then she fell sick. She was so bad they had to release her to go to the hospital in Cardiff. We thought she was going to die in there. Ann went down once and managed to get in to see her. She was so delirious she didn't know who Ann was ...'

Daniel stopped talking abruptly and Gwen looked round at him, shocked to see he was fighting back tears. He ground his cigarette stub fiercely under his heel.

'The worst thing was not being able to do anything. We were stuck. And the way people helped ... There was a lady along the road, a Mrs Morgan. Her husband was dying then. Miner's lung. Coughing and gasping all day long. She'd never been one to have much to do with us – chapel lady, and us being Catholics. But she came along every day after she heard, to see if we were managing, giving us a loaf she'd baked, or a pan of broth. And her hands were twisted and hurt her all the time. But she was like an angel to us, Mrs Morgan was. She died the next year after him, God rest them both.'

He couldn't hold back his tears then, as if a well of tension was waiting to be released, even though he was embarrassed by his emotion. It did not last long, but she held him until he was quieter, her forehead pressed into his shoulder as she stroked his back.

'My love,' she said, as he quietened. 'Dear one – you're so tender-hearted.'

'I just want things to be right.' He looked out over her shoulder, reaching up to wipe his cheeks again. 'For everyone. For our people not to suffer so much ...'

Thirty-Nine

They were back in Aberglyn by the late afternoon, the grey walls of the town bathed in mellow sunlight. There were some people about and one or two greeted Daniel. They passed the Bethel chapel and a few poor-looking shops with very little to be seen inside them. Then they saw a queue of people waiting outside a door, and across the road a man sat at a small table talking to a couple of others.

'Labour Exchange.' Daniel nodded at the queue. 'It's pay day. There'll've been a queue right along the road earlier on.' He then nodded at the man at the table. 'Uncle Anthony was there this morning.'

The NUWM offices were straight across the road from the Labour Exchange and Gwen knew that their officials gave advice to the unemployed workers collecting dole, or being refused it.

'He doesn't get paid for doing it, does he?' Gwen asked, watching one of the men standing in front of the table, talking emphatically to the NUWM official seated behind it.

'No, no,' Daniel said. 'People pay in a contribution every week . . .'

The official suddenly caught sight of him and waved. 'Hello there, Daniel!'

Daniel waved back. 'Hello, Mr Gallacher!'

'Coming to the meeting tonight with your uncle, are you?'

'I'll be there!' Daniel said.

Everyone was looking at them by now and one or two more called out greetings. They walked along to the main square, then round by the back roads towards Shân and Anthony's house. They walked side by side, but without touching. Gwen was conscious of feeling watched all the time. This was a small community and anyone different attracted interest.

Shân was at the stove cooking when they got back. She smiled wearily. Billy had not had a good day, she confided quietly to them both. He had not been feeling too well, his stomach upset. He was having a lie down when they came in and he looked up, unsmiling and said a curt hello. But Gwen couldn't help feeling also that their presence was upsetting for Billy. When would he ever be able to walk out over the mountain with a girl? Or work or give his energy properly to the party? It wrung her heart to see him lying there with all his young energy frustrated, such a cruel sight after the day she and Daniel had spent.

Anthony was sitting by the back door on a stool, leaning forward with his elbows on his knees, intent on his copy of the *Daily Worker*. He looked up long enough to nod at them and say, 'Coming tonight, boyo?'

Daniel, downing a long drink of water, nodded.

Gwen waited to be asked as well, but it became clear that this was considered men's work. She felt hurt and indignant for a moment. Wasn't she a comrade as well and a member of the party? She didn't seem to be considered worth asking to the meeting and she would have liked to see the NUWM in action.

I'm not going to beg, though, she thought proudly.

And anyway — I'll stay in with Shân and Billy, poor things.

Everyone seemed tired at the tea table and they ate mostly in silence. The evening had grown close and muggy, as if a storm was gathering. Billy seemed to liven up a little with food and company. As soon as they'd finished the stew, which seemed to consist mainly of potatoes plus additions from Theresa's parcel, Anthony stood up and picked up his cap from the sill.

'Best be off, Daniel.'

'See you later.' Daniel got up and Gwen struggled once more not to feel affronted by her exclusion.

She helped Shân clear up the dishes and afterwards they sat by the hearth with Billy, playing dominoes and drinking tea. It seemed to cheer him up and Gwen realized that he enjoyed her company. He was especially animated when she asked him about his reading and he showed her his copies of his favourites: Dickens, Jack London and Elizabeth Gaskell's *Mary Barton*.

'I wish we had a proper library here like in Tredegar,' he said wistfully. 'It's not often I get hold of a new book and I like it better than reading the papers, see. You get into the story and it carries you along . . .'

'I'll see if I can send you some,' Gwen said, 'when we get back home.'

'Oh, would you?' Billy lit up.

'Don't go giving Gwen trouble now, Billy,' Shân said, but Gwen could see she was delighted.

'Would you write me a letter now and then? Only I get ever so bored and fed up sitting here. I'd like to hear from you.'

He asked so sweetly that Gwen could only say yes. She liked him, as well as feeling so sorry for what had happened to him.

'Will you write back?' she asked. 'If it's not too much trouble?'

'*Trouble!*' He beamed. 'It'd be . . . *magnificent!*'

The evening passed companionably, though Gwen sensed at times that Shân seemed distant, as if she had something on her mind. She felt like asking if everything was all right, but as things were so obviously difficult all the time it seemed a foolish question and presumptuous of her to ask it, so she kept quiet.

'Well,' Shân said at last, yawning and stretching. She had put her shawl on now the evening was a little cooler. 'We'd better get you to bed, Billy.'

'Let me help.' Gwen stood up.

'All I need is a hand to the bed,' Billy said hastily. 'I can do the rest for myself, ta.'

Between them, the two women helped Billy manoeuvre over to the bed from his chair, his arms over their shoulders. Gwen felt the strength of them, the potential power in his upper body, and it made more poignant the dragging uselessness of his legs. With dignity he removed his arms, not wanting to be helped a moment longer than was necessary. There was a light sheen of perspiration on his face and she saw that the exertion of getting to bed had cost him more effort than she'd realized.

'Goodnight then,' he said, smiling.

'Those men won't be back for a while yet.' Shân stood with her at the bottom of the stairs, arms folded, looking very tired. 'You know what they're like. Might as well get some rest.'

'Goodnight.' Gwen felt she would like to kiss the woman's cheek, but Shân was not a demonstrative person and Gwen wasn't sure it would be welcome.

She was turning to go up the stairs when Shân, in a

lowered voice, called her back. Gwen went to her. In the dim light she saw a tight, anxious expression in the woman's eyes. Her arms were clenched tight across her chest. She seemed to be deciding whether to speak.

'Gwen . . .' She paused again, seeming to struggle for the right words. 'Has Daniel . . . has he told you anything much about himself?'

Gwen thought about that morning on the mountain, his tears. She had never felt closer to anyone than she had to Daniel that day.

'Yes!' She knew she sounded defensive, and she felt it. Of course she knew Daniel! They had shared so much, and he had told her some of the most painful memories of his life. Why did everyone feel they had to interfere?

'Why?' Gwen was polite, but she knew there was still a challenge in her voice. 'Is there something I should be told?'

Shân shook her head slowly. 'No, it's all right, Gwen *fach.*' She spoke in a conciliatory way. 'Don't you worry. I was only wondering. You know what boys can be like – never open their mouths to tell you a thing. You go up and get a good night's sleep.'

As she undressed upstairs, Gwen realized it had begun to rain. There was a low growl of thunder somewhere in the distance. The men would get wet walking home from the meeting, she thought. She felt glum. She would have liked to see Daniel before going to bed. But she comforted herself with the thought of spending more time with him tomorrow.

There was a bowl and pitcher of water in the room

this time, so she washed her face in the candlelight before she got into bed. All the fresh air and activity of the day had tired her and she felt drowsy already. Blowing the candle out she settled down, falling asleep almost instantly.

The next thing she heard was a great crash of sound. Her heart was beating fast, startled at being woken so abruptly. She got out of bed, moved the curtain aside and opened the window, feeling cool air on her face. There was nothing to see, the only sound the hard, steady fall of rain. Moments later there was a flash of white and the street was lit up for a second. Then came another wrench of thunder, then hard rainfall. She heard running feet and men's voices. Even at that distance she could recognize the timbre of Daniel's voice. He and his uncle were hurrying back from the meeting. She heard them reach the house and go inside. Immediately she wanted to go and see Daniel, have a goodnight cuddle. If she waited, maybe she could catch him on his own.

She pulled her cardigan on and stood by the window, enjoying the sounds of the storm. Before long she heard Anthony's lumbering tread on the stairs and the bedroom door across from hers open and close. Gwen dared herself to go down. The house was so small — surely they'd hear every sound she made!

Barefoot she went to the door, opening it as quietly as she could manage and crept down the stairs, wincing at every tiny creak. She stopped halfway down and listened. Something wasn't right. She could hear Shân's voice down there. Billy was asleep in the front, but Shân must be with Daniel in the kitchen. Gwen cursed under her breath. Curious though, she paused.

She heard Daniel say, 'What good will it do? That's the thing, Auntie. What's past is past.' He sounded angry and defensive.

'It's stayed past because I've kept quiet for you,' Shân said. 'And God knows there've been times it's weighed heavily on my conscience. There's ashamed of you I am sometimes – and of myself.'

'There's nothing for you to be ashamed of,' Daniel said.

'But plenty for you to be.' This sharp retort was followed by a silence. Then she said, 'This Gwen girl is very sweet and good-hearted. If you're serious about her, you can't keep her in the dark for ever you know, Daniel. Things come back to haunt you . . .' The rest of what she said was drowned out by a crash of thunder from outside. Gwen clenched her fists, desperately trying to hear.

'Don't go on, Auntie.' Daniel sounded weary, as if they'd had the conversation a number of times before. 'Digging it up. The damage is done – there's nothing more I can do about it now!'

'Nothing more! Daniel, for goodness sake!' Her voice rose. 'Sometimes I wonder if you've got a heart in your body, truly I do. The party isn't everything – there's a life to be led as well . . .'

'Oh, don't start on me again, woman . . . I'm going to bed.' Gwen saw a shadow move on the floor and she fled up the stairs and into her room. Holding the door open a crack she listened and a moment later heard Shân coming upstairs. Gwen slipped quietly into the lumpy feather bed.

She was wide awake now and wretched. She wanted to go down and have it out with Daniel. She felt suddenly as if she didn't know him at all: he was like a stranger. And after this morning, when they had seemed so close, it was a cold, desolate feeling.

Gwen slept later than she intended the next morning. It was Saturday, and she and Daniel were to travel back that afternoon, so she had wanted to make the most of the day. But it had taken her so long to get to sleep the night before that she did not wake until almost nine. When she went downstairs, Shân was kneeling sweeping dust from the hearth and Billy, already washed and in his chair, lit up at the sight of Gwen. But this was little compensation for Shân telling her that Daniel and Anthony had already gone out.

'Where's he gone?' Gwen asked, trying not to let her disappointment show too much. But she felt tired and close to tears. She needed to see Daniel, for him to hold her again and prove to her he was not the complete stranger he had seemed the night before.

'They've gone off to meet more of the party members at the movement's offices over in Tredegar. They're full up with the idea of this march . . .'

'Tredegar?' Gwen's spirits sank even further. Daniel hadn't thought to invite her to go, and now he wasn't even in Aberglyn!

Shân turned, hands resting on her knees.

'This is the life if you marry the party,' she said gently.

'Yes, I know,' Gwen said bleakly. But she thought, *I don't want to marry the party. I want Daniel . . .* She longed to ask Shân what she had been talking to Daniel about. What was he hiding from her? In another way though, she also did not want to know. Trying not to show how low she felt, she asked, 'D'you know when they're coming back?'

'There's no knowing with them, once they get on to party business. But Daniel said something about catching an afternoon train.' Shân got stiffly to her feet. 'Come on, Gwen *fach*. You know what I think of it all. But let's make a cup of tea, and you can spend the day with me and Billy. It's not much to make up for it, though, I know.'

Gwen gave a watery smile, trying to swallow down the lump in her throat. 'I'd love to spend the day with you both.'

By the time Daniel and his uncle came back that afternoon there was only just time to make it to the valley train. Gwen said fond goodbyes to Shân and Billy, with renewed promises to write to Billy. But as she and Daniel set off she felt tense inside with pent-up hurt and anger.

'Plans are coming on,' he said, full of excitement, as they walked down the hill. The day was dull, cooled by the previous night's rain. 'They're thinking about making it October. Nothing's getting any better here, whatever the out-of-work figures say!'

Gwen nodded, silent.

Daniel continued talking animatedly. His complete obliviousness to her misery made her feel even worse, and once more she found herself on the verge of tears, but she forced them away. How could she ask Daniel anything about what she had heard last night when she wasn't supposed to have been there to hear it? But how could Daniel just go off for the day like that without her, and not think now to apologize or ask her anything about her day?

Daniel was still distant, but full of talk. *And I'm just a willing audience for it all*, she thought bitterly. By the time they changed trains, she was so tense with hurt she was ready to explode.

They settled into a carriage in which there was only one other person: an old man, asleep by the window. As the train moved off, Daniel turned to her and went to put his arm round her.

'Don't!' she said, affronted. How could he start that, acting as if they were close when it felt as if he had never been further from her?

'What's the matter?'

'What's the *matter*?' The conversation was conducted in a venomous hiss so as not to rouse the old man. 'What d'you mean what's the matter? You're so caught up in yourself and so oblivious to anything else going on around you, you can't even see, can you?'

Gwen got to her feet. This time she couldn't push the hurt away, pretend she didn't mind.

'What . . .?' Daniel began.

'Oh, don't ask me "what" again! I just can't stand it. And I can't stand sitting with you for the rest of this journey, either.'

'Gwen – for heaven's sake!' He got up to stop her, but she pushed him forcibly aside and went to the compartment door.

'Just leave me alone!'

She found another compartment, empty except for a man reading a newspaper. She sat by the window and silently let the tears roll down her cheeks.

Forty

There was a playful breeze tickling his right cheek, and a sudden press of sun rays against his eyelids. He opened his eyes, rolled onto his back on the prickly straw bed and looked up into the high barn. He could hear the dogs, and a moment later a wet nose edged with black and white hair nudged at his face, the tongue licking him.

'Molly! Ugh – gerroff!'

He sat up, clinging to her. The dog's eyes seemed to smile into his. She was a shaggy, rumbustious, farm dog and, of all the good things here on Elm Tree Farm, to Joey she was the best.

'Time to get up, you lot!' Mr Belcher had swung open the barn door and dusty rays streamed in. Joey could see the man's round face beneath the brim of his hat, pink in the warmth. 'Come on – shake a leg!' They had been on the farm for a week and so far he had said that every morning, nothing more, nothing less.

Joey was stroking Molly, her hot, panting breath on his face, as the men woke around him. He kept touching the soft bit of black fur between her ears. Stroking that velvety spot made him feel nice. Next to him John sat up blearily, straw caught in his beard. Frank always woke very fast, was on his feet and moving within a couple of seconds, body a lean silhouette in the doorway as he went out to relieve himself. Steven lay curled up, as if he hadn't heard anything. He'd shouted out in his sleep again in the night.

Mr Belcher disappeared and a moment later they heard him whistle Molly, who obeyed instantly, pulling away from Joey.

'Molly . . .' he whispered after her hurrying form. He wrapped his arms round his knees.

All that week they had been picking potatoes, gathering them in sacks in the long, sloping field beyond the farmhouse, hands burrowing in the dry soil to uncover the dusty potatoes, the smaller ones pale, like buried eggs. They worked on their knees, sacks under them, to save their backs. Once they'd worked for an hour and a half or so, they gathered with the other farm workers in the yard – only in the house if it was wet – and Mrs Belcher handed out plates of food. The first time Joey saw what they were to have for breakfast, the other men laughed at him.

'His eyes're going to pop out of his head!' one of them teased. 'You never seen food before, then?'

'Don't look like he has to me – 'e's thin as a stick . . .'

Joey was too busy tucking into the porridge to respond. It was thick and creamy and topped with a spoonful of treacle and he felt it sliding down into his stomach, warm and utterly comforting. He licked every last bit off the big spoon and stared at his face in it, stretched into a funny shape. As if the porridge wasn't momentous enough, the next thing to appear was a great platter of curling bacon rashers, which they ate on hunks of bread, and white, thick-rimmed cups of tea into which he could put as much sugar as he liked. Joey ate until he thought he would burst. Later his stomach went crampy and he had to go and be sick at the edge of the field. After a couple more hours' work, one of the men brought round a basket of bread and cheese and more tea, then later every day there was dinner and tea, pies or roast meats with lashings of gravy and mashed potato and vegetables and big, filling puddings with jam or raisins or treacle and custard. Joey had never known there was this much food in the world, that it could taste like this! He was getting used to eating better food and at every meal he bolted down as much as he could possibly manage.

Mrs Belcher was a blunt, comforting person, with muddy-coloured plaits coiled round her head. Joey never saw her without a huge apron on, either white or made out of colourful flowery cotton.

'Why's this little 'un on the road with you, then?' she asked John on the first day. Joey and John had limped along the rutted track to the farmhouse and asked for food and water. She looked doubtfully at John with his filthy black clothes and wild beard, but then her gaze fastened on him. Joey saw a horrified expression in her eyes.

'He's with me,' was all John would say in his wooden way.

'Is he your boy then?'

'He comes with me.'

'Dear God – he's all skin and bone.' Joey saw her make a face when she came closer to John, though Joey could see she didn't mean to. Joey was used to John's stink. 'Are you hungry, boy?'

Slowly, Joey nodded. When was he ever not hungry?

'You'd better come on with me then.'

She had sat them down at a long wooden table in the kitchen, where there was a large range and lots of huge pots and a kettle bigger than Joey had ever seen. She fed them tea and bread and butter. On the table in front of them was a dish of brown eggs. She didn't ask any more questions. They needed help bringing the potatoes in, she said. And there was haymaking to do. They could sleep in the barn with the other men who were helping out.

'Wait there, before you go out.' She disappeared upstairs and appeared with clothes for Joey.

'These were my son's – don't fit him no more. They'll be too big on you, but you can't go round dressed like that! Give me them rags of yours and we'll put 'em on the fire. Here – you'll need a bit of twine to keep them trousers up.'

In the barn, Joey changed into the trousers. They were made of brown corduroy, well worn so that they were almost bald from thigh to knee, and were capaciously too large. Even tying them round the waist was not adequate – two or three Joeys could have fitted into them. John managed to rig them up by using the thick twine crossed over Joey's shoulders so that the trousers reached halfway up his chest, and turning the bottoms up. There was a blue-and-white checked shirt that reached below his knees and he rolled the sleeves up almost to the shoulder. The clothes felt heavy and awkward after the threadbare remnants he had been wearing and when he started work in the trousers he kept having to adjust the string on his shoulders. The farm workers started to call him Coco the Clown.

Later that day they'd met the two other migrant workers who had been taken on for the time being. Frank was a tall, lean, ginger-headed man who, Joey noticed, talked like Christie and had two fingers missing from his left hand, the little finger and the one next to it. All that remained were stumps with no nail and the flesh was stretched and shiny. Joey kept looking at them when they all sat at table together. When Frank used the rest of the fingers on that hand they looked like hooks. He had a scar on the side of his face next to his left eye. He joked with Joey, called him the 'little fella' like Christie had done. Sometimes he picked Joey up and spun him in the air. He was stringy thin, had prominent cheekbones and vivid blue eyes and Joey didn't feel safe with him. His eyes were hard, whereas Christie's had been soft and kind.

Steven was older, balding, with large, deep brown eyes. Frank called him 'the toff' as he had a soft, well-spoken voice. He was gentle and nervous and had bad dreams, crying out, screaming in the night. The first time it happened, a high, unearthly shriek out of the pitch black, it woke Joey and left him trembling with fear. Then Frank's voice came, blearily, 'Give it a rest now, Steven. It's all right, pal.'

Other things shrieked at night: owls, and rats which pattered and rustled through the straw. Joey lay on the soft stalky bed, stomach distended with Mrs Belcher's food, his back aching, limbs twitching with exhaustion after a day of hard work and sunshine. His face and arms, at first a raw pink, were turning brown. Occasionally at night the men walked three miles to the nearest pub, but usually they were too tired and sat outside the barn smoking. Joey would hear the rise and fall of their voices. Sometimes he heard them talking about life on the road, comparing spikes – the dirt-cheap doss houses – and characters they'd run into. John barely said anything and was always the first to come in. Joey knew, though nothing was said, that he didn't like Frank. He called him, 'that Frank'. Frank was always talking about Ireland and about guns and fighting, and he had a short temper which could whip out in a flash. Sometimes, as he drifted into sleep, Frank's voice would get muddled in his head with Christie's and Joey would have an ache in him to know why Christie had left them and where he had gone, and Siobhan too. And then he wouldn't think about it any more. Nor about his mother, nor Miss Purdy. He tried not to see their faces. In the daytime he didn't think about them.

He and John had left a few days after Christie failed to come back.

'I'm not staying here no more,' John said. 'We're going to get out on the road when I find some boots.' The next day he bought some in a pawn shop, and a hairy brown wool coat for Joey, which was too big and hung round his shins. They bundled a few things into the old red curtain: the pan, knife and spoon, the remaining candle stubs, matches and what little they had in terms of food and clothing. John carried the curtain over one shoulder, the contents clanking as he went along. Joey slung the coat round his neck, hanging forward over his shoulders.

They walked out of Birmingham along the Warwick Road.

That first day was very hot. They passed through Greet and Acock's Green, the glare of the sun in their eyes. The soles of Joey's feet began to burn on the hot road and each step hurt. The coat felt like a great weight and made his neck hot and prickly. In Acock's Green they stopped at a vicarage and asked for water. The woman gave it to them in jam jars and made meat-paste sandwiches. She told them to sit in the shade of the church. With the sandwiches were two pieces of fruit cake, and they ate them and lay dozing in the heat until a man came past and yelled at them to clear off. Later they got down onto the towpath along the cut, watching the boats go up and down, and moving out of the way of horses. It felt cooler there by the water. They sat for a while by a bridge and Joey took his boots off and dangled his feet in the filthy water. John didn't take his boots off. Joey wondered why not. He had never once seen John change his clothes. He barely ever even took his hat off. His beard was so tangled it looked as if it had melted into one big mass. They never said much to each other, just plodded on all day, Joey following behind John's black-clad figure. That night they slept in a park, the next tucked under a hedge in a field. It rained on the second night and the drops gradually trickled through the canopy of leaves, though the curtain and the coat, which Joey wrapped round him, helped keep some of it off. They woke the next morning and rolled out from under the hedge, looking out across a pasture of thistles and dock leaves dotted with black and white cows, all shrouded in a fine mist, which burned off as the day grew hotter. There were brambles woven into the hedge, but the fruits were still green and hard. Joey tugged one off its shoot. It was tough and gritty, and made his face twist at the bitterness, so he spat it out. The grass smelt so nice when you lay close to it that he tried eating that, nibbling at the young, green shoots.

'That ent no good,' John remarked. 'Only animals can eat that. You'll make yourself bad.'

After a lot of effort John lit a fire at the edge of the field and eventually they had a pan of black tea. They had spent almost a week on the road, wandering, begging from village rectories and farmhouses, sleeping in barns and hedgerows, when they walked up the track to Elm Tree Farm.

The potato crop was picked and they were put to haymaking. To save the horses from the hottest time of day, Mr Belcher began mowing soon after four in the morning. The others went out with him, still heavy with sleep, into the grey, uncertain light and the smell of night and dewy grass. A shred of moon still glowed in the sky. Joey was given a rake to gather in the long, damp grass, which dried in piles as the sun rose and the heat grew. The air was moist from the dew, then warm as a steam bath. In that early part of the day they worked in silence. All the men were quiet except Frank, who after breakfast would often whistle or hum lively, jigging tunes to himself. Joey liked the songs, his mind followed the thread of them, but for some reason they seemed to enrage John, who Joey sometimes heard mumbling that Frank should 'fuckin' shut up' or 'shut his cake hole . . . bloody Irish carry on . . .' Joey didn't understand what made John like this about Frank. You never knew with John. He had liked Christie.

The sun beat down on them as the days grew hotter. Mr Belcher stood the horse and cart in the shade of the one tree in the field for as long as possible. Frank and Steven flung forkfuls of hay up onto the cart and the mound grew higher and higher.

'You can get up there now.' Mr Belcher picked Joey up and almost threw him onto the pile, passing him a pitchfork. 'Get it spread out. We've a lot more to get on there yet.'

Joey stood, legs splayed, on the top of the cart. Molly was allowed to lie panting in the shade underneath. Part of the time Joey was busy with his fork while the others pitched up bundles of hay. As they went off to get more, he had time to stand and look around from the whispering green shade of the tree. The next field was full of waving heads of oats, which Mr Belcher said would be the next job. Beyond it, way down at the bottom edge of the farm, was the railway and every so often they heard the LMS trains chugging in the distance, puffing out clouds of steam to the blue sky, the sound building, then receding. Every time a train came by, Joey felt a thrilling sensation. He stood wanting to wave and shout. There were moments when everything seemed right, a perfection in the puffing of the train, the warm ease of his body fed with the morning bread and cheese, the smells of cut grass and horse, the animal nibbling at the grass and giving out loud breaths away to his left. There was Molly with her lovely soft head lying near him, only leaving the shade of the tree when she spotted a rabbit across the field and tore off after it. It was too quick for her and she returned with her tongue lolling to one side. He thought nothing could be better, ever.

There came a couple of days of rain, so heavy that they had to wait before anything else could be harvested and the Belchers found them odd jobs to do round the farm. Joey was put to cleaning the stiff, filthy harnesses in the barn. Afterwards it grew very hot again. They had a day's haymaking left. But the day was interrupted.

The heat built up. Even though they were gathering hay right from the top end of the field, Mr Belcher wouldn't move the horse. Frank cursed about this.

'The animals get treated better than us here . . . Treats her like a queen and us like scum . . .'

'No, he doesn't – you know he doesn't.' Steven reasoned with him. 'He's a very fair employer, Frank – you know he is.'

Joey liked Steven. He was gentle and kind. Steven had once worked in a bank. Joey didn't know why he was on the road now. He wondered if he ever screamed and shook when he was in the bank.

After a dinner of bread and meat pies, they rested for a while in the shade. Soon after they had picked up their rakes and pitchforks again, they heard a train coming up from the south. Joey watched it from the top of the cart. There was a heat haze across the pale oatfield and the train, dark and metallic, seemed the one thing with any definition in the landscape. Its steam was a cloud of white and the sound began to decrease. Then Joey saw something. Something which shouldn't have been there: flecks of coloured light. He narrowed his eyes. The light was leaping up, orange, dangerous.

'Fire! Down the oatfield. Get down there!'

At Mr Belcher's cry, everyone was running. Joey slid down from the stack, not knowing what to do but run. It seemed such a long way across the field. He was with Frank, John and Steven and Molly came with them too, her tail a flag amid the oat stems. Mr Belcher had disappeared, shouting that he was going to get some sacks. The four of them saw the fire take hold of a seam of the crop, licking hungrily at it.

'Thank heavens there's no wind,' Steven panted. 'Must have caught from a spark from the train.'

They had nothing but rakes and forks to beat at the fire. Molly circled, barking shrilly.

'Make a break round it!' Frank was shouting. They were all beating down the stalks around the fire, trying

435

to keep it from advancing any further. John beat at the flames with his pitchfork. Joey copied him. It frightened him hearing the crackling fire, feeling the heat of it on his face if he went too close.

'Help us make a break!' Frank yelled at him. 'It's no good doing that, you stupid fucker – get over here!'

Joey could see Frank was right, but John just ignored him and turned his back, thrashing away with his pitchfork, mumbling angrily to himself.

'Come and help us over here!' Steven insisted, but John ignored him as well. The others saw he wouldn't listen and left him. Joey joined them, beating down the crop in a semi-circle round the flames.

It seemed an age until both Mr and Mrs Belcher came running, staggering under the weight of rolled-up sacks. Joey saw the sacks were dripping water. They threw the sacks over the edge of the fire, stamping it out, then moving on, eating into it until it got smaller and smaller. Joey saw quite soon that they were going to beat it.

'What if we hadn't been there and seen?' Steven said as the last flames were stamped out.

'We'd've lost the crop,' Mr Belcher said. Both he and his wife wore sober expressions. Mrs Belcher wiped her puce face on the end of her apron. 'We try and plant away from the edge but it only takes a stray spark like that . . .' He looked round. 'You saved it, though. You're good blokes – thanks.'

''Cept for that feckin' idiot over there.' Frank nodded at John, who was standing, fully clothed as ever, in the heat. 'What's the matter with you, eh? Got a screw loose or something?' He tapped his head. Something had got into Frank. He seemed wound up and tremulous, his body tense with the need to goad John.

'Don't, Frank,' Steven said. 'It's over. It doesn't matter.'

'No, it doesn't matter,' Frank shouted. 'Except the man's an idiot – just look at him!'

Joey jumped as John launched himself abruptly from beside him and threw himself on Frank, punching him in the head.

'I'm not stupid!' he screamed. 'Don't call me an idiot!'

Of the two, John was the bigger and he caught Frank off balance, knocking him to the ground. But Frank was full of crazed, wiry strength and in a few seconds he hurled himself out from under John and over on top of him, snarling into his face, his teeth bared.

'Think you can push Frank Monaghan around do you? You stinking, shite-thick English bastard . . .'

Joey felt himself shrink with dread. He backed away as Frank began to punch John and Steven and the Belchers went to pull him off. Joey turned, hearing the blows and ran up the field away, away to the tree and its shade. He lay curled under the hay cart, eyes screwed shut.

Forty-One

Gwen spent the days after coming back from Wales feeling truly miserable. For part of the journey from Aberglyn she had sat in a separate carriage from Daniel, utterly hurt, weeping tears of anger and frustration. When next they changed trains, Daniel found her on the platform.

'Well, thanks for coming to find me!' she erupted at him.

'I just *have* come to find you,' he said, exasperated.

'I mean back there – on the train.' She was trying to keep from crying, but barely succeeding. There were people milling about on all sides of them. She pulled her hanky from her sleeve and blew her nose, feeling pathetic.

'But you told me to leave you alone!'

'I didn't mean *actually* leave me *alone* for the whole journey, I meant ... Oh, never mind. Forget I said anything.'

'Hey.' He went to put his arm round her waist. 'Come on – I don't know what I'm s'posed to have done, but I didn't mean to upset you.'

'That's the trouble though!' She flared up again. 'You've no idea, have you? You ask me to come with you to Aberglyn and then you spend nearly all your time off at meetings and ... I know it's important but you could just show a bit more consideration.'

Daniel sighed, pulling her closer. He looked dog tired and she began to relent a little.

'Sorry,' he said. 'Only – it's what I do down there, see. Habit really. And it's important.'

And aren't I important at all? she wanted to say, but she gave a stiff nod, swallowing her tears. *Why do I always have to come second?*

'We need to get to the other platform.' Daniel took her hand and she allowed herself to be led.

She hoped it would be better now, that they would sit close, talk again. And they did sit holding hands, but it was hard to begin. She didn't find the courage to mention the conversation she had overheard the night before. And very soon after the train left Hereford, Daniel's eyes closed and he slept until they arrived. By the time they had got on the last train, Gwen herself felt low, and sleepy and past talking about anything. They parted in Birmingham with a quick hug and kiss in the dark street outside Millie's and Lance's flat.

'See you tomorrow,' Daniel said wearily.

'Umm.' He saw her into the house and she stood at the door watching as he walked off along the street. A deep sense of melancholy came over her. She felt so close to him sometimes, as if they inhabited the same skin, yet there he was, a stranger heading off into the night without turning round.

I just need a good night's sleep, she thought. *I'm feeling tired and gloomy.*

She crept up the dimly lit staircase. At least Millie and Lance would be in bed by now and she wouldn't have to contend with them.

But she was wrong. As soon as she opened the door to the flat she heard Millie's angry voice raised shrilly in the sitting room.

'. . . but you don't – you never do anything except go to work and come back. It's bad enough now, but how are we going to get by once the baby comes?'

'Oh, do stop going on, darling . . .' Lance sounded plaintive and at the end of his tether. He evidently slammed something down on the table. 'Let's just go to bed – I can't keep this up.'

'No – that's just like you. Run away, go to sleep – anything to avoid me . . .'

Millie was crying. 'I feel as if I live on my own all the time! Gwen's never here and you have no time for me.'

'I do have time for you. But you're tired all the time – and so am I . . .'

'Well, it's not much of a life, is it? We haven't even been married a year and all you do is ignore me already . . .'

Their bickering voices went on and on. Gwen slipped quietly into her room, wishing the door would muffle the sound of their quarrelling completely. She was so tired she barely had the energy to get undressed before falling into bed, where she lay listening to Millie and Lance moving about, sniping at each other in an exhausted way before finally closing their own bedroom door behind them. She'd always felt sorry for Millie, but she didn't half go on. No wonder Lance got irritated. And he was such a drip! What on earth had Millie seen in him in the first place? Gwen lay there, fed up with the pair of them, resolving that she would never, ever get into a situation like that. But then her spirits sank even further. Hadn't she and Daniel sounded the same today? He had hurt her so badly by being blind to how she was feeling and she still felt sore about it. She thought of his parting words, 'See you tomorrow.'

No, you won't actually, she thought, as her eyes began to close. *Don't you take me for granted like that.*

The party was working towards another big demonstration in the Bull Ring with the the BCPL the following Saturday, in support of republican Spain. Gwen knew Daniel would be totally taken up with it and that all hands were needed, but she woke the next day even more sure she couldn't face going in. School would start again in a couple of weeks and she wanted a bit of time to herself. And – the thought that she kept trying to push away from her – that same Saturday she had been supposed to be getting married to Edwin.

In defiant mood she lazed around in bed with a cup of tea, then pottered about, doing her washing and catching up with odd jobs. Later in the afternoon she sat in the wicker chair in her room trying to read, but it was impossible to concentrate on the book. She found thoughts about her family and Edwin crowding into her mind. If the wedding had gone ahead, how would it have been? All out in the garden at the Shackletons' house, where they had planned their reception, tables with food, the children running up and down to see the pony in the paddock and her in that dress Mrs Twining had been making. She could hardly bear to think about Edwin and, more even than Edwin himself, his parents, whom she felt so guilty about. She knew Mr Shackleton had had a genuinely soft spot for her and she thought of him caring for Edwina so gently and unselfishly. What must they think of her? What kind of person was she, the way she had behaved? And she had cut herself off from her family completely now. The thought of this was both sad and frightening, yet when she thought about how it would feel to go home, to be back in her parents' house, with Edwin again, she felt the old sense of claustrophobia – panic even – wash over her.

Leaning over, she picked up the framed photograph of Amy Johnson, her handsome, inscrutable face looking out from under the goggles on her forehead. *How do you find freedom to fly in this world?* she wondered sadly. *Is it ever possible to do it without hurting someone else?* She thought, painfully, about Daniel. Here she was, trying to take off and fly and she had immediately got herself tangled, tied to him.

Impatient with herself, needing relief from her feelings, she put the picture away and went out, catching a tram into Birmingham. She went looking for books for Billy and, after a long time of musing along the shelves, found a translation of Victor Hugo's *Les Misérables*. It looked the sort of novel Billy would like and it would certainly keep him busy for a long time. Sitting in the sun near St Philip's Cathedral she wrote him a note to go with it, saying that she hoped he had not already read it.

Two more days passed and it became almost a matter of principle to stay away from the party offices. Gwen felt guilty, knowing how busy they would be, but she wanted Daniel to come and find her, to show he cared about her as well as politics and the party. She knew it was childish, but her feelings were hurt. She sat talking idly with Millie on those warm afternoons, listening to all her woes, the windows open to the street, the sound of voices and passing traffic floating up to them. They drank homemade lemonade and made toffee in a pan, as it was the one thing Millie 'just had to have!' and ate it until their jaws ached. Millie seemed to want to do nothing except eat and sleep, although the baby was not due for a few weeks yet. She always left her hair loose now and wore a succession of billowy cotton dresses.

By the third day there was no sign of Daniel coming to find her. *I could be ill*, she thought self-pityingly, *and he wouldn't know*. She felt restless, unable to settle, and longing to see him. Was he missing her? she wondered. Probably not – he would be too busy. In the end she decided she was punishing no one except herself.

If I want to see him, I should just go and do it, she thought. *I'm being ridiculous!*

Instead of going to the offices, she did the next best thing and walked to Alma Street. The school, when she passed it, was all locked up, silent in the sunshine. There was something sad, Gwen thought, about a school without any children. There were plenty of them about, though, out in the streets, playing.

Round the corner she found Lucy Fernandez sitting on the shop's front step watching Rosa and her brothers throwing a small rubber ball to one another back and forth across the street.

'It's Miss Purdy,' Gwen heard Rosa say as she approached. 'Daniel's not here, is he?'

Gwen was struck once more by how beautiful the girl was. Lucy was smiling shyly up at her.

'Hello, are you having a nice break?' Gwen said.

'Yes, thanks.' Lucy had on a skimpy, pale pink

frock, and sat with her good leg bent, the calipered leg stuck out awkwardly in front. She leaned aside to let Gwen into the shop.

'Hello there, Gwen!' Theresa called from behind the counter. Gwen felt cheered immediately. She was calling out a reply when she realized someone else was standing at the back of the shop. It took her a few moments to realize who it was.

'Afternoon, Miss Purdy,' the woman said. It was her soft, well-spoken voice that made Gwen realize.

'Oh – Mrs Wilson! Good afternoon.'

Alice's mother was wearing a pretty floral dress in pinks and greens and her hair had grown since the last time they met and was tied back. Unlike the last time, her face was calm.

'Mrs Wilson's just popped in to tell me the good news,' Theresa said.

'Oh, what's that?' Gwen asked.

'Well.' Louise Wilson blushed. She seemed unable to meet Gwen's eye. 'Just that I've got myself a little job.' She was going to be serving in a stationer's, she told Gwen. 'It's not much, but it's a start.'

'Well, I'm very pleased for you,' Gwen said carefully.

'Alice can come round here after school, see,' Theresa said. 'Lucy's pleased as anything.'

Gwen repeated her congratulations and looked gratefully at Theresa Fernandez.

'Daniel's not here, I'm afraid,' Theresa said. 'Course, you can stay if you want . . .'

'No, thanks, I'd better be getting along.'

Gwen smiled and parted from them. Her smile faded once she was along the street. She had to go to the party offices or she was never going to see Daniel!

Once more she went into town. As she did so her mood changed. Of course Daniel was busy! How could she be so self-centred? And she was supposed to be helping collect food and medicines for Spanish Aid, not sitting in Millie's flat feeling sorry for herself! Ashamed, she shook off her mood of gloom and resentment. She had to put other things before her own feelings. They were working for a cause and Daniel was very committed, very adult, about it. She strode along, full of new energy.

She was waiting to cross the street when she saw Esther Lane come out of the offices. *Good*, Gwen thought, *at least she's not going to be there*. But then she saw Daniel coming out after Esther. She didn't know why, but she shrank back, not wanting them to see her. In any case, they were not looking her way. Esther turned her head and said something to Daniel and Gwen saw him laugh. As they walked away, Gwen's saw Esther lazily put her arm round Daniel's waist. With equal casualness, he laid an arm across her shoulders. Then he reached down and kissed her in an easy, familiar way on the lips.

Forty-Two

It was like being punched. The breath seemed to have left her body. All she could do was stand at the kerb watching as Daniel and Esther went off along the road, wrapped round each other, talking away nineteen to the dozen, until they disappeared into the distance. Still she could not move, almost unable to believe she wasn't caught in a nightmare and would wake up.

'How could you?' She found her lips moving. 'How *could* you?'

When she managed to move away she almost collided with several people. It was as if no one else existed. In a dream she caught the tram back to Handsworth, but the thought of going home and facing Millie or sitting alone in her room seemed unbearable. Instead she wandered the streets until she found herself outside Ariadne's house. Unable to think what else to do, she knocked on the door.

It opened with a waft of cheap perfume and there was Ariadne, clad in a floaty frock, navy blue and covered in tiny white polka dots. Her hair was newly dyed and caught up in a loose chignon. Even in the state she was in, Gwen couldn't help noticing how hard and lined Ariadne's face looked in the bright light, all powdered and with her eyebrows pencilled in. But she beamed at the sight of Gwen, seeming quite overcome.

'Gwendolen, come in! Ooh, I'm so pleased to see

you. And I've just made tea! Fancy you coming to see me again!'

'I did say I would,' Gwen murmured. She felt quite disorientated. Ariadne immediately started complaining about 'that strumpet' Miss Hines and her perfume.

'I've told her about it,' Ariadne said, with a censorious sniff, leading Gwen into the back room. ' "I don't appreciate these odours," I said, but she gave me that look of hers.' The tea gushed out of the spout, narrowly making it into the cups. 'Have a cake, dear?'

'No thank you,' Gwen said. 'I'm sorry – I'm just not hungry.' It would have been a good time to eat since the Eccles cakes were obviously shop bought, but she felt too queasy with distress even to attempt it.

Ariadne sat herself down, smoothing her skirt under her in her affected way and proceeded to complain for some time about the indignities visited upon her by her lodgers. A travelling salesman called Mr Mealing had stayed for a couple of weeks with promises to be stable and long-term, and then upped and gone.

'You can't rely on people today – they've no staying power.' She bit resentfully into an Eccles cake and looked across at Gwen, who was cradling the cup between her hands, trying to warm them.

'You're not cold, are you? On a day like this? Perhaps you're sickening . . .' She looked more closely. 'You really look rather peaky, dear. Are you sure you're all right?'

Gwen had no idea it was going to happen. Afterwards she realized it was the look of real motherly concern in Ariadne's eyes that had done it, but suddenly she was sobbing, so hard that the tea started slopping out of her cup onto her skirt.

'Dear, oh dear!' Ariadne leapt up and took the cup

from Gwen's shaking hands. 'My dear girl, whatever is the matter?'

Gwen shook her head, unable to speak. All she could feel was pain . . . *Daniel, Daniel* . . . In her mind was fixed the sight of him with Esther, so comfortable and familiar as if they had walked that way, intimately entwined, many times before. And she could hear Esther's words, spoken in her superior tone when they were in Aberglyn, '*poor old you* . . .' The sense of hurt and humiliation was so great, she couldn't speak. She was beyond even embarrassment about having broken down in front of Ariadne.

Ariadne pulled her chair up close. Eventually, taking courage, she laid her arm round Gwen's shoulders. Even in the state she was in, Gwen was touched by the timidity of the gesture. She could smell Ariadne's perfume. It was quite pleasant, she realized, not like that smell in the hall.

'You can tell me,' Ariadne said, after letting Gwen have a cry. 'I know what it's like to be unhappy, dear, believe me. Has someone been playing with your heart?'

Gwen fished out her hanky and blew her nose, more tears coming as she did so.

'I've been such a fool and it hurts so much . . .'

She spilled it all out then, desperate to talk to someone, all about meeting Daniel, and Edwin and the wedding and the fact that her parents never wanted her home again and, most terrible of all, what had happened this morning.

'She's been chasing after him for ages. I've seen her. I've tried so hard not to be jealous, but every time we do anything, *any* meeting we go to, *she's* always there, making up to him, taking his attention . . . And she's so *bossy*, and she's older than he is,' she finished petulantly. 'Why would he want to go off with her when he's told me he loved me so many times? I can't understand him...' Once more she dissolved into tears. She realized Ariadne was lightly stroking her back.

'Poor child,' she said. 'Oh, what a thing. But that's men for you, dear. I've spent my life trying to get over men. You give them everything, pour your heart out to them and they run off and leave you, and you think: one day I'll find the one who's different, who'll be true...' The melancholy in Ariadne's voice cut through to Gwen and she wiped her eyes and turned to look at her.

'But you found your George, didn't you?' Both their eyes went to the photograph of George in its frame on the mantelpiece, with his moustache and military stance. 'He was different, wasn't he?'

There was a silence. Ariadne looked down into her lap. 'No,' she confessed miserably. 'He wasn't. Not in the end.'

Gwen stared at her, unable to make sense of this. Ariadne looked up, and Gwen could see the sad, defeated look in her eyes.

'I tell everyone I'm a widow, but it's not true. He left me – just like the others.'

'Oh, Ariadne!'

Ariadne withdrew her arm and looked down into her lap. 'You get over some of them. Most of them – but I've never got over him. Took the heart out of me, he did. Don't let this one do it to you. Look at you – your pretty face is all blotches! You're too young for all that.'

It's too late, Gwen thought, tears welling in her eyes

449

again. *He already has*. But she didn't say anything to Ariadne, just leaned over and gently touched her hand. Ariadne looked up at her, nodding gently, shame and hurt in her eyes.

'Your room's empty, dear, since Mr Mealing went,' she appealed. 'I do wish you'd come back and take it.'

Gwen thought of Millie and Lance's flat, the constant bickering and life with them at close quarters.

'Just give me time to give them notice,' she said.

Millie was not at all happy.

'But I thought you were going to stay and help me when the baby comes,' she complained. 'It's going to be ever so lonely, and I shan't know what to do!'

'I'm sorry, Mill – I've promised to go now. I'll come and see you whenever I can. It's not as if I've the faintest idea how to manage babies, you know.'

'Lance will be so cross – we need the rent, you see.'

But Gwen was determined. Now she knew she would be leaving in a couple of weeks, the realization came as a great relief, even though Lance was short and snappy with her. She was in far too much distress herself to care what Lance thought about anything.

Thursday and Friday she spent in a terrible state. She kept bursting into tears and lying on her bed, face pressed to the candlewick bedspread. She was so desperate, she thought sometimes she should go and find him, have it out with him. But her pride wouldn't let her. Nothing would have dragged her into the party offices. On Friday evening she was sure he would come to her, that he would want her there with him at the demonstration the next day. She waited all evening in a state of almost unbearable tension, thinking every sound was a knock on the door, but he did not come.

Saturday was the day of the demonstration. She decided that the only way to get through it was to try and keep busy, so she went out, buying food on the way, to Handsworth Park. In the afternoon a band was playing on the bandstand and she sat nearby amid the crowds sprawled on the grass, listening to marching tunes as they rolled across the sunlit grass, trying not to think about what was happening in the Bull Ring, the speeches, party members selling the *Daily Worker* and the BCPL banners. She should have been there with her bag of leaflets, one of the party's workforce.

Damn them – damn all of it, she thought savagely, hugging her knees and peering out from under the brim of her straw hat. They didn't care about other people – not really. All they cared about were abstract ideas, and slotting real people into them. Was that what she was for Daniel – an idea? A comrade so long as she thought as he thought, and joined the party and did as she was told? What if she had feelings and ideas of her own? Every time she thought about Daniel it was with a terrible lurch of pain inside. It was as if he had sucked her right in, body and soul, and then casually spat her out again.

That night she lay soaking in the bath. She had a good cry. When she got out her body was pink all over, her head felt muzzy and she had reached a point of numbness where she had thought about Daniel and dwelt on her feelings so much that she couldn't any more. Barefoot and in her nightdress she went into her room

451

and sat numbly on the bed. She didn't know how long she had been sitting there when there was a rap on her door.

'Gwen?' Millie sounded impatient. 'It's Daniel.'

She didn't have time to move. She had been in such a daze she hadn't heard the knock on the outside door of the flat.

His face, coming round the door, looked very dark. He obviously hadn't shaved for several days and his skin had tanned well in the sun. His white shirt hung outside his trousers and he looked generally dishevelled, but full of energy. He beamed at her in a way which indicated so clearly that he had absolutely no idea of her feelings, that she froze even further and just sat, staring at him.

Daniel closed the door quickly behind him. 'You missed a big day today! It went really well – crowds of 'em! Where've you been all week? We've been rushed off our feet!'

He sat on the bed beside her. 'Off to bed already? You been poorly?'

'No.' She kept her voice even and controlled. 'I just didn't come in. I had other things to do. Didn't you notice I wasn't there before today?'

'Yes – course. Only we've been non-stop all week before the big day today. I've barely been home, slept or anything! I fell asleep on the floor in the office once or twice. And today was big – crowds there. We got rid of hundreds of leaflets!' He talked on excitedly about the demonstration, the speeches and how it had all been. Gwen sat growing more and more tense with pent-up hurt and anger, yet she was already beginning to feel ashamed. She was being so trivial and womanish, being wrapped up in her own feelings when Daniel was spending himself every hour of the day for the party. If it had just been that it wouldn't have seemed so bad. But there was Esther . . .

'So –' he stopped at last – 'where've you been then?'

'Do you really care?' She stood up and walked away from him as he reached out to put his arm round her. 'Daniel.' For a moment she stared at him, feeling her cheeks burning red and a wave of tears barely held back. 'Don't come here and pretend to me.' He was looking up at her from under his curling fringe, frowning. She could see the dark rings of exhaustion under his eyes. She had trouble getting the words out. If she said what she had to say, it would change everything. But it had to be said. 'I saw you. On Wednesday. With Esther.' Tears rolled down her cheeks. Her throat felt as if it was about to close up.

Daniel was looking completely baffled.

'Oh, don't act as if you don't even know what I'm talking about! You and Esther came out of the offices together just as I was about to cross the road, and you were . . . you . . .' She began to lose control of herself. 'You put your arm round her and you kissed her on the lips. I saw you, so don't say you didn't! And then you both went along the road, all over each other . . .' She really began to weep now. 'And . . . why did you say you loved me, when all the time . . .' She put her hands over her face. 'I can't bear it!'

Daniel was beside her at once.

'Come here.' He pulled her into his arms and for a moment she tried to resist, but then she sank against him exhausted. She felt him press his cheek against the side of her head. 'What've you got yourself all upset for?' he said soothingly. 'Have you been fretting about this all week, silly?' She nodded against his chest, feeling his shirt button against her cheek. 'What, and worrying about old Esther? Gwen – you know what she's like – she's forever on at me. She's a strange one and I feel sorry for her, that's all.'

Gwen pulled back and glared at him. 'But you don't have to kiss her on the lips just because you feel a bit sorry for her!'

Daniel shrugged, comically. 'It doesn't mean anything – it's just easy come, easy go – we're comrades, that's all.'

'Oh, I see – is that it! So that's how it is with me as well, is it?'

'*No!*' His eyes held an intense expression which moved her. 'You know it's not, by now, don't you? God, Gwen, how much more do I need to show you?'

'You could have come and found me – this week,' she said bitterly. 'How am I supposed to know whether you care for me or not? Everything we do is when *you* want it or need it! I've been in such a state, and what do you care?'

He looked chastened. 'I just didn't have a minute . . . There's all the talk about the march at home and Spain, the demonstration . . . It's just been non-stop . . .' He looked deeply into her eyes. 'I'm sorry I've made you unhappy. But for heaven's sake don't let Esther be anything to worry about.' He laughed at the ridiculousness of it. 'I love *you*, girl. Like no one else. That's all.'

She leaned back into him with a sigh. She felt exhausted, foolish, wrung out. His hands were stroking her back.

'Oh, Daniel – you'll be the death of me.'

'Sorry. I'm sorry.' He put his face close to hers.

She could hear that he meant it. They stood close, absorbing each other's presence.

'You're lovely and warm,' he said.

'I had a bath.'

He moved one hand and cupped it round her breast. She could feel the heat of his hand through the thin nightdress. They stood like that for a moment, looking at each other, then he took her hand and led her to the bed, making love to her with a taut urgency which moved her. They lay holding each other in silence for a long time. Then Daniel lifted his head and looked down into her eyes, again without speaking, and she stared back in a moment of pure concentration.

'I never want to hurt you,' he whispered.

'You're hopeless.' Tears welled in her eyes again. Daniel gently wiped them from the side of her face with his thumb. He stroked her neck.

'Don't be so afraid. I love you.'

She held him tight to her. 'Not Esther?' It humiliated her asking this, but she had to know.

Daniel smiled. 'No. Not Esther. Absolutely not old Esther.'

'Stay with me tonight, Daniel, will you?'

He leaned down and kissed her nose. 'Course I will. You'll have to move over.'

She put the light out and they lay holding each other, talking very quietly for a long time. Daniel poured out his feelings about the work he was doing.

'Sometimes I feel I'm running round, but I never manage to be in the right place at the right time,' he said with a sigh. 'There's so much to get done, to make the revolution happen, and never enough people who've understood, who've caught the fire . . .'

Gwen felt a pang of guilt. She was working with him because she loved him, but had she caught the fire? Had she really?

'I'll be back at school in a couple of weeks,' she told him. 'I'm afraid I shan't have as much time.'

'No – what you're doing, educating the children . . . Sometimes that looks like a far more worthwhile thing to do – not like me . . . Sometimes I just wonder . . .'

'What're you talking about?' She lifted her head off the pillow in alarm. Never had she heard him express such self-doubt before. 'You're doing all the things you believe are right, aren't you? I thought you were pleased with how it's going?'

'I am.' She heard him let out a long sigh beside her. 'I s'pose I'm just worn out this week. But sometimes I think . . .' He faltered.

She stroked his chest. 'What?'

'That I'm not much of a person when you come down to it.'

'Oh, Daniel – you are! You're the best person I've ever met!'

'No – there are things you don't know about me, Gwen. Things I'm not very proud of.'

A twist of fear went through her at the sad tone of his voice. She remembered Shân's words downstairs that night in the house at Aberglyn. What was it Daniel was hiding? It sounded as if he had been in trouble at some time – with the police?

'What things?' she asked faintly.

'Oh, just – you know. We've all said and done things we're not proud of.' His voice was brisker now. He evidently wasn't going to tell her, and how much did she really want to know? 'It's nothing really. I'm just overtired and gloomy tonight.' He kissed her neck. 'Turn over, my lovely. I want to lie behind you.'

Pressed together, bodies fitting close, they slept.

Autumn Term

1936

Forty-Three

'Donald Andrews? Joan Billings?'

'Yes, Miss!'

'Ernie Davis?'

'Yes, Miss!'

The register held few surprises. A boy had left to be replaced by a new girl, but otherwise Gwen found she was facing the same set of faces as last year. Now, though, they had a new classroom upstairs, at the front of the school overlooking the playground. Opposite Gwen on the wall was a large picture of a cross-section through a flower. She kept seeing the word 'stamen' when she looked up.

'Lucy Fernandez?'

'Yes, Miss.'

Gwen was about to let out the fond smile which she would naturally have given Lucy had she been at her home, but she curbed it. She knew the children must have realized she was walking out with Daniel, but none of them had the impudence to say anything to her about it. She didn't want to be a teacher who had favourites.

She went on, past Ron Parks, who, she noted, had at last lost his two black front teeth, and Alice Wilson peering eagerly through her specs. She closed the register.

'Milk monitors . . .' she said, thinking aloud. She

looked round at the class. 'But first – I hope you all had a nice summer? You look bigger!' The summer months had made last year's Form Four sprout up to a size fitting for Form Fives.

'Anyway – it's very nice to see you all again. I hope you're going to work very well for me this year?'

There were a few scattered replies of 'Yes, miss.' Lucy was watching her every move. What a sweet face she had, Gwen thought. She looked so like Daniel it was almost unnerving having her in the class. She found she too was glad to be back.

The staffroom was its usual drab self and things were much as ever, except that Mr Lowry was no longer spending time there during the teabreaks, and last term's new teacher, Charlotte Rowley, often did not come in either. Miss Pringle announced that she had seen her going into Mr Lowry's office at the beginning of break in the first week of term, at which Miss Monk said nothing but swelled visibly with inner emotion. Gwen wasn't interested in whether Charlotte Rowley was in the staffroom or not. She thought she was a chilly woman anyway.

Lily Drysdale was in her corner of the room rummaging through a canvas bag which appeared to contain a collection of socks.

'Hello,' she said distractedly, giving Gwen a knowing look, which Gwen took to mean, 'I know you're a Communist, dear, but don't worry I won't tell anybody,' though it might not, of course, have meant anything of the sort. But having been mainly with party members all the summer, Gwen was conscious of coming back into a quite different environnment, where Daniel's passionate views might not have met with much sympathy.

'Are those for the children or for Spain?' Gwen asked.

Lily smiled, faintly. 'Oh, for the children. Though I do think as a staff we might think about gathering a few things together for the Spanish people.'

Mr Gaffney was nodding in his vague way, but Miss Monk looked up from her chair and said aggressively, 'Ah, but *which* Spanish people?'

'Well, which would you suggest?' Lily Drysdale asked.

'Oh.' Miss Monk sniffed. 'I have no views on the subject.'

'Perhaps it's time you had then,' Lily replied sharply.

Gwen grinned, her back to Miss Monk. Only Lily Drysdale could get away with treating Miss Monk like that. She perched on the table beside Lily, who told her more about her church's work in collecting medicines for Spain. There was talk of an ambulance going from Birmingham.

'Cup of tea?' Lily said after a while, about to move away.

'Yes – I'd love one. But I wanted to ask you – have you heard anything more about that boy – Joey Phillips?'

Lily bit her lower lip and shook her head. 'No. Poor little scrap. That was a very sad case.'

Gwen had moved out of Millie and Lance's flat at the beginning of September. Ariadne welcomed her back with enthusiasm, a newly repainted room and a meal which was almost edible and which they ate alone because, Ariadne said, 'that young trollop' upstairs had announced she wasn't eating any more meals in the house because – and here Ariadne almost pulsated with affrontery – the food was only fit for the pig bin!

'Oh dear, what an awful thing to say,' Gwen said, trying to suppress the powerful sense of fellow-feeling she suddenly developed with the hip-wiggling Miss Hines.

'No gratitude or consideration,' Ariadne said. But she gave a genuine smile at Gwen across the singular stew they were eating. 'But it's lovely to have *you* back. Like having a daughter come home, almost, dear!'

Gwen was startled at this, but also touched. Never could she have imagined anyone less like her own mother, but she knew Ariadne was genuinely pleased to see her.

'Thank you for making my room look so nice,' she said. Ariadne had had it painted a pretty shade of green, and had hung new curtains at the window.

'Well, it was getting so shabby. I thought it would brighten life up for you.'

Gwen hadn't been quite sure whether Ariadne was pleased or disappointed when she told her that Daniel had turned out not to have betrayed her after all and that they were as close as ever. Ariadne didn't say much, but gave her a look as if to say, 'You just wait.' But she had said she was glad Gwen was happy and indicated that a blind eye would be turned to Daniel visiting the house.

Those early weeks of the Michaelmas term were very happy ones for Gwen. She was busy at school and spent spare time when she could in the evenings and at the weekend working for the party, which was also a way of seeing Daniel. He barely ever stopped, but in the snatched times they did have together things felt good between them.

One night in late September they were walking, arms wrapped round each other, through the smoky evening. There was a nip in the air.

'They're closing the parks early now,' Daniel was complaining. 'Means we can't stay on late of a weekend. We're having to have meetings on street corners, village greens and all that. Bit of a pity.'

'Never mind – it's going well.' Gwen squeezed his arm. 'Think how many copies of the *Worker* we've sold already this month!'

'Any chance of smuggling a few into the school?' Daniel asked, teasing.

'Oh, I don't think so. There's a couple would be sympathetic – to some of the others it'd be a proper red rag to a bull!'

Daniel shook his head, as if unable to understand anyone who was not a Communist.

'I had another letter from Billy today,' Gwen said. 'He's already read *Les Misérables* and was pleased to get the other books I sent. He writes a good letter.' Despite his confined life, Billy wrote fluently and Gwen had found herself laughing at some of the descriptions of life in Aberglyn perceived from Billy's wheelchair.

'He's a gifted lad,' Daniel said wistfully.

'Perhaps he should be writing stories himself?'

'Well – you suggest it. It'd come better from a woman.'

'Why?' Gwen laughed.

'Well, not very manly, is it?'

'But Billy can't do man's work!'

'You suggest it, anyway.'

'I will!' she said. 'Honestly, I've never heard anything so daft.'

'I must get down there,' Daniel said. 'There's so much energy going on Spain now – we've got to make sure we keep up our solidarity with the miners instead of leaving them to the struggle on their own.'

'Are you going to go? Can I come with you?'

Daniel turned to take her in his arms and kissed the side of her neck.

'Oh, I think I might let you!'

Forty-Four

They were on the road again, between fields where the corn stubble had been burned black and the air smelled of ash. The hedgerows were full of haws and berries and Joey gorged himself from the brambles and damson trees. That day, as they walked, in the red curtain slung over John's shoulder, were stashed orchard apples and pears. But this was food that did not satisfy for long. It made their stomachs gurgle and churn and turned their bowels to water. Every hour pain clenched Joey's innards and he had to hurry into a field or wood. He walked mutinously behind John's black figure. John's hat was always worn at the same angle, his pace never varied, and he seldom spoke.

Joey didn't want to be with John. He wanted to be back at Elm Tree Farm. The morning after the fire in the oatfield and the fight with Frank, John woke him long before dawn, shaking him hard.

'Ow!' Joey yelped. It was pitch dark.

'Shurrup!' He recognized John's whisper in the darkness. 'Get up – we're going.'

'Where?'

'Just going – come *on*, will yer?'

Joey could hear from the faint clanking sound that John had their little bundle of belongings already gathered into the curtain.

'Bring that coat – don't leave it.'

Joey obeyed automatically. He just went where John went and that was that. He felt round for his boots and pulled them on, shook out the coat, hearing rats scuttle away over the straw, and pushed open the barn door.

There were still stars outside, and the moon, high and thin. As they crossed the dark yard, Molly set up a barking and came running out.

'Christ,' John muttered. 'The hound'll wake the lot of them. Shurrup, yer fuckin mutt!'

'Molly!' Joey called softly to her and she came and nuzzled at his outstretched hand. He stroked her head, fingering the soft spot between her ears. Feelings welled up in him. 'Can we take her?'

'Don't be stupid,' John said. 'Another mouth to feed. She won't come anyhow – she wants to stay here. C'm'ere – get moving.'

'Where're we going? I want to stay here.'

John took his arm and dragged him to the farm gate. 'Bloody get moving!'

Joey did not fully realize then that John was leaving for good, that this was the end of their time at Elm Tree Farm. They walked out as they had walked in and kept moving into a grey, mild day. It was only later, when he was exhausted and hungry, that Joey knew it was all over. He had had a glimpse of wonder and now it was snatched away. On the road into Warwick he flung himself at John's back, clinging on and kicking him in the backs of the knees, overcome with sobs.

'I want to go back to the farm! Why've we come here? I'm hungry and I hate you. I don't want to come with you!'

'Get off, you little fucker!' John reached round and wrenched him off, dropping the curtain bundle with a clunk as he did so. He seized Joey's hands. Close up,

Joey noticed afresh the matted state of John's beard. His eyes burned into Joey. They were stony grey.

'I hate you!' Joey shouted. 'I want my dinner!' All the other things he longed for stayed locked inside him. He had no words for loss, or for safety, comfort, kindness. For the feel of a soft spot between a dog's ears.

'There won't be dinner there no longer soon ... They'll finish with us and we'll be on the road again. And I ent staying with that mad bloody Irish fucker no longer.' John yanked on Joey's arms as if there was a switch in them that would silence him. 'Just shut it. Right?'

In Warwick John used some of their earnings from the farm to put new soles on their boots. Then they left the town again. John didn't like towns. The boots felt hard and rigid for a time but now they didn't let so much water in when it rained. The summer was waning, sunlight slanting across the fields onto the red-flecked hedgerows, picking out each fading leaf on the trees. In the morning there were drenching mists and the apples began to fall and rot. Every day they walked. They asked for work at another farm soon after leaving Elm Tree Farm, but the woman there was not round and comforting like Mrs Belcher. She looked thin and crabby.

'You can collect the eggs today as my boy's not here. Long as you don't go stealing them.' She had a pointed, suspicious-looking nose. 'Then you can be on your way. I don't want the likes of you hanging around.'

They collected all the eggs they could find, John

slipped four of them into his pockets and the lady gave them half a crown. She looked as if she wanted to search John for stolen eggs, but he was too revolting.

'Go on now,' she shooed them. 'Away from my door. And don't come back.'

The nights were spent in hedges and haystacks again. The hay was new and sweet smelling. Sometimes Joey asked where they were going, but he never received an answer. Then he stopped caring where they were headed. The days passed.

One evening, at dusk, they were close to the railway. They slid down into a siding where John had spotted an old railway carriage left to rust at the end of the track. They were approaching it, boots crunching on the stones by the edge of the sleepers, when a head appeared through the open door. In the gloom, Joey saw a man in a cap looking down at them. They could see the glow of his cigarette.

'Looking for a kip?'

John nodded. The man had a rough, gravelly voice.

'Thought you was trouble for a mo' there. Who'd come out 'ere poking about I don't know, but I thought you was it. Come on up – it ain't bad. Blimey – this is a young nipper you got 'ere. Running away to sea, are you, chum?'

Joey didn't know what to say so he said nothing.

'Is it just you here?' John asked cautiously. John did not trust people.

'Yep – just me, chum. I ain't the first to kip down in 'ere but there ain't no one but myself 'ere now.'

The man was stocky and bandy legged, and rocked from side to side as he walked. His face looked as if he'd had plenty of punches in his time and he had a rough beard. He led them into the first compartment.

The seats that were left by the window were in a terrible state and the rest, nearer the door, had all been ripped out leaving only the metal frame.

'There's places a-plenty to kip down out the wet. I've been 'ere a couple of nights, resting up. I'll be moving on tomorrow or the next day.'

The man told them his name was Bob Barron and he was from Catford.

'That's London to you, chum.' He laughed with a chesty wheeze and slapped John on the back. John sat woodenly. Joey knew the man had made a mistake. He shouldn't have touched John. But Bob didn't seem to notice the hostility of John's reaction.

'If we're careful we can have a little fire this side – no one can see. Got any grub? I've got a bit of bread and a couple of eggs ... There's a farm over there – easy as winking to get in of a night and get a handful of eggs. Nothing to it. Even got water from the butt ...'

As Bob and John built the fire, Joey explored the railway carriage. He'd never been on a train before. He forgot his rumbling stomach and sat in the compartment at the far end, where there was a seat on one side, half tilted off the frame. He thought about the noises the trains made as they went across the fields by the farm. He thought about the railway bridge by Ron Parks's house in Winson Green. He saw Ron's face suddenly, his black-toothed grin and the classroom, up close, like a picture. Thinking of that gave him feelings, so he got up and ran down the corridor and jumped out into firelight.

'Where's the fire?' Bob asked, then laughed his wheezing laugh. 'Blimey – look at them.' His gaze took in Joey's enormous trousers. 'Sure they're big enough for yer?' When Joey just stared, he said, 'It was only a joke, chum. Ain't you got big eyes, an' all? Like saucers, they are.'

They ate eggs, bread and potatoes and waited an age for the water to boil for tea. Bob had a billycan, which sat well on the fire. Joey saw John staring at it. Bob drank from a bottle of something and passed it to John. The nights were getting cold and Joey pulled the scratchy brown coat round him. Bob tried asking John questions, but didn't get anywhere until he mentioned that he'd been on the dole and sent to one of the camps to work, which set John off again about the camp in Brechfa, in Wales. Bob was just as scathing about it.

'The Labour Exchange made us sit through some bleeding picture about going there and what a cushy time we was going to have. *On the Way to Work*, it was called. Right bloody laugh. I ended up digging with a load of blokes – the underground. End of the Piccadilly line. Stuck it for a couple of weeks and I threw my pick down and I was off. Bugger that. I thought I'd be better off on the road – and I have been. Reckon it's three years now. Got everything I need, I have. Don't need nobody, me. How long you been on the tramp?'

'Just lately.'

'Been in the spikes?'

John shook his head. 'Not going in them.'

'Some of them're not bad. The Sally Ann – alleluia stew and all – better on me own, though, if I can. Some nights though, I've been in a spike or two.'

Joey knew John had a horror of the hostels, all of which he regarded as workhouses, offering a roof for the night for work in the morning. He remembered John saying to Christie once, 'I ent never going in one of them places. They took me mother in one and she never come out.'

'You want to get kitted up better if you're staying on the road in the winter,' Bob said. 'Need a reefer, mate – that jacket of yours'll let the cold in. Get some bacon fat on your boots – keep 'em supple . . .'

Joey was beginning to shiver as the two men talked on. The moon was rising. It was almost full, and its light poured down so he could see the railway track and the pewter-coloured fields stretching to their left. He went inside and fell asleep in the third compartment. Next thing he knew, John was shaking him awake again.

'Don't make a noise, right? Out of 'ere – now.'

Bob was asleep in the second compartment, snoring gently.

John's whiskery lips came close to Joey's ear. 'Go and get his stuff – that billy of his.'

Joey crept in, stepping round the man's body. But as he bent over to pick up the billycan, Bob Barron leapt up in a second and was on him. Bob didn't say a word, but Joey felt himself caught in two immensely strong arms, one round his neck, pulling tighter so he was soon fighting for breath. He struggled frantically, hearing himself gag as the man's forearm gripped his throat. In those seconds he became aware that John was there in the darkness with them, and there were thudding sounds, blows behind him and a grunt, and at last the arm loosed round his throat. Joey pulled away and heard the man slump down behind him, unconscious from John's blow. They took Bob's things: billycan, matches and the rest of the bread, and put them all in the curtain. A few moments later they were up the bank and away across the fields.

Forty-Five

Summer turned to autumn. Village after village across Spain fell to the nationalists. General Franco was now commander-in-chief of the nationalist forces, and the republicans were having to defend themselves mostly with pitchforks and a few old shotguns and blunderbusses. Neighbour turned against neighbour and groups of civilians were rounded up and shot.

The last evening before Daniel left for the valleys, Gwen had a few snatched hours with him in Ariadne's house. A few days before, on 2 October, there had been a big rally in the Town Hall for Spanish Aid organized by the Communist Party, the BCPL and the Labour Movement. Ellen Wilkinson, the MP for Jarrow, came to speak and there was a torchlight procession through the centre of Birmingham. Gwen marched beside Daniel, following the dancing train of lights through the streets. Esther was, as ever, nearby, but Gwen had got past worrying about her now. She knew Daniel loved her and her alone. He had shown her time after time. What did Esther matter?

'This should do us well!' Daniel's eyes were alight with enthusiasm as he looked at all the people and banners around them in the evening streets. By the end of the rally, to the excitement of the organizers, they had raised £120 for Spain.

Gwen knew Daniel was torn in two, never sure

where best to put his energy – in Birmingham for the Spanish cause, or in Wales. He had waited until after the rally – then he was going to leave for Aberglyn, where she was to join him at the weekend.

That night they were sitting on her bed, against the wall, arms round each other. The news from Spain was grim.

'They're killing people for not going to Mass,' Daniel said. He had one of her hands in his and his grip tightened on it sometimes to emphasize what he was saying. 'And for reading philosophers like Kant and Rousseau – or criticizing Hitler or Mussolini.'

'Well, of course they're going to criticize Hitler and Mussolini!' Gwen said heatedly. 'What do they expect?'

She could see how deeply the situation affected Daniel. Apart from his political views, Daniel had relatives on his father's side in Spain. She held him tightly, thinking that she didn't know anything about Kant or Rousseau or why the nationalists should get so agitated about anyone reading them. A few months ago she would have felt ashamed and inadequate about this and about the level of her own commitment to the revolution. She had begun to sense, though, that there was something about her very ignorance that Daniel needed: she provided him with a way out from the intensity of the struggle, another viewpoint, a refuge perhaps.

Though they had to snatch these times together, it seemed to Gwen that she and Daniel had never been closer. She felt borne up by love, humming with feeling for him, with a sense of passion and completeness which gave her almost endless energy. She was loving her work and one or two of the other teachers commented on how radiant she was looking. On Saturdays she went out with other party members selling the *Spain* leaflets and the *Daily Worker*. Ariadne not only allowed Daniel to be in Gwen's room but seemed to applaud it, and anything else that kept Gwen happy and in her house. Miss Hines had finally left, fed up with Ariadne's cooking and her endless criticism, so for the moment Gwen was the only lodger. Ariadne thought Daniel was 'a beautiful specimen of a man', and seemed to take pleasure in having the lovers in the house. So on their few evenings together they could relish each other's company, talk and make love and lie, warm and tired, in each other's arms.

Gwen only just made it to the station to wave Daniel off when school was over for the day. She tore from the tram stop through a downpour of rain and saw him waiting by the clock, where they had arranged, his jacket wet with rain, canvas bag thrown over one shoulder.

'I thought I'd missed you!' She flung her arms round him, face flushed, panting from running.

'Hello, comrade!' He laughed at her flustered state.

'I want to come with you now!'

He pulled her close and she could feel the beat of his heart. 'Only a few days. Billy'll be waiting to see you too.' He nuzzled her face. 'I think he's got a bit of a crush on you!'

'Poor Billy – he's such a nice boy. Will you come and meet me when I get there?'

'Course I will.' He hugged her. 'I'd better go.'

She saw him off, keeping the image of his face smiling from the window in her mind as she made her way back to Handsworth, thinking: *only four days and we can be together again.* How slowly those four days were going to pass!

Instead of spending her days longing only to be with Daniel, Gwen found that when she got back to school there was an unexpected distraction.

On the Wednesday morning, Ron Parks was late coming into the classroom. He missed the register.

'Ron? He must be poorly.'

Gwen was about to mark him down as absent, when one of the other boys said, 'No – he's here, Miss. I seen him.'

Gwen frowned. It wasn't like Ron to be late. He was still not there by the end of the register, so she left the space blank and began the lesson. They were learning about the life cycle of the butterfly. She was just trying to explain how a butterfly hatches from a chrysalis when Ron came in.

'Where have *you* been?' she was asking rather sharply, when she turned and caught sight of his face. Ron's cheerful, slightly eccentric demeanour had entirely gone and instead she saw a stony expression, as if he was struggling to control some deeply felt emotion. He also looked as if he had been crying.

'Are you all right? Has anything happened?'

'No, Miss Purdy.' His voice was subdued, and mutinous. Gwen stared at him perplexed, and saw him take his seat very gingerly, in the pained way the children did when they had had a thrashing from Mr Lowry, though nothing had happened at assembly. Realizing that the whole class was staring at Ron too and that his face had gone a deep, painful red, she said, 'Eyes to the front all of you – get on with your work.' She would get to the bottom of this later.

When the bell rang for break, she asked Ron to stay behind and he came cautiously up to her desk. Some of the others hung around curiously and Gwen shooed them away and closed the door. When she sat down at her desk, Ron just stood there, staring at the floor, whether in anger or shame she could not decide.

'This isn't like you, Ron.'

There was no reply.

'Will you look at me when I'm speaking to you, please?'

He raised his face to her and she could see his lips were quivering. His second teeth had come through and they made him look different, more serious.

'Why were you late this morning?'

'Because he gave me the cane!' Ron blurted, and Gwen could tell that he felt a terrible injustice had been carried out.

'Who – Mr Lowry?' Seeing him nod, she said, 'But you weren't in assembly?'

'Not in assembly – in his office.'

Gwen was silent for a moment, unsure what to say. As a teacher she should be loyal to the head of the school and not undermine his decisions. But she had great misgivings about Mr Lowry's version of punishment. Of course a lot of the children needed a telling off, maybe a slight taste of the cane if necessary. She had even done it herself, reluctantly, once or twice – a couple of strokes with a ruler on the hand perhaps – but not the sort of hard and humiliating treatment the headmaster meted out in front of the whole school. And what might he be like in the privacy of his office?

'Why did he do that, Ron?'

Again, Ron did not seem able to look her in the eye. He appeared to be really distressed. 'I'm not allowed to say.'

'Who told you that?'

'Mr Lowry.'

'I see.' Feeling she could hardly go against the head's wishes and ask directly, she said, 'Well, I'm sorry Mr Lowry felt he had to do that. Let's just hope that whatever it was for, it won't happen again.'

Ron was silent. Eventually, with obvious resentment, he squeezed out the words, 'Yes, Miss Purdy.'

She let him go, but throughout the day she felt troubled. Ron was obviously in pain and he was just not himself. She wondered if he would come back after the dinner break, but he did, and sat miserably through the afternoon classes.

At the end of the day, when Gwen went into the playground, Mr Lowry was standing just outside the back door of the school talking to Mr Gaffney. As she set out, Gwen caught sight of a small, dumpy woman coming in through the playground gate, hugging round her a big, brown cardigan as if she was cold. It took Gwen a moment to recognize her, but then she saw that it was Mrs Parks. She had only met Ron's mother once when she had bought sweets that day in the shop.

Mrs Parks never usually came to the school to collect her boys. She was not walking especially fast, but there was something determined, steely almost, in her manner. She put down her feet in her old flat shoes as if nothing was going to divert her from her path. Gwen said, 'Good afternoon,' as she passed her, but Mrs Parks didn't even seem to hear. Curious, Gwen turned to watch and could hardly believe her eyes when she saw what happened next. Mrs Parks made unwaveringly for Mr Lowry, brought her fist back and delivered a whacking great punch right into his face. There was a collective cry of surprise from everyone around. She gave him no time to recover before following up with another punch with the other fist, slamming it right into Mr Lowry's nose and knocking his spectacles off. Gwen gasped. The playground went suddenly quiet. Children stood staring.

'That's for what you did to my Ron,' Mrs Parks bawled. 'And don't you ever lay a finger on my boys again, you rotten bully!'

Mr Lowry was clutching at his face. His nose was bleeding. Mr Gaffney bent to pick up his specs and handed them back and Mr Lowry peered down to take them, trying to retain some dignity. He had no time to say anything, as Mrs Parks was already storming back across towards the gate, shouting back over her shoulder, 'You want to pick on someone yer own size next time! Think you can get away with doing anything you like, don't you? Bloody bullies, you teachers – that's what you are!'

And she was gone.

Gwen told Ariadne about the day's upset over a meal of lamb chops. She had started to give her landlady a hand with the cooking. Ariadne was so scatty that keeping an eye on anything was half her problem. Gwen stood guarding the chops under the grill to make sure they emerged a healthy, cooked colour rather than a singed mess.

'That sounds a queer carry-on to me,' Ariadne remarked, peering into the pan of potatoes, which was boiling so frantically that the room was already like a steam bath.

'It might be all right to turn those down now,' Gwen suggested.

'Oh . . . yes.' Ariadne fiddled with the gas stove as if she'd never seen it before, peering longsightedly at the dial. The fringe of her silky shawl hung perilously near the gas flame.

'There's certainly more to it than meets the eye. I'm going to see if I can get Ron to talk to me tomorrow.'

Once again, she called Ron to her at breaktime.

'Ron, I'm very concerned about what happened yesterday, and your mother obviously is too. Did you tell her why Mr Lowry gave you the cane?'

Ron shook his head, lips tightly pressed together.

'Why didn't you tell her?'

'Because . . .' Ron's face filled with emotion and his lips were trembling. 'He said he'd . . . he said I wasn't to say . . .' He wiped his eyes fiercely with his knuckles, smearing his grimy face. Suddenly he burst out, 'And it weren't my fault. I wish I'd never gone and seen what I seen!'

Gwen stared, at a loss.

'*Seen*? What did you see, Ron? Where?'

He gazed at her desperately and she could see he was close to telling her. But something was stopping him.

'I'm not to say.' He looked away, sullenly. 'Or I'll be in trouble.'

'What sort of trouble?' she asked.

'He said . . . he said he'd get me sent away.'

Gwen was horrified. What sort of a man was Mr Lowry to be making such threats to a ten-year-old boy?

'I don't think he can do that,' she tried to reassure him. 'Especially when you haven't done anything wrong.'

But she could see the boy was afraid and she didn't want to press him any more.

'Go on – go out to play,' she said. 'And don't fret.'

'What on earth am I to make of that?' she asked Lily Drysdale in the corner of the staffroom, where she hoped no one else could hear. 'The poor boy seems frightened out of his wits!'

Lily sat silently, a cup of tea held halfway to her lips and staring ahead of her almost as if listening to a voice that no one else could hear. Gwen began to wonder if she had heard what she said. Then Lily returned her cup to its saucer.

'Mr Lowry,' she pronounced, 'is almost certainly some kind of pervert. Though I've never managed to work out quite what kind.'

Forty-Six

They were chugging along the last few miles now, into Aberglyn.

It was dark outside the railway carriage. All Gwen could see in the window was her own reflection, her face, wide-eyed and solemn, gazing back at her, her hair tied softly back. She had taken her hat off and was holding it on her lap.

I look older, she thought. She remembered sitting on a train in just this way, pulling into Worcester, knowing that Edwin would be waiting for her under the platform lights. It seemed so long ago, another life in which she had been nothing more than a child. She wondered how Edwin was. Would he be bitter, or be putting experience behind him in his usual, blithely optimistic way? She thought of her parents. Sooner or later she would have to go back, to try and make peace. It was a dreadful thought and she pushed it away, pressing her face to the window to see something of the outside, but apart from occasional dots of light from houses and villages, there was nothing but the night. Sitting back, she closed her eyes for a moment. The air in the carriage smelled of smoke and dusty upholstery.

I'm someone else now. She swelled inside with joy. Daniel's girl. That's what the party members had finally started to call her, seeing them together. Apart from

Esther, of course, who treated Gwen in relation to Daniel with an arch irony. Gwen ignored her. She had also chosen to put out of her mind the conversation she had overheard last time she was in Aberglyn. It couldn't have meant anything much. And everyone did wrong things when they were young – herself for a start! She had jilted Edwin, more or less – she was a disgrace to her family! She and Daniel were both people who lived passionately, she decided, and were having to learn from their mistakes. That was why they were so well suited. They were Communists, revolutionaries: there was more to their lives than petty jealousies.

The train began to lose speed. They were pulling into Aberglyn and he would be there. In a few moments she would be in his arms!

As she stepped out of the carriage onto the darkened station, the train let out a great belch of steam, like a sigh of relief. There were not many people on the platform and she looked around, smiling in anticipation. She could not immediately see him, her eyes looking round hungrily, anticipating the sight of Daniel's beloved body, which she felt she knew as well as her own. But he did not appear. She stood by the little ticket office, keeping her lips turned up, trying not to feel deflated. He'd be here in a moment – he had said he would be. But the minutes passed.

'Gwen?' She turned to see a woman beside her, hair tucked under a little felt hat, and it took a moment to register that it was Shân Sullivan.

'Oh, hello!' After waiting alone, Gwen felt uplifted just seeing anyone she recognized. And she liked Daniel's auntie very much. In the dim lights, Shân looked pale and painfully thin.

'I came to meet you, Gwen *fach*. Daniel was coming, but he and his uncle have gone and got themselves tied up in a compo case . . .'

'A what?'

'Oh, it's over compensation for injury, like with Billy.' Shân sounded weary to her bones. 'There's another lad lost the use of his legs . . .'

'Oh, I see.' Gwen pushed away her feelings of disappointment. Of course a young man being crippled was more important than her. How could she argue with that? And, anyway, it was lovely to see Shân.

They began walking the two miles up from the station. Gwen couldn't help feeling cross with Daniel that his auntie had had to come all this way in her frail state.

'I could have come on my own,' she said. 'No need to drag you out.'

'Oh *duw*, no! There's a terrible thing, leaving you to walk on your own. Billy wanted to come and meet you as well, Gwen, but I hadn't the strength to push him all the way down here and back, so he's sitting stewing at home. He's been like a cat on hot bricks all day. You've been very good to him, girl, sending him the books and that.'

Gwen smiled in the dark street. She heard singing coming out of a little church on one corner. 'Oh, it's just something to keep him occupied. He seems to love reading so much.'

'Proper one for book reading, Billy is. Always has been, but of course since the accident it's meant everything to him.'

Gwen's arm was aching from carrying her case, but she tried not to show her discomfort. She asked after the rest of the family and Shân said Anthony was spending every waking moment at the NUWM offices making arrangements for the march, which was only two weeks away.

Daniel's absence was almost made up for by the radiant look of excitement on Billy's face as they came in through the door. He was in his wheelchair, a piece of blanket over his knees, which he snatched off impatiently as they came in.

'You're here – finally! Took you all evening to walk up the hill, did it!'

'Well, I'm an old lady now, you know that,' Shân retorted, going into the kitchen. 'I've made us a bit to eat – you settle in and talk to Billy, or he'll never forgive me!'

Even while Gwen was taking her coat off, Billy was already launching off enthusiastically about *Les Misérables*, what a fantastic story it was and how on earth had Victor Hugo managed to write such a *lot* and the chase at the end through Paris was so exciting! He said it was the best book he'd ever read and he was going to start at the beginning and read it all over again.

Gwen sat down beside him, laughing at his enthusiasm.

'Well, I'm glad you liked it so much! I'm having to guess what would be best out of what I can find.'

'Well, you found the best book ever written. Have you read it?'

She had to admit she hadn't.

'Oh, well, you read it! I've read lots of adventure stories and that – and Jack London's been one of my favourites, but I've never read anything like that before.'

'And I've never met anyone who loves reading so much.'

'Well, it takes you out of yourself, doesn't it? Sitting here all day – you know . . .' He looked crestfallen for a moment, but then smiled. 'Hope you don't mind me writing to you?'

'Mind? Of course I don't mind. It's lovely – and your letters are so nice to read. You've got quite a way with words, Billy.'

Billy looked so pleased when she said this that Gwen wondered whether to say more, to suggest that perhaps he might want to write other things, but she decided to wait. After all, she'd only just got in through the door.

They chatted as Shân heated the food. Gwen told Billy about her class, about how Lucy was getting on, and Billy laughed at some of her stories. She didn't tell him about Ron Parks. By the end of the week she had still not got to the bottom of what had happened to Ron.

'Those men won't be back yet,' Shân said, calling them to the table. 'We'll eat ours, or there's curling up with hunger we'll be before they decide to come home.'

Gwen pushed Billy's chair into the kitchen.

'Daniel's an idiot,' Billy said, as she walked behind the chair. 'I mean, I know the party's vital, and the march and everything – but if I had you here for me the way he has, I wouldn't be at any meeting tonight, I can tell you!'

Gwen felt a lump rise up in her throat for a moment, both for Billy's predicament and for herself. She liked being with Shân and Billy, though. It always felt cosy in the steamy little kitchen. She tried to relax, not to imagine each sound, every footfall, was Daniel and his uncle coming back.

'I hardly see Anthony these days,' Shân said. 'If it's

not problems with the dole or compo claims, it's the march ... I know they've got to do it, but I'll still be glad when it's over. Is anyone ever listening in the government? – That's what I want to know.'

'Now they've got the unemployment figures down in England they don't care two hoots about us here,' Billy said. 'You have to show them – *force* them to listen!'

Hearing the passion in his voice, Gwen immediately felt proud of Daniel again and all he was doing. After all, he could have gone to Birmingham and just looked out for himself. Instead, he was putting all his energy into his people and where he came from.

It was after eleven when the men came home at last. Daniel's eyes met hers as they came in and she beamed at him.

'Got here all right?' He came straight over and kissed her cheek. 'Sorry I wasn't at the station.'

'Not to worry.' She smiled, free of resentment now.

Before she went up to bed, Daniel came to speak to her in the little hall. Conscious of the others next door, they held each other close and he whispered into her neck, 'I'm going to have to be at a few meetings tomorrow.'

She had half expected this. 'It's all right.' She knew she had barely managed to sound as if that was true.

Daniel drew back and peered at her in the gloom.

'It's such a busy time. So much to do.'

'I know.' She hugged him tight. 'And they need you.'

'On Sunday we'll have time – we'll go out somewhere, start early.'

Her spirits rose. 'Promise?'

He kissed her. 'Course I promise!'

He won her round. He always seemed to be able to.

'Do you think Billy would like it if I took him out today?' Gwen whispered the question to Shân in the kitchen, out of earshot of Billy.

It was a brilliant, autumn morning. Daniel would be off and away. Why shouldn't she and Billy enjoy the day?

Shân looked doubtful for a moment, then smiled. 'Have you got the strength in you, girl? That boyo's heavier than he looks.'

'Of course – I'm sure I could manage, if you think it'd be all right?'

'Oh – he'd love you to, I know he would!' Shân looked wistful. 'He doesn't get out enough. To the odd meeting, or when his father's got the time. He'd be ever so pleased if you took him – for a little while, mind. Don't you go overdoing it.'

After breakfast, and when Gwen had kept tactfully out of the way while Shân saw to Billy's physical needs and helped him dress, they eased his wheelchair out through the door, and Gwen and Billy set out into the golden morning.

'Where would you like to go – up the hill?' She leaned down to talk to him and was suddenly uncomfortably aware of a blush rising in his cheeks. It only then occurred to her how much of an effect her physical presence had on Billy.

I must be careful, she thought, standing up again. She felt ashamed suddenly, realizing that it had never crossed her mind to think of Billy in that way, that he might be interested in her, because he was younger and because – it was an awful admission – he had been maimed, and seemed stripped of his manhood by his injuries. She had assumed somewhere in her mind that he was not whole as a man, that his body was numb, without a man's feelings. Now she was not sure and felt suddenly confused.

She leaned hard against the wheelchair, pushing Billy up the slope she had climbed with Daniel on that summer morning. There were a few crisp, brown leaves on the pavement, crackling underfoot. The air was full of the ripe smells of autumn: leaves and smoke and a hint of decay, sunlight pouring in at a low angle which seemed to make everything glow, the bracken a deep rust colour on the sides of the hills. Gwen pushed the chair on and on determinedly. The road curved round and, branching off it, she saw a steep track to the right. They had left the houses behind and were climbing steeply so that she had to lean all her weight into pushing the chair. The air was chill, but she was soon sweating with exertion.

'Shall we go on up there a little way?' she asked, trying not to let Billy hear how much she was beginning to pant.

'No – it's too much for you!' He sounded anxious and she wondered if he felt safe in her hands.

'I really think I could – just some of the way.'

'You can see a long way from up there,' he said and she could hear the longing in his voice.

'Well, we'll do it!'

Bracing herself, her chest level with the back of the chair, she heaved against it and slowly inched Billy up and up the steep incline. Once her foot slipped on a little stone; she almost lost her balance and let out a cry of alarm.

'What's the matter?' Billy tried to look round.

'Nothing – it's all right.'

After a time, there was a level resting place off the track. To one side was a rock, flattened on top to serve as a seat, and she pushed the chair over to it so that she could sit down beside Billy. They sat in silence for a few moments, each drinking in the great expanse of the green valley, smudged in parts with black, the little town nestled in its palm. The sound of a train whistle rose from the town, made soft by the distance and the gentle wind.

Gwen then became aware of Billy beside her, of the way his grey eyes were looking along the sweep of the valley with deep, almost meditative attention. She had been about to speak, but she sensed she might be interrupting his thought processes. His head was turned slightly away from her. Gradually, he looked back towards her again.

'The hills are so close – they seem to have a personality of their own,' she said.

'They do. They've all got names.' He pointed around the valley, telling her the names of the rusty peaks. Then he breathed in deeply, as if drinking the air. 'I've never lived anywhere but here.'

She nodded, understanding that the elevation of their position gave him a perspective on his home he rarely had, and of sensing the wider world beyond and all he might be missing.

'It's a good place,' she told him.

'It is.' He nodded emphatically, then laughed. 'Though I don't know anywhere else to put against it. Good people here, they are.'

'Daniel's always talking about it.'

'Is he?' He didn't follow this up, but just kept looking. 'I only know about anywhere else from book reading. You can go anywhere in a book, the way you can in a dream.'

'Billy, I've really enjoyed your letters.' She hesitated, and he turned to her with a candid, vulnerable gaze, and she saw, to her discomfort, in that moment the power of his feelings for her. It made her feel sad, flattered and uncomfortable all at once. She looked down in confusion, trying to hold on to what she had been going to say. 'It's just – well, the way you write – you've got a talent, you know. Describing things, bringing them alive. I wondered if you'd thought about writing other things, not just letters.'

'I do.' He was the one blushing now, with shy pleasure. 'Least, I've done a bit – a few stories and that. Don't know why. Something to do, I s'pose. No one'd want to read them.'

'I'd like to.'

There was a pause.

'I've never shown them to anyone – not even Mam.'

'Well, only if you want to . . .'

'Oh, I'd like to know if anyone – well, if they . . . If anyone else can read them and understand about them. D'you know what I mean?'

'I think so.'

'I keep them in a box. Under the bed.'

'Doesn't your mother ask what's in there?'

'Oh yes, but she's not much of a reader. She just calls it my scribbling. She doesn't want to read them.'

Gwen looked out over the valley to the mountain beyond. Clouds were beginning to gather.

'What about Daniel?' she asked. 'You've never thought of showing them to him?'

'No. Daniel's so clever with his book learning. I thought he'd laugh at me.'

'Surely he wouldn't.'

There was a silence, then, in a different tone, casual but solemn, Billy said, 'Daniel's not always straight with everyone, you know.'

A cold feeling gripped her. This warning that kept coming. She found she was angry. 'What d'you mean?' She heard the hostility in her own voice, but why was everyone trying to sow seeds of doubt in her mind about Daniel?

Billy looked into his lap. She could see him trying to decide what to say. 'I just mean I haven't felt like showing him my stories.'

Once she had pushed Billy back to the house, they had a bit of dinner with Shân and afterwards Shân went out to visit a neighbour at Gwen's urging.

'I'm so pleased Billy's got a bit of company,' she whispered to Gwen in the hall before she went.

Once she'd gone, Billy pulled a rough wooden box out from under the bed and showed Gwen some of his stories.

'You've done a lot!' she exclaimed, seeing him pull out a thick collection of dog-eared papers.

'You don't have to read them all.' He was excited. 'Look, take a couple. Will you?'

'Of course. I'd really like to.'

He handed her a sheaf of paper. All the stories were written on small sheets of cheap lined paper which had yellowed, in a tiny copperplate hand, as if he was trying to fit the maximum possible number of words on a page. The top one was called 'King of the Clouds'. As soon as she began reading, Gwen realized the story was about a boy who longed to fly aeroplanes. She looked up, smiling at him.

'I've always wanted to fly an aeroplane. Like Amy Johnson.'

Billy grinned, delighted. 'Proper heroine she is.'

He sat looking through his other papers while Gwen sat by the fire and read, sometimes having to stop and ask him to decipher a word for her. The story was quite simple, about a boy who dreams of flying and becomes a pilot, with his own plane. Something about the way it was written, though, drew her on. There was an intensity in the story which moved her. As she finished it, she kept her eyes lowered while she thought what to say. She could feel Billy watching her and his powerful need to know what she thought. She looked up into his hungry face.

'It's lovely, Billy. You could be a writer.'

And she could see she had said something which meant the world to him.

Forty-Seven

The next morning Gwen went with the family to early Mass in Aberglyn's small Catholic church. Anthony pushed Billy down the hill, well wrapped up as the morning was cold and wet. It all seemed very foreign to Gwen, the women's heads covered with lace or scarves and everything in Latin. When they came out into the narrow, grey street, amid the little knot of people, it was into bright, stormy sunlight which made them screw up their eyes.

'Still want to go walking?' Daniel teased. They had talked about going out after he got back the evening before.

'I've got my coat and hat – and my boots.'

'Welsh rain is wetter than English rain, you know,' Anthony teased.

Gwen laughed. 'I suppose I'll just have to get wet then!'

'You going over the mountain?' Shân asked. Her thin face was framed by a flowery scarf.

'We'll go to Tredegar,' Daniel said. 'It's a good walk.'

'You don't want to go tiring her out – she's got all that way to go back.'

'I don't mind,' Gwen said eagerly. 'I love walking.'

Daniel had, for once, put his greatcoat on and they set off for the head of the valley, then branched off on one of the steep paths over the mountain. To begin with, there was brilliant sunshine, but very soon, in the distance, clouds gathered like thick smoke over the mountains and moved towards them.

'Oh dear,' Gwen panted. 'We're in for it in a minute.'

'No doubt about that.'

Daniel seemed oblivious to the weather. When the rain started to come down, it was as if they were wrapped in water. Gwen laughed, as rivulets poured from her hat and down her neck.

'We're going to be soaked!' she shouted. Her lungs were straining. They were climbing steeply, barely able to see anything beyond a few yards all around.

'Never mind. The sun'll be back soon,' Daniel called to her. Suddenly he stopped and took her in his arms, kissing her fiercely, and the rain fell on her upturned face and ran down her neck. She broke away, gasping for breath and laughing.

'It's gone right inside my clothes – I'm soaked!'

By the time they reached the highest point, the rain was easing off. Gwen felt all-over warm and damp, clothes heavy and chafing, but there was a glory in reaching the top with the sun breaking through and everything wet and gleaming.

'Look now.' Daniel came and put an arm round her shoulders. 'There's Tredegar. Back there.' He pointed down at Aberglyn, from where they had just climbed. 'I was forever walking up and down across here at one time.' He stood, looking for a moment across the Sirhowy Valley. 'First deep pit in Wales was sunk here.'

The two towns below them looked small and defenceless with their straight little rows of houses. She felt a great rush of affection for them, of belonging.

With the sunlight and the mountain breeze on her face, the valleys spread out on either side, she was filled with certainty that she had been brought here for a reason. She saw her life spread in front of her: she would marry Daniel and he would come back to his home where he belonged and she would come to belong too. She would be part of this place, and have Daniel's children, even learn Welsh. It felt so right and meant for her. She turned and held him close.

'I love it here, Daniel. I love you.'

'Love you too, girl.'

She hoped he might say something more, that perhaps his thoughts had been the same as hers, that he might even make some promise for the future, but he was silent, just held her close.

After a time, Daniel said, 'All these valleys – there'll be men coming on the march . . .'

Gwen broke from him, stung, and walked a few paces away. She had imagined his thoughts might be running on similar lines to hers, but, as so often, she was wrong. Daniel was thinking about politics, as usual! *Can't you think about anything else, just for a moment?* she wanted to shout at him. *What about me? Don't you ever think about me and our future?* But then she thought of his tears over his mother and the lockouts, the poor pinched faces of the valleys, and she was ashamed. How selfish she was being again, when Daniel was always thinking about other people.

She went back to him and took his arm. 'They've got to make the government listen,' she said. 'And you *will*, all of you.'

'Everyone should listen.' His voice was low, passionate. 'The whole world.'

She watched his face as he looked out across the

landscape and for a moment she felt afraid for him. Would the world listen to the message of Communism? Were they even listening now?

'Shall we go on?' she said.

It was easier to talk on the way down since they were not so short of breath and the sun stayed with them. Daniel told her how he used to be back and forth over here to the library in Tredegar.

'One of the best socialist libraries anywhere. I was in the Socialist League here before I joined the party. Aneurin Bevan's family are all here – he was elected MP for Ebbw Vale in twenty-nine. Marvellous, it was. Talks on Marxism, philosophers – as good as any university, I'd say. Plato, Hegel, Kant – we had a genius of a man called Oliver Jones, gave us classes. It all started to make sense, fit together – all the injustices, what they'd done to us . . .' He held his hand out to help Gwen down from a rocky step in the path. 'Nothing was ever the same again. It's genius. And yet even here not everyone could see – wanted to appease the colliery owners, keep their jobs at any cost . . .'

'Like Hywel Jones?'

Daniel shook his head. 'Men like Hywel will never change anything,' he said bitterly.

The descent went quickly and soon they were walking through the narrow streets of Tredegar. The streets were quiet, except for a few people sitting outside their houses in the sun who nodded a greeting. The bright warmth stayed and Gwen was filled with a great sense of wellbeing after the exercise. Daniel lit a cigarette and showed her round: the library where he had spent so many hours, the NUWM offices, the square with its tall clock tower, which said that it was almost eleven o'clock. As they walked on, arm in arm, people started to come out of one of the chapels along the street in front of them.

'It's such a shame we don't have longer,' Gwen said. She had to catch a train in the afternoon and it felt like a pressure.

'Quick run up and down the mountain for you again,' Daniel teased, throwing down the butt of his cigarette. 'Good for you, that is.'

'I wish I could stay. It's gone far too quickly!'

'I'm no company. I'll be at meetings all the week, with the committee and that.'

'I know. And there's a class waiting for me.'

They crossed the street so as not to get tangled in the knot of people outside the chapel. Someone called, 'Morning, Daniel mun!'

'Hello, Albert – see you tomorrow!' Daniel raised a hand in reply as they walked on along the street. He exchanged greetings with a few other people, and was just saying, 'He's a good bloke,' about someone he had spoken to, when another voice called him from behind.

'Daniel? Daniel Fernandez?'

The voice was shrill and furiously challenging. They both spun round to see a dark-haired young woman, slim and in a pretty though shabby pink dress. On her hip she carried a little boy.

'So – deigned to come back here again, have you?' she demanded. Gwen could see she was quivering with such emotions that she could barely contain them.

'Couldn't come back when you were needed could you? Not to fulfil your responsibilities? You're a rotten, wicked man, Daniel – making your own son into a bastard. Going off without a hint of care for me – for us . . .'

Gwen was struggling to take in what the young

woman was saying. She could see that her taut demeanor was giving way to tears, however much she didn't want it to. There was obviously a great reservoir of pent-up emotion waiting to be released in her, even though she didn't want to lose her dignity. She didn't seem to care who heard her.

'Megan . . .' Daniel breathed.

'That's right – just stand there, nothing to say!' The woman turned to Gwen in a combination of fury and apparently looking for an ally. 'Are you the latest one, then? Well, all I can say is, I pity you, lovey. Don't believe a word he says – he's a cheat and a liar. Left me to bring up his son all alone without a word, ever. This is Evan, Daniel. He's nearly two years old now, and he's your son, remember?' She went as if to thrust the child into Daniel's arms, but then snatched him back, hugging him protectively to her. 'Not that you care . . .'

'I didn't know—' Daniel started to say. A couple of people had stopped to listen, tutting loudly.

'You didn't *know*? Course you knew! I came to Aberglyn looking for you, but no, you were never there, were you – always off somewhere else with your politics and your superior ways. You make me sick, Daniel. What about my letters? Didn't you get those either? What did you expect – for me to come to Birmingham chasing after you to make you see what you'd left behind? I didn't have any money, remember! Nothing but my drunken da and Auntie Beth. And not *once* – not one answer, or word, not one penny to help . . .' She was weeping now, angry with herself, Gwen could see, but unable to help it.

'You could have written back! What did you say those things to me for, Daniel? That's what I can't forgive you for. Why did you say you loved me and then treat me like that? Always politics, never people, that's you, Daniel. You're a cold, cruel man.'

A great chill went through Gwen. She was stunned, barely able to take in what was happening in front of her: the harsh words which, deep down, when she admitted it to herself, rang so true, the beautiful, brown-eyed boy who was so obviously related to Daniel. She stood paralysed, wishing with every fibre in herself that this was not happening, that she was dreaming.

'I couldn't,' Daniel was saying. His voice was neither apologetic nor defiant, just flat, as if his nature was an inevitability which he could only accept but not defeat. 'I couldn't just come back here and marry you, settle down in the valleys, Megan.'

The woman shook her head, more tears coming. The little boy was beginning to be upset too by his mother's emotion.

'I hate you, Daniel,' she wept. 'I love Evan, but I hate you. You've ruined my life. I was going to get away from here too – you know I was. And now I'll never be anything but the shame of Treherbert with the bastard child. D'you know why I'm here? With Auntie Beth again now she's had yet another baby, that's why. Good old Megan – she'll stay at home and be the skivvy. She'll come and nurse her auntie when no one else'll be bothered. That's why I was here in Tredegar, remember? Looking after auntie. Politics was my only way out. And *you* . . .' She looked up at him, wet cheeked, eyes searching his face as if trying to find hope, to understand. 'I loved you. And now I hate you more than anyone else alive. It's the only way I can get through.' She pulled her son close so that their cheeks were touching. 'That's your father, Evan. Take a good look at him – he's everything a man shouldn't be.'

'I could send you some money,' Daniel said desperately.

'Oho – talk about better late than never! I don't want your money, Daniel.' She almost spat at him. 'It'll be cursed, like everything else that comes from you. I just want you to know what you are – what you've done. I hope you rot for it.'

She turned away then and walked off, quickly, head down to shield herself from the staring bystanders, and in a few moments they saw her, in her pink frock, disappear past the chapel and round the corner.

Forty-Eight

'I can see something's upsetting you, Gwen *fach*. Is it anything you want to tell your Auntie Shân?'

Gwen could barely remember the walk back over the mountain, the having to be polite back with the family in Aberglyn, trying to eat thin stew and potatoes with them round the table. She could see, though, that the fact that she could barely swallow, or meet anyone's eyes for fear of bursting into tears, and the silence between herself and Daniel were not lost on Shân. After dinner, when they had moved from the kitchen to the front room to sit by the fire, and Shân was boiling the kettle for a cup of tea, she put her head round the door. 'There's a little bit of help I'm needing, Gwen. Can you come in here a minute?'

Once she was in the kitchen, Shân closed the door firmly behind them and spoke very softly. 'You haven't been yourself since you came back today.'

Touched by the woman's kindness, Gwen felt her eyes fill with tears again. She had cried on the walk home, trying to get Daniel to talk to her, to explain. All he seemed able to say was that he couldn't help it, hadn't meant to hurt her. But staying in the valleys, marriage and children – it seemed like a living death to him.

'The party, the movement – that's life and hope to me,' he said. 'I was only twenty-three when it happened ... My life had only just begun – I couldn't just be here and be tied down. It was a mistake. It's on my conscience – course it is! And it doesn't mean I don't love *you*, Gwen. I love you more than anyone I've ever met.'

'I bet that's what you told Megan!' She suddenly remembered his great anxiety that she did not fall pregnant. No wonder! Now she saw all too clearly just how familiar a problem that was to him.

'But I didn't love her the way I love *you*,' he said pleadingly.

She was so hurt that she could not think where to begin with Daniel's aunt. In the end she just blurted out, 'Did you know?'

'Know what, lovey?' Shân asked cautiously.

'About Megan? About the child – *Daniel's son*?' Tears ran down her cheeks and she put her hands over her face. The pain of it seemed enough to overwhelm her. She felt Shân's thin arms round her shoulders.

'Oh, my poor girl, oh dear, oh dear, So that's what's happened. Oh Lord, I knew she'd come back to haunt him one day.'

Gwen looked up at her. 'You *did* know?' The hushed conversation that night – of course she had known. 'Why didn't you tell me?'

Shân looked stricken. 'How could I? I'd only met the girl twice. She was staying in Tredegar, going to the League meetings there and that's how they met, but he never brought her back here. I think she was staying with an auntie, a strict young woman from what I hear of her. Megan Hughes is not from a good family – lots of trouble. I never knew Daniel was so involved with her then. Not until later. The family'd just left, see, Theresa and the rest, gone to Birmingham. Daniel wasn't coming back much at first – couldn't afford it. He even walked once, all the way. Come the time Megan knew she was expecting, she came here, trying it on, telling me she was carrying Daniel's baby. I mean, at first I wouldn't believe her. How did I know if she was lying? But she kept on – course, she was upset, see. In the end, I thought, well, Daniel knows the truth of the matter, whatever it is, so I gave her the address in Birmingham. I've asked him about it so many times. He wouldn't see her. Said what's done is done.' She shook her head, looking at the ceiling for a moment, as if in despair.

'She's not from round here, see, she's from the Rhondda. Once she'd gone back there and expecting a child, I suppose she wasn't in a position to keep running off trying to find him. After a time we all thought, let sleeping dogs lie. I don't think she kept on writing – she must have given up, poor girl. So you see –' she looked into Gwen's desperate face – 'that's our Daniel, I'm afraid. God knows I'm ashamed of him for this. I've told and told him he should face up to his responsibilities ... And then he came here with you, and you're lovely, girl, and I could see how he is with you, and what could I do? You're so good for him, Gwen, and how could I just destroy all that for you by bringing her up again? You must believe me – I've never seen Daniel be with anyone the way he is with you.'

Gwen started crying again. It was all impossible, the pain, the enormity of it. Looking up desperately into Shân's worn face, she said, 'But I can't be with someone who would deceive me like this! How could I ever, *ever* trust him again?'

As she was speaking the door opened and the two women realized that Daniel was standing looking at them. His face was filled with shame, and a sadness which wrung Gwen's heart. But in that moment she knew, really knew for sure, with a cold sense of reality. This was how it would always be, that he could hurt her so much then melt her with a look. She would come back again and again to burn herself against him, hoping it was safe, that she could love him and know deep, lasting trust – and that somehow, in one way or another, whether it was with women or politics, he would always let her down. Some women could live with it, but she knew she couldn't.

She drew away from Shân and went to him. She stood looking into his eyes, seeing that he was anguished, and sorry, but it was no good. He had betrayed her too badly this time.

'I'm going home, Daniel. I'm sorry. I love you too much and I can't live with what you might do to me.' She started to walk away. 'I don' t think I want to see you again.'

The train journey home was a blur. It rained much of the way so vision was limited, and along the way, after the extreme emotions of the day, Gwen shut down and sat numb and stunned. Parting with Shân, Anthony and Billy had been terrible. They already felt like family to her, but how could she ever see them again after this?

'Keep writing to me, won't you?' Billy asked, looking in a troubled way at her tear-stained face. And she could only promise that she would.

Shân embraced her silently and Anthony shook her hand and gruffly wished her well.

'I'm sorry, girl,' he said gruffly. 'Don't know what to say.' And this made her cry all over again.

Daniel accompanied her to the station and most of the way they walked through the drizzle in a cold, sad silence.

When they reached the station, Daniel stopped her outside. 'I can't let you go.' His voice was anguished. 'I've made a terrible mistake, I know, but I've learned my lesson. I'd never leave you, Gwen. I love you too much.'

She closed her feelings against this and looked up at him. 'As much as politics – the party? No, Daniel, I don't think you do. I've seen it, all the way along, although I've tried not to. I wanted to believe you could really love me and put me first in the line sometimes, but you can't. And I've seen you playing about with Esther. That was bad enough, but I tried to forgive you. But now this. You've got a *son*, Daniel, and you just walked away! I can't stay with you if I can't trust you. I can't keep giving you my heart and having you tear me to pieces.' She was dry eyed now, with a stony calm.

He looked down at her, and in that second's silence she saw that he knew she was right.

'I do love you.' He reached out to stroke her face but she pulled back.

'Don't, Daniel, please.'

Suddenly she couldn't bear it any more, being near him, even now the pain of being drawn back to him. She said an abrupt goodbye and walked away from him fast. She did not turn back, did not want to see if he left immediately or waited to watch her move out of his life.

She did not tell Ariadne what had happened. The next few days she taught her class in a stunned, automatic way, dressing herself in her role as teacher every morning and going through the motions. Seeing Lucy every morning in front of her brought home just how many connections she had made with Daniel's family, how she had come to love them. Breaking with Daniel was not going to be so simple. She couldn't abandon Lucy and Billy just because of what Daniel had done, could she? And what about the party? How could she bear to do anything connected with that now? She found it hard to pay attention to anything at school. What had happened to Ron Parks, for the moment, escaped her attention. The evenings she spent miserably in her room. Ariadne kept asking if she was sickening for something and Gwen told her she did not feel quite well. Somehow she could not face up to talking about Daniel to anyone yet.

Lying on her bed a couple of evenings after she had come back from Aberglyn, her mood sank very low. Everything she had wanted to do in coming away from home seemed to be cast into doubt. Look at what she had done! She had thrown away everything because of her love for Daniel: marriage to a good, decent man, her own family's approval and welcome, her own happiness and security. Here she was, in a room in a strange household, teaching the children of the poor. What was her life going to be now? More of the same, stretching ahead for ever until she was like Lily Drysdale? Or Agnes Monk? She lay for a long time, staring at the light above her and wondering how it would be if she admitted defeat and begged her parents to take her back. Even begged Edwin to take her back? For a few moments she longed for the familiar, its safety and security, imagined their wedding, as they had planned it at St Mark's, her home in a vicarage, children, Edwin talking over his thoughts and sermons with her, jigsaw puzzles on a table in the parlour to put visitors at their ease.

She sat up suddenly.

'No!' she said out loud, startling herself. Her heart was beating fast. She did not want that, had never really wanted it, but had not seen that there could ever be anything else. Whereas Daniel ... Caught between what she longed for in him, the passion of it, the sense of being so fully alive in his presence and the reality that it was never going to be possible to make a life with him that she could trust, she burst into tears. Hugging her knees, she sat rocking in distress on the bed. She felt torn up, as if Daniel had physically imprinted himself on her and then been ripped away, leaving her utterly bereft.

When she got home the next afternoon, Ariadne said, 'There's a message for you, dear. Came just after you left this morning.' And she handed Gwen a hand-written envelope. The looping script was unfamiliar and she opened it frowning.

Dear Gwen,
    Millie asked me to let you know that the infant has arrived and is a female. She's doing well and is at home. Millie would like some company so do come over.
        Sincerely,
        Lance

With a wan smile she showed it to Ariadne.

'A *female*?' Ariadne exclaimed. 'Well, isn't that just like a man – and not to tell you her name!'

'Perhaps she doesn't have one yet,' Gwen said.

'Or her date of birth, or weight or where she was born!'

'Well, that's Lance for you. He's not very sharp – not at this sort of thing.' She felt slightly cheered by the distraction and was glad all had gone safely for Millie.

'I think I'll go and see them now.' The thought of sitting alone in her room again was depressing. 'I don't have anything to take her.'

'Ah – now, I might be able to help you there,' Ariadne said. And she disappeared upstairs and came back with a soft parcel wrapped in tissue. 'It's a little matinée coat – I made it for my sister's baby, years ago now. She died a few days after she was born, poor little thing, and I've never had the heart to do anything with it.'

When Millie opened the parcel, the garment was a lovely pale pink, and Millie was delighted with it. She was sitting up in bed, the room in a great state of disarray because 'Lance is hopeless', as Millie kept saying. Lance, who appeared exhausted by the experience of becoming a father, was laid out in a chair in the sitting room. The baby was a dear little thing with a film of carroty hair like Millie's, and her name was to be Amy Jane.

'That's pretty,' Gwen said, perching precariously on a chair by the bed, on top of a pile of clothes.

'She's a poppet,' Millie said, looking down at the child in her arms, whose eyes were closed, the bluish lids flickering gently as if she was dreaming.

'How was it, Mill?' Gwen felt shy asking. Millie had been through something which put her beyond, into a new kind of adulthood.

'Pretty grim.' Millie made a face. 'Never mind – it's over now. Never again, though.'

'I bet everyone says that.'

'Maybe. I mean it, though.' She lowered her voice, leaning close to Gwen. 'What am I going to do? He just doesn't want to know.' Tears were rolling down Millie's round cheeks and they fell on Amy's tiny face as Millie looked down. 'She's so lovely – how can he not want anything to do with her?'

'Oh, Mill!' Gwen put her arm round her friend's shoulders. She had a warm, milky smell. 'I'm sure he does really. He's probably a bit shocked by it all. After all, he hasn't had to carry her round inside him all this time. It's early days.'

'But he's barely even been in to look at her! And he treats me as if I'm a terrible nuisance because I need help, and I'm so tired and sore . . .' Millie broke down and really cried now. 'Oh God, why did I marry him, Gwen? I wish I'd never set eyes on him! How am I going to bring up our little girl with him? I feel so hopeless – I just want to go home to Mum's.'

Gwen held her, stroking her back, desperately trying to think of something hopeful to say. Millie and Lance's marriage had been a disaster from the start: it was no good saying everything would all be all right.

'Men often don't get close to their children until they're older,' she said, dredging up something she remembered her mother saying.

'That's what Mum says. Course, she'll come and

help me, but he is her father – he should care about her, shouldn't he?'

Gwen sighed. She thought of Megan Hughes and little Evan. Daniel didn't seem to care a fig for his existence. As far as she could see, men were so different as to be an utter mystery. But it didn't seem helpful to point that out at this moment.

'Well, I think he should. She's beautiful, Millie. You'll just have to be very strong for her and hope he follows on. It's his loss if he doesn't.'

Gwen read about the Hunger March in the newspaper, sitting in her room at Ariadne's. Contingents of marchers were coming from all over the country. Ellen Wilkinson, the MP they had heard speak in the Town Hall, was marching with her constituents from Jarrow. The Welsh marchers, five hundred and four strong, had all assembled in Cathays Park in Cardiff to head east to London. She read the words spoken by the march's leader, Councillor Lewis Jones:

> We are going to London to meet the government and the House of Commons, and if they refuse to see us we will force ourselves upon the Cabinet and if necessary upon the King and we will force this pack of gangsters to abolish for ever the means test. They are ruining our country.

Gwen sat with the paper on her lap, staring ahead of her. She could see the great crowds of men in her mind, as they had been in Tonypandy: their poor clothes and caps, their Welsh accents, their hunger and the power of their determination. And among them, always, she could see Daniel's face, there with his people, alight with a passion that he could never quite find in anything else, not in her, not in his family, not in anything settled. And she ached with a pain that seemed to fill her whole body.

Forty-Nine

Day after day, they trudged on.

The days were cold now and the nights freezing, iron hard. Along roads and tracks they went, through towns and villages, begging food and sometimes work. Odd jobs came their way, on farms especially. Some people took one look at them and turned them away. But there had been work, along the road. They spent the best part of a week picking apples and pears and sleeping under the trees. They gathered late potatoes, mucked out horses and collected eggs when farms or stables were shorthanded. They helped pull down a rotting barn and burn the wood on a huge pyre. The farmer was kind and brought potatoes to cook buried in the heat. Many others cursed them and turned them away, especially when they left the country and tried begging round the towns. The days passed, hungry, cold, no beginning or end to anything except the daylight, the alternate rising of the sun and moon. Apart from that there was no shape or purpose. They just kept walking.

The night of the first frost they were sleeping in a barn, and in the morning stepped out to find the ground white, the cow-nibbled grass rigid underfoot. Joey walked round and round in circles, feeling the crunch of it under his boots. He had never seen a field covered in frost before. They had had to find him new boots when the soles of the others fell away from the uppers and he could no longer walk. These were old and too big, and inside he had wrapped his feet in rags. That day he remembered the name of the next village because they brewed up tea and walked on between icy hawthorn hedges, ploughed fields on each side, breath white, noses and ears frozen, and he saw a sign saying, ASTON.

Words spilled suddenly from his mouth. 'Aston – that's where my nanna's house was!'

John stopped, turned on the icy road and stared at him.

'This ain't Birmingham.'

Joey looked back silently. John's face looked pointed now, like a fox's.

It grew warmer again after that. Rusty leaves had rotted in drifts and the wind blew them into swirls. Nuts and haws rolled under their boots. There was no work now the summer was over. They passed through somewhere called Faringdon. People steered away from them as they passed. 'Dear me – look at them,' he heard. 'It's a disgrace.' Or 'How terrible.' In the main street Joey caught sight of a strange pair of people walking along: a boy with a head that looked too big for his body, staring eyes, clothes like a clown and a wild giant beside him, all black, bushy beard ... John, that was John, and it was only then that he saw he was looking in a shop window at his own reflection.

John sometimes mumbled to himself, but never looked anyone in the eye. Neither of them had the energy to say anything. They had no proper food, had not had a hot meal for weeks. John coughed a lot. Everything seemed distant, Joey felt, as if he was floating and not part of things. He had felt invisible and seeing himself was a shock.

The weather turned wet. One afternoon, on a stretch of open, chalky downland, they were caught in a downpour with no hope of shelter. The rain slanted down, turning the track to slippery clay which clung thick and heavy to their boots so that it became a struggle to lift their feet. They kept having to stop and try to wipe the caked mud off on the grass. John let out muffled curses. He had been even quieter than usual lately. He coughed, doubled up with it, making a racked, liquid sound. The sky was a thick swathe of cloud, no break in it and they were already soaked through. John put his head down against the wind and Joey walked in his shelter, the legs of his trousers sodden and heavy.

They stopped that day long before they normally would. There was a barn at the foot of a hill and they went into its hay-smelling gloom. Neither of them could stop shivering, their teeth chattering. Their clothes were soaked, and so were the contents of the curtain. Even the matches, which John usually kept safely stowed in the pan, had fallen out and were sodden and useless. Joey was surprised how quietly John took this. They could not build a fire, had no food, but he didn't shout and swear like he often did.

He just said, 'That's it, then,' and sat hugging himself, shaking.

Joey's clothes were so cold and uncomfortable that every move he made caused him miserable discomfort. They had eaten nothing that day. He stared out at the rain falling over the grey clay. When he looked round, John had lurched over sideways and stayed just where he was, fast asleep. In the end the hazy feeling Joey had so often filled his head completely and all he could do was curl on his side and let the darkness fill him completely.

    •

When he woke it was light and seemed to be morning, but he wasn't sure. He could hear rats moving in the barn. He lay for a long time in a dazed state, without the strength to get up, listening to sounds from outside, those big black birds calling in their scraping way from trees in the distance and a smaller bird somewhere nearer. He could not feel his feet. Perhaps he had no feet any more? He tried to wiggle his toes but felt nothing. After a time he thought about moving, about turning his head. Where was John? It was so quiet in here. It took a great effort of will to make himself move, having to think about it, to tell his neck to turn. When he did he saw John had shifted onto his back and was still asleep.

Now I'll move my arm, he thought. *Sit up, sit up . . .* His clothes were still wet. Moving was misery, barely seemed worth the trouble. In the past he might have sobbed but that took too much from him too. He hauled himself up and sat staring, hearing John's wheezy breathing coming to him faintly. John twitched, coughed. Joey pulled himself up and saw their bundle on the floor of the barn. He rifled through it, the pan and knife and spoon, the old rags, hoping there might be a morsel of food in there they had overlooked. Apart from a few crumbs, there was nothing. He looked at John again. In the end he went over and shoved at his arm, trying to wake him. John groaned, but his eyes did not open. Joey shook him but there was no response. He knelt, staring down at the man's face. There was dirt deeply ingrained in his forehead and nose. Joey saw yellow sticky stuff was coming out of the corners of his eyes. Everything else was hair, bushy, black and matted.

'John?' His voice sounded reedy and strange. No reply came.

Joey stood up, steadying himself, feeling light enough to float away, and wandered out of the barn, squinting as the light stabbed into his eyeballs. He set off across the field, but it was so wet that he was soon weighed down by the thick clay and he turned back and moved along the edge where there was a rough strip of weeds. In the distance he could see some farm buildings and he made for those. They were two fields away: another ploughed field, then a meadow for grazing, which was empty of animals. As he moved closer, he could hear cows bellowing in the farmyard, which reeked of manure. He crept closer and saw a wooden shed, which he took to be a henhouse. Keeping to the backs of the buildings, he edged round the farm until he was able to sneak over the iron fence and into the hut. It was, as he thought, full of the feathery warmth of hens, the stink of their muck and their fussy clucking noises. He groped around for eggs, found three and put them carefully in his coat pockets.

When he put his head out of the henhouse, though, he saw a man, walking across the yard in the distance. Joey froze, almost retreated into the henhouse – but he'd be trapped in there! He ran the short distance to the fence.

'Oi! What d'you think you're doing, you thieving little . . .'

Joey could hear that the man was running and he tore away across the field of cowpats, his lungs fit to explode, trying desperately not to lose his boots, grasping the ends of his coat to keep the eggs cradled and safe. He was convinced the man was chasing him and that he could hear shouting, but when he turned, there was no sign of him. By the time Joey got back to the barn he was stumbling, barely able to stand. He flung himself down and took out one of the eggs. Knocking the top off carefully with the knife, he slid the raw egg into his mouth, swallowing its slimy contents in two goes. There was no one coming outside, but he kept peering out just in case.

John was still asleep. He had not moved.

Fifty

People started disappearing from the school. First of all, Alice Wilson was absent for the register for two days in a row. Gwen assumed she was poorly and didn't give it much thought. She was caught up in her grief over Daniel, carrying her heart about inside her like a hard, painful stone. She kept thinking about going to see Theresa Fernandez. Had she known about Megan Hughes as well? Had they all made a proper fool of her?

But soon after, Charlotte Rowley vanished. Rumours started to circulate and days later Agnes Monk also failed to arrive at school. In the staffroom there was talk about nothing else. Mr Lowry did not issue an explanation, but one came, eventually, from an unexpected source. Lily Drysdale, as ever taking her own individual approach to the care of the school's children, had managed to get Ron Parks to talk to her.

'There was something not right about the boy, I could see,' she told Gwen. 'He looked troubled. And, my goodness me, I can see why now.'

What he had told Lily, in an empty classroom after the end of school, was that he had 'seen something he shouldn't have' and that was what had made Mr Lowry so angry. When Lily gently suggested that he might have been beaten unjustly and that it might be a good idea to get it off his chest, Ron looked deeply uncomfortable. He muttered that he had seen Mr Lowry 'doing something' to Miss Rowley in his office at the end of school the day before his beating. Lily felt it would be too delicate to ask what exactly Mr Lowry was 'doing' but Ron volunteered the information that she was 'lying across the desk, on her front' and they were 'fighting'. Ron said her face was 'all queer' and that it looked as if Mr Lowry was about to give her the cane just like he did the children, but he didn't hang about long enough to find out.

'But what were you doing up there?' Lily asked. 'Had he sent for you?'

Ron looked even more shamefaced at this point. He and his pals thought that Mr Lowry was out of his office after school. He often appeared downstairs, standing in the playground as they all left. A couple of Ron's pals had made a bet with him that he couldn't sneak up to Mr Lowry's office, pinch one of the canes off the desk, run down to them with it to prove he'd done it, and replace it without Mr Lowry ever knowing.

'Goodness – that would have taken some guts,' Gwen said admiringly.

'Well, quite,' Lily said. 'Except that he was so sure Mr Lowry wasn't going to be in there that he forgot to knock and find out and just went barging in.'

Gwen put a hand over her mouth, laughing in horror. What on earth had been going on?

'No wonder he's got shot of Charlotte Rowley . . .'

When Miss Monk failed to arrive at school a couple of days later their classes were run by last-minute replacements. It was the talk of the staffroom all week, and at home Ariadne was enthralled by the story.

'That poor Miss Monk,' she said.

'Poor be damned – she's a right old tartar,' Gwen said.

'But she was carrying a flame for him, from what you've said.'

'More fool her.'

'You're becoming very harsh,' Ariadne said.

'Well, the pair of them are just so horrid. I wish he'd leave as well and we could get someone else. It would make all the difference to the atmosphere in the school.'

Once things settled down, Alice Wilson still did not come back.

'Have you seen her?' Gwen asked Lucy.

Lucy Fernandez shook her head. 'Our mom went round to see her mom, but there was no reply when she knocked on the door.'

Gwen knew that she would have to go and see Theresa Fernandez. The pain of anything associated with Daniel was so great that she didn't know if she could bear it. But she knew that one day she was going to have to face her and ask the one question that she dreaded.

She went after school that afternoon.

'Hello, dear!' Theresa greeted her warmly. Gwen could still barely imagine this rounded, lively woman almost dying in a Welsh prison. Had Daniel been telling her the truth about that? Somehow she was full of doubt about everything now. It was achingly hard to be in this house again.

'Come in and have a cup of tea!' Theresa talked as she bustled about the back room, where most of the children were sitting or coming in and out. 'There was something I wanted to talk to you about – you've heard about Alice, I suppose? Mrs Wilson came round to see me today before they left. I don't know how, but her mother tracked her down and she seems prepared to take her and Alice in. I think it's up in

Staffordshire somewhere – the family are quite wealthy, I believe. Lucy will miss little Alice, though. She was ever so upset when she heard ... Don't s'pose you've heard from that lad of mine – the march is starting in a few days, isn't it, but he doesn't let me know anything!'

Gwen was completely taken aback. Theresa was treating her as if nothing at all had changed. Only then did it dawn on her that Daniel had been in Wales all this time and hadn't told his mother what had happened. It took her a few moments to cope with this. She felt as if the shape of the world had changed and become full of pain and sadness, yet Theresa had no idea! She kept chatting on about this and that, until Gwen could no longer stand it.

'Please.' She fought the tears she could feel rising. 'Could I have a word with you – on our own?'

Theresa looked startled, hearing the desperation in Gwen's voice.

'All of you,' she called to the children, 'out of here! Miss Purdy and I have something to discuss in private. Rosa, mind the shop, will you?'

The children scuttled out through the shop door.

'What is it, lovey?' Theresa said, and the comfortable tone of her voice suddenly filled Gwen with fury. She had been duped by the whole family! No one had told her the truth and she felt used and hurt and very foolish.

'You didn't think to mention to me –' she stood with her arms tightly folded, speaking in cold, clipped tones – 'that you already have a grandchild living in the valleys. Daniel's son.'

Theresa's face was a blank of bewilderment. She sank down on a chair at the table.

'*What?* What're you saying to me?'

Gwen stared at her. It dawned on her that Theresa's complete bemusement was real.

'So – he hasn't told you! And your sister-in-law hasn't let on either?' She couldn't keep the anger and bitterness out of her voice, even though none of this was Theresa's fault.

'Whatever haven't I been told? Look – come and sit down, love.' Agitated, Theresa pointed at the chair opposite her. 'I don't know what you're talking about – what's this talk about a grandchild? Whatever are you saying to me?'

Gwen stayed standing. 'Daniel has a son called Evan. He's the image of Daniel. His mother is called Megan Hughes and she lives in Treherbert.'

She could almost see Theresa Fernandez reading her lips, such was her need to make sense of what Gwen was saying.

'We came face to face with her – in Tredegar. Daniel's not denying it. He had an affair with her and she has a boy and now . . .' She couldn't hold back her tears any longer. 'And I can't stay with Daniel – not after this. He's betrayed me. I thought he was good and true and he's just lied to me all the way along . . .'

Theresa had been listening, apparently stunned, as if she couldn't make sense of what Gwen was saying, but seeing the girl's distraught state she got up and came closer to her, seeming unsure whether to touch her or not. Instead she stood wringing her hands.

'Are you telling me the truth? Gwen, you don't strike me as a liar but I can't believe what you're saying to me! You mean, my son . . .?'

Gwen nodded, sobbing. 'He didn't deny any of it. He knew because she wrote to him, but he didn't do anything, didn't go back to her or help her. I feel as if I don't know him at all.'

'Holy Jesus,' Theresa breathed. Gwen could hear how appalled she was. Staunch, Catholic Theresa. She could hardly have learned anything more distressing. 'If this is true ... How could I not have known? He never said a word ...' There was real anger in her voice now. 'I thought he was a good boy – he used to serve at the altar! I brought him up to be good that way ...' She sank back on to the chair again, in shock. 'What's the boy's name again?'

'Evan.'

'A grandson.' Theresa shook her head. 'How old is the child?'

'She said nearly two.'

'And all this time ... For shame. Oh my Lord, for shame ...'

There was a long, pained silence, then Theresa saw how it was for Gwen and said, 'You poor young thing. And Daniel thinks the world of you – you do know that, don't you?'

Gwen shrugged, looking down at the pitted surface of the table. 'Not enough to tell me the truth though.'

She looked up and the two women regarded each other for several moments in silence. Theresa's blue eyes held pity, shame, and an appeal to her.

'Can you forgive him?'

'I've told him it's over,' Gwen said flatly. 'How could I ever trust him again after this?'

Theresa shook her head, her face full of sorrow. She looked as if she was trying to decide whether to speak. Eventually, with difficulty, she said, 'It's the choice we often have, lovey. You forgive them or you lose them.'

'I can forgive him.' Gwen wiped her eyes. 'Least, maybe I will be able to one day. But I can't forget, and I'd never know again if he was telling me the truth about things, would I?' Gwen gave a great sigh and brought her hands up to cover her face.

'I love him so much, Theresa. I can't bear it!'

Fifty-One

The sun and moon rose and sank in the sky. Joey didn't know how many times. He felt hazy in the head, as if he was never completely awake. He stayed with John, waiting for him to surface. There was an old trough flung away at the side of the barn and he drank out of it. The water tasted of metal. He tried to dribble some into John's mouth, but most of it ran down into his beard. Joey ate the eggs. He hadn't the strength to go back to the henhouse to find some more. Most of the time he slept. After dark, rats scuttled and cheeped in the barn and sometimes he felt one brush past him, solid and sleek. At the beginning of the time in the barn, John coughed. Then his breathing rattled. Joey didn't like it and prodded John sometimes to make him stop. John's eyes and lips had white stuff round them. After a day or two he went quiet. At night the rats seemed to have come closer.

Joey woke sometime during a sunny day. It was bright outside and he felt a sudden increase in energy, like a flame drawn by the wind. John lay very still. He was silent now. His face looked different and sunken. When Joey went to prod him he saw the lobes of John's ears were nibbled away and there was blood. Joey didn't think about it any more. He left the barn and walked away without thinking of the curtain or the pan and knife. His clothes were dry by now. There was nothing to think about except putting one foot down, then the next, on and on along the fringe of the field, watching his feet because at first the slanting sunlight seemed too bright to look into and if he raised his eyes everything seemed to whirl and spin around him and the space was too wide, the sky so high and far it made him dizzy. He did not think about food now. There was no food. He had no memory of when he had last eaten. He stumbled on and on across the fields, lurching like a drunk, not looking for anything or heading anywhere.

Fifty-Two

It was drizzly the next day, and cold, and the men marched as briskly as they could, sometimes slapping their arms round themselves to try and keep warm. Some carried banners. At times they broke into song. The 'Internationale' was a good marching song and it helped pass the miles to sing. They sang political songs and songs from the valleys and in some places they earned money by singing. They had walked east, through Bristol and Bath and were now passing through Berkshire on their way to London, sleeping in church halls or workhouses, wherever hospitality was offered to them.

Two young men were marching together, talking, sometimes joining in the rich-voiced singing or discussing the impact the march would have when it reached Hyde Park. The government *had* to listen and abolish the means test.

'Catch you up in a mo', Dai,' the younger of the two said. 'Call of nature . . .'

'Careful now,' the other teased. 'Cold out, today!'

Despite the days of walking, the man vaulted with ease over a five-barred gate into the nearest field. He was dark-haired and lithe and had been toughened up by a collier's life. He disappeared behind the hedge, which glistened with water droplets. Having relieved himself, he straightened his clothes and turned to rejoin the marchers, but something caught his eye a short distance away in the field. It looked like a little heap of discarded clothing. This seemed a rum place to throw away clothes. He narrowed his eyes, peering at them. He thought he made out an arm, stretched out to one side of the bundle and, frowning, he moved closer.

For a few seconds he could not make sense of what he saw. The pinched face was obviously that of a child, though it had the worn, exhausted look of a very old man. There was a twig-like arm, and yet the creature seemed to have been stuffed, clown-like, into a set of clothes far too adult and bulky looking for him.

Leaning down, the man said, 'Hello, there. Can you hear me?'

There was no reply. He pushed gently at the body and assumed the boy was dead. Conscious of the march moving inexorably on ahead of him, he thought, well, nothing for it, and scooped the emaciated little body up into his arms. It was floppy as a rag doll, but not cold and stiff: there was still life in the skeletal frame, just. Poor little beggar looked close to death though! Whatever had become of him? The young man was full of rage suddenly. That was the reality of capitalism, of the country under this betraying government: children were starving to death, not just in the valleys, but all over!

As he began to walk, the child gave a slight moan and his big, prominent eyes flickered open for a second.

'It's all right, little man,' Daniel said. 'I'll take you somewhere safe. D'you know where you are?'

There was silence. What could he do? He'd have to take the child to the nearest house where they would have pity on him. A church perhaps, or a farm?

'Muur . . .' the boy groaned.

Asking for his mother, Daniel thought. God alone knew whether there was anyone for him in this world.

He was almost back to the gate now, and about to shift his stance and put the boy over his shoulder in a fireman's lift to climb over, when he heard something else which riveted him to the spot. No – he was imagining things – he could only have been mistaken.

'What were you trying to say then, lad?' he asked gently.

Quite clearly, just once, the little boy parted his parched lips and with a huge effort, murmured, 'Miss Purdy . . .'

Fifty-Three

'Gwen, dear, there's a letter for you – *and a telegram*!'

Ariadne was all of a flutter, the envelopes in her hand as Gwen came in from school.

'I hope it's not bad news!'

Ever since she had told Ariadne what had happened with Daniel, her landlady had adopted an even more motherly role towards her.

'Oh, you poor, poor young thing,' she had exclaimed with tragic eyes. 'And you thought he was the One didn't you? I know you did – I could see it in you when you were with him. And he was so polite and *handsome*.'

Gwen took off her hat and shook the rain off it, then hung up her coat, somehow not wanting to know what the news was. It was bound to be from home – her mother or father ill or some other unpleasant problem she would have to face. Wearily she took the envelopes and went into the back room, where it was not so dark. Ariadne followed like her shadow. The handwriting on the letter was Billy's. She smiled faintly. His letters were always bubbling over about something he had read and she found them uplifting. First, she tore open the telegram.

'Oh my dear – what is it?' Ariadne saw Gwen's first reaction, one hand going to her heart.

All she saw at first was the name at the bottom, DANIEL, and the rest took her time to make sense of, her eyes going over and over it:

HAVE FOUND JOEY PHILLIPS STOP IS IN WALLINGFORD WORKHOUSE STOP VERY SICK STOP WANTS YOU STOP DANIEL

Gwen looked up at Ariadne, completely bewildered. 'Where on earth is Wallingford?'

It was the middle of the next day when she stepped out onto Wallingford station and asked the way to the workhouse.

'We don't call it the workhouse any more,' one woman she made enquiries of told her severely, then instructed her to follow the Wantage Road.

All morning Gwen had been in a turmoil of emotion. The slightest thing made her tense and over-flowing with tears these days. It had not taken a second's hesitation to decide she would not be in school. Once she discovered that Wallingford was far to the south in Berkshire, though, her confusion increased. For Daniel to be there obviously had some-thing to do with the route of the march, but however had Joey got right down there? And hearing from Daniel again stirred up all the sad and bitter feelings which had not yet even begun to subside in his absence. Sitting on the train, she was full of her old hunger for him, as if his very being was imprinted on her, and yet the thought of him now gave her nothing but pain. Every time she thought of him, she could see the tired, pretty face of Megan Hughes, the hurt in it, and what

Daniel had done in leaving her and his son without any apparent regret or care.

She looked out at the damp autumn countryside and let herself think over all the close, happy times she and Daniel had shared together, allowed the sense of hurt and betrayal to overwhelm her for a time, and tears ran unstoppably down her cheeks. She was caught in a painful collision of emotions, longing both to be held in his arms and to punch him hard in the face.

Walking along to the workhouse, she wondered, had Daniel come here himself, carrying the boy? Had he left the march? She had no idea exactly where the route had gone. Or had Daniel handed him to someone else? How on earth had he found him?

The workhouse was a sturdy-looking brick building and she was admitted by an equally sturdy-looking woman whom she took to be the matron. In the hall inside, she explained that she was looking for a little boy, Joseph Phillips.

'I've come to take him back to Birmingham,' she said. 'I'm his teacher.'

'Birmingham?' The woman looked incredulous. Her tone was brisk but not unkind. 'Well, what's he doing down here?'

'I've really no idea. He disappeared from school months ago. We'd have to ask him how he got here.'

'Oh, I don't think he's in a fit state to tell you that at the moment. He's very poorly – I was surprised he lasted the first night after they brung him in.'

'Who brought him?'

She looked surprised by the question. 'A farmer, so far as I know.'

Not Daniel then, by the sound of things.

'I really want to take him back with me today,' Gwen suggested.

'Ooh no!' The woman pursed her lips and kept shaking her head. 'Oh, dear me, no – he's far too ill to be moved. Oh no, I don't think so.'

Gwen sighed. Perhaps the woman was right. How was she going to manage with a sick child all the way back?

'All right. I'll come back and fetch him when he's better. But may I see him? I've come a long way today.'

Well, I suppose that'd be all right. He's in the infirmary. I'll get someone to take you.'

A puny-looking young man was enlisted to lead her to the infirmary, where they walked between two rows of black iron bedsteads amid the sounds of coughing and hawking. From the far end came a terrible sound of groaning. On one bed she saw a tiny, crumpled figure lying like a fallen bird. It took her a moment to recognize the boy. Joey had always been a scrawny child, but now he was obviously extremely malnourished. His head looked disproportionately big, the skin tinged blue under his eyes, the rest of his face deathly pale. He lay prone, eyes closed, as if he had not an ounce of strength left to move. As she moved closer and leaned down to look at him, she saw his little hand, ingrained with dirt, the wrist so thin it looked fit to snap at the slightest touch.

'You poor little chap, what's happened to you?' she whispered. Tears filled her eyes once more as she stood looking down at him. The state of him! He was nothing but a bag of bones.

She wiped her eyes and knelt down beside the bed. 'Joey?'

There was no response. She could not see him breathing and, fearful, she hurried to check his pulse. But he was alive: she could feel a regular flickering through the veins. Gently she touched his hand, wrapping her fingers round his curled ones.

'Can you hear me? It's Miss Purdy.'

He seemed to breathe more deeply, like a little sigh.

'I've come to take you home, but they say you're too poorly. But I'll come back for you. All your class mates have missed you, you know – Ron and all the others. They'll be ever so glad to see you.'

She wondered if he could hear a thing she was saying. She looked at him, filled with gloom suddenly. Maybe he was too far gone. It looked as if he wasn't going to make it.

'Joey? It's Miss Purdy.'

And then she felt it. A movement in the wasted little hand, which gripped, at first almost imperceptibly round her finger, then clung on with a force which took her by surprise.

She knew then, with a certainty which filled her with dread, that she couldn't leave him here. He couldn't be abandoned yet again. Not surrounded by all these strangers, dying old men with phlegmy chests. How could he ever really know for sure that she was coming back? She knelt there full of tension, trying to decide what to do.

'Joey, listen to me,' she whispered. 'The matron says you should stay here because you're not very well. But if you want to go today, I'll take you with me. We'll manage it somehow.'

For the first time, his eyelids flickered. He did not speak, but the huge eyes looked at her suddenly with such urgent intensity that she knew the answer. Whatever the matron thought about it, they were going home. She was not leaving without him.

By the time the train pulled into Birmingham it had long been dark. She had argued her case with the matron, who caved in without too much protest, especially when Gwen pressed a ten shilling note into her hand. Joey was dressed in a roughly sewn sort of nightdress of coarse cotton, which was far too long so that it covered his feet, but not nearly warm enough for the October weather outside. Gwen paid the matron more to take the blanket from his bed to wrap him in. She bundled him up carefully and they went in a taxi to Wallingford Station. He was as light as a paper kite in her arms.

On the way back to Birmingham they found themselves near a kind, middle-aged lady, who introduced herself as a nurse, and helped Gwen to feed Joey a little of the milk diluted with water the matron had given her in a jam jar. It was a struggle to get him to take anything because he was barely conscious.

'His system won't be able to take too much at first,' she said. 'When you get home you'd be almost better off using a baby's bottle to begin with. You'll need to go very gradually. Dear me, what an awful thing – and in this country too! Where are you taking him to?'

'Well, I've got lodgings in Handsworth. My landlady was a bit unsure, but she said I can take him back there at least for now. She's not really used to children, you see.'

'He's not going to cause any trouble for a while, the state he's in, is he?'

When they got out at New Street Station, the woman helped Gwen lift Joey into a taxi.

'You can't possibly manage on the tram!' she said. 'Now let me give you a contribution to the fare. I think you're a very kind person indeed.'

She thrust a couple of half crowns into Gwen's pocket and barely waited to be thanked.

When the taxi reached Ariadne's house, she had evidently been waiting on tenterhooks.

'My dear – at last!' she cried as the door opened. Seeing Joey in Gwen's arms, her hands went dramatically to her face. 'Oh, my word! Oh, look at that little mite. The state of him! Don't you think he should be in the hospital? He looks . . . well, he doesn't look as if he'll last the night.'

'I think I should put him to bed,' Gwen suggested.

'Oh yes – of course! I've got the little room up at the back ready . . .'

It was no more than a boxroom, but there was a bed squeezed in which Ariadne had made up for him. Gwen told Ariadne of the help the nurse had given her and her suggestion about the baby bottle.

'I'll get one tomorrow,' Ariadne said. They were both talking softly. She kept staring down at the tiny, frail figure in the bed, seemingly unable to get over the sight of him. 'He's really rather beautiful, isn't he?'

'I'm very sorry, Ariadne. Maybe you're right about the hospital. I was so worked up about just getting him out of the workhouse and back here I hadn't thought how much work it's going to be looking after him . . . It's too much to expect you . . .'

'Oh, don't say that,' Ariadne burst out. She sounded really upset. 'No one ever expects anything of me – that's the trouble! They never have. And what have I ever done with my life, really? I mean I know I wasn't sure about him coming. I've no real knowledge of children – never had the chance. But I'll try – I want to! Poor little lad. It's the least I can do!'

Gwen hesitated, then dared to take Ariadne's hand for a moment. It was knobbly with all her rings, and Gwen gave it a gentle squeeze.

'Thank you,' she said. 'You're so kind.'

Fifty-Four

'Ron – stay behind a moment, please!'

The rest of the class were hurrying out for their first breaktime the next morning.

Ron came over to her desk and Gwen was disturbed to see a hunted expression in his eyes. It made her angry. He had always been such a carefree, sunny sort of boy. Whatever had been going on that afternoon in Mr Lowry's office, and the treatment he received as a result, seemed to have left him in a state of anxiety.

'Shut the door, Doreen!' she called to the last departing child, then smiled reassuringly at Ron. 'It's all right. You haven't done anything wrong.' He looked up at her in a hangdog fashion and she weighed up in her mind whether to say anything. The consequences of the headmaster's behaviour had affected Charlotte Rowley (though Gwen had very little sympathy for her) and Ron – not himself. How typical that was, she thought. She was on dangerous ground, she knew, saying anything against another member of staff to a pupil, but this was a question of justice.

'Look, Ron – all that's happened this term – nothing was your fault. It wasn't fair, and you shouldn't have to keep worrying. Try and put it behind you, eh?'

'Yes, Miss.' He stared at the ground, not seeming cheered by this.

'I've got some news to tell you. Good news.'

He looked up at her.

'I went down south yesterday. That's why I wasn't here.' She could feel her smile broadening. 'And guess who I brought back?'

Ron's brow furrowed.

'He's very poorly at the moment and won't be up to playing out for a long time. But tucked up in bed in the house where I live is your pal Joey.'

Ron looked blank for a moment, then his eyebrows shot up.

'Joey Phillips?'

Gwen nodded, delighted to see a smile spread across Ron's face once more. And some white teeth.

'Is he coming back to school, Miss?'

'Well, I hope so – eventually. He's got a lot of resting to do first, before he's well enough. But in a little while, a few days perhaps, I hope you'll be able to come round and see him.'

Ron was grinning now. 'That's bostin, Miss!'

Ariadne was a devoted, if rather agitated nurse. All Gwen could feel towards her was gratitude. Her life became centred round nursing Joey Phillips back to health. As she said, what else could they have done with the poor little mite? After all the lengths he had gone to to escape the orphanage, they could hardly just pack him back there now.

For the first few days, Joey lay fading in and out of consciousness. They managed to get him to drink a little: water with glucose powder, some diluted milk. He could manage to drink better soon, and open his eyes, and as soon as he had swallowed a few mouthfuls he would slip back into his long sleep again. Despite the doctor's advice just to keep him safe and warm, Gwen was worried, wondering if he should be in hospital, but to her surprise Ariadne took it all calmly.

'Do him good,' she said, tucking the blankets round him. 'Sleep is a great healer. And the doctor said we're doing all that can be done.'

'He reminds me of something in hibernation,' Gwen said. 'Like a hedgehog.'

As the days passed he became able to take more: milk with an egg whisked into it, and some thin soup. He was obviously going to get better. But although he was awake quite a lot, lying looking round the bright pink painted room, he barely ever said a word.

'D'you know,' Ariadne told Gwen, 'when you come into the room, his eyes never leave you, not for a moment.'

Joey was almost all their conversation now. Ariadne had taken to wearing flatter shoes so she could hurry up and downstairs easily, and her porridge making had come on no end. She often sat beside Joey, reading him stray snippets out of the daily papers.

By the end of the second week, Gwen told Ron he could come and visit after school and asked him to tell his mother where they were going.

'Just for a few minutes,' she said. 'He's ever so weak still, you see. He's not saying much. But I'm sure he'd be pleased to see you.'

She thought about asking Lucy if she'd like to come as well. Lucy had had another fit in class earlier in the week and Gwen thought it might be nice for her to feel chosen for something special. She felt awkward about it, though, not sure if Lucy knew of the rift between herself and Daniel, but the child showed no sign of it. The march was over – Gwen had read in the papers about the gathering in Hyde Park, the speeches. Aneurin Bevan had visited the marchers when they were sleeping in Reading cattle market and addressed them there. No one was sure if it was going to make any difference to anything. She didn't know where Daniel was, and was on pins in case he suddenly appeared to meet Lucy. She had said to him that she didn't want to see him, but she could hardly prevent him from living in the same neighbourhood as the school, could she? But the thought of seeing him again was very painful.

'Is Daniel home now?' she asked Lucy casually as they sat on the tram.

Lucy shook her head. She had a white Alice band holding back her long hair.

'He went back with the other marchers. I think he's coming soon.'

Ariadne had bought iced buns and lemonade for Ron and Lucy and laid the table with a lacy cloth. Gwen could see both the children looking round, overwhelmed by the big, cluttered house and Ariadne's fussing attention.

'I'll take them up to Joey before they have anything to eat, shall I?' Gwen said.

They followed her up, Lucy laboriously hauling her calipered leg up each step, and went into Joey's room. He was awake, and stared at them all as they came in. Gwen thought she saw a flicker of something in his eyes, but otherwise he remained expressionless.

Of course, the children found it difficult to know what to say.

Lucy said quietly, 'Hello, Joey. You all right?'

Ron was tugging at something in his pocket. He produced a squashed little brown paper bag.

'Here y'are, pal. Brought yer some rocks.'

He sounded so gruff and grandfatherly as he spoke that Gwen found herself smiling. Ron laid the bag of sweets on Joey's bed. There was a silence.

'I'm Ron,' Ron said. 'From school. D'you remember us?'

Gwen watched Joey's face. He said nothing, but his expression was not blank. She could tell there were thoughts going on.

'Well,' Ron said. 'Sorry you're bad. I hope you're coming back to school soon. Weren't the same after you went.'

There were no words, but Gwen saw something she had not seen before. There was a slight twitching round Joey's lips and, for the first time, a light in his eyes.

'Says here the king's been in Wales,' Ariadne said over tea one night. As usual she had a newspaper open on the table. King Edward had visited South Wales after the Hunger March.

' "Something must be done," he said,' Ariadne read. 'D'you know, it says here that *three-quarters* of the people in Merthyr Tydfil are on poor relief!'

'Yes,' Gwen said. 'Things are in a bad way there.'

Ariadne considered her across the table and said tragically, 'The least thing makes you think of *him*, doesn't it?'

Gwen kept her eyes on her plate of macaroni cheese. They had cooked it together. 'Yes.' It was no good pretending otherwise. She was so hurt that she wanted all thoughts of Daniel just to fade from her mind. Instead, he kept coming back to her. Ariadne was right. Any thought she had of Lucy or Billy made her think of him. And she couldn't forget, longed for things to be otherwise, for her to be able to trust him. But she couldn't and that was the truth of it. And yet she couldn't get past him either, couldn't get over him and feel better.

She swallowed down the lump in her throat. 'I've just got to stop thinking of him, that's all.'

It was getting close to the end of November. The weather was damp and unpleasant, but in spite of that Joey was getting better every day. He was still weak, but he was gaining weight, and once on a good diet, proved extremely resilient. He was soon able to get up and start moving about.

One Saturday afternoon Gwen sat with him up in his room, teaching him to play snakes and ladders. He was very withdrawn and she could still hardly get him to say anything at all. Trying to keep his attention focused on anything was difficult too.

'There –' Gwen pointed at the board – 'you've landed on a ladder. You can move right up there, look.'

Joey peered at it and solemnly moved his counter up the ladder, pressing his finger hard onto it.

'Joey?'

He looked up at her but wouldn't quite meet her eye.

'Can you remember your school? The class – Ron and Lucy and the others?'

Joey nodded.

'Would you like to go back to school one day?'

There was a faint shake of his head.

'No? Well, maybe not yet. You do know you can stay here for as long as you like? Ariadne's very kind and she likes having you here. And so do I.'

She heard a knocking on the front door, and, after a short delay, Ariadne talking to someone.

'It'll be all right, Joey. You don't need to run away again.'

'I'm never going to the orphanage!'

The words seemed to explode out of him. He was suddenly seething with emotion, eyes narrowed in an animal way, so that for a moment she found him almost frightening.

'The orphanage? No, of course we won't put you in an orphanage! Oh, Joey – that's why you ran away in the first place, wasn't it?'

'The man was coming. They took Lena and Kenny and Poll, but they weren't having me!'

To Gwen's irritation she heard Ariadne's tread on the stairs. She was just beginning to get something out of Joey and now they were going to be interrupted.

'Don't worry,' she told him.

'Gwen!' Ariadne hissed, poking her head round the door. 'It's Daniel – *your* Daniel. Downstairs!'

Gwen shot to her feet, in a complete panic.

'Tell him to go. I won't see him – I can't!'

'I can't just tell him to leave, dear. Do calm down! He wants to see Joey – he did rescue him after all.'

'Well, let me get into my room. I can't see him . . . Don't let him up here yet.'

She fled along to the front of the house and shut herself in her room, leaning back against the door. Through the blood pounding in her ears, she heard Ariadne calling from the landing, 'You can come up now, Daniel,' and his feet climbing the stairs. She stood with her arms folded, crushed against her, heart pounding, her breathing shallow. The longing to see him was so overpowering that it was all she could do to stop herself tearing the door open. Yet this collided head on with her dread of him, of the strength of her feelings, which gave him such power over her, a power which he had betrayed and could betray again and again. She closed her eyes, trying to make herself breathe properly, straining her ears to hear what was going on. She caught the deep timbre of his voice coming from Joey's room. He was speaking gently, reassuringly. Pain washed through her. How extraordinary it was that those two had been brought together, both so far from home – that it had been Daniel, of all people, who had found Joey. She still did not know the exact circumstances and she wanted to ask. Not long ago all this would have felt so right, as if it was meant – like her soft spot for Lucy, her rapport with Billy. As if all these things had brought her to Daniel, tied her so closely to him, given her that feeling she had of coming home every time she was with him, as if it had all been set in the stars. And now everything was wrong. There was no trust. It was broken.

She went to sit on the edge of the bed, and watched her hands trembling in her lap as if they belonged to someone else. She could think of nothing, nothing except that he was here, a few paces away from her, and that soon he would leave and the house would be empty of him. And how would it be, his not trying to see her? Seeing or not seeing him – which was the more painful?

Then she heard footsteps and before she could even move the door opened. She jumped. Seeing him again was such a shock, at once so familiar and so strange.

'Gwen – for God's sake . . .'

He sounded distraught, but somehow this enraged her instead of making her pity him.

'What?' She got up off the bed. 'For God's sake *what*? No – don't come any closer!'

Daniel turned and shut the door. 'Why won't you even speak to me?'

'Because . . .' She was having to hold on very tightly to her emotions. 'Because I can't stand it, that's why.'

'Please . . .' He walked a couple of paces closer. 'I know I've done something terrible, so wrong, leaving Megan like that – and the boy. I can't even make amends for that because she won't have me anywhere near . . .'

'You've tried, then?'

'I've been in the valleys. I went to Treherbert, but she wouldn't even let me in the house. But the thing is, Gwen, I was younger then and on fire for what we were doing. I never really loved her – not the way I love you. I've told you. I don't know what else to say . . .'

'She seemed to think you did.' Gwen felt suddenly overwhelmed with weariness. Here they were again, back in the same place, and it would always be like this. 'Look, Daniel – please, just go. I can't do this any more. I need to be by myself.'

Again, he came closer. They were only a yard or so apart, and she had to fight the feeling, the tingling that came over her when he came near. She stepped backwards.

'So are you saying you don't love me? All those months, all those words didn't mean anything. Was it just lies then, all you said, if it just disappears like this, like a puff of smoke?'

'You know it wasn't.' She could feel tears coming and loss of control and she fought them hard. 'I did love you – I do. I think I love you too much. What you do affects me *so much*. I can't live like that, never knowing if I can trust you – with Esther, or with whoever turns up next, or knowing that you had a woman and child all this time and never told me, never seemed to think it mattered!' She began to cry then. 'How could you, Daniel? I poured myself out for you, month after month and you just hurt me so much . . .' She put her hands over her face.

'I know. Don't you think I know? Look, I'm sorry . . .' He came close and gently put his arms round her, and she did not resist. 'But I want – I need – to tell you that it matters. That you mean more to me than any woman I've ever met before. I need to know whether you'll give me a chance?'

The feel, the smell of him, were so achingly familiar she longed just to surrender, to press him close to her, for everything to be back where it was and all right. But she was shaking her head. It was not all right. What they had had before had been ruptured.

'I want to know if you're with me.' His voice was very solemn and he drew back and looked into her tearful eyes. 'I'm going away.'

'*What?*' She stared at him. 'Where to?'

'There are volunteers going to Spain. Some have gone already – a few, here and there. The party is starting to get people signing up. They want to get something more organized going, when there are more volunteers.'

'You're going to go – to Spain?' Suddenly she laughed, incredulous, pushing him away from her. 'God, Daniel, you're the end. You come back here, playing with my feelings all over again and then announce that you're disappearing to heaven knows where!'

'We can do some good over there—' He was all fired up, she could hear. 'Something direct. Not like here, fighting against this cowardly government and all the apathy on the left! In Spain they're really making the revolution happen. They're up against it, see? It's so clear what's going on when you're fighting the fascist enemy face to face. I'll be leaving within the next week or two, to go to Catalonia.'

Gwen was lost for words.

'That's why I had to see you, my girl . . .'

'I'm not your . . .'

He laid his hand gently over her lips. 'Don't say that now. Think about it. Think of me when I'm fighting in Spain and see whether I matter to you. Because I know you'll be the light I carry in my heart . . .'

'Oh, Daniel, stop,' she said miserably.

'Will you write to me?'

She hesitated, then nodded. 'Are you really going so soon?'

'Within days. You know me – never sit still if I can help it.'

'It doesn't mean . . . It doesn't mean I'm just sitting here waiting for you to come back.'

He looked silently down into her eyes and she fought desperately not to be moved by his expression. She reached up and stroked his cheek.

'Give me a kiss for the leaving?'

His face moved closer to hers and she closed her eyes and kissed him back.

After he had gone she rested on the edge of the bed, lost in thought. Her emotions were completely different now from those of the previous weeks, and she realized to her surprise that she might reach a place of calm. The future held so many challenges. One day she would have to reckon with her family. There were the children in her charge, her life at the school. There was Joey to care for.

And there was Daniel ... She knew now some of the things she didn't want – with him or with anyone. She didn't want her mother's dead respectability, nor did she want to be trapped like Millie, who'd rather run home to her mother than be with her husband. She didn't intend to run slavishly after men like Ariadne had done either. She wanted to make a different way, deciding things for herself because she was learning from hard experience.

Daniel was in her life, and whatever difficulty and pain that involved she did love him. She believed that he also loved her. But he was going away and there was no knowing what it would mean for him. The future, for now, was without him and all she could feel was a delicate balance of the certainty of love and a surrender to not knowing whether she would ever be with him.

When she had sat for some time, a smile came to her lips and she reached across and picked up her picture of Amy Johnson. She looked into Amy's strong face.

'I'm learning to fly too,' she said.

Epilogue

February 1937

'It's from Daniel, isn't it?' Ariadne was full of glee as she handed Gwen the envelope. 'Boys, shoes off and sit by the fire. I don't want your slushy water all over the house! And there are doughnuts in the kitchen.'

Gwen had come home from school with Joey and Ron in tow. Outside, the place was bright with snow. She left the boys to Ariadne, who had been waiting to pounce on them and take charge.

In her room she read the letter, hearing his voice:

> *Albacete*
> 30.1.1937

Dear Gwen,

It was very nice to get your letter at last. I'm glad Joey is back at school and seeming more himself. I suppose his strange moods are not surprising, what with the time of it he's had. I wonder if he has talked to you any more about what happened and how he came to be all the way down there. Say hello to him for me, won't you? I'm glad Ariadne is 'like a new person' as you said. She must have been lonely and now you've given her a family, of sorts. Where would Joey be without her, eh?

Things are quiet here today so far, so that's why I'm taking the chance to write. Being here has given me so many thoughts, about the revolution and where we're all going. I don't possibly have time to write them all down. One thing that strikes me with great force is that when you hear about 'war' at home it sounds like something more organized and militarily set up than it ever is here. It really is neighbour against neighbour, men, women and even children. No one can escape and I've seen more inhuman treatment of man by man here already than I had ever imagined seeing in a lifetime. Even without extremes, there is so much misery, hunger, orphaned children etc. What we need desperately is more aid coming in to help the Spanish people. So, all of you – keep it coming to us. Your work is not for nothing! Even more than by the misery, I am affected by the courage, determination and self-sacrifice here in the face of Franco and his fascist thugs. The republicans are fighting for all the best things there are – freedom and justice and right. With all our efforts, these are the things we have to attain if barbarism is not to take over the world.

I am feeling especially melancholy though today, as a terrible sad thing has happened. I think I told you in my last letter that I had palled up with an Irish lad, Christie O'Brien? He'd come from England, but he said he'd been training as a priest in Ireland and left the seminary. Wouldn't say why, but he seemed to have had it hard. He was killed by a sniper yesterday – hiding out in the church tower they were. Got him straight through the head. I feel badly as I have no address to let his family know. He didn't talk much about where he came from. I'll miss Christie, though, God rest him. He was a good *compañero*.

I'm going to have to stop, when I feel I've barely

begun, there's so much to describe and there's so much to feel. But this is to let you know how we are so far. Go and see Mam now and then for me, will you? And keep up those letters to Billy – you've done wonders for him.

All I want to say is too much to put down, about how you're in my heart and all the bad I've done I'm ashamed of. But I'm rushing now and it's coming out wrong. I do love you, however hard it is for you to believe me. You're my light. I hope I'll get another letter from you soon, dear Gwen.

Anyway, *Salud!* as they say here.

My love,
  Daniel